UNSTICKY

Sarra Manning

CORGI BOOKS

TRANSWORLD PUBLISHERS
61–63 Uxbridge Road, London W5 5SA
A Random House Group Company
www.transworldbooks.co.uk

UNSTICKY
A CORGI BOOK: 9780552167765

First published in Great Britain
in 2009 by Headline Review,
an imprint of Headline Publishing Group
Corgi edition published 2012

Addresses for Random House Group Ltd companies outside the UK
can be found at: www.randomhouse.co.uk
The Random House Group Ltd Reg. No. 954009

The Random House Group Limited supports The Forest Stewardship Council (FSC®),
the leading international forest-certification organisation. Our books carrying the FSC
label are printed on FSC®-certified paper. FSC is the only forest-certification scheme
endorsed by the leading environmental organisations, including Greenpeace.
Our paper-procurement policy can be found at www.randomhouse.co.uk/environment.

Typeset in Sabon.
Printed and bound by
CPI Group (UK) Ltd, Croydon, CR0 4YY.

2 4 6 8 10 9 7 5 3 1

Dedicated to the memory of Kate Jones,
who mentored both book and author.

thanks

To Gordon and Joanne Shaw, Sarah Bailey and Kate Hodges for all their long-suffering support. My aunt, Lesley Lawson, for shared writerly woes. And Pavel Zoubok of the Pavel Zoubok Gallery in New York for allowing his brains to be picked.

My agent, Karolina Sutton, Laura Sampson and all at Curtis Brown. Catherine Cobain, Harriet Evans and Sara Porter.

'I seem fated to pass through the world without colliding with it or moving it – and I'm sure I can't tell you whether the fate's good or evil. I don't die – I don't fall in love. And if other people die or fall in love they always do it when I'm just not there.'

Where Angels Fear to Tread, E.M. Forster

chapter one

'I just don't love you,' he said.

It was the most brutal dumping Grace had ever had. And she'd had a few.

But if Grace was being honest with herself, which didn't happen often, then it wasn't a complete surprise. She'd seen the light gradually dim in Liam's eyes like a torch with dying batteries. He'd begun to look at her in this bemused way, as if the actual dating was a major letdown after the months they'd spent skirting around each other and snogging furiously as they waited for the night bus. He'd even stopped holding her hand when they crossed the street, so Grace didn't need to be a cartographer to read the signs: being dumped was inevitable.

But she'd never expected it to happen on her birthday. In Liberty's. Right by the new season's Marc Jacobs bags.

'You're finishing with me?' Grace clarified, her voice metronome-steady. 'On my birthday?'

Finally Liam found the balls to look her in the eyes, before his gaze skittered away to rest on the tomato-red, outsized Hobo she'd been admiring before he turned up and crunched the day under his tatty Converses.

Grace should have known better than to arrive at Liberty's all quivery and expectant that maybe, just maybe, Liam had finally got his shit together and was going to buy her some serious designer real estate as a birthday present. She wasn't picky; she'd have settled for a key fob or a marked-down hairslide.

'I wasn't going to split up with you. Not today, anyway. But then, I don't know ... I just saw you standing there and I couldn't hold it in any longer,' Liam said heavily, shoulders slumping under his leather jacket. It was too hot for leather jackets even if you were a wannabe indie rock star in your very wildest dreams.

Grace had often wanted to tell Liam that writing whiny mope-rock anthems for teenage boys to listen to in their breaks from wanking and GCSE revision wasn't something to aspire to, and now she watched with satisfaction as little beads of sweat sprang up on Liam's pretty face even though it was cool and closeted in Liberty's. That was one of the reasons why it was Grace's happy place. There was something civilised and genteel about the thick wood panelling that hushed the merciless, hurrying world outside. Well, that and the rail upon rail of pretty frocks, the spindly shoes that looked too delicate to walk in and the beauty hall where she wanted her ashes scattered when she died. Except Liam had just gone and trashed her happy place as well as ruining her birthday.

'Why? Why are you splitting up with me? Should I mention that it's my birthday again, or is that getting boring? Jesus, Liam, what is wrong with you?' Grace's voice was slowly edging towards the red end of the dial marked 'hysterical', but really – extenuating circumstances.

Liam gingerly touched her arm as he gnawed on his pouty bottom lip because she was making this harder than he'd expected. Generally, Grace was the kind of girl he could leave in a corner and not have to worry too much about.

'Gracie, c'mon,' he said helplessly, running a hand through dirty-blond hair, his eyes shutting tight. 'I was going to wait a few days, but it all just got too much. Things aren't good between us, y'know?'

'Is it something I did?' Grace asked, taking pity on him and scrabbling in her bag for her Miu Miu shades to shield her accusatory glare. 'What did I do wrong?'

'You didn't do anything wrong. We just don't fit.' For the greatest undiscovered singer/songwriter of his generation, Liam was being annoyingly vague. Grace could see he was searching wildly for an excuse. 'Your hair,' he mumbled finally. 'I don't think you should have dyed it black.'

'You're splitting up with me because of my *hair*?'

They both knew that it had only five per cent to do with Grace's hasty decision to go from honey blond to blue black after watching a series of Bettie Page shorts at a Burlesque all-dayer. It was meant to have signalled a new, edgier Grace but it had just made her look peaky and stained her Cath Kidston towels.

'No,' Liam prevaricated. 'Yes – I don't know. Look, we can still go out tonight and hook up or whatever, but I just don't think we're heading anywhere serious, so what's the point of pretending any more? But I got you a card – here.' He proffered a creased pink envelope like it was all done and they could just move along because there was nothing to see here. She was good for a 'hook-up or whatever', but she was never going to make his heart go pitter-patter.

'You're an arsehole,' she hissed, voice quivering with the threat of tears. 'You could have picked any other day and cobbled together some lame excuse but instead you do it now, *here*, and you don't even have the decency to be screwing someone behind my back.'

'Don't make a scene, Gracie . . .' Liam said in a shocked whisper.

'I'll make a bloody scene if I want to.'

Liam was shuffling his feet like he was about to bolt but Grace wasn't done with him yet. Not when she could shove him square in the chest with two puny fists because he really, really deserved it. Liam rocked back on his heels, arms

3

pin-wheeling to keep his balance, and knocked the Marc Jacobs bag off its Perspex plinth.

It tottered for one terrible second before dangling forlornly from its security chain and setting off a shrieking alarm, which would have made Grace clamp her hands over her ears if she wasn't hunting in her pockets for a ratty tissue. She could feel her mascara slowly descending as tears began to trickle down each cheek.

'You want a reason for me to break up with you?' Liam snarled, deigning to lower his head so he could get all up in Grace's face. '*This* is a reason to dump you. You can be so fucking embarrassing.'

After that pithy summing-up, he gave the hapless Marc Jacobs bag a vicious punch before stalking away.

Grace carefully rubbed her thumbs under her sunglasses, not surprised that they came away streaked with black gunk as a bevy of shop assistants hurried over. Usually, Liberty's staff could be relied upon to be discreet yet friendly. Not like in Harvey Nicks where they called her 'Madam' in a condescending manner as she fingered dresses that she couldn't possibly afford. Mind you, they didn't seem quite so friendly now.

Grace had been dumped, seen her boss taking the new, suck-up intern out for coffee and had had an email from her mother, all of which added up to make the worst birthday ever. Being barred for life from Liberty's would put the icing on the cake. A mythical cake though, because no one back in the office had any plans to take her to Patisserie Valerie this afternoon.

She swallowed hard to dispel the sob that was rising up her throat. But the next one and the one after that were all cued up and Grace's frantic gulps made her start coughing and spluttering and—

'Stop crying,' someone behind her said sharply. 'You'll make everything worse.' The voice had an arm, which curved

4

around Grace's shoulders and ushered her towards the exit. Both his tone and grip left no room for resistance. 'Let's get out of here before they have you tried for crimes against expensive handbags.'

There were feet too, in highly polished brown brogues. Still coughing, Grace watched them walk alongside her scuffed ballet flats as she was steered past the flower stall and towards Regent Street. Her bag was banging against her hip with every step and this was just ridiculous – letting herself be frogmarched out of Liberty's, eyes watering now rather than tearing, by some nameless, faceless man who was cutting a swathe through the jostling crowds as if he was going into battle. Grace slowed down as a prelude to dodging into the oncoming traffic to escape but was propelled forward by a decisive hand.

As he delivered her safely to the other side of Regent Street, Grace ground to a halt and tugged on his sleeve. 'I'm all right now, thank you,' she said, sniffing to get rid of the snot – she'd never felt so gross and disgusting as she did at that moment.

She glanced up then, because curiosity trumped tear-streaked vanity every time. He had a thin, clever face that was all angles, blue eyes creasing up against the glare of the sun slanting between the buildings; lips quirked in something that wasn't quite a smile. Dark-blond hair peaked into little tufts that rippled in the slight breeze. It was easier to focus on his suit: cream, summer-weight wool by Dries Van Noten if Grace wasn't mistaken. And Grace never was when it came to matters of fashion.

'You don't look all right,' he noted crisply in etched-glass, public-school English. 'You look as if you need a drink.'

He was old-fashioned looking, Grace decided. Not just the suit, which made him look as though he should be taking the air in one of those fifties movies set on the French Riviera, but as if he was the second male lead in one of those same films. Not matinee-idol handsome enough to get the girl, but good enough to be the best friend of the one who got the girl. Or the arch nemesis of the one who got the girl, who had his comeuppance ten minutes before the end credits began to roll.

Also, he was old. Or *older*. Late thirties, early forties, which made this whole situation even weirder than it already was.

'Look, I'm really sorry about causing a scene and thank you for getting me out of there, but I'm OK now. Really.'

'Where shall we go?' he mused, looking around. 'Which street are we on?'

'Conduit, and I can't—' But she could – for the simple reason that his arm was back around her shoulders and he was setting off with a long-limbed stride so she had to scurry to keep up or get dragged underfoot. 'I have to get back to work,' she panted. 'My boss gets really pissy if I take longer than an hour for lunch.'

'Really? He sounds very tiresome.'

'He's a she,' Grace corrected him as she struggled to keep up with his long-limbed stride. She was being abducted, not to mention manhandled, in broad daylight, and wasn't fighting or flighting. In fact, she was even glancing in the window of Moschino as she hurried past, but obviously the shock of being dumped and now being kidnapped had made her cognitive thought processes misfire.

'Come on, chop chop,' the man said, pulling Grace round one corner and then another until he came to a halt outside an unmarked black door and started tapping a security code into the keypad. The fight or flight part of Grace's brain was finally firing up and telling her to run screaming for the hills or to the nearest police station. She took a tentative step to the right but his hand, which was still on her shoulder, tightened. 'Through here,' he said.

There was a buzzing sound and the man slowly pushed the door open and Grace was ushered over the threshold into a dark space, walls painted a rich ruby red, polished wood under her feet and a large set of doors slightly ajar to the right. No way was she going any further than right here where she stood, unless it was back out the way she'd come in.

Someone was walking towards her, a smiling woman in a ruffly black dress and pinny, which brought to mind Laura Ashley – if she'd ever had a Goth period. 'Good to see you again, sir,' she said to the man standing behind Grace. 'Are you here for lunch?'

'Just drinks, I think. Maybe afternoon tea,' he said, finally taking his hand off Grace's shoulder and stepping forward. His sleeve brushed Grace's arm and she flinched.

The front door finally shut with a soft but decisive thud so she had the sensation that she was cocooned in this dark red place, where people only talked in low, soothing tones as if anything louder wouldn't be tolerated. It was strangely comforting and suddenly, inexplicably, Grace started to cry again.

Or cry properly, because the tears in Liberty's had just been the warm-up act and this was the main event. Being abducted had been a great diversion, but it was still her birthday and she'd still just been dumped and her life was still sucking beyond all measure. Grace felt her chest shuddering, and then the sobs that she'd managed to mute down ten minutes before were back for their encore presentation. They sounded like death rattles as they ricocheted off the walls.

'Oh dear,' the man said softly, cupping Grace's elbow and steering her carefully down the corridor, the black-clad, ruffly woman bringing up the rear. 'I'm sure he's not worth crying over. Magda will take you somewhere to get your tear ducts under control, while I order you a glass of champagne.'

Grace shrugged, or would have, if her shoulders weren't heaving, and let herself be led through a small side door and up a narrow, curving staircase. The place was like a very red, very twisty rabbit warren. 'Bathroom's through there,' she was told in that same modulated murmur.

7

Diving for the nearest stall, Grace sank down on the loo so she could finally, properly, get her weep on.

The attendant averted her eyes as Grace emerged, as if she hadn't heard the muffled howling coming from the cubicle, and dabbed furiously at the shiny chrome taps as Grace washed her hands and stared despondently at her reflection in the mirror. There were dirty grey rivulets running down her cheeks, which she scrubbed away before evaluating the raw material carefully, a tube of tinted moisturiser poised and at the ready.

Parts of her face Grace liked, other parts not so much. She liked that her eyes were grey, a dark, school-uniform grey that couldn't be mistaken for blue or green or hazel, and framed by long lashes so close-edged that she always looked as if she hadn't taken off her eyeliner the night before. There were freckles, the bane of her teenage years, but which she now hoped made her look younger, and a mouth that drooped downwards, even when she was smiling. Her grandmother had constantly told her to stop pouting when she was little but actually the sulking had paid off in the permanent jut of her lower lip.

But Grace's nose was too pronounced to be excused, especially in profile where it looked alarmingly Roman; her forehead wore a deep furrow right between her brows and her chin was in a state of confusion between square and pointed.

It wasn't a face that anyone could get lost in. It was a face that needed a splash of red on the lips, a little animation to give it some distinction. Right now, it would have to settle for some light base coverage, more mascara and a dab of berry lip-stain.

'That's better,' he said when Grace arrived at his table. She'd been all ready to make a dash for the front door, but there had been another smiling, murmuring woman stationed at the foot of the stairs to guide her into the room behind the big doors Grace had glimpsed before. The promised glass of champagne was waiting for her, along with her bossy abductor. He prodded the cleft in his chin with one long finger as she sat down with her knees tightly pressed together, back straight.

When she'd dressed this morning, Grace had been delighted with the bold seventies' floral graphic on her tunic dress. It was the perfect outfit for grubbing around all day in the fashion cupboard before spending the night crawling from one barstool to another. Now it clashed with the orange velvet of her over-stuffed armchair and made Grace feel less like she was working the Pucci revival and more like she'd failed the auditions to become a C-fucking-Beebies presenter.

'I really have to go back to work,' she muttered, glancing out of the window, almost unable to believe that there was a normal London street outside and not Munchkin Land. His amused smile, as if Grace was a performing seal with a beach ball balanced on her nose, was beginning to grate on her already frayed nerves.

'Don't be so silly,' he said lightly, as if going back to work was an alien concept. 'Drink your champagne.'

Grace decided to stay but only because she didn't want to struggle out of the sinking embrace of the chair like a demented Jack-in-the-box. Besides, she really did need a drink.

'I'm Grace,' she said, her voice sounding rusty as if she hadn't used it for weeks. He gravely shook the hand she was holding out, his fingers warm, brushing against her palm just long enough that she snatched her hand back.

'Vaughn,' he offered, before turning back to the menu.

'Is that your first name or your last name?'

He shrugged. 'Does it matter?'

It didn't really. Grace raised her glass in silent thanks before taking a sip. The bubbles, light and effervescent, evaporated on her tongue as she took three good swallows.

'I have no idea what *fleur de sel* or *grue nougatine* are,' he remarked conversationally as he looked at a menu. 'Do you?'

'*Fleur de sel* is just a fancy kind of sea salt and *grue* are pieces of roasted cocoa beans – don't know about the *nougatine* though. I like baking,' she added defensively as one of his eyebrows arched up because second male leads always had voluble eyebrows.

'Shall we just have chocolate cake instead? And tea. We should definitely have tea. But not Earl Grey, it's too watery. Darjeeling?'

Grace instinctively knew that there was no point in arguing. 'Darjeeling's fine,' she said, picking up her glass again.

All he had to do was raise a finger, quietly and unobtrusively, to have the waitress breaking the world speed record and start scribbling away his order for four different kinds of chocolate cake.

Grace crossed her legs as the waitress scurried away. The champagne was fizzing its way down to her empty stomach, making her restless enough to jiggle her ankle and wonder what, exactly, she was doing here making stilted conversation in a polite voice that didn't sound as if it belonged to her. Her stilted conversation was all used up now anyway, so Grace looked around her.

They were sitting in a room which seemed to have been imported straight from the kind of crumbling country manor that the BBC used for period dramas. There were mismatched chairs, some upholstered, some hardbacked, gathered around scratched and scarred but deeply polished tables, yet the whole effect shrieked money rather than genteel poverty. Maybe that was down to the clientèle. Grace glanced at the last stragglers from the lunch setting as they lingered over coffee and brandy as if they had all the time in the world and no recession to worry about. Nothing to worry about at all, in fact. Grace's gaze came to rest on Liam's crumpled pink envelope lying on the table and she couldn't help the tiny but heartfelt sigh that leaked out of her mouth.

'I'm glad that you're not crying any more,' Vaughn said, with one of those not-quite smiles. 'If you cry on your birthday then you cry every day for the rest of the year.'

'My grandmother used to tell me that too,' she confided with a not-quite smile of her own. 'Also, that it was bad luck to put new shoes on a table.'

'I think our grandmothers must have been related. Mine was quite evangelical about the dangers of chewing too fast.' It was freaky how he managed to affect such ease while pinning her down with that intent blue stare. 'So, how old are you today?'

'Twenty-three.'

When he smiled properly, Grace got an echo of what he could be. Younger, handsomer; someone that she'd get a totally inappropriate older-man crush on because he smiled as if Grace was the only other person in the world who got the joke. 'And on the twenty-third of July? That's very propitious. Did you know the number twenty-three is meant to have mystical qualities? There are twenty-three letters in the Greek alphabet, twenty-three seconds for blood to circulate around the body . . .'

'David Beckham was number twenty-three when he played for Real Madrid.' Great. Now she was talking utter shite. 'Not that it ended well for him.'

'Twenty-three is a good number,' Vaughn said emphatically, as a teapot and delicate doll-sized cups and saucers were reverently placed in front of them. 'This is going to be a very interesting year for you, I can tell.'

'Was twenty-three an interesting year for you?'

'Yes,' he said shortly. 'Will you pour? Milk, two sugars.'

Grace lifted the teapot and tested its heft before she carefully poured tea, added milk to the exact colour of a pair of American tan tights and dropped in two spoonfuls of sugar. 'Do people always do what you tell them to?' she asked, before her courage exited stage left. 'People never do what *I* tell them to.'

Vaughn peered critically at the cup she pushed towards him, then obviously decided that it met his exacting standards. 'By people, you mean your ex?'

She considered the question. 'Not just Liam. Everyone. People just push right past me like I'm not even there.' She shook her head. 'I'm sorry, I'm not usually like this. I mean, I'm not so mopey. I guess I've got a bad case of the birthday blues.'

'You just haven't learned how to make people take you seriously yet,' Vaughn said lightly, leaning forward. 'I find not saying please or thank you helps.'

'I'm genetically programmed to say please and thank you even when I'm not pleased or thankful.' And not to rest her elbows on the table or put the milk in first or any of the other life lessons she'd had drummed into her under the pain of death of her grandmother's most disapproving look. No weapon forged could defeat *that*. 'So, do you make a habit of abducting young women from department stores?'

'I was wondering when you were going to ask me that.'

'Well, I should probably have asked during the abduction but I was too freaked out,' Grace said just a little snottily, so Vaughn would know that she had some backbone.

'Anyway, I wonder if I could ask you for a small favour?'

The way he cut right across anything Grace said was annoying. Not as annoying as the sudden lightbulb moment that *this* . . . the being taken for tea and cakes and awkward chit-chat . . . had some sinister ulterior motive, which probably involved schoolgirl outfits, whips, and possibly a wife with lesbian tendencies while he filmed the whole shebang.

Grace dragged herself out of the voluminous depths of the chair as their cakes arrived. Which was a pity because the milk-chocolate tart looked deadly. 'I'm going,' she announced icily. Well, it had sounded icy in her head; the reality was a little more sullen. 'I know *exactly* what kind of favour you're talking about and the answer's no. A world of no.'

Vaughn flashed her a smile, which was bordering on a smirk. Grace was starting to dislike him in the way that she disliked Kiki, her boss, and Mrs Beattie, her landlord, and Dan, Liam's best friend, and a whole cavalcade of other people who looked at her with that same blend of sneering condescension. 'Be a good girl and sit down,' he said calmly. 'Haven't you caused enough scenes for one day?'

'Just who do you think you—'

'I saw you in Liberty's and decided that you were the sort of person who'd know her way around a French cuff.' He was already pulling a small, dark purple box out of his pocket as Grace snapped her mouth shut so quickly that she bit her tongue. 'I lost one of my favourite cufflinks this morning, popped out to buy some new ones and I think the least you can do after I've bought you a glass of champagne is help me attach them.'

Grace sank back down in an ungainly sprawl. 'How did you fix your cufflinks this morning then?' she asked suspiciously, because there was probably still a wife lurking.

'Ineptly,' Vaughn explained, holding up one hand so she could see an untethered shirtcuff. 'I'd be for ever in your debt.'

Grace risked an eye roll as she snatched up the Liberty's box and made a vague gesture in the direction of his arm. Vaughn lowered his eyes contritely, which Grace didn't find remotely convincing, as she slipped the pair of Paul Smith cufflinks, which were the same blue as her favourite denim mini she'd lost at Glastonbury the year before, neatly out of the box. Then she took his hand.

It was a strangely intimate moment. Grace scraped her chair forwards and awkwardly patted her knee so Vaughn could rest his hand on it while she gathered up the excess sleeve. She'd done things, countless things with countless boys under cover of darkness, then conveniently forgotten about them the next morning, but now, with her head lowered, Vaughn's pulse thudding steadily against her fingers, she could feel a blush staining her cheeks.

She did not have a father fixation. Or a thing for older men. Or the need for a strong paternal signifier. She was not that sad kind of cliché. No, she was just a girl having a bad day who'd drunk a glass of champagne on an empty stomach.

'All done,' Grace said crisply, pushing Vaughn's other hand away. He had beautiful hands – long-boned and elegant as if they spent most of their time conducting symphonies with lots of complicated arpeggios in them or performing delicate surgery on previously no-go parts of the brain. Though he had very knobbly wrists. 'I really have to get back to work,' she told him now, 'or they'll think I've been kidnapped.'

'Would you like a cake to take back with you?'

She really, really would. But . . . 'No, thank you,' she said primly, standing up.

Cutting her nose off to spite her face was a vocation with Grace. And she suspected that Vaughn knew it too, by the wry twist of his lips as he paused to admire his gleaming cufflinks. 'Well, I hope you enjoy what's left of your birthday,' he said, like he really couldn't care one way or another.

And now, Grace wasn't walking away but hanging back, the hem of her tunic catching against the arm of his chair. 'I shouldn't have snapped at you,' she blurted out. 'I'm sorry.'

'Another reason why people take me seriously is because I never apologise even when – no, *especially* when I should,' he told her coolly. 'No pleases, thank-yous or sorries – remember that and you might have that interesting year I was talking about.'

It seemed like the right time for a brisk handshake, but when Grace extended her hand, Vaughn bent his head and kissed it. It was a proper kiss, brief and warm, that made her pull her hand away with a grunted goodbye.

Grace took her bag, hurried through the room and down the long, red corridor until she was out on the street. She stood there for a moment to get her bearings. If she could feel the pavement under her feet and smell the exhaust fumes, then she wasn't dreaming. Through the big picture window, she could see Vaughn's tufty head bent over his plate of chocolate cakes. She hoped that he fell into a fatal sugar coma right there.

Vaughn suddenly looked up to catch her staring at him. He held her gaze until Grace felt the need to raise her hand in a limp wave. Vaughn didn't wave back, but kept on looking at her as if he was taking an inventory until it suddenly occurred to Grace that she could simply walk away.

Though she tried to ignore it, the place where his lips had touched tingled for the rest of the afternoon.

chapter two

The offices of *Skirt* magazine were on the seventh floor of a high-rise block at the southernmost end of Oxford Street, which looked like it should house a branch of the Civil Service circa some time in the seventies. Their distinctly shabby building was a source of much irritation to the staff of *Skirt*, who lived and breathed the magazine's mantra of 'Fabulous is a right, not a privilege'. Not only did they have to share lift space with the other magazines of Magnum Media's empire, a motley collection of teen mags and downmarket weeklies, but they were also on the wrong side of Oxford Street to pretend they worked in Mayfair.

'Oh, we're just round the corner from Selfridges,' was a phrase heard in *Skirt*'s huge open-plan office at least twenty times a day, but in reality Selfridges was a couple of blocks away and they were actually just round the corner from one of the largest KFCs in the country. It was a sorry blot sullying the view from the office windows but Grace didn't really care as she sat in the *Skirt* conference room. She was deciding that, if she had a superpower, it wouldn't be anything useful like the ability to turn people into stone for crimes against fashion, or the possession of a highly tuned spider sense to weed out boys with severe emotional problems. No, her superpower would be a telepathic gift to sense that she'd got stuck with the rickety swivel chair *again* and was nanoseconds away from hurtling floorwards.

Face flushing, she picked herself up off the floor and ignored the hissed 'What a *dis*-Grace' comments that the other members of the *Skirt* fashion team never tired of, even after two years.

'Did you have a good weekend?' asked Courtney, the bookings editor, who obviously wanted something done in the way of filing because normally she didn't much care whether Grace had had a good anything.

'It was OK.' Grace pulled a bruised banana out of her bag as Courtney delicately picked her way through a box of sushi that cost twenty pounds from the Japanese place next door. The truth was that she'd spent every waking hour since her birthday last Thursday either drunk or hungover. In fact, for one brief, unpleasant hour on Saturday afternoon, she'd been both. 'I went to this club and—'

'Sounds wonderful.' Courtney didn't even pretend to pay attention, but shook back her shiny blond hair. 'Do you notice anything different about me?'

Grace stared blankly at Courtney's face, which was the same as it ever was: all cheekbones and expensive dental work. 'Collagen filler?' she ventured timidly.

'No! I went to this amazing spa . . .' Ten minutes later, Courtney came to the end of her spiel about the freebie spa weekend that she'd won in a raffle at some charity ball, and gave Grace a rueful smile.

'Sorry, I bet you had an awesome weekend too,' she said, and looked thoughtfully at Grace's Primark blouse. 'That hard-times chic thing is so adorable.' Grace suspected that she was taking the piss but it was hard to tell with Courtney. She was an ex-pat American who didn't see anything morally reprehensible about voting Republican. Or telling people that she voted Republican. Or saying that she was 'post-humour'.

'Well, I did a test shoot on Saturday with a photographer's assistant and some Polish model.' Courtney didn't need to know that Sam and the model had got intimately acquainted in a toilet cubicle while Grace had been throwing up in a fire bucket. 'Then I went to this club in Hackney, where you can hook up your iPod to the sound system and they had this dance-off with the best tracks.' Again, Grace decided to gloss over the fact that she was the only person in the Western world who didn't have an iPod. 'And I got free tickets to the fashion exhibit at the V and A on Sunday and did some sketches of the Worth gowns.'

'Oh, we found some of those in the attic when Granny died,' Posy, the junior fashion editor, chimed in. 'Flogged them at Sotheby's.'

'You *auctioned* off a Worth dress?' The fashion department all winced in unison at Grace's shrill middle-class tones.

'You're such a fashion geek,' Posy wagged a chopstick reproachfully in Grace's direction. 'I've told you a million times that people only wear vintage if they can't afford new clothes or they have crippling death duties.'

There was a plethora of crushing retorts that Grace could have barked out but she contented herself with taking an angry bite of her manky banana as Kiki Curtis sailed into the room on a cloud of *Fracas* and bad vibrations. 'I've spent all morning in a merchandising meeting. Go and get me some lunch, Grace – a Caesar salad with a very light dressing and grilled salmon, not chicken.'

Kiki Curtis (though Grace had seen her passport and she'd been christened Kimberly) was the kind of brittle-thin, over-groomed fashionista who avoided direct sunlight and had never met a neutral colour that she didn't love. Grace had been recruited by Derek, the former style director after six months slaving away as an unpaid intern and getting paper-cuts from huge amounts of photocopying, filing and cutting up magazines. It had been the happiest six months of Grace's life because she also got to spend large parts of every day with her hands on silk, chiffon, duchesse satin and cashmere so fluffy and soft that she'd hold it up to her face and sigh rapturously. She'd probably have carried on working at *Skirt* for free, but a junior position had opened up and lovely, lovely Derek had given Grace an interview, which involved sending her out on a complicated coffee run. When she'd returned with his soy milk, bone dry, caramel *macchiato*, he'd given her the job on the spot.

It was strange when all your dreams came true. Or Grace's new dreams – because her old dream was to become the new wunderkind of British fashion but she'd screwed that up by abandoning her course at Central St Martin's days before her final degree show. But *still*, her new dream to become a super stylist like Katie Grand was the next best thing, and fashion assistant on *Skirt* was the first step. Grace could still remember the victory jig she'd done when Derek had told her she was hired. 'There was absolutely no one else I could even consider giving the job to,' he'd said, when he'd taken her for an alcohol-soaked celebratory lunch at The Wolseley. 'Stick with me, kid.'

Grace had stuck with Derek for a whole two days before he'd been suddenly poached by German *Vogue*. She'd been inherited by Kiki, who'd been trying to disinherit her ever since. *Skirt*'s famous 'no-fur' policy had lasted a week under Kiki's reign, but Grace was made of stronger stuff. Also, she was the only person in the fashion team who knew the postroom's extension number.

These days they had a simple understanding. Kiki made Grace's life a living hell with some abject misery served up on the side. And Grace took it like a dose of castor oil, because sooner or later, it had to be good for her.

Grace brandished her folder of ideas like a protective talisman in a to-the-death *Dungeons and Dragons* game. Her hands were still aching from wrestling with unwieldy Japanese fashion magazines the day before. 'I've got some ideas that I really wanted to put forward for the next issue.'

'Did you type them?' Kiki asked sweetly.

'Yeah, double-spaced like you told me to.'

'Well, as long as they're not written in your usual illegible scrawl, I'm sure we'll manage to decipher them somehow.' Kiki held out an imperious hand for the folder, which was making Grace's shoulders sag under the weight of all the tear sheets and sketches she'd painstakingly collated.

'But I really wanted to explain them myself,' Grace said doggedly. She was sick of being sent off on some low-carb errand, only to find that her ideas had been divvied up in her absence.

'Really, Grace, I think I can take it from here,' Kiki said firmly. 'You do what you're really good at and buy me lunch.'

There was a flurry of activity from all corners of the room.

'If you're going out, can you get me some organic chocolate, Gracie?'

'And I'll have some orange juice – make sure it's freshly squeezed but they've got rid of the pulp.'

'Oh, and I want . . .'

Grace snatched up some Post-its and started scribbling orders down. Even Bunny, the work experience girl, was getting in on the act. And Kiki could glare as much as she wanted, but no way was Grace adjusting her surly expression or her demands for cash upfront. If Lucie, the senior fashion editor, expected her to trawl the streets looking for organic Mexican chocolate then she could bloody well pay for it first.

Grace got back to the office in time for a riveting discussion about how nasty suburban girls shouldn't be allowed to ruin the Hermès brand name and how dear, sweet Bunny was super-keen to write something super-fun about fashion and how it would really raise her profile on *Cherwell*.

'Grace!' Kiki snapped, clicking her fingers for the salad container. 'I thought you'd gone all the way to Scotland to get that salmon. There's been no one to take notes – poor Posy had to do it.'

'Sorry about that.' Hadn't someone told her recently that she should never apologise? Mind you, *he* wasn't here to face Kiki's wrath. 'There was this queue out of the door, and then—'

'I have things for you to do,' Kiki decreed, and just for once Grace wished that someone, somewhere, would let her finish a complete sentence. Just once. 'We're done here anyway.'

Grace could already see that her tear sheets were resting on various laps. She knew young and hungry fashion obsessives were the lifeblood of any magazine, but she was still on £14,000 a year and getting hungrier by the week so she wasn't going down without a fight. 'I'd really like some feedback on my ideas,' she said to Kiki's pronounced shoulderblades, clad in the Michael Kors cashmere jumper that Grace had called in for her, as she exited stage left, her team trailing in her wake like a family of ready-to-wear-clad fluffy ducklings. 'You said you'd think about letting me style the accessories still-lifes for this issue.'

'Oh, we're getting Bunny to do that,' Posy told her brightly. 'Turns out that her godfather has a non-executive seat on the board. And she really is very visual for an intern.'

Bunny had to die, Grace decided as the other girl shot her a perky smile. 'I'd really like to set up a time to go through my ideas this week,' Grace insisted weakly. 'Your diary isn't too full.'

Kiki pursed her lips as much as the Botox would allow and Grace couldn't stop the heartfelt and desperate 'Please' that popped out.

'Oh, go on then,' Kiki capitulated, opening her office door with a slightly put-upon air. 'Ten minutes and then I want you giving Milan some serious phone. But first, let's take a moment to appreciate your ensemble.' Kiki collapsed elegantly on her big, squidgy leather chair and waved a hand in Grace's direction. 'Go on, talk me through it.'

Kiki's incisive analysis of Grace's outfits was a daily routine that Grace bore without a murmur of protest. She suspected that it was the main reason why she was still on the payroll. It certainly wasn't for her awesome styling skills. Grace put down her folder and obediently struck a pose.

'The blouse is from Primark. It cost seven pounds,' Grace said, and watched as Kiki shuddered from being in such close proximity to a cheap, poly-cotton blend. White T-shirts from Gap were as High Street as she went. 'And I made the tulip skirt from an old vintage dress because modern anti-perspirant tends to rot out the armpits.' Kiki twirled her index finger and Grace slowly rotated so she could get the full 360-degree view. 'The fishnets are from Tescos and these are Marc Jacobs flats I got on eBay.'

Kiki's eyes raked Grace up and down more thoroughly than any man ever had. 'Your fashion choices are very . . . *brave*,' she cooed, eyes glinting with malice. 'I knew there was a reason why I wasn't doing volume this season and I'm telling you this as a friend, Gracie, but that skirt is doing your arse no favours.'

Grace decided that Kiki's smug, satiated look meant she was done critiquing, so she placed her folder timidly on the desk.

'Well, these are very edgy,' Kiki finally remarked, gesturing at the fan of papers spread out on her desk. 'You might want to dial that down. We're doing that *Day in the Life of a Changing Room* idea as one of the main fashion stories – should get the ad department off my back. We're going to pretend a model wrote the piece about fashion-related injuries and we all loved the vintage idea. Maybe it could be shot on geriatric models – there are always a few lurking about from the fifties.'

Grace nodded eagerly to show that she was totally flexible.

She was so flexible that if Kiki wanted her to back-flip out of the office, she'd do it. 'Well, Posy's gran modelled for Hartnell back in the day, so I could call her . . .'

'But you don't have any shoot experience,' Kiki sighed, as if she'd been foisting shoots on Grace from day one, only to have them thrown back in her face. 'And now that little Bunny is going to be let loose on the accessories page . . . Well, you're going to be stuck with a lot of admin this month and I need you to file three months' worth of expenses before I miss the deadline. I do like that vintage story though. Maybe I could get Posy to shoot it. I'm sure she'd let you help her,' Kiki added kindly, opening the lid of her salad box and scrutinising the contents. 'We're shooting in New York next month and so if you're a really good girl and manage not to lose a very important Proenza Schouler dress *like you did last time* then I'll let you come along too.'

'One of the make-up girls stole that dress,' Grace muttered under her breath because God, when was Kiki going to let that drop? Then she realised that she wasn't focusing on the important part of Kiki's last sentence. 'I'm going to New York?' She had to will herself not to start clapping her hands in glee. 'You're taking me to New York with you? Oh God, that would be so cool. Thank you so, so much. I promise you won't regret it.'

'I'm regretting it already,' Kiki said, but there was a tiny smile just poking through the set line of her lips, like she appreciated Grace's genuflection. 'Don't think you're going to be swanning about the Village and stocking up on cheap Ugg boots, though. It will be hotel, studio, Starbucks, then back to the studio.'

'I know, but it would still be totally ace and I really appreciate you taking me with you. I mean, thinking about taking me with you,' Grace amended hastily at the warning glint in Kiki's eyes. She couldn't blame the woman though; Grace found her own breathy sucking-up equally irritating.

Kiki poked at the salmon with her fork. 'Well, we'll see. And I need you to call Paola in Milan and sweet-talk her into lending the feathered dress from the runway show. She seems to have a soft spot for you. Oh, and book a table at The Ivy for nine p.m. on Saturday night and send flowers to my mother-in-law for her birthday with a note that sounds as if I actually give a damn.'

'I'll get right on that,' Grace said brightly because she was going to be on her very best behaviour until she had her place on the New York trip locked down, though being perky 24/7 would probably kill her.

'Best assistant ever.' Kiki nodded regally. 'It's your own fault, Grace, you make yourself far too indispensable.'

'So if I was less good at my job, you'd let me shoot and write and get non-gutter credits?' Grace asked incredulously, as she straightened up the teetering pile of magazines on top of the filing cabinet. Kiki, for all her expensive beauty treatments, was a slob from way back.

'No, I'd give you a massive bollocking and if it persisted, I'd fire you,' Kiki said with too much bloodlust for a woman who hadn't eaten red meat since 1997. 'There are dues that need to be paid, Gracie. We've been through this. And you don't even have a degree, do you?'

'I *nearly* have a degree. I was two weeks away from getting it.'

'And then you fell at the final fence,' Kiki pointed out. 'Which doesn't exactly inspire confidence, especially as you've never managed to come up with an explanation which sounds even vaguely convincing.'

There was an explanation. Of course there was, but it wasn't one that Grace was going to share with Kiki. Not just because it was so private that she wouldn't even be able to stutter out the words, but because Kiki would bring it up at every available opportunity: that was the kind of thing she did. Grace would rather have Kiki think that she was a quitter than know the truth, though Grace had worked like a dog at St Martin's. There had been many, many times during her three years there that she'd wanted to throw it all in. There was the feeling that she didn't really belong; she wasn't like the other wannabe fashion designers in her year who all had unswerving self-belief, while Grace was riddled with self-doubt. There had been the three part-time jobs she juggled to try and stave the flow of money she was spending on rent and food and bolts of fabric. And there had been the harrowing day when she'd broken the overlocking machine and been chewed out by her entire class. But she'd stuck out her chin and stuck out the course until she was two weeks away from her final show. Ten outfits ready to send down the catwalk after months of draping and cutting and sewing and unpicking and starting all over again – and Grace had gone out with the puniest of whimpers for reasons that were nobody else's business but her own.

On the plus side, Grace would never be able to fuck up anything else as stupendously as she'd fucked up her degree. It just wasn't possible. Now she returned Kiki's malevolent glare with a completely blank face. 'It's been two years already,' Grace reminded her quietly. 'When will my dues be paid up in full?'

'When one of the other girls goes to *Vogue* or gets pregnant and I don't have some daughter of a board member or one of the landed gentry waiting to take her place,' Kiki snapped as she speared a cherry tomato and glared at it, her sunny mood clouding over for some inexplicable reason. Her face trembled with effort as she tried to pull her eyebrows together. 'And when you can actually get a lunch order right. I specifically told you no dressing.' She thrust her salad box at Grace, even though she'd already scarfed down half the contents. 'I can't possibly eat this. Get me some sunflower seeds and be quick about it. I'm getting a hunger headache.'

'You said a *light* dressing,' Grace insisted, snatching up the salad and considering the leftovers. Her banana really hadn't hit the spot. 'There were actual witnesses, you know.'

'If you argued less and worked a bit more, you'd probably be editor by now,' Kiki hissed, throwing the minutes of the last planning meeting at Grace. They missed completely but the point had been made. 'Now get out and close the door behind you. You've wasted enough of my time.'

chapter three

The fashion team sat right at the end of *Skirt*'s large open-plan office space; the fashion cupboard was a small, windowless room that extended into an L-shape behind them. After Liberty's, it was Grace's favourite place in the whole world, her little sanctuary where she was queen of all she surveyed – the groaning clothes rails lining the walls, shoes and bags carefully arranged under them, and the shelves above where she kept the accessories, from handfuls of brightly coloured tights and scarves and belts to plastic see-through crates crammed full of costume jewellery.

It had been a mess when Grace first arrived but now she had a system and the fashion team respected that system. Maybe respect was too strong a word but when Grace issued an edict about fashion-cupboard etiquette the rest of the staff listened to her. After months of lectures, they even wrote stuff down in the *Fashion Cupboard Book of Comings and Goings*. When they were doing a lot of shoots and there had been a lot of deliveries, there was only enough space in the cupboard for a maximum of two people, which suited Grace just fine. She'd mutter some vague excuse about 'doing inventory', which would make everyone else suddenly try to look industrious, and Grace was safe to shut the door and try on dresses.

After her pep talk with Kiki, Grace sequestered herself in

the cupboard, jumped up and down twice at the prospect of going to New York, then curled up in a corner so she could start pairing up wedge sandals. She was completely engrossed in her task when the door burst open with a loud bang.

'Gracie, did you tell me that you'd broken up with Liam?' Grace's best friend Lily demanded with her hands on her thirty-four-inch hips. 'I have absolutely no memory of it.'

'I told you on Thursday night.' Grace stashed the last pair of sandals under the day-dresses rail. 'But I was pretty drunk and you were absolutely hammered. I think I cried, though.'

'I remember you crying but I thought that was because you'd drunk too much vodka and you were regretting the black hair dye. Oooh, shiny!' Lily's attention was momentarily distracted by a pink sequinned shift dress, which she began to wriggle into over her jeans and Cacharel top. 'I was sure we talked about your hair at great length . . .'

'I was crying about being dumped but Liam dumped me because of my hair so I can see why you thought that.' Grace hadn't thought about Liam for at least an hour but it was already corralling the New York happiness to the furthest corners of her mind. 'Or he said it was my hair when we both knew it was just a lame excuse. Hey, Lils, I love you but if you keep trying stuff on without undoing zips, I swear to God, I will kill you.'

'Sorry! It's just so sparkly.' Lily stopped wriggling and stood stock still as Grace struggled to her feet so she could unzip the pink dress and carefully ease it down Lily's sylph-like frame. There was a full-length mirror against the one piece of wall that wasn't obscured by a clothes rail. Grace had spent hours tilting it by micro-degrees for the optimum flattering angle and now Lily smiled serenely at her reflection for a split second, then schooled her features into something more sympathetic.

'OK, I'm done. Now, back to this whole dumping thing. I

think Liam's regretting his extreme lameness. He seemed very angst-ridden last night before he went to the pub with Dan. I can't believe he dumped you on your birthday. That's just *rude*.'

'And did he tell you where he dumped me? In Liberty's – *and* he punched a Marc Jacobs bag in a fit of temper.'

'That's awful,' Lily breathed, eyes wide. 'Was it one of the new season's quilted totes? Why would he do that? Me and him are going to be having serious words. Oh poor Gracie, do you need a hug?'

Grace shook her head. 'I'm OK. But if you really wanted to make me feel better you could call me in some *Crème de la Mer* lip balm.'

'Consider it done. I'll get them to send over some hand lotion too,' Lily promised, and even though Grace had nixed the whole hugging thing, Lily gave her arm a quick squeeze.

There was something to be said for having a best friend who was a junior beauty editor. There was also something to be said for having a friend like Lily, though sometimes Grace felt as if they came from different planets. Maybe even different solar systems.

Grace could still remember the first time she saw Lily, because Lily's celebrity lookalike was Marianne Faithfull before the Rolling Stones had got their grubby paws on her. She had the most perfect silvery-blond hair, which owed nothing to Clairol and everything to really good genetics, and she'd been wearing a tiny gold dress that shimmered in the strobe lights. So when she saw Lily hanging out in the DJ booth at a little hole-in-the-wall club Grace used to go to in Hoxton, Lily had made an immediate impression.

It had been strange because after that, Grace had seen Lily everywhere she went: rifling through a box of button badges at the next stall along when Grace was working at Shoreditch market, buying a bag of Haribo Starmix at Grace's local Co-op, and even doing a sedate and elegant breaststroke at the

Gospel Oak Lido with her head at an odd angle so she wouldn't get her hair wet.

Grace didn't normally go in for girl crushes but she'd had an out-of-control pash on for Lily because Lily was the stuff of dreams. The kind of girl you wanted to be if you weren't the girl you were. But Grace had never even smiled at Lily, let alone spoken to her, until her first day at *Skirt* when she'd been skulking in the kitchen too scared to drink a cup of tea at the ramshackle intern desk in case she spilled it on some vitally important piece of paper, when Lily had strolled in.

'Hey, it's you! God, I see you everywhere I go!' Lily had yelped in her breathy Surrey tones, while Grace had stared at her feet and felt her cheeks heating up. 'Last time I saw you, you had the most adorable leather bag. Did you get it in Topshop?'

Grace had looked up to see Lily staring at her, blue eyes wide and friendly. 'I found it in a Cancer Research shop in Worthing,' she said shyly.

'Oh, you're one of those girls who have a freaky ability to source the really good vintage,' Lily had sniffed. 'I hate charity shops. They smell of old people who don't wash properly. We should do lunch and maybe if I sit next to you, I might absorb some of the vintage ability. Y'know, like a radio signal.'

It had been the start of a beautiful friendship, because Lily and Grace had everything and nothing in common. They were both lowly magazine assistants, but Lily's boss, the beauty director, adored Lily and regularly insisted that she accompany her to St Barts in the French West Indies to sip cocktails while they shot skincare stories.

Both girls had managed to run up thousands of pounds in credit-card debts, but Lily's father, owner of several successful used-car dealerships in Surrey, loved writing huge cheques so his little princess didn't have to put on a Polish accent and a quizzical expression when the bailiffs came round.

They both dated boys in the same band, but after three months, Dan had declared his undying love and moved into Lily's Tufnell Park flat, which her father had bought her, while Liam had just dumped Grace.

They both wore a size eight, but Lily had a super-fast metabolism whereas Grace couldn't afford to eat anything other than bananas and ramen noodles.

Yes, they were both the same. But different. And though Grace sometimes found it teeth-grindingly irritating that Lily was like some modern-day Pollyanna whose life was all puppy dogs and free spa treatments, she still couldn't believe how much she'd lucked out in the best friend lottery.

'So, if Liam realises that he's been an arsehole, would you get back with him? If he really grovelled?' Lily wanted to know, as she started wriggling out of the pink dress without unzipping it.

'Stop right there!' Grace growled, turning Lily round and sliding down the zip herself. 'Me and Liam are done. My three months were up. I'm, like, the queen of the three-month relationship.'

'Grace, don't go all dark side on me. One day you'll meet some foxy boy who'll worship the ground you walk on. Seriously. He'll get down on his knees to kiss your feet on a daily basis.'

'Does Dan kiss your feet on a daily basis?' Grace asked with a grin, as she made a concerted effort to shuck off her Liam-sponsored bad mood.

'Not yet, but I'm working on it.'

Lily's unwavering optimism was interrupted by the arrival of two guys from the postroom, wheeling in a trolley heaving with garment bags.

Lily clapped her hands in delight. 'New clothes!' she squealed.

Grace glanced at the trolley. The sight of an expensive cardboard bag with a designer name printed on it in an interesting font always perked her up no end. Perched precariously right on top was a gift box from Liberty's.

'This isn't ours,' she started to say because she hadn't called the press office . . . then she saw the label: *For Grace, aged 23 c/o* Skirt *Magazine.*

Curious.

Kneeling down, Grace placed the box on the floor so she could snip away at the taped sides with her scissors. Then she lifted the lid and burrowed through the tissue paper until she caught a glimpse of tomato-red leather.

Curiouser.

Grace's hands were shaking slightly now as she picked up the bag. The unfortunate Marc Jacobs bag which had been stroked, patted, punched, then wept over.

Even curiouser.

Maybe Liam had seen the error of his ways, knocked over a bank and was offering restitution. And maybe she was delusional. Grace ran reverent hands over the bag and her fingers closed round a piece of card tucked into the side pocket.

The tear stains have seriously compromised its resale value, someone had written in a slashing black scrawl. *Happy belated birthday. V.*

Vaughn. It had been four days since the strangest lunchhour of her life. Grace hadn't forgotten a single moment of her forced abduction but she'd been trying not to remember, because every time she replayed the memory of his unwavering stare, his cut-glass drawl, her stomach would lurch and she'd get the shivers.

She turned the card over.

J. Vaughn
Acquisitions Consultant

There was a Mayfair address and a mobile number prefixed by the international country code.

What the hell was an acquisitions consultant? An arms dealer? A white slave trader?

'Let me touch it!' Lily was already snagging the bag so she could see what it looked like hanging from her arm. Grace had to concede that it looked better. Everything always did. 'What story is this for?'

Grace looked furtively over her shoulder. 'It's not for a story. It's for me. From that guy.' Her voice was an urgent whisper to match the gravitas of the situation.

'What guy?' Lily asked shrilly. 'What guy has just bought you a one-thousand-pound Marc Jacobs bag? Why have you been holding out on me?'

'Jesus, Lils, you have to start remembering the stuff I tell you when you're drunk! The guy! The guy I met in Liberty's two seconds after Liam stormed out, who dragged me off for champagne and cake and was just . . . *weird*.'

Lily's face registered ten out of ten on the blank scale.

'He was wearing a Dries Van Noten suit,' Grace prompted.

'No! *Nuh-huh!* I would have remembered that.' Lily's inner turmoil was written in each wrinkle in her forehead, even though she'd sworn off frowning the month before as a last-ditch attempt against preventative Botox at the suggestion of Maggie, the beauty director. 'Wait! Something's coming back to me – something about cufflinks . . .'

'He asked me to help him out with his cufflinks,' Grace reminded her, as she started to tick off items on the post docket.

'Yeah? Then what?' Lily was almost vibrating with the need to know.

'Well, first he asked me to do him a favour and I thought he meant . . . well, I told him to fuck off. Well, I didn't actually say it but I got really snippy.'

'You give great snip!' Lily hung up the discarded pink dress on a spare hanger. 'Tell me everything and don't skip bits.'

There wasn't much to tell, Grace thought sadly – just a

handful of details, which had been rattling around her head like Smarties in a tube. But she couldn't wait to tell Lily every single one of them. Even if it was for the second time.

'. . . and he was the most obnoxious person I've ever met,' she finished ten minutes later.

'Even more obnoxious than Kiki, because surely that can't be done?'

Grace was forced to correct her last statement. 'It would be a photo finish as to which one of them was more obnoxious.'

Lily was now lying on her back with her legs in the air so she could work her core muscles while she listened. 'You have to admit, Gracie, it's a little bit sexy.'

'It wasn't sexy.' Grace's face was a perfect match for the bag. 'He was old.'

'George Clooney old or, like, Hugh Hefner old?'

'He wasn't as old as The Cloonster,' Grace admitted unwillingly, 'but he wasn't at all sexy. He was pointy. His face, the way he talked, and he just stared and stared at me.'

'At your tits?' Lily asked, sitting up so Grace got the full benefit of her horrified expression. 'What a perv!'

'Not at my tits. Just my face,' Grace said, covering that part of her body with her hands in an effort to cool it down.

'Well, I'd put up with some pointy creep staring at my face if I got a bag like that afterwards,' Lily sighed. 'Maybe it was birthday karma. The fashion gods sent you a Marc Jacobs bag to make up for Liam dumping you.'

'He wasn't a creep. Well, he was a little bit creepy. Oh God, I don't know. It was all completely weird with added bits of weirdness and there's no way I can keep the bag.'

'Why? Because you're worried that he'll turn up and want to do more than stare at your face as payment for the bag?' Lily giggled, because really the whole situation was ridiculous. Things like this didn't happen to girls like Grace.

Grace didn't giggle though as she waited for a wave of horror to knock her over at the thought of those long fingers on her, but no, she was still standing there on her own two feet.

'Nothing like that,' she insisted. 'I'm probably going to eBay it for some spare cash.'

chapter four

The bag went home with Grace in a Peacock's carrier.

It was like the designer equivalent of a heart buried under the floorboards. After Grace had wrapped it in plastic (a lesson learned the hard way after the damp in her flat had claimed a pair of Sass & Bide jeans as its first victim) and stashed it in her broken oven, which was doing time as an overspill accessories closet, she could still hear it. It seemed to emit a low-level static hum that left her twitchy and restless. As if something that had been asleep for a long time was slowly unfurling in the pit of her stomach.

For the next five nights, Grace would roll off her rickety sofabed and pad across to the kitchen so she could open the oven door and stare at the bag, as if it contained the mysteries of the universe. Not just a piece of card that she'd left in the side compartment.

It was still in the oven the following Saturday night. And even though Grace was six miles away from her flat in a grimy bar on the grimy Kingsland Road in the grimiest part of East London, it still had a freaky ability to make her palms itch.

'You haven't listened to a single word I've been saying,' Lily announced querulously, and it was true. Over the ironic strains of Bing Crosby coming from the DJ's decks, which were perched on orange crates, Grace had only caught every seventh word. *Chemical. Square. You. Directional.*

'What's directional?' she asked, trying to sit up and look alert even though the sofa was sagging to the floor and was determined to take her with it. She gathered her hair in a loose ponytail with one hand in the vain hope of a cooling breeze on her neck.

'Directions! I was talking about going to Bestival this year,' Lily said. Her forehead was damp with perspiration, which was a Lily first. Normally she didn't do anything as uncouth as sweat. 'But my dad has to give me a car with Sat Nav first. Remember what happened last year.'

Last year they'd ended up in Devon en route to the Isle of Wight. 'Yeah, Liam called me a stupid bitch because I screwed up the mapreading and we weren't even going out then. Remind me why I dated him again?'

'Because you fell in love with each other,' Lily explained kindly.

But that wasn't it. Not even close. Grace had fancied Liam and pestered Lily to set them up because he had dirty-blond hair and a dirty grin to match. (Once she'd got to know Liam, there had been dirty other things – like his standard of personal hygiene.) And he was in a band, which made up for a hell of a lot. Especially when they could curl up on her sofa on rainy afternoons and he'd strum Beatles songs on his guitar while Grace knitted and the rest of the world passed by outside. That had been nice, but it hadn't been love.

'I didn't love him. I *liked* him. A lot. Really a lot, for the first two months. Then I didn't like him quite so much but it wasn't bad enough for us to split up over it, you know?' Grace didn't wait for Lily to agree because when Lily was seeing someone, they usually swore their undying devotion within the first five minutes. 'Anyway, I don't believe in love. Never have done. Never will.'

'I've already told you that you just haven't met the right guy yet,' Lily said. 'And I don't think it will be awkward tonight if Liam turns up, because I really think he's been missing you. Well, he *seems* like he's been missing you.'

'Whatevs. If he does turn up then I need more alcohol than the human body can usually withstand. Hold that thought.' Grace fished around in her purse and came up with a handful of coins; none of them pounds. 'That's all I've got,' she announced sorrowfully, counting them out. 'Seventy-eight pence. Let's buy a bottle of wine and put it on my card.'

Technically Grace only had one credit card left out of the eight wedged into her purse that wasn't maxed out, but amid the scary brown envelopes that she never opened, there'd been a letter from a finance company offering her a shiny new one with only thirty-five per cent APR, whatever the hell that was.

Lily folded her arms and tried to look disapproving. 'Are you having money problems again?'

'When am I *not* having money problems? It will be OK. No one's phoning up yet . . .'

'And if they do, you just change your phone number. That's what I'd do if I was you,' Lily said blithely, as she stood up. 'I'm going to the bar. I'll get the drinks.'

'No, you always get the drinks,' Grace said doggedly, because if there was one thing worse than being broke, it was being tight. Anyway, she was used to being broke – the word had long ceased to have any meaning. And spending a tenner on a bottle of bad white wine wasn't going to make much difference to the ungodly amount of money she owed. 'Just take my card.'

'Gracie, I don't mind. Honest.'

'Lily, I appreciate the offer but take my card or else I'm only going to drink tapwater and you'll have to get pissed on your own,' Grace said triumphantly and slapped her card down on the table.

'God, you're annoying sometimes.' Lily scooped up the card with an aggrieved air because there was no truer sign of friendship than a shared pin number.

Grace watched Lily walk to the bar with an automatic

sway to her hips, which made every man in the place, even the too-cool-for-skool boys with their mullets and fugly trainers, look longingly at her like she was a Siren about to lure them on to the rocks and not a former Pony Club stalwart from Godalming who *still* couldn't pronounce Nicholas Ghesquiere's surname properly, no matter how many times Grace drilled her. Boys never seemed to care about stuff like that though.

J. Vaughn
Acquisitions Consultant

She wondered what the J stood for. Jeremy? Jonty? Jacob? Jonathan? Justin? Jezedbiah? Julian? Job?

Lily was flirting with the Aussie barman as Grace tucked her itchy palms under her arms and looked up. The door burst open and a crowd of people came in: a crowd of lanky-arsed, floppy-haired, unwashed people. And as usual, that first sight of Liam made her heart flip over because he really was pretty, but the stubble and the tattoos gave him a dangerous edge. God, the bad boys were Grace's kryptonite.

Grace steeled herself to smile faintly at Liam. She needn't have bothered. He was too busy attaching his mouth to the neck of a waifish girl wearing a ratty rip-off of the Alexander McQueen skull scarf, which, hello, was beyond three years ago.

'Gracie! How's life in the fashion fast lane? Let you out of the cupboard yet, have they?' Dan, Lily's boyfriend who was the Mick Jagger to her Marianne Faithfull, bellowed as he strode over and took the bottle straight out of Lily's hand before she could put it on the table. 'I'll get some more glasses, shall I?'

'Hey, baby,' Lily cooed, patting his bottom with a proprietorial air. Grace couldn't blame her – The Waif was travelling in a pack.

'This is Grace,' Liam said, sitting down and almost pushing her off the sofa so he could make room for his little friend. 'She's in fashion.'

Grace assumed a nonchalant expression as she was scrutinised by four sets of eyes all clocking her vintage Ossie Clark sundress and finding it sadly lacking.

'Nice dress,' Waify smirked. 'I think my mum has one just like it.'

'Oh, do you still live with your parents?' Grace asked sweetly. 'That's so retro of you.'

She got a glittering smile in return and then Waify played her winning hand. 'Well, duh. Of course I live with my parents, I'm only seventeen.'

'You utter, utter bastard! You replaced me with a younger model!' Grace screeched much, much later. Two bottles of wine and a really ill-advised burger from a dodgy kebab shop on York Way later. There had been a vague plan to flag down a taxi but the glowing orange light of an empty cab had been an elusive sight as they trudged past bleak industrial sites and even bleaker council estates. Still, it had given Grace plenty of opportunity to get her rant on. 'I had to sit there and slowly metamorphose into Patricia Routledge. What time is your curfew, young lady?'

'Who the fuck's Patricia Routledge?' Dan asked and Grace wished that he and Lily would piss off so she could scream at Liam in peace.

'Hyacinth – someone you don't know because you weren't brought up by two people in their seventies,' Grace snapped. 'And I was talking to Liam.'

Liam was staring at the peeling toe of his sneakers and looking as if he wished he had an elsewhere to be. No one had asked him to walk home with them, but Heather and her public-school posse had piled into a parental people-carrier so they could go home and braid each other's hair.

Or whatever it was seventeen-year-olds did for kicks these days.

'Have you fucked her?' Grace grabbed Liam's arm. 'Did you dump me because you're hitting that fashion-backwards teenybopper? It didn't stop you from trying to get into my pants last week, did it?' Being drunk really brought out her inner vicious bitch.

Liam obviously thought so too because he shook free from her grasp and gave Grace a thoughtful look. It was strange to see something pensive flash across his face for once. 'I've been trying to figure it out all week,' he said. ''Cause you're cool and stuff, but you know what? You really want to know why I broke it off?'

'Go on! Enlighten me with your amazing insights, Dr Freud.'

'It's because you're not any fun, Grace.'

'Grace *is* fun,' Lily protested loyally. 'She dressed up as a chav last Halloween, and that was hysterical.'

Dan was forced to agree, even though he wasn't Grace's biggest fan, because her shellsuit and Croydon facelift had been a comedic *tour de force*.

'We did loads of fun stuff,' Grace insisted as they crossed over Brecknock Road. 'I came round and baked you brownies. And, hello, I invented the *Ugly Betty* drinking game. And what about the time you played that gig in Brighton and we dropped some E and I made you go on the waltzers . . .'

Liam nodded dumbly as Grace gave him example after example of what a fun-loving girlfriend she'd been. 'Yeah, yeah, I know all that,' he conceded. 'But that's it. You're funny, but you're not happy.' He nodded again, a short, decisive dip of his head. 'You have no happiness in you, Grace. You just fake it.'

The four of them had come to a halt by a zebra crossing so they could watch the bus they should have caught sail past, making a faint breeze out of the hot summer's night so

Grace's dress fluttered against her legs as she felt the warm gust of the exhaust envelop her. The faint shrieks from a gaggle of drunken girls stumbling home echoed in her ears and she looked over Liam's shoulder at the City stretching out in the distance. She'd never get used to looking up at the London sky and not being able to see the stars, but the neon and the streetlights would do instead.

'You're the fake,' Grace said bitterly. 'You're just a lame, tenth-generation copy of Kurt Cobain in your dreams.'

'Why can't you two just kiss and make up?' Lily begged. 'You wouldn't be getting so mad if you didn't still care about each other.'

'The only thing I care about is the three months I wasted on him,' Grace sulked, taking a sharp left. 'Fuck this!'

Lily's hand was in hers before she could take another step. 'Come back to ours for tea and toast. You shouldn't walk home on your own.'

'I'll be fine,' Grace hissed so Liam and Dan wouldn't hear. She tried to pull free of Lily's hand but Lily just tightened her grip. 'I can't do this. I can't pretend that everything is OK and I'm not bothered about Liam being here, because I am. He dumped me so he doesn't get to flaunt his new girlfriend in my face then act surprised when I call him on it.'

'He could have handled it better but maybe he was just trying to make you jealous,' Lily whispered. 'Or he wants to be friends. That wouldn't be so bad, would it?'

'It would be beyond bad.' Grace succeeded in tugging her hand free and tried to smile to soften the blow. 'I just want to go home and be by myself for a bit. I still have at least a week's worth of wallowing time.'

'Are you sure? It's not really safe . . .'

Grace rummaged in her bag. 'Look, I'll have my keys in one hand and the rape alarm my gran bought me in the other.' She took a step away from the concerned expression on Lily's face. 'I'll call you later and I'll take a break from wallowing so we can go out for a fry-up.'

Another step, then another until there was a huge expanse of pavement between them. 'OK,' Lily agreed grudgingly. 'But you're still going the wrong way.'

Lily was right, but there was no chance of Grace retracing her steps and having to walk all the way down Brecknock Road with the three of them until they parted ways. 'I fancy some fresh air,' Grace lied, and finally Lily was nodding and she was able to walk away.

Going home via a three-mile detour to Kentish Town hadn't been one of Grace's better ideas, she thought as she finally reached Junction Road. As far as her grandparents were concerned, Grace lived on the 'Highgate borders' but actually Junction Road was firmly situated in Archway and was a great greasy smear of late-opening convenience stores, workmen's cafés and shops selling a variety of plastic household goods and non-brand detergents, even if it was hemmed in on all sides by Highgate and Dartmouth Park, which the estate agents of North London called 'charming enclaves' or 'bustling cosmopolitan villages' or 'in the catchment area for several outstanding local schools'.

Grace turned into Montague Terrace and ran the last few yards home just so she'd get there that little bit quicker, then slowed down so she could quietly open the front door and creep down the hall and up the stairs without waking Eileen on the ground floor.

Although Mrs Beattie, her landlady, charged Grace £140 a week for a one-bedroom flat, it was a bedsit with ideas way, way above its station. Grace had two rooms, which were meant to be separated by a screen door but it had shifted off its castors. One room was the kitchen and dining area but the stove was so old it had vents rather than gas rings, and the other room was where Grace slept on a sofabed, which threatened to give up the ghost each time she transformed it from bed to sofa or back again – it mostly stayed a bed.

The flat could have been lovely. It had high ceilings and a huge bay window behind her bed, but the damp had taken hold and wouldn't let go. The place had been freshly painted when Grace handed over her deposit, but now there were streaks of moisture staining the walls and mildew collecting on the insides of the windows, and Grace had packed all her worldly goods from clothes to books to magazines to handbags, in huge vacuum-sealed plastic storage bags so they wouldn't rot.

If she wasn't always six months in arrears with her rent, Grace could have found somewhere else to live, except she remembered the poky rooms in shared houses she'd looked at when Dan moved into Lily's and she'd moved out. Still, it would have been nice to have her own bathroom rather than sharing the one on the ground floor with Eileen and Anita and Ilonka, the Polish girls who had the flat above Grace's.

She could hear the two of them clumping up the stairs now as she realised that drunk and depressed had become sober and depressed and actually it was too cold to be standing in her underwear eating peanut butter straight out of the jar with a teaspoon. It was almost four in the morning and staying up so late that the dark was turning into smudges of light always made Grace feel the chill.

Grace licked the teaspoon thoughtfully and tried to find her happy place, though according to Liam she didn't actually have one. Liam wasn't big with the perception, but he'd half-glimpsed something that she thought no one else ever saw. A girl who drifted through life without ever touching the sides. A girl who didn't get the most cake, because she was something less than all the other girls.

Then again, there was a Marc Jacobs bag in her oven that said otherwise.

Maybe she hadn't sobered up completely. She definitely

had the early morning blahs. That's why Grace was opening the oven door, her phone clutched in the other hand. If he hadn't wanted her to call, then he could have just ixnayed on the business card.

And before she could pontificate on the wheres and whys and the absolutely spectacular *what-the-fuck-are-you-thinking-Grace?* she punched in the number.

The plan was that she'd leave a message. A breezy, insouciant 'thanks even though you don't do thanks' voicemail because . . . because . . . because it was rude not to.

'Hello?'

Grace took the phone away from her ear so she could stare at it in disbelief. Why was he answering on the first ring? That wasn't part of her plan.

The next 'hello?' was tinny and tetchy.

'Hi,' she said quickly, mind racing through possibilities of why he was up and why she was ringing before the cock crowed. Not that Archway had a huge number of crowing cocks. 'It's Grace. We met in Liberty's.'

'Oh yes, I remember.' There was a delay on the line, which threw Grace into even more confusion.

'I'm sorry to call you so late. I was just going to leave a message,' she babbled, her words sticking together in a garbled rush.

Vaughn gave the tiniest chuckle. 'It's not that late where I am.'

'Where are you?'

'In Miami, just coming back from a very boring business dinner.'

'For real?' Incredulity won out over breezy and insouciant.

'Yes, for real. I could stick the phone out of the car window to see if I can pick up some salsa music if you need proof.' Vaughn snickered again and God, Grace thought, this had been such a bad idea.

'OK . . . I'll take your word for it,' she said, flicking the corner of a postcard she'd pinned to the corkboard in the kitchen, as an alternative to hurling herself out of the window. 'Well, I just—'

'But it's very late where you are,' Vaughn continued, and now Grace remembered how he'd constantly interrupted her mid-sentence when she'd been sitting across from him in that red room. 'Why are you still up?'

'Oh, I only just got in and I wasn't ready to go to bed yet. Thought I'd catch up on my outstanding correspondence.' That was better. It was almost breezy and insouciant. 'So anyway,' Grace rushed on, 'how did you find out where I worked?' That two-second pause after everything she said while the fibre optics sent her words over two continents and several time-zones, made Grace feel as if her tongue was this cumbersome thing that had found its way into her mouth by accident.

'Would you buy that I put a tracing agent in your champagne? No? You had a very fetching security laminate around your neck,' Vaughn replied. 'What do you do on *Skirt* magazine?'

'Well, technically I'm the style director's assistant but mostly I live in the fashion cupboard.'

'In the fashion cupboard?'

'Yeah, the fashion cupboard. It's where we keep the, er, fashion.'

'And do you like it?'

'I love the fashion part but the cupboard bit, not so much. What do *you* do? I've narrowed it down to a weapons supplier or human trafficking.'

The chuckle upgraded to a full-throated laugh and Grace wondered what Vaughn looked like when he did that. 'Oh, it's much worse than that. I'm an art dealer.'

That would be Grace's cue to say something incisive and intelligent about the modern art world gleaned from all the articles she'd flicked through but not read in the *Evening*

Standard. But she was too busy nervously twisting her legs around each other, until she banged into the side of the fridge. She settled for a hesitant: 'Cool.' The two-second delay stretched to five and counting. 'So, like, anyway, I wanted to thank you for the bag but you don't do the thanks thing, so can I take you out for a drink sometime instead?'

Where the fuck had *that* come from? Vaughn was saying something and she didn't really want to hear what it was. 'You're offering to buy me a drink?' He didn't sound at all repulsed. 'That's . . . well, rather charming. You lower-middle-class girls do have beautiful manners.'

'I am *not* lower middle class,' Grace gritted immediately. 'I come from Worthing and my grandfather was a bank manager, for God's sake.' Vaughn laughed again and being mad at him made the nerves and the awkwardness melt away. 'I'm sorry, did I ask you out for a drink? I must have taken huge amounts of drugs at some point during the evening.'

It would have been easier to just hang up the phone instead of walking into the lounge/bedroom/ecosystem for mould and flinging herself down on the sofa, which creaked in protest, but Grace still hadn't figured out how to do easy. She also wished she hadn't got undressed because this wasn't the kind of conversation she wanted to have while she was wearing a pair of rainbow-patterned knickers and a bra that had been through the wash too many times.

'Are you pouting?' he asked.

'No,' Grace lied. 'And I take back the drink thing. Revoked. Never happened.'

'You can't take it back,' Vaughn said smugly. 'You said it, it's out there. I'm checking my BlackBerry right now.'

'Well, I'm going to New York the week after next so I'm very, very bu—'

'I'm in New York then too.' Of course Vaughn would be in New York too. He probably spent loads of time in New York; it was like a second home to him and he had a favourite deli, bought his cufflinks in Barney's, and he'd go to a New York version of the club he'd taken Grace to where all the staff knew his name and his favourite brand of champagne.

'I've never been to New York before,' Grace heard herself confess haltingly, because there was something about Vaughn that made her feel so nervous that she just blurted out the first thing that came into her head.

'Well, how fortunate that our schedules have us there at the same time,' he said smoothly. 'Fine, we'll do drinks there if you can find a window in between doing the Circle Line tour and trying to find the Empire State Building. Where are you staying?'

And Grace had just been imagining that her gaucheness was going to pass unnoticed. 'Did you hear what I just said about the drinks thing being totally revoked?'

'Give me your exact dates.'

'God, you're pushy.' Grace sighed without much bite, because there was something to be said for a man who got what he wanted and didn't just wheedle and whine until she did it for him. Like, say, Liam.

'Determined,' Vaughn corrected firmly. 'Dates: sometime before the end of the year would be preferable.'

Grace rattled off the relevant information after a few false starts because Kiki had been changing the dates and times on an hourly basis. 'I probably won't return your calls,' she warned him. 'Just so you know.'

'Of course you won't,' he agreed cheerfully. 'It's very late, you should get some sleep. Being tired obviously makes you cranky.'

And then he rang off before Grace could give him an example of just how cranky it made her.

chapter five

When she was little, Grace used to think that there really was a big apple hidden somewhere in New York. She imagined a maze in Central Park, and glowing somewhere right at the very heart of it was a golden apple waiting for her to take great, sweet bites of it.

But she was older now. Not wiser, but definitely jaded. She knew that the golden apple of her childhood was false advertising, but still it would have been nice to get to Central Park and see for herself. And it would have been even nicer to do all the touristy things that Vaughn had sneered at, like taking the Circle Line tour or falling down on her knees and kissing the ground outside Bergdorf Goodman and eating cupcakes at the Magnolia Bakery and going drinking at this bar that was styled like a fifties beauty parlour and all the million other things that Grace had promised herself she'd do when she finally took Manhattan. But the only remotely touristy thing she'd done was to see the steam rising up from the manhole covers just like it did in the movies and be verbally abused by numerous cab drivers as she forgot which way the street numbers ran.

So far, New York had been three days of fetching, carrying, faxing and phoning. That was usually before Grace even got to whichever studio they were shooting at. Then she'd steam clothes, coo over skittish models and put out every single one of Kiki's fires. Grace had already resigned herself to the fact that her boss's voice would never register below a scream for the duration of the trip.

Grace was currently star-fished on the roof of the Industria Studio Complex in the Meatpacking District, which was the centre of the NY fashion universe and only a hop and a five-minute dash to the Marc Jacobs shop on Bleecker Street in the West Village, not that Grace had visited its hallowed portals. And she was also smoking, because she'd had to hurl herself back into the loving arms of the Marlboro Lights as an alternative to a stress-induced heart attack. It was either that or crying – and Grace knew that once she started, she wouldn't be able to stop.

The day had got off to a good start. Grace had loved the cavernous space that was Studio 5 with its vaulted ceiling and the sun beaming in through the huge skylights. It even had a decent-sized dressing room and not the usual alcove with just enough room for a clothes rail and a really skinny model. Kiki had a breakfast meeting so Grace could wolf down several cherry Danishes without being screamed at for having grease smears on her fingers. And Michael, the photographer's junior assistant, was a foxy, tousle-haired boy who recognised her as a kindred spirit from the global put-upon assistants' club.

Even the huge number of satin dresses that had all needed to be painstakingly steamed to get the creases out couldn't put a damper on her day. The stereo had blared early Motown, Michael had totally been checking out her arse in her skinny jeans; all was right in Grace's world.

When Grace had first started coming to shoots, she'd been amazed at the vast number of people involved. Then she'd been amazed that they didn't actually do any work but lounged on the leather sofas that every photo studio had, drinking coffee and leafing through German fashion magazines. Today was no exception. There were two make-up artists, two hair stylists – none of whom had even opened their cases. The photographer had two assistants. There were three guys from the studio fiddling with Coloramas and computers. Two catering assistants. One handyman. And a fat bloke in a baseball cap who'd wandered in and started making himself a sandwich but didn't seem to have anything to do with anyone.

The day had started to career downhill soon after Kiki had arrived and proceeded to spend hours arguing with the photographer over the position of a teeny, tiny sidelight. Grace had made a mental note to keep out of her way as she wrangled the models: three lanky teenagers who had collective annual earnings of £5 million and about five brain cells apiece. Grace had spent the next couple of hours on her knees pinning hems, helping them on with their shoes and holding mobile phones and cigarette lighters and generally genuflecting at regular intervals.

It was the same old, same old, but at least Grace was doing it in New York, rather than in some draughty studio on an industrial estate near King's Cross, which automatically made it more exciting. Even when one of the models had a high-volume argument with her boyfriend on her iPhone, then locked herself in the toilet, Grace had managed to keep her cool. Or rather she'd got Lucie to coax the girl out with the promise of some Xanax, after all of her own pleading and threats had fallen flat.

Finally there were no more frocks left to steam, no more models to pander to, and Grace had just been looking forward to sitting unobtrusively on one of the sofas so she could watch the shoot, when Posy had hurried over with a grim look on her face. 'Gracie, Kiki wants you,' she said urgently. 'There's a problem with one of the Marchesa gowns.'

The words 'Kiki' and 'problem' in the same sentence didn't bode well. Grace hurried into the dressing room to find Kiki tapping the floor with one pointy toe. 'What colour is this?'

she demanded without preamble, carelessly grabbing a handful of dress that Grace had spent ages steaming.

'Red?' Grace asked uncertainly, because Kiki liked trick questions almost as much as oxygen facials.

'It's not red – it's scarlet.' Kiki thrust the dress at Grace. 'I told you to call in the crimson!'

'It is the crimson,' she said, without first weighing up the pros and cons of disagreeing with Kiki. 'It looks scarlet but it photographs as crimson. I had a whole discussion with the publicist about it.'

'It's not the same dress I specifically marked in the LookBook,' Kiki growled, which was a nice change from the continual screaming. Maybe that was why Grace was lulled into a sense of false security and kept making words come out of her mouth. 'It's practically orange when I wanted a bluey red!'

'Look, it's got the same beading on the bodice,' Grace enthused eagerly. 'Same gathers, even has the pleating detail at the back. It's Number Seven in the LookBook – I'll show you.'

'Are you arguing with me?' Each word was an ice cube tumbling down Grace's back. 'I just wanted to be clear, because after two decades in fashion, I think I know the difference between crimson and scarlet.'

'I'm not saying that you're wrong,' Grace clarified quickly, when actually she should have just shut the fuck up. 'Just that the dress photographs a different colour, and if you let me get the LookBook . . .'

Grace had been one nanosecond away from rummaging on the counter for the right brochure, only to be stopped in her tracks by a box of costume jewellery flying through the air. She just had time to think that Kiki normally had too much respect for Kenneth J Lane to use any of his pieces as projectile missiles, then she'd ducked.

It was too late. A chunky ring had glanced off the bridge

of her nose and a bracelet narrowly missed her right eye, but a turquoise, tendrilly necklace hit her square on the cheek. The sharp edges of the strands whipped and scratched enough to surprise a squeaked, 'Fuck!' out of Grace as the necklace clattered to the floor in several separate pieces.

Kiki had the decency to look ever so slightly shocked as Grace clutched her cheek and felt something wet coat her fingers. Kiki might have looked even more shocked if she hadn't had her biannual Botox a week before. 'Oh, don't look at me like that. It barely touched you,' she said in a voice that wasn't quite so filled with loathing. 'I really can't deal with you right now, Grace.' She stalked out and left Grace staring in dismay at her bleeding face in the mirror. It wasn't a gushing wound that required stitches but it still counted as actual maiming.

'Shit! Are you all right?'

Grace turned to see Posy standing in the doorway with a gratifyingly horrified expression on her face.

'It doesn't matter what kind of bloody red that dress is. She'll get one of the art team to Photoshop it anyway.'

'I know, I know.' Posy was all right when the rest of the fashion team weren't around. She gave Grace a quick, surreptitious hug. 'You know Kiki really gets her bitch on when she's shooting.'

'God, I always have to open my big mouth and make a bad situation even worse,' Grace lamented. 'And now I'll have to call the press office and tell them that we've damaged some of the jewellery.'

'Actually, Gracie, I think you'd better stay out of Kiki's way for at least an hour,' Posy advised. She rummaged through the debris on the counter top. 'Look, take my ciggies and make yourself invisible for a while. I'll get Lucie to talk Kiki round. I think she's got some more Xanax.'

And so there Grace was, lying on the roof with gravel digging into her back as she tried to remember how to blow smoke rings. She wasn't going to be allowed to watch the shoot now, which sucked. Sometimes she thought it was the only part of her job that she liked, apart from the clothes, which never argued back.

Grace loved standing on the sidelines, watching the nuts and bolts of the production – the ornate sets they built which were usually held together with staples and sticky tape, the models seamlessly switching poses in clothes that she'd painstakingly steamed and pressed, the photographer seeing something extraordinary through the camera lens that wasn't apparent to anyone else. It all seemed like a lot of effort for not much and then Grace would sneak a look at the Polaroids and there would be this fantasy, fairytale world of beautiful girls in beautiful outfits. And she'd remember why she was sticking this out; so far down on the fashion food chain that she wasn't even an amoeba – maybe just the waste product of an amoeba. But one day, if she was really good and managed to get out from under Kiki's Prada jackboot, she'd be the one who made the fairytales happen. The one who got to sprinkle magic dust over the whole mind-numbing process. Who'd create these inviolate, unworldly images so that girls like she used to be would rip out the magazine pages and stick them on their suburban bedroom walls and to hell with the Blu-Tack stains.

Grace drifted back from her very favourite daydream, the one where she shot couture at a Roller Derby, to find her phone ringing. If it was Kiki or someone else from downstairs bitching about *anything*, she was going to order a bottle of Valium and some razor blades on room service when she got back to the hotel, and expenses be damned.

She groped for it one-handed. '*What?*'

There was a startled cough. 'Grace? It's Vaughn.'

Grace sat up as her mood went from dejected to excited to nervous and back to excited in nanoseconds. 'Oh! Hey! Hi! How are you?'

'All the better for you sounding so pleased to hear from me.'

Grace turned on her side, so she could roll her eyes more effectively without sun glare. She really had to start engaging her brain cells before she opened her mouth. 'Been to any good gallery openings?'

'One or two and several very bad ones. Talking of which, are you free tomorrow night?'

'Hang on,' she mumbled so she could light another cigarette and not check her schedule. 'What's happening tomorrow night?'

'You owe me a drink and then I'm going to take you to dinner,' Vaughn said smoothly. 'Maybe Pastis – I'm not sure what I'm in the mood for right now.'

Grace didn't want to be impressed, but she so was.

'But first, there's an exhibition opening. It will probably be dull as mud, but that can't be helped.'

There was another pause because for the life of her, Grace didn't know how to respond. This kind of situation had never come up before.

'So, Grace, how's your diary looking?'

She made some rapid mental calculations. A friend of a friend's boyfriend was DJ-ing at a bar in Williamsburg, which meant no free food and one comped drink if she was lucky. 'Well, maybe I could shift a couple of things around,' she hedged, because she didn't want to sound too eager.

'Good. I'll pick you up at eight,' Vaughn said. 'It would be helpful to know where you're staying.'

Something was seriously wrong when Grace couldn't muster a snappy comeback. 'Soho Grand,' she answered dully. 'Y'know, I could just say thank you for the bag and then we wouldn't have to—'

'I'll see you tomorrow then.'

Half an hour later when she was enjoying her enforced exile to the dressing room and silently contemplating the chipped polish on her big toe, she realised he hadn't even waited for her to say yes.

Yesterday, the cut on Grace's cheek had simply been an angry red mark, but during the night it had scabbed over nicely. The thing that made it the best wound in the history of work-related accidents was the look of horror on Kiki's face the next morning as she stared at it in all its crusty glory.

'I just wanted to thank you for all your hard work this week,' she said carefully, both eyes fixed firmly on Grace as if she expected her to bolt at any loud noises. 'You've really been a star.'

Kiki was never going to apologise – she just didn't roll that way – but this was the closest she'd ever come and Grace was going to savour every last sweet second of it.

'Just doing my job.' Grace absent-mindedly reached up to prod at the cut with the tip of one finger and allowed herself one tiny, ouch-laden shudder. Anything else would have been overkill. 'So, what dresses do you want for the first shot?'

'Why don't we get Posy to do all the prep work and you can help me with the styling?' Kiki suggested, as she patted Grace's shoulder without visibly wincing. 'And I want you out of here no later than five tonight. You deserve some time off.'

Grace had had many hours to whip herself into a state of near-hysteria about spending the evening with Vaughn. The sheer giddy thrill of wining and fine dining had slowly ebbed away to be replaced with white-knuckled terror at the thought of Vaughn staring at her and making sarcastic remark after sarcastic remark while she babbled and burbled. Finally at dawn o'clock, Grace had come to the happy conclusion that Kiki would have her slaving over a warm iron all day and most of the night too, and she'd have no choice but to leave Vaughn an apologetic message and bail on him. Because assignations with arrogant older men were one thing when they led to Marc Jacobs bags, but a dinner date was something else entirely – and who knew where *that* would lead. Nowhere good.

However, Kiki was as good as her word and as the studio clock edged towards five, Grace was frog-marched out of the door by an indignant Posy.

'Kiki says you have to go now,' she informed Grace sourly. 'And I have to pack up all the returns. God, I wish she'd inflict GBH on me occasionally!'

Grace tried to keep the fear at bay as she swiped at her legs with a razor, while she lay up to her neck in Malin+Goetz's bergamot-scented bubbles. At least she was getting a night out in New York instead of returning clothes to designers' ateliers until the only place that was open and that she could afford was the Duane Reade on Broadway where she'd buy a bag of Doritos and a jar of salsa dip for dinner. So why not get gussied up and have her first square meal in six days and get to see the bright lights of the big city in the company of an enigmatic and not-so-bad-looking man who probably didn't even look at the prices on the menu? Why the hell not? And just like that, she was excited all over again.

Half an hour later, Grace stepped back to stare down her reflection in the mirror. Her dress for that evening was a raspberry chiffon number from Moschino Cheap & Chic, which she'd 'borrowed' from the rail of shoot clothes in her room. It was a demure, polite frock in theory. But there was something special about designer dresses that could silk purse even the most pig-like of ears. It rippled down Grace's body, which hadn't seen the inside of a gym for several months, skimmed politely over her tummy and clung gently to the curve of her hips in a way that was suggestive and promising. But not, repeat not, slutty.

Even the colour did wonders for her skin, transforming it from bedsheet white to the creamiest shade of porcelain. Or maybe it was just the lighting in the room. Her hair was already pinned up with a handful of sparkly clips so Grace concentrated on applying a sweep of liquid eyeliner and some lipgloss that was exactly two shades darker than the dress. If she wore anything brighter, then Vaughn was bound to get the wrong idea.

But ultimately this Grace was just a reflection in a mirror. In reality there was tit-tape sticking the bodice to her chest so Grace didn't flash her Love Kylie bra at the wrong moment, while her feet were being crunched into a shape they weren't meant to go by her peeptoe heels. It wasn't very feminist, but Grace fervently believed that a girl had to suffer to look this good.

The phone suddenly rang and Grace's stomach slam-dunked at the prospect of what might happen in the next few hours, but as long as she kept it light and frothy and managed not to say anything stupid, what could possibly go wrong? Grace scooped phone, lippy and purse into her vintage clutch bag and at precisely 8.01 p.m., the lift doors swooshed open and she stepped out into the lobby to find Vaughn waiting for her.

chapter six

Vaughn was a little taller and leaner and scarier than she remembered. Maybe it was the slim-cut charcoal suit and black shirt, which made him look grim and forbidding. Or maybe it was just the way he stared at her, head tilted, without saying a word.

'Hey, it's me,' Grace said uncertainly as her eyes swept over Vaughn's unsmiling face. Considering she'd been wearing Primark and tear stains the only time they'd met, maybe he didn't recognise her.

'I know it's you,' he murmured, stepping forward to graze her cheek with a barely there brush of his lips. Grace took a hasty step back to get away from him and the faintly disconcerting scent of limes.

She was meant to be light and frothy, not skittish. Grace clasped her hands in front of her and gave him a cool smile, even as her heart thumped out a warning tattoo. 'Do you want your contractually obligated drink first or do we have to be at this exhibition thingy soon?'

'Drink first, exhibition thingy second,' Vaughn decided, finally smiling as he spread his arms expansively. 'So where are you taking me?'

Somewhere she could put the bill on her room tab and swear blind, even under the toughest interrogation, that he was a fashion PR. Grace pointed at the stark metal steps. 'Hotel bar,' she said firmly.

Vaughn's hand was already curving around her elbow so he could guide her up the stairs as if she was a delicate flower of a girl who couldn't walk unaided.

'How did you get that cut on your cheek?' he asked as they walked into the lounge.

Grace marched determinedly to the bar, ignoring the plump, cosy sofas and chairs in favour of hauling herself up on to one of the stools. 'There was this whole thing with a box of costume jewellery,' she said vaguely. 'It looks worse than it is. What do you want to drink?'

It wasn't so bad. *He* wasn't quite so bad as they sipped vodka martinis, so dry that the first taste made Grace's tongue recoil in horror. If she was light and frothy, then Vaughn had decided to be charming and urbane. They talked about the weather because they were English people abroad. Then they talked about New York. Vaughn mentioned an apartment with a view of the park and an ancient next-door neighbour who was one of the Kennedys and never went out without her sable coat, 'even when it's ninety degrees humidity like today'.

And Grace told him the thing she liked most about New York so far. Which had been her first glimpse as she drove along the BQE and looked over the water to see the tiny island of Manhattan, rising up from the Hudson like some mythical, enchanted forest of skyscrapers and neon.

Grace was just munching on the three olives she'd begged from the barman in a futile attempt to mop up some alcohol, when Vaughn slid gracefully off the stool. Not that he had far to slide.

'Shall we?' he said, taking her arm again and this time it didn't feel so strange. Besides, men with good manners who held doors open for you and walked on the road side of the pavement were a dying breed.

There was one startling moment of damp heat as they stepped outside before Grace was nestled in the back of a sleek expensive car on soft leather seats with the air conditioning turned up so high that she could feel goose-bumps hatch along her arms. Vaughn slid in next to her because he had a driver. An actual driver. In an actual uniform. Man, if the folks back home could see her now.

'Where are we going?' she asked, a hint of suspicion creeping into her voice because she hadn't entirely ruled out the human-trafficker idea.

'Chelsea,' Vaughn sighed. 'I always end up in Chelsea in some poky little gallery drinking rancid white wine. Now, there are some things you need to know.'

He started to give her a rundown on his resumé. A gallery in London. A gallery in New York. Up-and-coming artists 'nurtured and mentored', as if they were little furry pets who'd been abandoned by their birth mothers and had to be bottle-fed by Vaughn. 'They're so needy,' he complained. 'Especially the older ones. The younger ones have business managers before they've even graduated.'

When he wasn't hand-rearing artists, he bought and sold art for private clients and collectors, and advised several museums and national galleries. He obviously did it very well, if the chauffeur-driven car and the whimsical purchase of Marc Jacobs bags was anything to go by.

Grace cast her mind back to her Art History A-level, but all she could remember was the drone of Mr Mortimer's voice as she'd ignored the words in her textbooks and looked at the pretty pictures. Vaughn must have noticed the rising panic she was giving off like white noise because he gave her a reassuring smile and squeezed her fingers so briefly that when she looked down at his hand, it had already gone. 'The whole world seems to know that I'm in acquisition mode at the moment so I need you to do one thing for me,' he said calmly.

'I won't have to bid on anything, will I?' Grace asked uncertainly.

'No, no, nothing like that,' Vaughn said. 'If I get cornered by the gallery owner or, God forbid, the artist and his agent, you have to rescue me. I'll tap my chin and you can come rushing over and spirit me away.'

Actually, that sounded like fun. She could even use a foreign accent and play up the part of the spoiled girlfriend. 'I can do that.' Grace grinned, turning to him. 'I give really good glare.'

'You do,' he agreed. 'But when you smile properly, then you're very beautiful.'

They were already nudging into 23rd Street so Grace didn't have to reply. The car pulled up to the kerb and instead of scrambling out like she normally did, Grace waited for the driver to open her door and as she stepped out, Vaughn was there to take her arm again and carefully lead her up the six steps to the gallery entrance.

The second that they entered Blax Gallery, the excited hum of opening night became an expectant silence, as if someone had suddenly pressed a cosmic mute button. Grace looked up and saw a sea of curious faces, sliding right past her to fix on Vaughn.

'Anyone would think they'd never seen an art dealer before,' he muttered in her ear, his hand around her wrist as he strode into the room. 'Let's be daring and actually look at the art.'

'Are you well known?' Grace ventured, stepping around a rapier-thin blonde woman who was making absolutely no attempt to stop staring at Vaughn and get out of her way.

'I'm very good at what I do,' he said simply. 'And that has its advantages and disadvantages.' They were fighting through the jostling epicentre of the crowd now to get to one of the far walls so they could look at the pictures. Vaughn grabbed two glasses of wine from a waiter holding a tray aloft and handed one to her. 'Remember if I make the signal, you're to come and extract me,' he warned her before he was swallowed up into the gaping maw of the throng, leaving Grace on her own and utterly out of her depth. There was only one way to get through this and it wasn't sober.

Vaughn was right. The wine was gross. It left an oily aftertaste in Grace's mouth as she squinted at the tiny pictures hanging on the wall. They were bigger than postage stamps; not as big as an iPod shuffle. With all the art groupies milling about and push, push, pushing because they were New Yorkers and it was their God-given right to annexe as much space as they could, it was hard to get a proper look. Grace even resorted to elbows when she was boxed in by two plastic-faced trophy wives screeching about the macrobiotic diet responsible for their size double zero figures.

Vaughn was really tall. She hadn't realised that before, because when you were five feet three inches everyone was tall – but she could see wheat-coloured tufts of hair bobbing above the crowd and she made sure to keep him in her eyeline as she replaced her empty glass with a full one. He might claim to hate snobby art openings but Vaughn sure knew how to work a room: shaking hands, kissing cheeks, face all smiles as he clapped a short, sweaty man in glasses on the back.

Vaughn didn't look like he needed rescuing; he looked like a man who'd executed a sneaky cut and run on her. During the third glass of wine, which was becoming more palatable the more that she drank, she saw him press a finger to the cleft in his chin. He did it so casually that at first Grace thought it was an involuntary gesture. But then he did it again, eyes scanning the room. Besides, the woman clinging to his arm didn't look like she had much truck with personal space boundaries.

Grace took a step towards them. In her head she had a Russian accent all good to go, but as soon as she opened her mouth, she realised that it sounded more Mumbai than Moscow so she settled for giving Vaughn a sharp poke in the ribs with her clutch. 'I'm hungry,' she said plaintively. 'You promised me dinner.'

Vaughn's eyebrow winged all the way up to the ceiling as he

slowly tried to raise the arm that the other woman was clamped to. Reluctantly she let go, so he could wrap it around Grace's waist and pull her gently towards him. 'There you are, darling,' he said. 'I'd almost given up on you.'

OK, she was halfway to hammered, which had to be why Grace leaned against Vaughn and brushed a proprietorial hand over his jacket lapel. The woman, another emaciated forty-something in an understated black dress with hair practically the same colour as Grace's Marc Jacobs bag, smiled thinly. 'I don't think you've introduced me to your new girl.'

New girl? Did she think Grace was an office junior that Vaughn had taken on to help with the filing? Grace looked pointedly at Vaughn in the hope he'd correct the woman pretty damn sharpish. Instead he said, 'Deirdre represents Ben Myers.' Who the hell was Ben Myers? 'Deirdre, this is Grace, she's in fashion.'

Grace extended a hand and had it almost crushed between Deirdre's skeletal fingers. 'What do you think of Ben's work?' Deirdre asked, gesturing at one of the micro-sized portraits on the wall behind them.

The seconds passed with agonising slowness – only Vaughn's thumb rhythmically stroking the indentation of her waist anchored Grace to the spot. 'Well, they're kinda small, aren't they?' she said finally.

'That's because they're miniatures,' Deirdre sniffed. 'Ben's reclaiming them as a vibrant twenty-first-century genre.'

What*ever*. Through the alcoholic haze, Grace dimly remembered an essay she'd written on *The Practical Uses of Painting Before the Twentieth Century*. 'But, hey, weren't miniatures meant to be carried about?' she asked. 'Like, they were the camera phones of the olden days, y'know?'

She was slurring her words, but Vaughn's hand was still smoothing down the material of her dress so he couldn't be that pissed off with her, even though Deirdre looked like her face had just been coated in hydrochloric acid.

'And your point *is*?' the woman asked.

'Well, they're just, like, really *small*.' Grace tried to tap the tip of her nose and nearly poked her fingernail in her eye. 'I had to get *that* close to work out what was going on, and—'

'Look, Deirdre, if Ben started to work on a larger scale, I'd love to have another look,' Vaughn added. 'But Grace is right. Can you imagine any gallery letting the public get so close to the exhibits? And we both know that most private collectors prefer something a bit more showy.'

Deirdre gave Grace an all-encompassing once-over. 'I'm giving you the opportunity to get in on the ground floor,' she said, though her gimlet gaze was still locked on Grace, as she paused deliberately. 'After all, you have a wonderful talent for . . . smoothing out the rough edges.'

Somewhere in there was a major diss aimed directly at Grace, as if Deirdre had X-ray vision and could see right through Grace's borrowed finery to the tit-tape that was holding her dress together. Grace longed to shut her down, even opened her mouth – but the hand at her waist administered a warning pinch and when she looked up, Vaughn was smiling tightly.

'That's very sweet of you, Deirdre,' he said with a careless shrug. 'But I'm going to have to pass. I have my hands full at the moment.'

'Well, you're letting go of a wonderful opportunity,' Deirdre hissed, before striding off with her nose in the air.

'Was I rude?' Grace asked Vaughn worriedly, but he was looking amused. 'I was aiming for diplomatic but it sort of came out as rude.'

'A little forthright, perhaps?' he suggested. 'But really, she's so aggressive.'

'I don't know if you want to leave yet, but it wasn't just a line. I'm starving and my stomach is making all sorts of gurgling noises . . .'

'And you need food inside you to soak up some of the

wine,' Vaughn finished for her with an indulgent smile. 'Shall we get out of here?'

Grace tried not to loll in a drunken sprawl on the back seat of the car as they drove further downtown. Apart from the demands of her gut, she felt like the whole world was in soft focus, the bright glitter outside the tinted windows muted to a delicate shimmer, the low murmur of Vaughn's voice as he took a call, a soothing accompaniment to the hum of the air conditioning. She really had drunk quite a lot.

When the car stopped with a gentle lurch as a cab pulled out in front of them, it shocked her out of her stupor. Grace peered out on to Bank Street, eyes flickering in disbelief as the frontage of the Waverly Inn came into view. Owned by Graydon Carter, editor of *Vanity Fair*, the Waverly Inn was so now, so hip, so on trend that even Kiki couldn't get in. Or actually she'd been offered a table on the terrace and had turned it down because apparently the terrace was New York shorthand for social Siberia.

Grace tried to play it cool, aware of Vaughn's eyes on her, as they were waved past the bouncer, ushered through the bar and into the tiny inner sanctum of New York's power players. The dining room wasn't much bigger than Grace's bedsit and decorated with what looked like a pile of tatty old junk; battered books, old baseball photos and some really tacky paintings. Grace knew she'd just been admitted into the Holy of Holies and she wanted to stop and drink it all in but she forced herself to keep moving. Vaughn's hand was at the small of her back, and she was sure he could tell that she was trembling as if a whole colony of butterflies had taken up residence in her stomach as she and Vaughn were led right to the back of the room while all eyes rested upon them.

Grace slid on to the empty banquette and tried not to bounce in excitement as Vaughn sat down opposite her. 'Graydon lets me have his table when he's out of town,' he told her, not bothering to explain who Graydon was and Grace was grateful that she knew and didn't need to ask for subtitles. There was a conveniently placed mirror next to her so she could see the entire room and didn't have to shamelessly rubberneck the other guests to see if she could spot a stray Scarlett or Gwyneth. She'd even have been happy with a Sienna.

'This is amazing,' she breathed when the ability to speak finally came back to her. She wanted to wince at how starstruck she sounded but Vaughn didn't seem to mind. He simply smiled and then raised his hand at someone a couple of tables across who was sitting with a woman who looked a hell of a lot like Jennifer Aniston.

'The food's good,' Vaughn said. 'I hope you're not a picky eater.'

He made 'picky eater' sound like code for 'kiddy fiddler', and Grace was pleased she could shake her head. 'I'll eat anything. Well, apart from artichokes.' Now she could smell the surprisingly homely scent of food and remembered how hungry she was; her stomach gave another warning rumble. As a waiter had come over with the sole intention of serving them alcohol, Grace could feel herself start to relax ever so slightly.

Dissecting and discussing the menu kept the conversation grooving along and by the time Grace had gulped down a glass of water and they were sharing a starter of crab cakes, she was beginning to enjoy herself.

Normally Grace treated conversations as awkward silences punctuated by whatever she could think of to fill the pauses. But Vaughn chatted with a practised ease and when Grace realised that they'd lapsed into quiet, he was ready with an anecdote about a Texan oil baron who'd spent millions on a Picasso and then put his elbow through it while he was showing it off at his birthday party.

By the time Grace's forty-five-dollar macaroni and cheese

with fresh truffle shavings was just a few smears on her plate, they were on to the subject of twentieth-century art.

'Your favourite painter's Paul Klee?' she clarified, remembering to pronounce his surname 'clay' so she didn't come across as a total philistine. 'That's such a boy thing to say.'

'Well, who do you like?' Vaughn laughed and he needed to do that more often because it transformed the angular lines of his face into something almost friendly. 'Georgia O'Keeffe? What a girl thing to say.'

'Erté,' Grace said immediately. 'Mostly his fashion illustrations for *Harper's* – that girly enough for you, Mr Vaughn?'

'Just Vaughn will do,' he said mildly, refilling her glass from the second bottle of Sauvignon Blanc. 'You know a lot about art.'

'I did Art and History of Art for A-levels and I must have been dragged round every gallery in the country before I was ten.' Grace reached for the bottle of San Pellegrino as her teeth were going numb, which was a warning sign that she was well on the road to ruin.

'Your parents are art lovers?'

'Grandparents,' she corrected, carefully pouring water into her glass with a hand that barely shook. 'And not really art lovers, they just wanted to find a way to occupy me that didn't involve video games or watching too much TV.'

Vaughn's ever-changing face had changed again; eyes narrowed in contemplation. 'And what do your parents do?'

'My father does something in an office in Worthing. Sells insurance, I think,' Grace conceded, looking hopefully around for their server. There was still enough room for dessert and if she was chowing down on something chocolate-based then she didn't have to answer any more questions. 'My mother lives in Australia.'

'So you were brought up by your father then?'

Grace put down her glass with enough force that water slopped over the rim. 'I don't like talking about my family.'

Vaughn gave a careless shrug. 'Evidently.' He smiled with just the tiniest hint of cruelty. 'Why did your mother leave?'

He was un-fucking-believable and blind if he couldn't see that Grace was scowling ferociously. But judging from the way Vaughn hadn't taken his eyes off her, he'd noticed but simply didn't care. 'My personal life isn't a free gift that comes with the purchase of dinner,' she told him crisply. 'My parents married young, they divorced young. I went to live with my grandparents. Satisfied?'

Vaughn calmly rearranged his napkin as if the brief recap of Grace's toxic formative years had barely registered. 'I was only asking. I didn't mean to upset you.'

'I'm not upset! FYI, I had a happy childhood. I baked cakes. I learned to knit. There were books everywhere. The worst thing was they only had a black and white TV and it was embarrassing when I had friends over.' Grace made a concerted effort to lower her volume knob. 'My grandparents are amazing. They put their life on hold for me.' She tried to smile. 'OK, they were kinda strict sometimes and there was a lot of 'when I was your age there was a war going on' but I'd have been much worse off if my parents had stayed together.'

'And what do your grandparents do? Are they retired?'

Grace couldn't help but smile now. 'Grandy plays golf and my grandmother's a pensioners' rights activist – she writes angry letters to the *Daily Mail* when they're mean about Marks and Spencer.' She paused for thought. 'And they go on a hell of a lot of walking holidays.'

She smiled again, expecting Vaughn to smile back but he was studying her so intently that Grace was tempted to cover her face with her napkin. 'I'm getting used to your huge repertoire of filthy looks,' he remarked idly. 'But like I said before, when you smile, you're really quite beautiful.'

'You are *so* weird,' Grace muttered, before she could stop herself.

'Most people just call me an arrogant bastard and have done with it.'

'I never said that . . .'

'And I'm most grateful.' The smile he gave her was slightly cracked. 'I'm just curious about you. Also, I have a theory that the most interesting people have the most interesting pasts. Don't you agree?'

Grace twisted her lips. 'I'm not sure we have the same definition of what makes an interesting past,' she said carefully.

'You're probably right.' Grace must have imagined that cracked smile and the shadowed cast to his eyes because now Vaughn was curling his arm over the back of the banquette and giving every impression that he was relaxed. 'Now why don't you tell me what you get up to in that famous fashion cupboard?'

There was a line being carefully drawn through the last ten minutes so Grace could take her cue and rattle on about her thwarted plans to become the greatest stylist that never was. Instead, she flagged down their waiter and after a little dithering ordered the apple crisp with vanilla *gelato*, then she turned back to Vaughn. 'Well, hang on, do *you* have an interesting past?' she asked coolly. 'Want to tell me about *your* childhood?'

Vaughn shifted fretfully and drew his arms in so he could trace patterns on the table with his long fingers. 'There's really nothing to tell.'

'Have you always lived in London?' Grace persisted.

Vaughn lifted his head and, even in the soft light, Grace spotted the warning glint. 'Off and on,' he bit out.

She'd always been the kind of girl who liked to pick her scabs instead of leaving them to heal on their own. 'Like, how?'

'Like, I grew up there when my family weren't abroad and then I went to boarding school in Hampshire.' Vaughn hesitated, before throwing caution to the wind. 'My father was in the Diplomatic Corps.'

Grace could feel him pulling away from her so that the little throb of connection between them, which had been waxing and waning all night, was abruptly severed. Besides, being the sole focus of his most glacial stare wasn't much fun at all. Grace decided to stop scab-picking and go back to her original plan to be light and frothy.

'I heard that if you meet someone at an embassy party and they say that they're a cultural attaché, then actually they're really a spy. Is that true?' she asked mischievously.

Vaughn's eyes stopped trying to bore holes into her and he laughed softly, the tension melting away like the pool of ice cream in the bowl, which had just been placed in front of Grace. He even stretched out a hand towards her arm resting on the table, but thought better of it and fiddled briefly with the salt-cellar instead.

'I do know some cultural attachés, and I don't think any of them are involved in international espionage. Another illusion shattered?'

Grace nodded, her attention temporarily distracted by her pudding, which was the fifth best thing she'd ever eaten. 'They all get shattered sooner or later.'

'I still want to know what you get up to in your fashion cupboard and why you were so tetchy when I spoke to you yesterday,' Vaughn said, his gaze riveted on her bowl-to-mouth motions.

There was no way Grace could give Vaughn any of the highlights of yesterday's shoot, so she settled for a highly edited version that made her appear to be indispensable and ingenious in a demurely sexy *His Girl Friday* manner and had the added bonus of coaxing deep-throated chuckles from Vaughn. 'My boss calls me "the Model Whisperer",' she concluded with bashful false modesty, but Vaughn's attention was on her pudding, which she pushed away after only a few spoonfuls. 'Too much,' she complained. 'My eyes were bigger than my belly.'

Vaughn hesitated for almost a nanosecond, then snagged the bowl nearer and licked his bottom lip. 'You don't mind?' he asked, spoon already halfway to his mouth.

'Go for it.'

'I don't usually have that much of a sweet tooth,' he remarked. Grace nearly believed him, then remembered how he'd eagerly ordered four variations of chocolate cake on her birthday.

Thinking about that also made Grace remember how she'd become so flustered when they'd said goodbye. She wondered what 'goodbye' would be like this time. The evening's non-date status was still undefined. There had been no sly touches of his hand on her leg under the table, no accidental banging together of knees. But there had been the waist-stroking at the gallery and he'd called her beautiful twice.

Probably when she was getting out the car, she'd brush her lips against his cheek, Grace decided. This time she'd totally own the goodbye and leave him wanting more.

Vaughn was currently scraping the bowl clean with a dreamy little smile on his face. For the first time he seemed like a real, live boy and not a man who was a combination of expensive suiting and huge amounts of sarcasm. He looked up and blinked as if he'd forgotten she was there.

'You should have just ordered a pudding for yourself,' she said.

'Oh, I never have pudding,' he declared loftily. 'Do you want coffee?'

Grace didn't wear a watch but it felt as if it was late. 'Not really, thank you,' she said, standing up. 'Would you excuse me for a moment?'

At least she wasn't lower middle class enough to make

polite noises about having to powder her nose, she thought, as she took in her flushed cheeks, which were a perfect match for her dress, in the restroom mirror. She also looked a lot drunker than she felt, though that wasn't saying much.

By the time she walked back to the table, rather steadily, all things considered, Vaughn was pulling a black Amex card out of his wallet. She hadn't known they existed for real outside of books. Grace watched as he signed his name and gave their waiter a $100 bill for a tip with a subtle sleight of hand.

Vaughn didn't try to touch her as they walked alongside each other, but when they reached the door, his hand grazed her hip. It felt like a million tiny fires igniting, just from one incidental touch. Grace cannoned into the door with a small, 'Ouch!' and she knew that Vaughn *knew*.

Walking to the chauffeur-driven car felt like wading through treacle and as soon as the door closed on them and the car eased away from the kerb, Vaughn was reeling her in. Hand gently cupping the back of her neck, he was pulling her in closer, closer, closer.

He didn't kiss her. Not at first. But stroked the back of his hand against her cheek and it felt scratchy and wrong. That Grace could ever be with someone . . . be with someone like Vaughn, and just sit still and be touched.

There was only one way to get him to stop. So Grace kissed him for the lack of good reason not to. And Vaughn kissed her back.

It was different from the kisses that she usually got. Vaughn kissed her just like he'd eaten her dessert, like her mouth was a thing to be savoured, enjoyed slowly.

It was as if Vaughn's kisses were saying all the stuff that he couldn't – and when it really came down to the cold, hard facts, there was something between them. Had been ever since she walked out of the lift earlier. Grace didn't know what it was, but when Vaughn's hand closed over her breast, thumb rubbing and pressing, she made a sound in the back of her throat that she didn't think she'd ever made before.

There weren't many things that Grace knew for certain. But she absolutely and unequivocally knew that sex with Vaughn would be good. More than good. It would be sheet-tearing, limb-flailing, screaming-loud-enough-to-wake-the-neighbours good. No one could be as tightly wound as Vaughn and not unravel when the lights were on low and the stereo was set on smooch.

His hand slipped from her breast to her waist, mouth worrying at a spot behind her left ear that seemed to be connected by some complicated system of veins and blood vessels straight to her clit. Then it was an undignified tug and scramble so Grace was half in his lap, half-kneeling on the seat, one foot on the floor for balance. Making out in the back of a limo was just as ergonomically challenging as making out in the back of an unlicensed minicab, though thankfully the driver was behind a screen and not able to ogle them in his rear-view mirror.

Vaughn whispered something but Grace was too busy finally curling her fingers through his hair to hear. She realised that she'd wanted to do that for hours. He was coaxing her closer now, so one hand could slip under her skirt, up her thigh, and one hand was edging along the neckline of her dress.

Grace felt him hesitate then but she pushed her tongue into his mouth so she could taste vanilla ice cream and expectation. His fingers were still dancing against breast and thigh and she wanted something more forceful but made an inarticulate sound of protest instead. How could you say this stuff with words, when you never knew what you really wanted?

Then Vaughn's fingers grazed the edge of the tit-tape, which was starting to come unstuck. Grace tensed at the thought of being found out but he was already pushing her sideways on to the seat so she was no longer riding his thigh like a Grand National jockey hopped up on speed pills, but sliding clumsily over leather with legs akimbo.

And OK, she could deal with a moment's regrouping to pull down her dress where it had ridden up and surreptitiously prod her tingling lips to make sure that the *Harlot* lipgloss wasn't smeared around her—

'Thank you for a lovely evening,' Vaughn said, straightening his jacket and crossing his legs so it was hard to believe that a minute ago he'd had Grace writhing on his lap.

Rewind! thought Grace in horror. That hadn't been some polite kiss good night – that had been foreplay. Or was this just some tactical retreat to ascertain that Grace had no intention of crying 'date rape' and embroiling him in a messy court case a couple of weeks from now?

Bold from the endorphin rush and the huge amounts of white wine still racing through her system, Grace reached for his stiff hand. 'It's OK,' she assured him, with a coy sideways sweep of her lashes. 'Let's go back to yours.'

He was already disentangling her fingers. 'I don't think so,' he said, patting her hand in an almost avuncular manner. 'It's very late and I'm sure you have an early start tomorrow.'

Her brain could register the snub but instead of passing a message on to her body, Grace was pressing up against him and taking in tiny sips of air as she brushed her breasts against Vaughn's arm. 'I don't need much sleep,' she husked, and reached up to kiss the flushed plane of his cheek. And she couldn't believe she was doing this, going *there*, but her hand was curling around the twitching length of him, relishing his shocked gasp. 'I know you want me.'

'It's late,' he repeated mechanically, firmly removing her hand and looking straight ahead. 'We've had a wonderful time and you're a very sweet girl, but this is not going any further.' And while Grace was still processing this, he added censoriously, 'You've had far too much to drink.'

Of course, it made perfect sense. Even though, one minute ago, it had seemed like the best idea ever. But then it would be an hour later or morning and Grace would be creeping home in the same clothes with that same dry-eyed, dry-mouthed feeling she always had when she'd slept with someone and knew she was never going to see them again.

Apparently she wanted to see Vaughn again.

But that wasn't why he wouldn't take her home and have his way with her on sheets with some super-numerical thread count. It was because Grace had been pretending all night; trying out the part of another girl who was more upper class than Upper Holloway, at ease rather than easy. And Vaughn must have seen right through it as soon as the lift doors opened and she'd tripped out in her uncomfortable shoes that she'd got for fifty per cent off because there was a tiny nick on one heel.

And if she'd really been that other girl, she'd have laughed this off, but she was Grace. So she made the time-honoured 'talk to the hand' gesture and snarled, 'Fine, what*ever*' as she slid so far across the seat that the door handle dug painfully into her side.

Vaughn sighed and shot her a grimly unamused look. 'You're being ridiculous,' he said sharply, which finished the job of completely piercing her drunken miasma, so she was left feeling miserable and nauseous. And yeah, completely mortified. 'There's no need to take this so personally.'

He was right again. She was being stupid again. Getting way ahead of herself *again*. 'Can you drop me off at my hotel?'

Vaughn didn't even look at her but smoothed down the lapels of his jacket. 'Fine,' he said. 'Of course. You don't mind if I catch up on my messages, do you?'

Grace did mind but she wasn't in a position to argue, so she stared out of the window and concentrated on the exquisite agony of her pinched toes and the itchy tit-tape and how she wanted to puke every time the car hit a pothole. Or was it from shame? She couldn't tell either way.

When they pulled up outside the Soho Grand, the driver opened the door for her and the only acknowledgement she got from Vaughn was a brief and dismissive glance as he looked up from his BlackBerry.

There was no need for him to be so huffy. After all, she was the injured party. 'Look, maybe we could . . . ?'

But the door had closed and the driver was already behind the wheel and pulling away from the kerb. Grace was left standing on the sidewalk outside the Soho Grand on West Broadway with even the doorman giving her a disparaging look as he took in her dishevelled hair, crumpled dress and the way she was scrunching up her face to stop the tears from falling.

chapter seven

Grace did a lot of knitting during the next two weeks. It was now late August and London was still in the thrall of a relentless heatwave. The sun beat down on her bent head as she purled and plained and moss-stitched on buses and in cafés and, on one occasion, in Waterlow Park in Highgate until she got harassed by a gang of hoodies. Knitting was good for soothing her soul, and as Grace had sworn that she was never going to use a sewing machine ever again after jacking in her fashion degree, knitting would have to do.

She liked the rhythmic click of the needles, the feeling of the wool wrapped tight around her fingers, and the satisfaction as row upon row of perfect stitches emerged. Technically she was lapsed C of E, but Grace liked to think that knitting was her version of the Rosary – but without all the Hail Marys and vows of chastity. Besides, she'd been in a state of extreme agitation for a fortnight and it was either knitting or Prozac. As she'd never get time off for a doctor's appointment, Grace knitted a pair of gloves with *love* and *hate* stitched across the knuckles, a peaked cap for her grandfather because his ears got cold when he golfed in winter, and a stripy jumper to use up all her odd ends of wool. Now she was sketching out patterns for a range of knitted accessories including an iPod holder and a make-up case with a vague plan that she could make enough money to pay off a fraction of one of her credit-card bills.

She'd come back from New York to find that the pile of brown envelopes that Anita and Ilonka from upstairs had thoughtfully left on her doormat, stamped with friendly warnings like *Final Reminder!* and *Immediate Action Needed!* had reached critical mass. Grace had an inkling that things might get ugly again, like they had last year when she'd been tailed by a private detective from a debt collection agency who'd wanted to repossess her credit cards. Fun times.

It wasn't as if work could distract her either. Even though it was August, they were already working on the November and December issues, which were always light on both editorial and ad pages so it wasn't as if Grace was busy calling in clothes for shoots and assembling the fashion credits. Instead she was busy listening to a newly single Posy regaling her with tales of horrific blind dates with old Etonians and getting quotes for granite worktops for Lucie's new kitchen.

Worst of all, Lily was spending her annual fortnight at the family villa in the non-chav part of Majorca and Dan had sent Grace a pointed text message before they left, instructing her not to contact Lily. And Grace needed to contact Lily so they could have a long, drunken night out and Grace could tell Lily about the art exhibition and the Waverly Inn and dinner with Vaughn. But mostly she'd spend hours reliving and dissecting those ten minutes in the limo afterwards. Then Lily would say that he sounded like a total bastard and that Grace was well shot of him and all the bad thoughts would stop tormenting Grace. Or they'd lessen at least.

Because the bad thought that made all her other bad thoughts seem like the most microscopic of potatoes, all centred on the moment when she'd got out of that car and watched the tail-lights fade into the distance as he'd driven away from her. If she didn't concentrate really hard on other things, all she could hear was the way Vaughn had drawled out, 'This is not going any further' in the face of her most determinedly sluttish behaviour. Which had been moments after he'd taken her hand off his dick.

So skulking in the fashion cupboard and shunning human contact had become a valid lifestyle choice until the summons from her grandparents to come to Worthing for the weekend. It didn't matter that it was sweltering, there'd be a mammoth cake-baking session on Saturday afternoon, roast chicken for Sunday lunch and a twenty-pound note slipped into Grace's hand as she said her goodbyes so she could 'buy herself something nice'. It was routine, safe, a little boring. But boring was OK sometimes.

So Grace was confounded to find herself leaning against the counter of the Worthing branch of Carphone Warehouse on a Saturday morning because her elderly parental signifiers had decided to dip a toe into the twenty-first century and buy his 'n' hers mobile phones. She watched as her grandmother harangued the spotty Saturday boy with querulous enquiries as to the benefits of a monthly tariff versus pay as you go.

'Gran,' she sighed, 'get the pay as you go phones.'

Her grandmother frowned. 'Pay as you go?'

'You're only going to use the phone for emergencies, and maybe in six months' time, you might have figured out how to send a text message,' Grace explained patiently. 'I promise it will take a year to use up ten pounds' worth of credit.'

There was no rushing her grandmother, who never drove at more than thirty miles per hour and could make a portion of peas last fifteen minutes. 'I'm not going to let your impatience influence my decision-making, young lady,' she said grandly.

'I'm gasping for a cup of tea,' Grace wailed, but her grandmother was now asking to see phones with larger keypads, 'Because my eyesight isn't what it used to be.'

Later – much, much later – in the first-floor café in Beales department store, with a pot of tea and a scone each, her grandmother went on the offensive.

'You need to do something about your hair,' she announced, à propos of nothing. 'It doesn't suit you at all. Really, Grace, I don't know why you meddle with what nature gave you.'

'Because nature gave me mousy-brown hair,' Grace said without much bite.

'You're very listless,' her grandmother continued. 'Are you in trouble with the bank again? You're sticking to the monthly repayments?'

There were so many monthly repayments that Grace was meant to be sticking to. 'Yeah, of course I am. All that stuff is in the past, Gran,' Grace assured her blithely. She'd decided long ago that lying to her grandmother for the sake of a quiet life barely even registered on the wrong scale. 'It's just super-hot and I'm really busy at work.'

'Too busy to write to your mother?' If ever the CIA were doing research into new interrogation techniques, they should send some scientists to Worthing to work out how her gran did that thing with her eyes. 'She said you never replied to the email she sent on your birthday. Did you get the photos of Kirsty? Sweet little thing, we thought.'

'You've seen one toddler in a pink fairy outfit, you've seen 'em all,' Grace muttered.

'She's your sister.'

'*Half*-sister,' Grace reminded her, yanking out her knitting from her bag. 'Gran, Mum left me. In fact, she didn't just leave – she went to the other side of the world to get away from me. Then it took her – what? – twelve years to suddenly feel bad about it. Honestly, I'm glad she got married and that she's having another bash at motherhood, but I don't see why I have to get regular updates by email.'

Her grandmother's attention was momentarily diverted by the skull and crossbones pattern on the scarf that Grace was knitting, before she efficiently distributed the last of the tea. 'Well, it wasn't as cut and dried as that. If you remember—'

'I don't want to talk about it! I just want her to leave me alone.'

Grace's voice was rising, which was usually her grandmother's cue to tell her to calm down, but this time she just stared at the nosy middle-aged couple on the next table until they looked away, and squeezed Grace's hand. 'She's trying, dear. She's making an effort.' There was the most delicate of pauses. 'You might as well know that Grandy and I are thinking of flying out this Christmas, to meet our youngest granddaughter, and Gary. He seems nice.'

Gary was the new husband. 'You know it's a twenty-four-hour flight, right?' Grace blustered. 'Plus it's going to be the middle of summer in Australia and they have snakes and, Gran, they're all Republicans. You'd hate it.'

'We thought you might want to come too if we bought you the plane ticket as a Christmas present. What do you think?'

'Do I really need to answer that?' Grace snapped, watching her grandmother's lips tighten and relenting immediately. 'If I have a spare second, I'll bang out a thank-you email, OK? That's it. End of discussion. Now, can we change the subject? *Please?*'

Her grandmother patted a stray crumb from her mouth. She looked older. Her skin was thinner, like creased brown paper, her rigid curls more liberally doused with grey, and it weighed heavily on Grace. Like, her gran was a little old lady to the outside world and earlier, when they'd strolled down South Street, she'd had to glare at a couple of teenage girls who'd knocked into them and not apologised. Both her grandparents had become nothing more than doddery, vulnerable targets for muggers and . . .

'So, are you seeing anyone nice? It's about time you settled down. I was married by the time I was your age.'

Correction. There was nothing vulnerable about her grandmother. 'When I said change the subject, I thought we'd talk about whether we should make chocolate cake or gingerbread.' Grace suddenly giggled and her grandmother smiled too, with a naughty twinkle that made Grace reach across the table so she could squeeze one liver-spotted mitt gently. 'I was seeing someone but we split up. He had no prospects.'

Her grandparents were big on people with prospects. Her grandmother nodded sympathetically. 'Can't stand a man who dithers,' she said stoutly. 'So – any other admirers?'

'Oh yeah, I have a whole string of besotted boys lining up to mark my dance card. Sometimes I think I go for the wrong guys, like, maybe I'd be better with someone older, more focused.' Grace hadn't been thinking that at all, but there was no harm in putting it out there if only to see her grandmother's face wrinkle up in consternation.

'I used to think that an age gap was quite romantic until that horrid business with Charles and Diana,' was her crushing verdict.

As weekends in the loving bosom of two seventy-somethings went, it hadn't been too bad, but Grace was glad that she was back on the train to London by seven on Sunday evening. They'd wanted her to stay the night and catch a morning train at some horrifically early hour, which really was a case of hope over experience.

Even knitting couldn't make the train move faster or the air circulate more efficiently. Grace was just unpicking her last row when her phone started to ring. Her grandfather had already rung five times as he pressed buttons on his new phone and tried to work out how to access his voicemail.

'Grandy? You need to hit star, then number one,' she squeaked in exasperation. 'How many more—'

'Am I speaking to Grace Reeves?'

It was a woman, her voice polished enough to immediately put Grace on edge. Usually they phoned in the mornings, pretending to be a long-lost friend, and as soon as Grace confirmed her identity, it was threats and counter-threats and bailiffs and debt specialists and, 'It would just be easier if you signed over your firstborn.' Phoning on a Sunday evening was underhanded even for them. And surely there were laws that prohibited them from working on the Sabbath?

Grace contemplated switching off her phone, then thought of her grandparents panicking when she didn't answer the next ten of their misdirected calls. 'Who's speaking?' she asked, her accent becoming crisp in a crisis.

'My name's Ms Jones, I'm calling from Mr Vaughn's office.'

'Vaughn? As in J. Vaughn, art dealer?'

'This *is* Ms Reeves then?' The woman sounded irritated, but then if she'd had to work Sunday evenings, Grace would have had a strop on too.

'Yeah. Is there something I can help you with?'

'Mr Vaughn would like to arrange a meeting with you. Are you free at eleven tomorrow morning?'

Er, why? Grace thought. 'Well, I'll be at work,' she said out loud. 'I guess maybe lunch-time or . . .'

There was a muffled conversation on the other end of the line. 'Seven thirty in the evening? Shall I give you the address of the gallery?'

'But what's the meeting about? Why doesn't he just call me himself? Is he there with you?' Grace could have fired questions without pause until the train pulled in at Victoria. But she was stopped by a terse cough.

'I'm going to give you the address. Have you got pen and paper?'

'Hang on.' After a quick rummage, she found an old flyer and an eyebrow pencil. 'OK.'

The Mayfair address from the business card was reeled off. 'It's just off New Bond Street.'

'Could you just tell me—'

'Mr Vaughn will see you at seven thirty. I hope you enjoy

the rest of your evening.' There was a decisive click as the connection was severed.

Grace decided she wasn't going to answer the imperious summons. Not after Vaughn had dumped her on the street like a broken fridge. Well, technically it had been the entrance to her hotel but same difference.

When she woke up the next day, she planned to be on the 134 bus heading back to Archway at seven thirty that night, but just to keep her options open, Grace put on her black and white, fifties polka-dot sundress that smooshed her breasts right up to her chin. She even took the Marc Jacobs bag out of the oven with the idea that she'd stalk in, place it on Vaughn's desk and walk out without saying a word. Just to show him that she had some pride.

But Vaughn obviously had a reason for wanting to see her again. Maybe to tell Grace that he couldn't stop thinking about her and he'd been beating himself up for the callous way he'd spurned her advances. But no, that wasn't Vaughn's style. Which was a pity, Grace thought, as she spent the morning doing a Google image search on 'j vaughn + art dealer' and turning up photo after photo of Vaughn, usually stiff-backed in a dinner jacket, standing next to Icelandic ambassadors and YBAs. He was much better looking in the flesh.

By lunch-time, Grace had decided that Vaughn was going to offer her a job. Because she'd totally rocked when it came to scaring away aggressive agents, and his current assistant had a very poor phone technique. That was why Vaughn hadn't wanted to succumb to Grace's blatantly offered charms. She rehearsed the moment when she'd turn him down with a cruel smile playing around her mouth. Then he'd know *exactly* how it felt.

During her mid-afternoon Diet Coke break, Grace toyed with the idea of asking what the salary and benefits package would be. Just to satisfy her curiosity. And by seven, she was slowly walking up Bond Street towards Mayfair, pausing to stare at artful window displays of expensive bags shiny with gilt hardware, dresses that would change her life the moment she slipped them on, shoes that were the very epitome of 'fuck me', until she could practically hear her one solitary credit card begging to be allowed out to play. It simpled things up though. She loved fashion. And she was going to stay in fashion for as long as it would have her – or until Kiki pushed her down several flights of steps for calling in an unphotogenic belt.

chapter eight

17 Thirlestone Mews was a pretty, stucco townhouse with a discreet brass plaque to the left of the imposing black door. Grace wiped her hands on the skirt of her dress and pressed the bell. She heard the sound of a bolt being pulled back and steeled herself for a face-to-face confrontation with the unpleasant Ms Jones but it was Vaughn standing there in shirtsleeves, a pair of grey suit trousers with razor-sharp creases, and a harried expression on his face which suddenly disappeared as he saw her.

'Grace,' he said smoothly, as if that horrible scene in the limo had never happened. He stepped aside, so she could enter. 'Glad you could make it at such short notice.'

Grace was all set to walk past him, but Vaughn took her arm, fingers sliding into the crook of her elbow, and pulled her towards him. So this wasn't a job interview, Grace thought, as she tilted her head so Vaughn could kiss her on the cheek.

But he didn't. His lips found the corner of her mouth for one fleeting, unbelievable moment and then he was stepping away as Grace touched her fingers to the tingling spot where his lips had just been, because when she wasn't saying something dumb, she was doing something dumb instead. She risked a glance at Vaughn but he wasn't half-smirking as she expected but giving her a long, considered look that she

87

couldn't begin to decipher but which made her feel like her blood was coming to a slow boil.

'Let me show you the gallery,' he said in exactly the same voice he'd used to greet her and didn't even try to touch her as he gestured to the right.

A huge skylight at the back of a long room spilled mellow evening sun over the stark white walls. The canvases on display were bold splashes of electric blue and shocking pink, sludgy reds and a stinging acid green that made her eyeballs itch.

'Our current exhibition,' Vaughn said from behind Grace. 'An Austrian artist called Wilhelm Bauer. I've been buying up his work for years.'

'Oh, are they for sale or just, like, a retrospective?' If he could pretend that nothing had happened, so could she. Though he was far better at it.

'They're for sale, of course,' Vaughn said, standing next to her so that, out of the corner of her eye, Grace could see his bemused smile.

'Does it bother you to have to sell them after you've spent so many years collecting them?' Grace asked, thinking of the time she'd had to eBay most of her vintage dresses because her former landlord was threatening to take her to the small claims court. It had been like a death in the family. 'It must be horrible to get attached to some pictures, then have to pack 'em up and ship 'em off.'

'If I had that attitude I'd be destitute,' Vaughn laughed. 'I don't get attached to pictures. I foresee their potential, collect them discreetly so that I don't drive up the price, and sell them several years later for a lot more than I originally paid. Liking them really doesn't come into it.'

'You must like some of them,' Grace protested, following him back into the reception area and up a sweeping flight of stairs. Did he live above the shop? Should she try out a really tasteless joke about coming up to see his etchings? Probably not.

They arrived at the second floor just as Grace was starting to fight for every breath. Her flip-flops slapped against the parquet as Vaughn ushered her into a minimalist sitting room: all white leather seating and black walls. There was a Bauhausy desk to one side with a sleek little laptop perched on it. 'This is my office,' he said, rifling through some papers. 'Sit down.'

Grace chose one of the high-sided, cubed armchairs and sank down on it. She felt as if she was being swallowed whole.

'Do you want something to drink?'

'May I have some water? Still, if you've got it,' she added, forestalling yet another question.

Grace watched Vaughn get a big blue bottle of Ty Nant out of a fridge, along with two glasses. Keeping glasses in a fridge was just the kind of effortlessly stylish thing that impressed the hell out of her. Sometimes Grace wished that she wasn't so shallow.

When she was clutching the glass in her sweaty hand and hoping it wouldn't slip to the floor, Vaughn sat down on the sofa opposite her and placed some papers down on the long, low table between them. 'I need to discuss something with you but before I do, I'd like you to sign a non-disclosure agreement,' he said reasonably. So reasonably that Grace was already nodding her head before her rusty internal alarm system blared into life.

'Why? You know, I half-wondered if you were going to offer me a job, but—'

'Grace, I know this all seems very cloak and dagger but you have to sign an NDA before I explain anything else.'

'Why do I need to sign anything?' Grace suddenly had a horrible suspicion that maybe this, *all of it*, was some elaborate sting operation by a big financial conglomerate that had bought all her outstanding debts. She dismissed the thought. There was no way she could owe *that* much money. She tentatively pulled the two sheets of paper closer and flicked her eyes over dry legalese. 'The only bit I understand is my own name!'

Vaughn muttered something under his breath, but when he turned to her, it was with a disarming smile, despite the little tic twitching by his left ear. Grace watched it in fascination. 'There's really nothing to worry about. Just a confidential proposition.'

'You could just ask me not to tell anyone,' she suggested, wrinkling her brow at all the *henceforths* and *indemnifications*.

The tic in Vaughn's cheek picked up speed. It looked painful. He thrust a pen at her. 'Just sign it. Now.'

It wasn't a tone of voice that Grace was brave enough to argue with. She put down her glass on a little side table and signed on the dotted line that was neatly marked with a cross, then handed the agreement back to Vaughn.

Vaughn studied it intently, possibly to check her penmanship. She wasn't too sure and he didn't seem in a hurry to fill her in about, well, anything.

'So, what did you . . . ?'

'You're very pretty.' He breathed hard and steepled his fingers together.

'Well, thanks . . .'

'You're well-educated, you have a good layperson's knowledge of the art world,' he continued listing her plus points, though it was going to be a very short list so he might get to the point soon. 'Though it occurs to me that you may be back with your ex.'

She'd barely thought about Liam at all in the last fortnight. 'God – as if!'

'And you're not involved with anyone else?' he asked, tapping his fingers nervously against his knees.

'Well, no,' she said slowly. 'Not that it's any of your business, and actually this is all slightly inappropriate after New York, and—'

'It's not,' he said briskly. 'It's not at all because I'd very much like you to be my mistress.'

Grace stared at him in disbelief. Her mouth opened to let out a few wheezy gasps.

'That was a little forceful, wasn't it?' Vaughn smiled, like he was trying to put Grace at ease. She didn't return the smile but stared at him without blinking. 'I'd really like to spend more time with you on an exclusive basis.'

'Huh? What? Like, you want me to be your girlfriend?'

Vaughn shook his head. 'Not exactly. Do you remember in New York that I told you I looked after young artists? Spotted their potential, nurtured their talent? Well, that's what I'd like to do with you.'

'But I'm not an artist.' Grace picked at a hangnail on her thumb, then gave in to the urge to stick it in her mouth and nibble. And if she was biting her nails, then she was still herself, still the same old Grace. And the same old Grace didn't sit in fancy offices in Mayfair as a wealthy art dealer asked her if she fancied being his mistress. 'I don't understand what you're talking about.'

'I'm talking about going into partnership together,' Vaughn said softly, as if the impatient, sarcastic man she'd met before had just been an illusion. 'What I'm proposing would be almost like a business agreement.'

'Christ! You think I'm a tart!' Grace spluttered indignantly. 'I'm not some kind of rent-a-skank, thank you very much.'

'Of course you're not,' Vaughn said, and he sounded so offended at the idea that Grace was mollified – just a little. 'I'm not explaining myself very well. I'd like to take you to all sorts of places – Art Basel in Miami, the Art Cologne show, the Tokyo Design Festa . . . I'd introduce you to interesting people, give you new experiences and I'd have someone to talk to at some very dry functions. On a more practical note, once a month I give a dinner-party with a very exclusive guest-list and you'd act as my hostess, provide some colour while I discuss business. I do my biggest deals at these dinners.'

He could dress it up any way he wanted to, but he'd said 'mistress'. That was what he'd started with and that was where Grace was still stuck. Yes, the travel sounded wonderful – there might be a private jet involved and she'd always wanted to go on one of them – but she'd been brought up to be a nice girl, and just thinking of exactly how she was brought up gave Grace a mental picture of her grandmother's horrified face.

'No,' she said firmly. 'No.' This time it was definite. 'I can't.'

Vaughn gave an elegant, ophidian shrug. 'I realise that I'd be taking up a lot of your time, so of course there'd be a monthly retainer and a clothing and grooming allowance.' He was purposely misunderstanding her and as diversions went, it was effective, but the mention of allowances made the whole tart scenario loom large again.

'I'm going,' Grace said as she struggled to get out of the depths of the chair. 'I'm sure you could find a discreet escort agency that—'

'I was thinking five thousand pounds a month – and what? – an additional two thousand pounds for the clothing allowance,' Vaughn said before Grace could even get fully upright.

'Fucking hell!' She sat down again, or rather collapsed heavily back into the chair. 'That's a lot of money. That's way too much money.'

'Not for someone like me,' Vaughn said smoothly.

'Well, it is for someone like me.' Grace hunched forward, elbows on her knees, and ran her fingers through her hair. 'Just how rich are you anyway?'

'Well, I could provide five years of accounts but this isn't about the money, Grace. It's about you and me and what we can do for each other.'

She could hear Vaughn getting up, walking over to her, but

it was still a shock when he squatted down so he could take one of her limp hands. 'I can see that this has all been rather discombobulating.'

Grace wished that he'd stick to words of two syllables or less, as she tried to think. £5,000. £5,000! She could start paying off her most outstanding debts. Like her Topshop store card or the consolidated loan she'd taken out to pay off her creditors although she'd never got round to making any of the payments. Or the new credit-card debts she'd incurred in the meantime. Or even the months of back-rent she owed so she wouldn't have to live in fear that one day she'd come home from work to find all her belongings in the front garden because her landlady would no longer accept IOUs . . .

'You're very quiet, Grace,' Vaughn prompted, and he reached up to touch her, maybe stroke her cheek or push back the hair that was falling into her face, but she shied away from him and he blinked rapidly before he could check himself.

Grace squinted at him. 'So that evening in New York – was that meant to be a dry run?' And if she sounded pissed off, then good. 'Did I get a black mark or a gold star?'

'It was more of an informal interview,' Vaughn said carefully. 'And you don't have to be embarrassed about what happened. I was very flattered and it clarified a few grey areas.'

Grace stared at him. 'Well, that would probably fall into the category of apologising and you told me that I shouldn't do that.'

Vaughn dipped his head in acknowledgement but didn't fight back with the acid-dripping sarcasm that she was sure he'd have had all good to go. The urge to giggle and to check the plant in the corner for a hidden camera was hard to avoid. Somebody was *Punk*ing her – they had to be.

'This is not fucking happening,' she said quietly. 'I know what you think. You think because I was up for it in New York that I'm easy, but I'm not. You kissed me first! And then you made me feel like a complete . . .' She'd been planning to say 'twat' but at the last second improvised with 'idiot'.

'That wasn't my intention. It was just . . . well, don't you think you're worth something more than a one-night stand?' Vaughn stood up in one easy movement and toed a little leather footstool nearer so he could sit on it, his shirtsleeve brushing her leg.

And yes, Grace did think she was worth something more than that, but it didn't really make much difference. 'Well, yeah, but—'

'Do you remember how we first met? You were crying your eyes out in the middle of Liberty's. I saw him, Grace.' Vaughn paused to shake his head as if the memory of Liam was causing him all sorts of inner turmoil. 'Why are you wasting your time with pitiful losers who don't appreciate how special you are?'

Grace felt compelled to stick up for Liam, and by definition, herself. 'Oh, come on, he's not that bad. I mean, it was good at the start and then . . . He's just, like . . . he . . .'

'He was trying to crush your spirit,' Vaughn supplied, as if it was an undeniable fact. 'Men like that haven't got the intelligence or the imagination to appreciate how extra-ordinary and vibrant you are. You deserve so much more than that, Grace, and I can give it to you.'

Vaughn's voice was low and urgent, his eyes bright with fervour as he sold a shiny, new version of Grace to the current model who was leaning forward eagerly so she didn't miss a single word. He didn't just want to get in her pants, he seemed to actually want the whole package, which was a first. It was also insanely flattering because he was rich and successful and attractive, and for some inexplicable reason he wanted *her*.

Grace couldn't think of anything vibrant and extra-ordinary to add. 'Well, so we'd date then or something?'

'It's a partnership, an agreement with a contract – say for a six-month period . . .'

It had been much better when he'd been playing to her strengths. Now panic flared up again. 'I'm not signing anything else!' Grace burst out, white-knuckled hands clutching the sides of the chair because she might bolt at any moment. 'This is not how you do things. It's so calculated and it's cold. You'd be paying me – and last time I checked, that was prostitution.'

'Sshhh.' He placed a finger on her mouth and it was only to get her to shut up but it made Grace shiver because there *was* a connection between them. It was why she was here, after all. 'It's better this way with clear-cut boundaries, so we both know exactly where we stand. Aren't you tired of constantly stumbling about in the dark?'

Vaughn couldn't know that she felt as if she'd spent all her life blindfolded, hands stretched out in front of her to feel where she was going. Nobody knew that, but his eyes were boring into hers, not judging but as if maybe Vaughn knew how that felt too.

'I can't think. Honestly, my head feels like it's about to explode,' Grace said weakly. 'None of what you're saying is making any sense.'

'I don't think I'm going out on a limb here to say that we get along,' Vaughn explained patiently, as if she was purposely not getting a clue. 'There's absolutely no reason why we can't enjoy each other's company and let things run their natural course. You certainly didn't find me that repugnant in New York.'

Vaughn wasn't repugnant. There were men who made Grace's flesh want to crawl off her bones, like Ron from the postroom who always smelled of mouldy cheese and never took his eyes off her tits. Or even Alfie, the drummer in Liam's band, who was textbook good looking but had really small feet and chewed with his mouth open.

The leather seat was sticking to the backs of her thighs and Grace hoped that when she stood up again there wouldn't be any embarrassing noises. She leaned over and picked up the glass of water because there was so much to process that speaking would finish her off altogether.

Vaughn was watching her keenly and, even though it was very immature, Grace angled her upper body away from him so she could stare at a picture on the wall that looked like splattered guts.

There was a firm grip on her chin, so she had no choice but to turn her head and look right into those big, blue eyes. She'd never got such a close look at them before with the benefit of really good lighting. There were little flecks of gold breaking up the blue, and near to the pupil, they were almost navy. 'I don't know why you want me to be your m-mistress.' Grace stumbled over the word. 'I'm nothing special. And six months is a long time. You'll be sick of me after three, I guarantee it.'

'We could take the six months under advisement,' Vaughn offered, and Grace had the feeling that that was all he'd be willing to concede. 'I happen to think you're a very singular young woman. You won't bore me, for one thing.'

'Yay me,' Grace said solemnly, as the hand that had been on her chin brushed back her hair in a way that could be misconstrued as tender.

'Your roots are coming through,' Vaughn murmured, his fingers tensing as they smoothed over her crown. 'So, why don't I take you out for dinner and we can discuss this in more detail. What are you in the mood for?'

Grace had almost been lulled into calm by the rhythmic movement of Vaughn's fingers in her hair. Almost. But now she imagined two hours of sitting across from Vaughn in another expensive restaurant where she'd feel ill at ease and vulnerable enough that she'd probably let him talk her around. She'd let herself be persuaded that it was all right for him to *pay* to sleep with her. And it wasn't. It so wasn't.

'Will you please move so I can get up?' Grace clung to the

arm of the chair as she hauled herself to her feet. 'This is, like, really fucked up.'

Vaughn didn't seem that perturbed by the hysteria Grace was transmitting like some high-frequency bat sonar. 'Grace, you're overreacting. I understand that, but there's no need. It all makes perfect sense if you look at it logically. Would you like a week to think about it?'

Grace was already halfway to the door but she whirled around, in a flutter of angry polka dots. 'What makes you think that a week is going to be enough time for me to agree to this insane and actually really humiliating proposal?'

Vaughn looked surprised that she was dumb enough to ask. 'Because you haven't said no.'

She nearly broke her neck running down two flights of stairs in her flip-flops and for one awful moment, Grace thought she was going to have to go back to Vaughn's office and ask for his help because she couldn't figure out how to open the front door, but finally she was free and pelting down the street, not even caring if Vaughn was watching from his office window.

Grace was still out of breath as she sat on the top deck of the 134 and placed a steadying hand over her frantically beating heart. She'd done the right thing though, she thought. She did actually have a strong moral code, which was news to her, though it had never really been put to the test before. She stared out at Camden High Street, which was far more her speed than Mayfair. She was charity shops and picking up a ready meal from Sainsbury's Local. She was drinking until two in the morning in pubs with sticky floors and really good jukeboxes, then stopping to get a bag of chips on the way home.

She might have to live cheap, but that didn't mean that she *was* cheap, which was what Vaughn obviously thought. Grace sighed so heavily that the two teenage girls sitting behind her burst into giggles, even when she turned and gave them the evil eye. But she couldn't help sighing again because it had all been too good to be true; there really was no way a man like Vaughn would be interested in her without there being an ulterior motive. If she'd just sent him a polite little thank-you note for the Marc Jacobs bag, then none of this would have ever happened.

Grace tugged her foot free from the gooey blob of chewing gum that was stuck to the bottom of her flip-flops and closed her eyes.

chapter nine

Lily was back in the office the next day, her skin sun-kissed to the exact shade of toasted almonds because she even tanned perfectly. Grace didn't think she'd ever been so pleased to see anyone. Lily was going to have to cancel all her social plans for the rest of the week so they could properly do justice to the whole Vaughn débâcle.

'I missed you so much and I've got so much to tell you!' Grace exclaimed when Lily walked into the fashion cupboard, and Grace hurled herself at her friend. It was a moot point which one of them was most surprised, as they had a standing joke that Grace had cuddle deficiency syndrome. Now that Lily was hugging her, Grace wasn't sure what to do; Lily always felt so fragile but she patted her back enthusiastically before wriggling free. 'Did you have a nice time?'

'It was the best holiday of my life.' Lily beamed, and even without the tan, she would still have looked radiant and glowy. 'And I've got something to tell you too. Well, something to ask you.'

'Ask me what?'

Lily took Grace's hands and assumed a serious expression, which made Grace both intrigued and nervous. Lily only did serious in the most extenuating of circumstances, like the time she'd wanted Grace to let her cousin stay in her flat while she was in Worthing for the weekend.

'You're my absolute best friend, Gracie,' Lily began nervously, then stopped for a swift intake of breath.

'Lily, just spit it out. The suspense is killing me! Is your cous—'

'I want you to be my maid of honour. Look!' Lily started waving her left hand around like she was trying to put out a fire.

'Is that . . . ?' Grace squinted at the ring on Lily's third finger and the little stone that might possibly once have slept next to a diamond. 'Are you *engaged*? To Dan?'

'Who else would I be engaged to?' Lily said, as she held up the ring for closer inspection. 'It was so romantic, Gracie. We'd been smoking spliffs on the beach in the moonlight and Dan asked me to roll another one and he'd put the ring in the bag of weed.'

'Totally romantic,' she agreed, painting on a smile that drooped a little at the corners because her best friend was going to marry a guy that she really didn't like and who really didn't like her right back. She and Dan just weren't mixy, like stripes and polka dots. It wasn't anything that Dan had done in particular, apart from the fact that Grace thought that Lily could do much better and when Grace had started going out with Liam, Dan had told him that *he* could do a lot better. About the only thing that Grace and Dan agreed on was that Lily didn't need to know about their mutual antipathy because it violated all sorts of boyfriend and best friend codes of behaviour. So Grace put her game face on.

'I'm so happy for you,' she added with a lot more feeling, and gave Lily another hug. 'Wow, you're going to get married! You know you're going to be a proper grown-up now and you'll have to get a pension and at least three sets of bedlinen.'

'I know. I can't believe it.' Lily grinned. 'And you're not just maid of honour, you're also my wedding-dress consultant.

We'll have to go to Browns Bride so my mum doesn't force me into a meringue.'

This time, Grace's smile was one hundred per cent genuine. 'I promise your wedding will be a meringue-free zone,' she said solemnly.

'I'm counting on you.' Lily whirled around so the light caught her ring. 'I'm thinking of a spring wedding but Dan says that he wants to do it really quickly so I don't fall in love with anyone else. He's so sweet! Oh, but hey, so what were you going to tell me?'

Grace was sure that there was a scarlet letter branded on her, Hester Prynne style. A big H for Ho. But apparently it was invisible to the rest of the world. So she was just on the verge of launching forth with a million words a minute about drinks with Vaughn and dinner with Vaughn and being propositioned by Vaughn. She even opened her mouth to unleash them – but then she paused and shut her mouth.

It suddenly occurred to her that this was Lily's moment in the sun and it wasn't right to tarnish it with her tawdry tale. Today was and should be all about Lily. Grace looked at her friend, who was gazing down at her engagement ring with a look of wonder like she couldn't quite grasp how it had got there, and felt that unwelcome pang of envy she sometimes got when she thought about how different she and Lily were. Like, Dan wanted Lily to marry him because he thought she was priceless, whereas Vaughn had asked Grace to be his mistress because he thought she had a price.

'Gracie?' Lily prompted, tearing her eyes away from her third finger, left hand. 'Give me gossip. Now, please.'

Grace placed her finger on her chin so she could strike a thoughtful pose because she knew it would make Lily giggle. 'Where do I start? Kiki inflicted GBH with a Kenneth J Lane necklace when we were in New York,' she said breezily. 'I saw Ethan Hawke walking his dog. Also, fried shrimp and dirty martinis are a really bad combination, when you're throwing up three hours later. And Posy's single again but I think she's been doing stuff with Martyn from Subs in the wheelchair toilet.'

And that was how the last few weeks had been. Apart from the other stuff that Grace wasn't going to share with Lily right now. She'd wait until the excitement over the engagement had died down a little and find the right moment.

'Are you OK, Gracie?' Lily wanted to know. 'I'm not going to become a bridezilla or anything, if you're worried about that.'

'I wouldn't let you,' Grace assured her, tucking her arm into Lily's then wishing she hadn't because she was never normally this touchy-feely and Lily was bound to realise that something was well and truly up. 'I was just thinking that we should do something to celebrate. I could ring up the Hat and Fan and see if they'd let us have the back room this Saturday, if you like?'

'I like! I'm sure my dad would stick some money behind the bar for drinks,' Lily cried happily. 'Oh, that's so sweet of you. Could you help me set up one of those event things on Facebook?'

Organising an impromptu engagement party was just what Grace needed to take her mind off things. Her grandmother was a great advocate of keeping busy in times of crisis, and if Grace was faffing about with Facebook invites and having tense negotiations with the landlord of the Hat and Fan, then she didn't have time to obsess about Vaughn.

Obsessing about Vaughn was a strictly post-work, unable-to-sleep activity as Grace replayed the scene in his office over and over again and tried to sift through all the different feelings it raked up. Mostly, there was the feeling of rejection because Vaughn didn't want her for good, simple reasons like thinking about kissing her made him feel all shivery. But he had wanted her enough to pay her to slide between his sheets. It went round and round in Grace's head until each night she gave up trying to sleep and sat on the windowsill drinking mugs of tea and smoking cigarettes and trying really hard not to play 'what I would do with £5,000 a month'.

The next Saturday morning, Grace would have liked nothing more than a monster lie-in to try to pay off some of her sleep debt, but instead she was standing on a ladder pinning up Tord Boontje-inspired paper streamers in the back room of Lily's favourite pub. If only she could translate her completely random life skills into cold, hard cash, she thought to herself for the gazillionth time.

Once again, Grace mourned the loss of that sweet, tax-free £5,000. She kept seeing a fat wad of cash with little arms and legs that did a lopsided soft-shoe shuffle when she thought about it. Which she did – all the sodding time, though she kept telling herself not to. £5,000 would mean no more brown envelopes, no more harassment from loan companies and the really snippy woman who kept phoning from her bank. Three lots of £5,000 would be enough to put down a deposit on a little flat. And the clothing allowance would buy the kind of designer dresses that she normally only came into contact with when she was putting them on skinny models or ambling through Liberty's . . .

'Christ, you must have been here for hours!'

Grace glanced over her shoulder as Lily and Dan walked in, almost buried under a weight of Tupperware containers. She'd spent Friday evening using their oven to bake hundreds of cupcakes.

'Hey,' she said through a mouthful of drawing pins. 'You can put them in one of the big fridges in the kitchen.' Dan walked back out again, muttering under his breath as he did so.

'Oh, it looks so pretty in here!' Lily exclaimed, turning slowly so she could see the Chinese lanterns and fairy lights that Grace had already placed around the room. 'It's adorable!'

'You're sure it's not too cheesy?'

'No, it's lovely,' Lily said, and she sounded close to tears. 'I can't believe you did all this in four days.'

'I learned from the best. My gran can organise a sit-down dinner for twelve at twenty-four hours' notice,' Grace said lightly. 'It was no biggie.'

'Thank you so—'

Grace held up her hand because she didn't really deserve Lily's effusive thanks. It wasn't as if she'd done the party planning entirely out of the goodness of her heart; it was more about trying to wipe out that hour in Vaughn's office by being so busy she couldn't think straight.

'You don't have to do the big speech,' she said. 'I was happy to do it.'

'God, Gracie, when will you learn to take a compliment?' Lily looked up at her in exasperation, which just made Grace feel more guilty. 'Can you come down from there, because I want to talk to you.'

Grace jumped down the last step and stood with hands planted firmly on her hips. 'What's up?'

'You. You've been in the dark place all week,' Lily said, plonking herself down on a chair. 'I know something's bothering you.'

'I'm fine,' Grace said automatically, then amended it because Lily always got understandably touchy when she said that. 'I just have some stuff on my mind. Really, it's too boring to even talk about. Work, money, the usual.'

'Oh Gracie, I wish you could be as happy as I am. I really do,' Lily said fervently, and her kindness always killed Grace a little bit. Of course, it was easy to be sweet and understanding when nothing bad had ever really happened to you. What Grace knew, and what Lily couldn't ever fathom, was that suffering didn't improve you; it just made you miserable and gave you a really bitter outlook on life.

'I'm OK,' she assured Lily. 'You know what I'm like when I go to the dark place. Give me a couple of hours to get over myself and if that doesn't work, just give me a good slap.'

'I would never resort to physical violence,' Lily mock-sniffed, and Grace could tell she was relieved that Grace had hauled herself back from the brink enough to crack a joke. 'Well, actually I might pull your hair a little.'

Thankfully, Lily didn't have time to probe any further because at that moment Dan came back into the room, giving a long, low whistle as he took stock of Grace's DIY party decorations. 'Nice,' he stated. 'Very nice, Gracie.'

'Dan, you could be more wordy with the thanks,' Lily pouted. 'Grace has been slogging her guts out all week.'

'Yeah, but then Grace would do that passive-aggressive thing she does when she won't let anyone say nice things to her.'

'I don't!'

Lily threw her hands up in the air; even her bountiful supply of good cheer wasn't infinite. 'Why is everyone being so scratchy today? Dan, say something nice to Grace and Gracie, for God's sake let Dan say something nice to you.'

Grace raised her chin in a challenge that made Dan's eyes flash but then he grinned. 'How about I don't say something nice and I give you some champagne instead?' he asked, pulling two bottles of Moët out from behind him. 'It's just our way – well, Lily's dad's way 'cause he's paying for it – of saying thank you.'

Champagne she could handle. Grace grinned right back and for a few scant seconds she and Dan were in perfect accord. 'Yes, yes. Champagne. Now, please.'

Lily was back to sunny smiles and hair flicks. Dan still wasn't good enough for her and never would be, but was there any better sound in the world than a champagne cork popping? Hell, no.

Grace held the bottle to her mouth and took a long swig before she brandished it at the happy couple. 'Come on, let's start the toasts early.'

Grace was a genius. She was stardust. She was one carbon in a billion. She was a Martha Stewart for her generation, with the witty fish-fingers-and-oven-chips hot buffet, and her intricate Dutch streamers. She'd even told the DJ to only play songs with 'love' in the title.

If the knitted accessories range didn't pan out, then she could easily be a party planner. People were happy. People were having a good time and it was because Grace totally rocked when it came to creating the perfect party vibe. Well, that and the free bar.

Grace was startled out of her reverie and aimless swaying to 'Peace, Love and Understanding' when Liam looped an arm round her shoulder. 'Can we have a chat?'

She was in that mellow, toasty drunken state that wrapped her up in a cocoon, unplagued by negative thoughts about her cupcakes being trodden underfoot or treacherous ex-boyfriends.

'Yeah, sure,' she slurred, letting Liam lead her out of the room and into the little backyard outside. 'What gives?'

Liam perched on one of the metal beer barrels. 'Is Lily knocked up?'

'Well, if she is she shouldn't have been drinking since eleven thirty this morning.' Grace frowned. 'No, she'd have told me.'

'So why are they getting married?' Liam asked. He was sober, which was a novelty but he spent Saturdays working on a bootleg DVD stall at Camden Market and he needed to be able to count change. 'Like, if they don't need to.'

Grace hauled herself on to a neighbouring barrel. 'Well, they're in love and neither of them are very bright. Is this the wrong moment to let slip that Lily wants you to play a medley of Burt Bacharach hits at the wedding reception?'

'Jesus, kill me now!'

'Could be worse, baby. Lily has a couple of Boyzone CDs tucked away!' Grace tried to give Liam a friendly punch on the arm and nearly fell off her perch. She settled for groping in her bag for fags and lighter. She'd started smoking again in earnest this week.

'Are you pissed, Gracie?'

'Beyond pissed and verging on paralytic,' Grace announced proudly, as she managed to light her cigarette on the fifth attempt. Then in a fit of alcohol-soaked cunning, she realised that she had a Get Out of Jail Free card to say whatever she liked. Tomorrow she could just pretend that she didn't remember. In fact, tomorrow she probably wouldn't be able to remember. 'So, who are you with tonight? Some barely legal Trustafarian, I'll bet.' Grace exhaled smoke with what she hoped was haughty disdain.

'You jealous?' Liam asked with a hint of that smirky grin that had used to make her come over all unnecessary. He'd also washed his hair in the last twenty-four hours, which was a huge deal and not to be taken lightly.

'Hardly, but, like a month to get over an ex is standard. You could have pretended that you were a bit cut up about it.' All the hurt was welling up again and it was almost a relief to think about something that hadn't occurred in Vaughn's office.

'Look, I was upset,' Liam said, leaning closer so Grace could see the deep hollows under his eyes which she'd used to stroke with her thumbs when they were in bed. 'You have to know that those first few weeks that we were together, I was so into you.'

It wasn't what she wanted to hear. 'Then why did you stop?'

Liam shrugged. 'Don't know. It's what we keep coming back to, isn't it? Something wasn't right.'

'You mean *I* wasn't right?'

He was trying; Grace had to give him that. 'You just weren't there, Gracie. Like, I never got to see the real you and it didn't even seem like you were that into me until I broke it off. I really didn't think you'd be this bothered.'

Grace felt as if Liam had stuck a pin in her and she was slowly deflating until there'd be nothing left but a little pile of skin and hair and one hundred per cent cotton. 'Well, I thought I put some serious effort into our relationship,' she said in surprise, and she must have been looking all kinds of hurt because Liam gave her knee a gentle pat.

'Maybe relationships shouldn't be such hard work,' he mused. 'Like, if you're right for someone then shouldn't everything fall into place really easily?'

'Don't ask me. I realise I don't know a thing about making someone else happy. Like, I knew you were going off me but I was powerless to do anything about it.' It was probably because she was drunk and her defences were down, but Grace was pleased that she and Liam could give their three months a proper goodbye. 'I'm going to end up alone, I just know it.'

'Don't be such a drama queen,' Liam drawled, giving her another sideways smirk, and Grace remembered how he could usually tease her out of her bad moods. 'Yeah, we didn't work out, but some other guy will come along and he'll think you're ace. And we should be friends, Gracie. I need to have someone to bitch to when Dan starts trying to make me plan stag weekends and write best man speeches.'

They sighed in tandem at the hell that awaited them as the wedding got nearer. 'Well, I s'pose you can never have too many friends.' Grace paused as she debated whether she should roadtest Liam's declaration of friendship. 'So, if we're friends, then can I ask you something as a friend? Something guy-related so I can get a male perspective on it?'

'What guy?' Liam asked suspiciously, like he was suddenly having trouble letting go of the boyfriend mindset.

'This rich, older guy who bought me a designer handbag.'

'Lily told me about that perv who picked you up in Liberty's,' Liam snapped. 'He's only after one thing.'

His reaction wasn't exactly encouraging but Grace wanted to tell somebody, even if it was Liam. *Especially* as it was Liam. 'If I tell you this, then you have to promise you won't blab to anyone. Which mostly means Lily and Dan.'

Maybe it was the conspiratorial, low voice Grace used or the hand on his leg but Liam nodded, his mouth hanging open.

So Grace hit him with the highlights, drawing a discreet veil over anything that might have happened in the back of a limousine, and concentrating on the moral implications of letting the rich, older, strangely attractive, art-dealer guy who owned successful businesses in London and New York pay for the pleasure of her company.

'So, what do you think?' she asked anxiously. 'It's kinda surreal, isn't it?'

Liam looked like he'd just witnessed a ten-car pile-up, which was deeply satisfying because it would be a while before he became a friend rather than a former boyfriend. 'I think it's fucking degrading. You're not going to take him up on it, are you?'

'Well, no . . .'

'You can't fuck someone just because they're going to buy you some expensive shoes!'

'I fucked you and all you ever bought me were a couple of cans of Stella and the condoms if I really nagged.'

'But . . . but . . . but at least I . . . respected you!'

'Oh, come on, Liam! You never took me anywhere nice, you never paid for anything, you took a picture of my tits on your camera phone and showed it to all your mates – how was that respecting me? At least he's being honest about it.'

'So you are going to do it, then?'

'No!' Grace pulled her fingers through her hair and

groaned. 'I don't know. I'm hammered and thinking is really hard right now.'

Liam stood up solely so he could look disapprovingly down at Grace. 'I might not have been the best boyfriend in the world but that's no reason to give up on relationships and get into something this shady. He's treating you like a whore.'

'No, he's not!' Grace snapped immediately, though hadn't she been thinking exactly the same thing? 'You're making out that it's sordid and all to do with sex, and it's not like that at all. He happens to think that I'm talented and he's giving me sort of like a . . . an Arts Council grant to develop myself.'

The champagne had made everything glitter. Now it was wearing off, leaving Grace as flat as the dregs in her glass. Liam stopped boxing her in and took a step backwards. 'God, it's a fuck of a lot of money though. Five grand a month?'

Grace nodded frantically. 'Plus a clothing allowance. And it would be, like, maybe six months out of my entire life, which is nothing really. I could pay off all my debts and—'

'You are not doing this, Grace,' Liam growled. 'C'mon, babes, you're too good for a creep like that.' He was looking at her like he used to during those few weeks when she was the centre of his world.

'You're right,' Grace sighed. 'I know you're right. I was just saying, is all.' She drained the last mouthful of champagne. 'But it's not that bad being a mistress. 'Cause half the women on the party pages in the *ES Magazine* are mistresses and they don't seem like skanks. Or what about those girls who go out with fugly guys just 'cause they're Premier League footballers? They get given newspaper columns and no one judges them for anything except their crappy dress sense. And it would have been cool in this Holly Golightly way – we're not even talking about fifty dollars for the powder room but five grand! Hey, did you know that Marilyn Monroe was meant to be in that film instead of Audrey Hepburn, but then she died?'

He didn't know and couldn't have cared any less. 'You're

totally rat-arsed,' Liam stated, sounding pleased that it was the alcohol talking and that common sense would prevail once the hangover kicked in.

'Whatever,' Grace mumbled listlessly. 'I'm starting to sober up and I feel like crap.'

He held out his hand. 'Come on, let's share a cab home.'

chapter ten

Grace wasn't sure what woke her. It could have been the need to glug down three pints of icy cold water because it felt as if someone had emptied a slagheap into her mouth. Or the sun glaring in through the open curtains. Or Liam's hard-on digging into the small of her back.

Actually it was all of the above, but mostly Liam's hand dive-bombing between her legs.

Grace had very little recollection of events after she'd staggered out of the bar wrapped around Liam, who'd been the only thing between her and the pavement. But somehow he'd managed to put her in a taxi (Grace was pretty sure he'd rifled through her purse to pay for it), got her home, took off all her clothes, pulled out the sofabed and was now trying to have sex with her. To think she used to accuse him of not being goal orientated enough.

'What are you doing?' Grace's voice was muffled by the pillow, as she tried to wriggle away from his fumbling hand.

His mouth latched on to the back of her neck in a hot-breathed, wet kiss that made her flinch. 'C'mon, Gracie, for old times' sake.'

'Shut up and go back to sleep.' Grace grabbed the edge of the bed and hauled with all her might because Liam was slobbering over her shoulder and it was too early for this. 'I'm tired and I'm trying very hard not to throw up.'

Liam kept butting his dick against her like a dog with a wet nose that wanted stroking. 'I've got condoms,' he offered generously, because going bareback was a Grace deal-breaker. Considerate of him to remember.

'Go back to sleep,' Grace rasped, and now she was wide awake and wishing she wasn't.

'Grace . . .' Liam was whining now and trying to find her clit, though he was a good few centimetres off. 'Look, this was always good between us.'

Yeah, keep clinging to that illusion, Grace thought to herself, but she wriggled free of Liam's hands so she could roll over. 'What happened to just being friends?'

Liam was already trying to fit their bodies together, entwining his legs with Grace's. 'Friends with benefits,' he clarified, leaning in to try to kiss her, though Grace winced as the smell of morning breath assaulted her. She was pretty sure that her own didn't smell much better.

'Don't "friends with benefits" me,' she said, rubbing the back of his neck to take the sting out of her words. 'Look, you go and brush your teeth, then I'll brush my teeth and if you make me a cup of tea while I'm doing it, we can have a cuddle. But I'm putting my knickers back on.'

'Cuddle with knickers off and I'll make you toast too,' Liam offered, clambering out of the sofabed, which creaked alarmingly.

'It's not a negotiation, Liam,' Grace said, as she watched him pad across the room. He did have a nice arse – malleable yet firm, even though he lived on fried food and did absolutely no exercise. 'And two sugars, please.'

They'd ended up having sex, because the cuddling just hadn't worked out. Contrary to popular belief, sometimes Grace did like to hug and cuddle and just be held in someone's arms for the sheer comfort of being held. But it hadn't worked this time. Something had come between them – Liam's penis, which had made its presence felt and Liam's face contort like he was in pain until Grace had taken pity on both of them.

'Go on,' she'd sighed, pulling free of Liam's embrace so she could slide her knickers off. 'Just this once, but don't think we're going to make it a regular thing.'

Sex with Liam certainly wasn't good enough to ever become a regular thing, and he'd given her a lovebite. Grace only noticed it once he'd left after a brief hug and a promise to call her.

Then she'd had to wait ages to get into the bathroom as Eileen from the ground-floor flat was doing her weekly scrub with her bucket of cleaning fluids, though Grace didn't know why she bothered. When she finally heard Eileen trudge back to her own two lonely little rooms, Grace locked herself in the bathroom and as she waited the twenty minutes for the tub to fill up, there was nothing to do but either stare at the lovebite in the cracked mirror above the cracked sink or stare at the avocado tiles and stained grouting.

Once the bath was full of water that was a few degrees too hot for comfort, Grace carefully lowered herself into the tub and sat there, knees hugged to her chest and a slight ache between her legs. She knew she'd never be able to forgive Liam for this. Which was a strange but effective way to move forward.

And in some ways, a grudge fuck with Liam simpled things up. There was no way she should feel this dirty and used and have nothing to show for it but a dark, throbbing bruise in the wrong season for polo necks.

Vaughn had been right – she was worth so much more than this.

Once she was scrubbed clean, Grace dug out her emergency credit card, unsullied in its never-been-used splendour, from where she'd wedged it down the back of the fridge. Then she headed for Oxford Street.

Grace hadn't shopped like this in months. She started at

Liberty's and worked her way down to Marble Arch, not even bothering to stop in Primark or New Look because ten-pound dresses couldn't soothe the hurt inside. She didn't look at the price tags or try anything on, just snatched up something satin in her favourite shade of emerald green, which slithered between her fingers. Grabbed a pair of shoes with that buttery leather smell that always made her feel high. A necklace here, a Balenciaga bag there.

Grace didn't want to know how much she'd spent and actually she didn't really care. She just wanted to fill up the gaping chasm inside her with pretty things. Grace always told herself that these occasional shopping binges, which only happened in the most dire of circumstances, didn't matter too much in the grand scheme of all her many debts. She'd still owe thousands and thousands of pounds anyway just from not being able to live on what she earned at *Skirt*, so what difference did a few more thousand make to Mr Visa or Mr Mastercard? Though it was odd that she'd chosen an out-of-control shopping habit for her emotional disorder when her grandparents were the poster OAPs for frugality.

Seams were let out, hems were taken down, and when an item of clothing was deemed beyond repair, her grandmother would cut it up and find fifty different uses for it. The stale end of the loaf became bread and butter pudding. They saved on petrol and walked any distance that was less than three miles. These were lessons that had been drummed into Grace from the age of eight, but they obviously hadn't stuck, she thought as she collapsed on to one of the stone benches outside Selfridges, the fancy ribbon handles on all the stiff cardboard bags cutting into her hands. She sat there for several minutes staring at the welts criss-crossing her palms, then pulled out her phone.

Vaughn answered just as Grace hoped it would roll over to voicemail.

'It's Grace,' she said flatly.

'Oh, I was beginning to wonder if I'd ever hear from you again.' She could hear the caution carved into each syllable. 'Is it yes or no?'

That was the only thing she liked about him right now. He wasn't into bullshit; he just got straight to the point.

'I need to ask you some stuff. About, like, this arrangement,' she ground out and she could practically *hear* him arching an eyebrow.

'Now? Over the phone?'

'Yup.' Flippancy seemed like the best way to go. As if this was the kind of conversation she'd had a million times and in her experience over the phone was just peachy, thanks for asking.

'I don't th— Where are you? You sound as if you're at a football match.'

Grace paused as a bus vibrated noisily behind her. 'Oxford Street,' she admitted unwillingly because she knew, in a freakish sixth-sense sort of way, exactly what Vaughn was going to say next.

'Perfect. I'm finishing some work at the office. Come straight over.'

Which was reasonable and made sense, if she didn't have a skanky bruise on her neck and the net worth of several Third World nations in her bags. 'Well, now's really not a good time,' she prevaricated. 'I have stuff to do.'

'What's that? I can't hear a word you're saying.' He *so* could. 'Just be a good girl and come over.'

'But I'm not a good girl,' Grace said, bristling angrily. 'Isn't that the whole point?'

'I'll see you in the next half-hour,' Vaughn said crisply, then he had the fucking nerve to hang up on her.

Half an hour and well, seven minutes later, Grace was standing in front of the gallery and looking down doubtfully at the black clam-diggers and sleeveless pin-tucked blouse, which had officially gone 'missing' on a shoot and never been returned to the press office. Then she adjusted the scarf she'd just bought and knotted round her neck, choker-style, to make sure it was still covering the bite.

She couldn't put off pressing the door buzzer any longer. 'It's me, Grace,' she said, when Vaughn's disembodied voice floated through the speaker.

There was an awful 'push me/pull me' as she tried to open the door in the allotted time but there was no sign of Vaughn, so Grace stashed her bags behind the reception desk and took a few deep breaths.

'There you are,' said a voice behind her and Grace turned around, face flaring up as if she'd been caught stealing from the till rather than foofing up the limp strands of her hair. 'I'd almost given up on you.'

Grace's hand was already creeping up to make sure that the scarf was secure but she forced it down and feigned an indifferent shrug. 'Slow-moving tourists,' was all the explanation she could come up with. She hoped Vaughn would stay on the half-landing and she'd stay cowering behind the desk and launch into her speech but he was already tripping down the last flight of stairs.

He was wearing dark blue jeans and a faded green T-shirt with a disintegrating logo on it that Grace couldn't identify but didn't want to get caught staring. So she concentrated on his feet, even though the Camper shoes were another tiny mind fuck. Vaughn did casual Sundays? Who knew?

Not that it made him less intimidating but maybe Vaughn realised that Grace was seconds away from a major freak-out because he stood a few feet away and gestured at the stairs.

'It's almost as hot as New York. I've been working on the roof terrace – the view's quite incredible.' He was talking too much, giving Grace too much explanation – could he be as nervous as she was? 'Shall we go up there?'

Grace nodded and followed Vaughn up the stairs. On the

second floor he paused. 'Does this merit a glass of champagne?'

'God, no! I'm still recovering from last night,' she amended at a less shrieky volume, fingers worrying at the edge of the scarf again. 'Actually, I've given up alcohol. I'm taking the pledge tomorrow.'

And that was the right note because Vaughn smiled ever so slightly. 'I've come to the same decision many times but it never lasts more than twenty-four hours. Do you want a cold drink?'

Grace really wanted a mug of builder's tea brewed so strong that she'd need a hand-whisk to stir it, but she couldn't imagine Vaughn boiling up a kettle and dunking tea bags. 'Diet Coke, if you've got it.'

'The terrace is through those French doors at the end of the corridor.' Vaughn tipped his head in the general direction before disappearing to find her a can of caffeiney goodness.

The terrace was perfect. A little rooftop oasis of cool and calm; a water feature trickling away in defiance of the hosepipe ban, gravel crunching under Grace's ballet flats as she picked her way through succulent green plants, their leaves brushing against her legs until she came to a spindly and delicate wrought-iron table with chairs gathered around it.

Grace stared out over the rooftops and chimney stacks. There were little patches of green here and there, other gardens in the skies, and if she really craned her neck, she could just make out the tops of the plane trees edging Hyde Park. She'd only ever seen the park from eye-level, never from this high up, and – without the hordes of tourists and the danger of being mown down by skateboarders and over-excited small children – it was peaceful. Almost calming. And a timely lesson that money could buy you anything: even a better view.

'It's so beautiful up here,' she said, because she could hear

Vaughn's footsteps behind her. 'Like a secret little camp or something.'

'Well, it's wonderful on days like this but it doesn't get much use, I'm afraid,' Vaughn said shortly, setting two glasses down on the table. He pulled out one of the chairs so Grace could sit down, and the tight, binding feeling was back in her stomach. She took a quick gulp of the Coke to rinse the metallic taste out of her mouth, while Vaughn watched her closely. 'OK, what would you like to ask me?' He looked intrigued, as if she was going to ask him if he had a dungeon or if he wanted to dress her up as a French maid before he fucked her. Not even close.

'Are you married?'

There was a moment's startled silence, before he cleared his throat. 'Divorced. For quite a while now.'

That was just the warm-up question; the ones after that were harder, especially when Grace felt as if she was having to fight for every breath. She swallowed nervously and turned her head to gaze at a water feature. 'See, I was thinking about the terms of the agreement, that we could . . . that you could . . .' She trailed off, not exactly sure how to phrase it, and shrugged helplessly.

'That I could what?' Vaughn prompted, and Grace didn't think she'd ever heard him sound that gentle. It helped a little.

'Couldn't I just help you with your parties and be your hostess and that would be it?' She looked up to see Vaughn frowning, though surely he had to understand what she was saying. 'That we wouldn't, y'know, have sex. It would just be like a part-time hostess job.'

She looked down at her hands, which she was clasping tightly so she wouldn't start wringing them, and waited for Vaughn's reply. She didn't have to wait very long.

'No, that doesn't work for me,' he said simply. 'Correct me if I'm wrong, Grace, but surely you're here because you wanted to have sex with me.'

Grace had been heating up steadily and now she was sure that she was so red she could be seen from outer space. 'Yes, but . . . I did, but that was before you started talking about agreements – and I was really, really drunk that night!' Her voice was straining higher and higher and she took another gulp of Diet Coke and nearly choked on it. All the while, Vaughn watched her as if she was some kind of science experiment and it made Grace resentful enough that she found her second wind. 'What I'm trying to say is, this whole sex thing: I just don't know that I could do *it* without being in love.'

'Oh, do you only fuck people you're in love with?' Vaughn asked tartly, and actually the snark was easier to handle, familiar territory. 'That's novel.'

'No, but there's usually an emotional involvement . . .' Grace tailed off again because she was tying herself up in knots. Usually there *was* an emotional involvement, but sometimes it was just because it was easier than saying no and she didn't want to be on her own.

'Interesting as it is watching you have a crisis of conscience, I need a decision,' Vaughn said sharply, and if Grace thought he'd be charming and persuasive to get her on side then obviously she was wrong. 'In the next five minutes, otherwise I'll rescind the offer. Would you like me to set my watch?'

'No! I can't think properly. You could at least try to see this from my point of view.'

'Well, I'm trying, but your point of view is a little cloudy,' Vaughn murmured. He made a big show of looking at his watch. 'Four minutes now . . .'

'Jesus!' Vaughn hadn't said anything about her having to squirm under his relentless gaze so Grace stumbled to her feet and crunched over the gravel until she was looking down at Hyde Park again and trying to herd her scattered thoughts. She could go back the way she'd come in so she was at ground level, chugging along at the same old pace. Or she could stay up on the roof where even the air seemed purer.

And really, she would have slept with Vaughn in New York. So if she just remembered that and also remembered that the money wasn't for the sex but for being Vaughn's hostess, then it immediately became less shady. Because sleeping with your boss wasn't that bad on the wrong scale: loads of women did that. Or married for money. In fact, all the *Skirt* fashion department had rich husbands. Kiki was married to a hedge fund manager and he was really plug ugly so it wasn't like Kiki had been knocked off her Jimmy Choos by his good looks. And Posy and Lily had rich dads. Grace frowned as she suddenly realised that practically every woman she knew was being bank-rolled by a man in some way. Well, except her grandmother who would have fifty fits if she ever knew what she—

'Time's up, Grace,' Vaughn said behind her. 'Are you in or out?'

Was she in?

Was she going to say yes?

Grace closed her eyes and stepped nearer to the edge of the roof. She could stay exactly where she was, still and stagnating, or she could jump. She took another step, until she felt the guard rail dig into her waist.

Of course she was going to say yes. If she really thought about it, she'd been planning to say yes ever since last Monday. Being Vaughn's mistress was the something that would one day turn up and take her out of a life of colossal, mind-churning debt and nagging discontent. She'd been waiting for this, for something to change because she felt that she was walking through life in slow motion. Liam was moving on. Lily was moving forward. And, as usual, Grace was stuck in the same place and she couldn't fucking stand it.

'I'm in,' she said finally, glad that her voice didn't shake or sound squeaky. Nothing happened, which was weird. There should have been a sudden loud clap of thunder at the very least. But she'd been here before, and when your life changed, everyone else's life carried on the same as before. It was like the long minutes of silence after her mother and father had had their most ferocious row ever about who *wasn't* going to get custody of her. They'd sat glaring at each other from either side of the table in the little anteroom in the family court, terrified that one of them would get the short straw. Finally, the social worker had asked Grace who she wanted to live with and rounded it off with a volley of encouraging smiles and she'd heard herself say, 'I don't want to live with either of them.'

The buses had carried on trundling past the window, someone had laughed in the corridor, the sun had continued to shine, even though something inside of Grace had been smashed into little pieces that could never be put back together. So, really, no matter how scary Vaughn was, he couldn't break her. She was already broken. In a way the joke was on him, because he was buying damaged goods.

'I'm in,' Grace said again because Vaughn hadn't responded and she wasn't sure if he'd heard her.

'Good. Now come away from the edge before you break your neck and we can go over a few details.'

Grace followed him back to the table and this time she was able to sit down, cross her legs and sip at her Diet Coke without feeling like she was about to burst into flames. She wasn't relaxed, not at all, but now she could fake being relaxed.

Vaughn didn't say anything. Nor did Grace as she stared at the heat haze suspended above the city. 'OK, you need to start talking,' she said finally, because the silence was torturous and she was clutching the can of Coke like it was a life-raft again. 'You're totally having second thoughts now, aren't you?'

'Don't be so fatuous,' Vaughn snapped quickly enough that her ego undented itself. 'Could you bring yourself to maybe look at me?'

Grace inched forward so she could meet his eyes, but

Vaughn was staring at the thrust of her breasts in the fitted blouse, which was unexpected, but strangely validating.

'So, how does this work then?' she asked curiously. 'Would I have to live with you?' She had a sudden vision of herself handing Vaughn a perfectly mixed vodka martini as he came through the front door and asking him in a seductive purr, 'Hard day at the office, dear?'

Vaughn gave a snort of laughter, which nixed that idea. He even slapped one hand against his knee, which was completely unnecessary. 'There aren't enough incentives in the world to persuade anyone to put up with me seven days a week.'

Grace let out tiny sips of air. 'Are you really that bad?'

'Yes, I am. I hope it's going to be an exciting experience for you, but I'm not the easiest man to be with. You should think very carefully about what you're agreeing to,' Vaughn advised, his eyes fixed unwaveringly on hers. 'I'll give you one last chance to back out, but then all bets are off.'

Grace thought of the bags stashed behind the desk downstairs. Compensation for how shitty Liam had made her feel this morning. At least with Vaughn, it wouldn't be messy. No more grey, which had never been a colour that went well with her complexion. Might as well be with someone who wasn't going to pretend that she was the one girl he'd never get enough of. At least he'd buy her things to make up for it.

'I'm not going to back out,' Grace said firmly, fingering the knot of the scarf to make sure it was still secured.

'Even when I make you cry every day? Twice daily on weekends?' Vaughn's voice was airy but he was drumming a tattoo with his fingers on the tabletop and his fierce blue glare didn't falter. 'When I tell you that I hate what you're wearing or force you to flirt with some malodorous Russian oligarch, or I don't want to talk to you because I've been on conference calls all day. Are you sure you're up to it?'

Grace didn't scrape back her chair and flee in squealing horror. Vaughn's catalogue of horrors were nothing compared to what she'd had to put up with from past boyfriends. There was Paul Gold who'd taken her virginity and given her a score out of ten on the wall of the gents in Burger King. Or the graphic artist in her freshman year who'd dumped her on the side of the M6 after they'd had a row on the way home from visiting his parents. Or the cokehead DJ who'd nicked her TV, DVD player and stereo to buy drugs. And there was Liam . . . So, yes, Grace was sure she was up for anything Vaughn wanted to throw at her.

'You've been nothing but honest with me and I think that's a good basis for this, like, partnership,' Grace said. 'There are boundaries, which means I have less chance of screwing things up, but I still think you might regret the whole six months thing.'

Vaughn waved a dismissive hand. He was already snaring the edge of a pad with his finger and pulling it closer so he could make notes. 'Why don't you let me worry about that? What kind of holiday allowance do you get?'

'Six weeks and public holidays.' Grace was lucky if she took half of that because, despite all appearances to the contrary, when it came to signing her holiday booking forms, Kiki was always reluctant to let her go.

'We can work around that, though I have to insist that your days off belong to me now.'

All sorts of warning bells should have been ringing, but all Grace could hear was a solitary car horn beeping from a long way away. 'OK. I'll work out how many days I've got left and email you or something.'

'I'll get my assistant to set up an account for you at a spa. Now do you want the other allowances paid into your bank account or would you prefer cash?' Vaughn's voice was bland, like he was asking her if she wanted another Coke.

'What?'

'How do you want to be paid?' Vaughn repeated, tapping the edge of the notebook with an impatient finger.

Grace thought quickly. The second that money hit her bank account it would disappear, snatched away by greedy hands belonging to several large, loan-clearing companies and she would need to spend some of it on some suitable hostessy clothes and other luxuries like food and topping up her Oyster card. 'Um, cash will be fine. You know, you don't have to give me so much money!' she exclaimed. 'I don't need that much. It's seven thousand a month – that's like having a part-time job that pays nearly a hundred grand a year.'

'I know. And really, if I gave you any less I'd be short-changing you,' Vaughn assured her carelessly, but his eyebrows had risen up in surprise. 'If you can't spend it all, then give some of it to charity. Really, it's no concern of mine.'

He had to be really, really rich, Grace thought. The kind of rich where almost a hundred grand a year was pocket change – money that didn't matter one way or another; the multi-millionaire equivalent of coins down the back of the sofa, even though it was enough money to instantly change her life beyond all her expectations. It was impossible to process and Grace had this strange out-of-body sensation, as if she was floating high above the clouds, watching a girl who looked like her and sounded like her. Because stuff like this just didn't happen. Life – *her* life – didn't work like this.

'So, what happens now?' Grace was half-expecting, half-dreading Vaughn to have her naked in the next five seconds.

But he just underlined something on the page in his crabby scrawl, before he closed the pad decisively. 'I had my lawyer start to draw up the contract. It will be with you later in the week.'

'So you knew I'd say yes?' Grace couldn't help the slightly peevish tone. Was she really that predictable?

'I hoped you'd say yes. Now you have, so it's worked out well for both of us.' There was a slight bite to Vaughn's voice and his lips tightened, but when Grace tried out another tentative smile, he relaxed. She just needed to figure out the right way to handle him – and quickly. 'Anyway, I won't see you for a while. I'm flying to Moscow in the morning for a week and you're going to be rather busy. My assistant will be in touch about the specifics.' He stood up and held out his hand so Grace had no choice but to let him pull her to her feet. 'Your top priority is to do something with this.' His hand brushed her cheek as he lifted up a hank of hair. 'It really isn't the right image.'

There wasn't a person in the world that approved of her daring and bold choice of hair colour. 'I'll see what I can do,' Grace said demurely, though her words lacked conviction.

'You do that.'

They were just sounding out words now as a way to avoid the fact that it was time to make things official.

It was weird, especially when Vaughn's hands rested on her hips, that they could stand so close, touch each other, but still feel so far away. Grace shifted, her knees banging against Vaughn's legs, and giggled.

She expected Vaughn to smile back again but he lowered his head and kissed her.

It started out as a perfunctory kiss, something a little more symbolic than a handshake. But it was so different from the way that Liam had dribbled into her mouth that morning, that Grace rose on tiptoe and put her hands on Vaughn's shoulders so she could tentatively kiss him back. Both of them were just testing the water but there was a part of Grace that wanted to close her eyes and dive right to the bottom.

Grace was certain that this wasn't a kiss that was going to lead anywhere. Vaughn's grip relaxed and loosened but he didn't slide his hands a few crucial inches down but up to trace the violin curve of her waist as he caught her bottom lip between his teeth, tugging lightly before he pulled away. A tiny whimper of protest leaked out of Grace's mouth before she could hold it in.

Desire was so complicated.

'Well, I guess I'm your mistress now,' Grace said, and wished she hadn't because it was a totally dumb thing to say.

Vaughn obviously thought so too because he ignored her but lightly traced the edges of the scarf. 'You've been worrying at this ever since you got here,' he remarked idly, as Grace flinched away from his touch. 'Why did you change your mind?'

The scarf felt as if it was still fulfilling its remit to cover up the evidence of the night before but Grace really wanted to fiddle to make sure. 'I just did, is all,' she muttered. 'It made sense once I thought about where my life was going and where I really want to be.' Which was anywhere but where she'd been that morning.

'I was very disturbed after our last meeting. You seemed to think that it was all a nefarious scheme so I could have my evil way with you. That you were being used for sex,' Vaughn continued, tucking a lock of hair behind her ear. These involuntary caresses were starting to freak Grace out. He was so tactile. 'Which you're not, by the way.'

'Well, actually I kinda *am* – but I'm using you too,' Grace countered, staring at the cleft in his chin which was right on her eyeline, as his hands dropped away. 'We both need something from the other one. And for me, it's not just for the money, but that I get to live in a different world, get treated differently. Or at least people will—'

'You should stop talking now,' Vaughn warned her, and it was amazing how chilly his voice could get. 'Nobody's being used. We're just entering into a mutually beneficial arrangement.'

Grace decided to see if she felt like the user or the used when it was the morning after and she had £5,000 in crisp banknotes in her hand.

Vaughn stepped away and she waited for him to call the whole thing off but he just looked at her thoughtfully. Like he'd stripped off everything – clothes, skin – and was the first person to ever see her for what she really was. Apparently, the vision wasn't too horrific because he smiled. And if Grace thought there was something a little sad, a little bruised in the quirk of his lips, she put it down to the light playing tricks.

'I told you this would be an interesting year,' was all he said.

chapter eleven

Grace thought the attack of conscience would kick in on the way home, but it didn't. In fact, she had an entirely different attack of conscience when she unpacked the spoils from her shopping binge. Even the prospect of actually being able to afford them in the very near future wasn't enough, and the panic was rising like bile. So she did what she always did; stored them in vacuum-sealed plastic bags and buried them right at the back of her wardrobe where she wouldn't see them. Then even though it was early, only five o'clock, Grace got into bed and slept. It was monster sleep. Fourteen hours of oblivion and when she woke up, in those few split seconds before her synapses fired up, she'd forgotten what had happened the day before. But as she opened her eyes and sat up, it all started to come back to her.

It wasn't until she was in a cab on the way to work (because girls with £80,000 per annum part-time jobs didn't take the bus) that Grace was fighting for breath and frantically tugging at the window because throwing up seemed like a definite possibility.

It was horrific. Yesterday, she'd given Vaughn an Access All Areas pass to her body and he could call it what he wanted, and throw in a few fancy long words for good measure, but it was what it was. She was his mistress and nothing would ever be the same again, Grace told herself. She'd stop being *her* and become this other creature completely subject to Vaughn's whims and demands. It was the demands that worried her the most.

But then the cab was pulling up outside the *Skirt* offices, and Grace was popping into Caffè Nero for a triple-shot latte, no foam and a blueberry muffin, and she realised that technically she might be a mistress but actually nothing had changed. Grace wasn't sure what she'd expected – maybe Tiffany's boxes being couriered over and there were definitely strawberries dipped in chocolate, which she ate while lounging on oyster-coloured satin sheets – not holding the lift for a couple of girls who worked on the teen mag on the floor below and exchanging pleasantries about the weekend. It was all the same as it ever was, and if God was planning to strike her down with a thunderbolt then He was taking His sweet time about it.

The only new development was a barrage of emails from Ms Jones, Vaughn's assistant, when Grace turned on her computer. There was an itinerary of art exhibitions that Grace was meant to toddle along to in her lunch-hours and reading lists to occupy what was left of her waking hours. Grace stared balefully at a catalogue of books on modern art with fun titles like *Primitivism, Cubism, Abstraction: The Early Twentieth Century.* She felt less like she was having her potential harnessed and more like some Gen-Y Eliza Dolittle.

'Hey, what you doing?' Lily asked, coming up behind Grace as she was morosely selecting art books on Amazon and hoping her credit card wouldn't be declined.

Grace hurriedly clicked the screen away and turned to Lily, who was looking a little peaky for once. 'You can't still have a hangover?' Grace asked.

Lily grimaced. 'Had a hangover, started drinking again yesterday to get rid of it, now I have a shiny new hangover to take its place. Couldn't even think about breakfast this morning.'

Grace clucked sympathetically. 'Breakfast is overrated. I only eat breakfast the week after payday.'

'Gracie,' Lily sighed, 'I'd lend you some money but with the wedding coming up . . .'

'No! No! No! That's not what I meant at all. 'Sides, when am I not absolutely skint?'

Lily settled for a non-committal murmur because in all the time that they'd known each other, Grace had always been careering from one financial crisis to the next.

Then, in a sudden flash of inspiration, Grace had the answer to a problem that had been bugging her for the last sixteen hours. 'Actually, there's something I've been meaning to tell you,' she said casually, looking Lily right in the eye. 'I had an interview for a part-time job.'

'Oh? Doing what?'

'It's this private members' club thing,' Grace replied, grateful that she'd had years to turn being vague into an art form. 'If I get it, it will be a lot of evenings and weekends so I might not be around so much.'

That merited the new issue of *Vogue* being thrust aside. 'But you promised you'd help me with the wedding prep!' Lily gasped. 'I was just going to ask you if you'd managed to blag me a discount card for Browns Bride yet?'

'You're not getting married until next spring and this is just a short-term contract. Probably be fired in three months anyway,' Grace assured her, hoping these weren't the first few faltering steps on Lily's road to bridezilla-dom. 'And I'm not sure they do discount cards,' she added.

'So, do you think you'll get the job?' Lily wanted to know. 'You said you always go to pieces in interviews.'

It was true, Grace did. She'd interviewed for three junior-stylist positions in the last year; screwed up two of them with her utter lack of a famous father or perkiness, and had turned up fifteen minutes late to the other one because the bus had broken down. 'They seemed pretty keen so maybe,' she mumbled. 'And the money's really good. Unbelievably good.'

'Thank God the wedding won't be until next year,' Lily sighed, and Grace wished that Lily wouldn't make this all about her. But then for this not to be all about Lily, Grace would have to tell her the truth and she wasn't ready to do that just yet. It could all be over in a couple of weeks (and wasn't that a welcome thought?) so there didn't seem to be any point in rocking Lily's world off its axis until Grace knew exactly what being a mistress entailed.

'Sucks for you, though,' Lily went on. 'Kiki's going to get really pissy when you can't work late.'

'Kiki's always pissy about something,' Grace said heavily, and she couldn't help but slump over her desk. 'God, how do I manage to get myself into these situations?'

'Gracie, could you try and cheer up a little bit?' Lily said imploringly. 'You were in a weird mood all of last week and Liam said that you completely freaked him out on Saturday night.'

Grace's head shot up. 'What exactly did he say?'

Lily shrugged. 'Just that you got really drunk and were all over him.' She brightened. 'It would be so cool if you two got back together. Just what you need to cheer yourself up.'

'Going to take more than that,' Grace said dryly, and marvelled that she hadn't even thought about Liam until now. She'd had far more pressing matters to angst about.

Lily rummaged in her Chloé handbag. 'You can have this,' she said cheerfully, offering Grace a glossy leaflet. 'It's a free consultation with this make-up artist who's just launched a new range of mineral cosmetics. You get a fantastic bespoke goodie bag with all these products tailored to your skin type. It's this lunch-time but I can't go 'cause I've got a perfume launch and the PR said there'd be champagne.'

It was amazing how the thought of free beauty products could make everything seem better. 'Thanks,' Grace said, taking the leaflet from Lily, then rustling the nearest pile of press releases ostentatiously. 'I'll try my best with the discount card, but I've got a ton of work to do first.'

As soon as Lily was out of range, Grace picked up her phone.

Liam sounded satisfyingly groggy when he answered on Grace's fifth attempt to get through.

'I'm so sorry,' she cooed. 'Did I wake you?'

'Well, yeah . . .'

'Good,' Grace said savagely. 'Listen to me, if you breathe a word to Lily about *anything* that we talked about on Saturday night, I'm going to use my spare key, come to your flat and smash every single piece of vinyl you own. Including your Nick Drake boxed set. Got that?'

'What the fuck is wrong with you?' Liam spluttered. It was a fair question. It seemed to Grace that she'd been mainlining the crazy ever since that first tear-soaked meeting with Vaughn in the accessories department of Liberty's.

'Do. You. Understand?' Grace bit out. She was all set to hang up on Liam's sleep-fuddled response, which mostly involved the words 'psycho bitch' when another thought occurred to her. 'And if you tell her that we had sex then I'll smash your guitars too.' She did hang up then, almost spraining her index finger as she pressed down on the 'end call' key with maximum force.

Grace arrived back at the office after her consultation clutching a sweet little wicker basket full of pots and vials. The make-up artist had been really insistent that she was a winter person, though Grace still thought she was a spring. She'd also had to surrender her make-up bag and its grimy contents, which had been chucked unceremoniously into the nearest bin. 'Time for a whole new you,' the make-up artist had said, and Grace wondered why everyone was so down on the old Grace. She hadn't been *that* bad.

'Someone's waiting in Reception for you,' Lucie informed her cheerily as Grace stared at the new Grace in her pocket mirror. The new Grace didn't seem to have quite so many open pores, thanks to the mineral make-up. 'Says he has to have your signature and no one else's will do. We think it might be the new Chanel pumps, so get a wiggle on.'

Grace squinted at her fringe. The black hair dye looked even harsher now she was wearing the correct base colour for her complexion. 'Hey, what do you think I'd look like as a blonde?'

'He's been there *ages*, Gracie,' Posy chimed in. 'I think that might be a human rights violation.'

'OK, OK, I'm going,' Grace said, clicking her compact shut.

When she got down to Reception, there was no courier waiting for her, but a delicate-looking boy about her age wearing a Dior Pour Homme suit and flicking through a copy of *Real Women*, Magnum Media's most downmarket title. He seemed pretty engrossed and it wasn't until Grace cleared her throat that he looked up.

'Are you from Chanel?' she asked.

'Are you Ms Reeves?'

They were talking over each other and Grace was painfully aware that she had green eye-shadow smeared over one lid and not the other. She gestured jerkily to indicate that they should try again.

'I'm Piers,' he said in a low voice. 'From Vaughn's office. He asked me to deliver a few things.'

Grace looked down at the thick white A4 envelope, which bulged promisingly, on the sofa beside him. Then shook the hand Piers was offering.

'I'm Grace,' she said, trying to ignore the way Piers's eyes had widened as he looked at her, although he was now gazing at his shoes. Despite the impeccable suitage, Grace had a feeling that Piers felt as out of his depth as she did – the tips of his ears were bright pink. 'Shall I take that?'

They both looked at the envelope. 'I need to get your signature first,' Piers said, swallowing convulsively. 'The contract . . .'

It was a mutual blush-fest. Grace glanced over her shoulder anxiously but the two receptionists were obscured by a gigantic floral display and too busy fielding calls to pay any attention to her. 'Why don't I take it and pop it in the post once I've signed it?' she suggested, but Piers was already opening the big envelope and pulling out a couple of pieces of paper.

'Vaughn wanted it signed now. He was really insistent.' Piers grimaced. 'He expected me back ages ago. He's meant to be flying to Moscow today.'

Vaughn seemed very keen to have everything sewn up – almost as if he was worried that Grace was going to back out. She knew he wanted her, that was what the contract and the money were about, but all of this would be so much easier if he'd just told her how much he wanted her, instead of getting one of his minions to do it.

'So, if you could sign it now?' Piers continued. 'It's just I've been waiting for ages and Vaughn's already called twice and, quite frankly, my life's not worth living if I go back empty-handed.'

Grace suspected that Vaughn didn't know how fabulously indiscreet Piers was, but she'd been made to do Kiki's dirty work often enough (and going to the dry cleaners was the very least of it) that she could empathise. 'God, my boss would be baying for my blood too if she wasn't on holiday. I've just taken a two-hour lunch-break,' Grace confessed, and now she and Piers shared a mutual eyeroll. 'OK, let me just have a quick look at it.'

There were only two sheets of papers and the second one didn't have much on it except a dotted line where Grace's signature was meant to go. Grace scanned her eyes over what appeared to be a pretty standard employment contract. In fact, it was very similar to the one that she'd signed when she'd started at *Skirt*. It even included that catch-all: *Other duties, as required*.

Piers was now fiddling with three smaller envelopes and Grace was sure she could make out the outline of a wad-like object, which made her concentration waver.

'Ms Reeves . . . Grace . . . I don't mean to rush you,' Piers almost moaned as something in the inner pocket of his jacket began to ring. 'Here's a pen.'

Grace had only skim-read the top sheet, but it was enough to decide that there didn't seem to be anything particularly sinister in the contract. She quickly signed her name and watched as Piers signed as a witness.

'Do I get my own copy?' she asked, because there'd been two copies of her *Skirt* contract, but all she could really think about was the three envelopes that Piers was withholding.

'I'm not sure. I'll ask Madeleine when I get back to the office,' Piers said, as he tucked the contract away. 'OK, these are for you. Vaughn said you'd know what to do with them.'

He'd got that right. Grace tried really hard to contain herself and not squeak like an overexcited little piggy as Piers finally handed over the envelopes. 'Thank you,' she breathed.

Grace saw Piers to the main doors, then ran up seven flights of stairs so she could lock herself in the wheelchair toilet before she eagerly ripped into the largest envelope. Inside were two stiff bundles of money; ten- and twenty-pound notes so shiny and new that Grace couldn't resist holding them up to her nose. She then opened the second thickest envelope, which had *Clothing Allowance* helpfully written on it, and found another £2,000 inside. She plopped down on the toilet, then quickly stood up when she realised she hadn't put the lid down first. Finally, she sank down and stared at the money spilling in her lap.

£7,000! Suddenly all the indignities of the past week didn't matter. *Pffft!* Not when she had cold hard cash in her hot little hands. There was no doubt or hesitation now that the money was real. Through a sequence of events that she still didn't completely understand, Grace was going to live the life that she'd only read about in the pages of *Skirt*: parties, champagne receptions, first-class travel and lots and lots of lovely frocks. And shoes. And bags.

Yes, there was the whole *thing* with Vaughn, but he was probably on his way to Moscow right now for a whole week, and if he was hardly ever going to be around, then Grace could deal. She'd be jetted off to some glorious locale once every fortnight, be glittering and witty, shag him then fly home again. There were worse ways to earn £5,000 and allowances a month. Hell, she'd worked in a pub in Dalston for four pounds an hour and had the landlord trying to shove his hand down the back of her jeans when his wife wasn't looking. This was completely different. It was practically respectable.

If the nagging doubts hadn't completely disappeared, then the contents of the third envelope would have made them melt away like drops of water on a hot griddle. Inside was a membership card to a spa equidistant between the *Skirt* offices and Vaughn's gallery. It was the beauty equivalent of those invitation-only, private members' clubs that wouldn't even give out a street number. And thankfully, Kiki wasn't a member. In fact, Grace remembered how Lily had spent weeks trying to sort out Kiki's membership and they'd point blank turned her down.

Grace had been worried that the spa staff would give her knowing looks when she rolled up for her first appointment – that she was just the latest in a long line of Vaughn's girls and they'd seen it all before. But they couldn't have been nicer, even sending someone out to Pret a Manger to get her a sandwich when they'd realised she was on her lunch-break, though the spa was so luxurious that Grace had been terrified of getting mayonnaise on the white leather that seemed to coat everything from the walls to the couch that she lay starkers on while her pasty flesh was worked on.

Over the next few days, a new Grace started to emerge. It wasn't just the best efforts of trained aestheticians with their tri-enzyme facials and bleach baths, but as if they'd also taken a rubber to Grace's face to smooth out the frown and the pinched look from worrying about money, Kiki, and why none of her relationships ever lasted.

She was never going to be a beauty, but her grandad always said she scrubbed up all right and Grace was beginning to scrub up to the nth degree. All the little flaws that she'd catalogue as she stood naked in the bath and twisted and contorted so she could get an all-round reflection in the mirror above the sink were becoming a thing of the past. The little bumpy spots on the back of her thighs and arms had been pummelled away, her blackheads obliterated and her hair had recovered from its bleach bath and was now a glossy chocolate brown. Every time she passed a shop window, Grace couldn't resist preening a little, then shaking her head to see her hair give a little shimmy then settle back down without ever losing its shape.

Still, Grace faced her first bikini wax with trepidation. She had heard tales of the close bond that formed between waxer and waxee. Mainly from Lily as she was the only one of Grace's friends with a spa membership and she got on with everyone – but Grace wasn't expecting a short, squat woman who eyed her up and down as she entered the waxing chamber and barked, 'I'm Galya. Take off your knickers' in an Eastern European accent.

Lily hadn't said anything about her waxer snorting in

disbelief either, but then Lily didn't wear boy-cut panties with the Superman logo on them.

'On the table,' Galya demanded, staring at Grace's pubic hair. 'You do this yourself, huh?'

Grace raised herself up on her elbows and nodded. She wanted to defend her trimming skills but realised it would be futile as the woman snorted again and started heating up the wax.

'You want the Brazilian?' Galya asked after a few moments of fraught silence.

'Is that the one with the little landing strip?' It had been a while since *Skirt* had done anything on the latest trends in waxing.

Galya approached Grace's spread legs with a pot of wax. 'New boyfriend,' she sniffed. 'First-timers always come for the new boyfriend.'

Grace looked helplessly up at the ceiling. 'Well, yeah. Kind of. It's hard to explain,' she added as she eyed Galya and her spatula warily.

'What's he like?'

How to sum up Vaughn in one sentence to a woman whose first language wasn't English. 'Er . . . older,' was the best she could do.

Galya cackled knowingly. Grace was rather warming to her. 'How old?'

Grace picked a number. Any number. 'Thirty-nine,' she said decisively.

'Then I take off everything. The older ones like that. Lift up your leg.'

It hurt like a bitch, though Grace wasn't going to give Galya the satisfaction of even the smallest 'Ow!'. By the time she was ordered on to her hands and knees so Galya could wax a place where Vaughn would never go (not for £5,000 a month, not for all the couture gowns in Paris), Grace realised that all the times she'd known embarrassment before had just been a dress rehearsal for this moment.

There were other parts of her life that were in desperate need of a makeover too, but Grace had been putting it off until a week had passed and all that money was still stashed in the Marc Jacobs bag in her oven. Finally, Grace took it out. Then she hauled out one of the shoe boxes and started sorting through the bills – there were so many of them and none of them were in the right order. Grace couldn't remember which ones were pending and which ones had been shunted over to a debt consolidation company and then promptly forgotten about. There was the interest and the late fees and the penalty charges and in the end, it was easier to go with gut instinct and prioritise the two most important debts.

The next day, Grace couriered over six months of back-rent to her landlady and ambled down to Topshop in her lunch-hour so she could pay off the £2,318 and 35p she owed on her storecard. That was the £5,000 completely gone and then some, but she dipped into the clothing allowance to buy a fitted tuxedo jacket from the new Kate Moss collection. Then she paid twenty pounds for a box of mediocre sushi from the place around the corner just like the rest of the fashion team.

On the Saturday, Grace bought a Zac Posen silk jersey dress in almost the same shade of green as one of the pictures she'd seen hanging up in Vaughn's gallery, and a pair of Oscar de la Renta peeptoe slingbacks. That took up the rest of the clothing allowance and Grace was back to bananas, noodles and trying to scare up enough loose change to top up her Oyster card. Next month, she promised herself, she'd make another sizeable dent in the bills before she even thought about shopping.

Now she only had one thing to worry about, but another week rolled by and Vaughn had become nothing more than a shadowy Fairy Godfather, just lurking at the edges of her mind. So even Kiki at her most vicious couldn't wipe the beatific smile off Grace's face. Kiki had returned on the Monday from her annual fortnight in St Barts with the devil on her shoulder and had actually ripped up Grace's ideas and flung them in her face during the monthly fashion and beauty brainstorm. Grace clutched the BlackBerry that had been couriered over that morning by Ms Jones as if it was a Kevlar shield and decided to rise above it. Keeping calm in the face of Kiki's most savage mood yet would be great training for when Vaughn did put in an appearance.

'I don't know what you're smirking about, Grace,' Kiki hissed as Grace stared resolutely at her feet, which had been treated to their third intensive pedicure that lunch-time and were, for the first time in years, devoid of calluses and hard skin. 'And your hair looks even more ridiculous than usual. Get out!'

Grace was only too happy to escape to the cupboard. They'd just had a delivery from Milan and were about to start work on the January issue (that actually went on sale in December), which meant parties, which meant party frocks. There was no harm in trying on a couple in preparation for next month's clothing allowance. It was probably tempting fate but Grace was powerless to resist in the face of Miu Miu.

She was just easing up the zip of a little Roland Mouret number when she realised that her discarded jeans were humming and vibrating. Bending down carefully so she didn't split the tight seams, she retrieved her new BlackBerry. It hadn't done anything since it had been couriered over and she hadn't given the number to anyone, so that meant . . .

'Hello?' It was hard to make your voice husky and alluring when you were wearing a dress so tight it was cutting off your blood circulation.

'Grace. I need you to come with me to a party on Wednesday evening,' Vaughn said, like it was a perfectly reasonable request for 12.35 p.m. on a Monday, when she hadn't spoken to him for a fortnight.

'Um, OK,' she mumbled, her face flaring up because simply talking to him felt illicit. Grace made a mental note to phone her spa (*her* spa!) and book an emergency bikini wax, and a mani/pedi and maybe they could fit her in for a wash and blowdry after work on Wednesday and Jesus, two weeks ago all she'd ever had in the way of regular beauty treatments was a peel-off face mask as she watched *Project Runway* . . .

'Grace,' Vaughn said again, terse enough to cut right through all of Grace's breezy notions that handling him would be just like handling Kiki. All of a sudden her mouth was dry and she had that funny taste at the back of her throat again. 'You could try to be a little more articulate.'

'I'm sorry.' Grace clamped the phone under her ear while she made sure the cupboard door was shut. 'Anyway, like, how are you?'

'How am I?' Vaughn echoed, sounding surprised that she'd even asked. 'I'm fine. Have you done the reading? What did you think of the Karvovsky exhibition?'

Grace squirmed as much as she could in skin-tight silk crepe. She had bought one of the boring art books from Borders (the only one they'd had in stock) but mostly her research had involved reading a biography of Madame Pompadour. There was a long, fraught silence. 'I went to the Tate Modern,' she said at last.

There was a long sigh. 'It's not enough to just stand about looking pretty,' he said through what sounded like tightly gritted teeth. 'I thought I was perfectly clear about that.'

He'd said she was pretty before but now he dragged it up like an accusation. 'I'm sorry,' she said apologetically. 'I got a bit carried away with spa appointments.'

'Fine,' Vaughn said, as if it really wasn't fine. 'Madeleine will send you some notes about Wednesday. She'll try to keep them to bullet points, given your hectic schedule.'

'Um, who's Madeleine anyway?'

'I believe you know her as Ms Jones. So, Wednesday. Come to the gallery for seven and be on time.'

'What kind of party is it? Do I need to dress up? Is it really swank?'

'Grace, I don't have time for this. Call Madeleine and she can fill you in,' he said, and she could sense his impatience to finish the call. 'I'll see you on Wednesday.'

chapter twelve

At precisely 6.57 p.m. on Wednesday, Grace stood outside 17 Thirlestone Mews. She looked down at her perfectly polished toes peeking out of her vintage Roland Cartier silver sandals and told herself that everything was going to be all right.

The door was opened by Piers, his face pinking up as soon as he caught sight of her. He was the only person she'd ever met who blushed as much as she did, and if Grace's gaydar wasn't shrieking at a very high frequency, she'd have begun to wonder if he had a crush on her.

'Hi. I'm expected . . .'

'Hi. I think he's expecting you . . .'

Grace felt a little ragged standing there in her expensive new dress, which was starting to stick to her clammy skin.

'So, do I just go up then?' she asked, though the moment it popped out, she wondered if she was meant to be more blasé. It wasn't the sort of dilemma that had been covered in the Madame Pompadour biography. And Madame Pompadour had never turned up to meet Louis XIV with a spare pair of knickers, a toothbrush and her multi-vitamins stashed in her clutch bag or have to plan a sneaky cut and run from the office half an hour early so she could get to the spa for a quick wash and blowdry.

Grace followed Piers up the stairs, casting an interested

glance at the two other girls who were standing behind the reception desk. Posh girls – she could tell immediately. Something about the self-assured way they held themselves and their shiny hair and crisp dresses that looked as if they'd been freshly pressed and put on five minutes earlier. They barely looked in Grace's direction, though Grace couldn't tell if they were following orders or monumentally not interested.

'He's through there,' Piers told Grace, pointing down the corridor, when they'd finished the long climb to the second floor. Grace slowly walked up to the door and knocked softly on it.

'Enter.'

Grace wriggled her shoulders and opened the door.

Vaughn was sitting behind his desk and frowning at his computer screen as Grace walked in. She hesitated, thought about perching on one of the Cubist armchairs but then he looked up and frowned a little bit harder.

'Hey,' Grace said, raising one sweaty paw in a salute.

'Hello,' he said, pushing his chair back so he could walk towards her. Grace wanted to inch back but she stayed where she was.

Vaughn was wearing one of his snowy-white shirts and impeccably tailored trousers, but he'd caught the sun on the high planes of his cheekbones, which made his eyes seem bluer as they fixed on Grace's face and didn't waver.

'You're on time,' Vaughn murmured as he reached her, brushing her cheek with his lips, his hand just skirting her hip and slip-sliding off the jersey silk in a proprietorial gesture that made Grace give a nervous start before she could stop herself. He was frowning again. 'I don't like your hair.'

'You told me to change it.' Grace ran a defensive hand over her new cut, which she happened to love, from the blunt fringe to the long, razored layers that actually gave her cheekbones. 'I got rid of the black.'

'Why didn't you just pick a new colour and stick with it? It looks like a Mars bar,' Vaughn said flatly, moving his head so he could get a better angle to see the lowlights in Grace's hair, which had been far too brown without a few streaks to give it some oomph. Vaughn ran an appraising eye over her new Zac Posen dress with its asymmetrical hem, which had cost most of her clothing allowance. 'The rest of you looks very lovely,' he said. 'Green suits you.'

Then he picked up his suit jacket from the back of a chair and marched out of the room, without bothering to see if Grace was trotting after him like an obedient little dog.

There was a long, sleek car waiting for them outside with its engine running. A uniformed driver opened the door and Grace sank back against the plump leather and tried to will herself to unclench.

Vaughn crossed his legs and looked at her. 'I don't want you to drink too much at this party,' he said. 'Just one glass of wine, I think.'

'What's that supposed to mean?' Grace immediately bristled.

'It means that the first time we met, you downed a glass of champagne in one,' Vaughn informed her. 'The second time you phoned me drunk. You were absolutely steaming in New York and last time you admitted you had a hangover.'

When he put it like that, Grace felt like she should ask the driver to drop her off at the nearest AA meeting.

'Fine,' she said, her lips thin.

'You can drink afterwards, when we have dinner,' Vaughn conceded and Grace's heart lifted, then sank to her knees. Ms Jones hadn't mentioned anything about dinner. Grace had imagined that Vaughn would want to skip right to the sex part. But, no, he was determined to prolong her agony.

'You're annoyed with me,' he went on, 'but really, there was no polite way to say it.'

Grace looked at him from under her lashes. 'Well, actually there was but you chose not to use it.'

Vaughn shrugged carelessly. 'I gave you fair warning about what you'd be dealing with. *Who* you'd be dealing with. So there's really no need for the sulky face.'

It took a great effort to rearrange her features into something less pouty. 'I'm sorry. I'm just a bit nervous.'

That should have been Vaughn's cue to say something nice to help Grace tamp down the rising hysteria, but he just gave her a bland smile that she didn't like one little bit and didn't say a word for the rest of the journey.

The party, given by a Russian businessman who collected art and trophy wives, was being held at his home in Kensington. It wasn't a home like Grace knew homes, where you kicked off your shoes by the front door and were offered a cup of tea by your host. This was a home where a line of limos were gridlocked outside, and once Grace and Vaughn had hurried up the stone steps of the immense Regency townhouse, which took up most of the block, there was a uniformed flunky to take their names and announce them.

As Grace stepped over the threshold she was momentarily dazzled by the huge amounts of gilt and crystal that covered every surface, including the banisters of the sweeping staircase, and the sparkling stones dripping from the necks of every other woman present. A mêlée of guests milled over the imported marble floor and a hundred different French perfumes fought it out for olfactory supremacy. Grace counted five Roberto Cavalli dresses, which made her decide that the gathering was mostly former Eastern Bloc. Kiki was always banging on about how only rap stars and Russian gangsters' wives wore Cavalli.

Grace caught sight of herself in a huge ormolu mirror that took up most of one wall and inwardly shuddered. When she'd left the spa, she was certain that she'd never looked this good, this pretty, in her entire life. But now, she looked all wrong hanging from Vaughn's arm, though that could be because Vaughn was still frowning. It was more than that; Vaughn looked at ease. He wore his suit with the same assurance as he'd worn jeans and a T-shirt, while Grace felt horribly contrived in her £1,000 plus change dress, like it was a costume rather than the most beautiful frock she'd ever owned. And Vaughn was right: her hair *was* stupid – and so were her tatty sandals. All of a sudden, vintage was just another word for secondhand.

Grace took a panic-stricken step back and nearly trod on the foot of the woman behind her, who took it in really bad humour.

'Let's get out of this scrum.' Vaughn took Grace's elbow so he could lead her away from harm. 'The ballroom's through those doors.'

'They have a ballroom?' Grace whispered frantically. 'Ms Jones didn't say anything about a ballroom. Will there be dancing? Will I have to waltz?' Grace had taken some Lindy Hop lessons when she'd been trying to ensnare a beautiful boy with a quiff and a pair of dice tattooed on his biceps, but she'd stopped going when he'd tried to get off with Lily instead.

'Don't be ridiculous,' Vaughn whispered back, steering Grace adroitly through the crowd into a larger room with, yes, a sprung floor. 'This is where Boris displays some of his art.' Grace cast a cursory look around at the hideous canvases, then to the point where the huge doors at the other end of the room opened out into a garden. She wouldn't have been surprised if it turned out to be a landing strip or an Olympic-sized pool.

'I need my one drink now,' Grace breathed as she watched a woman walk past swathed in fur though it was a hot and balmy late-summer night. She snagged a glass of champagne from a passing waiter and took a small sip because it was going to have to last her hours.

Grace stared at a trio of girls, who looked like they might

be trannies, before her attention was diverted by a fat, sweaty man in a pink suit. 'Like blancmange,' she muttered under her breath as Vaughn raised his hand and waved at someone on the other side of the cavernous ballroom.

He tried to take a step forward and they both realised that Grace had his arm in a death grip. 'Let me go, Grace,' he said evenly. 'I'm going to talk business.'

'OK,' she said. 'Can I come with you?'

'No, you're going to mingle and absolutely not have any more to drink,' Vaughn informed her, skilfully detaching himself and disappearing across the floor.

Grace made a face at his departing back and wondered how she was supposed to mingle when usually her two conversational gambits were, 'Where did you get your dress?' or 'Didn't we meet at Glastonbury?' Neither one would work here.

Slowly she ambled down the room, smiling vaguely, which she hoped made her look as if she was perfectly at ease.

Eventually she sidled up to a middle-aged woman who was staring, almost disconsolately, at one of the paintings. 'It's a great piece, isn't it?' Grace chirped. 'Some people prefer his earlier work, but whatever.'

The woman turned and stared at Grace for a moment with great consternation, then walked off without saying a word. Still, Grace had made the effort and, more importantly, she was now out of sight of Vaughn's beady eye so he wouldn't be able to see what an utter failure she was at being a people person.

Her mind made up, she wandered out into the garden. The sky was a smudgy dark blue somewhere between dusk and twilight, and there were hundreds and hundreds of candles in votive holders illuminating a path across a gently sloping lawn to a canopied seating area. Grace sniffed the air appreciatively. She'd found the official smoking area.

There was a couple huddled in conversation and a man

quietly barking on his phone, but apart from that the place was deserted. Grace gratefully sat down on an overly padded gilt chair, swapped her empty glass for a full one on a tray and fished out her cigarettes.

Grace smoked the first one right down to the butt, then started on the second one at a more leisurely pace. She used to be a social smoker, but that had recently upgraded to a packet a day.

'Hello,' a voice drawled.

Grace looked up into the heavy-lidded eyes of a young man standing in front of her.

'Hello.'

'Mind if I cadge a fag?' he asked, and didn't wait for Grace's answer, but sat down next to her and reached for the cigarettes she'd left on the side table. He ignored Grace's huff of indignation as he lit up, inhaled extravagantly and then puffed out a series of smoke rings.

Grace disliked him on sight. He looked like he'd just stepped off-stage from a local rep revival of a Noël Coward play.

'I'm Alex,' he said.

'And I'm so not interested,' Grace rapped back because his arrogance was as overpowering as his cologne.

He laughed in a way that made her want to slap him. Repeatedly. 'Don't flatter yourself, darling. I'm gay.'

Grace gave him her best bitch goddess glare. 'And I'm still not interested.'

'No, actually you're the new girl,' Alex said with a sly smile. 'You're not his usual type.'

Curiosity meet cat. 'Oh yeah?'

'They're usually older,' Alex explained kindly. 'Not to worry though. A few months with him and you'll lose that dewy glow.'

'You mean Vaughn?' Grace tried to disguise the note of dread in her voice. 'What exactly are you talking about?'

Alex wagged a finger at Grace. 'You should have done some digging first, darling.'

It was a little late to try and save face but Grace decided to give it the old college try. 'I don't know what you're talking about,' she lied. 'Vaughn and I met, we had a ton of stuff in common, and we're enjoying each other's company. End of.'

'You know something? You're adorable, we should really do lunch.'

'Oh gee, I wonder why? Maybe it's because you'd like to patronise me a little bit more,' Grace said, snatching her packet of cigarettes away from Alex's marauding hand. 'Go away.'

'You're a lot more fun than the others. Mostly he goes for these chilly Fembots who smile politely and nod at all times. I think Vaughn has Social Anxiety Disorder but he's too much of a control freak to give in to it. Don't you agree?' Alex had the audacity to nudge Grace like they'd known each other for ages and he could invade her personal space without risk of injury.

'He's actually a very nice man,' she insisted stoutly. 'He's super-nice, and we couldn't be happier.'

Alex snorted, which didn't work when you were attempting to be effete. 'Whatever you say, darling. Why not try it again with a little more sincerity?'

Grace was saved from the lack of snappy comeback when Vaughn suddenly appeared through the billowing netting at the entrance to the smoking area, with a scowl on his face. 'Grace,' he said thinly. 'There you are.'

'Here I am,' she agreed, jumping to her feet because she couldn't get away from Alex fast enough. She even slipped her hand in Vaughn's to complete the picture of girlfriendly devotion. It was like holding a piece of wood, until he squeezed her fingers in an almost imperceptible gesture. 'There's a freaky picture in the ballroom that I need you to explain.'

'You do?'

'Yes, the one with the penguins. Or they might be men wearing bowler hats. It's hard to tell, which is why you'll have to provide subtitles,' Grace said, almost leaning against Vaughn. There was only a wafer-thin gap between them and she could sense the heat and density of him in a way that made her feel grounded for the first time since she'd arrived at this horrible party.

'I think I know the one you mean,' Vaughn said gravely. Finally he acknowledged Alex, who'd been watching the whole exchange with a faint and supercilious smile playing about his lips. 'Alex. Harry's looking for you.'

'Oh, he'll find me soon enough,' Alex assured him airily. 'Grace, we'll do lunch.'

It was a dismissal and one that Grace wasn't even going to bother responding to. Instead she started marching up the candlelit path, almost dragging Vaughn in her speed-walking wake.

'You're not having lunch with him,' Vaughn said, like it was an absolute incontrovertible truth.

'I know I'm not,' Grace muttered.

'He's the one person at this party that I didn't want you to talk to,' Vaughn continued as if Grace hadn't spoken. And now they were away from Alex's avid eyes, he let go of her hand pretty sharpish too. 'The one person, Grace. And yet you managed to hunt him down.'

'I was the hunted, not the hunter,' Grace informed him indignantly. 'What has he ever done to you?'

They'd reached the open doors of the ballroom by now, but Vaughn pulled Grace into a shadowed alcove on the patio. 'He's unashamedly vicious. He hurts people, and the person he's choosing to hurt this time just happens to be a . . . a business associate of mine.'

Grace had thought Vaughn was going to say 'friend'. But having business associates suited him better. 'I can handle myself, you know. And I had his number as soon as he opened his mouth – and no, before you ask, I didn't give him mine.'

It was harder than usual to read Vaughn's expression in the gathering shadows, but he reached down and tugged on the one piece of Grace's fringe that wouldn't lie flat for longer than five seconds. 'I know you pride yourself on being waspish but he's way out of your league.'

Then he stepped back, gestured with his hand and walked back into the ballroom, calling something about the car over his shoulder.

The party must have been her official début and she'd failed miserably, Grace decided as she sat in the back of the car, while Vaughn talked rapid French to someone on the other end of his BlackBerry. It was annoying, because couldn't he just be made of fail at something? And also annoying because talking French in a low and urgent voice was textbook sexy. Grace had had an out-of-control crush on Monsieur Taylor, her French teacher even though he'd had hard-boiled-egg eyes and lived with his mother.

'*D'accord, oui, d'accord.*' He was practically purring now, and for the first time that evening, for the first time since that rooftop kiss, Grace felt the start of that little tickle she got deep down in her belly. The tickle that, if nurtured, would turn into Grace's blood thickening, her pulse racing and their deal being sealed.

Grace stared resolutely out of the window.

The car wound through the back streets of Kensington, until it stopped outside a restaurant that Grace vaguely recognised from reviews in the Sunday supplements.

Vaughn finished his call as the door was opened by the driver and he stepped out. Vaughn's hand was waiting for her as Grace got out and this time he didn't let go as they were ushered into a foyer, the only focal point a huge arrangement of lilies on the reception desk; their pungent scent clung to everything so that Grace wanted to clamp her hand over her nose. The constant, almost thrilling edge of nerves, which had got her through the first part of the evening, was now transforming itself into stomach-churning fear. Tightening her jaw to stop her teeth chattering, she concentrated on the maître d's ramrod-straight back as they were led through a dining room that was a cold, white paean to minimalism.

They arrived at a secluded corner table. Grace's chair was pulled out first, and before her bottom had even made contact with brushed steel, an impossibly white napkin was laid reverently across her lap. It was so much more formidable than the other meals, the other drinks, as if Vaughn was showing Grace what his world was really like.

A world which was waiting for her to quit being such a wet blanket and show some backbone.

It was only the arrival of a waiter cradling a bottle as if he was about to present his firstborn for Vaughn's approval that chased her nerves away.

'I ordered champagne,' Vaughn said smoothly. 'So we can celebrate properly.'

Grace watched intently as her glass was expertly filled. But instead of downing it in one quick swallow, she settled for curling her hands around the delicate stem and waiting until Vaughn was holding up his own flute.

'What shall we drink to?' he asked, with just the faintest hint of a challenge. 'New beginnings?'

'Sounds good to me,' Grace agreed, raising her glass and sipping gingerly as if she suspected that the Louis Roederer had been liberally laced with Rohypnol.

Vaughn tried to be charming after that. Grace found it almost endearing as he guided her and her rusty A-level French through the menu, enquired after life in the fashion cupboard and shot her an approving look when she asked him about the new Damien Hirst exhibition. However, by the time her goat's cheese salad and his langoustines arrived, the conversation had dried up like a stale sandwich.

Grace looked helplessly around the room and decided that Vaughn wouldn't want to bitch about the sallow woman at the next table's brave decision to go with mustard satin. She settled for a non-controversial: 'So, how're your langoustines?' and tried not to wince.

It wasn't the worst meal ever. That distinction still went to the last Christmas dinner before Grace's parents had called in the lawyers, which had ended with cranberry sauce on the ceiling and her father putting his foot through her new Barbie dream house, in his rush to exit the premises. But it was definitely in the top five.

Somewhere around the main course, Grace and Vaughn came to an unspoken agreement to stop speaking and concentrated on rearranging their food in pretty patterns. The waiter gave them a reproachful look as he whisked away their plates, food barely touched. All Grace could focus on was her heart banging against her breastbone like it wanted out. It was a perfect match for that telltale tic in Vaughn's cheek.

There was only the faintest trickle left in the second bottle when Vaughn signed the credit-card slip without even bothering to look at the total.

'Shall we leave?' He sounded hesitant, which had to be a first. Grace knew that there was only one possible answer. Just as she knew that that, 'Shall we leave?' was not-very-secret code for, 'Let's take our clothes off and have sex when we get back to mine.'

'Sounds like a plan.' It came out of her mouth like she was all primed and ready for action. And after the best part of two bottles of champagne, she should have been. But apart from her teeth, which had gone numb, the rest of her felt alarmingly sober.

Vaughn's hand burned through the silk jersey as he touched the small of Grace's back to skilfully guide her through the tables. Grace bit her tongue hard enough for her eyes to water when they reached the door and Vaughn untucked a stray strand of hair that was caught under the strap of her dress. She needed to stop acting like a virgin about to be sacrificed for the sake of the crops, she thought as she kept her gaze fixed firmly on the floor so she wouldn't have to look at Vaughn.

In the back of yet another chauffeur-driven car, Vaughn sat closer than usual, his arm almost touching Grace's even though he seemed shadowy and remote as the car circled Regent's Park, the trees and hedges indistinct blurs against the night.

For once, Vaughn wasn't on the phone, but he seemed to be waiting for her to make the first move. Grace thought of at least three really lame conversation starters and quickly abandoned them. Why couldn't his stupid BlackBerry ring or buzz or . . .

'You know your BlackBerry: does it do this really annoying thing when you send an email?' Grace heard herself squeak.

Vaughn turned to her with a startled look as if he'd forgotten she was sitting there. 'What annoying thing?'

'It leaves this signature line that I sent the email from my BlackBerry. It makes me feel like a gigantic poseur.' Grace briefly closed her eyes and wondered when her brain would finally make her mouth shut up. 'I wish I knew how to get rid of it.'

'Yes, I can imagine how annoying that would be,' Vaughn muttered, running a hand through his hair. 'Have you tried reading the instructions?'

'Yeah, well, sort of,' Grace said vaguely, wishing that she'd never gone down this road. 'I guess I'll work it out eventually. I know loads of models who have them so, like, how hard can it be?'

'But apart from that, it meets with your approval?'

Christ, she hadn't even thanked him for it. Her

grandparents would be appalled. 'Oh, don't get me wrong, I love it,' Grace assured him hastily, and in the dim light, she was sure she saw him smile. 'It was really kind of you.'

They were climbing up the hill towards Hampstead, the driver suddenly veering left to wind along narrow, crooked roads until they came to a pair of gates, which slowly swung open. This was the part where the very stupid and impressionable fashion assistant was taken to an unknown location, hacked into little bits by a man who had an initial instead of a first name, and was never heard from again.

Grace peered curiously at the elegant Georgian house, while she remembered to stay seated like she didn't have full use of her limbs, until the driver opened her door. Actually, no, not her door, but Vaughn's door.

'I'll be in touch soon,' he said, brushing his hand against Grace's cheek and leaving her open-mouthed, astonished and unkissed as he got out.

The next day, as Grace sat at her desk desultorily opening the post, she wondered if she'd ever hear from Vaughn again. It wasn't like she'd been panting to get her hands on hot, naked Vaughn flesh but she'd have honoured the terms of their agreement, whereas he'd obviously decided that she was sexually repulsive. When Grace had got home the night before, she'd stood on a chair in the bathroom to look in the mirror and had realised that the dress made her arse ginormous. That was it. She was a great, fat bloater with stupid hair and no conversational skills and Vaughn was going to call the whole thing off. Which was fine by her, though if he wanted her to return some of her monthly retainer she'd have to write him an IOU.

It seemed best to skulk in the fashion cupboard until she'd got her head straight. Or straight-ish at any rate. There had been several deliveries over the last two days, which Grace hadn't got round to sorting out, and as she surveyed the messy rails and shelves she decided that it was no surprise that her life was in such disarray: she was surrounded by chaos.

She was happily colour-coding tights when one of the interns stuck her head round the door. 'You've got a delivery.'

Grace didn't even look up. 'Be a love and shove it under my desk so no one pinches it, please.'

'You have to come and look!' the girl exclaimed breathlessly. 'They're so pretty.'

Grace took the bait, jumped off the kick steps and stuck her head round the door. Her desk was completely obscured by a huge bouquet of flowers wrapped in brown paper – a humble affectation employed by all the really chichi florists. Grace approached cautiously, the peppery, delicate scent of freesias assaulting her nostrils before she'd even taken two steps out of the cupboard.

'They're beautiful,' the intern chirped. 'Must have been one hell of a row if your boyfriend's sending you flowers from Wild at Heart to say sorry.'

'I haven't got a boyfriend,' Grace muttered, snatching up the flowers and rooting through the freesias and tiny bud-like roses, all in the duskiest shades of lilac, to get to the prize. Her fingers closed around the card.

Thank you for a lovely evening, it read in an unknown hand. Not his heavy black scrawl but whoever Ms Jones had dictated the message to over the phone. It was probably a task she had programmed into her calendar for the morning after each one of Vaughn's dates.

'They're from a PR,' Grace said shortly, tucking the card into the back pocket of her jeans. 'You can take them home, if you like – my hay fever is way out of control at the moment.'

It was the first sensible thing that Grace had done since her birthday. And although when she got home that night she questioned the wisdom of stashing the card carefully in one of the side pockets of the Marc Jacobs bag, she wasn't going to waste time angsting about it.

*

Over the next few days, there were other things to angst about. Like a daily torrent of official-looking envelopes or Kiki rejecting every single piece that Grace had called in for a winter coats story. And there was Lily turning into a bridezilla before Grace's very eyes.

'Would you hate me if I made you wear a buttercup-yellow bridesmaid dress?' she asked Grace as they headed into Sainsbury's after work.

Grace didn't even have to think about it. 'Yup. And while we're on the subject, that goes for puce, mustard, khaki and brown too.'

'I would never make you wear mustard,' Lily insisted. 'But my bridesmaids have to look a bit crap so I outshine them.'

Grace considered braining Lily with a wire basket for one brief moment. 'You know you're beautiful,' she said baldly. 'No one is going to be looking at your bridesmaids.'

'They'd better not,' Lily said as she groped avocados. 'I've already refused to have Dan's nieces and my cousin's kids anywhere near the aisle. Toddlers would look sweet in the wedding photos but they don't follow direction.'

'Selfish little bastards,' Grace deadpanned, selecting three Granny Smith apples and heading over to soups. 'I'm done,' she called, picking up a carton of carrot and coriander.

'Is that all you can afford?' Lily asked, pausing her bridely woes as she took in Grace's evening meal. 'I could treat you to a ready meal, one of the posh ones.'

'I need to lose some weight,' Grace admitted, because if Vaughn did want to see her again, she'd probably have to get naked and she wanted to banish her lardy arse before that happened. 'See, it's hot so if I make soup, I can only manage half a cup and apples are the model-approved snack food of choice.'

'Really? You don't look like you need to lose weight,' Lily

said as she poked her friend's belly with one cautious finger. If it had been anybody else, Grace would have had their hand off. 'You're looking pretty hot actually, Gracie. Who did your hair?' she added in a slightly annoyed tone. 'I could have got you in somewhere for free.'

'Oh, I slapped some L'Oréal on and then there was this hairdresser on a shoot who did the highlights and the cut,' Grace said hastily, turning to stare at the salad bar. 'You were right about the black dye; it really wasn't doing anything for me.'

'But your skin is looking amazing too – even Maggie said.' Maggie was the beauty director and Lily's boss who didn't tolerate blackheads or open pores in much the same way that Kiki wouldn't tolerate bootcut jeans or flip-flops. 'Is it your apple and soup detox?'

Grace had been relying on Lily not noticing anything that didn't have the word root 'bride' so she could only stand there and flap her mouth and wait for sounds to emerge. 'It's that mineral make-up, Lils,' she said weakly. 'It's amazing.'

'It really is,' Lily agreed, peering at Grace's face. As she was a trained beauty professional who might be able to spot the signs of a tri-enzyme facial, Grace reared back in alarm – but Lily obviously didn't see anything suspicious on her friend's unusually blemish-free face. 'So, anyway, let's talk bridesmaid dresses again,' she continued. 'What about a pale lemon sherbet if you don't like the buttercup?'

Grace was saved from having to answer by the distant trill of her usually silent BlackBerry, which was just as well because she was on the verge of agreeing to pale lemon sherbet because she felt so guilty about lying to Lily. 'Hi,' she said, her voice breathy with anticipation.

She needn't have bothered. 'Miss Reeves?' enquired the frosty tones of Madeleine Jones. 'This isn't an inconvenient time?'

Lily was now reading the nutritional information on a

packet of spaghetti Bolognese, her lips moving soundlessly. 'I can talk for a bit,' Grace said.

'I'm couriering over rail tickets tomorrow morning,' Ms Jones announced. 'What time do you finish work on Friday?'

Grace sagged against the chiller cabinet in relief – she wasn't completely and utterly disgusting, after all. 'Tickets to where?'

'Vaughn wants you to meet him at Babington House,' came the answer. 'Miss Reeves? What time can you get to Paddington?'

When Kiki had had a row with her husband, she often got Grace to book a room at Babington House in Somerset so they could spend the weekend making up. Or Kiki could spend the weekend having spa treatments. Either way, if it got the Kiki Curtis seal of approval then it was absolutely fine with Grace. More than fine. 'You can call me Grace and I can probably be there by five.' Kiki always left early on a Friday.

'A car will pick you up at Bath Spa. They'll be expecting you at Babington but I'll email over all the details.'

'Is this, like, a whole weekend kind of deal?' Grace asked hesitantly, because the prospect of forty-eight hours with Vaughn took the lustre off the whole country-house thing. Also, it would be good to know how many pairs of knickers to pack. 'Is Vaughn travelling down with me? Do I need to meet him at Paddington?'

'Until Sunday afternoon and Vaughn will be flying in to meet you at Babington,' Ms Jones said icily. God knows what her issue was.

'Flying?' Grace echoed.

'Yes, in a helicopter.'

Lily had finished counting up carbs and was looking at Grace curiously.

'OK, fine. Thanks for letting me know,' Grace muttered. 'Oh, and by the way, thank you for the flowers. I thought you probably sent—'

'You don't have to thank me,' Ms Jones said quickly, but it sounded as if the ice had slightly melted. 'Have a good evening, Grace.'

'You too. Work,' she added to Lily, hoping to forestall her, but . . .

'*Work?* How's it going? Is that why you need to lose weight? Do you have to wear a uniform? What are the tips like? When did you get a BlackBerry?'

'Yes, work. It's going OK, I'm still on probation. No, that's not why I need to lose weight because there isn't a uniform but I do have a dress code. No tips as yet and Carphone Warehouse were doing a special promotion.' Grace smiled blandly as Lily opened her mouth to fire off another rally. 'Really, it's just a crappy old bar job but a bit posher than when I used to work at the Queen's Head.'

Lily chortled happily. 'Do you remember on your last night you were so pissed by eight p.m. they had to send you home in a cab?'

'Yes, and halfway down the road we had to stop so I could puke my guts up,' Grace finished for her. 'And I haven't drunk gin since.'

'Only old ladies drink gin anyway.' Lily tucked her arm into Grace's as they ambled towards the checkout. 'Now, if you're really anti-yellow, how do you feel about a very pale orange?'

chapter thirteen

Grace opened the window of the light, airy attic room she'd been shown to when she arrived at Babington House and stuck her head out as far as she could without plunging to her death. Her internal organs felt as if they'd tied themselves together, making it hard to breathe, so she took deep gulps of country air and peered into the fading light at rolling lawns and, further in the distance, green fields and hedgerows dotted with wild flowers. She was sure that if she strained her ears, she'd be able to hear the lazy buzz of bees punch-drunk on their own pollen, or the faint mooing of cows in far-off pastures. Then the smell of something farm-like wafted around Grace's nostrils and she slammed the window shut.

It was eight o'clock, and she had an hour to get her gameface on before Vaughn arrived at Babington House. Unless his helicopter crashed on the way, because helicopters had a habit of doing that. Not that Grace wanted Vaughn to die, but while it didn't have a Vaughn in it, the room was lovely. Grace had never been inside a Swedish farmhouse but she imagined it would have similar exposed beams, minimalist fixtures and fittings, and carefully distressed furniture. Grace bounced experimentally on the huge bed whose pristine white sheets were probably going to get seriously rumpled later, then turned her attention to the roll-top bath.

It was 8.50 p.m. when Grace wriggled into a white broderie

anglaise frock, then caught sight of herself in the mirror and made a horrified face – she looked far too virginal. In the end, she pulled on her trusty Ossie Clark sundress, because when in doubt she always went for vintage. She arranged her hair in a messy bun, and settled for a slick of lip-stain, a couple of coats of mascara and some powder to take the shine away. It was so hot that any more make-up would simply slide off her face.

Half an hour later, there was still no whirring of blades, no light tread on the stairs, no one coming into the room with some well-meaning constructive criticism about her outfit. Grace picked up her new copy of *Vogue Italia* and the Michael Chabon book she'd been picking at for the last two months and headed for the door. Amazed by her own daring, she texted Vaughn as she walked down the stairs. *Waiting for you on the terrace. Hope everything is OK*. Grace didn't think he would appreciate smiley faces and missed vowels.

Once she was seated at a quiet end table on the terrace, with a faint breeze stirring the sticky night and candles to keep the midges away, Grace felt less like she was about to hyperventilate. A tureen-sized glass of Sauvignon Blanc helped too. She flicked through *Vogue*, and made no attempt to even open *Kavalier & Clay*.

All the other tables were occupied by a large pre-wedding-party. Grace surreptitiously stared at them from behind her menu and tried to work out if it was the future groom who was looking as if his whole world had turned to broken biscuit. The bride-to-be was book-ended by two older women, who had to be mother and mother-in-law-to-be, and appeared close to tears. Grace gave the couple two years at best, but before she could start pontificating on the topic of marriage, which usually left her in a foul mood, Vaughn appeared through the French doors.

He looked around slowly, but didn't smile as he caught sight of Grace. He still wasn't smiling as he wove his way through the tables to get to her, and Grace's heart sank. She'd screwed up. He'd been expecting some decadent buffet of oysters and lobster laid out in their room so they could get straight down to the shagging . . .

'You look very Daisy Miller sitting there,' Vaughn said as he reached her, and leaned down to brush his lips across her cheek.

Grace took a moment to get the reference. 'That's probably one of my favourite books,' she lied. It wasn't, but she'd contemplated having her hair cut into a Mia Farrow crop when she'd seen the film.

'Are you enjoying this?' Vaughn asked, picking up her ragged copy of *Kavalier & Clay* as he sat down.

'It's all right. Long though,' Grace admitted. 'I always get intimidated by big books before I've even started them. Is this all right?' She gestured at the candlelit terrace. 'Eating out here, I mean. It's so hot and they said they could hold the table if you were late.'

Vaughn nodded. He was wearing jeans and a white shirt – untucked, Grace was pleased to note – but his casual clothes didn't make him seem friendlier. Instead they highlighted how stiff he was, his face pinched in the soft light.

'Are you OK?' Grace asked, before she could stop herself.

He nodded again. 'Long day,' he elaborated. 'And then we were last in a queue to take off. I don't like helicopters. They're too flimsy.'

Grace had been thinking exactly the same thing. 'You should have a drink,' she decided firmly, because it was her answer for everything. She picked up the bottle of Sauvignon Blanc from the ice bucket and reached for his glass. It was a very mistressy thing to do – maybe that was why Vaughn smiled approvingly as she carefully tilted the condensation-slicked bottle.

'It's nice to get out of London,' Grace ventured once he'd taken a small sip of wine. 'It's really pretty here.'

'Let's order.' Vaughn summoned a hovering waiter with a flick of his hand. Grace wasn't in any rush to go upstairs, and she could have stretched out the meal to all three courses and suggested that they linger over coffee, but wary of Vaughn's hard gaze, she ordered a mozzarella salad.

'As my main course and with a side order of chips.' Anything more solid would never have got round the lump that had suddenly materialised in her throat and she needed the carbs to soak up the alcohol, because, once again, she wasn't exactly sober.

None of Grace's carefully prepared conversational forays worked. 'Don't ask,' Vaughn sighed painfully when she enquired how the global art market was faring. And her thoughts on the new exhibition at the Tate Modern, that she'd prepped on the train, met with a dismissive, 'It's just for the tourists. All that gimmicky rubbish goes down well in the cheap seats.'

Forty-six hours, Grace thought to herself. It's forty-six hours out of your entire life. You can get through this. But then she could imagine another forty-six hours next weekend, plus a couple of evenings during the week; that would be eight more hours. Her whole life for the foreseeable future would be made up of blocks of time when she didn't know what to say or how to act, or how to do anything that might possibly please him.

Vaughn was picking at his Dover sole, brows knitted together. Grace put down her knife and fork and pushed away her salad. Across the terrace, the blushing bride was gulping down a cocktail with a haunted look on her face as she was harangued by the Mamas. For a second, Grace thought about whipping out her phone and taking a picture to send to Lily with the caption *Behold your future!*

'What are you smirking about?' Vaughn asked, startling Grace from her evil plans.

'Oh, it's nothing,' Grace mumbled hastily. Vaughn didn't

sound like he minded the smirking, but she was terrible at reading his moods. 'Really. Just this silly idea I had.'

For the first time that evening, she finally had Vaughn's full attention, though Grace wasn't sure that was a good thing. He was looking at her as if she might actually have hidden depths, so he was doomed to be disappointed. 'Do share,' he drawled, with just enough challenge that Grace couldn't back down.

'It's so dumb.' If she started with the disclaimer then Vaughn wasn't allowed to hold anything Grace said against her. Well, he could, but he'd been warned. She gestured discreetly at the other tables. 'That's a wedding-party over there. The bride's getting aggro from what can only be her mother and her soon-to-be mother-in-law and that bloke who's wearing the blue shirt – I think he's the groom – he looks like he wants to call the whole thing off.'

'Their obvious distress gives you pleasure?'

Grace thought about sticking her tongue out, but that could be misconstrued. 'No! It's just my best friend Lily's getting married and I thought it would be funny to take a picture on my phone and send it to her so she could see what she was getting herself into.'

Vaughn was smiling now. Not one of his chilly smiles but something warmer that opened the shutters a little. 'She's having cold feet?'

'As if!' Grace snorted inelegantly. 'She's been banging on about centrepieces and trying to bully me into a buttercup-yellow bridesmaid's dress. I swear, she's going to put me on a diet so I don't ruin the wedding pictures.'

Vaughn gave her a lazy appraisal. 'You know you don't need to lose weight,' he said mildly. Which was sweet of him, but the empire line of Grace's Ossie Clark dress was very forgiving and he was making major inroads into Grace's chips for someone who claimed she didn't need to cut the carbs. 'So the future doesn't look good for our fellow guests?' he added, inclining his head in the direction of the other tables.

'I give them a year,' Grace stated firmly. 'Two years if she gets knocked up on the honeymoon.'

And making Vaughn laugh like that, really laugh so he shook silently and pinked up, was going to be added to the list of Grace's ongoing projects, which currently included finding the perfect LBD and learning to make lace. It took at least ten years off him.

'Why the gloomy forecast?' he asked, after the laughter had ebbed away so the only reminder left was a softening of his voice.

Grace swept her eyes along the table. 'The bride has the potential to grow into a real harpie – just look at her mum.' She grinned. 'And I think the groom's gay for his best man. Jesus! Don't stare! They'll know we're talking about them.'

'You're quite right,' Vaughn agreed, standing up so he could pick up his chair and sit down next to Grace. 'And I couldn't really see properly anyway. Which one's the groom again?'

Halfway through Grace's character assassination of a woman they'd decided had slept with the groom's father after a Masonic dinner dance in 1987, Vaughn draped his arm around Grace's shoulder, fingers ghosting across her clavicle, and the rush of sensation was as unexpected as Vaughn's laughter. When he tugged on a stray tendril of hair escaping from her topknot, Grace almost turned her head to kiss him. Instead she picked up her glass with a not-quite steady hand and said, 'I'm pretty sure the woman in the nasty red dress is a Russian mail-order bride.'

Vaughn shook his head. 'Actually I think she's from the Ukraine.' He gestured for a waiter. 'You should order pudding.'

'Not for me, I'm stuffed,' Grace protested.

'You must, Grace. They do a wonderful sticky toffee pudding,' Vaughn urged her. 'You really didn't eat much dinner.'

Grace looked at him incredulously. Sticky toffee pudding in this heat? Maybe Vaughn was a feeder and his endgame was locking her in a basement, tying her up and pouring liquid lard down her throat. She'd seen a documentary about it on Channel 4. 'Two spoons, please,' she yelped at the waiter once Vaughn had ordered the pudding and two glasses of brandy.

The waiter left and Grace wondered if she should carry on describing the wedding-party from hell before they lapsed into another uncomfortable silence, but the other diners were starting to head indoors. The groom's Uncle Bertie (a secret cross-dresser, they'd decided) ambled past their table and Vaughn suddenly raised his glass.

'Are you here for a wedding?' he enquired.

'My god-daughter,' the man replied, slurring his words because Grace had already identified him as a heavy drinker from his bulbous red nose and crumpled white suit. 'Can't say I like the fella she's marrying though.'

'Well, I hope they'll be very happy together,' Vaughn murmured. 'We were just remarking on what a beautiful couple they are.'

Grace smiled weakly, which was hard when she was biting her lip at the same time. The moment that the man unsteadily tottered off, she picked up her napkin and swiped Vaughn with it. 'Give me a warning next time,' she spluttered through her giggles.

'He wasn't anyone's uncle. You were wrong. You'll have to pay a forfeit later,' Vaughn said, his fingers rubbing circles on the back of her neck, and Grace swayed a little closer as the waiter presented her pudding with what she thought was a very unnecessary flourish.

She looked at the bowl without much enthusiasm. Then she quickly swallowed a mouthful of ice cream to cool her down. It didn't work. 'No, it's too much.'

Vaughn was already pulling the bowl closer. 'Are you sure?'

he asked perfunctorily, and Grace didn't even have time to nod before he brought the spoon to his mouth.

Every time he swallowed, Vaughn would close his eyes and purse his lips, like he was having these tiny moments of rapture. It was the cutest thing Grace thought she'd ever seen, though Vaughn wasn't at all cute. He was, like, the Anti-Cute.

Still, when he'd scraped up the last sticky pools of melted ice cream, she vowed that, when he was being his most intimidating and infuriating, she'd remember him like this – with a smear of ice cream clinging to his bottom lip.

And, quickly, before she could wimp out, Grace leaned in and kissed him clean, snaking out her tongue to lick away a stray crumb. She felt Vaughn tense – and just when he gave in and opened his mouth . . . she pulled away and smiled at him. She could *so* do this.

'Shall we have the brandy in our room?' she suggested.

Vaughn didn't touch Grace during the climb upstairs. With one hand cradling her glass of brandy and the other holding up the hem of her dress so she didn't trip, it made coordination tricky. Especially as Grace could feel Vaughn's eyes etching a pattern right between her shoulderblades.

She stumbled through the door and took a second to catch her breath, before she turned to face him.

Vaughn shut the door with a decisive thud and leaned back against it. 'This will do,' he said, so blandly that Grace wasn't sure if he was talking about the room or her. 'Have you been smoking in here?'

Grace sniffed the air. She'd had the window open the entire time and she couldn't smell any lingering traces of Marlboro Lights. 'I had one,' she said defensively, hoping he wasn't going to give her a lecture on the perils of smoking because that would damp down the little spark that was still smouldering.

But Vaughn just smiled. 'You shouldn't. You'll get wrinkles

on that pretty face,' he purred, taking her hand so he could pull her towards the bed.

It was going to be like that. No stilted conversation and tentative kisses – and anyway, Grace had had enough of those to last several lifetimes. Vaughn sat on the edge of the bed and tugged her between his legs so she could feel the heat coming off him and felt sure it was mirrored in her own rosy cheeks.

She took a gulp of the brandy and felt the burn sizzle its way down to her belly. Before she could gulp the rest of it down, Vaughn was taking the glass from her and leaning over to place it on the nightstand.

'I'd very much like to see you undress,' he remarked conversationally, the picture of poise apart from that familiar tic pulsing away.

'OK,' Grace whispered, and she flexed the hand he was still holding and waited for him to let her go. Without Vaughn's touch, Grace felt slightly disorientated as she took a step back. Then another. She could keep taking steps as far as the door, she thought, then down the stairs and out into the night.

She could . . . but instead with clumsy fingers, she reached for the concealed zip and inched it down. Staring at a point approximately six inches above Vaughn's head, Grace started to wriggle out of the diaphanous chiffon folds.

'Slowly,' Vaughn said quietly, though Grace didn't remember asking for any audience participation. But she decided it didn't matter when he breathed in sharply as her breasts emerged.

They shimmied in the dim light as the dress got stuck on her hips. Objectively Grace knew that her breasts were damn fine. They still aced the pencil test every time and had a few good years left before they started a gradual descent and she'd have to start sleeping in a bra like Marilyn Monroe. So she concentrated on stepping out of the puddle of material rather than clamping her elbows to her boobs, and kicked free of her flip-flops so she was standing there in nothing but her M&S

cami-knickers. Then, before she could stop herself, Grace bent down to pick up her dress and placed it neatly over a chair.

It wasn't seductive but Grace had blown an entire term's student loan on the Ossie Clark dress when she'd found it languishing in the back of a vintage shop in Manchester and she couldn't just leave it on the floor. Nope. That wasn't the way she rolled.

Maybe that's why Vaughn was staring at her like she'd just back-flipped across the room but Grace simply shrugged, which sent his eyes right back to her chest, and hooked her fingers in the waistband of her tap pants.

'No,' Vaughn said suddenly. 'Come here.' And he tapped one finger against his thigh.

Grace approached with some apprehension but Vaughn wouldn't have been looking at her like that, with something approaching awe, if he wasn't pleased with her performance so far.

'Hey,' Grace said, as she straddled his thighs and wound her arms round his neck, their faces so close that if she leaned forward a couple of millimetres they'd bump noses.

'Hey,' Vaughn said, hands coming to rest on her hips, eyes almost closed so Grace couldn't tell what he was thinking. 'There's no need to look so anxious.'

Grace frowned. 'I'm not,' she denied hotly. 'Do I look anxious?'

But Vaughn didn't answer because he was kissing her.

His kisses were as contradictory as he was. Forceful, demanding but also concise, even sweet as he bussed the tip of Grace's nose with his lips as he settled her more securely on his lap. They were the kind of kisses that made Grace come slightly untethered because good kissing, really good kissing, wasn't about being in love with the person you were with. It was all about the technique of the person you were with.

And Vaughn was right up there in her Top Five Best Ever

Kissers. In with a bullet, when he did something with his teeth and her tongue that made Grace sigh into his mouth and almost swoon if she hadn't been grinding herself against his cock.

Vaughn's lips left hers to nuzzle a path along her neck, lifting her up again like she was much lighter than 123 pounds so he could mouth her breasts, sucking at one tightly budded nipple while Grace ran her fingers through his hair.

She tensed momentarily when Vaughn's hand crept between her legs but he made an approving noise when he discovered how wet she was and she thought that maybe she'd never been quite this turned on before. It was a potent combination of being with a man who actually knew what he was doing and knowing this was just an arrangement, which had seemed sordid but was now edging firmly towards the door marked *illicit thrill*.

'For fuck's sake,' Grace muttered as she tried to undo his shirt buttons with clumsy hands. 'Jesus.'

'Don't be so hasty,' Vaughn said against her skin. 'Stand up for a minute.'

Grace slid off his lap, and even the floorboards beneath her bare feet felt like sensory overload as Vaughn slid down her panties and cupped her bottom to bring her close again.

Maybe the waxer she'd seen had been right because Vaughn pushed Grace down on the bed, arranged her as if she was one of his pieces of art, and started to explore her pussy like it was his new, absolutely favourite thing in the world.

'Do you like it when I do that?' he asked Grace, propping himself up on one elbow from between her thighs, and she felt dismay wash over her. She didn't do dirty talk and she'd been percolating nicely when his fingers were delving, mouth too busy for questions.

All of a sudden it felt ridiculous to be sprawled out, legs scissored, sheet wrinkling underneath her. 'You still have your clothes on,' she pointed out, and rubbed the back of her knuckles against his cock. She felt it give a little leap of excitement; it distracted him beautifully.

Vaughn's hand curled around hers and together they dragged down his zip.

When he came, Vaughn said her name like it was a prayer, then he was silent, burying his head against her breasts as Grace stroked the thick hair that he'd never grow long enough to become curls.

Grace had the scent of Vaughn on her, a little bit citrusy, a little bit sweaty, the taste of toffee in her mouth from their kisses and a slight ache between her legs because he'd been inside her. He'd fucked her. And she'd been fucked enough times for it not to mean very much. But when Vaughn finally disentangled himself with one last clinging kiss, Grace was glad to be free from his embrace because lying skin-to-skin, his arms around her so she could feel his pulse slowing down to a steady thud, had been much harder than she expected. It was intimate in a way that had nothing to do with sex or their names signed on a legally binding agreement. Why hadn't she realised that? Because she was stupid, stupid, stupid.

Grace shifted away from him but Vaughn pulled her back into his arms so she could feel his softening cock against her arse as he dotted her shoulderblades with kisses and petted her belly with lazy fingers. 'Don't go,' he whispered in her ear. 'Let's stay like this for a while.'

Afterwards was always messy and sticky in Grace's experience but she lay against Vaughn quietly, fingers curled around his upper arm.

'What this?' she eventually asked, when her fingers traced around the edge of a plaster.

Vaughn made an odd snuffly noise. 'Nicotine patch.'

'I didn't know you smoked.'

'Well, I haven't for three years hence the nicotine patch.'

'You know that you're not meant to wear them for that long, right?'

'Yes, I'm well aware of that.' There was no need for him to sound quite so snippy. This was traditionally the time when you really looked at each other, swapped stories about childhood scars and . . .

Grace inched her head closer because now she'd opened her eyes and adjusted, wincing, to the light he'd left on because he'd said that he wanted to look at her, she could see that the nicotine patch wasn't the half of it. Vaughn had a tattoo. Not some tiny Chinese letters that probably spelled out *I'm a gullible wanker*, or an equally risible tribal band. This was a big, no-holds-barred inking, only half-lasered off. Grace could just make out the edge of a flush of cards, maybe a dice . . . and was that a skeleton or a rabbit?

But if he got that pissy about a nicotine patch, then Grace guessed that his bigass greaser tattoo was also another no-fly zone.

They stayed like that for a few more minutes, Vaughn's hands slowing until they rested on her hips. Grace tried to ignore a tickle somewhere around her left ankle. She'd never been one for snuggling and eventually, when the tickle became an itch, she shifted out of Vaughn's loose embrace and leaned over so she could scratch her ankle.

'So, are you all right?' Grace asked as she sat up and tried to casually wrap the sheet around her. Really, she wanted to ask if she'd been all right but that would have violated all kinds of unspoken first-time rules.

'Never better,' Vaughn assured her with a lazy grin. 'Do you mind if I have the bathroom first?'

'Go ahead.' Grace ran a hand through her hair, which felt very birds' nesty. 'It's all yours.'

'If you open the window, I won't say anything if you want to have a post-coital cigarette,' Vaughn murmured and Christ, Grace thought, sex really brought out the best in him. She could see that wrangling Vaughn into a sunny mood would involve spending a lot of time horizontal, and she wasn't sure how she felt about that.

Grace watched him lope towards the alcove with the bath in it. His body was a testament to the benefits of having your own basement gym, which he'd mentioned the other night. Or at least the back view was. He was long-limbed, she'd already guessed that, and his arse was just as pert as any of her much younger boyfriends. Actually more pert than about fifty per cent of them because they drank too much lager and didn't have basement gyms. Grace would reserve final judgement until she'd seen the front, she decided as she groped frantically for the free bathrobe because she hadn't grown up in a naked house.

Curled up on one of the armchairs, sucking down a medicinal cigarette, Grace wondered if she felt used. But mostly she felt disappointed because at one stage, when it had been all kissing and hands pressing her into the mattress with a firmness that was just the right side of forceful, she'd thought that she might come.

There was no way Vaughn could have known she hadn't. By the time you were twenty-three, you were meant to have the sex thing sussed, in the same way that you were meant to have memorised the fat units, carb content and calories in every M&S Ready Meal and know what time each morning Topshop got their new deliveries.

It was a small comfort but Grace prided herself on the quality of her fake orgasms. Unlike other girls she'd talked to, she didn't go for the whole porn-star routine of flailing limbs and, 'Yes, yes, fuck me, yeah fuck me, like that, just like that' histrionics. Instead she'd fling her head back, give these little airless gasps and when the critical moment came, she'd clench everything she had in the way of pelvic-floor muscles. Grace liked to think that her performance was subtly sincere . . . and it had always got her rave reviews.

She quickly stubbed out her cigarette as Vaughn emerged from the bathroom nook and seemed to sniff the air appreciatively. 'All yours,' he murmured, now clad in boxer shorts. The front of him looked OK too, now that Grace was in a position to pass judgement. He didn't have a six-pack, but Grace had never actually met a boy who did. Vaughn did have a spare, lean look to him, like he could actually order his own desserts and not have to rely on the kindness of other people's sweet tooths. And she'd already felt the muscles in his biceps taut under her fingers as she'd clutched at his arms . . .

'Seen anything you like?' Vaughn enquired archly and Grace realised she'd been staring at him, possibly with her mouth hanging open as she often did when she zoned out.

She settled for a non-committal, 'Hmm,' as she edged past Vaughn, but he pulled her closer so he could kiss the top of her head. 'Today was absolutely horrendous but you turned it around, so thank you.'

'I thought you didn't ever say thank you,' Grace reminded him, as she stood in the cradle of his arms. Without heels, she was on an eye-level with the cleft in his chin, close enough to pout her lips and kiss it.

'Well, I'm not going to make a habit of it,' Vaughn said lightly, letting her go so she could scurry to the wash area.

He barely looked up from the book he was reading when she emerged in her Primark vest and shorts combo. As she climbed into bed and pulled the covers around her, Vaughn put down his book and reached over to turn the bedside lamp off.

Grace could feel her breath hitch in her throat as Vaughn settled down, plumping up his pillows and stretching out. She steeled herself for the inevitable arm hauling her in but it turned out that Vaughn wasn't a cuddler. Or a sprawler. He arranged his limbs like a question mark and when Grace was sure he'd settled, she curled up in her usual foetal ball and willed herself not to fidget. Why was it that sleeping, just sleeping, with Vaughn made her feel more vulnerable than when he'd been *fucking* her? It made no sense.

'Are you a light sleeper?' he suddenly asked.

Grace had spent the last two years of her life sleeping on a sagging sofabed, or sometimes the floor, when she couldn't find the optimum position not to get poked by the springs. She figured that a firm mattress and Egyptian cotton might take some getting used to, but she could deal with it. 'Not especially. Are you?'

'Yes, very,' Vaughn replied emphatically. 'So don't move around too much.'

'OK, I'll try not to,' she said, trying to get in some prime burrowing time before Vaughn threw a fit.

Which didn't take long. 'I can't believe you're comfortable under the covers when it's so hot,' he muttered peevishly.

'I like to be tucked in,' Grace grunted, because she was tired, she'd drunk most of a bottle of wine and she didn't want to be pulled out of imminent slumber by Vaughn deciding that her sleep preferences were contravening some obscure clause of the mistress code. 'Good night.'

Vaughn turned over and muttered under his breath but Grace ignored him in favour of shutting her eyes and falling asleep.

chapter fourteen

The other side of the bed was empty when Grace woke up nine hours later. She followed the trail of clothes that Vaughn had been wearing the night before to the bath alcove, where a mound of damp towels were heaped on the floor and his wash things were strewn across one of the counters; he'd even left a blob of toothpaste clinging to the side of the sink. She'd never have guessed that Vaughn was a secret slob, nor that he'd spend most of the night thrashing about so that only grim determination had made her go back to sleep each time she'd been knocked by a flailing limb.

She was drying her hair and wondering what to do about breakfast when he appeared positively glowing with exertion.

'I've been up for hours,' he said, with too much smugness for Grace's liking. 'I've been to the gym *and* had a run around the tennis courts.'

That would be why he was dripping sweat over the floorboards. £5,000 a month wasn't enough to get her out of bed early so she could kill herself on a treadmill. 'I don't do exercise,' she growled, because she didn't do talking before eleven either.

'I'm going to jump in the shower,' Vaughn told her, toeing off his trainers, 'then I'm going to be working for most of the day so you need to make yourself scarce. I should be done by six.'

Of all the things Grace had expected from their first weekend away together, her absence wasn't one of them. She stared at Vaughn blankly and hoped that she didn't look offended or hurt that he found it so easy to resist her charms. 'Oh,' she said. 'OK.'

'There's no need to sound quite so forlorn. They're expecting you at the spa after twelve, once they've finished buffing and polishing the blushing bride,' Vaughn said over his shoulder. 'You'll just have to find somewhere out of the way until then. Oh, and ask someone to send up some coffee.'

Finding somewhere out of the way took ages. After Grace choked down her usual breakfast of two cups of tea, a muffin and a banana, the staff kicked her out of the House Kitchen so they could start preparing for the wedding. The terrace was equally out of bounds. The Pool Room was full of braying men in morning coats. The Study was a hubbub of women adjusting hats and cooing over outfits. Thankfully, the Library's only occupant was an elderly woman in a lilac dress snoring loudly on one of the sofas.

Grace pulled down a copy of *The Great Gatsby* and tried to speed-read it in case Vaughn quizzed her on it later, but mostly she worked on version five of her knitted iPod holder, which was proving tricky, until it was time to head spa-wards.

It was 6 p.m., and from the sounds of carousing drifting in from outside, as Grace slowly climbed the stairs, the bride and groom were joined in god-holy matrimony. She knew she was being an ungrateful wretch, but she was starting to feel spa-ed out, though three and a half weeks ago she'd never even stepped inside one. She didn't have an inch of skin left that hadn't been poked, prodded, pummelled, exfoliated, depilated, oiled, moisturised and thoroughly pampered. *Skirt* were very big on spa treatments – in fact, Lily had been working on a spa special for the January issue – but never once had anyone written a piece on how exhausting being beautified was.

Grace stretched tiredly as she pushed open the door to find Vaughn sitting on the sofa, laptop on the coffee-table and a phone clamped under his ear. He was talking in rapid Italian, and as he motioned her into the room, he held up a finger to his lip. She could take a hint and tiptoed across the room to the bed, because that last deep-tissue massage had left Grace as limp as a bowl of day-old noodles.

Vaughn was still chattering away as she kicked off her flip-flops, eyed *Kavalier & Clay* warily and decided there was no harm in lying down quietly until Vaughn had finished doing art-dealer stuff.

Grace was woken up by a sharp knock on the door after what felt like hours. Disorientated, she sat up and saw a member of staff wheel in a trolley, which she hoped was dinner because breakfast had been a long, long time ago.

Vaughn sat down on the edge of the bed. 'You've been dead to the world for the last three hours,' he murmured, cupping her cheek. 'I didn't have the heart to wake you.'

Grace squinted at the clock; it was gone nine. 'I always have a disco-nap before I go out on Saturdays.'

'You barely moved. I thought about holding a mirror in front of your mouth to check that you were still breathing.'

Grace was profoundly glad that he hadn't. 'Is that dinner?' she asked hopefully. 'You didn't want to eat on the terrace again?'

Vaughn's hand was trailing absently along her jaw and she wasn't sure whether she should lean into the caress or ignore it. 'I'm afraid we're confined to quarters. I thought we could have a little picnic in here.' His thumb pressed against her bottom lip. 'You're all rosy-cheeked.'

'I'm blotchy. I've just had a ninety-minute facial,' Grace pointed out.

'Rosy-cheeked,' Vaughn insisted. 'It suits you. Usually you're so pale.'

'My grandmother made me have two spoonfuls of cod liver

oil every morning because I was so pasty,' she found herself admitting, though she didn't know why. 'It tasted absolutely gross.'

'You need to learn how to accept a compliment.' Vaughn held out his hand and Grace let him lever her off the bed, so they could sit on the sofa and eat dinner, as they watched a DVD from the pile the staff had thoughtfully provided. Grace suspected that it wasn't Vaughn's usual speed for a Saturday night but he didn't seem to mind. On the contrary, he was more relaxed than Grace had ever seen him; feet propped up on the coffee-table as he enthusiastically munched his way through a ham and cheese sandwich and swigged from a bottle of designer beer.

The film, something in black and white with subtitles, wasn't really holding Grace's interest, but mindful of Vaughn at the other end of the sofa, a decorous twelve inches between them, Grace tried to keep the fidgeting and the running commentary down to a bare minimum. Vaughn was OK with the odd, 'So is he one of the good guys?' and, 'I thought she was dead', but Grace was just wondering out loud if the person who'd written the subtitles was on crack when he suddenly got up without warning.

Grace was about to start apologising when Vaughn opened the mini-bar and called, 'Milk or plain?' – even though he allegedly didn't do carbs after six.

'Whatever. I'm not fussed.' Grace paused. 'Actually, have they got anything salty? Peanuts or crisps or something?'

When he got back, hands full of calorific treats, which he dumped in Grace's lap, he sat down next to her, and patted his leg. 'Let's make ourselves more comfortable,' he said, and Grace thought about sitting on his knee, which actually would be incredibly uncomfortable for both of them. Instead, she swung her legs up and into his lap. His hands immediately encircled her ankles, his grip warm and strangely comforting.

Grace tore open a bag of Kettle Chips and pressed 'play' again.

By the end of the film, Vaughn's eyes were almost closed, teeth gritted, his head flung back. It had started off innocently enough, her feet in his lap, which actually worked out really well because it meant she could nudge him when he tried to bogart the Kettle Chips.

He'd been surprisingly docile about it, until Grace had poked him with her foot and discovered that Vaughn was hard. Correction: rigid. Grace had frozen for a second, then a sudden wicked impulse had made her flex her foot. Vaughn had swallowed compulsively, fingers tightening around her ankle. Grace had known she was on dangerous ground, but when did she ever err on the side of caution? Since never.

Now, as the final credits rolled, Grace was still curling her toes round the stiff outline of Vaughn's cock and taking great pleasure in watching him lose every single ounce of self-possession as he bit his lip and tried not to groan.

'For God's sake, will you stop that?' It was almost a growl, and before Grace could begin to retreat in panic, one of Vaughn's hands was clamping round her thigh and tugging her closer.

It was only when he kissed her and Grace willingly mashed her mouth against his, that she realised that goading Vaughn beyond his endurance got her seriously hot. There was no hesitation, no reticence; she kissed him right back, only pausing so she could help him pull off her dress and slip out of her knickers.

'Don't stop kissing me,' she ordered breathlessly, once his T-shirt had joined her frock on the floor.

Vaughn didn't snap to it, but stared at Grace for a moment probably because she was every nympho cliché made flesh, what with the straining breasts, the flushed cheeks and the way she was undulating against his dick like a professional lap dancer. 'I can't wait to fuck you,' he enunciated very precisely, despite the urgency of the moment.

Grace planted a line of kisses against his set jaw as she lifted herself up slightly, so she could unzip his jeans, reach one hot little hand into his boxers and close her fingers around the thick length of his cock. 'Then fuck me,' she said, because she was *this* close, closer than she'd ever been, and she didn't care that normally she hated going on top because she didn't like the way her tits bounced or her belly rippled.

Thigh muscles screaming with the effort, she slowly lowered herself on to Vaughn as he let out the breath she was still holding. Grace took a moment to savour the feeling of him buried deep inside her, but Vaughn was already raising her up so she could slam back down, jarring her so she lost the rhythm. Lost the insistent 'fuckmenowfuckmenowfuckme now' pulse of her clit. Her feet, splayed in an ungainly fashion on either side of Vaughn's thighs, were crunching over discarded sweet wrappers and the moment was gone as swiftly as it had appeared. So Grace did what she always did – closed her eyes so they wouldn't give her away, and pretended that what she had was enough.

It was the insistent buzzing of a phone that woke Grace up. She'd been sleeping fitfully anyway because Vaughn had tossed, turned, thumped his pillows at regular intervals and sighed in a way that had her twitching with irritation. But she'd pretended to stay asleep because she had a hunch that if she so much as fluttered an eyelash, Vaughn would accuse her of keeping him awake.

She heard Vaughn grunt before he sat up and answered the phone in a terse whisper. Grace risked rolling over on to her tummy to get more comfortable. Then the mattress shifted as Vaughn inched back his half of the duvet so he could swing his legs over the edge of the bed and reach for a bottle of water on the nightstand.

'Get a driver here no later than five thirty.' His voice was at normal speaking volume now and there was no point in feigning deep slumber any more. Grace sat up and peered at the time on the digital clock as she pushed her hair out of her eyes and yawned. It was four in the morning and only God should be awake. Vaughn glanced over at Grace and his face twisted in a grimace that she hoped wasn't aimed at her. 'No, you did the right thing in calling me,' he said tersely. 'I just wish Grant would schedule his creative crises on Greenwich Meantime. Come and meet me at JFK and you can fill in the blanks.'

He put the phone down and got to his feet so he could stretch in a half-hearted way. 'Go back to sleep,' he told Grace.

Grace experimentally shut her eyes but they wanted to stay open. 'I'm fine,' she said, stifling another yawn.

'Well, that makes one of us,' Vaughn said, and going back to sleep was the safer option because right now he was made of cranky.

However, she couldn't resist saying, 'You've got some uppity artist who needs talking down from the ledge?'

Vaughn started gathering up his clothes, which were liberally scattered around the room. 'At this precise moment I'm thinking about pushing him *off* the ledge. Do wonders for his resell value and I'm sure I could find a lawyer who'd plead justifiable homicide.'

'Do you want me to make you a cup of tea? I'm going to have one.'

Vaughn paused on his way to the bathroom. 'I'd love one, and if you wanted a cigarette I could probably get a sizeable hit from your second-hand smoke.'

That was all Grace could do to help, though she yearned to stage an intervention and do Vaughn's packing herself because he had to start all over again when he couldn't get the zip to close, which almost sent him over the edge.

Grace had reached the wired, teeth-grinding stage of being

awake, when there was a discreet tap at the door. She managed to get to her feet and retrieve Vaughn's phone, which was still on his nightstand.

'Don't forget this,' she said, walking over to place it on his outstretched palm.

Vaughn frowned, as if he was discarding some of his opinions about her and creating shiny new ones in their place. 'If I'm still in New York at the end of the week, maybe you can fly out and join me?' he murmured, tugging a lock of Grace's hair so he could pull her closer and press a kiss to her forehead. 'Go back to bed. There's a car booked for midday that will take you home. We were going to stop for lunch on the way but I'll be somewhere over the Atlantic.'

'Have a good flight.' Grace nudged Vaughn with her hip, but decided a kiss on his cheek was more appropriate. 'Don't take any crap from uppity artists.'

It teased a smile out of Vaughn. A small, forced smile that showed up the tiredness around his eyes, but it was a smile nonetheless. This mistress thing was a piece of cake, Grace thought smugly, before he said curtly, 'And if you're not going to sleep naked, then buy some slips or something. The vest and knickers is really doing nothing for me.'

chapter fifteen

Grace relished the journey home in the sleek car that smelled of expensive leather. It sure beat getting the train and being shunted on to sidings for half an hour because it was a Sunday afternoon.

Grace wondered why she didn't feel skanky or slutty or any of those other words that described how you were meant to feel when you were coming back from a dirty weekend with a rich, older man. What she did feel was hard to describe. She was glad, relieved even, to have survived the weekend. The sex had been as OK as it ever was, and once or twice had even headed towards phenomenal – and though Grace didn't think that she'd ever get over being freaked out and intimidated by Vaughn, there had been times when she'd enjoyed herself; enjoyed being with him, enjoyed the moments when he seemed to be enjoying being with her too. Really, he wasn't so bad in small doses – and it looked like small doses was all that she was going to get.

Back in Archway, Grace had time to walk to the Co-op and buy stuff for packed lunches for work, because it would be another week before the next batch of crisp twenty-pound notes arrived. There were going to be no more Zac Posen dresses in future, she decided, if she wanted the clothing allowance to cover more than one outfit and to save the five grand for paying off her bills. Now that she'd paid off her Topshop card and the rent arrears, she needed to make a dent in her overdraft. She couldn't be sure because she made a point of not opening the brown envelopes very often (or the white ones, come to that), but she had a sneaking suspicion that the bank were charging her daily interest. Then, once the overdraft was cleared, there were the credit cards, and the student loan, and the other loans ... and really, it was just as well that the weekend had gone OK, because she needed Vaughn's money, much more than Vaughn needed her.

For a moment, when she got back to her flat, Grace felt fired up enough to maybe pull out one of the shoeboxes so she could do sums and make a plan of action, but just the mere sight of one pink box poking out from the side of the sofa made her stomach flip over. Housework was a more appealing option.

Grace was on her knees, scrubbing the kitchen floor, when Lily rang. She knew it was Lily because her name popped up on the screen, although all she could hear was hiccuping.

'Lily? You all right?'

The hiccups morphed into snotty sniffs. 'No, I'm not. You have to come round right now.'

'Why? What's up?' If it was something to do with bridesmaids' dresses or fricking centrepieces, then no, Grace really didn't have to trudge over to Lily's house, especially as there was a bonnet drama on BBC1 that evening and her video player was wonky. Maybe next month she could splash out on a DVD recorder or even a Sky+ box, once she'd paid off some of the overdraft ...

'Grace!' It was an ear-perforating wail. 'Please, please, *please* come over! I am freaking out so badly right now!'

Grace dabbed at a mark on the lino that refused to budge. 'Give me a clue at least. Bet it starts with a D.'

'I'll see you in ten minutes,' Lily choked out, and hung up.

Grace stopped at the convenience store that was exactly halfway between her flat and Lily's Tufnell Park love nest, to buy ice cream and vodka. All of Lily's problems could usually be soothed with Grey Goose and Häagen-Dazs.

'Hey, cutie, turn that frown upside down,' Grace drawled five minutes later, holding up the bottle of vodka when Lily opened the door.

Lily burst into tears. She tried to say something, but it was impossible to understand with all the sobbing.

'Hey, Lils. What's up?' Grace stepped over the threshold and gently nudged her arm. 'What's Dan done now?'

It was a safe bet that Dan had done something heinous. Grace shut the door behind her and put an arm around Lily. 'Come on, I'll pour us a drink and you can tell me all about it.'

Lily cried a little harder and resisted Grace's efforts to lead her into the lounge. 'No, bathroom,' she choked.

'OK, bathroom it is,' Grace conceded, casting one covetous look around. Lily's flat was gorgeous – a huge two-bedroom place that not even Lily's bland décor by way of IKEA could ruin. Having a rich dad was wasted on Lily. If Grace's father had bought her a flat, which was unlikely when he didn't even send birthday cards, Grace would have painted the floorboards white, run up curtains from some vintage fabric she'd been hoarding for years, haunted car-boot sales and architectural salvage yards for *exactly* the right kind of pieces for each room and some wrought-iron furniture for the garden, which she'd carefully tend, rather than paving it over like Dan and Lily so they'd have somewhere to put their barbecue.

'Grace! Why are you standing there like that?'

Grace snapped to attention. 'Sorry,' she soothed, because Lily was still crying and this didn't seem like a simple case of Dan staring at some random girl's boobs for longer than ten seconds. 'Will you please tell me what's going on?' she added, following Lily into the bathroom.

'Look!' Lily gestured wildly as Grace's eyes swung this way and that. Dan had left a pair of boxers on the floor, which didn't seem that terrible in the grand scheme of things, but on the sink surround . . .

'Are those what I think they are?' Grace enquired dubiously, staring at the little white sticks lined up in a row.

Lily picked one of them up and waved it wildly, as Grace took a hasty step back. 'I'm bloody pregnant, aren't I?' she spat. 'Look!'

'Don't make me touch something you've peed on,' Grace squeaked, peering at the stick and for what she guessed was a blue dot or a pink line or a picture of a baby. She was far too sperm-phobic to ever have had a pregnancy scare herself. 'Are you sure?'

'Yes, I'm sure,' Lily gritted, throwing the stick back down. 'I knew I should have stayed on the pill.' She had come off the pill because she was convinced it was making one of her breasts larger than the other.

'But you were using condoms or a cap or something, right?' Grace asked.

'Usually, but sometimes we just got carried away and it would have killed the mood,' Lily sniffed, sitting down on the edge of the tub. 'You know what it's like when you're in the moment.'

No, Grace didn't, but she sat down next to Lily and put an arm round her. 'Those home pregnancy kits can be totally suspect.'

'I did twelve of them! And I've drunk about fifty litres of water! They can't all be faulty. My period's a week late. I'm never, ever late. It comes every twenty-nine days, except this month.' Lily began to cry again. 'And Dan was horrible about it, called me a stupid bitch and stormed out, like it was nothing to do with him.'

At last Grace could empathise. 'God, he really is a total wanker.' She unscrewed the bottle of vodka and took a generous gulp, then offered it to Lily. 'I think you need this more than me.'

'I'm pregnant, Grace!'

'Oh my God! You're not going to *keep* it?'

Lily almost vibrated off the bath in indignation. 'It's not an it, it's a baby. *Our* baby.' It sounded as if the tears were rallying for an encore performance.

'Right now it's just a few cells mushed together,' Grace insisted, taking another swig of vodka. Lily should have called someone else, because this situation was stretching her limited people skills to breaking point. 'Sorry, I don't mean to sound so callous. This is just . . . Jesus, Lily. I don't know what you want me to say. You're *pregnant*!'

'No, it's all right,' Lily said in a small voice. 'Not like it's going to stick around. I did some coke the night of the engagement party and I've been pissed at least five times since my last period. It will probably be born with foetal alcohol syndrome or something. I might have a crack baby!'

'Don't talk shit. When my gran was pregnant, the doctor told her to have a pint of Guinness every day.' Which explained a hell of a lot. 'And French women knock back the red wine when they're pregnant.'

'This was not part of the plan. This is, like, skipping five pages of the plan. I'm not meant to be having a baby right now.'

Grace hugged Lily a bit tighter. Her friend was so ethereal-looking and felt so fragile that it seemed impossible that she could be with child. 'What plan?'

'Y'know, *the* plan! Everyone has one and I don't have a baby until I'm married and we've moved to an actual house in an area with good schools and I've been promoted twice at work so I'm a beauty editor and after I've had the baby, I can get freelance work or maybe even get a book deal to write one of those yummy mummy beauty books. I had it all worked out!'

It was a plan. Maybe it was a little far-fetched in places, but still Lily, whom Grace's grandmother had always described as 'flighty', had a plan.

'Well, you might have to shift a few things around, but life never happens like you think it will,' Grace said feelingly.

'But this is not the right time,' Lily wailed. 'I can't have a baby now. Dan and I kill plants, we forget to pick up our dry-cleaning and we're always running out of milk. That's why you have to stick to a plan.'

'I don't stick to a plan,' Grace said. 'Sometimes you have to kick it freestyle, Lils.'

'But you must have, like, this timetable of stuff you want to do and when you want to do it by, like having kids and buying a flat.'

'I'm never having kids,' Grace said flatly. 'And unless the property market keeps crashing so I can find a flat that costs five quid, I don't really see flat-owning in my future. Honestly, Lily, I'm pretty much plan-free. I mean, I dream about finding the perfect black dress or being spotted by Marc Jacobs who asks me to style his ad campaigns, but that doesn't really count, does it?' Grace asked sheepishly. She'd been toying with the idea of coming clean to Lily, now that the weekend could be counted as a success, but Lily's big life moments kept getting in the way. How could Grace tell Lily that her only plan was to be someone's mistress for six months so she could pay off her creditors?

Lily gave Grace a watery smile. 'Thanks for trying to cheer me up.'

'All part of the service,' Grace assured her. 'Oh God, why are you crying again?'

'I don't know,' Lily sobbed, and she even cried beautifully – tears clinging to her lashes before gently rolling down her cheeks. 'I keep thinking all of these stupid thoughts, like what if I'm one of those women who can't shift the baby weight, like ever?'

Grace got up and held out her hand. 'Let's go and sit out in the garden. I have ice cream with Baileys in it. The alcohol content is pretty low so you should be OK.'

Lily let herself be guided slowly through the kitchen as if she was just approaching the ninth month of a multiple pregnancy. Grace snagged a couple of spoons and they sat on Lily's extremely naff but extremely comfortable canopied swing and gently rocked as they ate the rapidly melting ice cream.

There wasn't much Grace could say but she liked to think that just being there for Lily in a companionable silence was enough. Also, she was still trying to process the shock, because Lily didn't ever fuck up. The fuck-up gene was missing from her DNA. And was it wrong to be gloating just a little bit that Lily had well and truly fucked up this time? Probably.

'Is that top from Paul and Joe?' Lily asked eventually.

Grace looked down at her grey cotton smock. 'Yeah, I got it at the sample sale last year.' She chased a stubborn scoop of ice cream around with her spoon. 'Too hot to wear anything clingy, isn't it? God, this weather is so unBritish.'

Lily nodded. 'I called round for you last night but you weren't in.'

'Oh, I was working.'

'Doing what?'

'There was some wedding going on.' Grace was just congratulating herself on not actually lying, technically speaking, when Lily gave an anguished sob.

'I'm not going to get to have my special day now.'

'You can move the wedding up, Lils.'

'I've been planning my wedding since I was thirteen, and me waddling down the aisle wasn't part of the picture.'

'Look, it's September now. You won't be showing that

much if you have the wedding in, like, November or December. That will still give you enough time to organise everything.' Grace held up her hand to ward off the protests that Lily had good to go. 'You might have to downsize a little, but it would be kinda cool to get to share your special day with it – the baby, I mean.'

Lily nodded slowly. 'I s'pose. I hadn't thought about that.'

Grace knew that she wasn't a particularly good friend, that she never did the right things or said the right words or responded in the right ways. But just this once, she wanted to buck the trend. 'Remember when we went to *The Golden Age of Couture* at the V and A and they had that gorgeous draped gown by Madame Grès? You get married in winter and we can find you something like that in a really heavy silk jersey and it will skim, not cling. You'll look beautiful, Lily.'

It worked. A proper smile was lighting up the other girl's face for the first time that evening, chasing away the tear-tracks and the trembling bottom lip. 'I do look good in white,' she said. 'Though maybe white would be pushing it. Do you think I could get away with ivory?'

They sat in the garden until dusk started creeping in, bringing a slight chill with it. Grace made scrambled eggs on toast and they were broaching the ever-thorny topic of bridesmaids' dresses when Dan stumbled through the door, full of apologies and mixed blooms from the garage.

'I'm so sorry, babe,' he blurted out, managing to look shamefaced, while simultaneously shooting death rays at Grace.

'Let's hope the baby gets Lily's looks and *her* disposition,' she hissed out of the side of her mouth, as she brushed past Dan.

Life was happening all around her, Grace mused as she unlocked her front door. Lily would have the baby, her dad would buy them a bigger place, and no way would she come back to work. Grace's visits with hand-knitted baby clothes would become less frequent and then Lily would disappear into the sunset with the other yummy mummies she'd met at her NCT classes. But for the first time, Grace didn't feel like she was stuck where she was, being who she was, without any hope of ever changing.

This *thing* with Vaughn wasn't built to last, but while it did, Grace felt as if it was giving her the potential to change; to be the Grace she wanted to be or at least, more like the Grace she wanted to be. It wasn't just the outside stuff, the spa-ing and the pretty clothes and the posh weekend breaks. It was being with a man like Vaughn, who'd obviously seen something in her that she still couldn't see herself. If she took her cues from Vaughn, let him guide her, got used to being in his world, then it would all rub off on her. She'd have that glossy patina that the posh girls, the successful girls, the sophisticated girls had that was nothing to do with how shiny their hair was but came from walking in a world which was always good to them. Grace wanted the key to that magic kingdom and Vaughn could give it to her for the next six months – or until the next pretty girl caught his eye.

Grace filled the kettle on auto-pilot, put a tea bag in a mug, got the milk out of the fridge and all the while she imagined the unspecified point of time in the future when Vaughn wouldn't be able to recall her name or the shape of her breasts or what she'd been wearing the first time they met.

The kettle boiled at the same time that the BlackBerry let out one impatient buzz. Grace picked it up and opened the email she'd just been sent.

Please click on the link to view your travel itinerary for next weekend.
  Regards
  M Jones

Grace clicked on the link and discovered that she was booked on a flight to New York at 7.30 p.m. the next Friday. She took a ruminative sip of her tea and winced as she burned her tongue.

chapter sixteen

Time seemed to speed up over the next few weeks so Grace felt as if she was always arriving, or leaving, but never staying still long enough to remember to breathe in and out. Or get the eight hours' sleep a night that she needed to resemble anything close to a human being the next day.

Grace was so tired that she'd taken to napping at the spa when she was getting her hair and nails done. She'd even set up an alarm system with her two favourite interns so she could have a power snooze in the fashion cupboard first thing in the morning, as the rest of the fashion team rarely put in an appearance much before eleven. Kiki was still suspicious though, and didn't have a good word to say about her hair. 'I think I preferred the black,' she'd sniped when she'd caught Grace fingering her newly restreaked hair in a meeting. 'And I absolutely hated the black.'

What with Kiki cranking the handle on the bitchometer, Lily overloading her with wedding prep and her contractually obligated dates with Vaughn, Grace was feeling a little ragged. But there were compensations. Not just the allowances, but the sleek black car that was always waiting to take her to work on the mornings after she'd been out with Vaughn. Or flying business class, not cattle class, on her three trips to New York, and staying in an Art Deco suite at the Plaza Athenée when they'd gone to Paris. It was all a blur really. When she tried to think back to the places she'd been, Grace could recall very few details, just the same things that kept cropping up over and over again. The delicate flutes of champagne, which now tasted as familiar to her as Diet Coke, the scent of expensive perfume as women she didn't know leaned in to almost brush their lips against her cheek, the flat airless atmosphere of airport departure lounges.

The only detail that stood out in stark relief was Vaughn. It was early November now, and though Grace had swapped bare legs for woolly tights and had got used to the way her hair swished about her shoulders, her feelings about Vaughn hadn't changed much from the first day they'd met.

He still had her on the freaked-out setting and Grace couldn't imagine that changing any time soon. She'd started to think of him as two separate people. There was Good Vaughn, who was as elusive as a rainbow after a rainstorm, but was funny ha ha rather than funny weird and had bought her a £3,000 crystal-embroidered Marc Jacobs dress in Paris. Then there was his far more ubiquitous evil twin, Bad Vaughn, who found fault with everything that Grace said, did and wore, from letting her phone roll over to voicemail instead of answering it in five rings or less, inserting the word 'like' at random intervals ('It's not like anything, Grace. It either is or it isn't') to her wearing flat shoes because 'I never realised just how short you are.'

During the second trip to New York he'd been outbid at an auction and had sunk into such a dark mood that he hadn't spoken to Grace all evening. He'd only started speaking to her again when they were back in his huge but spartan Central Park apartment, and that was to tell her to relax because she'd been far too tense to even think about having sex with him.

Bad Vaughn was definitely her companion for this evening, Grace thought glumly. She'd wanted to go to the restaurant at the Pembroke Hotel for weeks after she'd read a review in *ES*

Magazine. She'd even sent Madeleine some beauty freebies as a thank-you when she'd managed to book them a table, and Piers had emailed her that afternoon to say that he'd heard Madonna was going to be there. But Bad Vaughn was doing everything in his power to ruin it for her.

' "Amish organic free-range chicken with foraged mushrooms",' Vaughn recited from the menu with a sneer. 'Ridiculous. And this fashion for truffle fries is getting very boring.'

'What about the lobster?' Grace suggested brightly, looking at the daily specials. He'd obviously had a stinker of a day and Bad Vaughn didn't deal with stress very well. 'You like lobster, right?'

'I'll have the lamb,' Vaughn decided, as if he was ordering his last meal. 'And don't try to humour me. What are you going to have?'

Grace flushed. He had this uncanny knack of sounding like her grandmother telling her to stop showing off when she was little. No put-down since had ever taken the wind out of Grace's sails quite so effectively. Though Vaughn came a close second.

'I'm going to have two starters instead of a main. Maybe the crab cakes and the country salad or something.' Grace watched Vaughn wince at her mumbling. 'No dessert,' she added pointedly, because if he was going to keep on being mean to her then she wasn't going to order dessert solely so he could eat it. 'I'm not that hungry.'

They got through the meal with the barest minimum of conversation. Every time Grace tried out another amusing *bon mot* to show Vaughn that she'd done the required reading for that week, it was met with a grunt until he finally told her that she was giving him a headache. She could tell he was seething about her decision not to even look at the dessert menu, but his BlackBerry kept ringing with calls that he just had to take so he couldn't bring pressure heaping down on her.

'Oh, for fuck's sake,' he hissed as it rang again, and he picked it up with a white-knuckled hand. 'Now what?' he barked into the receiver.

Grace looked at her reflection in the back of her spoon and tried not to eavesdrop on a very tense conversation about a collection of photographs for a new exhibition, which had been impounded by Customs for being obscene. Vaughn's head sank lower and lower until he looked like he had no neck and he kept rubbing the bridge of his nose the way Grace did when she was getting a headache. He pushed his plate away virtually untouched and stood up.

'Finish your dinner,' he said shortly. 'I'll be waiting outside. I need to take this call. We'll have to stop at the gallery on the way home.'

'Um, do you want me to ask the waiter for a doggie bag?' Grace asked, but Vaughn just scowled at her and walked off.

He was still scowling when she finally emerged from the restaurant.

'I was beginning to think that you'd climbed out of the bathroom window and disappeared into the night,' he snapped, as he held the car door open for her.

'I had to get this.' Grace handed him a little box containing a generous portion of bitter chocolate cake that she'd sweet-talked from their waiter. She really wished she hadn't bothered now. 'Thank you for taking me out to dinner.'

Vaughn peered at the contents of the box and Grace peered at his face and the warring emotions on it: surprise, delight and, inevitably, rejection. 'It's very kind of you,' he said stiffly. 'But I can't eat this.'

'You can watch me eat it then,' Grace replied in exasperation. 'Might even let you have a bite if—'

Grace didn't even have a chance to finish the sentence with a sassy little quip, before Vaughn was hauling her into his arms so he could kiss her. He'd never kissed her like this before. Biting, hungry kisses, as if he couldn't get enough of the taste of her, his hand tangling in her hair to tip Grace's head back to meet his mouth.

His other hand was already sliding up her skirt in a possessive way, and just as she was about to protest because she didn't want their driver to get an eyeful, Vaughn pulled away to talk to him. 'Take us to the gallery,' he ordered in an unsteady voice.

Grace turned to Vaughn who was now staring out of the window and looking as remote as hell. Before she had time to chicken out, Grace's hand covered Vaughn's so she could squeeze his fingers. The pressure was returned immediately though neither of them spoke for the time it took the car to wend its way through the Mayfair streets.

Vaughn didn't let go of Grace's hand until they were climbing the stairs up to his office. It should have killed the mood, but Grace didn't feel out of the moment because the look in his eyes was heating her up from the inside.

She was already closing the gap between them as he beckoned her with one long finger. In the movies when the hero and heroine kissed in a frenzied, passionate way while they manoeuvred around the various obstacles that were between them and the nearest horizontal surface, there were never banged elbows and jostled limbs.

Grace, however, cannoned off the wall and knocked her hip on the fire extinguisher as Vaughn danced her down the corridor, arms tight around her. There was a brief pause as she fumbled with the door handle, his hands under her skirt so he could tug down the Agent Provocateur knickers that had cost her (well, him) sixty-five pounds. Grace heard the silk tear but she was already falling through the open door and being marched across the room.

Vaughn bent her over the back of the Cubist sofa, and before Grace could even wriggle out of her jacket, she heard the rasp of his zipper and he was inside her in one deep, hard stroke.

It was everything Grace hated about sex: undignified, messy, desperate – but this time she was getting dragged under. Her fingers gripped handfuls of leather cushions as she bent her head and took deep breaths in time with Vaughn's thrusts, each one surprising a moan out of her as she ground back against him.

It was hard to move with Vaughn's hands tight on her hips, and if she could just get one hand free to rub at her clit, then . . .

'Are you close?' His voice was slurred, not clipped and cut like usual, like his control was hanging by the most frayed of threads.

'Nearly,' Grace managed to grit out and he pushed her further into the sofa, changing the angle so she clenched around him in delighted surprise and then it was game over.

He groaned, like he was lost, as his rhythm faltered, then Vaughn was driving into her so fast and hard and all Grace could do was hold on and hope for the best. He came with a gasp that may or may not have been her name, and Grace's elbows, which had been keeping the whole show upright, collapsed under the strain and she sprawled against the back of the sofa, Vaughn on top of her, still inside her.

It was kind of nice to be like that for a minute or two. There was something comforting about the weight of Vaughn all around her, solid and reassuring. But then he was simply heavy and Grace stirred and shifted until Vaughn took the hint and set her free, taking hold of her hand again so he could sit them both down. Just this once, Grace curled herself against him so she could muss his hair. She decided to be philosophical about the sex; she'd had more near misses with Vaughn than with anyone else. Tonight she'd been closer than ever and, as an added bonus, Vaughn was still pleasingly non-verbal.

He stretched lazily, eyes closed as Grace rubbed her fingers in a slow circle against his scalp. 'What happened to the chocolate cake?'

It was a really effective mood-killer. Grace immediately took her hand away and flopped back against the cushions with a furious little huff. 'It's probably still in the car.'

'Pity,' Vaughn sighed, completely unaware that Grace was trying to burn holes in his skin with her eyes. 'You'll have to put something similar on the menu when you're planning the dinner.'

Grace sat up because snuggle-time had just been cancelled. 'What dinner?'

Vaughn opened one eye. 'Didn't Madeleine mention it?'

'No. *What dinner?*' Grace repeated, her voice growing shriller.

'You're hosting a dinner for me on the nineteenth. Or did we move it back to the twenty-first?' Vaughn finally sat up and adjusted his shirt, which had sustained only minor creases in all the excitement. 'There's no need to look quite so panic-stricken, Grace. I've given you two months to find your feet and this is easing you in gently. It's just a little dinner-party for eight people, nothing that alarming.'

'Say what?' Yeah, he'd mentioned something about parties at the beginning but Grace hadn't been listening that hard and she thought that she'd just wear a pretty dress and order a bevy of good-looking waiters to keep people's glasses filled.

'Are you unfamiliar with the concept of a dinner-party?' Vaughn asked, his voice dripping with condescension. 'I did mention this right at the very beginning of our arrangement, Grace, so I'm not sure why you need clarification. It's very simple. There'll be a Russian client of mine, another art dealer and an artist about your age, plus their significant others who I'm relying on you to entertain while I do business. You'll plan the menu, organise the seating, gift bags and such.'

Grace wished that her knickers weren't currently a damp,

torn scrap of satin on the floor. This wasn't a conversation she wanted to have bare-arsed. 'I can't. I just can't,' she insisted, hysterical now winning out over shrill. Home-made streamers and cup-cakes were not going to cut it, and no one she knew actually had a dining room to have a dinner-party *in* – apart from her grandmother who'd been entertaining members of the Rotary Club with a menu that she hadn't deviated from since 1995. She could just imagine Vaughn's white-hot fury if she served his guests smoked salmon mousse and duck *à l'orange*. 'Don't make me do this. I'll ruin it and it'll be crap and your guests will think I'm useless and no one will buy another painting from you ever again.'

Vaughn was staring at Grace as if her head was spinning around *Exorcist*-style. 'I don't understand why this is such a surprise,' he said, derision curling around each syllable. 'I'm not asking you to split the atom.'

'God, can't you see what a terrible idea this is? I'm a twenty-three-year-old girl who spends most of her days hanging up clothes in a fashion cupboard. Do you really think I'm the best person to organise a fucking sit-down dinner for eight people?' Grace put her hands over her hot face. 'If you make me do this, I will fuck it up. End of.'

Vaughn stood up; all the better to stare down at her with icy disapproval. 'No, fucking it up is not an option,' he said with grim finality. 'I thought we might go back to my house after I've made a few phone calls, but actually I'm not in the mood to listen to any more of your melodramatics.'

'I'm not being melodramatic! You could try to understand where I'm coming from.' It was hard to flounce seated so she settled for wriggling her shoulders furiously. She had a feeling that tears weren't far off.

'At the moment, Grace, you seem to be coming from another solar system.' Vaughn was already striding towards the door. 'I'm going to New York tomorrow. I'm back in London on Wednesday – I'll talk to you then.'

*

Three days later, after a series of increasingly terse phone calls between herself and Vaughn, Grace was officially summoned to meet Madeleine Jones outside the offices of a private catering firm in Bloomsbury. Grace saw a tall, well-preserved redhead who looked like she bought all her clothes and shoes in LK Bennett sales, glancing impatiently at her watch, even though Grace was actually two minutes early. Grace thought about ducking around the corner and having a sneaky cigarette because she was dreading meeting Madeleine in the flesh, though the most recent emails and phone-calls had been almost cordial. Plus she was also freaking out about menus and temperamental chefs.

Grace got as far as pulling out her trusty Marlboro Lights but in the end steeled herself to walk up to the other woman with a perky smile. 'Madeleine? Hi, I'm Grace.' Maybe she should have called her Ms Jones. It suited her better than Madeleine, which was too French and frivolous and cake-related for someone who always punctuated her emails so perfectly.

Grace was being given the once-over too, Madeleine's eyes widening slightly as she took in Grace's jeans and jumper. But she'd been doing returns all week, and grubbing about in the cupboard in a little black dress would have been totally impractical.

'Good, you're on time.' There was something about Madeleine Jones that reminded Grace of one of her lecturers at St Martin's who'd been teaching textiles since God was a boy and had looked at each new intake of students with the world-weary air of a woman who'd seen it all before. But at least Madeleine was smiling. A polite, reined-in kind of smile, but it was a smile. 'Shall we go in?'

They were shown into an empty dining room and took a seat at a table laid out with six different place settings. Grace stared at them in dismay. Vaughn had said nothing about cutlery and crockery – though he'd had plenty to say about Grace's can't-do attitude when she'd spoken to him on the phone the night before. However, he'd finished the lecture with the news that Ms Jones had kindly volunteered to lend her services just this once.

'I really appreciate you helping me out like this,' Grace said with her most winsome look. The look that even disarmed Kiki sometimes when she was getting difficult about Grace's very long lunches, which doubled up as spa appointments. 'Thanks for sending me the list of all those dietary requirements. God, I can't believe that anyone's still doing the South Beach diet. It's so three years ago. And what's the difference between macrobiotic and vegan?'

'Grace, you're bright red. Please calm down.'

'So, can I ask you some questions about the guest-list?' Grace persevered, pulling a piece of paper out of her jeans pocket, because she'd long gone past calm and was edging towards hyperventilation. 'This Russian guy's girlfriend, I knew her name was familiar and I Googled her – and she's practically a supermodel!'

Madeleine didn't seem to share Grace's distress. 'I'm sure you can talk about fashion and all the other exciting things you do at work. Vaughn thinks the two of you will get along really well.'

Grace paused at the thought of Madeleine and Vaughn spending a cosy coffee-break discussing her and her many failings. 'And this art dealer's boyfriend, Alex . . . I don't know anything about him.'

'Vaughn says you've already met him. At Boris Volkova's party in September.'

September seemed light years ago. Then Grace had a memory of an effete, annoying person blowing smoke rings in her face with her own cigarettes. 'But Vaughn told me to keep away from him, that he was trouble – so why is he on the guest-list?' It would have been helpful if Vaughn had filled her in on some of this information himself instead of telling her to stop having hysterics and leaving it to Madeleine.

'Because Vaughn wanted to invite Harry and sadly, Alex is part of the package,' her mentor explained. 'If he starts causing trouble, which Vaughn seems to think he might, you're to shut him down. Politely, but don't stand for any nonsense.'

As if organising the party wasn't bad enough, now Grace was expected to do crowd control as well. 'I am *so* out of my depth,' she whimpered, and Madeleine was looking very disapproving – but oddly, it didn't seem to be directed at Grace, more at Vaughn, as if she was going to give him a piece of her mind at their next coffee klatch.

'Really, what were you thinking?' Grace could imagine her saying to a chastened Vaughn. 'It's obvious she isn't mistress material.'

'Alex and Nadja aren't your priority,' was what Madeleine actually said. 'Noah Skinner and his girlfriend, Lola, are. It's the first time that they've been invited to one of these dinners and they'll probably be very nervous too, so I suggest you put them on either side of you. Sergei is close to finishing a deal with the gallery so Vaughn needs to talk to him, but Nadja doesn't like Alex so don't sit them next to each other. Put Nadja next to Noah, Alex next to Lola and Harry and Sergei on either side of Vaughn. Would you like me to go more slowly?'

Grace had only just started scribbling notes with a leaky ballpoint pen. She didn't answer at first as she was busy drawing circles and arrows on the list. Finally she looked up. 'It sounds like a Mike Leigh film,' she remarked, and got another tiny smile from Madeleine. 'So, like, does the catering firm sort out the flowers – and what about the goodie bags? Should it be lots of little things, or one big thing? What's the budget? Do you have an account or do I need to pay for gifts and keep the receipts? Oh God, sorry. I don't mean to keep bombarding you with questions.'

Madeleine waved a dismissive hand as if mistress-whispering was all in a day's work. 'I suggest you choose the flowers once the menu's locked down. We have an account with a florist; I'll email you. Vaughn prefers the gift bags to be individually tailored to each guest. I'll send you some details about each one. Aim to spend about one thousand pounds.'

'For all of them?'

'Each. There's a one-thousand-pound budget for each one. I have the money with me. Grace, I really need you to calm down before Henri starts bringing in the sample dishes.'

'Sweet Jesus,' Grace muttered under her breath, then tried to find her happy place. Or a happier place. 'I haven't seen you at Vaughn's gallery, have I?' she asked, to show she was now calm enough to make polite conversation.

'I have an office at the gallery,' Madeleine revealed somewhat unwillingly, 'but I'm Vaughn's personal assistant, so my hours are flexible.'

Grace processed that information. A lot of Madeleine's flexible hours were filled in with sending emails to Grace containing reading lists, travel itineraries and links for articles that she needed to read. 'Have you worked for Vaughn long?' she asked.

Madeleine looked at her watch again. 'Almost twelve years.'

Grace wondered how many other women's reading lists and travel itineraries Madeleine had arranged in twelve years. 'I hope I didn't pull you away from anything important,' she said sweetly. 'This is all so new to me, but I bet you've done this for Vaughn's other, um, girlfriends – right?'

Grace really couldn't blame Madeleine for pursing her lips so tightly that it looked painful. 'My duties are varied,' was all that she would say.

But Grace never knew when to leave well enough alone. 'When I met Alex at that party, he said I was younger than the others. Were they a lot older than me? Like, really sophisticated and could organise a sit-down dinner without breaking a sweat?'

But it worked because Madeleine was giving the matter some thought. 'Well, none of them talked this much,' she clarified, fixing Grace with a steely look.

Grace was saved from having to come up with a suitable response, when there really wasn't one, by the arrival of a man in chef's whites, followed by two lackeys wheeling in a trolley. And actually planning a menu was almost like fun, once Grace realised they'd brought samples to taste, and Madeleine would purse her lips even tighter than usual when Grace was veering towards the wrong decision.

Grace played it safe and chose the plainest crockery and silverware. She'd chosen a selection of *amuse-bouches* to be served on trays with drinks, and a starter of *mahi-mahi carpaccio*, before nixing a game entrée ('too fiddly and too gamey') in favour of a posh version of surf and turf with scallops and tournedos of fillet steak and asparagus and ricotta ravioli for the two vegetarians. As she sipped from a selection of mineral waters that all tasted the same, she couldn't remember why she'd been getting so hysterical.

'Shall we do desserts now?' she asked brightly, pushing her preferred water in the direction of one of the assistants who was tapping notes into a PDA.

Madeleine and the chef exchanged looks. 'Usually we provide a selection of artisan cheeses,' the chef explained carefully.

'Cool,' Grace shrugged. 'And what desserts have you got?'

'Vaughn never serves a dessert,' Grace was told firmly. But remembering Vaughn's passionate reaction to a slice of bitter chocolate cake and seeing the currently scandalised expression on Madeleine's face made ordering puddings absolutely the right way to go.

'Well, I never got that memo. Have you a menu I can see?'

The dessert menu was placed in front of Grace who took her sweet time running an eye down it. 'Can you do the lemon meringue flan, the apple tart and the *pot au chocolat* as miniatures for each guest?' she asked. 'With crème fraîche on the side? Oh, and maybe some fresh fruit or a sorbet as a palate cleanser?'

'Are you sure about this?' Madeleine muttered as an aside. 'Vaughn doesn't care for dessert.'

There were a lot of things that Vaughn didn't care for, and Grace knew that dessert wasn't one of them. 'Quite sure,' she insisted. She might not be anything like his other women, but if none of them had wised up to the fact that Vaughn turned into a pussy cat when the sugar rush was on him, then maybe they hadn't been all that.

Apart from a brief trip on Saturday night to Lily's, ostensibly for a Chinese takeaway and an *Ugly Betty* marathon, but actually to do the unthinkable: present a united front with Dan to persuade Lily that she had to tell her parents she was pregnant, Grace spent most of the weekend assembling the goodie bags. Despite her extreme doubts, it hadn't been that difficult. When she phoned the contact numbers on the guest-list, there had been assistants only too happy to provide shoe sizes, fashion preferences and the names of obscure brands of malt whisky.

Mindful of her put-upon assistant karma, Grace had used Vaughn's florist account to send each of them a huge bouquet when she ordered table centrepieces of white camellias, which would match the corsage on the little black Chanel dress that she'd blown practically all of that month's clothing allowance on. It was a little too staid for her but if she fucked this up, then at least she'd have got a Chanel dress out of it.

Only two people proved a problem – the artist, Noah Skinner, and his girlfriend, Lola. Neither of them had an assistant, though Madeleine had sent Grace a brief biography. They'd both studied at the Slade and were part of a collective of edgy artists who lived in Dalston and showed in Shoreditch, and Vaughn was very keen to represent Noah. Madeleine had bolded the last part, just so Grace got the message that Noah and Lola were to become her two new best friends.

Grace didn't know a lot about edgy artists but she knew enough to realise that £1,000 goodie bags might be misconstrued as a flimsy attempt to bribe them. Especially as Grace had done a Google image search and found a painting Noah had done, which looked like a pastiche of a Gainsborough with the words *Fuck Global Capitalism* graffitied over it. A Smythson portfolio case really wouldn't go down too well. She'd also found a couple of photos of Noah and he had a carefree grin and looked like Robbie Williams when he'd been hanging out with Oasis, which made her feel nostalgic. She missed flirting with boys who had carefree grins, and if Vaughn had a carefree grin, she'd yet to see it. Grace knew precisely nothing about Noah's girlfriend, Lola, except she was a very lucky girl.

The problem of what to get Lola and Noah cast a shadow over the whole weekend. Which was a pity because it was Grace's first weekend off since she'd signed on with Vaughn. She knew he was in London, but he was still so angry with her that he was maintaining BlackBerry silence, which suited her just fine. Madeleine had told Grace she could call her if she needed help, but Grace was determined to get something right on her own. She wanted the dinner-party to be a success as much as Vaughn did, just to prove to him, and to herself, that she wasn't completely useless.

By Monday morning, Grace was still devoid of inspiration as she updated her status on Facebook. And then she had a lightbulb moment. Even edgy artists were on Facebook and, amazingly, Noah had three friends in common with her: a boy who had dated her flatmate in her first year at St Martin's, a French girl she'd worked with on a vintage clothing stall in Spitalfields in her second year, and a random DJ that she'd hooked up with two summers ago. Lola, the girlfriend, played bass in some shouty, faux riot grrrl band and had a thing about snakes, so Grace bought her a platinum guitar pick, an adoption certificate for a boa constrictor at London Zoo, and a spa day at a new holistic place that had just opened up in Hoxton.

After serious trawling through weeks of Noah's self-important status updates, Grace eventually hit paydirt. *Noah is appalled at the cost of hand-made oil paints from the London Graphic Centre. Especially Vermillion Series 7.* God, she *hated* fine artists, carefree grins notwithstanding, but in her lunch-hour she went to the London Graphic Centre in Covent Garden and ordered him twenty tubes of the stuff at fifty pounds a time.

By Wednesday, D-Day – D for Dinner-party Day or Doomsday, depending on your politics – Grace was vibrating, rather than existing. She'd had an 8 a.m. hair appointment and had left the salon with an elaborate updo, which meant that she had to hold her head at a really awkward angle so she didn't dismantle it, and try to bat off curious comments from both the fashion and beauty teams.

Lily had spent ten minutes staring at Grace's hair with a perplexed expression, her own woes temporarily forgotten, as she kept asking, 'But how did you manage to do the plait thing by yourself? Is that a hairpiece at the back?' Even Kiki had come out of her office to stare in disbelief, but she was working on budgets with the editor, who wanted to know why Kiki had hired a helicopter for a safari-themed fashion shoot she'd done in Kenya, and that took precedence over Grace's elaborate coiffure.

By lunch-time, Grace had stabbing pains right between her eyes as she fitted in a quick bikini wax and pedicure while fielding calls on her BlackBerry. The chef had a million questions about chafing dishes and the exact timing of each course. The florist couldn't make Vaughn's Bulgarian housekeeper understand that he needed a fridge to put the camellias in and the artisan cheesemaker had had a problem with his goats. It made Grace long for the halcyon days of cupcakes, DIY streamers and a fish fingers and oven chips hot buffet. In fact, she was surprised that her brain wasn't slowly leaking out of the holes in her head where hairpins were currently skewering her scalp, as Galya ripped off strips of wax and kept up a running commentary on the regrowth of Grace's pubic hair.

When Grace got back to the office to find Bunny on Facebook rather than getting prices so two fashion stories could be sent down to the repro house, she couldn't be blamed for anything that she said. Which was a very loud and venomous: 'Are you completely retarded or just incompetent?'

Bunny gave a nervous start. 'Everyone I phoned was at lunch,' she whined. 'And usually *you* ring and get the prices.'

'I am busy,' Grace growled. 'I am busy with all sorts of important stuff and I ask you to do one thing and you're playing Scramble and I just had a call from Prada who said you hung up on them.'

Bunny had never seen Grace's fight face before and she didn't seem to like it very much. 'They were really rude and—'

'They're Prada; they can be as rude as they bloody well want,' Grace screeched, grabbing the list of fashion credits and slamming it down on the desk in front of Bunny. 'Get on the phone, be polite to people and you're not to leave the office until every last fucking shoe and hairclip has a price. OK?'

'OK, Grace,' Bunny whispered. 'I'm really sorry.'

'Sorry isn't good enough!' Grace looked up slowly because

she couldn't make any sudden movements and realised that the entire fashion team were staring at her in amazement. Or was it awe? It was something beginning with an a. Grace never shouted – usually furious pouting was her only form of attack.

At 4.55 p.m., with the dress bag hanging over her shoulder, Grace was ready to clock on at her other job. She grunted a goodbye at Bunny, who'd responded really well to being held up for public ridicule and had even made Grace two cups of tea. There was a salient lesson in there somewhere but Grace's mind was too crowded with fun facts about her guests and reminding the chef that he was going to serve apple slices rather than grapes with the cheese, to ponder it further.

As she stepped into the lift, Kiki was hot on her heels. 'I have an appointment as well,' she murmured, though they both knew it was a lie. Kiki had never actually seen 5 p.m. in the office, ever. Even on press day. 'What's in the bag?'

They both stared at the interlocking c's on the dress bag. 'Chanel sent this dress over even though we hadn't asked for it,' Grace quickly improvised. 'It's got to go to New York tonight so I promised I'd personally deliver it to the press office. Keep them sweet, you know?'

Kiki inclined her head in tacit acknowledgement of Grace's dedication. 'Courtney said that Bunny was sobbing her little heart out in the kitchen after you tore into her,' she informed Grace, with a faint note of praise in her voice. 'I didn't know you had it in you, Gracie.'

'She's useless,' Grace muttered bitterly. 'She spends all day on Facebook, and I'm pretty sure she nicked a D and G bikini from the cupboard last Friday. How come she's not needed back at Oxford?'

'Oh, she's on sabbatical. I really wish she'd do something about her weight,' Kiki sniffed. 'She's a good stone too heavy for a bikini.'

It was the most cordial exchange Grace had ever had with Kiki. Plus it looked as if Bunny's days were well and truly numbered. It put a spring in Grace's step as the lift doors opened.

chapter seventeen

Grace had been to Vaughn's house before. Many times actually, but it was always as a coda to an evening out and she'd follow him up the stairs to his bedroom, which was a symphony of grey, on the second floor, stay for an hour or so and then climb back down the stairs to a waiting car as Vaughn said she fidgeted too much in her sleep to stay the night.

Although her mind was on other things and she was constantly being interrupted, this was the first time Grace had been able to explore it properly. It was just like the gallery and his New York apartment: spacious, with stunning views (from the top floor she could see Hampstead Heath and the whole of London laid out before her), but all period features and interesting architectural quirks had been ruthlessly gutted. The whole place was an antiseptic advert to the joys of minimalist living, Grace thought as she walked into something that wasn't a living room or a lounge or anything other than an art gallery with some really uncomfortable furniture in it; a couple of bendy leather pieces that hadn't been designed to be sat on. Only a room on the first floor at the end of a long corridor looked halfway lived in; it had softly curved walls, more pale wood, two fairly comfy sofas, even a rug adorned with blue and grey circles that probably didn't come from IKEA and, hallelujah, praise be, a bar. It was practically a den.

Back downstairs, the servers were setting up the crockery and cutlery Grace had selected on a vast table in the dining room. Grace wished she hadn't gone with the camellia centrepieces now she'd properly seen the house; they were completely overshadowed by a huge painting of a Japanese girl wrapped in a flag with her mouth open in a silent scream, so Grace actually felt a moment of fondness for her grandparents' collection of Capo Di Monte figurines. She should have gone for something more modern and eclectic like lemons or cacti because her centrepieces didn't belong in this cold, impersonal house any more than Grace did. She felt a wave of panic wash over her like dirty grey water, and had to grip the back of a chair with icy hands.

She honest to goodness screamed when someone touched her lightly on the shoulder.

'Well, there's no need to ask if you've got everything under control,' Vaughn said tartly in her ear.

'Everything *is* under control,' Grace panted, hand clutched to her heart as she turned round to face him. 'You just surprised me.'

Vaughn ran an assessing eye over her, starting with her hair, which Grace was hating more with each painful moment that passed, lingering over her breasts and hips, which were nicely showcased in boned satin, and finishing at her toes, which were wiggling nervously in her Oscar de la Renta slingbacks. He nodded but didn't say anything so Grace guessed she'd passed muster. If she hadn't, Vaughn would have been sure to let her know. And Christ, she really needed a cigarette and a stiff drink.

'Don't let me down, Grace,' Vaughn said softly, as she stood there and waited for the inevitable 'shape up or ship out' pep talk she was certain was coming. But it seemed that was all she was getting.

'I'll try not to,' she said. 'I mean, I'll really try not to.'

'You do well tonight and I'll buy you a present. What

would you like? Jewellery? Maybe a tiara if you're going to wear your hair up more often?'

Grace had always wanted a tiara, ever since she'd seen *Breakfast At Tiffany's* at the tender age of eleven and decided that she was going to be Holly Golightly when she grew up. But when she'd actually read the Truman Capote novella much later on and realised that Holly was a prostitute, her fictional heroine had lost a lot of her allure. And now, when she was coasting a tsunami of stress and standing here in a dress paid for by a man with whom she had sex on a regular basis even though she didn't like him very much, it was all too close to home.

'You don't have to buy me presents,' she burst out, and knew she sounded like an absolute ingrate, but the mention of tiaras had hit a nerve. 'You're paying me to organise this and that's enough. The allowances are enough.'

Vaughn's eyebrows had shot up, but now he'd schooled his features into the slightly sneery, but otherwise impassive expression that always made Grace nervous. *More* nervous.

'You're in a very strange mood this evening, Grace. I hope you snap out of it before our guests arrive,' he said lightly, turning away. 'Where are you serving pre-dinner drinks? In the drawing room?'

Then he strode out, leaving Grace with no option but to follow him.

It wasn't a perfect evening. Grace constantly had to leave the table with a murmured, 'Would you excuse me?' to run interference between two of the waiters who'd had a lover's tiff five minutes before the first guests had arrived. Or to listen to the latest thrilling instalment of the chafing-dish saga. Then she'd sit down again to find that the conversation at her end of the table had ground to the grinding-est of halts because Lola and Nadja, the eighteen-year-old almost-supermodel girlfriend of a Russian oligarch, had absolutely nothing in common.

Luckily, Nadja had taken one look at Grace's Chanel dress and decided that both it and Grace met with her approval. She'd tucked her arm into Grace's as they walked into the dining room and confided, 'I'm so glad you're not old. These dinners, they're so boring. You smoke, da? Good, then we go out for fags in between courses.'

Grace had nodded shyly because Nadja had replaced Lily as the most beautiful person she'd ever met in real life. Most models in the flesh were tall, skinny and nothing much to look at until the camera lens did something magical with their angles, but Nadja was so gorgeous that she seemed to suck all the light and colour from the room. She was the only thing you wanted to look at. From the way she tossed back her toffee-coloured hair and smiled with a feline grace, she knew it. But she was more than her beauty; she was also a straight-talking, take-no-shit-and-no-prisoners girl who'd been discovered by a scout when she was bunking off school to beg on the Moscow Underground.

'Alex, you sell any more stories about me to the gossip men, I have you offed,' she'd hissed when Alex had taken his place opposite her at the table. Within seconds they were quite happily swapping scurrilous stories about people they'd met at other dinner-parties. Meanwhile, Vaughn was sitting at the other end of the table looking like a drawerful of daggers because Lola and Noah were a no-show.

They'd finally turned up half an hour late, claiming they'd got lost on the way to Vaughn's house, which to be fair was set far back from a narrow twisty road that snaked around Hampstead Heath. Noah walked in with a cocky swagger and a shit-eating grin, which accessorised perfectly with his paint-splattered jeans and a T-shirt with *Fuck Art, Let's Dance* emblazoned on it. Lola, on the other hand, looked as if she'd come straight from a Punk Rock Aerobics class because she was in running shorts, metallic leggings, vile pink trainers and a deconstructed vest. She was also sallow and sour, but Grace could tell that if she'd been able to crack a smile, she might have looked a little like a young Bianca Jagger. But it was academic because Lola looked like she hadn't smiled since 2001.

Grace got the whole 'eat the rich' shtick, she really did, but she'd wanted to smack them as they stood there in the doorway. Noah had eyed everyone up with a disdainful stare while Lola had scowled, but her grandmother always said that good manners was making people feel comfortable no matter what the circumstances. What her grandmother had meant was when guests turned up for dinner without even a box of Milk Tray or a bottle of Liebfraumilch, but it was the same thing.

Vaughn slowly got up, brows beetled in irritation, but Grace had beaten him to it, leaping to her feet and exclaiming, 'Did you get turned around on the way out of the tube? It sounds like you should get out at Hampstead but actually Belsize Park is nearer. Let me get you a drink and introduce you to everybody.'

She'd been so jolly hockey sticks that she'd actually grabbed Lola's hand to escort her to the table and felt the other girl's fingers trembling. Immediately, Grace guessed that Lola was putting a brave face on sheer terror – that she was regretting the statement outfit and wishing she'd never come. Grace knew exactly how she felt. And if she'd never met Vaughn and had found herself suddenly catapulted into this dining room, straight from the fashion cupboard, she'd have covered up her nerves by giving it some serious attitude too.

It turned out that Noah knew Alex (who seemed to be one of those annoying people who knew everyone), Nadja had taken advantage of the diversion to go out for a cigarette, and Grace decided that her energy was best spent getting Lola to withdraw the stick she had lodged in her rear end.

Grace longed to keep refilling her own glass until the sharp pang of nerves was replaced by numbness, but she didn't dare. Not when keeping the conversation going had been like wading through treacle in gumboots.

At one stage, Grace had heard herself ask manically, 'So, who else is angsting about their carbon footprint?'

But the puddings had been received with rapturous little ooohs of delight and the gift bags had been a monster hit. By this stage Noah had lost the sneer and could only smile in dopy stupefaction at the tubes of paint. 'How did you know?' he asked Grace.

'I Facebook stalked you,' Grace revealed, and he looked even more stunned.

'Didn't know girls like you used Facebook.' He grinned.

'Are you kidding?' Grace spluttered. 'And what do you mean, "girls like me"?'

'Posh girls.' Noah waved his hand to encompass the poshness that was Grace. 'Thought you'd be too busy getting your nails done to check Facebook.'

Grace had wanted to tell them that the elaborate hair-do and the designer frock were just window dressing. Really, she was like them, but with better manners and much, much better dress sense. That she ate peanut butter straight out of the jar and could find her way through Shoreditch blindfolded, but tonight she was playing a part and she guessed her performance had verged on flawless. But if Vaughn wanted her to suck up to edgy Shoreditch artists then maybe Chanel dresses and elaborate updos weren't helping.

'We have three mutual friends,' she informed Noah smugly. 'You know Laetitia? We worked on a vintage clothing stall in Spitalfields together.'

'I know Laetitia,' Lola offered, but she looked at Grace suspiciously. 'What were you doing working on a vintage clothing stall?'

Grace made an executive decision then to stop channelling

her grandmother and be more like herself. 'Mostly we spat in the owner's tea because she was a heinous bitch. Like, she'd make me sew fake Biba labels into this Chelsea Girl dead stock she used to get really cheap.'

'Laetitia told me about her,' Lola said, nodding her head slowly as if maybe there was slightly more to Grace than met the eye. Not much more though, and Grace wasn't sure why, but it hurt a little that Noah and Grace thought she was slumming it in Spitalfields and on Facebook, when actually it was much more her scene than catered dinner-parties in Hampstead.

Now, though, as Sergei and Nadja (still cooing about the Cavalli shoes) finally left, Grace could feel herself wilting, head hanging heavy under the weight of all the expectation and hair products.

Vaughn walked back into the big open space that Grace would never consider a living room, where they'd taken coffee and dessert, to find her slowly and methodically taking apart her chignon.

He didn't say anything, but watched Grace run her fingers through her hair to try to smooth down the lacquered hanks. Then she leaned over to the side table to pick up a half-full brandy snifter that Sergei had left and knocked it back.

'For God's sake, Grace, that's disgusting,' Vaughn snapped. 'If you want a drink, I'm sure we can find an empty glass.'

All the stresses and strains of the last week were still there with a side order of anti-climax that Grace hadn't expected. She blinked teary eyes as one of the servers came in with a laden plate, which Vaughn told her to put on the table next to Grace.

'You barely touched your dinner,' he chided, once the woman had closed the door behind her. 'I think you had maybe one scallop.'

Keeping the ball of conversation firmly in the air had completely destroyed Grace's appetite, though she'd been too aggravated to choke down anything that wasn't a banana over the last few days. In fact, she was seriously considering pitching her patented Banana Diet to the health editor. 'I was too nervous to eat,' she explained, rubbing a hand over her empty stomach, which didn't feel quite as squidgy as usual. 'You know what I mean?'

From the envious look on Vaughn's face, he was a comfort eater from way back. 'You should eat something,' he insisted. 'And there was no need to worry. You handled everything beautifully. I was so proud of you.'

She did? He was? Grace wondered if there was an apocalypse just around the corner, because Vaughn's affirmative statement had contained absolutely no traces of sarcasm. 'That's cool,' she decided, staring at the plate. 'That you're pleased, I mean. I thought it was all going to go horribly pear-shaped just before they served pudding. Lola, Noah's girlfriend . . . God, she was hard work.'

'She could have made more of an effort,' Vaughn agreed, coming to sit on the end of the futuristic chaise longue on which Grace was perched.

'Tell me about it,' Grace nodded, surreptitiously easing off her right shoe, which was a good half-size too small. During an awkward lapse in the chatter, Grace had mentioned that she'd been at St Martin's at the same time that Noah and Lola had been at the Slade. Lola had narrowed her pale blue eyes. 'Did you know that girl who bailed on her final degree show at the last minute?' she'd asked. 'My cousin's at Glasgow School of Art and even she heard about it.'

Grace had felt her heart do a painful fandango, but she'd forced herself to muster a bland smile. 'Not anyone I know,' she'd lied. 'I think that was just an urban myth.'

Lola had refused to let it drop. In fact, it had been the first time she'd really relaxed. 'No! It's true! One of my friends was studying fine art at St Martin's and it was all anyone talked about for weeks. They were doing renovations in one of the studios and apparently she dumped all her outfits in a skip and walked out.'

It hadn't been a skip. It had actually been a common or garden bin in the corner of the sewing room, but Grace had just stared at Lola, aware that her face was going redder and redder. Surprisingly, it was Alex who'd come to her rescue, though it was more a case of out of the frying pan and into the fire.

'So, Gracie, I'm dying to know how you and Vaughn met,' he said with a sly smile, and maybe her greatest triumph of the night had been the way she'd managed to recover and spin that first fateful meeting into a wry little anecdote that made everyone, even Lola, laugh.

Now she pulled a face at the memory of Lola. 'I felt sorry for her,' she admitted, as Vaughn tilted his head and looked surprised. 'She was really nervous and it just made her aggressive. You know, like fight or flight. She couldn't run away so she went on the attack. She was OK by the end. She even said she was going to friend me on Facebook.'

Vaughn was dipping his finger into the *pot au chocolat* that Grace would have quite liked to eat herself. 'And what about her boyfriend? What did you make of him?'

'Noah? He's not as working class as he pretends to be,' Grace mused, finally kicking off her other shoe so she could curl her legs under her. 'Like, he and Alex went to the same public school so I don't know why he got all up in my grill because he thought I was one of the landed gentry. I mean, he's called *Noah*, for goodness' sake,' she summed up scathingly. 'And he totally took a moment to appreciate the expensive brandy.'

'So you think he was impressed?' Vaughn was now stealing little forkfuls of lemon pudding, and closing his eyes blissfully every time he sneaked a piece into his mouth.

'I think he was impressed, but maybe they were out of their comfort zone. Just a little bit.'

'But that was the whole point of having dinner here; it was more intimate.' Vaughn frowned. 'Usually I just book a table in a restaurant, it's a lot less bother.'

And he'd said that he was easing her in gently? Grace decided that it wasn't worth seething about. There'd been that line in the contract about *other duties: as required* and Vaughn was entitled to ask her to do anything he saw fit, considering the amount he was paying her. Besides, he was being nice to her for once so she also decided that there was no point in telling him that she'd been in airports that were more intimate than his home. 'I guess Hampstead is a long way from Dalston,' was all she said. 'Like, in this metaphorical way 'cause it's only a few miles as the crow flies.' This relaxed debrief and watching Vaughn have multiple foodgasms wasn't helping to make Grace any more lucid. Her brain had packed up shop for the night.

But he just gave her another lazy smile. 'Duly noted. This pudding is rather good. Do you want to try some?'

He waved the fork temptingly in front of Grace's mouth and part of her job was to put things in there when he told her to so she obediently opened up to let Vaughn feed her a huge piece of surprisingly sugary sponge.

'Too sweet,' she complained, squinching up her face as she chewed, then took a huge gulp of champagne to wash it down. 'I can feel my back molars protesting.'

There was something sticky clinging to her lip and before Grace could discreetly dab it away with her napkin, Vaughn was cupping her chin so he could rub his thumb slowly at the offending glob of sauce. 'That's better,' he said, stroking the pooch of Grace's lower lip and smiling when she flushed.

'So how did things go at your end of the table?' Grace asked, in a voice that sounded as if she smoked at least forty Gauloises a day.

His hand hadn't left her face, but was trailing a path along her neck, where her pulse was thundering away like she was a prime candidate for a pulmonary embolism. 'Boring,' he confided. 'We had to talk about Third World debt but I think I managed to offload a painting I hate for a lot more than I originally paid for it.' Then his fingers moved down and curved around the swell of Grace's breast and they were both surprised when she relaxed into his touch.

'That's cool,' Grace whispered, and it was even more surprising that she was closing the gap between them so she could get to his smiling mouth but Vaughn was leaning towards her like he was totally down with that.

Grace kissed him slowly because she wanted to savour the lemon-tart taste of him. Vaughn's lips clung to her and she could feel the faint scrape of his stubble against her cheek. When Grace shifted restlessly, hips circling against him, he was hard. Sometimes it seemed like his dick was the only part of him that never played games. And sometimes it seemed as if she spent all her time veering from not liking him to liking him a lot.

Vaughn was still stroking her breast, rubbing his thumb against the spot where Grace's nipple was peaked and aching. 'There are three people standing outside the door waiting to clear up,' he remarked conversationally. 'Shall we go upstairs, because I'd like to get you out of this pretty dress as soon as possible.'

The parquet felt rough under her bare feet as Grace stood up and stretched languidly, aware that Vaughn's eyes were resting on her body as it undulated under the black dress. Just the way he was looking at her, like everything she did tonight was perfection wrapped up in a big bow, was making Grace itch inside her own skin.

Apparently, approval really turned her on. Who knew?

And when Vaughn stood up and took her hand, Grace let him pull her bonelessly behind him as he opened the door and startled the servers who were lounging against a Corbusier table that cost more than their combined annual earnings.

The small blonde Polish girl flicked a glance at Grace, at her perfectly polished toenails, understated dress that still managed to shriek its net worth and Vaughn clutching her arm in a death grip, before turning away with a knowing smile, while he murmured platitudes about their silver-service skills. For the second time that evening, Grace marvelled that simply looking the part made up for what really lay underneath.

The split second that the door closed behind them and Grace heard the first clink of china, Vaughn pushed her up against the wall.

Usually he tried to show some restraint for the first few minutes of kissing and caressing, but this time he was fucking her mouth with his tongue, his skin feverish hot beneath Grace's fingers. The warm glow from a job well done had gone, not to her head, but between her thighs, or maybe that was Vaughn's hand sliding up her leg to press and knead.

Getting upstairs became an undignified stagger. Vaughn hauled Grace down the landing and through a door then pushed her down on his bed so enthusiastically that she bounced a couple of times, then lay there momentarily stunned as Vaughn pulled his shirt over his head without bothering to unbutton it.

'How much did that dress cost me?' he asked, voice muffled as he bent down to take off his shoes.

Grace didn't like the sound of that. Talking about payment in kind was very tacky when they'd been thundering towards the kind of dirtybadwrong porno-sex that she'd remember on her deathbed.

'Two thousand and change,' she said, feeling that little hiss as the fire in her belly went out.

'You'd better take it off then,' Vaughn drawled. 'Before it gets damaged.'

His eyes were all pupil and Grace scrambled to her knees and yanked at the zip. She could have slowed it down, drawn the moment out, but she wanted the dress off and Vaughn's hands on her.

The Chanel dress was thrown into one of the far corners of the room as if it had been a ten-pound Primark number, but Grace didn't care – which was a fashion first because Vaughn was on the bed, pushing her down again and pausing to kiss and suck at every piece of skin that distracted him along the way. Grace hadn't even known that the area above her left knee was an erogenous zone.

She gasped every time Vaughn touched her until she wanted to scream because it was happening too fast. Or maybe it was happening too slowly? Vaughn made a pleased sound when Grace grabbed his hand and shoved it between her legs. 'You're ready?' he muttered in surprise.

Grace didn't answer, just sank her teeth into his shoulder in the universal language for, 'Yes, now, don't make me wait', and Vaughn must have understood because he was inside her in one sudden thrust.

It might have been when she wrapped her legs round his hips or scored a path down his back with her nails but Vaughn's control upped and left. He surged into her harder and faster than before, hitting this perfect little spot that made Grace arch her back and swear that she'd just seen God.

And it was suddenly OK that it was messy and sweaty because sex was supposed to be. And when the sex was this good, the mess and sweat didn't seem to matter so much.

Grace was drumming her heels against the small of Vaughn's back when she realised that she was going to come. All she needed was one more lip-biting kiss, one more bruise blossoming because Vaughn had pinned her arms over her head, one more hungry rasp in her ear about how much he loved fucking her and she . . .

There was a groan and a quick jerk of Vaughn's hips and apparently they were done. Move it along, nothing to see here.

Except Grace was still trying to remember how to breathe

and had to be persuaded to unlock her legs and let Vaughn pull free. Just the feel of his still half-hard cock sliding slowly out of her, had Grace closing her eyes as another shudder of almost-there hit.

'Are you all right?' Vaughn asked solicitously, like he wasn't some selfish wanker who'd just fucked her into the mattress and left her stranded. He'd done this many times before, with many other women, so how could he not know that Grace hadn't reached the finishing line? 'You look exhausted.'

'I'm OK,' Grace said flatly. Or it would have been flatly, if she wasn't still panting like she was halfway through the London Marathon. 'You go and have your shower and I'll get on the cab thing.'

The proprietary stroke of her thigh was new, but the lack of orgasms was alas, getting very old.

Grace listened carefully for the shower then picked up where Vaughn had left off. It only took one stroke and all those delicious nerve-endings were thrumming insistently again because at least she knew how to get herself off. Grace's fingers worked busily as the memories of the last fifteen minutes ricocheted through her brain's pleasure centres. It was all there in glorious HDTV: Vaughn's sweat-slicked skin skittering against hers, his ragged breaths, his cock driving into her . . . and Grace screwed her eyes tight shut and worked her hips a bit faster to get that good old orgasm thing going.

She wasn't entirely sure when she registered the fact that the shower had stopped. Maybe it was the moment her eyes flickered open and she caught a glimpse of Vaughn standing in the doorway staring at her.

Every single millimetre of Grace was blushing. She knew that for certain because she was lying on Vaughn's Frette bedlinen, stark naked. Her sticky hand was removed so she could curl into a ball and will herself to telepathically transport to another dimension.

'Don't stop,' Vaughn said hoarsely, unbelievably, and the

bed dipped as he sat down next to her. 'You should have said that you hadn't come. I'd have taken care of you.'

'It's no big deal,' Grace mumbled, trying to press her face into the sheet but Vaughn's hand was insistent on her hip as he forced her to turn over.

'Look at me,' he ordered, in that low, commanding tone that she was always too scared to ignore.

Grace's eyelids fluttered open so she could watch Vaughn watching her. He didn't look disgusted, repulsed or as if he was about to throw her and her sexual conflict out on to the street. He looked pretty horny actually. His eyes couldn't decide whether they wanted to look at Grace's nipples, which were standing to attention or her newly waxed snatch.

'Really, it's OK. I don't normally, like . . . I don't . . . not from sex,' Grace blurted out. 'God! Will you stop staring at me?'

Vaughn ignored her heartfelt plea, and stroked a finger along Grace's arm. 'You seemed to be managing just fine by yourself,' he commented, and he was smiling and she didn't know why. 'And I can't help but feel responsible.'

Now really was not the time for his inappropriate humour. 'Go away,' Grace said. 'If you care anything for me, you'll stop talking and go back to the bathroom.'

Vaughn moved but it was only to shove Grace across the bed so he could lie down and rest his damp head against hers. 'Show me what you do when you're alone,' he whispered in her ear. 'So I'll know for next time.'

But there wasn't going to be a next time because Grace was joining a nunnery the next morning. 'I *can't*!'

'Yes, you can,' he said firmly, leaning over to bite the inside of Grace's thigh at the same time that he took her hand and put it back where it had been, his fingers glancing over her clit so she had to force every muscle she had not to shiver. 'Let me watch.'

Grace sighed because there was no way out, short of

climbing over Vaughn, and he had a good four stone on her. She started moving her fingers cautiously until Vaughn took his hand away. She figured that she could do that for three minutes before she faked an orgasm, got dressed and went home to scrub her brain with bleach.

She couldn't believe that she was letting Vaughn have a courtside seat while she prodded gingerly at her clit. There wasn't a designer dress in the world that was worth this humiliation.

'Do it properly,' Vaughn suddenly snapped. 'Or do you want me to do it for you?'

'Shut up!'

But Vaughn didn't shut up. He carried on talking, saying filthy little things in Grace's ear until her fingers were rubbing frantically against her clit and she was lolling her head back against his shoulder.

'You're such a good girl, Grace, and you're going to come, aren't you? Because you want to and you really do deserve it . . .'

And that was all it took to have Grace arching for an eternity, a harsh little cry escaping as the world seemed to stop for one split second and she was reduced to nothing but sensation.

But another second passed and she was Grace again. Vaughn stroked the hair back from her heated face. 'How old are you again?'

He knew exactly how old she was, but Grace didn't have the energy to call him on it. 'Twenty-three. Why?'

'Because I'd have thought you'd have grown out of these hang-ups by now. And I have to say, I think you've had some very selfish lovers – oof!' Vaughn added when Grace elbowed him in the ribs as she strove to put as much distance between them as possible. And God, she really wanted to tug the quilt over herself too.

She settled for glaring ferociously. 'Maybe I should have

said something, but it's not the kind of stuff that you can just bring up casually . . .'

'I'm going to make a note in my BlackBerry.' Vaughn cut right through her heated defence. ' "Make sure Grace comes every time we have sex." '

And it was such a stupid-sweet thing to say that Grace got over herself for the time it took to giggle and flop back on the bed, because Vaughn had seen everything now, several times over and there was no point in false modesty. She reached out a hand so she could prod him in the ribs again. 'Oh, whatever.'

'Whatever is right,' Vaughn murmured, and he lifted her hand so he could press a kiss to her knuckles. It was an oddly gallant gesture after what Grace had just done, what he'd just asked her to do, and Grace was touched by it. Tonight was all about firsts so she scooched up the bed so she could rest her head on Vaughn's shoulder and let him wrap an arm around her pleasure-heavy body.

Grace was just getting into the cuddling and thinking that maybe a little kissing would be nice too when Vaughn started gently extracting himself from her limbs, which had gone all limpet-like. 'You can shower in the guest room, if you like.'

chapter eighteen

The next morning, Grace was more relaxed than she'd been in weeks. It helped that there was a Facebook message from Lola thanking her for the night before and apologising . . . *if I acted like an arsehole. I was seriously freaking out for most of the dinner, then we got lost again on the way back to the tube. Anyways, you, me and Laetitia should go out for a drink sometime.*

It was a relief to know that Lola had seen the real Grace peeking through, and it fortified her for an emotionally draining lunch with Lily, who was steeling herself for a weekend visit to Godalming to tell her parents that they had to move up the wedding because their precious only daughter was in the family way. After that, there was the big biannual fashion and beauty brainstorm to suffer through.

Grace could feel her eyelids drooping as Kiki wittered on about the It bag and how rumours of its untimely demise were the work of dumpy features writers who could never get on a wait list. Courtney was surreptitiously messaging someone on her iPhone, Lily was hiding behind her bigass Alberta Ferretti shades and absent-mindedly stroking her stomach, and Posy was nodding her head in agreement with every single thing that Kiki said.

Grace looked down at her folder of ideas, which were uncharacteristically sparse. She didn't have the free time any more to do test shoots, mooch around Shoreditch sourcing new designers or leaf through obscure fashion fanzines. Not that that was going to stop her.

'Maybe we could do a special on the new accessories,' she piped up, when Kiki finally had to stop to draw breath. 'The new It shoes or sunglasses or those killer skinny patent-leather belts. Like, the It bag is dead, long live the It shoes or whatever.'

There was a deathly silence, because the first rule of the biannual fashion and beauty brainstorm was that you didn't speak until Kiki spoke to you. It was the second and third rule too. Grace cowered on her usual rickety chair, as she waited for Kiki to tear into her.

'The advertising department would resign if we mention death and It bags in the same sentence,' Kiki reminded Grace icily. She paused to glance down at her taupe-clad bosom as if she expected to see a garish fluorescent accessory nestling there, before giving the assembled throng a wintry smile. 'Then again, they do love accessories. Courtney, can you get on that? And don't use the in-house digital studio . . .'

Grace's shoulders slumped. *Plus ça* fucking *change*.

'. . . and have a bash at the copy, Gracie. Just extended sells for each spread and keep it cliché free, please. If I read "belt up" or "best foot forward", I'll fire you.'

Grace's head shot up so fast that she bit her tongue and could only nod eagerly. It was the first piece of writing that Kiki had asked her to do in two years. Apart from making Grace draft emails to the *Skirt* staff to inform them that Kiki would be a guest judge on some tacky TV model show. 'Sure th-thing,' she stammered, beaming at Posy who'd just given her the thumbs-up.

But what made it the best day ever wasn't Bunny then getting reamed out for mucking up Kiki's soy latte order but the flat, square turquoise box that Ron from the postroom handed to Grace, two minutes after she got out of the meeting. 'You have to sign for it,' he grunted, eyes fixed firmly in the vicinity of Grace's nipples.

Grace knew for an absolute fact that no one had ordered anything from Tiffany's and suddenly any similarities between her and Holly Golightly didn't seem to matter so much. She quickly untied the white ribbon, lifted the lid and scrabbled through tissue paper to unearth a tiara. A tacky plastic tiara that still had a Claire's Accessories price tag on it.

'You shouldn't have,' she said when Vaughn answered the phone. 'You really shouldn't have.' She couldn't hold back her gurgle of laughter.

Of course, Vaughn delivered the punch line, which just made Grace laugh even harder. 'I offered to buy you a tiara and I'd hate you to think I wasn't a man of my word.'

'It's beautiful,' Grace giggled. 'Really makes my highlights pop, thank you.'

'I always send you flowers but a three-pound gag gift is the only time you phone to thank me and don't send me a text message instead?' Vaughn enquired idly. 'Actually, I think this is the first time you've called.'

The flowers always put in an appearance each morning after a Vaughn night before, apart from the last couple of weeks when he'd been furious with her. Grace had asked Madeleine to stop sending them to the offices but to Montague Terrace instead, because the PR excuse was wearing thin. She divvied up the bouquets between Ilonka and Anita on the floor above her and poor Eileen on the ground floor, who always told Grace that no one had bought her flowers since her husband died. Grace kept every third bunch for herself and even if she knew the flowers were nothing more than a fake token for a fake relationship, it always lifted her heart a little to wake up and see her Murano vase crammed full of delicately shaded flowers that tried hard to give off a scent in the dankness of her flat. But she couldn't tell Vaughn any of that so Grace decided to keep this light before it veered off down dark paths. 'Well, fake plastic diamonds are a girl's best friend. I thought that warranted a phone call.'

'I'll remember to buy you fake plastic diamonds more often then.' They were flirting, which hadn't happened before. It was a shame because Grace had a feeling that Vaughn could be an incorrigible flirt if he tried hard enough. 'But actually I'm glad you called. There's something I wanted to talk to you about.'

God, that sentence never led to anything other than tears and recriminations. Grace shoved the tiara under a pile of invoices. 'Oh? What was that?'

'Last night, when I was in the bathroom – the *first time* I was in the bathroom – I remembered that I needed to say something to you, but then you distracted me.' Vaughn sounded wistful, as if the memory of how Grace had distracted him was a very pleasant one.

'Hey, you did your fair share of distracting too,' Grace pointed out, relief washing over her because he wouldn't have brought *that* up if he'd been planning to terminate her contract. Probably.

'I'm going to be away from London for a couple of weeks and I'm afraid I'm not going to ask you to fly out on the weekends,' he said, and it was enough to have Grace tensing up all over again. 'I'm going to be constantly on the move; lots of loose ends to tie up before December.'

Grace was still holding herself very still because this was beginning to sound a lot like an official brush-off, even though she'd thought she'd rocked the dinner-party. 'OK,' she said hesitantly.

'Madeleine will send you the itinerary for December. It's not pretty. There's a party or a dinner or a reception every night; sometimes two or three, just to give you fair warning. Though if you're as charming as you were last night, then you'll sail through.'

Vaughn wasn't big with the compliments so when they did

come, it meant more to Grace than all the bouquets he'd asked Madeleine to send. 'Thank you, and I'm really sorry I was such a pain in the arse about organising the party. Look, I know it's taking me a while to learn the ropes,' Grace added, lowering her voice as she stood up and walked towards the cupboard because Bunny was hovering nearby, 'but I'm trying, I really am.'

'I'm starting to think that I should buy you plastic tiaras every week and that we should have all our conversations over the phone. You can be very reticent.'

'And you're not?' Grace all but gasped in outrage.

'I am not. I'm enigmatic,' Vaughn insisted with that hint of a chuckle back in his voice. 'Often verging on mysterious. Occasionally inscrutable.'

'Did you eat a thesaurus for lunch?' Grace asked sweetly. 'With a dictionary for dessert?'

'I didn't, but as you're in such a forthcoming mood, I'd like to ask you something. Can you talk for a little while?'

'Yeah, sure.' Grace shut the door of the cupboard and steeled herself for news of another party she needed to organise. Maybe a ball for 500 guests, with an international pop star flown in to provide the entertainment. 'What's up?'

'Well, I'd like to know what gets you off,' Vaughn said smoothly, like it was a perfectly normal question to ask someone over the telephone on a Thursday afternoon.

'Excuse me?' Grace asked weakly as her face went from white to crimson in a split second.

'You heard me perfectly well the first time. Obviously, the sex isn't as good for you as it is for me. I'd like to know how I can rectify that situation.'

'I'm at work! I'm in the fashion cupboard!'

'I'm sure the frocks won't tell anyone.'

They probably wouldn't, though Grace had often suspected that Kiki had planted a bug in the cupboard so she could find out what the rest of the fashion department said about her. Posy always came in exactly ten minutes before six each day so she could vent. 'Please, Vaughn, can we just not?' Grace begged and she thought it was maybe the first time that she'd called him by his name because it sounded really weird coming out of her mouth.

'I thought you'd prefer to do it over the phone but we can do it face-to-face, if you like,' Vaughn offered graciously, and she could hear the laughter lightening his voice, though Grace was failing to see anything funny about her orgasms or lack thereof.

'I enjoy it,' she whispered fiercely, because it seemed very important that Vaughn knew that. 'Not saying it to spin you a line. I like it even if I don't come. It's really not that big a deal. Like, I bet there's loads of women who don't.'

'Why don't you think of it as harnessing some of that potential we talked about?' Vaughn said smoothly. 'I always tell you what I like in bed, but you never do, so now's your opportunity. I'll be making notes.'

Vaughn always told her what he liked and what he didn't, in bed and out, but it had still been something of a shock to discover how vocal he was when he got naked and would rasp filthy little nothings in her ear. That seemed as good a place as any to start.

'Well, I like it when you say stuff to me,' Grace muttered, sinking to the floor so she could sit under one of the rails of clothes and let the trailing hems hide her blushes. 'You know, the dirty talk,' she added.

Thankfully, Vaughn didn't ask her to enlarge on that topic. 'OK, what else?'

'Oh God, I don't know!'

'I always try to go down on you, but you wriggle away from me as if I'm trying to perform a depraved act on your poor, innocent flesh. You react in the same way when I try to touch your—'

'I thought you were just trying to be nice,' Grace

interrupted lamely, because she had to get him to shut up.

'Surely you've known me long enough to realise that I never do anything just to be nice. I like touching you. I'd like to taste you, and I'd particularly like to know you weren't just lying back and thinking of England or what Marc Jacobs is doing for Autumn/Winter. So, once again, I'm going to ask you what gets you off?'

He'd tried to make a Marc Jacobs joke, which Grace thought was kind of adorable, even if she was dying of shame. And it touched her that Vaughn was making such an effort to try to discover the workings of her pleasure centres. She rested her elbows on her knees. 'I don't know. And I'm not sure why I can't come. I just thought it would happen eventually, like when I was learning to knit: one moment I was dropping stitches and getting my needles criss-crossed, the next I just got it. I thought sex would be like that.'

'And what is it like?' Vaughn's tone was light and impersonal and it made it easier to say stuff that she never thought she'd say to anyone.

'I just feel too much like me,' she confessed. 'Like, I can never get carried away or swept up in the moment. I'm worried that I'll look fat from the wrong angle or that I'm doing something stupid and it just kills the mood.' She sighed. 'If it makes you feel any better, there were a couple of times that you got me really close – but then I got distracted.'

'Well, you do have the attention span of a fruit fly,' Vaughn countered, and it was the honest truth so Grace couldn't get offended. In fact, she was even smiling. 'You don't have to worry. I don't have some elaborate seduction in mind with props and a ten-point action plan.'

'Glad to hear it,' Grace said fervently, and although there was a mountain of returns to get through, for some reason she was in no rush to start on them. She'd much rather talk to Vaughn, especially since he was in such a freakishly good mood. 'So, when am I going to see you again then?'

'Not until we go to Miami for Art Basel. It's the first weekend in December. You'll have to take the Thursday and Monday off work.'

'We're going to Miami? No way!' Grace tried to lower her voice because she was squealing so loud that they could probably hear her downstairs on the teen titles. 'I've always wanted to go there.' It was all she could do not to drop the phone and start clapping her hands in joy. 'And it will be really sunny and hot.'

'But you'll be too busy looking at mediocre art installations to take advantage of that,' Vaughn reminded her, but she could hear him smile. He was right. They really should just do all their talking on the phone. 'I'll see if Madeleine can pencil in half an hour's sunbathing every day. Now I have to go.'

And Vaughn went, not even bothering to say goodbye, but Grace was starting to get used to that.

Winter was coming on fast now. Every morning as Grace crunched through a carpet of crisp leaves on her way to the office, she felt that the colder weather should be all the impetus she needed to move to a new flat; a new flat with central heating and absolutely no damp spores. Because the old flat really didn't suit the new Grace.

The new Grace who was greeted with open arms and welcoming smiles by the Spa. The Grace who was on first-name terms with a Russian almost-supermodel and the most frightening sales assistant at Miu Miu. The Grace who was beginning to feel like she wasn't just playing a part, but was starting to become the confident girl she pretended to be when she was with Vaughn.

Kiki had major issues with the new, confident Grace who no longer dyed her hair ridiculous colours or wore homespun ensembles from charity shops. If ever Grace felt she was getting a little too full of herself by preening in front of the fashion cupboard mirror or leafing through the *Time Out Guide to Miami* to bookmark restaurants when she should have been working, she could always rely on Kiki to throw some finely honed vitriol her way – almost as if her boss was determined to rid Grace of her new-found perkiness with each barbed remark and insult. 'Just because you've finally learned, after two years, to put together a passable outfit doesn't mean you can wear horizontal stripes with your hips, Gracie' was practically motherly advice compared to her querulous demands as to why Grace was no longer working through her lunch-breaks. She also snorted derisively every time Grace invoked the part-time job that meant she couldn't work later than six.

Nor did she approve of Grace working smarter, rather than harder, so she could fit all her work into an eight-hour day, rather than the pre-Vaughn days that stretched to twelve hours, or even fourteen if the fashion team were going on a trip. Bunny was still around and getting paid for it, unlike the other interns, so Grace decided to make the most of her. There was also a new intern, Celia, who'd been at American *Vogue* for a month until she got deported for overstaying her student visa, and she could actually be trusted to call PRs for prices and do returns as long as Grace bought her chocolate and let her try on new deliveries when they came in. It left Grace free to minister to Kiki's every need and surreptitiously work on Lily's wedding prep.

But just when Grace felt like she really was kicking arses and taking names, the old Grace would pop up to remind her that she was still dogged with debt and that the new Grace needed to pull her finger out if there was ever to be any hope of her becoming debt-free.

If someone had told Grace a few months ago that £7,000 a month wasn't enough to manage on when you were a rich man's mistress, she'd have laughed hard enough to snort liquid out of her nostrils. But £7,000 a month had a completely different ring to it when you were moving through a world where people thought nothing of ordering £600 bottles of champagne or booking a suite at Claridge's like Nadja did because she couldn't be bothered to make the long drive from Mayfair to Kensington one night when she'd asked Grace to dinner. Grace had got the night bus home still reeling from the £100 tip Nadja had asked her to leave because she'd paid for the meal.

Was it any wonder that the allowances, which she kept in an envelope in her handbag, seemed to dwindle at an alarming rate? Or that she spent most of her money on clothes? Not sensible, versatile outfits that would take her from desk to dinner either. These days she wasn't popping out after work for a bottle of white wine in All Bar One with Lily but going to a ball or a gala or a museum reception, which were fancy words for a black-tie event where the women wore couture, and a dress from Zara just didn't cut it.

Vaughn didn't really know anything about fashion. Grace was pretty sure he couldn't tell Primark from Prada, but when she'd turned up in her Zac Posen dress for the third time, he'd given her a long, hard look and said, 'Oh, you're wearing that again.'

Then there was the time he'd taken her to Paris for the weekend and Grace had worn a dress from the Kate Moss Topshop collection to meet some friends of his for lunch. It had been during the few first, fraught weeks of their arrangement, and she'd been horrified when Vaughn and his friends, two couples in their forties, had all started speaking French and she'd had to muddle through, though she'd remembered enough from her A-levels to understand perfectly when Guillaume, a heavy-set man sitting next to Vaughn, had tilted his head in her direction and shrugged expansively. *'Elle est trop jeune pour toi, mon ami.'*

Vaughn hadn't commented at first, he'd been too busy gazing at his dessert like it was the Eighth Wonder of the

World. Then he'd smiled ruefully. '*Mais elle est très jolie.*' Grace had still been reeling from that little bombshell when Guillaume's wife, Solange, had taken her to one side in the powder room and said, 'You're a very sweet girl and I understand how new this all is, but darling, this really won't do.' Then she'd fingered the sleeve of Grace's dress as if it was made from the nastiest of nylon. Grace suspected that she'd said something to Vaughn, or else his dessert had really sweetened him up because afterwards he'd taken her to Marc Jacobs and bought her the most expensive dress she'd ever owned.

It was then that Grace had realised that you had to be creative to keep up with women who weren't on first-name terms with the girl at Miu Miu, but with John Galliano and Karl Lagerfeld. The kind of women who'd sneered at Grace's last season Diane Von Fürstenberg that she'd got on sale when she'd worn it to a gallery opening in New York.

Vintage was always a safe bet and Grace had found a place that hired out evening gowns for £100 a day. She'd even forced herself to forage at the back of her wardrobe so she could do an inventory on the ill-gotten gains she'd acquired from her shopping binges. But as luck would have it, she'd never once purchased a formal dress. She tended to go for bags and shoes – and just unwrapping them from their plastic shrouds had been enough to make her start dry-heaving.

The first week that Vaughn was away, Grace received her itinerary for December, which looked more daunting than she could have possibly imagined. There were a hell of a lot of parties hosted by ambassadors and Russians who owned Premier League football teams, and she needed to assemble twenty-five party outfits on £7,000. It was just as well that Grace loved solving fashion conundrums as much as her grandfather enjoyed playing Killer Sudoku. She'd even made a complicated flow-chart diagram in her Google documents when she realised that she'd pretty much worn every vintage dress that the hire place had in her size and they had nothing left in stock that hadn't been booked months in advance for Christmas parties. Grace figured that she could double up at least five outfits if they were black dresses, three of which she could borrow from Celia, Lily and Posy as the four of them had made a pact to pool frocks to get them through the party season.

Luckily, Courtney and Lucie had a raft of discount cards between them and would let Grace borrow them 'for Christmas presents and I totally need some statement dresses for all the parties coming up' if she did their Christmas shopping while she was at it, which netted her a Chloé dress, a ballerina skirt and a Burberry coat, which would draw people's attention for long enough until she took it off to reveal a borrowed black frock.

Then there were other put-upon assistants employed by various fashion companies dotted all over London who'd give Grace hefty discounts and occasionally even lend her dresses, especially when she started calling in favours. A whole year's worth of favours, and she owed fashion credits up the wazoo, but Grace was pretty proud of herself for doing designer on a limited budget, even though Kiki often complained that Grace always brought her problems and never solutions. But if this was a problem, then it was one that Grace didn't mind having.

'It would be like Cinderella moaning about getting blisters from her glass slippers,' she told herself as she hung her newly acquired, begged, borrowed and heavily discounted dresses on one of the rails in the fashion cupboard, then struck a pose in front of the mirror. 'Oh Grace, you poor thing, having to make seven grand go a long way because you've got so many high-falutin places to go and people to meet. Sucks to be you.'

She wondered how Vaughn's other mistresses had coped and decided that they must have all been independently wealthy or that he'd had different arrangements with them; either way, Grace didn't want to know.

Even though December was panning out to be the cruellest month, Grace was still determined to earmark at least £1,000 to pay off some of her creditors. When she received her allowances on the first of every month, she used a scientific method to select which bills to pay: this involved opening a shoebox, shutting her eyes and rooting around until she had three pieces of paper in her hand. Then she'd toddle off to the Post Office. So far, she wasn't even paying the actual amounts she owed, but trying to make a dent in the interest and penalty charges and late fees so it felt like she was throwing a glass of water at a forest fire but it was a start. More than that, it was the endgame, it was the reason why she'd got into bed with Vaughn in the first place. Though at this rate she'd have to stay in his bed for at least three years before she was out of the red and luxuriating in the novelty of being in the black.

All in all, it had been a very fruitful fortnight. December's outfits were half-assembled. She'd made major inroads into getting the fashion department on track to clear their Christmas deadlines, paid some bills, started getting her body bikini-ready and spent some quality time with Lily.

'I've been given two weeks off before the Christmas rush,' Grace told Lily when she'd asked why Grace wasn't at her part-time job.

It had sent a pang of guilt hurtling through Grace at how pathetically grateful Lily was that she had time after work to come round and write lists and insert magazine tears in her wedding folder. And it was that same guilt that made Grace agree to Sunday lunch in Godalming so Lily could finally tell her parents she was up the duff and the May wedding that her mother thought she was getting caterers' estimates for was going to be moved up. Way up.

It wasn't just guilt though. Grace had been lured by the promise of roast potatoes cooked in goose fat too and stayed to make sure that Lily's dad didn't get down the shotgun above the mantelpiece and use it on Dan, who was now in Grace's eternal debt.

'Gracie, I think if you hadn't been there, her dad would have broken my legs,' he kept saying all the way back to North London. 'I never dreamed they'd react like that.'

Lily had just smiled beatifically because the bad news was out of the way, the wedding was set for Christmas Eve and now Grace could get on with briefing the seamstress she'd found and a million other tasks she'd agreed to, because that pesky guilt made it impossible to say no. It was also why she'd spent two hours of her last free Saturday tasting cakes with Lily, not that it was a hardship, before rushing off to meet her grandparents outside John Lewis on Oxford Street.

She couldn't help but smile when she saw them approach, refusing to be buffeted by crowds of Christmas shoppers. They rarely came up to London, which Grace was hugely grateful for, and the occasion warranted dressing up. Her grandmother was wearing the Betty Barclay suit that did for funerals, AGMs and occasional stints as a Justice of the Peace. And her grandfather was wearing a trilby hat and a three-piece suit. They were so adorably retro. Grace was overcome by tenderness as she skipped over to them.

Her grandmother gave her the usual peck on the cheek and perfunctory hug, but her grandfather squeezed her tight and scrubbed at her face with his whiskers, even though Grace wasn't five any more and no longer squealed in delighted disgust.

'It's so good to see you!' Grace exclaimed, hugging them again.

'We hardly recognised you. You've got some colour in your cheeks for once.' Coming from her grandmother, this was high praise. 'Now, I just need to pop into Liberty's and get some wool.'

'There's not much to buy,' Grace said. 'They've shrunk the yarn department right down but there's this great little shop in Islington. You can get the bus back to Victoria really easily.'

'We always go to Liberty's for wool. Then we'll go to that little café round the corner for some tea.'

'It closed down,' Grace said firmly, though she had no idea whether it had or hadn't. But they had really horrible cheese scones in there and didn't know how to make a proper latte. 'I'll take you to Patisserie Valerie. You'll love it.'

It was hard shopping with her grandparents. They tended to make very loud observations about how expensive everything was and what a pity it was that Marshall & Snelgrove had closed down. They also needed regular bathroom breaks.

Finally, Grace managed to herd them to a corner table in Patisserie Valerie, and before they could start interrogating her on the state of her debts, career prospects and hair, presented them with the chocolate and pralines she'd bought in Paris two months ago. She had had to exercise every last drop of willpower not to eat them herself.

'That's very thoughtful, dear,' her grandmother said. 'I don't like to cook with anything other than eighty-five per cent cocoa solids. But can you really afford to go to Paris? Remember the monthly spending spreadsheet Grandy drew up so you wouldn't get into debt again?'

'Maybe you got a pay rise at the office?' her grandfather ventured. 'Or you've been walking to work to save money?'

'I went with a friend,' Grace said quickly. 'And we split the costs.' Or, to be far more accurate, she'd bought Vaughn a coffee as penance for dragging him into a yarn shop. 'And I have been making monthly payments, I swear.'

'A *friend*?' her grandmother queried, in the same way that Lady Bracknell would ask about handbags.

'Yup, a friend. A mate. A pal.' Grace took a sip of her coffee and tried to make her eyes look extra big and guileless. Her grandparents stared right back at her, like the time they'd known Grace had been drinking cider in the park because she'd been spotted by Mrs Singh from next door, even though she'd denied it vehemently. 'A friend who's a boy,' she added, because she always cracked under pressure. 'He's very nice and I like him a lot and we totally had separate rooms.' Which wasn't a lie because it had been a suite with two bedrooms, two bathrooms and a sun terrace.

'What does he do?' her grandfather asked, actually putting on his spectacles, all the better to scrutinise Grace's every facial gesture.

'He's in art,' she muttered.

'Oh Grace, not another artist!' Her grandmother sighed loudly, as she surreptitiously pocketed some packets of sweeteners. 'Why can't you find a boy with prospects?'

'Not an artist,' Grace insisted doggedly. 'He's *in* art. It's a big difference.'

'And how long have you been courting?'

Why couldn't they say 'dating' or 'seeing him' like anyone else who was actually living in the twenty-first century? Grace shrugged. 'A few months.'

'How long is a few months?' her grandmother enquired and Grace wished that she'd never started this.

She did some quick-ish mental arithmetic. 'Nearly three months.' Had it really been that long? Their three-month anniversary was coming up and actually things were improving, not going steadily downhill like they usually did at the three-month mark in Grace's relationships. Not that it was a relationship, but still . . .

'And you never mentioned him once during our phone calls.' Her grandmother warranted this important enough to put down her cup. 'Is it serious?'

'Gran, we're just hanging out. It's not a big deal so don't make it one.'

'But he took you to Paris . . .'

'No, we *went* to Paris together . . .'

'Going away with someone is a big commitment, Grace.' Her grandmother paused and seemed to be having slight trouble finding the right words. Maybe it was the first signs of Alzheimer's. 'I'm sure we'll meet him at Christmas.' Or maybe it was simply her grandmother moving in for the kill.

She made it sound so reasonable, so sensible, that for one brief moment Grace actually gave the idea serious consideration. Then she thought of Vaughn in their front room being ruthlessly interrogated by her grandmother and ignored by her grandfather, while he gazed at her toothy school photos, the antimacassars, the hideous reproduction of Gainsborough's *The Blue Boy* which hung over the mantel-piece.

Then Grace realised she was focusing on the wrong part of her grandmother's sentence. 'Hang on, you're going to Australia for Christmas. It's all you've been talking about for weeks.'

'There's been a change of plan,' her grandfather piped up. 'Doctor said it could be risky flying such a long way with my angina.'

'And someone from the Mothers' Union got deep vein thrombosis when she flew to Florida,' added her grandmother. 'Besides, it can be very hot in Australia in December, you know.'

'I did tell you that but you said—'

'So that's why Caroline and Gary are going to fly over here,' her grandmother continued, though she wasn't looking at Grace any more, but at a fixed spot on the table. 'With little Kirsty, of course.'

Grace immediately felt something in her chest clench so she wasn't sure she could even breathe. She could still talk though. 'You have got to be bloody kidding me!'

'Don't swear, dear,' her grandfather said reflexively, but he patted her suddenly icy-cold hand. 'Once you're over the shock, I bet you'll secretly be pleased to see your mother again.'

'You think?' Tears were falling fast and Grace tried to wipe them away with the back of her hand, until a crisp square of white cotton was handed to her.

'Come on, Gracie, don't make a scene,' her grandmother said, her voice soft now she'd delivered the killer blow. And God forbid that Grace should make a scene. Making a scene was right up there with tax evasion and mass genocide. 'You're both very different people to how you were fifteen years ago. If you'd talk to your mother, then you'd realise that.'

Grace curled her arms around herself protectively. 'I can't believe that you just spring this on me and think I'll be cool with it. Because I am not! I don't even want to be in the same room with her so I don't really see us pulling crackers and passing the gravy over Christmas lunch. I'll stay in London. Anyway, I told you Lily's pregnant and she's getting married on Christmas Eve now, so there wouldn't be any way I could get from Godalming to Worthing after the reception.'

Her grandmother put down her cup of tea so forcefully that she spilled a little. 'Nobody gets married on Christmas Eve; it's so thoughtless. And she's *pregnant*? I hope it's not going to be a church service.'

'Well, it is. Apparently the vicar's really progressive about these things and her dad made a massive contribution to buy a new church organ or something,' Grace said as tetchily as she dared. 'So, I'll see you between Christmas and New Year, just the two of you.'

'Now wait a minute, young lady,' her grandfather snapped because her grandmother might huff and puff but he was the one who laid down the law. 'You're coming home for Christmas and you will be civil to your mother and we won't have any upsets. Is that clear?'

'I'm *not* coming,' Grace gritted, because defying her grandfather when he got all Wrath of God on her was very hard. 'I don't ever want to see her again and, believe me, I'm sure the feeling's mutual.'

The three of them glared at each other for a while, until her grandmother picked up her tea cup again. 'People are staring,' she stage-whispered. 'There's no point in anyone getting upset about this. We'll talk about it another time, Grace. Now eat the rest of your scone.'

And Grace knew that there would be daily phone calls in which her grandmother would cajole and threaten and probably play the trump card that she and Grandy weren't in the best of health and it could be their last Christmas. And Grace would eventually bow to the relentless pressure and give in, because that's what she always did.

chapter nineteen

It was only the prospect of a long weekend in Miami Beach that turned Grace's frown right way round again.

It was lovely to wake up on Thursday morning and realise that in a few hours she'd be soaking up the sun, putting on new fancy clothes that she could never wear to work, and seeing Vaughn again. That thought unexpectedly popped into her head while she was waiting for the kettle to boil and she examined it carefully. He'd sent her a text message – something innocuous enough about having an exciting weekend ahead of them – but then when Grace thought of their last phone call and the things Vaughn had said he wanted to do to her in his quest for her elusive orgasm, she shivered. It was a shiver that owed nothing to the fact that her plug-in radiator was taking for ever to heat up and more the thought of Vaughn single-mindedly pursuing his goal.

It felt good to shut the front door of 17 Montague Terrace and leave everything behind as she climbed into the back seat of a toasty warm car that smelled of leather, and ask the driver to crank the heating up just a little.

By the time Grace was ushered into the Business Class cabin by a smiling stewardess, she was shrugging off all the worries of the last week, along with her new Burberry coat. The woman behind her was complaining bitterly because she normally flew first class, but as Grace sipped her complimentary champagne and tried to decide which of the many films on offer she'd like to see first, she didn't think she'd ever take travelling Business Class for granted.

As she obeyed the announcement to turn off her mobile, Grace realised she was free from Kiki, who'd been an absolute nightmare and had almost refused to sign Grace's holiday form, Lily and her crazy baby hormones, Lily's mother, her own grandmother's increasingly hectoring calls and some woman from a debt collection agency who'd started calling up and leaving ominous messages. In fact, she could switch off her phone until Monday evening and pretend that her non-Vaughn world didn't exist.

The world that did have Vaughn in it was pretty fucking fantastic. Grace had slept on the plane and was wide awake as her driver took her the scenic route along Ocean Drive so she could see rippling waves frothing along the shore on one side and, on the other, bright lights and people spilling out of clubs and open-topped cars, and she could hear the insistent thump of music. It felt like the city's pulse was connected straight to the exhilarated beat of her own heart. Grace could remember standing in her kitchen in her underwear calling Vaughn for the first time and he'd been here in Miami. Maybe even driving along the same stretch of road – and all of a sudden she couldn't wait to see him. She was dying to see him.

But when she was shown into their bungalow at the Delano, which was five steps away from an Olympic-sized pool that shimmered electric blue in the dark, Vaughn wasn't there. Grace looked around the cool white space, arms clamped to her sides because it was so pristine and perfect, she was sure she'd leave dirty fingerprints over anything she touched.

She wandered from the lounge into the bedroom where there was a note propped on the pillow. *Gone to dinner. Hope you had a good flight. See you later. V.* Anyone else would have told her not to wait up, but Vaughn wasn't anyone else and besides, Grace was too wired and excited to go to sleep. She even thought about having a dip in the pool, but decided she'd indulge in her own patented, post-plane ritual – because she had a post-plane ritual now.

Lighting the Diptique fig candle she'd brought with her 'cause she'd read somewhere that Madonna always did that, she poured all of a bottle of Korres bubble bath into the huge tub as she took a bottle of wine out of the mini-bar. This made her think of Vaughn's incredulous reaction when they'd stayed at the Plaza Athenée in Paris and she'd asked if it was OK to get a Diet Coke out of the mini-bar. Actually he'd looked at her like she was certifiably crazy and snapped, 'Yes – and don't let me *ever* catch you asking something so ridiculous again.'

Five minutes later, she was immersed up to the neck in bubbles, sipping at a glass of Pinot Grigio and wiggling her toes luxuriously, because in Vaughn world you never had to wait for the boiler to fill up again and all bathrooms came with heating as standard. And in Vaughn world, there was now a Vaughn standing in the open doorway, not smiling, not saying anything, just looking at the surprised expression on Grace's face. The silence only lasted a few seconds, but it seemed to go on for ever, until Vaughn shook his head, then stepped into the steamy, scented bathroom.

'Hello, stranger,' he murmured, bending down to kiss Grace briefly on the lips before he straightened up. 'Can I share your wine?'

' 'Course you can,' Grace said, and if she was pink-cheeked it was because she was in a hot bath, but then Vaughn sat down on the bath's tiled surround and they took turns sipping from her glass as he told her about the places he'd been, turning what sounded like a nightmare blur of meetings and difficult artists and agents into a long stream of funny anecdotes. Soon there wasn't much left in the bottle and it didn't seem so weird to be naked when Vaughn wasn't.

The bubbles were melting away and Grace could see her body slowly coming into focus. She glanced up to see Vaughn looking too, then he reached down and deliberately trailed his hand through the water, dispersing the last of the bubbles so he could see Grace's breasts: her nipples a deep, dusky pink compared to the paleness of her skin.

'I think it's time you got out of there before you turn into a prune,' Vaughn said casually, but he was swallowing hard, so if Grace was nervous then he was too. 'I never did care for prunes.'

Grace gently levered herself out of the water and let Vaughn wrap her in a snowy-white towel, because in Vaughn world nothing ever went grey in the wash. Standing up in the tub, she was the same height as him for once and she wrapped her arms round his neck so she could rub her nose against his and tease a smile from him. 'You promise you won't get mad if I can't come?' she whispered in his ear.

'Well, we're not leaving that huge bed in the other room until you do, so let's hope there's twenty-four-hour room service,' Vaughn said, as he lifted her out of the bath.

Grace had always imagined that the secret to good sex was like an algebraic equation or a chemical formula. There was a complicated sequence of manoeuvres, positions and breathing exercises that other girls knew about but she didn't because she'd overslept the day they were being given the printed handout.

It had to take more than a pillow under her hips and a simple combination of tongue and fingers building her up and then easing her down so Grace was digging her heels into the mattress, tears of frustration spilling down her cheeks.

'No, you're not ready yet,' Vaughn said to every one of her desperate pleas, until she was beyond mere words and reduced to these high-pitched moans that would make Grace shudder with embarrassment when she thought about them later.

But not then. No, then, she grabbed handfuls of Vaughn's hair so she could tug him upwards and he had no choice but to give in to her growled, 'Now. You have to fuck me right now', or emerge from their battle with half a dozen bald spots.

As soon as Vaughn slid inside her, it was inevitable. Grace went from not-quite to all-the-way-to-happyland instantly, clutching at Vaughn's arms, his shoulders, anywhere she could reach as he lifted her legs so her knees were almost touching her ears and drove into her again and again. The world seemed to break around her, shattering into a million different pieces and it only seemed whole again, reshaped by Vaughn's hands and mouth, long minutes later.

Grace sprawled carelessly on the bed, still fighting to catch each breath as tiny and delicious after-shocks rippled through her.

'Are you all right?' Vaughn asked, his voice equally unsteady.

The ability to form words would have required way too much effort, so Grace just sighed instead. A little, rapturous exhalation that sounded odd coming from her mouth. She raised her head slightly so she could confirm that her skin was sheened with perspiration and she had a mottled flush on her chest and collapsed on the bed again. Yup, she'd definitely had an orgasm. A monster, no-holds-barred, satisfaction-guaranteed-or-your-money-back orgasm.

She rolled on to her side so she could curve herself against Vaughn and haul one heavy arm around her waist. 'It was probably just a fluke,' she murmured. 'A Miami-sponsored fluke.'

'Well, why don't we check again in the morning, just to be on the safe side?'

'Usually I can't come more than once in a twenty-four-hour period,' she shared, and felt Vaughn's chest rumbling against her back. She reached around so she could dig him in his shaking ribs. 'Don't laugh at me! I'm being serious.'

'It can all wait until tomorrow,' Vaughn decided, as Grace yawned and rested her head on his shoulder.

By 5 p.m. the following afternoon, Grace was forced to admit that the whims and workings of her own body were a complete mystery to her. Vaughn had coaxed another two orgasms from her: the first before breakfast, and later as he fucked her over the distressed white table in the corner of their suite, his palm grinding against her clit, number three hit. Grace vowed that she was going to try out a cartwheel when she got home. She'd never been able to get the hang of them either, but maybe with the right kind of application, she'd soon be a cartwheeling pro.

'What are you thinking about?' Vaughn asked, as he cupped Grace's breasts with soapy hands because showering together now seemed entirely innocent after the positions Vaughn had had her in.

Grace shook wet strands of hair out of her face. 'Nothing.' She turned herself round in the circle of Vaughn's arms so she could look up at him. 'You're, like, my favourite person in the world right now.'

Vaughn tried not to look smug but failed. 'I've got a few years on you and I don't think your past boyfriends knew what they were doing.'

Grace thought of all those guys who had never gone down on her in return for lengthy blowjobs that had given her lockjaw. Boyfriends who'd been more interested in trying to persuade her to forego a condom, than get her off. 'Well, they didn't pay as much attention to detail as you do,' she sniffed, coiling herself sinuously around Vaughn, because, hell, right now, she *was* his biggest fan.

But Vaughn was holding her firmly at arm's length. 'Do you realise that I've blown out at least three meetings and two exhibitions today? I'm not cancelling dinner too. I'm a mere shell of the man I used to be.'

*

Art Basel, Miami was the most important event in the American art calendar. Over 200 galleries exhibited work from their best artists, put on shows and introduced new talent to the industry. That was Vaughn's official line, but as far as Grace could tell, Art Basel was like an end-of-term school disco with art installations.

It seemed like the art world had converged on Miami for a weekend of drinking, partying and getting off with each other. Grace found that she wasn't propping up the wall any longer and trying to look animated at parties when Vaughn disappeared in the direction of museum directors or stinking rich hedge fund managers. At Art Basel it was easy to talk to people – or maybe it was because she was giving off a post-sex glow and was so chilled out that she was beaming at anyone who strayed into her field of vision.

Mostly she talked to gallery assistants and other girlfriends, but Vaughn was delighted when he came to find her on the Saturday night and she'd palled up with a rock-star daughter who styled herself as a DJ and was looking to invest in some 'really whacked-out light features' for a club she was opening in Las Vegas. But then, Grace was starting to feel as if everything she did that weekend delighted Vaughn because they had been back at the Delano by eleven the last two nights so he could show her just how delighted he was, which involved stripping her clothes off as soon as the door shut behind them and coming up with new ways to make her lose her mind.

Although they were three months and then some into their partnership, Grace felt like this was a honeymoon. Vaughn's face was creased into a permanent smile and he didn't feel the need to snark about anything. They'd even found a way to sleep together, curled round each other at first before moving to their separate sides of the bed, but that could have been because they were both too exhausted to worry about who was fidgeting. Vaughn wasn't and never would be her boyfriend, but Grace decided when she woke up on Sunday morning to find him trailing kisses down her stomach that she liked him a lot better than she'd liked most of her old boyfriends.

Later, after Vaughn had gone down on her for half an hour and she'd reciprocated with probably the best blowjob of her life, they went to a brunch buffet at the Biltmore, courtesy of some bigass, environment-damaging, art-sponsoring oil company. The crowd was older and stiffer than the other Basel parties and Grace soon found that she was hugging the walls again.

Finally braving the crowd to get a refill of guava juice, she suddenly found herself surrounded by Alex, who was always popping up like tie-dye as a trend prediction, and a gaggle of beautiful but vicious-looking boys.

'This is Grace, Vaughn's new girl. She looked far more fresh-faced a few weeks ago,' Alex informed the cheap seats, then had the nerve to lean in for an air kiss.

'Alex,' Grace said thinly. 'Don't brunches interfere with your creature-of-the-night lifestyle?'

There was a collective snigger because Alex's pallor was truly vampiric and he always wore black, which Grace considered to be the sign of someone who had no true fashion nous.

'Nice dress. How much did Vaughn pay for it?' Alex sniped back, with a pointed look at the Marc Jacobs dress Vaughn had bought her in Paris.

'About the same amount it cost you for that last batch of dodgy Botox,' Grace sniffed because she'd worked with Kiki long enough to spot the telltale signs of an immovable forehead. She saw Vaughn across the room, and as if she was sending out a distress signal, he immediately turned his head and stared directly at her.

Grace tried to telegraph an urgent 'Rescue me, right the hell now!' message, and it was a miracle on the same level as turning water into wine because Vaughn was moving towards her.

'. . . and I ask every time we bump into each other, but Grace still won't have lunch with me. Not even early evening drinks.'

'Are you sure you're gay, Alex?' she asked sweetly. 'Because you're awfully fixated on being alone with me.'

Vaughn had now arrived at her side. He was wearing the cream-coloured suit from that first encounter in Liberty's and he'd brought reinforcements.

'Am I interrupting something?' he asked, barely even acknowledging Alex's presence.

'Nope, absolutely nothing,' Grace said. 'Oh hi, Nadja. *Love* your shoes.'

Vaughn was flanked by Sergei and Nadja, who'd become Grace's text buddy, though Grace was still a little scared by her: not just her daunting beauty but the way she said the most outrageous things in such a deadpan manner that Grace could never tell if she was joking or being serious.

'From Cavalli,' Nadja said, tucking her arm through Grace's and pouting furiously as the A-gays melted away. 'Grace, I need fur.'

It was currently a very agreeable seventy degrees in the shade. A touch too warm even for the purple opaque tights Grace was wearing. 'You sure about that?' she asked.

'This afternoon, we get me fur,' Nadja insisted. 'But where?'

'Sergei and Nadja are heading back to Moscow tomorrow, where it's currently snowing,' Vaughn translated. 'Would you mind going shopping with Nadja?'

Grace could shop with the best of them, even Russian almost-supermodels. 'We could try Fendi or Gucci?'

'Anything Nadja wants,' Sergei grunted. All he ever did was grunt and run his eyes over people, like he could tell exactly how much they had invested in stocks and bonds.

'Cool,' Nadja opined. 'But first you change your tights, Grace. Is too edgy for South Beach.'

'I don't mind,' Grace assured Vaughn later, as she removed the offensive hosiery and changed out of Marc Jacobs and into American Apparel. 'I mean, I don't approve of wearing fur . . .'

'Do you actually own anything made of fur?' Vaughn asked lazily, as he peered at his laptop screen.

'Well, no, but I work for a magazine that shoots fur and advertises dead animal pelts, so shopping with Nadja isn't that much of a problem.' Not for the first time, Grace marvelled at just how wonky her moral compass was.

'I was considering buying you a fur jacket for Christmas but obviously I shall have to rethink that,' Vaughn said, lifting his head so he could waggle an eyebrow at her, which meant he was still in playful mode. 'Are you sure you won't change your mind? Whistler can get very cold.'

'We're going to Whistler?' Grace decided that jumping up and down would not be cool. She'd do it in the bathroom where Vaughn couldn't see her. 'I know you promised me foreign travel but you do realise that taking the bus into work on Tuesday morning is going to be a major comedown?'

'Poor Grace,' Vaughn murmured, his attention already back with his latest acquisitions. 'I always go to Whistler for Christmas, but we left it off the itinerary until I got a few dates locked down.' He tapped some keys. 'We'll fly out on the twenty-third, then go off to Buenos Aires on the twenty-eighth for the New Year.'

It sounded wonderful. The answer to all her prodigal-Mum-sponsored Christmas nightmares. Except . . .

'I can't.'

'Can't ski? Really, Grace, *everyone* can ski. I'll get Madeleine to book an instructor to take you out on the nursery slopes. And on Christmas Eve, we've been invited to—'

'No, you don't understand,' Grace burst out. 'I can't *go*! There's a lot of stuff happening around then.'

She tried to explain in a matter-of-fact way because they'd been having such a great weekend and Vaughn really hated it when she whined. She couldn't bring herself to mention her mother, but her grandmother wanted her home for Christmas and, short of Grace contracting the Ebola virus, no excuse was acceptable.

Vaughn listened to it all, eyes so narrowed that Grace didn't know how he could still see out of them. But he let her ramble on, becoming more and more disjointed, until she got to the Lily part of her set-in-stone Christmas plans. Then he got his scathe on.

'No one gets married at Christmas – it's so inconsiderate of other people's plans.'

Lily had been told exactly that countless times, by countless other people, but she refused to budge. 'She's severely hormonal and she wants the day to be *special* and *romantic*.' Even though Grace had heard Lily use those exact adjectives at least three times every day for two weeks, they sounded equally lame coming out of her own mouth.

'Either she's mentally deficient or colossally self-involved,' Vaughn shot back, standing up so he could loom. He did so love to loom.

'Look, I can fly out on Boxing Day. I'll fly out late on Christmas Day if there's a flight but I can't miss my best friend's wedding.' Grace wasn't capable of unemotional any more. She got out of range of Vaughn's looming so she could fling herself down on the bed in a fit of pique. 'Please, Vaughn, I'm chief bridesmaid and I promised Lily that I'd—'

'You're not going. I have a lunch on Christmas Eve that could bring in millions of pounds. I think that takes precedence over a shotgun wedding for a girl who's too stupid to use birth control.'

'Please don't talk about my best friend like that! Look, why can't you meet me halfway? Why can't *you* compromise just this once?'

Vaughn had given up on looming, in favour of prowling towards her.

'Because we have a contract and I made it perfectly and explicitly clear that our arrangement would take up all your free time, all your vacation allowance and any public holidays. You are flying out to Whistler on the twenty-third and that's it. End of discussion.'

It wasn't the end of the discussion as far as Grace was concerned but she was too busy fuming to think of anything to say. So she picked up the nearest pillow and threw it at him. Of course it missed. She watched it sail through the air and land at Vaughn's feet but her intention had been unmistakable.

That was when he got really angry. 'You are coming to Whistler when I say so. You will go where I tell you to go. You will do so with a smile on your face while wearing clothes that don't include ridiculous pairs of tights that make you look as if you've escaped from the nearest clown school *and I do not want to hear another bloody word about it.*' He hadn't shouted once. Hadn't even raised his voice but Grace still felt as if someone had tipped a bucket of ice down her back.

He stormed out of the room after that and Grace barely had time to sag back on the bed, when he poked his head through the door again.

'And if I want you to have lessons at a bloody dry-ski slope every night from now until the twenty-second of December, you'll bloody well do it,' he growled.

chapter twenty

Grace was used to the inexplicable but small events that led up to life-changing moments. There was the congealed cranberry sauce that had started the final row that had led to her parents' divorce. Or the rainy Sunday afternoon when she'd first seen *Breakfast At Tiffany's*, fallen in love with Audrey's black Givenchy shift dress and decided that she wanted to work in fashion. There was the Marc Jacobs handbag that had led her to Vaughn and now, there was a pair of Fendi shearling boots altering the course of her destiny.

Nadja had bought her the boots. Even though Grace had been wearing a huge pair of Chloé sunglasses, it was obvious that she'd been crying and could only splutter, 'Me and Vaughn just had a little spat.'

'When Sergei is a pig, I buy expensive things on his card,' Nadja had said, tossing back her hair, though she bought expensive things on Sergei's card even when he wasn't being a pig.

Grace didn't have a Vaughn-sponsored credit card, just a monthly allowance that was mostly gone even though it was only 7 December, so Nadja had bought her the boots. Which hadn't made Grace feel even the tiniest bit better.

When Vaughn had finally shown up at one the next morning, Grace had been in bed but was still too upset to sleep. She'd kept her eyes shut and tried to make her breathing deep and slow, even when Vaughn sat down on the bed and stroked her hair.

'The dry-ski slope was a bit much,' he said softly. 'I'll make sure you get to see your grandparents on the twenty-third and then I'll have a car take you from Worthing to Gatwick. Now, did you and Nadja have fun?'

It wasn't even a second-cousin to an apology but then Vaughn didn't do apologies. What he had done was trail his hand down her spine so he could cup her arse.

Grace had given up feigning sleep. 'I have a headache,' she hissed, and that had been the last they'd spoken. Vaughn had left again and hadn't come back when the car arrived to take her to the airport.

But the fact that Miami was now Grace's least favourite place on earth hadn't been the Fendi boots' fault, so when she'd woken up on Tuesday morning, fuggy with jet lag and with a sick feeling of dread about the conversation she needed to have with Lily, she'd put them on to cheer herself up – in direct contravention of her rule that Vaughn clothes and work clothes were to be kept strictly separate.

Which, in retrospect, hadn't been big or clever. But Grace only realised that five minutes into a crisis meeting about Christmas deadlines. The production editor was droning on about the repro house and Grace was wondering if anyone would notice if she shut her eyes and had a doze, when Courtney sat up and stared at Grace's legs in amazement.

'Those are Fendi,' she announced. 'Where did you get them?'

Grace looked down at the boots and then back at Courtney while her sluggish brain came up with and discarded several not-very-plausible lies. Bottom line was that fashion assistants without trust funds couldn't afford Fendi shearling boots.

'Don't say you got them in Paris or Milan because they're wait-listed there too,' Lucie piped up, also staring at the boots.

'I was going to fly to Berlin but they only had the size forty-ones.'

There was a murmur of excited chatter. Even Kiki was looking as Grace placed her legs as far under her chair as they would go. 'They are *so* not Fendi,' she protested, throwing in a little eyeroll. 'They're fakes I got on eBay. Like, seriously! How could I afford Fendi? Hel*lo*!'

That crisis had been averted and Grace could get on with the real crisis, which was lunch with Lily. Grace had decided that the only solution was to tell the truth. Or as close as she could come to telling the truth without actually *telling the whole truth*.

But the first thing Lily had said was, 'Those are the Fendi boots that were in *Vogue*, aren't they? I thought all your credit cards were maxed out?'

Grace took a deep breath because Lily had provided her with the perfect opener. 'You remember that guy I met in Liberty's on my birthday who bought me the Marc Jacobs bag?'

Lily nodded. And kept on nodding. Then Lily stopped nodding and her eyes widened comically as Grace got to the part where, 'So we have this arrangement where I'm kind of his official escort. Like, how famous gay guys have beards except he's not famous or gay. How can I explain this? It's dating but with benefits.'

'How long has this been going on and why are you telling me about it now?' Lily sat back and folded her arms, which wasn't exactly encouraging.

'I'll get to that in a minute,' Grace said, and the only way to do this was quickly, like ripping off a plaster super-fast so it only hurt for a second. Though she wasn't entirely sure if quick was for Lily's benefit or her own.

'Lils, I can't make the wedding. I won't even be at my gran's for Christmas. Vaughn's got a really important lunch on the twenty-fourth in Canada and I have to be there. But I can still help you with all the planning. It's just the wedding itself that's going to be a problem.'

Lily slammed her glass of carrot and pear juice down so hard that Grace flinched. 'What? *What?* What the fuck are you talking about?'

Grace summed up her agreement with Vaughn in a few pithy lines, stressing the benefits of foreign travel and parties, which Lily would appreciate, and glossing over contracts and really bloody-minded older men, which she wouldn't. 'I know it's a lot to take in.' Grace reached out to touch Lily's arm but she slapped Grace's hand away, as the people sharing their table turned and stared. Served them right for communal dining.

'I can't believe you'd do this to me!' Lily shouted, tears streaking her mascara. 'You've ruined my wedding day because you're a skanky, disgusting bitch who fucks men for money and I hate you.'

Then they were thrown out of Wagamama.

Grace tried to reason with Lily all the way back to the office because Lily was too scared to run in heels now that she was pregnant and couldn't get away from her. 'C'mon, Lils. It's not the end of the world. You'll still have a special and romantic day and I'll be there with you right up to the twenty-second.'

'Fuck right off,' Lily said in a cold tight voice. 'You've been lying to me for weeks, haven't you? Making me feel sorry for you because you had to get a part-time job when basically you've pretty much become a prostitute.'

Lily stopped crying, just as Grace started. 'I'm not. That's not at all what it's like.' Grace grabbed hold of Lily's coat-sleeve so she could force her friend to a halt. 'He pays me to act as his hostess, not to sleep with him.'

'Yeah, right.' Lily snorted in disbelief. 'You're screwing someone you hardly even know, Grace! He's put you on a salary. It's the skeeviest thing I've ever heard. How could you?'

'You're not listening to me! The screwing and the money are completely separate from each other.'

'Yeah, it really sounds like that,' Lily said icily, her nostrils flaring. 'God, what the fuck is wrong with you, Grace? It's like you can't do anything normal.'

'It is normal. Girls do this all the time,' Grace protested. 'What about when big Julie was going out with that really horrible DJ just because he'd fly her out to Ibiza every weekend over the summer? You didn't think there was anything wrong with that. You laughed about it!'

'That was different,' Lily said quickly. 'She said he was really funny once you got to know him.'

'Yeah, that was why she dumped his funny arse the moment that his residency finished,' Grace snapped before she could stop herself, because she didn't have any right to get angry at Lily, not when she was bailing on Lily's wedding day and sending her blood pressure sky high, which couldn't be good for the baby. 'And what about Dan? He does nothing but mooch off you. He sure as hell doesn't work for a living.'

'Dan's a web designer . . .'

'Oh, I'm sorry. I just thought he sat on his arse all day playing computer games.'

'You've never understood how me and Dan work because you're incapable of being in a proper relationship,' Lily informed Grace, patches of red staining her face. Even as Grace gasped in shock it occurred to her that if she and Lily weren't such good friends then they wouldn't know exactly what to say to cause maximum hurt. Though that wasn't much comfort right now, but it was just what she needed to remind her to rein in her temper. She was in the wrong here. Elbow deep in the wrong.

'Look, Lily, I was going to tell you right from the start but you'd just got engaged and then you found out you were pregnant. And the longer I left it, the harder it got to tell you, because—'

'Because I would never do what you're doing, but then I guess I have a stronger moral code than you – not that it's hard.'

Grace was still holding on to Lily's sleeve; now she clutched her arm even tighter. 'We've both had one-night stands so don't you dare try and pull that crap on me. Vaughn's all right – we're not having the love affair of all time but we get on, most of the time.'

'Well, you kind of have to when he's paying you. God, why can't you just stop shopping and save some money so you can pay off your own credit cards? If you can't afford stuff, then just don't buy it,' Lily said sanctimoniously, trying to shake Grace off though she was clinging on for dear life.

Grace let go. And she wasn't going to get angry with Lily – not when she was going to get absolutely bloody furious instead. 'You have no fucking idea what it's like to try and manage on your own,' she shouted, rage bubbling up and spilling over so Lily took a step back from the twisted expression on Grace's face. 'No, you'd never do something like this because you don't have to. You've never had to solve your own problems because your dad's always there to bail out his precious little darling. Well, I don't have that luxury – and if you didn't have Daddy funding you, you'd be in way worse debt than me.'

'I don't have problems?' Lily screamed back, her face red with rage as she pointed at her stomach. 'I'm pregnant and the one person I need is too busy fucking some dodgy old bloke to come to my wedding. You could have said no to him, Grace. You could have finished it, but you chose him over me! Well, I hope all the dresses and stuff he gives you for spreading your legs is worth it.'

The argument was running away from them, careering out of control as they stood on a narrow Soho street shrieking at each other as people had to step into the road to get round them. Grace tried to take a deep breath and calm the hell down because this was Lily and they would get over this, they'd carry on being best friends for ever because—

'You know what you are, Grace? You're a fucking slag,' Lily spat, and it was the single worst thing *ever* to call your best friend. It wouldn't have hurt as much if Lily had called her a C U Next Tuesday, and it meant that calming the hell down wasn't an option any more.

'And you know what your problem is, princess? You can't handle the fact that I'm not your sidekick any more. I'm going out and doing exciting things and being flown all over the world and I have a three-thousand-pound Marc Jacobs dress . . .'

'Yeah – and what did you have to do to get it? I bet—'

'And you're pregnant and you're getting married and you know that your life is over, so don't take it out on me!' As soon as the words came tumbling out of her mouth, Grace realised that she wasn't just saying them as payback but that she actually meant them. Had been thinking it for months.

'Oh, fuck you, Gracie,' Lily hissed, and she might have been pregnant but she was still perfect, so when she stuck out her hand a black cab immediately came to a halt beside her in a furious grinding of its gears.

'We are done. I'm never speaking to you again, not after what you've just said.'

'Yeah, but *you* said—'

But Lily was slamming the cab door and she'd obviously told the driver that she'd tip him extra if he lead-footed it because he took off with an audible squeal, leaving Grace standing there.

It took half an hour to walk back to work, smoking five cigarettes in quick succession because Grace had this awful feeling that she and Lily were broken beyond repair. She couldn't begin to imagine how they could work their way back from this, and she wasn't sure she even wanted to after the things Lily had said. Horrible, hateful things that were forcing Grace to confront all the aspects of life with Vaughn that she tried not to think about any more. Because Lily hadn't said anything to her that Grace hadn't thought herself when Vaughn first propositioned her – and the ugliest truth of all was that she hadn't even considered telling Vaughn to stuff his arrangement. Not even during their fight in Miami when he'd spelled out her duties. Leaving him simply hadn't been an option. Or maybe leaving his money hadn't been an option, Grace wasn't sure.

There was no opportunity to dwell on this when she got back to the office. Lily was still crying, the other beauty girls crowded around her, but they all looked up as Grace walked through the door and she was surprised that she didn't immediately shrivel up and die from the condemning looks being thrown her way. Meanwhile, Maggie, the beauty director, was slipping out of Kiki's office just in time to send Grace a glare of utter loathing.

The effort nearly killed her, but Grace reached for the nearest box-file and started sorting invoices. Or rather she made three piles of invoices on her desk just for something to do as the beauty department must have told the art desk, who'd told the subs, who'd passed it on to the features team who'd filled in the fashion girls. Everyone was staring at Grace's reddening face, although Posy had just sent her an email with the subject heading: OMG!!! We HAVE to talk!!!

'I can't believe it,' Grace heard Bunny hiss in a fierce whisper. 'I mean, Grace isn't even *that* pretty.'

Grace heard Kiki's door open behind her. Out of the corner of her eye, she saw Maggie sweep back down to the beauty department where Lily was still sobbing, but in this muted, understated way that would have tugged at the heart of an Al Qaeda suicide bomber.

'Grace. In my office now.'

There wasn't one solitary sympathetic look as Grace got up and shuffled to where Kiki was standing in the doorway. She let Grace sidle past her, then slammed the door.

'Take off the boots,' was Kiki's opening salvo, which wasn't what Grace had been expecting.

'Um, why?' Grace mumbled, folding her arms behind her back, like she used to when she was called in front of her old headmistress.

'Because I told you to,' Kiki said coolly.

Grace knew that arguing would be futile. Awkwardly balancing on one leg, she unzipped a boot and carefully eased it off, then did the same with the other.

Kiki took them from her and didn't need longer than a second to ascertain their origins. Kiki had many faults but her ability to spot luxury leather goods wasn't one of them. She didn't give the boots back, but gestured to the hard-backed chair in front of her desk.

'Four is such a boring number,' she remarked as Grace sat down and noticed there was a hole in the toe of her polka-dot socks. 'Don't you think?'

Grace eyed her warily. She knew that the explosion was going to happen really soon, she just didn't know what the number four had to do with, well, anything really. 'Never thought about it.'

'Because when I add two and two together, I keep coming up with at least double figures.' Kiki smirked at her own cleverness. 'Care to fill in the blanks?'

Oh, where to begin? 'I'm not sure what you're talking about,' Grace hedged.

'I've had Maggie in here, which is always a pain, insisting that I have you court-martialled by HR while the entire office waits to see if little Lily miscarries due to the stress of finding out her best friend is a high-class call girl who'd rather entertain clients than attend her wedding. So, it's not really a surprise that you've got a pair of Fendi shearling boots, though I'm dying to know how you got fast-tracked up the wait list.'

Grace gulped and exhaled at the same time, which

immediately led to a choking fit. She was going to fucking *kill* Lily. She couldn't think of anything to say that didn't involve grisly details of just how she'd bring about Lily's demise, so she settled for answering the last question. 'I was in Miami this weekend and the Fendi there had a pair delivered by accident. And actually they were bought for me by a friend. A girl. Not a girlfriend. A friend who's a girl . . . fucking hell!'

'Oh Gracie, what mess have you managed to get yourself into now?' Kiki asked, and it still wasn't the whipcrack bark she'd been waiting for. It was amused, maybe even a little concerned, which completely spun Grace off her axis.

'I . . . it's hard to explain . . .' Grace spluttered, and typically, predictably, the tears began to punctuate what she couldn't even begin to explain. Not *again*. It was much easier to cover her face with her hands and give in to sobs that felt like they were being torn out of her.

It was humiliating to cry in front of Kiki, but every time Grace tried to stop, a fresh wave of tears began to spurt out. Then she felt a hand pat her head and looked up through tear-spiked lashes to see Kiki perched on the desk in front of her.

'Stop it right now,' she ordered brusquely. 'Everyone will know you've been crying and you don't want to give them that satisfaction, do you?'

Grace really didn't. She took a series of shuddering deep breaths, finished off with a couple of hiccups and blinked in surprise as Kiki pulled a bottle of champagne out of the mini-fridge under her desk and popped the cork.

'I don't have any brandy and you look like you could do with a drink,' she said, carefully pouring some champagne into a mug. 'Now what you say in this office stays in this office – unless you've done anything to bring the *Skirt* name into disrepute, in which case I'll have to fire you.'

Grace took the mug and knocked back the champagne in one long gulp. 'I am not a hooker. Or a whore. Or a fucking slag, as Lily put it,' she said fiercely. 'I'm just seeing this guy . . .'

Getting it off her chest took half an hour and the whole bottle of Taittinger. Grace stuck to the facts. That girl met rich, older man. There was mutual attraction and a Marc Jacobs bag. Which led to spending time together exclusively, designer dresses and very swank parties on both sides of the Atlantic, which were fantastic networking opportunities for a lowly fashion assistant.

'It's just a simple arrangement,' she said, though really it was anything but simple. 'And the places we go, well, I couldn't exactly turn up in a New Look dress, and he takes up a lot of my free time, which he reimburses me for. It doesn't mean that I'm a prostitute!'

'Hardly,' Kiki drawled, leaning back with a look of disappointment as she realised that Grace had reached the end and that further details wouldn't be forthcoming. 'Charles's main attraction was the large mutual fund that he manages, so what does that make me?'

'But you're married to Charles!'

'Well, that's neither here nor there,' Kiki said. 'And I wouldn't even have had one date with Charles if he hadn't sent me a single Christian Louboutin shoe with a note telling me I wouldn't get the other one until I had dinner with him.'

That sounded better than a tear-stained Marc Jacobs bag. Not better, but romantic. 'I wouldn't have thought that Charles would do something like that,' Grace said carefully because she'd met Charles only once and he'd been stodgy of build and personality.

'He has to – he's ugly but rich.' Kiki laughed. It wasn't her usual cackle but something warmer, more affectionate. She was full of surprises this afternoon. 'Come on, Gracie, you know exactly what I mean.'

'No, I don't,' Grace said indignantly. 'Vaughn isn't ugly at all. He's pretty OK looking. Kinda handsome, actually.'

'Rich and kinda handsome? Well, you've either hit the jackpot or you're in for a world of trouble.'

It was exactly half and half, Grace thought to herself. 'Well, let's say that one makes up for the other.' And it was the sort of clever thing that she never thought of to say very often and she could tell Kiki was impressed because she did her secret, amused smile that she usually only pulled out when she'd been sent something fabulous like a pair of Prada skis.

'Well, you weren't lying when you said you were working evenings and weekends. So, as a matter of interest, how much are you getting?' she asked without preamble, not even blinking or blushing though Grace imagined that the Botox had probably paralysed her blood vessels.

'He doesn't pay me to be his girlfriend,' Grace protested. 'Why does no one believe me? He gives me a monthly allowance and something on the top for clothing because he takes me to lots of parties and I need to dress the part and—'

'Yeah, yeah. How much?'

It was impossible to remain tight-lipped when Kiki's eyes had to say everything that her facial muscles couldn't. Her eyes were currently saying, 'Tell me, or I'll have you filling in Customs forms until you're ready for retirement.'

'Five thousand for the allowance, two thousand for clothes and I have membership to this spa. It's why I've been taking lunch-breaks – you wouldn't believe how much personal grooming I need,' Grace added rashly, because Kiki was giving her the oddest, most unnerving look. Like she was trying to circumnavigate the frozen face to show surprise. 'I know it's a lot of money. Like probably too much money, but—'

'And I imagine that at least twice a month you have to go to a gala or a ball and you need the kind of dress that you're not going to find in Topshop – formal, floor-length, ready-to-wear though you could get away with couture. And obviously you can't wear the same dress twice. Then there's cocktail dresses, day dresses, at least two pairs of designer jeans, bags, shoes, really good costume jewellery and a new coat every month. Coats are very important. They're all about that first impression . . .' It seemed as if Kiki was lost in her own private daydream, she'd even shut her eyes, but then she opened them again so she could fix them on Grace. 'I bet you have to use all of that monthly allowance too. In fact, how the hell are you managing on just seven thousand a month? Even fifteen grand would be a stretch.'

'Are you kidding?' Grace asked incredulously. 'It's a huge amount of money! It's like I was earning an extra eighty grand a year.'

'So, you've got money left over to spend on wool and sweeties every month, have you?'

'Well, no . . .'

'And just how rich is he anyway?'

'I don't know. I mean, I guess he's really rich,' Grace said helplessly, because talking about Vaughn's money and how much of it he had felt so tacky. The Business-Class travel, chauffeur-driven cars and fancy hotel suites were testament enough to Vaughn's riches, but once when she was waiting for him to finish a call so they could go out to dinner, she'd heard him say, 'Push him up to twenty-five if you can, but I won't go under twenty-three.'

Grace had thought he was talking thousands, until she'd glanced at the pad Vaughn was doodling on, counted up the noughts and realised he was talking millions. So even if his commission was only ten per cent, he'd cleared over two million just on one phone call. 'Really, really rich,' she amended.

'Then he's undercutting you,' Kiki said flatly and God, she was loving this, Grace could tell.

'He's not. He's been very generous.'

'Oh, he's been *very* generous and I bet he's got a nice bridge he could sell you too,' Kiki said, and this time she did cackle. 'Please tell me you at least tried to negotiate with him, Gracie.'

'Of course I didn't! He's giving me more money every month, in cash, than I've ever seen and he's taken me to Paris and Miami and we're going to Whistler for Christmas.' And the thought of that made Grace remember why she was having this bizarre heart-to-heart with Kiki in the first place. 'I get that Lily's upset, but I don't know how she could say all that stuff about me,' she burst out.

'She's a lovely girl but rather stupid,' Kiki announced. 'But really, Grace, why didn't you just tell people you'd bagged a rich boyfriend, instead of being so secretive?'

It was another freaky aspect to an exceedingly freakish day: Kiki being nice and understanding and making complete sense.

'Do you think Maggie will go to HR?' Grace asked anxiously. 'What did you say to her?'

'That you and Lily were both silly, self-dramatising girls and we should leave you to sort it out between the two of you,' Kiki recalled with relish. 'You know, Grace, this is the first bit of initiative you've shown. Of course, we all noticed that your hair no longer looked as if it had fallen on your head from a great height and Courtney said you were spending a lot of time in the cupboard on a BlackBerry, but we all thought you were looking for another job.'

Grace raised her eyebrows. She'd imagined that her day-to-day doings were not worthy of speculation. 'I'm not,' she assured Kiki. 'I love *Skirt*, you know that, right?'

'Don't think for one moment that just because I approve of your expedient relationship, you can start angling for a raise. Or a promotion, for that matter,' Kiki snapped – and it was almost comforting that she'd put her bitch back on.

'I didn't tell anyone because I thought they'd judge me,' Grace explained, and her shoulders sagged a little. 'Bit late for that now though.'

'They can judge you all they like, but there aren't many options for girls like us who are expected to maintain a certain lifestyle and don't have huge trust funds,' Kiki said bitterly. 'When I met Charles I was living on spaghetti hoops and fashion party canapés. I've been poor and I've been rich, and rich wins out every time. So don't you dare let any of those girls look down on you when they're being bankrolled by their families.'

Grace had never heard Kiki sound so passionate about anything that wasn't fashion-related. She knew her real name was Kimberley and Kimberleys didn't usually have huge, unearned incomes, so maybe Kiki did know where she was coming from because they came from exactly the same place.

'It's really hard sometimes when everyone runs out to get twenty-pound boxes of sushi and they think I shop at Primark as some kind of fashion statement,' Grace said.

Kiki leaned back in her chair and looked at Grace thoughtfully. 'Your problem is that you have to overcomplicate everything. Your outfits, your copy, your styling, your faux relationships – you're always adding too many embellishments, when you should just keep it simple. Simple is always better. As I just said, if you'd told people you'd bagged a filthy rich boyfriend from the start, then none of this would have happened.'

It was the first piece of really constructive criticism that Grace had ever had from Kiki. 'I suppose I should have,' she agreed. 'It would have made everything so much easier.'

'Well, "rich boyfriend" has a more respectable ring than "sugar daddy". I'm sure they'll all get over the shock eventually.' Kiki looked pointedly at Grace, then at the door. 'Go on, shoo!'

Grace got up, grabbed the boots, which Kiki was pointing at with an imperious finger and steeled herself for what lay behind the office door.

It was obvious they'd all been talking about her because as

Grace emerged, the chatter stopped and everyone appeared to be typing industriously. Which wasn't something that happened very often in the *Skirt* office.

Grace sat down at her desk, aware that the entire fashion department and most of features were half-expecting George, the security officer, to appear and escort her from the premises. She made an extravagant show of pulling out her BlackBerry and hit no 1.

Vaughn answered on the third ring. 'Grace, if you're about to launch into another fit of hysterics about Christmas, I don't want to hear it.'

Grace gritted her teeth. 'Yes, it's me,' she cooed, knowing that everybody was listening. 'I just wanted to thank you again for taking me to Miami this weekend. It was wonderful.'

'Are you on crack?' It was a perfectly reasonable question, Grace thought as she racked her brains for something to say that would let the entire office know that she was dating a rich man and wasn't a prostitute. Besides, it would mean she no longer had to hide her weekend case in the postroom or keep extolling the virtues of mineral make-up.

'Yeah, I miss you too,' she sighed loudly. 'Now don't forget you were going to email me with some Christmas gift suggestions for your mother 'cause I'm drawing a total blank.'

'As she's been dead for ten years that might be a little difficult,' Vaughn said dryly, but Grace could hear his voice softening slightly. Like he was amused and intrigued, against his better judgement. 'I take it that all festive obstacles have been removed?'

'All but one. I'm going to get on that now.' She dropped her voice to a whisper so she could add: 'But I'm still really, really mad at you. And I'll wear whatever colour tights I bloody well want to.'

Vaughn had something to say about that, but Grace didn't care to hear it. Instead, she hung up and went to the cupboard to call her grandmother. The day couldn't get any more horrific so it was as good a time as any to categorically state for the record that Worthing would have to manage without her over Christmas.

chapter twenty-one

When she woke up on 23 December, Grace was still tired and aching from the night before. She'd been to Vaughn's Christmas party, held at the gallery and, thankfully, arranged by his staff rather than herself, as she'd already hosted two dinners in London and New York for favoured clients. They'd been formal affairs in trendy restaurants, but the gallery party had been a strange cross between a sophisticated art soirée and an office knees-up.

Madeleine Jones's teenage emo daughter had been a really amusing diversion and Piers had got pinker and gigglier the more he drank, and he'd even tried to foxtrot with Grace in the back office when they'd gone to get some more glasses. It had felt a lot like fun until an hour into the party, when Madeleine had been despatched to Grace's side to tell her that Noah had arrived, already half-cut, and in dire need of a babysitter.

Since the dinner-party, Grace had seen Noah and Lola across the room at a couple of crowded parties. She'd spoken to Lola both times but only waved at Noah, though they were Facebook friends. That might have been why he'd greeted her like they were buddies from way back when she'd hurried over to the bar where he was trying to persuade the server to let him take a bottle of whisky.

'Gracie, I can't get through this sober,' he said, mournfully scratching what looked like three days' worth of stubble on his chin. 'Vaughn hasn't stopped glaring at me, even though I put a suit on.'

The suit consisted of a pair of paint-splattered jeans, an old Ramones T-shirt with a tie half-knotted round his neck and a blazer, complete with school logo stitched on the pocket. 'Vaughn's not glaring,' Grace lied, though he was definitely scowling. 'Why don't you start with just a couple of shots of whisky and I'll introduce you to some people.'

Then Grace had wheeled Noah around the room, pausing to talk to a couple of Vaughn's pet artists, then she'd snuck him on to the roof terrace so he could have a cigarette. He kept calling her sweetheart and teasing her about how her voice went up a couple of notches every time she talked to someone important, and Grace had let herself flirt back. Just a little, because for once it was nice to have some simple, uncomplicated boy do a little simple, uncomplicated flirting that wasn't going to go anywhere. Not until Noah had tried to stick his hand down the front of Grace's draped Derek Lam dress.

Grace had gently intercepted his paw. 'Dude, you're completely pissed and tomorrow you'll realise that trying to grope me was a bad move.'

'You and him exclusive then?' he asked, breathing whisky fumes in Grace's face. 'You just being sweet to me because you're under orders?'

'I'm a sweet girl,' Grace had insisted. 'And I'm Vaughn's girl so nothing's going to happen. Anyway, what about Lola?'

Noah shrugged. 'We have a communist relationship, you know?'

Grace didn't know, but she doubted it was anything to do with Marx or Lenin, and she didn't want to ask Noah what he was talking about and have him think she was stupid. 'Whatever. Let's have one more cigarette than we have to go back downstairs.'

Noah had backed off and they'd huddled against the wall

as they'd shared Grace's last Marlboro Light, Noah's bulk shielding her from the bitter wind. He had the build of a boxer who was on the verge of going to seed, but apart from that, he was precisely the sort of cocky, toxic bad boy that Grace used to throw herself at. It wasn't that her tastes now ran to richer, older and better groomed. It was more like she just didn't dare.

Especially when she'd seen Vaughn standing on the path a little distance away from them. It was too dark to see his face, but there was something very purposeful and still about the way he stood there which made Grace slide a few inches away from Noah.

'Grace, I need you,' he said mildly.

He hadn't moved as Grace hurried towards him, her breath crystallising in front of her. Vaughn followed her back on to the landing and, as they passed his office, he'd suddenly grabbed her wrist and pulled her inside. Didn't say a word, but pushed her up against the wall and kissed her with more passion than he'd shown her for weeks.

Now, hours later, as Grace hopped from foot to foot in the icy-cold bath in her icy-cold unheated bathroom, she saw that she had bruises on her hipbones from where she'd been pressed against the edge of his desk as Vaughn had fucked her. Not that she'd minded at the time. God, she'd moaned and whimpered until Vaughn had put his hand over her mouth because she was making so much noise and Noah was still out on the terrace. And when he'd done that, Grace had come faster and harder than she ever had before.

Since the row in Miami their *entente* had been less than *cordiale* – in fact it was as chilly as the cold December nights – but Grace's body had been so well trained, that just a firm stroke from Vaughn's hand or a whispered suggestion in her ear and it knew it was in for a treat. Which was infuriating.

Her life was definitely better since she'd met Vaughn but it was also a lot more complicated.

Grace's phone started ringing at the exact same moment that she had to leave if there was any hope of making it to Victoria to get the midday train to Worthing. She hoped it might be Lily finally getting over herself and calling to thank Grace for the £500 espresso machine she'd bought as a wedding gift with a loan she'd got from a finance company advertising on Facebook. December's allowances had run out around the fifteenth, despite all her creative solutions to the problem of party dresses. There had also been Christmas presents to buy and that old gnawing ache in her stomach that didn't go away even when she had brushed the dust off her credit cards, so she'd faxed the loan company her latest pay slip and they'd given her £2,000, most of which she'd blown on a Bottega Veneta bag she couldn't even bear to look at now.

Private number was flashing on Grace's phone so it could be Lily, Grace thought as she answered with a tentative, 'Hi?'

'Hi! Is that Grace?' asked a friendly voice, so obviously it couldn't be Lily.

'Yup, who's this?'

'Ms Reeves, I'm calling from North South Finance. We've sent you several final demands and left several messages for you about immediate repayment of—'

Grace's first instinct was to throw the phone at the wall. Hard. 'I've never heard of you,' she squeaked.

'We took over your debt from two of your credit card—'

'How can you do that? That can't even be legal!' Grace yelped as she shrugged into her Burberry Prorsum coat. 'Anyway, I've started paying off my cards. So if you tell me which one it is, I'll pay a thousand off next month. On the first, I promise.'

'We tried to contact you by email and post but, Ms Reeves, you've accrued so much interest and penalty charges that I've been instructed to call in the entire amount. I need an immediate payment of just over four thousand pounds or we'll have to use a collection agency to recover . . .'

Grace went with her first instinct and hung up. Then she switched off the phone, got on her knees and shoved it as far under the sofa as she could.

Vaughn had withdrawn his offer of a car to take her down to Worthing, but Grace wasn't that bothered about having to take the train. It didn't hurt to have a reminder that just as Vaughn gave, so Vaughn could take away as the mood suited him. Still, it was a mad scramble to make the train with two heavy suitcases, and it took most of the journey to Worthing before Grace stopped feeling as if she was about to hurl, though she didn't know if it was her hangover, the phone call she'd just taken or terror at the ordeal that lay before her.

Grace felt her skin grow clammy as she rehearsed The Speech. She'd been working on The Speech for fifteen years, like most people rehearsed their Oscar acceptance. The Speech would succinctly and scathingly reduce her mother to tears, before she admitted that she'd got back in contact, not for Grace's benefit, but just to make herself feel better. Then she'd get on the plane back to Australia and that would be that. Over. Done. Never to be heard from again after Grace had delivered The Speech in all its awe-inspiring, terrible beauty.

But when Grace was ushered into the front room, normally reserved for non-family guests, all she could manage was a wave limper than her own second-day hair and a muttered, 'Hi.'

Grace's gaze rested on her mother for two seconds before she lost her nerve but it was long enough to take in a tanned blonde with a slightly anxious smile. She felt her body give a quick jerk of recognition even though her grandparents had taken down all the photos when Grace had first come to live with them. All she had were hazy mental pictures of a thin, pale woman with mousy hair and a harried face, so the woman kneeling in front of the fire was an anomaly and

Grace's memories and grudges shifted and rearranged themselves to account for this slightly plump woman who had eyes the same colour as her own. She was holding a wriggling child in a ballerina outfit on her lap. 'Look, Kirsty, it's your big sister, Grace.'

Kirsty gazed at Grace in that mulish, 'I'm a toddler and I'm going to stare at you for as long as I want' way. Grace stared right back and waited for their shared DNA or irrevocable flesh and blood bond to kick in. It didn't. Also, someone needed to wipe Kirsty's nose.

'I'm Gary,' said a voice behind her. There were introductions to the second husband, and her grandmother wanted to know why she hadn't called from the station and it was still awkward half an hour later when they were balancing cups of tea and plates of mince pies on their laps. Her grandmother wouldn't stop harping on at Grace for her Christmas Day no-show while her grandfather grilled Gary and Caroline about the current state of the Australian economy. When that topic had been exhausted, Caroline kept asking Grace questions: how had her journey been? Had she been going to lots of Christmas parties? What part of London was she living in? Under her grandmother's most steely glare, Grace was forced to answer politely. Monosyllabically, but politely, as Kirsty lay on the floor and kicked her legs in the air – Grace knew just how she felt. Then she remembered that she'd bought a bagful of pink, glittery tat from Claire's Accessories, because her grandmother would have killed her if she'd turned up empty-handed and besides, none of this was Kirsty's fault.

Three-year-olds were very easy to please. Kirsty put on everything in the bag from fairy wings to bangles, beads and bracelets, so she looked like a pre-school drag queen. After that, she climbed into Grace's lap, though Grace tried to dissuade her, and launched into her entire repertoire of party tricks, which consisted of tuneless renditions of 'Row, Row,

Row the Boat', and some knock-knock jokes, which were mostly gibberish. Actually it was a godsend because it meant that no one could really talk about anything significant, and when Kirsty moved on to 'Twinkle, Twinkle Little Star', her grandmother went for a lie-down.

Grace could finally excuse herself 'for a bit of fresh air', and scurried outside to sneak a crafty fag behind the shed in the back garden. She'd barely taken the first drag when she heard the kitchen door open and saw Caroline coming down the path. She steeled herself for a confrontation, or worse, platitudes, but Caroline merely smiled and gestured at Grace's hand.

'Can I nick one?'

Grace proffered the packet, making sure that their hands didn't touch.

'This used to be my secret smoking place too,' Caroline continued at a breathless pace so Grace guessed that she was nervous as well. 'One year they dismantled the shed to put a new one up, and found piles of fag butts by the fence and a couple of empty Bacardi bottles. I blamed it on next door, but they didn't believe me.'

She really didn't want to, but Grace could feel her face stretching into a grin as she answered: 'It never mattered how much perfume I sprayed on myself or gum I chewed on the way home – and one time I even used mouthwash – the minute I got through the door, Gran would be all, "You've been smoking. I can smell it all over you."'

'So, Mum says your best friend's getting married tomorrow?' Caroline leaned against the fence and blew a few experimental smoke rings, as if she wasn't sure that she still had the knack.

'Yeah.' Grace had decided that Lily's wedding was the best option for a Get Out of Worthing Free card, followed by a winter skiing holiday, which was a surprise gift from her newly acquired, doting boyfriend. The fact that she wasn't actually attending the wedding was a mere technicality.

'And you and this guy – is it serious?' Caroline asked, like it was any of her business.

Grace stared at her feet. 'Still early days.' She glanced up to see Caroline watching her, and not even Vaughn looked at her so hungrily, like he was committing every gesture and grimace to memory. It wasn't much and it didn't make Grace hate her any the less, but it was something. 'Don't say anything to Gran, but he's older than me. A lot older than me.'

Caroline pursed her lips as she processed that information. 'I meant to ask, do you ever see Mark . . . your dad?'

Jesus! She'd only volunteered the information about Vaughn to be charitable. Not because she had a daddy complex. 'No,' Grace said shortly. 'Never. Guess there's a lot of that going round. Or there used to be.' She threw her cigarette end away and viciously ground it into the path with her foot. 'Why did you have to come back?'

From the calm look on her face, Caroline had been waiting for Grace to get down to business. 'Because I haven't seen my parents for fifteen years and they've never even met Gary and Kirsty.'

'So?'

'It was time. They're not going to be here for ever. When I talk to Mum, she spends ages going on about their various hospital appointments.'

Grace shoved her cold hands into her coat pockets. 'What? You talk to her regularly?'

Caroline sighed and pushed herself away from the fence so she could stand up straight because Grace was obviously in attack mode. 'Every week.'

'She never told me that,' Grace said sullenly, though having secrets was a family trait, like not being able to whistle or feeling the cold. 'Have you been asking Gran to butter me up? Because, you might as well know, I don't want you in my life. I don't want you calling me and emailing me with photos that totally clog up my inbox. You made your choice – just stick with it, will you?' It wasn't The Speech. It wasn't even The Speech Lite. It was like a badly recorded version of The Speech, but Grace could still feel herself trembling as hard as the tea towels her grandmother had pegged to the washing line.

'Grace, you've managed fine without me. Mum and Dad are so proud that you went to college and have a job on a magazine. They're always going on about you.' She pulled a face. 'Though I think they're just relieved that you got through your teen years without a pregnancy.'

It was the God's honest truth. In fact, Grace was convinced that on the day before her twentieth birthday, her grandparents had let out such a huge collective sigh of relief that it had caused a tidal wave somewhere off the coast of South-East Asia.

'You might be right there,' she conceded with a mere hint of a smile.

Grace had thought that seeing Caroline again would whip up fifteen years of hurt and resentment into white-hot fury, but now that her mother was standing in front of her, it was proving impossible to even maintain an icy dignity. Maybe her best revenge was simply that she was making more of a success of her life at twenty-three than Caroline ever had. Then Grace remembered that actually she didn't have a degree, her grandparents thought she earned £10,000 more than she really did and also thought that the reason it still said *fashion assistant* on the *Skirt* masthead was because the subs hadn't got round to changing it to *senior fashion stylist*. If they really knew, they wouldn't be even a little bit proud of her.

'For what it's worth, I'm glad you came down today,' Caroline said, because she'd mistaken that glimmer of a smile as proof that Grace was softening. 'I picture you as a little girl and now you're standing here all grown up. God, there's so much I want to say to you and I don't even know where to start.'

Grace opened her mouth so she could issue a furious disclaimer but her grandfather called from the back door: 'Gracie, the taxi's here to take you to the station!'

There was no time for anything other than a hurried goodbye while she prised Kirsty's arms from around her leg and insisted that no, she didn't need a lift to the station, that's why she'd called a cab.

They all stood on the doorstep waving, as if Grace was going off to war. As if they were one big happy family.

Grace buckled her seat belt before her grandmother could come hurrying down the path to tell her to do just that, and waved back. 'Please, can we go now?' she begged the driver.

She'd had this idea that as soon as the car had turned the corner of Linden Way, she'd start to bawl and never stop. But Grace's eyes were dry and itchy, as if she'd stayed up three nights straight in a really smoky room. It had to be her hangover coming back for an encore that was making her stomach lurch and her temples throb as if she was in for a world of pain once the headache kicked in.

chapter twenty-two

'You look very pale,' Vaughn announced when Grace finally arrived at Gatwick, dragging her suitcases behind her and inwardly berating herself for never being able to pack light. 'I didn't think you'd had that much to drink last night.'

'Enough,' Grace said weakly, checking herself before she could grab her suitcase. In Vaughn World you paid a uniformed airport employee to do all the shlepping for you. Luckily her feet could find the British Airway Business Travel check-in all by themselves, until Vaughn hauled her back.

'We're travelling first class,' he said shortly, and strode off before she could even thank him. Grace couldn't believe that he was still angry with her for trying to amend his Christmas schedule. Or maybe her wide-eyed ingénue routine was getting a bit boring and he hoped that she'd have acquired a more blasé attitude by now. Bearing this in mind, she kept her delight about the first-class lounge, complete with dining room and waiter service, to herself and hoped that she hadn't lowered the tone by detouring via the Duty Free shops to get fags, gossip mags and some lozenges because the dry, itchy feeling had migrated to her throat.

Grace wondered if she could risk a little doze as they waited for their flight to be called, but Vaughn was already opening his briefcase and presenting her with a stapled sheaf of papers. The itinerary, prepared by the ever-loving hand of

Madeleine Jones, ran to several pages and involved far too much ski instruction from some chump called Chip for Grace's liking. But mostly, Vaughn was fixated on tomorrow's lunch-party and finally, Grace got what the big deal was.

'Oh my God!' she hissed, when she saw the first name on the guest-list. 'Even my grandmother knows who he is!'

'If you act like some starstruck groupie, I'll tell Chip to take you down the black run,' Vaughn snapped, one finger tapping impatiently against another name. 'This is who you need to be concerned about.'

'Lucy Newton. Never heard of her.'

'Well, she used to be a model, though I think the highlight of her career was probably draping herself across the bonnet of sports cars at motor shows,' Vaughn said waspishly. 'What's important about her is that she's been with Martin Halpert for two years.'

Grace read the dry facts supplied. *Martin Halpert. Venture capitalist.* She was never sure what that meant, other than being richer than God. *Philanthropist. Art collector.* 'OK.'

'Poor Lucy's been given her marching orders; Martin has rather a short attention span, but he likes to make sure his companions will be financially solvent until the next billionaire comes along.'

When Grace got dumped, it was usually with a text message asking for the return of borrowed CDs, articles of clothing and duplicate keys. 'What do you mean by financially solvent?'

'Lucy's been with him for nearly two years so I imagine about two million dollars' worth of generous. Hopefully, in art, though I hear she's been seen in several Beverly Hills car dealerships, which is not something that makes me happy.'

'Why doesn't he just give her the money?'

Apparently the tax implications of giving your ex-girlfriend two mill in cash were very complicated. The pounding headache finally arrived as Vaughn explained the

finer points. 'I'm relying on you to get her on side,' he concluded, as their flight was called. 'You can be very disarming
when you put your mind to it.'

Grace doubted that very much. Vaughn seemed pretty
immune to it anyway. 'Well, I'll do my best,' she offered feebly.

'We'll talk more about it on the plane,' Vaughn promised,
as Grace started hunting through her bag for passport and
boarding card. 'You asked me to look after them. For God's
sake, Grace, focus!'

Spending Christmas in Worthing was starting to look like
the better option, Grace thought to herself until she turned
right when they boarded the plane and had to revise all her
previous notions of air travel.

There was an actual lounge with comfy bucket chairs and
a stewardess who couldn't wait to brandish a glass of
champagne at Grace, before she'd even found her seat. Some
hair of the dog that had savaged her the night before couldn't
hurt, Grace reasoned, and as Vaughn was offloading his coat
and briefcase, she downed it in one, but classily.

Then they were shown to their seats, although there wasn't
anything as prosaic as seats but pod-like demi-cabins with
wallpaper and loungers that folded out into full-sized beds.
There was no climbing over other passengers to sit down or
entering into tense negotiations on discovering that someone
had nicked her blanket either. Grace lovingly stroked the Anya
Hindmarch wash bag and velvet slippers that had been
provided and decided that there was something to be said for
the sugar that made the medicine go down that little bit more
easily.

Vaughn was being carefully cajoled into turning off his
BlackBerry and going to his own pod for take-off. 'We'll talk
more once we're in the air,' he told Grace as she snuggled
gratefully under her blanket. From the speculative gleam in his
eye, Grace suspected that he planned more than just a little
light conversation.

*

'Grace! Wake up!' A hand was stroking her face. Grace opened one eye to see Vaughn squatting down in front of her; a stewardess hovering anxiously behind him.

She opened the other eye and wished that she hadn't as the dim lights of the cabin made her head throb. 'Why haven't we taken off?'

Vaughn rolled his eyes. 'We've taken off, flown across the Atlantic and landed again.'

Grace stretched cautiously and realised that her seat belt was still fastened. She must have slept the whole seven hours with her mouth open as it felt like something had crawled into it during the flight and died. She'd never even got to experience the turndown service. 'You should have woken me,' she groused, trying to undo her seat belt with clumsy fingers.

'I did try but you were dead to the world,' Vaughn said, freeing Grace from her restraints and offering her his hand so she could stand up.

Being vertical made Grace feel dizzy and disorientated. It was only as they stepped out of the airport, after being whisked through Customs, that she regained full consciousness.

'God, it's freezing,' she whimpered, as an icy blast of air rushed to meet her, the cold scouring her face and hands as she scrabbled for her gloves. 'Did the plane drop us off in the Arctic Circle by accident?'

Vaughn was already hustling them towards a car and Grace decided that she'd never think another uncharitable thought about the sleek, black cars he had on standby, as she was cocooned in blissful warmth within seconds.

'You have brought proper cold weather gear with, haven't you?' Vaughn asked, giving Grace's Burberry coat a disapproving look.

She had. For London cold weather, which now seemed like

a tropical heatwave compared to the icy hinterlands of British Columbia. As they cleared the airport, all Grace could see out of the window was pitch-black night and white snow heaped as far as the horizon. 'I have lots of stuff I can layer,' she improvised. 'And I can hire a ski suit.'

Grace was saved from the inevitable lecture by Vaughn's BlackBerry. He spent the rest of the two-hour drive to Whistler on the phone, getting increasingly ratty as he tried to track down a painting that had last been seen in a packing crate in Berlin airport.

By the time they got to the hotel – yet another modernist, upscale boutique – his face was set in a painful-looking grimace. Even the unctuous reception they got from the hotel manager only managed to downgrade it to a scowl.

'This will do,' he remarked tersely, when the door shut behind a kow-towing porter and they were alone in a two-bedroom loft suite. He was already unzipping his laptop bag and checking the wi-fi access.

Absolutely no idea of priorities, Grace thought as she found the tea bags she'd stashed in a Ziploc and put the kettle on in the fully fitted kitchen. She walked back into the lounge and shuddered. The fire was roaring away but simply looking at the glittering white view from the big picture windows set her shivering.

'Do you want a cup of tea?' she asked Vaughn and got a nod in reply.

There was milk in the fridge but not much in the way of food. Grace tore open a carton of raisins, gave Vaughn his tea and began to unpack.

She was just hanging up the last dress, when she felt Vaughn's hands around her waist. 'Dinner in or shall we go out?' he asked, kissing her ear.

Grace could feel the beginnings of a really promising hard-on against her buttocks and Vaughn's hands were already creeping up to cup her breasts. For once, she wasn't turning into a puddle of formerly Grace-shaped gloop because the mere thought of getting naked and exposing her body to the elements made her shiver again.

Vaughn mistook the shiver for incipient lust and gently but firmly turned her around. Grace knew that she had to stop behaving like the soggiest of blankets just because her mother issues were still unresolved and it was a bit nippy outside. 'I don't mind ordering in,' she husked, though that was less about sounding seductive and more that her throat was still dry.

'Good girl,' Vaughn murmured, and it was the nicest thing he'd said to her in days so Grace leaned up for a kiss.

The moment that his tongue slid between her lips, Grace's head started to swim. Not in the usual swoony way that meant her insides were getting ready to melt but more like fainting was a possibility. All of a sudden, Vaughn's arms were holding her up rather than holding her tight as Grace slumped against him.

'What's wrong?' he demanded sharply, touching a warm hand to her forehead which, if it was anything like the rest of her, felt cold and clammy.

'Nothing, I'm OK,' Grace said quickly, as the world came back into focus. 'I'm probably just hungry from missing dinner on the plane.' She punctuated the sentence with a sneeze that morphed into a cough, which did nothing to ease the tickle in her throat.

'Are you going down with something?' Vaughn asked suspiciously, as if Grace was feeling peaky out of sheer wilfulness.

'I'm fine, really,' Grace assured him, swallowing down another cough. 'It's just the change in climate and sleeping too long. Get a hot meal inside me and I'll be back to my usual chipper self.'

'You're many things, Grace, but chipper has never been one of them.' Vaughn took her arm and led her back into the lounge as if she was an elderly relative who might keel over and break a hip if left unattended.

After a gourmet pizza that had shaved parmesan on it instead of the unidentifiable stringy cheese that Grace was used to, she went to bed.

Grace could have sworn that she didn't sleep at all. She spent the night on a constant repeat cycle of burning sweats, then convulsions as too hot suddenly became so cold that it felt like her blood had been replaced with liquid nitrogen. She must have dropped into a fitful doze at some stage, because she woke when suddenly the drapes were wrenched back, throwing beams of blinding sunlight across the bed. It felt like a million pointy implements stabbing at her cranium.

'Go away,' she croaked in a voice that was barely audible.

'What's the matter with you?' Vaughn was already dressed in an immaculate YSL charcoal suit, which made Grace feel even more like something that had been chewed up and spat out. She sat up, despite the painful protest of her aching muscles and pushed a lank lock of hair out of her eyes.

'I'm dying!' She flopped back and put her hands over her eyes to block out the light. 'Seriously, I think I've got flu.'

'Nonsense,' said Vaughn crisply. 'Probably just a head cold. You'll feel much better once you've had a shower.'

That was obviously meant to be Grace's cue to shake a leg but she curled up under the duvet. 'I can't.'

But she could for the simple reason that Vaughn pulled back the quilt, yanked a hand under her arm and hauled her up on to her own very unsteady feet. 'I don't need this today of all days. I let you have a lie-in. Now you've got two hours to get ready for this lunch. I don't need to tell you how important it is.'

Because he'd already spent hours doing just that – in mind-numbing detail. Vaughn made an impatient sound in the back of his throat as Grace stumbled to the bathroom, clinging to pieces of furniture as she went.

Grace sat on the floor of the walk-in shower as she washed

and conditioned her hair and figured that her body was clean enough from the shampoo to skip the soap part and move on to levering herself to the vertical position and slathering on moisturiser.

'What's taking so long?' Vaughn called, rapping sharply on the door. 'I want to go over some notes with you.'

'Go away,' Grace hissed to herself. 'Why can't you just leave me alone?' She tucked a towel around her and shuffled back into the bedroom to find Vaughn rifling through her wardrobe.

'Maybe this,' he decided, tossing her beloved Marc Jacobs frock on the bed with scant regard for its designer status. 'Or maybe this.' A purple Uniqlo sweater dress followed it.

Grace sank down on the nearest chair and huddled deeper into her towel. 'Vaughn, will you listen to me?' she said in a raspy whisper. 'I'm ill. Something is very, very wrong with me.'

Finally her words penetrated. Vaughn strode over, face squinched up like he thought she was faking and pressed a hand to her forehead. 'You're very cold,' he announced. He peered at her curiously. To show willing, Grace stuck out her tongue and croaked out an 'Aaaahhh,' that sounded like someone trying to kickstart a motorbike.

'When did you last have a flu jab?'

'Um, sometime like never.'

'Oh, for fuck's sake!' Vaughn whipped out his BlackBerry, stabbed at a couple of buttons and waited to be connected. 'Why the fuck didn't you sort out Grace's flu jab?' Grace looked on in amazement as he proceeded to give Madeleine Jones a vitriolic tongue-lashing, the likes of which even Kiki had never been able to achieve.

'Vaughn! It's Christmas Eve. Stop shouting at her.' Grace paused to cough – a wet phlegmy rattle that didn't stop even when Vaughn held his phone to her face.

'Can you hear that?' he ranted. 'Does that sound like a

little chill? I want a doctor here in ten minutes or you can start the New Year by looking for a new job.'

Vaughn was done ranting. Grace threw off her towel as the hot flush started and watched him cause havoc in her drawers as he rummaged through her underwear. She had a horrible feeling that she knew where this was going.

'Put these on!' he ordered, throwing bra and knickers at her, followed by a pair of tights. 'Where's your hair dryer?'

'I can't go,' she protested weakly, even as she hooked an ankle into her Coco Ribbon panties.

'Don't be such a baby,' Vaughn snapped, crouching down to help her. Desperation was not a good look on him. And he was much, much better at getting Grace out of her clothes, than into them. She was leaning against him as he pulled the sweater dress over her head when they heard a knock on the door.

'Doctor,' Vaughn said eagerly, rushing to answer the summons, as Grace tugged at purple wool that was going to slowly boil her insides. She collapsed back in the chair, strangely calm now because Vaughn would have to listen to a trained medical professional.

The doctor looked too young to be a trained medical anything. Grace suspected that he mostly strapped sprained ankles and referred more serious skiing injuries to the nearest hospital. Still, he shoved a thermometer in Grace's mouth, shone a light in her eyes and ears and throat and passed judgement. 'Flu,' he diagnosed succinctly. 'I'll prescribe you an anti-inflammatory but really you need bed rest and lots of fluid. Guess you won't be skiing this vacation.'

Grace smiled wanly and gave up a silent Hallelujah. 'Guess not.'

'But she's well enough to attend a little lunch-party,' Vaughn insisted forcefully. 'It's flu. It's not as if she has pneumonia.'

'Well, flu can be pretty serious . . .' the doctor, and Grace's current favourite person in the world, started to say, when Vaughn put a heavy hand on his shoulder.

'Can I have a word in private?' he asked in that silky smooth voice he always used when he was trying to persuade Grace to do something she wasn't sure about, whether it was ordering dessert or letting him bind her wrists to his bedposts.

Grace decided to dry her hair while the doctor told Vaughn in no uncertain terms that whatever he was proposing was against the Hippocratic Oath.

Vaughn returned on his own and with cheeks so flushed that Grace wondered if his own flu jab was up to date. 'You look much better,' he insisted, like if he said it then it had to be true. 'Now, let's get some war paint on.'

'What's the point? I'm not allowed to go, the doctor said.' It was really hard to sound authoritative when you had to choke at the end of each sentence.

Vaughn crouched down again to take her hands in his as he gazed at her so unwaveringly that Grace didn't even dare to blink. 'I've booked a car so you'll only be outside for a matter of seconds and when we come back here, I'll hire you a nurse, find you Lemsip – anything you want. But I need you to do this one thing for me, Grace.' He gave her hands a gentle shake as she tried to protest. 'You're going to be fine. The doctor left a little something to make you feel better. But put some make-up on first.'

'What is it?' Grace asked warily, but she knew that she was going to lunch, probably with some black market flu remedy in her, because Vaughn's force was far greater than her resistance. Besides, she didn't have any fight left in her. It took all her last reserves of strength to dab on a little highlighter and some lipgloss. The finished effect screamed crack whore.

'I suppose you'll have to do,' Vaughn sighed, surreptitiously producing what looked like a yellow pen from his breast-pocket. 'This will only hurt for a second,' he added, as he flicked off the top and grabbed Grace's leg in a tight grip.

'What wi . . . Fuck! What did you just do to me?' Grace gasped as she gave a sudden jolt, just like Uma in *Pulp Fiction*. She could feel her heart flipping over several times as the blood surged through her veins.

Vaughn didn't even have the decency to look embarrassed as he threw the empty syringe at the wastepaper basket. It missed. 'Just an adrenalin shot,' he murmured. 'It will give you some pep.'

Grace felt like she was having a heart attack – it was all she could do to take in huge gulps of air and listen to the faint gurgle of the central heating and stare at the patterns in the deep pile of the carpet, because as an added side-effect she had surround sound and extra-sensory vision now. It felt a lot like her one and only foray into acid and that hadn't ended at all well.

But then she could move, picking up her handbag and stuffing some tissues in it, grabbing lipstick and lozenges, and the effort no longer made her want to puke.

'See? You're feeling better already,' Vaughn looked out of the window. 'I think that's our car.'

Grace stared at him for as long as it took until he turned away from the snowy vista and met her eyes. 'I fucking hate you,' she enunciated slowly and clearly.

Vaughn shrugged and his lips quirked maybe a half of a millimetre upwards. 'I know,' he said, sounding not the least bit surprised.

chapter twenty-three

'I think it's a combination of jet lag and being in such close proximity to a film star,' Vaughn said to Robert Simmons, when he unsuccessfully tried to bring Grace out of her energy slump. The adrenalin shot had long since worn off. 'She's not normally so shy. Quite the opposite. Usually I can't get a word in.'

Grace tried to send him a dirty look but just thinking about narrowing her eyes made her head hurt. She didn't even have the energy to hate on the eight other people, who all laughed at Vaughn's comment as they sat in the private dining room of a restaurant that called itself a bistro, even though everything came heaped with black truffle shavings (including Grace's onion soup, which was the only thing she could swallow).

Vaughn was glaring at her from across the table, while simultaneously sucking up to Martin Halpert, who was an able-bodied Doppelgänger for Stephen Hawking. Then there was Robert Simmons, star of stage and screen, and a UN Ambassador who helped starving orphans and had an old skool Hollywood glamour that brought to mind Cary Grant by way of the Ratpack. In the flesh, he was so devastatingly handsome that Grace finally understood the meaning of over-trumpeted clichés like charisma and star quality. But his lunch-date wasn't his quirky, indie actress girlfriend but a quiet, homely-looking man in his forties who made Grace's Gaydar ping. And when Robert Simmons shook her hand (Vaughn had advised him not to kiss her because 'she's just getting over a cold, Rob'), Grace's Gaydar had practically vibrated. It was probably just as well that Vaughn had made her sign a non-disclosure agreement all those months ago.

The other two men were standard-issue, moneyed douche-bags. Both of them had blatantly checked Grace out, eyes lingering on her boobs and bottom, when they were introduced, but compared to the three other women at the table, Grace didn't measure up. Two of them had the slightly glacial features that Americans mistook for class: hair carefully streaked to what Maggie, the *Skirt* beauty director, called heiress blonde. Their breasts were maybe half a cup size too large for their frames and perky in a way that breasts aren't after the age of seventeen, without the efforts of a really good surgeon. Kelly wore Calvin Klein. Anna wore Gucci and both of them ordered the winter greens as a main course and had only one glass of the 1995 Gosset Celebris Brut champagne.

But Lucy Newton? She was one hot mess of an ex-motor show model. Everything about her was too much, from the Day-Glo tan, to the pneumatic tits, to the leopard-print Dolce & Gabbana dress she was almost wearing, to the huge amounts of vintage champagne she was knocking back like it was fizzy pop. If Grace hadn't felt like she had only twenty-four hours to live, then she'd have definitely wanted to hang out with Lucy. She was the kind of girl who was made for bar-hopping.

As it was, Grace couldn't even bring herself to make eye-contact. That would have required all her powers of concentration, which were currently being employed so she didn't collapse across the table. Even The Last Supper couldn't have taken so long, she thought forlornly, but finally they cleared away the cheese course and one of the douchey men said, 'You ladies might want to take coffee in the lounge while we talk shop.' It was like fifty years of feminism had never happened. Kelly, Anna and Robert Simmons's maybe-boyfriend were making noises about touring the wine cellar, but all Grace wanted to do was find the nearest sofa and fall down on it.

Grace had just made it to the door when Vaughn's arm clamped round her waist. 'Be back in a minute, guys,' he said jovially in a very unVaughn-like manner. Then it didn't matter that Grace was having trouble walking because Vaughn marched her down the hall so quickly that her feet barely touched the ground.

The waitress in the lounge looked up in surprise as Vaughn pushed Grace through the door. 'Get out!' he demanded. One glimpse at the thunder and lightning on his face and she was gone.

Grace stared longingly at the couch but before she could negotiate the five steps to get her there, Vaughn practically lifted her up and threw her down on it. Then he placed his hands on the cushions on either side of her head so he could get right up in her face. Grace could have individually counted each one of his pores if she'd had a mind to.

'You're not even trying!' he said menacingly in her ear. 'You've had an adrenalin shot, so why the hell are you sitting there like a wet weekend in Wigan?'

Grace leaned back as far as she could, which was a matter of mere millimetres. 'I'm ill.'

Vaughn's smile was as icy as the view of snow-capped mountains out of the window. 'Boo hoo. You're ill.' He cupped Grace's chin so she couldn't look away from the uncompromising, couldn't-give-a-fuck set of his features. 'If you screw this up for me, Grace, then God help you.' He didn't specify just what assistance the Almighty would provide but Grace got the message.

She turned her head and before she could start to splutter, Vaughn let her go. He watched her hack out another cough with his arms folded, then turned on his heel and left.

She was beyond tears, which was a Grace Reeves first. Instead, she popped another lozenge in her mouth and curled up in a tight ball on the couch, as the shivers seemed to turn her body inside out, then back to front.

The door opened just as Grace was struggling to get her shoes off, and Lucy Newton staggered in, a bottle of champagne clutched in one red-taloned hand. 'Oh, I think we just had lunch together,' she said in a high-pitched breathless voice, like she'd been inhaling helium.

'Yeah,' Grace agreed. She was meant to be launching into the hard sell right about now, but she couldn't remember her Abstract Expressionists from her YBAs. 'I'm Grace.'

Lucy was fiddling with her Louis Vuitton clutch. 'Have you got a light?'

For the first time that day, Grace managed to do something right and handed Lucy her disposable lighter. Then she pulled out her own crumpled pack of cigarettes. The nicotine could hardly make her feel any worse and it might even numb the ache in her throat.

Lucy came and sat next to Grace so they could share a saucer as a makeshift ashtray. The other girl was clutching at herself and rocking slightly as if she was having a psychotic episode rather than just being very, very drunk.

'Are you all right?' Grace ventured softly.

Lucy gave Grace a limpid look from artificially blue eyes, then the foundations of her face began to crumble. 'No,' she said, fighting back tears. 'I'm pretty fucking far from all right. That bastard, I gave him the two best years of my twenties!'

It wasn't difficult getting Lucy on side. Though Grace wasn't sure that's what she was doing as she stroked the other girl's surprisingly soft platinum-blond hair and told her not to cry. She was just down with her pain.

'Look, you can do so much better than him,' she advised when Lucy had come to the end of a long, tear-soaked rant about how Martin's lawyer had told her that she had to vacate the Bel Air mansion no later than 15 January. 'You're gorgeous and he looks like he fell out of the ugly tree and hit every branch on the way down. No offence.'

Lucy stared at her in amazement. 'But I love him!'

Grace stared right back. 'Really?'

'I know he's not much to look at, but the handsome ones don't try so hard. And Martin looked after me. He made me feel safe but now he's sniffing around some preppy bitch who looks like she came off the WASP assembly line, and siccing his lawyer on me. I can't believe he's doing this!' Lucy finished on an anguished wail that made Grace's headache feel like a migraine. 'You should be taking notes, honey. Don't think this won't happen to you.'

It would happen to her, Grace knew that. Probably sooner rather than later, if her performance today was any indication. But, on the other hand, she'd gone into this knowing she had an expiration date because Vaughn had never lied to her. In fact, he'd spelled out just what an objectionable wanker he was in unflinching detail, but Grace had been too distracted by the shiny things she was going to buy, to pay attention to the small print.

'Speaking of Vaughn . . . look, Lucy, he wants me to talk about your . . . your . . . leaving gift. Like, maybe you might want to think about investing in some art?' She pulled a face, as Lucy's eyes glazed over, then coughed and said, 'Fuck art! Where are you going to live?'

'Well, my boyfriend before Martin bought me some property. I have a place I sublet in New York and this sweet little condo in Silverlake but it's not a Bel Air mansion with a room just for my shoes.'

Lucy Newton might walk and talk like a Barbie doll, but she knew how to pick her boyfriends. 'OK, so what are you going to ask Martin for?'

Diamonds. A limited edition Bugatti sports car designed by Hermès. Part share in a private jet. 'Oh, and I definitely want a new fur but mostly I want Martin to realise that he's in love with me.' Lucy swigged from the bottle of champagne. 'Fat chance of that, isn't there?'

Grace squeezed her hand. Having a front-row seat to Lucy's pain and humiliation was really taking her mind off her own impending death. 'Do you think you might be interested in some art though?' Grace wished she wasn't sucking quite so badly at the hard sell. 'I can't even remember who the good artists are, but Vaughn buys stuff that isn't worth shit, holds on to it, then flogs it a few years down the line for a gazillion times what he paid for it.'

The door had opened in the middle of Grace's speech and Kelly, Anna and the maybe-boyfriend of Robert Simmons trouped in, yapping on about some dude who'd just sabred a bottle of champagne.

'But I don't know anything about art,' Lucy protested, as the man sat down with a cup of coffee.

'It's Grace, isn't it? I'm Eric,' he said, turning to Lucy. 'Sweetie, invest in art. I wouldn't put a dime into a hedge fund with the economy the way it is, but the art market's still pretty buoyant. I bought a Basquiat for twenty thousand dollars fifteen years ago and just had it valued at nearly three million. And don't even ask me how much my Keith Harings are worth.'

'Not diamonds?' Lucy breathed.

'You get a good uncut stone worth a few carats and your money's all gone,' Kelly declared, leaning against the arm of the couch. 'So, what does Vaughn think the next big thing is?'

They all turned to look at Grace, who tried to visualise the words on the crib sheet that Vaughn had made her memorise. But she couldn't remember and it had become cloyingly hot in the room, so she settled for clawing at the neckline of her dress, which felt like it was choking her.

'You should talk to him,' she croaked. 'He's here for the next few days and I know he closed on some big acquisitions before we left London.' Vaughn was *always* closing on some big acquisitions and it sounded better than pleading ignorance.

Anna was already brandishing her phone. 'Let's swap digits,' she commanded. 'I know Al is after a particular light installation but I'm really into figurative pieces, y'know?'

Grace didn't know. Didn't much care. But she had one phone number.

'Robert's going to talk to Vaughn about some pieces for the place we just bought in Aix-en-Provence, but I'll give you my number too.' Eric sighed. It was conclusive proof that Robert Simmons was a far better actor than Grace could ever have imagined. 'If I leave it to him, he'll bring home yet another Jeff Koons.'

Lucy was definitely wavering. 'But I already made an appointment to look at a jet,' she said. 'It has hand-embroidered leather seats.'

'Give Grace your number,' Anna snapped. 'And don't buy any piece just because you like the colour.'

Grace tipped her head back and took in tiny sips of air, as the room tilted around her. 'I'm getting property this year. It's so cheap at the moment,' Kelly was saying. 'I'm just about to close on a sweet little apartment building in Florence, on the good side of the Arno.'

Grace didn't think she'd ever felt so out of place as she did right then in her stupid itchy chainstore dress, with no severance package in place for her imminent severing and a head that felt like it had swelled to twice its normal size.

The waitress came back with fresh coffee. 'Can I get anybody anything else?' she asked.

Water. Or tea with honey and lemon. Anything to lubricate her parched throat. Grace tried to get the girl's attention and lifted up her arm only to watch it fall back down as it deliberately ignored the messages her brain was sending.

'You're bright red,' someone said. 'Are you OK?'

Grace had only fainted once before and that was after she'd taken a dodgy E at Glastonbury. That time, the friends she'd been with had left her in the tent to sleep it off. This time she had many, many people whose combined incomes probably added up to the GNP of a small country fussing around her. The restaurant owner was insisting loudly that it couldn't have been anything that she'd eaten, as Grace lay flat on the sofa, Vaughn holding her hand, while a man in chef's whites felt her pulse.

'Poor thing,' Vaughn murmured, brushing Grace's hair back, and he was only being nice to her because he had an audience, but Grace nuzzled against him. He was the only familiar thing at hand and she needed to keep him close.

'She should probably go to ER,' the chef said and Vaughn nodded.

'I just want to go home,' Grace whispered, but home was across an ocean and wasn't really a home, just a place where she slept.

But Vaughn seemed to know what she meant. 'Can you help me get her to the car?' he asked the chef, who was twice Vaughn's size and scooped Grace up like she weighed nothing and carried her out.

It seemed to take ages, and a cast of thousands including their driver, the hotel manager and another doctor who was waiting for them when they got back, before Grace was lying on the sofa in their loft suite.

There were too many questions being fired at her but Grace just lay quietly trying not to cough because when she did, all she could taste was the consommé she'd had for lunch. She was never going to have onion soup again for as long as she lived.

Finally the doctor left and Vaughn was the last man standing. 'Bed,' he said firmly, and Grace wanted to clean her teeth and have a shower and get out of the bloody dress and burn it but she let him gently tug her towards the downstairs bedroom.

He took off her dress and tights, even sponged her down, but all the time Grace could sense something expectant about him. Like, he knew this wasn't the time or the place, but he just couldn't help himself.

Vaughn closed the curtains, put a bottle of water on the nightstand, even tucked the duvet around her, and when there was nothing left to do, he still lingered. 'Is there anything else you need?'

Grace took pity on him. He couldn't help what he was and maybe she was finally starting to understand that. Besides, the sooner he went away, the sooner she could sleep. 'My phone,' she whispered hoarsely.

'Your phone? Do you want to speak to your grand-parents?'

'There are numbers on it. Lucy's, one of the blondes', and the guy – I said you'd call them.' Talking hurt. Really hurt, but she wasn't finished. 'Didn't even remember the cribs – they talked Lucy round, not me.'

'Grace . . .' Vaughn's usually impeccable posture had deserted him and his body hung limp. 'I . . . I don't know what to say. You must think—'

'Whatever,' she sighed, not even having the energy to hit the beat on the second syllable like she usually did. 'Just promise me that you'll look out for Lucy and not dump her with some shitty painting you've been trying to offload for ages.'

'I wouldn't do that!' Vaughn sounded indignant, which actually was rather comforting. Contrition really didn't suit him.

'Yeah, you would,' Grace mumbled, fighting to keep her eyes open for a couple of seconds longer. 'I know you.'

*

Usually when Grace was under the weather she loved to curl up with some DVD boxed sets while doing a languid impersonation of Camille. This time around, there was far too much snot and sweat for that and when she wasn't sleeping, all she wanted to do was go back to sleep.

Vaughn popped in at regular intervals to get updates but left the heavy lifting to Blessed, the day nurse he'd hired, a cheerful, middle-aged Jamaican woman who sat by Grace's bed reading crime novels with really lurid covers and couldn't make a decent cup of tea.

It was late afternoon on the third day of Grace's confinement when she woke up and thought that she might be feeling a little better. The fact that she wasn't lying in a pool of her own sweat was a good indicator and her head felt like it was almost normal size again.

Vaughn was on the phone in the living room but he turned round instantly when Grace opened the bedroom door after a slightly shaky shower. 'I have to go, I'll speak to you later.' He blocked Grace's path to the kitchen where she was hellbent on making a brew so he could cup her face. 'How are you?'

'Like I just have a cold instead of pleural pneumonia,' Grace said. 'I'm dying for a cup of tea.'

'I'll make it. You go and sit down.' Vaughn was already brushing past her and Grace was tempted to exploit his guilt for all it was worth, but still . . .

'Please let me make the tea,' Grace begged him once he'd put the kettle on and was about to add the milk first, which was an offence punishable by death. 'You won't dunk the bag enough times.'

'You're definitely feeling better,' Vaughn snorted, moving to open the fridge, which was full to bursting with cartons of soup, juice, eggs, bread and fruit. 'Madeleine faxed the hotel over a list and they got one of the local shops to deliver.'

'So you're not firing her?' Grace squeezed the tea bag

against the side of the mug with a spoon. 'Or was that her last duty before she put her belongings in a cardboard box?'

'Madeleine's put up with much worse from me,' Vaughn said slowly. He took the mug that Grace pushed towards him. 'I was rather keyed up on Christmas Eve and you bore the brunt of that. Come on, let's go and sit down and you can tell me what you'd like to eat.'

If you squinted really hard, and possibly used a microscope, it was Vaughn saying sorry, without actually saying sorry. 'You were horrible,' Grace told him, as she sat down next to him on the couch. 'A complete bastard, who cares more about earning his commission than anything else. You have severe emotional problems but whatever, I'm over it.'

Vaughn looked sceptical. 'You don't sound as if you're over it.'

But she was. Grace had had nothing to do over the last few days but think, and she kept coming back to the same conclusion. 'I can't believe you stabbed me with an adrenalin shot,' she sniffed, because she wanted to see him squirm a little. 'But y'know, if I had stayed in England and had flu there, Lily would still have forced me into my revolting bridesmaid's dress and up the aisle. Her mum would probably have held a gun to my head, just to be on the safe side.'

'I never asked how that all went,' Vaughn said casually, and they both knew that he hadn't asked because the thought hadn't occurred to him. 'How did she take it?'

Lily and Dan had been joined in holy matrimony at about the time that Grace was doing her dying swan act. Actually, having flu had taken her mind off all sorts of things that Grace hadn't wanted to think about, and now they were leaking back and taking up all sorts of neuron space that could be better used for cataloguing her shoes. 'Lily went ballistic, which was understandable, but when I told her about you she said a whole bunch of stuff and then I said even worse stuff and she went back to the office and told everyone that I was a prostitute.' She gave Vaughn a lopsided smile. 'Well, at least I'm out at work now.'

'You should never let secrets fester,' Vaughn admonished, but that was easy enough for him to say. There was a small moment of excruciating tension between them and then he traced a line from the tip of Grace's nose to her chin. 'You missed Christmas. I could probably persuade someone to rustle up a turkey dinner if you wanted.'

'Rather have scrambled eggs on toast.' Grace looked at Vaughn from under her lashes. 'I could make you some too, if you like.'

Normal service had been resumed. Grace pretended to forgive Vaughn and Vaughn pretended to be penitent and in the gap in between they bickered gently about the correct way to make scrambled eggs so they were moist rather than runny. And later when Grace was the good, mellow kind of drunk from the generous amounts of single malt whisky with which Vaughn kept topping up her hot honey and lemon, they opened their Christmas presents.

Obviously it was better to receive than to give. Much, much better – but Grace liked the giving too. Maybe buying perfect presents was another one of her superpowers. She had a knack for the quirky and the unusual and the gag gift that didn't actually make the recipient gag, but Vaughn had been Grace's hardest challenge yet. She knew all sorts of dark secrets of his: the emphatic little grunt he gave when he came, the sour-sweet smell of his morning breath, the nicotine patch he still wore, but actual facts that could lead to the buying of actual presents was harder. It had been a Herculean task, but she was proud of the little cache of beautifully wrapped presents she placed on the coffee-table. Wrapping gifts was another one of her nascent superpowers.

Grace suspected that Vaughn's presents had all been gift-wrapped by shop assistants under Madeleine Jones's watchful gaze – but she was still secretly thrilled by the sheer size of her haul. Her grandparents had never spent more than fifty pounds total on Christmas and birthdays so she couldn't help but bounce a little as she unwrapped Agent Provocateur underwear that was maybe a little too coquettish for her tastes, another Marc Jacobs handbag with matching purse and key fob because it had been quickly established that he was her favourite designer, and two boxes from Tiffany's.

'Open the larger one first,' Vaughn said, watching her closely as if he didn't want to miss a second of her reaction.

Grace didn't have to fake her sharp gasp. 'It's beautiful,' she breathed, carefully lifting up the delicate necklace of aquamarines, diamonds and pearls randomly strung on a platinum chain. There was a bracelet to match.

'Tiffany's don't actually sell tiaras,' Vaughn informed her. 'And you have no idea how hard it is to buy jewellery for someone with grey eyes. Turn round so I can put the necklace on.'

Grace scooched round and lifted her hair so Vaughn could fasten the clasp. Then he was leaning forward to fasten the bracelet too. Grace allowed herself to rest against Vaughn's chest because it felt so nice to lean on someone else for a little bit. She still had a slight fever and the necklace and bracelet felt cool against her skin, but not as cool as Vaughn's fingers, as he encircled her wrists with his hands, and all of a sudden she didn't feel quite so safe, more like she'd been collared and cuffed.

She blinked and everything that had been soft focus in the glow of the fire and the haze of the whisky shifted and became sharper. Then Vaughn kissed the nape of her neck – a sweet, unnecessary gesture that made Grace will away the dark thoughts. She lifted her arm and turned it this way and that so she could see how the stones in the bracelet sparkled as they reflected the light.

'I've never had so many presents and they're all so beautiful,' she said, wriggling out of Vaughn's hold, so she could turn round and kiss him very gently on the cheek, which made him smile. 'Thank you so much. Now open mine.'

Her presents seemed a little shabby now: an Art Deco pair of cufflinks, a fancy pedometer, *The Thin Man* boxed set because Grace liked to think they had a Nick and Nora Charles vibe, a box of hand-made chocolates . . . but Vaughn tore into his presents, like he couldn't wait to get to the toy surprise, scattering paper and ribbons on the floor.

Grace could tell instantly that he was delighted with her gifts, turning each one over carefully, eyes soft with pleasure. He came to the last present and pulled out the scarf she'd knitted him with wool she'd found that was exactly the same shade of blue as his eyes. Even though things had been pretty awful between them since Miami, she'd still spent hours making the scarf on tiny delicate needles using tiny delicate stitches that would probably result in her being officially blind by the time she was thirty.

Vaughn pored over the scarf without saying a thing, holding it up to his cheek to gauge the softness, running a finger over the edges. 'You made it yourself,' he announced. 'Grace, it must have taken you ages.'

'It was no big deal.'

'It is a very big deal.' Then Vaughn wrapped the scarf around his neck and smiled a big, dorky smile. It was the single, most adorable thing Grace had ever seen him do. 'No one's knitted me anything before.'

Grace returned his smile and they were almost having a moment, which didn't happen very often. 'If I'd had enough wool, I could have made you a matching hat or maybe gloves.'

'You've already given me quite enough,' Vaughn said, piling up his presents so carefully that Grace wondered how often he was the giftee and not the gifter. Not very often, she decided, and made a little promise to herself that on the weeks when he wasn't driving her to utter despair she'd get him a little present. Nothing fancy, but she was a firm believer in giving gifts, and not simply to celebrate special occasions, but just because.

Vaughn was ripping the shrink-wrap off *The Thin Man* boxed set and Grace snuggled deeper into her corner of the couch as he got up and walked over to the TV. It hadn't been her best Christmas ever, but it hadn't been the worst either, so she was still ahead on points. She also had a feeling that Vaughn was still feeling guilty about the way he'd behaved on Christmas Eve, so he'd probably be on his best behaviour until 2 January at the earliest.

chapter twenty-four

Four days later, Grace sipped a mojito on the terrace of a penthouse apartment overlooking the Recoleta in Buenos Aires and watched the Eurotrash party hard around her.

The people around her had an over-glossy, over-groomed, so-over-everything look and everyone danced as if everyone was watching – Grace always danced as if no one was watching. She saw a petulant girl snap her fingers in a waiter's face because her champagne wasn't chilled enough, while her friends had a competition to see who could hoover up the most lines of cocaine off a glass coffee-table, the way Grace downed shots of tequila when it was payday.

Grace sighed as she saw the same oily guy who'd tried to chat her up twice already, heading in her direction. She put down her drink and went to find Vaughn.

The penthouse belonged to a photographer who'd made his fortune from semi-pornographic, highly stylised ads for cigarette and car companies. Maybe that was why there were so many barely legal, barely dressed girls in attendance. Grace glanced through an open door to see a girl on her knees sucking off a man while people stood around and watched, their expressions bored rather than titillated. The whole scene made Grace feel contaminated, as if the skeeviness was an airborne toxin and she needed to hold her breath to stop inhaling great big whiffs.

She finally saw Vaughn at the other end of the huge open-plan living space. He was talking to a large man who was red in the face and sweating profusely, bulbous belly straining against his white shirt. In fact, there wasn't a lot of talking because the other man was too busy jabbing his finger into Vaughn's chest.

As she got closer, Grace saw Vaughn lean in to say something. She could tell from the set of his jaw and his humourless smile that it was something if not outright rude, then flippant, obnoxious and guaranteed to get a rise. She'd been on the receiving end of those barbed remarks enough times to recognise the signs.

It wasn't really a surprise when the man lunged at Vaughn, shoving him up against the wall as Grace broke into a teetering run.

'You undercut me like that again, I will fuck you up!' the man spat in Vaughn's face. 'You're an arrogant piece of shit.'

'Vaughn? I want to go. *Now!*' Grace planted herself firmly between Vaughn and his attacker without even thinking about it. If she had thought about it, she'd have kept her distance because, well, she'd never been made of brave. 'Please. I'm getting a headache.'

Vaughn made a great show of whipping out his pocket square and wiping his face, as if the other man had spittle issues. 'Of course we'll go,' he said easily. 'Carlos's parties aren't what they used to be. He invites the most appalling people.'

Grace heard the other man snarl and she was sure he was going to lunge again and she'd be crushed to death between Vaughn and the other man's beer gut. Trust Vaughn to goad him a little bit more, rather than making with a speedy getaway.

But then the snarl turned to a laugh and the man took Grace's hand, which she'd been holding up in a gesture that she'd totally stolen from Diana Ross. 'The new girl,' he drawled, planting a fleshy kiss on Grace's knuckles, which made her want to squirm. She *did* squirm when his eyes moved to her breasts and stayed there.

'That's quite enough, Raoul,' Vaughn clipped out, because the man would have to have a really tacky name.

But Raoul wasn't done yet. Still not taking his eyes off Grace in her shocking pink Preen minidress, which still showed approximately seventy-five per cent less skin than the other girls' dresses, he sneered: 'You always did go for the mundane, Vaughn. I've never been able to fathom your choices.'

'And yet, two years down the line you're happy to jump on the bandwagon and tell anyone who'll listen that you got there first,' Vaughn said smoothly. Grace let Vaughn take her hand and pull her away from Raoul and his really powerful body odour.

Grace could feel Vaughn's fingers trembling slightly and for the first time she felt sorry for him. Confrontations weren't so much fun when you were the one who was being confronted.

'Well, that was bracing,' Vaughn said in her ear, and even above the music and the chatter, Grace could tell that he was striving for a lightness of tone and falling short.

'This party is completely creeping me out,' Grace said, shuddering. 'I don't want to see the New Year in here.'

Vaughn wasn't moving towards the door, but towards the bar, and short of digging in her very spindly heels, Grace had no choice but to follow as he still had her hand clutched tight. When he did let go, it was only to grab two bottles of champagne.

'Glasses,' he said to the barman, who didn't miss a beat but handed Vaughn two flutes. 'You should probably take a third bottle,' he told Grace, who frowned but did as she was told because when Vaughn was being this bossy, it was easier to follow his commands and not talk back. 'OK, now we can go.'

*

The streets of Buenos Aires were dark and deserted. Restaurants were shuttered, bars were closed and apart from a few cars speeding past, intent on getting to their destination before midnight, there was an unnatural stillness to the night. Vaughn had told her that most places were closed because the Argentines preferred to celebrate at home.

They couldn't find a cab so they started walking. It was hard to balance with two fragile glasses in one hand, a chilled bottle of champagne in the other and her clutch bag tucked under her arm, and in four-hour heels that had passed their comfort threshold forty-five minutes ago.

'Don't pay any attention to Raoul,' Vaughn said, breaking the silence that had fallen between them. 'He's a vulgar arriviste with more money than sense. There's no need to look so upset.'

'I'm not upset,' Grace told him, swaying slightly. 'Not now, but I don't like scenes and that party was one gigantic, horrible scene . . . and my feet are killing me.'

Vaughn glanced down at Grace's silver Roland Cartier sandals. 'Are they what you call limo shoes?'

'More like taxi shoes,' Grace said with a wince because the balls of her feet were on fire and she had a blister blossoming on her littlest left toe that chafed painfully every time she took a step. 'Is it nearly midnight?'

'We've still got an hour,' Vaughn replied, glancing at his watch. 'It's not exactly an auspicious start to the New Year.'

Grace opened her mouth to agree with him, then paused and looked around at the wide avenue and the ornate edifice of the Alvear Palace Hotel looming behind them. But it was more than that. It was New Year's Eve and a warm night in Buenos Aires with a man she'd only known for four months, but he bought her diamonds, treated her orgasms as a top priority and drove her absolutely, teeth-clenchingly mad at least once every day. 'Could be worse. I spent one New Year's

Eve on a night bus, another one throwing up from a dodgy curry, and definitely one in A and E.'

'Well, when you put it like that, I suppose wandering the streets of Buenos Aires does have a certain exotic appeal,' Vaughn said, like he wasn't exactly sure what it was.

'We have champagne,' Grace reminded him, 'and we'll still be able to see the fireworks. If we could just find somewhere to sit and drink, we're golden.'

Vaughn gazed around the empty street. 'You're not particularly religious, are you?'

'God, no! Why?'

'Church steps.' Vaughn tilted his head to the left and Grace didn't need to ask directions, she was already hobbling over to the Nuestra Señora del Pilar. Vaughn got there first and was already laying down his jacket with a flourish for Grace to sit on, in one of those gallant gestures that seemed innate, no matter how annoyed he was with her at any one time.

Grace wanted nothing more than to sink down but, 'Vaughn, that's your Dries Van Noten jacket.'

Vaughn was already sitting and tearing the foil off one of the bottles. 'It's only clothes.'

'Why would you say something like that when you know it upsets me?' Grace pouted, as she sat down with a grateful little sigh. 'Only clothes? It's never only clothes.'

'I think this is one argument that I'm not going to win.' Vaughn eased the cork out of the bottle carefully but the champagne still spurted out frothily from being jostled. Grace squealed in genuine alarm as a few drops landed on her dress.

She held out the glasses but Vaughn was already swigging straight out of the bottle. He grinned when he caught the scandalised expression on her face as he handed Grace the bottle. 'I promise I didn't backwash,' he said solemnly, eyes twinkling. 'Oh, stop being such a princess and have a drink. I think we should both get disgustingly drunk.'

As a plan, it got Grace's vote. She made a big show of wiping the neck and then took a generous gulp. They sat there for long moments, hardly talking until something occurred to Grace. 'How come I've never seen you drunk? You must have a very strong tolerance to alcohol,' she mused.

Vaughn leaned back on his elbows. 'I just don't drink as much as you.'

'Whatever! You always order wine with dinner and brandy afterwards.'

'Yes, but I never refill my glass and you're too busy refilling yours to notice,' Vaughn explained without any note of censure. 'But tonight I'm going to match you swig for swig and we're not going back to the hotel until all the bottles are finished and one of us gets arrested. Probably you, as it will be a first offence and they'll be lenient.'

'Second offence, actually.'

'Don't even try that one, Grace. You've never been arrested – you have absolutely no follow-through,' Vaughn stated with utter certainty.

'Well, shows how little you know because I have. Fingerprinted and everything,' Grace said smartly before she remembered that it wasn't a charming, funny story to see them on their way to inebriation.

'Admit it, you once got a stern look from a policeman and that was as far as it went,' Vaughn drawled, when Grace refused to be drawn on the details. He was already a good halfway down the first bottle, his usually impeccable posture the first thing to go, as he lounged back on his elbows. Then he had the audacity to nudge Grace so she nearly spilled her own bottle, which he'd made her open after he'd decided she might still be contagious.

'Don't do that!' Grace snapped as she slopped champagne, at ten dollars a swallow, over her leg. And she must have been a little drunk by now because she instinctively raised her knee and licked it off. 'It's a really lame story . . .'

'Tell me.' Vaughn lifted his elbow again and Grace sighed in defeat.

'OK, then.' She kicked off her shoes, even though she was pretty sure she'd never be able to get them on again. 'I was in town one day, Worthing, because this was, like, six years ago . . .'

'So, you were seventeen?'

'If you're going to interrupt then I'm stopping right now.'

Vaughn mimed zipping his lips shut because he was a surprisingly amiable drunk and she continued. 'So, it was a Saturday afternoon and I was in town and I saw my dad coming towards me.' She grimaced at the memory of her father with his two little boys, one on his shoulders, one swinging on his arm. 'And I hadn't seen him for ages because there was this whole thing with the custody and child support, so I'm getting ready to smile and he just walks right past me, like I wasn't even there. I knew he'd seen me because he'd been looking right at me . . .' Grace tailed off and took a huge medicinal gulp of champagne.

'What happened next?' Vaughn gave her an expectant sideways look.

'Nothing much. I went home but I was really mad about it and that night I was out with my friends and I got really pissed and went round to his house to break his windows.' None of Grace's friends had thought it was a good idea, apart from Angie whose own home was equally broken and was the bad seed best friend you always had when you were seventeen. Grace's grandparents had hated her, which had just made Angie even more alluring.

'You should so do that,' she'd enthused as they'd sat on a park bench drinking cider.

Grace had tried to chicken out until they got to the house and she'd seen the windchimes hanging up in the porch and the two cars parked on the drive and a swing-set in the back garden – all proof that her father didn't want reminding of what a cock-up Happy Families v.01 had been. That was when she'd taken the brick Angie had found in a skip and lobbed it through the front window.

Her aim had been straight and true. The window had shattered inwards with a deafening crash.

'Angie ran off as soon as the window broke but my big mistake was waiting for him to come out so I could call him a wanker,' Grace said with a shaky, self-deprecating laugh. 'And he shouted at me, and his wife, who's a fucking heinous bitch, called the police.' Grace paused for more champagne. 'The cops didn't even want to press charges but he insisted. Said I needed to be taught a lesson.'

They hadn't put her in a cell because it was obvious, despite the caked-on make-up and the perilously short skirt, that Grace was a nice girl from a nice part of town who had Daddy issues. Mainly that her daddy was standing outside the interview room, where Grace had been put by an understanding WPC, and demanding that she was charged with aggravated assault and criminal damages.

It had ended two hours later when her grandfather turned up wearing a raincoat over his pyjamas to persuade all parties concerned that Grace should be let off with a caution. 'Then I was grounded for six months,' Grace told Vaughn, who was now sprawled on the steps, his head in her lap. 'The only reason I did so well in my A-levels was because I wasn't allowed to watch TV and they took the plug off my stereo.'

'Poor Grace,' Vaughn murmured. 'If it's any consolation, your father sounds like an utter bastard.'

'Yup, he really is. My mum's even worse.' Christ, the champagne was like truth serum. 'Y'know she was there when I went back to Worthing the day we flew to Whistler? I have this cute little half-sister who my mum's going to fuck up because that's what she does. But sometimes I wonder if she did fuck me up or if I just use it as an excuse.'

'Grace, don't,' Vaughn said, reaching round with an unsteady hand to pat her back, which seemed to unlock something inside her so the words were spilling out unchecked.

'You know, I didn't graduate from St Martin's, right?' Grace tugged a lock of Vaughn's hair to make sure he was giving her his undivided attention. 'I walked out just before my final show because that was the week she had Kirsty and she decided to get in touch for the first time in years. I remembered that she wanted to be a fashion designer too but she got pregnant with me and didn't take up her place at art school. She taught me to sew. I had this little dress form and she'd help me cut out patterns and sew them up. I've always told myself I walked out because I was scared I was going to turn into her, but maybe, secretly, deep down, I knew I wasn't good enough and it was easier to jack it in than fail horribly.'

'You could always go back and finish if you wanted,' Vaughn said carefully, as if he knew he was crunching over eggshells. 'I have some sway at St Martin's.'

Grace shook her head. 'No, there's no point. I even got rid of my sewing machine – dumped it on the side of the road and took up knitting instead.' She wiped her hand across her eyes, not even caring that she was smudging her mascara. 'God, I don't know why I'm telling you this. I've never told anyone before.'

Vaughn glanced up at her and sighed. 'I think if you cry at New Year, it's the same as crying on your birthday. You'll have bad luck for the whole year.'

It was sweet, Vaughn trying to jolly her out of her funk, but Grace ignored him. 'I swear to God, that's why I got flu. It was being so stressed out about having to breathe the same air as her. Bad shit always happens around my parents. They're like lightning rods for bad shit.'

'Don't be so melodramatic. You got flu because you smoke too much and you never button your coat,' Vaughn said, turning his head so he could press an unexpected but sweet kiss on Grace's forearm. She ruffled his hair and decided that Vaughn needed to get drunk more often.

'I think I've officially overshared,' Grace said, because the situation needed lightening up before she smashed the bottle and tried to slit her wrists. 'Try not to judge me too harshly, OK?'

Vaughn didn't say anything, just craned his neck at what had to be a very awkward angle so he could have another swig. Then he rested his head back on her thighs with a blissful sigh. 'I used to be a fat child,' he announced. 'A very fat child. I had no friends and I was bullied at school. Hiding my clothes when I was showering after PE, then forcing me to run naked around the Quad, was a very popular pastime.'

'That's awful!' And actually explained a hell of a lot, from the faint cobwebbing of silvery stretchmarks across his hips to the machinations when it was time to order dessert.

'I don't drink very much now because when I hit my growth spurt at the very advanced age of eighteen and slimmed down, I decided to spend what was left of my youth acquiring all sorts of bad habits.' Vaughn's lips twisted. 'I got sent down from Oxford and at twenty-three, I was shipped off to rehab after I'd signed my trust fund over to my drug dealer. Apparently, I have a very addictive personality.' Vaughn sat up and reached for the last bottle of champagne.

Grace instinctively placed a hand on his shoulder. She didn't pet or stroke him but tried to convey what she was feeling: empathy, tenderness and maybe a little pity through her fingertips. 'C'mon, Vaughn, it's in the past. You're a fine, upstanding member of the community and you got over your addictions, didn't you?'

Vaughn sat up and popped the cork of the last bottle and drank steadily like a man who was determined to reach oblivion. 'Now I'm addicted to making money but that's acceptable.' He paused to take another swig of champagne.

'I'm starting to remember what it feels like to be drunk and it's not as much fun as it used to be.'

Grace didn't know what to do. She needed Vaughn to be in control because God knows, she wasn't capable of being the designated adult. And she couldn't handle him sitting several feet away from her with this awful lost look on his face that she didn't know how to wipe away. But she could try at least.

'I do have some funny stories from my teen years,' she said desperately. 'Ask me anything about the age of fifteen, when I dyed my hair pillar-box red and my grandmother came into the bathroom and thought I had a head wound, through to nineteen, when I did acid at a party and thought I had multiple personality disorder for six months afterwards.'

Vaughn turned his head and, yay for her, he was smiling, though Grace could tell that he didn't want to be cheered up, but he was a heterosexual man and when she pressed him ('Come on. One-time only offer – ask me anything'), she knew what he'd choose.

'How did you lose your virginity?' It was dark, but Grace would have bet her new diamonds that Vaughn was blushing because honestly, how predictable.

She took a deep breath. 'I was sixteen and it was with Paul Gold because we'd been going out for two weeks and he said he'd dump me if I didn't.' Even at sixteen, Grace had had an unerring knack for finding boys who would treat her like crap. 'We did it in his dad's Ford Mondeo while it was parked on the drive and, yes, it was a major disappointment. Then the next day his mum was giving their elderly neighbours a lift to Tesco's and they found the used condom down the back of the seat.'

Vaughn snorted with laughter just as Grace had intended, which was why she'd glossed over the part where Paul had told all his friends what a crap shag she'd been and how she'd cried at the crucial moment. 'I don't think anyone has a good first time,' he remarked, finally putting down the bottle.

'How did you lose yours then?' Grace asked. She was starting to feel as if she'd drunk her way to sober.

Vaughn gave in without a struggle. 'Well, it was in Saint Tropez, which sounds glamorous, but the venue for my deflowering – can boys be deflowered? – was an abandoned, ant-infested ice-cream hut. I had bites all over me for weeks afterwards.' He smiled and Grace smiled back though it wasn't a happy smile. But then, maybe neither of them had many happy stories to share. 'What else? I was eighteen, a late developer as I said, and she was older than me, the sister of someone I was at school with.'

'See? You did have some friends!'

'He wasn't my friend. That's why I fucked his sister.'

'But you were into her for a while, right?' she asked, because she wanted it to be true. Vaughn could be a bastard, for sure, she knew that better than anyone, but he wasn't a stone-cold bastard.

Vaughn shook his head. 'No, I just fucked her and made sure I told her brother about it afterwards.' He put his head in his hands. 'It wasn't one of my finer moments.'

They sat there in silence, both steeped in memories of the bad times. Eventually Vaughn closed the distance between them so he could loop his arm around Grace's shoulders and hold up his watch so she could see the second hand getting closer to the twelve.

The fireworks started with thirty seconds to spare. There was an avalanche of bangs and the entire sky lit up so one moment it was glowing a ghostly, smudgy pink, the next it was streaked with a rainbow of sparks.

'Five, four, three, two, one.' When the hand hit the twelve, Vaughn chastely kissed Grace's cheek. 'Happy New Year,' he said flatly.

Grace didn't want the year to start on such a despondent note, soured by past regrets. 'C'mere,' she slurred, and lifted her face so she could kiss him properly, which involved hair-tugging, tongue and a lot of enthusiasm even if the champagne had completely destroyed her technique. 'And Happy New Year to you,' Grace said firmly, when she pulled away. She looked around the empty square and sighed. 'Argentines really don't get the whole New Year thing.'

Vaughn staggered to his feet like a comedy drunk and Grace thought he might topple down the last three steps. 'I never used to get a headrush.'

Grace stood up and yes, she was definitely on the way to sober and it didn't feel that great. She shoved her throbbing feet back into shoes that felt as if they'd been lined with razor blades and limped after Vaughn, who was standing in the middle of the road and trying to flag down a passing police car that he'd mistaken for a taxi.

After walking for what felt like hours but could only have been a few minutes, they found a cab. Vaughn had recovered from the bad trip down Memory Lane and was attempting to snog Grace, while she tried to make sure that the driver, who had shifty eyes, took them to the Four Seasons and not to a scrub of wasteland where he'd steal their money and leave them for dead.

As soon as they were in their suite, yet another suite with incredible views and two bathrooms, Vaughn had Grace pressed against the door and his hands up her skirt. His usual finesse was lacking, but he more than made up for it with eagerness. Grace knew from bitter experience that he'd never get beyond half-hard and wildly optimistic.

'Let's get more comfortable,' she suggested, wriggling free and tugging Vaughn towards the bed because if they had sex against the wall he'd probably drop her. She flopped down, Vaughn following so excitedly he almost fell off the bed. 'OK, how do you want me?'

Vaughn didn't answer. He had a deep frown of concentration on his face. Grace prodded him with one finger. 'Vaughn? Do you want me to go on top this time or . . .'

'Oh, *crap*!' Vaughn was already jack-knifing off the bed, one hand clamped over his mouth, as he cannoned off an end table in his rush to get to the bathroom. Grace sat up as she heard the unmistakable sounds of the contents of his stomach being regurgitated. That seafood dinner earlier probably hadn't been a good idea.

It seemed to go on for ages. Just when Grace thought Vaughn must be finished, it would start all over again. She knew he'd want his privacy so he could retain maybe, like, a shred of dignity, but she couldn't ignore his pain. He'd looked after her when she'd had flu. Well, technically he'd made her feel a lot worse by giving her an adrenalin shot, then he'd paid someone else to look after her, but he'd tried.

Stopping en route to grab a bottle of water from the mini-bar, Grace tentatively knocked on the bathroom door. There were a few more retching sounds by way of a reply. She sent up a silent prayer and pushed open the door.

Vaughn was on his knees, hugging the toilet. He looked up briefly so Grace got a good view of his red face and streaming eyes, then bent his head again.

'Oh, poor Vaughn,' Grace cooed, crouching down so she could rub circles on his back. He'd be furious about the baby talk as soon as he'd got all the booze and lobster out of his system, but right now, he could just suck it up. 'Come on, better out than in.'

Grace was philosophical about throwing up. First you got pissed, then you puked, then you passed out. But Posy and Liam and Ilonka from the flat upstairs always freaked out, and from his groans and gasps, Vaughn was too.

Eventually Vaughn was done and leaning against the wall to try and get his breath back. The skin around his eyes was a mottled purple from all the burst blood vessels and he was covered in a fine film of sweat – and definitely off his game because he let Grace run a flannel over his face.

'Are you all right now?'

Vaughn closed his eyes. 'No.'

'You should probably brush your teeth, that always makes me feel better. Then I drink as much water as I can so I don't get such a bad hangover.' Grace peered at Vaughn's contorted face.

'Stop hovering,' he bit out, getting to his feet with all the grace of a day-old elephant. 'I'm going to have a shower.'

That would have been Grace's next suggestion. Vaughn started to unbutton his shirt, then stopped. 'I don't need an audience.'

Grace held up her hands and backed away. 'OK,' she said, fighting to keep the hurt out of her voice. 'Just yell if you need me.'

Vaughn was already turning away. 'Shut the door on your way out.'

chapter twenty-five

They flew back to a London that was carpeted in a thick drift of snow. Grace stared out of the car window at pavements covered in sludge, sooty banks of ice heaped against the side of the road and pasty-faced people trudging grimly through it with their hoods up and their heads down. After the icy white majesty of Whistler, it was kind of lame.

'So I guess it's been snowing while we were away.'

Vaughn didn't even dignify Grace's comment with a response. Though he came pretty close to an eyeroll. But then he'd been monosyllabic ever since he'd emerged from the bathroom after his pukeathon.

He'd woken up the next day with a killer hangover but that had been twenty-four hours ago and he was still treating Grace like it had been her idea for him to fall off a wagon that she didn't even know he'd been on. On the plane he'd avoided Grace's first-class pod after the seat-belt sign pinged off and when she'd eventually sought him out, he barely looked up from his laptop. 'I'm busy,' he said. 'Go away.'

And so they came to the end, not with a bang, but with an absolutely deafening silence. This wasn't how Grace had imagined it. She would have fucked up in some huge, colossal way sooner or later. A fuck-up that would have made all her other fuck-ups seem trivial in comparison. But what had she done that was so terrible, apart from soothing Vaughn's fevered brow and not once complaining about the stale smell of vomit in the bathroom the next day? It was because the power balance had briefly shifted in her favour for maybe half an hour – and for Vaughn that seemed to be an absolute deal-breaker.

By the time the car nosed carefully into Montague Terrace, Grace's lips were sore from all her worried nibbling. 'You can just let me out here,' she called to Jimmy, the driver. 'You'll never be able to turn the car around.' If she'd been concentrating instead of angsting, then she'd have made him stop on Junction Road.

'Don't be stupid. You can't drag all your luggage through the snow.' Vaughn wouldn't speak to her but apparently arguing was a completely different story. 'What number is it?'

Grace gave in to the inevitable. She was on the outs – it didn't really matter if Vaughn saw where she lived. 'Number seventeen, it's right at the bottom.'

Number seventeen was the red-headed stepchild of the street. All the other houses had been gentrified by the assorted Chloes and Jacks who did something at the BBC or the *Guardian* and had moved in with their antique brass door knockers and job lots of Fired Earth paint so they could restore their mortgaged-to-the-hilt Victorian terraces to middle-class splendour. Whereas Mrs Beattie, the slum landlady of North London, had simply got her octogenarian handyman to come round and paint Grace's front door a fetching shade of electric blue last year.

Cringing slightly, Grace was painfully aware that Vaughn was peering over her shoulder. At least the peeling paint, crumbling masonry, and even the mattress, which had been dumped in the front garden long before Grace moved in, was buried under heaps and heaps of lovely snow. It almost looked respectable.

'Well, I guess I'll be seeing you,' Grace said in a voice devoid of hope.

Vaughn nodded in agreement or dismissal but just as Grace started her usual awkward scramble for the car door, his arm curved around her waist, his intention unmistakable.

Vaughn's mouth moved on hers as gently as his hand traced the curve of her cheek. It said all the words he hadn't spoken to her over the last two days, but most of all it said goodbye. Grace held herself very still until it was over and Vaughn tapped on the window for Jimmy to open the door. 'Don't leave anything behind,' Vaughn said pointedly.

As she stepped out of the car, the wind tore at Grace's face, which was the only reason why her eyes watered instantly. It took her two trips to get all her luggage and yank it up the steps, carefully avoiding the middle one which was on the verge of collapse. Grace made sure the car was slowly reversing up the Terrace before she opened the front door and watched her frozen breath curling in the frigid air of the hall. Central heating was for pussies and people who didn't pay their rent weekly in cash.

As ever, Eileen had thoughtfully left Grace's post, the usual teetering pile of envelopes, on the hall table. She scooped them up and stuffed them in her duty-free carrier bag.

Even that wasn't enough to send her back to reality with a jolt. That happened when she shouldered open the door to her flat, flicked on the light switch and realised that the electricity had gone out. A quick rummage in her purse and then a frantic search through her collection of fifties china pots netted the grand sum of seventy-two pence – not enough to nip out to the newsy's and charge up her PowerKey.

Standing there in her £2,000 coat, Grace wondered for the millionth time why her life was such an abject lesson in irony. Still, she decided wearily, she could manage until tomorrow without electricity. She could light some candles, climb into bed and think warm thoughts . . .

But before anything else, like sorting out her laundry and unpacking her presents and railing at the injustice that flavoured every single part of her life, Grace needed a bath. Even travelling in first class didn't prevent the scent of eau de plane clinging to her.

Getting undressed was no fun. Each strip of flesh exposed to the air sprang to life with painful goosebumps so her skin looked like an oven-ready chicken.

Bundled into a thick bathrobe and with woolly socks and Uggs on her feet, Grace stumbled down the stairs on tiptoe because she wasn't in the mood for Eileen beetling out of her lair to start jabbering on about the binmen, the suspicious comings and goings of Ilonka and Anita on the second floor or, God forbid, her late husband, Alfred.

Grace made it to the safety of the unheated, shared bathroom and its bilious green tiles, which no amount of Cillit Bang could ever buff up, set her wash bag down on the windowsill and mentally prepared herself for the ordeal ahead. When you lived in third-world conditions in a first-world country, a girl learned a few tricks. Like, if she ran the bath with only hot water, within minutes it would be warm enough to sit in for the time it took to soap up, rinse off and then be back shivering on the freezing cold lino.

'This is good for your soul,' Grace muttered under her breath. Her grandparents were very pro things that were good for the soul or character building. They were always things that Grace hadn't wanted to do, like getting up at some ungodly hour to do a paper round or taking a GCSE in Physics. Grace's soul had to be practically glowing with all the good she'd done in its name, she thought glumly as she grappled with the taps. The hot one was always a little stiff, unless you jiggled it slightly to the right. A sudden wrench, which nearly dislocated her wrist, and Grace was good to go.

There was an ominous gurgle, followed by a rattling in the pipes, before a drip of rusty water trickled out of the taps. Grace stared at it transfixed, waiting for a hot gush to spill forth. Instead the pipes kept clanking like an ex's of Lily's who'd been really into body piercings.

That was when Grace noticed that the water in the loo was frozen over. There was a solid block of ice in her toilet bowl. A solid block of *yellow* ice. Her life was not meant to be like this.

There was nothing else to do but plonk herself down on the edge of the bath, the cold enamel chilling her skin even through the plush terry towelling, and burst into tears. She was all out of other ideas.

Eventually the pity party in her head was penetrated by a loud ringing sound. Some thoughtless bastard was leaning on the doorbell, and if it was Anita or Ilonka who'd forgotten their keys *again*, they were going to get a high-pitched lecture about frozen pipes and not phoning Mrs Beattie, and peeing in iced-over toilets.

'What are you doing here?' Grace yelped in surprise, when she yanked open the door to see Vaughn standing there. For a second her heart rallied – maybe he'd seen the error of his extremely conflicting ways.

He held up her knitting tote. 'You left this under the seat,' he said, eyes everywhere all at once: on her tear-streaked face, her Uggs, and over her shoulder at stained wallpaper and torn carpet and oh God . . .

'Thanks,' she grunted, making a swipe for the bag, which he adroitly hoisted out of her reach.

'What's the matter? Have you been crying?' he asked sharply, stepping past Grace into a building she'd vowed he'd never enter and striding towards the bathroom, where the pipes were still making clanging noises.

'You can't go in there,' Grace squawked, catching hold of his sleeve, but Vaughn brushed her away as if she was made of air.

When Grace caught up with him, he was staring at the toilet as if he'd never encountered modern plumbing before. Or plumbing that was modern sometime in the 1940s.

'Good God,' he whispered. 'Why isn't there a radiator in here? No wonder your pipes are frozen.'

Grace flapped her hands but said nothing.

'Why aren't you using the bathroom in your flat anyway?' Vaughn continued and it was hard to distinguish between the icy fingers of fear trailing down Grace's spine and the onset of hypothermia.

'I'm having it done up.' The lamest lie ever came shooting out of Grace's mouth at a rate of knots. 'I should have told you. The whole place looks like a building site.'

Vaughn was already turning. 'What floor are you on?'

'No, you can't go up there,' Grace pleaded, and panic was making her voice catch so Vaughn looked at her suspiciously. 'There's really no point in getting dust over your coat.'

'I asked you what floor?' It was the voice Vaughn had used when he was being spat at by Raoul; the voice that Grace had never wanted to hear when he was talking to her. 'I can tell when you're lying. You're not very good at it and you're turning into a block of ice in front of me so, again, *what floor?*'

The tears rallied for an encore presentation, which just made Vaughn sniff contemptuously, his elegant, aquiline nose rosy red in the Arctic wastes of the bathroom. 'It's the first floor,' she said, 'but I don't see why you need to go up . . .'

Grace was talking to empty space, so all she could do was trail up the stairs after him as Vaughn took the steps two at a time. He really wouldn't have been in such a hurry if he knew what lay in store for him.

With mood lighting coming from a million little candles, Grace's two rooms looked cosy, like a little country cottage kitted out in retro soft furnishings that she'd snagged from the bi-monthly *Period House* magazine sales at work. Shabby yes, but shabby chic. When there was actual electricity so the plug-in radiator was working and Grace could iron her sheets before she got into bed to warm them up, it was almost homely.

But with harsh winter sunlight spilling in so she could watch Vaughn slowly take it all in, it looked like a dump. Because he made it look like a dump with his polished brogues on her threadbare rug and his beautifully cut Prada suit sharing space with the damp patches on the ceiling and the mould collected around the windowsills. Vaughn couldn't take his eyes off the neatly stacked piles of plastic-wrapped clothes and magazines, sealed tight so the damp wouldn't get at them.

'This is a pit. Why do you live here?'

Grace could have bluffed her way through some explanation. A trust fund that hadn't quite come through yet, money needed to pay for her grandfather's hospital bills because 'actually didn't I tell you he's got some mysterious ailment that has the medical community completely foxed?' She could have come up with *something*. But the way Vaughn was standing there, with his mouth clenched so he wouldn't inhale the clotting whiffs of mildew, huddled into his coat so he didn't brush against any contaminated surfaces, meant that all Grace could muster was a tight little voice, which made her throat hurt because the truth was always painful. 'I earn fourteen thousand a year,' she said dully. 'Y'know, what you'd spend on a really good bottle of wine.'

That made the mask slip off Vaughn's face so he was flaring his nostrils and flushing with something that wasn't guilt or shame or anything that Grace could properly identify.

'No one earns fourteen thousand a year,' he stated unequivocally. 'Not in the media. What have you been spending your allowances on?'

Grace shut her eyes but when she opened them again, she was still standing in her freezing cold flat with Vaughn staring at her like he was seeing her for the very first time.

'I had a lot of clothes to buy,' she started, but she could tell right away that a long, garbled explanation about how expensive it was to maintain a certain sartorial standard wouldn't go down too well. That she was blaming Vaughn for not giving her enough money, when that wasn't the case. But she couldn't find anything else to say, so she simply shrugged and hoped that might say it for her.

'If I were you'd I'd have worried less about shopping and more about finding somewhere else to live. Not to put too fine a point on it, this place is a shithole,' Vaughn said crudely and deliberately.

'Excuse me?'

'Or maybe slumming it is what all the cool kids are doing this season.'

It was hearing him drawl that out, as if her pitiful living conditions were actually a lifestyle choice, instead of a source of misery and frustration, that made Grace forget her shame. 'You patronising bastard!' she hissed, fists clenched at her side. 'You have absolutely no fucking idea what it's like to be born without a silver spoon rammed up your arse. You live in this little cocoon where nothing touches you and if it does, you throw money at it until it goes away. Well, I can't do that – and how dare you fucking judge me for it!'

'Grace, don't talk to me like that,' he clipped out, and usually that was enough to have her toeing the party line again. But not this time.

'Why the fuck shouldn't I?' She was shouting now, while her arms flailed helplessly. 'Apparently I live in a shithole but it's *my* shithole and I can say what I bloody well like.'

'You're getting hysterical,' Vaughn noted, like that was any newsflash. Grace felt as if she'd done with hysterical and was quickly approaching a full-blown psychotic break as she dropped to her knees and began hauling out her collection of shoeboxes from the side of the sofa so she could hurl them at him.

Vaughn stood there motionless, even when one of the boxes glanced off his shoulder, and watched the mess of final demands and bailiffs' notices float around his feet. 'You want to know the really funny thing?' Grace screamed, and she knew she was screaming because she could hear herself screaming, but she didn't know why or how to stop. 'I've got no money, I never have any money but I'm really, really good at spending it. I spend hundreds of pounds on stuff I don't even want but I can't even afford to top up my fucking electricity meter. Go on! Try the light and see if it works. Put on the television that I'm not going to pay off until I'm eighty, and—'

'Pull yourself together,' Vaughn snapped at her, crunching over paper so he could take Grace's shoulders and give her a good, old-fashioned, teeth-rattling shake. 'Stop crying, stop screeching like a fishwife and get dressed. You're absolutely freezing.'

Vaughn gave Grace a little push in the direction of the pile of clothes she'd discarded half an hour ago while he crouched down and began picking up the debris from the floor, eyes scanning all those numbers and words that she always studiously avoided.

There was nothing remotely sexy about the way he watched her pull on her clothes, though he'd once told her that watching her do a reverse striptease was far more seductive than when she was getting naked. This time he was already tutting with impatience. 'Get me something to put all this in,' he ordered.

He snatched the Selfridges bags Grace offered him, and nudged the mobile phone that was on the floor with his foot. 'What's this?'

Grace didn't have the energy to come up with another lie. 'I got a phone call from a debt collector before I left so I switched it off and shoved it under there,' she admitted limply, all the fight gone out of her now as Vaughn tucked it into his coat pocket and hefted up two of her suitcases.

'Get the rest of what you need,' he barked over his shoulder. 'I'll be waiting in the car.'

*

Grace sat in front of Vaughn's tubular steel Marcel Breuer desk, its surface slowly being covered in neat stacks of financial documents, and watched as he pulled out a calculator from a drawer and started tapping away at the keys. Being dumped was now the least of her worries, as judging by the furious, skin-stripping looks Vaughn kept giving her, he was planning to pencil in a little light whipping before bed.

A lot of the envelopes, and the white ones too come to that, hadn't even been opened, and Vaughn handed her his letter-opener and told her to get to work. He ground his teeth as her fingers fumbled with the handle and she stuttered and stumbled over the numbers he wanted her to read out loud, until he sighed.

'Give them to me,' he ordered, and Grace was only too happy to hand over the mounds of paper, which hadn't seemed quite so mountainous when they'd been hidden away out of sight.

'Shall I make some tea?' she offered hesitantly, because watching his fingers press down, again and again unrelentingly, and the piles of paper never getting any smaller, was torture.

'Stay there,' Vaughn said sharply, and Grace had no choice but to sit there on an uncomfortable chair and concentrate really hard on pretending she was somewhere else until Vaughn started talking.

'You do know that when you go to – what is it? – the Co-Op and buy something for two pounds ninety-nine and get fifty pounds cashback on your credit card, they charge you at two point five per cent? And when you use the same credit card to get money out at an ATM, there are also another two separate charges?'

'I didn't know that,' Grace finally mumbled, when Vaughn glared at her until she answered, because she'd thought they were rhetorical questions. Turned out they weren't, and as he went back through five years of Grace's bills, she was expected to fill in the blanks.

'How did you manage to have absolutely no income coming in for a year after you graduated? What did you live on?'

'I had to intern for six months before I got a staff job at *Skirt*, but I had some cash-in-hand bar work in the evenings, and on the weekends I worked in a vintage clothes shop. And I didn't have to pay rent,' Grace added, as Vaughn kept tapping her bank statements with his pen. It made her nervous, made her want to keep talking to ward off the silence that would mean he'd have time to think of more questions.

'Why not?'

'Lily let me stay in her spare room when her dad bought her flat, but then Dan her boyfriend moved in. She didn't ask me to leave,' Grace said, rushing to Lily's defence as Vaughn's top lip curled, 'but I could tell they wanted their privacy, so I moved out.'

Vaughn nodded and lowered his head and didn't raise it again until he'd reached Grace: The College Years. He threw question after question at her about why she had had to buy her own dress-making materials and about student loans until Grace was wriggling on her chair because it was like being cross-examined under oath. She couldn't lie, not because she'd sworn on the Bible, but because Vaughn seemed to have this sixth sense and knew immediately when she was getting seriously economical with the truth so Grace began to wonder if her eyelids were twitching or she was scratching her nose in a giveaway manner without even realising it.

'I don't know how your grandparents let you get into this mess,' he announced censoriously, and for the second time that afternoon Grace felt herself getting angry, rather than intimidated.

'They paid my tuition fees,' she said hotly. 'And FYI, they have four other grandchildren whose tuition fees they paid.

And they gave me a thousand quid after St Martin's to sort myself out.'

Vaughn snorted just once and that single, inelegant exhalation said very plainly that they could have given her ten times that and she still wouldn't have been sorted out.

'Do they have any idea at all?' Vaughn asked, and his voice was softer now, which strangely made Grace feel worse. She didn't deserve his sympathy. She didn't deserve anyone's sympathy. Lots of people her age were in debt and they found a way to get out of it. Or at least not get themselves into an ever-increasing shame spiral of yet more debt.

'My grandad made me a spreadsheet,' Grace admitted unwillingly, 'with a monthly budget so I could start paying back my student loan and the overdraft, but that kind of depended on going straight into full-time paid employment, and if I'd told them I was interning, then they'd have offered to fund me and I didn't want them to.'

'It's only natural that they'd want to help you,' Vaughn said.

Grace shook her head. 'They're both retired and I know that some of their pensions or investments or whatever took a beating in the credit crunch, so I didn't want them to worry about me too.' It sounded a little too selfless and Grace winced, but Vaughn was nodding. He even threw in a head tilt like he understood where she was coming from.

'I'm not surprised you're in so much debt. Your salary is just enough for rent, utilities, travel and, let's see . . .' He ran his eyes down one of his neatly penned columns of figures. 'Yes, twenty pounds a week for everything else, including food, entertainment and clothes. It really isn't any surprise you've accumulated so much debt and haven't been able to pay it off.'

'But I started to, with the allowances . . .'

'Yes, which was admirable if you'd spread the payments over several of your most outstanding creditors instead of continuing to make payments on a Topshop store card that you'd already cleared and a credit card that had already been taken over by a debt clearing agency.'

'Well, I just kind of grabbed the first pieces of paper I came across . . .'

'I thought as much,' Vaughn said, and he still sounded calm and had stopped with the filthy looks and Grace hoped that they were nearing the end of this – whatever 'this' was. 'So as I said, it's no wonder you owe so much, given the lack of funds coming in against the funds going out, which is why I don't understand these particular statements. Maybe you could enlighten me.'

He handed over a wad of papers that Grace took, then really wished she hadn't. 'What seems to be the problem?' she choked out.

'I can see you've been living off your Visa and Mastercard cards for the last three years, but as far as I can tell you've gone through ten other cards and managed to exceed your credit limit in one day on each of them. I'd like an explanation.'

Grace stared at the numbers on the statements but didn't see them. Like, they were those 3D Magic Eye pictures and she didn't have the knack of getting through the swirly pattern to what was buried underneath. She looked a bit harder and saw one payment for an £800 Mulberry bag that she couldn't even remember buying.

'I'm waiting, Grace.' Vaughn had put down his pen so he could look at her, as if she'd just peed on his pristine white rug. 'Why do you spend money you haven't got on things you can't possibly afford?'

She could feel crimson staining her cheeks though her shopping binges weren't any worse than Vaughn being packed off to rehab when he was her age. But having to say the words out loud, describe how shitty and worthless she felt so that there was no other choice but to go out and buy the outer trappings that would make her shiny and perfect, was too hard. Even harder than trying to articulate the revulsion she felt once she got home and realised how much money she'd spent on an impossible task because she was never going to be anything other than shop soiled.

'The clothing allowance . . . it barely covers one outfit and shoes,' she heard herself insist weakly. 'And then I started having to buy clothes from the general allowance and there was always something every week that I'd have to buy a new dress for.' That at least sounded much better than admitting that she binged on designer goods like he wanted to binge on cake.

Grace realised that Vaughn hadn't really been angry before, he'd just been reeling her in, softening her up, because he was blisteringly angry now, eyes blazing away in his pinched white face.

'You're breaking my heart, Grace,' he sneered and God, at the moment, she'd never hated anyone as much as she hated him for doing this to her, for raking up things that were best left buried in shoeboxes under her bed. 'Don't lie to me. All but one of those statements in your hand dates back to before I met you, so why don't you try again?'

'If I hadn't left my knitting tote in your car, then you wouldn't know about any of this and quite frankly, it's none of your business. You were getting ready to dismiss me for, like, gross misconduct so just do it and then I can go and I can take my stuff with me.' Grace couldn't quite believe it but she was on her feet and grabbing handfuls of paper so she could stuff them back into their boxes and bags so they wouldn't be out on display, where she had to see them and talk about them and—

'Sit down!'

Vaughn had never shouted at her before. He never had to because his coldest, quietest voice was like a scream, but he was shouting now and it was enough to shock Grace into sitting down so suddenly it felt like she'd jarred every bone in her body. 'I'm going,' she said defiantly, but she was still sitting down with crumpled pieces of paper clutched to her chest.

'Put the paper back on the table,' Vaughn said like she hadn't even spoken. He wasn't shouting any more but looked as if he was grinding the enamel off his back molars. 'So, what's your solution?'

Grace looked at the paper covering Vaughn's desk, then she looked at Vaughn who was staring at her grimly. Looking down at her feet was the better option. The arrangement with Vaughn was meant to have been her solution and all it had done was get her deeper into debt. 'I don't know,' she said at last. 'I guess I'll declare myself bankrupt.'

'Do you know the consequences of declaring yourself bankrupt?' Vaughn asked her, and as long as it made the envelopes stop coming and the people from finance companies stop calling, Grace didn't really care.

'I'll Google it,' she said exasperatedly, because she was fresh out of other ideas, and really what was the point of Vaughn getting his hands dirty with her mess, other than getting a sadistic kick out of watching her squirm with shame? 'I know I've fucked up and yes, my credit rating is probably screwed for ever, but I'm not really in the market for a mortgage so who cares if I declare myself bankrupt? It just doesn't matter. There's no other way out. So are we done here?'

'Don't you want to know your magic number?'

'I. Don't. Care.' It was surprisingly easy to sound as if she meant it, as if she'd never spent weeks living on ramen noodles or had countless sleepless nights worrying about bailiffs.

Vaughn tore off a sheet of paper from a pad and wrote something on it, then pushed it across the desk. 'Read it out loud.'

Grace shoved it back at him. And then they were playing

push me, pull me until Vaughn stood up so he could tower over Grace, and force the piece of paper into her hand. 'Read it out loud,' he repeated in a growl that made every single hair on her body stand up.

What was written on the piece of paper was scary but when Vaughn was like this, hanging on to his temper by the most gossamerlike of threads, he was even scarier. Grace's fingers curled round the finest linen bond paper that Smythson had to offer and scrunched it in her fist.

'Just . . . I can't. Please don't make me.'

Vaughn was already prising open her fingers, one by one, so he could retrieve the crumpled ball of paper and smooth it out.

'Read it out loud.'

Grace knew that he'd never hit her in anger. Bent over his knee as foreplay didn't count, not when she was giggling madly. But she could tell that Vaughn was dangerously close to wrapping his hands around her throat and throttling her for a little bit because she'd reached the absolute zenith of infuriating.

Grace forced herself to focus on the piece of paper. There were a lot of numbers; it almost looked like a phone number. Then she read them out loud and after she'd done that, she pushed Vaughn away so she could slowly walk to his bathroom and throw up.

chapter twenty-six

The office was quiet the next morning. Kiki and the rest of the fashion team were skiing, Lily, who hadn't even texted a thank-you for the espresso machine, was still on her honeymoon, and practically everyone else had either taken the short week as holiday or called in sick. Only the various assistants to the various section editors were in and Grace was the only one who wasn't on Facebook.

Grace had made a To Do list the moment she got into work and was steadily ticking off items on it. So far, she'd called her bank manager to make an appointment to discuss her overdraft, though now that she wanted to speak to him, he was nowhere to be found. She'd also called a debt hotline, but after spending half an hour on hold, Grace went on eBay and began estimating how much money she could make if she sold off her shopping-binge trophies. There was no point going to see her bank manager or phoning up her creditors unless she had some money to give them. All she could think about was her magic number in all its five-figure glory. Seven figures if Grace added the forlorn eighty-three pence at the end of it. Now she knew exactly how much she owed, it couldn't be hidden away any more. It was her mess and it was up to her to clean it up, because there wasn't anyone else to do it for her. Certainly not Vaughn, or his allowances. He'd banished her to the guest suite last night with this tone of grim finality to his voice that had made Grace realise that he didn't even have the energy to make her dumping official.

After Googling 'bankrupt' Grace logged on to net-a-porter.com for five minutes just to cheer herself up and take the nasty taste out of her mouth. She started to add things to her wishlist on autopilot and came to with a start as she realised her mouse finger was just about to click on the *proceed to purchase* button. Christ, she thought, what the hell was wrong with her?

As if on cue, her BlackBerry started to ring, almost as if Vaughn knew she was up to no good, but when she answered it with a very tentative, 'Hello?' it was Madeleine Jones.

'Happy New Year, Grace,' Madeleine trilled. 'I hope you're feeling better.' She probably wanted to make sure Grace was fighting fit and unlikely to relapse when she told her she was fired. Because Vaughn would so get her to deliver the news.

'I'm fine. And Happy New Year to you too,' Grace said by rote. 'I take it he didn't sack you then?'

'He threatens to sack me once a week on average. After the first year, I stopped worrying,' Madeleine said dryly, and Grace couldn't imagine her taking shit from anyone, not even Vaughn. 'I really am sorry that I forgot to organise your flu jab. It's horrible being ill when you're in a foreign country.'

'Well, it got me out of having loads of ski instruction from the infamous Chip so it worked out OK,' Grace said, because that had been one hell of a silver lining. Madeleine laughed, and Grace appreciated the fact that she and Madeleine had moved past the frosty phone calls of last summer, but she wished that they could just cut to the chase. 'Can I help you with something?'

There was the most delicate of pauses. 'Vaughn asked me to call you . . .'

Grace closed her eyes and wondered why she was

dreading what Madeleine was about to say. It wasn't as if it was unexpected, and even a fake relationship couldn't last if you spent most of the time moving from one argument to the next.

'He's going to be in Berlin for the rest of the week,' Madeleine continued. 'I'm sending a courier over with the security codes so you can get into the house. Please don't lose them. In fact, if you could memorise them, then destroy the paper, that would work.'

'OK.'

'That was a joke, Grace,' Madeleine sighed. 'I'm also sending some cash to tide you over.' She was talking in rapid bursts as if she was uncomfortable with the conversation and wanted to get it done with as quickly as possible. 'Not the full allowance – you'll have to talk to Vaughn about that when he gets back. I think that's everything, but please set the alarms before you go to bed each night.'

'He didn't say anything else?' Grace asked tremulously, but she was already resigned to the agony being prolonged for a few more days and it would give her time to tick off a few more items on her To Do list.

'Well, he wanted me to remind you to button your coat,' Madeleine said.

'Because really it would be best if I just went back to my place . . .'

'I don't think that's a very good idea, Grace. In fact, I don't even think that's an option right now.'

It was comforting to know that even though Vaughn was done with her, he hadn't been planning to send her back to Archway and the yellow ice straight away. 'He's really furious with me, isn't he?' she asked Madeleine before she could stop herself.

'You know I can't answer that,' Madeleine said gently. 'Now do call me if you need anything, and please remember to set the alarms, because if the house is ransacked while you're at work, then he really will be furious. We'll all have to emigrate.'

It might have been the first time that year that Grace had actually smiled.

She wasn't going to stay in Hampstead – Grace was adamant about that. It wouldn't kill her to not have any hot water, it would be character building, but when she got back to Vaughn's house that evening, she found every single one of her possessions stacked neatly in packing crates in the hall. Every single one. There was even a balled-up pair of socks, which she didn't recognise but might have been Liam's, listed in the inventory provided by the removal company. It was a perfectly executed moonlight flit, except there was a receipt from Mrs Beattie for January's rent, plus a month in lieu of notice.

It narrowed Grace's options down considerably. Sure, she had friends with sofas, but twenty crates and twelve garment bags wouldn't be quite so welcome. All she could do was wait for Vaughn to come back and savour the pleasure of having the whole house to herself, including Vaughn's premium cable package and a state-of-the-art kitchen.

The week drifted by and Grace felt as if she spent most of it on hold trying to speak to her bank manager. She also set up an appointment with a debt specialist who wouldn't see her until she could find the contents of her shoeboxes, which had gone AWOL. They weren't in Vaughn's study, and it seemed ironic that now she was ready to face facts and all those little red figures, she was stuck in at least three different holding patterns.

But on Friday Grace no longer felt as if she was drifting. Suddenly the real world was beginning to intrude again. Madeleine had woken her up with a text message telling her that Vaughn would be home that night, and Lily arrived back at work that morning with another perfect suntan and a look of utter disdain each time she glanced Grace's way. Lily had reached the stage of gestation where she just looked fat, rather than pregnant, which made Grace feel slightly vindicated, but she still wished she hadn't run to squeeze into the lift just as the doors were closing, and had to share a confined space with Lily for thirty seconds.

'Look, you have to talk to me eventually,' Grace sighed in exasperation as the lift doors opened and they both headed out to get some lunch. As soon as she'd seen Lily breeze into the office that morning, she'd realised all the little things that were missing, like swapping bitchy emails and checking the Eat website to see what the Soup of the Day was and how many fat units it had, and the times they'd pretend they had appointments so they could go to the cinema. Grace wasn't prepared to have a Lily-less existence just yet, even though she was still pissed off with her. 'We work in the same office and I still have your DAY Birger et Mikkelsen blue tunic.'

It was the one thing guaranteed to force a reaction out of Lily. 'I've been looking for that everywhere!' she gasped in relief before she remembered that she'd put Grace on no speakers. 'I want it back and that doesn't mean you need to talk to me. Not after what you did. Not after what you've been doing. With *him*.'

'Look, we don't have to talk about *him*.' Grace touched Lily's sleeve lightly and tried to avert her eyes from the two bottom buttons on Lily's coat, which had been left undone because her hips were getting themselves ready for the childbearing. 'Tell me how the wedding went.'

She'd already heard in mind-numbing detail about the wedding from everyone else in the office. It had been a beautiful day. Lily had looked like Velvets-era Nico. Dan had cried when he'd recited his vows. But Lily seemed to have forgotten all about that. 'Your dress was way too short on my cousin,' she said, elbowing Grace out of the way so she could be first through the revolving doors. 'And why did you get us a stupid espresso machine when you know I can't drink coffee?'

After that stressful encounter, Grace was relieved to come home to a house that still didn't have Vaughn in it. She tended to camp out in the upstairs living room that had a massive HDTV mounted on the wall and sofas that you could actually lie on, like she was doing now as she worked her way through a huge plate of shepherd's pie and watched the *America's Next Top Model* marathon she'd persuaded Vaughn's Sky+ box to record.

Grace was snickering gently as Tyra Banks exhorted one of the girls to smile with her eyes, when she caught a movement in the doorway and looked up to see Vaughn standing there.

'Oh, hey,' she said, through a mouthful of potato.

'Hello.' Vaughn stayed in the doorway as Grace heaved herself up and started straightening the cushions. 'You don't need to do that.'

Vaughn thought that the floor and the backs of chairs were where his clothes and accessories lived but she was a guest in his house, so she carried on fussing and primping. 'I wasn't sure what time you'd be back. Madeleine said it would be late.'

'A couple of meetings got cancelled so I pushed up my schedule.' Vaughn dumped his briefcase, coat and laptop bag on top of a Frank Lloyd Wright sideboard, which was far too old to take their weight. 'Where are you going?'

Grace was on her feet, dinner tray in her hand. 'Going to put these in the dishwasher.' Though actually she was getting out of his hair, which was standing on end like he'd spent the last six days pulling on it.

She wasn't expecting Vaughn to follow her out of the room, down the stairs and into the kitchen, and she could feel the back of her neck tingling, just from being so close to him, though she wasn't sure if it was from fear or longing. And in the end she had to turn around.

Vaughn was leaning against the door, like he wasn't sure if he was welcome in his own kitchen; it was an uncharacteristically humble gesture and Grace let down the defences she'd spent all week building up. 'You look like you slept in a wind tunnel,' she said with a strained smile so Vaughn would know she was trying to lighten the mood and not being snarky.

'I had a very long, very arduous meeting as soon as I got back to the office this afternoon that made me tear my hair out, quite literally,' Vaughn explained, and there was all this stuff she had to say to him, but Grace didn't feel as if she could struggle her way through to the finish line. From the way that Vaughn was leaning against the door, he didn't either.

'Have you eaten anything?' she asked.

'I had something on the plane.'

'I made this huge shepherd's pie. There's tons left, if you want some.'

Vaughn ate two helpings, but refused to drink Grace's wine. Instead he opened a bottle of Merlot that was probably older than she was and sipped a glass as Grace loaded the dishwasher, wiped down the stove top and the counters and packed what was left of the shepherd's pie away in a Tupperware container.

'We need to talk, Grace. Come and sit down.' Grace had to give him credit for not dragging this unbearable arrangement out any longer. She pulled out a chair and sat down opposite him.

'I'm sorry,' she said, because it was as good a place as any to start. 'That you got dragged into all this and I whined on about how it was hard to manage on thousands of pounds every month. I want you to know that I am grateful for all of it and I shouldn't have thrown it back in your face the way I did.'

Vaughn had looked startled when Grace first began to speak, but now he was steepling his fingers and staring at her over the top of them. 'Did you agree to this arrangement because you needed the money?'

He wasn't biting his words out like he usually did when he was mad at her, but Grace still cringed because she knew the truth would make him angry.

'I just want us to talk,' Vaughn said, as if he could read her mind. 'You've stuffed me full of carbs so I doubt I could find the strength to start shouting, not that I'm going to. We need to do this, yes?'

Grace nodded slowly and bit her lip until she'd worked out what she wanted to say instead of blurting out the first thing that came into her head. 'I wouldn't have become your mistress if I hadn't been so broke, but you were the one who wanted an agreement. It wasn't my idea. If you'd just asked me to be your girlfriend with no contract, no allowances, I'd have said yes, because I fancied you. You know I'd have slept with you in New York.'

'Those allowances were just pin money,' he said. 'A little sweetener. It wasn't meant to be a lifeline.'

'Pin money? You were giving me more in two months than I make all year!' Grace exclaimed and once again, there was a table and several worlds between them.

'I had no idea you were barely earning minimum wage. I assumed you were making at least ten times that, and that you walked out of work every day with armfuls of clothes foisted on you by grateful fashion houses,' Vaughn protested.

'Well, they kind of make us give the clothes back once we've shot them,' Grace said wistfully. 'I have a New Look discount card, but that's about it.'

'You should have come to me if you needed more money. You know I'd have given it to you without question.' He'd promised he wouldn't get angry, but he was starting to sound a little peeved and Grace realised Vaughn was offended at the implication that he was tight – and of course he wasn't. He'd been unstintingly generous – but he wielded his generosity like a weapon sometimes. 'You should have told me about this, confided in me. Why didn't you?'

There were so many reasons that Grace didn't know where to begin. She started with the obvious. 'Because I don't want to think about it, even though it's *all* I think about. It's why everything was tucked away in boxes under my bed. If I talk about it, then it's real and I have to start dealing with it, and I didn't want to. And I hardly know you . . .'

'What do you mean, you hardly know me? You've been sleeping with me for the last four months.'

'That doesn't mean I know you,' Grace said. 'Just like you didn't really know me until all this exploded in your face on Monday.'

Vaughn's face tightened and Grace suspected that his promise that this wouldn't turn into another fight was a case of hope over experience. 'I told you things in Buenos Aires that I haven't told anyone,' he said stiffly.

'Then you were furious with me because I'd seen you let your guard down. But, God, Vaughn, you've seen me make a total idiot of myself so many times. The first day we met, and when you caught me masturbating . . .' Grace covered her cheeks with her hands, though that memory managed to raise a smile from Vaughn. 'You've seen me dripping with snot, and then last Monday . . . I was so ashamed and you just wouldn't stop making me look at those pieces of paper and trying to make me tell you things, my dirtiest secrets . . . and you got so angry with me.'

'Do I frighten you?' Vaughn asked, and Grace looked at his clenched jaw, his white-knuckled fingers tapping on the table-top, and . . .

'A little bit,' she admitted. 'Not frightened, exactly, but you're kind of scary sometimes.'

Vaughn stretched out his hands and tried to relax

his posture, like a marionette suddenly coming to awkward, jerky life. 'Surely you know my bark is much worse than my bite.'

But I don't, Grace thought, and she shrugged helplessly. 'Look, it was horrible but I'm glad because I couldn't keep ignoring it. I've spent all week trying to straighten it out. Like, I'm going to sell some of my stuff and see a debt specialist because he thinks he could get the loan companies to forget the interest. And I might even move back to Worthing and commute in to save some money, and I've left a ton of messages for my bank manager but I think he's breaking up with me too, but I need my papers back . . .'

'Just stop. Slow down,' Vaughn demanded. He scraped his chair back and stood up and walked over to where Grace's handbag was perched on the worktop. 'Give me your credit cards.'

Grace looked at him warily. 'But didn't you hear what I said? I'm sorting it out and I'm not going to do *that* any more.'

'So give me your cards then,' Vaughn replied imperturbably.

Giving Vaughn her cards for safekeeping made perfect sense. That way she wouldn't be tempted, no matter how low she got, but . . . 'I need one card, in case I—'

'All the cards,' Vaughn repeated, and it worked out really well that she was a little scared of him because Grace took the bag he was holding out to her and started rummaging through it, pulling cards out of her purse and side pockets.

'My Topshop card has actually got credit on it,' she protested, almost wincing as she heard her voice getting shriller, but she slapped the cards into Vaughn's outstretched hand and watched him sift through them.

'Grace, I said we wouldn't have an argument, but there are two cards missing,' he said. 'You have twelve in all – there's only ten here.'

With shaking fingers, Grace unzipped an inner pocket and

sifted through receipts until she closed her hand around an all too familiar plastic rectangle. Once she gave it to Vaughn, she could feel terror rising in her like bile. Losing the cards was like suddenly being thrown from a plane without a parachute, so she had the sensation that she was freefalling with nothing to cling on to. She could actually feel herself fighting for each breath while Vaughn stood and watched her. He waited until she'd managed to pull herself back from the brink, then said gently, 'Where's the last card?'

It took Grace fifteen minutes to sort through the crates, looking for a big cake tin while Vaughn sat on the bed in the guest room. Then she knelt on the floor with the cake tin on her lap and with her nails started slicing through the tape that was sticking down the lid. Inside was another tin, also taped down, and another, and another, and another . . . until she finally got to the last tin – a pretty little Art Deco-inspired box that had once contained some caramel pastilles – and prised it open. 'It's my emergency card,' she told Vaughn defensively as she handed it over, even though everything in her was screaming to snatch it back.

Vaughn fanned the cards out and looked at them. 'Just pieces of plastic and computer chips,' he remarked, before he tucked them away in his shirt pocket. 'You're practically vibrating – come and sit down.'

Grace guessed they'd reached the stage in their discussion where Vaughn was going to break up with her, very gently, very nicely and with her pieces of plastic and computer chips in his custody. She kept a good metre of bed between them as she sat down and looked at him from under her lashes expectantly.

'I'm paying off your debts,' he said evenly, and it was the last thing Grace expected him to say. 'My accountant is contacting all your creditors and he expects to have all the loose ends tied up by the end of next week. And I got you this.'

He pulled something out of his trouser pocket and placed it on the bed between them.

Grace didn't dare touch it because this had to be some bizarre game and she wasn't sure of the rules. Or if there even were rules. 'What's that?'

'It's a credit card, Grace – one of those Black Amex numbers that you've always been so taken with. I thought you'd have recognised it immediately.'

'I mean, why does it have my name on it?' Grace pushed it away from her with the tippy tip of one finger, because she didn't trust herself not to grab it and run off into the night to the nearest place where she could exchange it for goods and services. The restraint was fucking killing her.

'Because it's yours,' Vaughn said with just a hint of gritted teeth, like he couldn't believe she was being so obtuse. 'I'm only going to give you £200 a month in cash for incidentals from now on. Everything else you put on the card. If you have to buy a dress or a birthday card or knitting needles, you put it on the card. I'm not going to pore over the statements but please run any big purchases past me first. Speedboats, tiaras and such.' Vaughn took Grace's shell shock as permission to carry on. 'You're not to touch your wages: they go into the bank and stay there earning interest.' He picked up the card and pushed it into Grace's hand. 'Think of this as a set of training wheels.'

Grace looked up at him. 'But why . . . I mean, why would you . . .' Vaughn seemed very soft-focus and was getting blurrier by the second, and as Grace blinked her eyes, she realised that tears were streaming down her face. She tried to scrub them away with an impatient hand, but more appeared to take their place.

'Don't cry,' Vaughn warned but it was too late.

Grace bent forward so her forehead was almost touching her knees and started to cry. Not like the crying Vaughn had seen before, when she was trying to hold back her sobs; this time she could feel her body shuddering and shaking as it birthed out each howl. At the periphery of her senses, she was vaguely aware of Vaughn shifting, but then his arm was around her shoulder and he was scooping her on to his lap and holding her while she cried, softly murmuring words as he stroked her hair but didn't try to stop her until finally the sobs began to diminish in ferocity and volume.

Slowly Grace felt herself begin to emerge from the dark place she'd disappeared to, back to the here and now where she was clinging to Vaughn, her face buried in the warm hollow where his shoulder met his neck, shirt soaked with tears and . . . God, she couldn't even cry properly. Her nose was running as she sat up and wiped it with the back of her hand because she was disgusting. Vaughn wasn't recoiling with horror but still smoothing her hair with steady, even strokes.

'I've never met anyone who cries as much as you do,' he said, brushing his fingers over the last few tears trickling down her hot cheeks. 'I wasn't trying to upset you. I thought I was doing something nice.'

'You were,' Grace hiccuped, and she thought about wriggling off his lap, trying to regain some tiny semblance of dignity, but it was so comforting just to be held without any kind of expectation. 'But I don't deserve it. It's my own fault that I got into such a mess, that I owe so much money.'

'We've been over that. I told you there was no way you could live on what you earned, especially when you had to fund yourself for—'

'No, not that.' Grace scrunched up her face as she tried to summon up the courage that she always had in very short supply. 'Those credit cards . . . when you asked me why I bought all that expensive shit and I got angry, it wasn't at you, it was at myself. I just feel like, like . . . I'm just not good enough, not ever. I'm not worth anything. And sometimes I feel it so much, like there's this big hole inside me and I don't know how to fix it so I go and buy all this stuff because if I have these pretty, expensive things then it must mean that I'm worth something. But when I get them home, I realise it's not going to work and I can't bring myself to look at them and then I feel even worse and it's just this never-ending loop that I can't break. Do you know what I mean?'

It was a garbled explanation and Grace wasn't even sure if it was particularly coherent as she was still crying a little bit. Vaughn didn't say a word because why should he? It was a lame excuse for something that Grace was only just starting to figure out, but then he kissed her on the cheek. 'Yes, I know exactly what you mean,' he said softly. 'But I'm giving you the chance for a do-over. Because I also know how rarely those come along. Don't fuck it up.'

'I won't,' Grace assured him. 'And I'll pay you back. We can sort out a schedule and it will take me a while, a long while, but . . .'

'You don't have to do that,' Vaughn said quickly, and Grace could feel his muscles tensing.

'But I want to – I should. It's the right thing to do,' Grace insisted, and she thought that now it probably was time to slide off his lap, but Vaughn's arms tightened around her as soon as she tried to move. 'It's so much money.'

'It's just money, and money only matters when you don't have any. I have lots of it and it's up to me what I spend it on,' Vaughn said. 'Besides, I didn't pay back the full amount, I negotiated. I made them take off all the interest and the penalty fees, and really what I was giving you in allowances wasn't enough. In the past – well, let's say I had different arrangements. Let this be a lesson to you to never accept the price on the ticket.'

'What do you mean, in the past?' Grace asked, curiosity triumphing. 'What did you do for your other . . . ?'

'We don't talk about our others,' Vaughn snapped, before he softened his voice again. 'We're talking about you. Really,

Grace, what you've earned me in commissions on Christmas Eve completely cancels out what I've just paid several loan-clearing companies, so I don't want you to feel that you're beholden in any way.'

'But it can't be that simple,' Grace protested. 'Nothing is ever that simple. It shouldn't be.' But it was if she remembered back to Christmas Eve and why Vaughn had gone to such lengths to get her to that lunch. 'But I thought . . . when you said we needed to talk, I thought you were going to end things. God, I can't believe you'd still want me around.'

'You do love to jump to conclusions. Your bank manager didn't break up with you – he was under strict instructions that he was only to deal with me – and I'm not breaking up with you either. Despite all evidence to the contrary, I've grown very . . . fond of you.'

'You have?' Grace knew she sounded sceptical but she didn't really think she'd done very much to warrant any fondness on Vaughn's part.

'Well, when you're not driving me to the very end of my tether. Though you seem rather less fond of me,' he pointed out, even though Grace was on his lap and resting her head on his soggy shoulder. 'You said you hated me.'

'You were vile to me that day,' Grace reminded him, sitting up so she could look him in the eye. 'But most of the time I like you. When you're nice to me, I like you. It's that simple.'

'So you like me right now because I'm being nice to you?' Vaughn clarified.

'Super-super nice, but I don't know why because I don't deserve it. I spent money that wasn't mine when I knew I couldn't pay it back, and there should be consequences. My grandparents are always going on about consequences. You have to let me pay you back somehow because I can't—'

'Grace, all the reasons why we started this are still there. I need a hostess and God knows, I need your help with Noah. You're about the only person he bothers to be civil to. And after your quite miraculous shepherd's pie, I expect you to make me dinner one night a week.'

'It was just a shepherd's pie.'

'It was the first home-cooked meal I've had in years,' Vaughn said, jiggling Grace to make his point. 'And I want you to promise not to mention the money again. I think you've been torturing yourself enough over it the last few years and I really don't see what purpose it would serve to keep bringing it up. It's over, Grace. Clean slate.'

For a moment Grace thought she might start crying again, out of sheer relief, because no matter how much Vaughn might protest, she knew she'd got off lightly. Too lightly. Not just because she didn't have to pay him back but because he knew all her grubby little secrets, but his arms were still around her and he was looking at her with concern, not condemnation or judgement like she expected.

Grace cupped his face in her hands so she could kiss him softly on the lips. 'Thank you,' she said. And she wanted to dress it up, make it sound more fervent, but she didn't know how. 'Thank you so much. I know you say it doesn't mean anything, the money, but what you've done, it means the world to me.'

'I can't cope with any more tears tonight, Grace. You've already ruined one shirt,' Vaughn sniffed, but Grace could tell he was faking.

'I think I'm all cried out for the rest of the month,' she said, finally tipping herself out of his lap so she could flop back on the bed, her hand reaching out to touch his back because she didn't want to lose this lovely connection they had tonight. 'God, I'm exhausted.'

Vaughn grunted in agreement and lowered himself so he was lying next to her. 'Tomorrow, you should unpack,' he said casually. 'You might as well stay here. I have all these empty rooms and I can't bear the thought of you finding another fetid pit and immediately starting to skip the rent payments.'

There was no point in Grace trying to deny it. Well, the first part anyway. 'I'm not going to skip any type of payment ever again,' she said fiercely. 'But my intern says she might have a spare room in her house soon, and—'

'It's easier for you to stay here where I can keep an eye on you,' Vaughn said, rolling on to his side so he could rest his arm on Grace's belly, as if he was going to anchor her to the spot in case she planned to leave there and then. 'Really, we're going to be so busy in the next few months, and it's silly for you to come back here for an hour or so, then get a car home.'

It *was* silly and again, everything Vaughn was saying made sense, except now that Grace wasn't quite so overwhelmed by gratitude and the threat of tears, she was beginning to feel as if she'd been taken over by a conquering army. 'But this time last week, I was on the outs and now you want me to move in.' She hoisted herself up on her elbows so she could see the discomfited look on Vaughn's face.

'Well, that was last week,' he said obliquely. 'Everything's changed now.'

'Are you sure?'

'Absolutely positive,' Vaughn stated firmly. 'I think as long as I don't get drunk again and bare my soul, we should be fine.'

Grace lay back down on the bed. She wished she could take Vaughn at his word, but he seemed to come with so many disclaimers. 'But you like your own space,' she reminded him. 'And I've never lived with a boyfriend before.'

'Well, you'll have to stay in one of the guest rooms because you're the most impossible person to sleep with, you fidget so much,' Vaughn complained, brushing Grace's fringe back so he could catch her rolling her eyes.

'I don't fidget that much – you're a very light sleeper.' Just the mention of the word was enough to make Grace yawn. It had been the most intense, emotionally draining two hours of her life.

'We've hit the highlights, shall we save the small print for the morning?' Vaughn suggested as he peeled back the duvet. 'You're tired, you should get into bed.'

Grace crawled under the quilt, pleased when Vaughn spooned against her back. 'Nobody's ever been this good to me,' she whispered, when he'd snapped off the light on the nightstand. 'Or had this much faith in me. I don't want to let you down.'

'You won't. Now shut up and go to sleep.'

Although she'd insisted she never fidgeted, Grace couldn't help but wriggle uncomfortably as Vaughn hissed in annoyance, which actually was strangely comforting. 'I hate going to sleep with my clothes on. When I wake up I feel really grungy.'

Grace could have sworn she heard his jaw clench. 'Well, take them off then.'

But once Grace had pulled off her clothes, there was something charged about Vaughn holding her, and she could feel his cock hardening. There was something even more charged about turning over so she could kiss him, when the credit card was still lying on the floor where it had fallen. She knew that, but she still couldn't hide her hurt when Vaughn pushed her away.

'It wouldn't be appropriate tonight,' he said, and it would have sounded more convincing if he hadn't bitten his lip as Grace closed the gap he'd made between them so she could coil herself around him.

'So, it would be appropriate tomorrow?' she pouted. 'It's been a week. Over a week and I just want us to be close.'

'I don't want you to think that I'm taking advantage of you.'

'And I don't want you to think this is me showing you my gratitude. It's just me wanting to have sex with you and I know you want to have sex with me. We'd never have started any of this if we hadn't wanted to have sex with each other.'

Vaughn tried to squirm out of the reach of her marauding hands and Grace discovered that she got a kick out of being the seducer and not the seducee for once.

'I thought you were tired,' Vaughn complained, but Grace could tell that he was just one more bitten-off groan from giving in. 'You said you were tired.'

'I'm not *that* tired,' Grace insisted, and this time when she wrapped her arms and legs around him and threw in a little shimmy for good measure, he stopped pulling away.

It was different to all the other times they'd had sex. Slow, silent, pausing for these long, devastating kisses that made Grace feel as if Vaughn was sucking the heart right out of her and she did cry a little when she came, as if she'd needed the release to wash away the last few dirty smears on her soul.

Later, much later when she was finally drifting off to sleep, wrapped round Vaughn like a quilt, he was the one who shifted restlessly. 'We still have an arrangement, Grace. No matter how close we've become, this isn't a relationship.'

Vaughn's timing was terrible, Grace thought sleepily, but she knew he was right. 'It can be a friendship. I want us to be friends.'

'Friends?' Vaughn echoed like it was a concept that he wasn't familiar with. Friends probably wasn't the right word but it would do for now.

'You did something amazing for me and I'm beyond grateful, but you don't have to worry that it's going to make me fall in love with you. I'm not a falling-in-love kind of girl.'

'Aren't you a little too young to have given up on love?' Vaughn wanted to know as Grace burrowed against his side because she'd found the perfect place in the crook of his arm to rest her head.

'Nothing to do with being young,' she mumbled. 'Never believed in love anyway, so how could I give up on it?'

'Then we'll be friends.' Vaughn dislodged Grace, making her whimper in protest, as he retrieved the duvet from the floor so he could tuck it around them. 'We're a good team, though neither of us is particularly house-trained, are we?'

She knew exactly what he meant. Despite their differences, *because* of their differences, they were a perfect mismatched set. Two sides of the same tarnished penny. An out-of-step Fred and Ginger. Vaughn was just as fucked up as she was – he was just so much better at hiding it.

chapter twenty-seven

It used to be that when Grace woke up in the morning, she'd have a few scant seconds of contentment, before her brain kicked into gear and she remembered exactly who she was and what she was doing in the world. She knew that when she got out of bed, feet dancing on cold lino, there would be bills on the doormat. There would be a boyfriend who was on the verge of dumping her, who'd never called the night before. There'd be clothes that smelled of damp when she went to get dressed, and a colony of ants marching across the kitchen floor as she put the kettle on. So when Grace woke fully and took stock of her life, she always wanted to close her eyes and go back to sleep again.

Now when she opened her eyes, she still thought those exact same things but as her eyes adjusted to the new day, she'd see that she was waking up in a different room. One painted in a soft shade of blue, with three Bridget Riley stripe paintings hanging on the wall: Vaughn had let her pick them out when he'd taken her to his temperature-controlled storage facility in King's Cross. They reminded Grace of the stripy bags from Paul Smith and were a perfect foil for the bookshelves, where she'd arranged her nicest shoes, including her black velvet Christian Louboutins, which were her new favourite things in the world.

Her clothes were hanging neatly in the huge walk-in closet,

not hermetically sealed in plastic bags. Vaughn's house was never cold, hot water never ran out, and as soon as her clothes hit the laundry basket, they were whisked away and reappeared neatly pressed and folded on her bed, which was turned down every day by Vaughn's housekeeper. As Grace's feet sank into plush white carpet as she wandered into her en suite bathroom, it felt like she was living in a dream.

It wasn't just the outer trappings of her life that had changed, swapping a squalid bedsit in Archway for a three-storey mansion in Hampstead, it was the whole rhythm of her life. Her old routines and habits had had to shift and coalesce with Vaughn's. On the days that he was working from home, that meant he'd come and wake her up after he'd pounded the footpaths of the Heath with Gustav, his trainer, even though she could have an extra half-hour in bed and still be at work almost on time. On the nights when they weren't out, he was unswerving in his belief that Grace needed eight hours' sleep a night, which was as sweet as it was annoying. Ever since she'd left her grandparents' house, there hadn't been anyone to give a toss about how much sleep she had or if she was bothering to eat a proper breakfast.

It worked both ways, the taking care of someone else. Grace realised she was equally unwieldy on the subject of how a protein bar didn't constitute a proper evening meal, even if Vaughn had had a big lunch. And though they never mentioned the money, Grace felt as if there was a debt that had to be repaid and cooking one meal a week didn't begin to cover it. The way she felt about Vaughn now was so complicated. She wanted him, that was a given, but liking him, looking forward to seeing him when he'd been away for a few days, not being so scared of him, was new and confusing. But it was her gratitude and her frustration at not being allowed to express that gratitude which underpinned everything.

Grace tried to say how she felt in the stroke of her fingertips along the back of Vaughn's neck when she kissed him or when she smoothed down his jacket lapels and in a hundred tiny, inconsequential ways, from packing his suitcase when he went away to withdrawing money from her own bank account and not using his credit card, so she could buy him little presents. She remembered how touched he'd been by his Christmas presents and how she'd vowed she was going to get him small 'just because' gifts. Nothing very special – a book that had been reviewed in the *Observer* that weekend, which he'd mentioned. A bottle of Trumper's Extract of Limes cologne because she'd noticed his was running low, and an Ealing Films DVD boxed set because she couldn't be friends with anyone who didn't love *Kind Hearts and Coronets*. Grace would leave each gift on Vaughn's bed when he wasn't at home, and when he tried to thank her she'd just shrug and say, 'Really, it's no big deal, I just saw it and thought you might like it.'

There were times that Grace missed the chaos of her old life – little things like going to bed as soon as she got home from work because it was cold, and eating bowls of cereal as she watched TV and adjusted the position of her three hot water bottles. Or just slotting one of her favourite CDs into her battered old Discman and going for a long walk and finishing up in Little Venice, where she'd hole up in a café and knit. There wasn't so much time for those kind of indulgences any more.

Vaughn hadn't been joking when he said they were going to be busy. There were dinners to organise and parties and exhibitions to attend, but even if the stomach-churning fear hadn't completely disappeared, Grace was much better at faking it. It helped that Vaughn's people weren't strangers any more, waiting to laugh at Grace's clothes and catch her out as she tried to remember the name of the artist whose exhibition she'd seen the night before. Now, some of Vaughn's people were becoming *her* people: Nadja always wanted to go shopping when she was in town, Grace and Piers had a secret

Facebook friendship, and her new best friend was an elderly curator at the V&A who'd sneaked her into the costume archives and let Grace try on a Vivienne Westwood Watteau-inspired evening gown.

It seemed to Grace that her new world was about doors opening, rather than slamming shut in her face. Like, it wasn't just enough to have shampoo-commercial shiny hair and the new season's clothes to be admitted, you had to know the secret handshake and the password. No longer being the new girl but the girl who was living with Vaughn was all it took for the doors to slowly creak open so Grace could step through into a world she'd only half-glimpsed before.

Grace understood now why the celebrities they shot for the front cover of *Skirt* generally acted like complete wankers. It was because they glided through that same world, so that when they rolled up for a shoot three hours late, they expected Grace to put on their earrings and shoes for them, because they were used to never having to do anything for themselves. It would be really easy to let the high life go to her head when she was being chauffeur-driven into work by Jimmy, who'd get out of the car and unfurl a huge umbrella because it was pissing down with rain and something terrible might happen if one single raindrop landed on Grace's head.

It was just as well she had her job to keep her humble. Not as humble as she used to be, because Lucie and Courtney were treating her with a new respect now that she brought her weekend case and garment bags into the office, instead of hiding them in the postroom. She didn't have to do their filing any more, which suited Grace just fine, but they expected her to provide a blow-by-blow account of where she'd been that weekend or who was on the guest-list for the Tate Modern exhibition opening she was going to that evening. Grace made sure that she still went on chocolate runs and kept a tight rein on the cupboard comings and goings, because she wasn't going to let anyone accuse her of getting too full of herself. Not that she could while Kiki was around.

'I don't want your social life interfering with your work,' she snapped each time Grace went into her office with another holiday form for her to sign. But instead of throwing random hoops at Grace so she could jump through them, Kiki now presented her with a list each Monday morning. It was a list that made the Treaty of Versailles look like light reading, but it meant that Grace could plan out the week's work and even call in clothes for shoots while she was getting a pedicure.

Kiki had also taken it upon herself to give Grace's daily outfit critiques a shake-up. She'd suddenly appear in the cupboard, which was unheard of, and demand to know where Grace was going that night and what she was planning to wear. After Kiki's savage condemnation of several of her outfits, it suddenly dawned on Grace that she could save a lot of time and having to return things unworn by asking Kiki for advice. The latter had feigned complete indignation the first time Grace had asked, 'Do you think I need to wear a long dress for this thing at the US Ambassador's place?' but ten minutes later she'd emailed Grace a list of frocks from Net-a-Porter. She'd even given Grace the number of her own alterations woman because, 'Everything you buy is too big on the bust and far too small on the hips.' It was almost as if Kiki had become a surrogate mother, albeit in a dysfunctional Joan Crawford way. Grace didn't doubt that Kiki would get medieval with a dress hanger if she persisted in buying dresses with asymetrical hems.

The only problem left to worry about was Lily. The rest of the beauty department had stopped with the filthy looks and the stony silences the day after Grace got a 'beige wash', which *Vogue* called 'the new blonde', from Marc, her hairdresser. When Maggie, the beauty director, saw the caramel, champagne and honey highlights woven into Grace's now shoulder-length hair, she couldn't stop herself from cooing, 'Love the beige wash, sweetie.' But it had been exactly twelve weeks since Grace and Lily had fallen out, and her friend still showed no signs of softening.

'I say hello to her every morning and I always compliment her on what she's wearing or ask how the pregnancy is going and she looks at me like I've just stepped in dogshit,' Grace complained bitterly to Vaughn one rainy evening at the end of February, as they stood in a draughty room that had once been a church hall when the residents of Bow were still God-fearing folk, and tried not to shiver.

It wasn't just the cold but a shudder of sheer revulsion as she tried not to look at any of the canvases. It was the opening night of Noah's new exhibition, pretentiously titled *The Killing Fields*, and it consisted of painting after painting of what looked like blood-splattered poppies. Though when Grace got closer she realised that they were actually mutilated girl parts. At least that's what they looked like to her, but it could just be that Noah was a really rubbish artist who didn't know how to draw either flowers or vaginas properly.

'Maybe it's time to cut your losses then,' Vaughn said, but Grace could tell that she didn't have his full attention. She never did when there were paintings in front of them. 'A lot less aggravation that way.'

'She can't ignore me for ever,' Grace mused, looking around the room. It was a very different scene to the parties they normally went to: acid wash jeans, limited-edition Japanese trainers and fitted caps had replaced dinner jackets and cocktail dresses. Grace waved at a guy who'd been two years above her at St Martin's and had given her flatmate crabs. 'Noah's trying to get your attention,' she added, nudging Vaughn so he looked up to see that Noah was at the makeshift bar in the corner of the room and aiming frantic hand signals at him.

'He probably wants me to stick vast sums of money behind

the bar,' Vaughn noted sourly, but he gave Grace's waist a quick squeeze before he strode off.

Three months ago, Grace would have found the nearest wall to lean against and practise becoming inconspicuous, but now she surveyed the room, caught Lola's eye and hurried over to where she was sitting with a bunch of people that Grace didn't know, although they looked familiar. When you'd been out of circulation for a while, all Hoxtonites looked the same.

By the time Vaughn had sorted out the bar bill, Grace had found a seat, a bottle of beer and some scenesters she'd used to hang around with in her student days when she'd been doing the club kid thing. She looked up to see Vaughn standing there at the edge of the crowd looking completely out of his depth. He shouldn't have worn a suit, Grace thought. It made him stand out like a fake Chanel bag in a front row.

Grace smiled encouragingly but he still hung back so she was forced to half-rise off the bench. 'Vaughn! This is my friend, Laetitia.' Laetitia was in grabbing distance and not too controversial. 'We used to work on a market-stall together.'

Vaughn looked absolutely appalled, but his attention was riveted, so Grace could tug him nearer before he could protest.

'What did you sell?' he asked. 'Fruit and vegetables?'

'Vintage clothing,' Laetitia supplied, scooching along so Vaughn could sit down. She looked him up and down then smiled knowingly at Grace in her impossibly foxy, impossibly French way which always made Grace think of illicit trysts in dark corners of Parisian bars with Serge Gainsbourg leaking out of the speakers. 'For this woman who was a horrible, horrible bitch. We used to take turns to spit in her tea.'

'Oh, Grace.' Vaughn's shoulders shook. 'Why doesn't that surprise me?'

'She used to accuse us of chatting up boys when we were meant to be working,' Grace explained, which actually had been a fair point. 'And she said I was stealing her stock, which

I would never have done because it was all disgusting eighties' stuff that wasn't even a little bit vintage.'

'And what do you do now?' Vaughn asked Laetitia, crossing his legs and almost looking relaxed.

Grace sat back with a little sigh of relief as Laetitia and Vaughn began to talk about her art therapy course and funding for non-profit organisations, keeping one ear cocked in case the talk veered towards ex-boyfriends. Gradually Vaughn was pulled into the general conversation. He was a little stiff for the company Grace was keeping, and although she was used to his precise, slightly fussy way with words, it was odd to hear him talk to people who'd made it their life's work to drop their aitches.

He lasted a good half-hour before his foot started knocking against Grace's shin every few seconds. 'Do you want to mingle?' she whispered in his ear.

'Yes, please.' He was on his feet in an instant, as Grace retrieved her bag and coat and promised that she'd ring Laetitia and, 'Yeah, straight up, Lily's married and pregnant.'

The crowd was beginning to thin out as the alcohol dried up, making it easier to look at the pictures. Which was a pity. Vaughn gestured at the largest canvas, which was a mess of smeared crimson and reminded Grace of a used sanitary napkin. 'What do you think of Noah's work?'

Usually Grace didn't voice a strong opinion on art because usually she didn't have one, but the reaction Noah's paintings provoked in her was too extreme not to pass judgement. 'They're revolting! I don't even want to look at them!' she exclaimed, pulling a face in case Vaughn needed a visual too. 'They're obscene and totally misogynistic. Honestly, if you stick one up at home I'm moving out.'

She'd said 'home', which generally she tried not to do, but if Vaughn was bothered by the idea that Grace was getting too comfortable he didn't let it show. 'Misogyny always sells very well. Though Noah says they're not for sale.'

Grace sniffed. 'He's only saying that because he knows that no one in their right minds would want to buy one.'

'The pieces he did for his degree show were more nuanced than this – delicate pen and ink sketches on a very large scale,' Vaughn said thoughtfully. 'I'm not sure if he's simply being provocative or whether this is the direction he's moving in.'

'Well, why don't you just visit him in his studio?' Grace was already bored with talking about Noah. Lola had been bending her ear for the last half-hour about how she suspected Noah of screwing someone else. If they had a communist relationship then it seemed to be news to Lola, and Grace had longed to give her a heads up.

'Because he's made it very clear that I wouldn't be welcome. He really doesn't like me very much.'

'I wouldn't lose any sleep over *that*,' Grace said scathingly, and she knew that Vaughn liked to bitch, did he ever, but she wondered how he felt about gossip. 'Apparently he's been seeing someone behind Lola's back.'

'Really?' Obviously Vaughn was down with gossip too.

Grace scouted the room. 'That girl over there in the pink dress at your nine o'clock. Don't look!' She punched Vaughn's arm before he could turn round. 'She's cute. Think she's about sixteen though.' Grace was starting to realise that once a guy hit twenty-five, he always went at least five years younger.

'Stay there and don't move.' Vaughn casually strolled to the next canvas then pretended to look around in astonishment when he realised that Grace wasn't glued to his side. He gave the girl in the pink dress a cursory up and down, made an unimpressed face and beckoned Grace over. 'At least this one can actually smile,' he remarked, putting his arm around her waist.

She hated looking at pictures with Vaughn. He'd stare at them for ages, whereas all Grace needed was two seconds to tell whether something sucked or didn't. She suspected that Vaughn was faking being engrossed but let herself lean against him as she had only about an hour of standing time left in her heels before she lost all sensation in her toes. She counted, 'One elephant, two elephant,' in her head until Vaughn touched her arm.

'This really isn't my scene. I feel very old,' he said, helping Grace into her coat.

'You're not old,' she protested, because she didn't think of him like that any more. He was older, but that wasn't the same thing. 'Age ain't nothing but a number and all that.'

'I suspect that inviting Noah to intimate little dinner-parties with influential buyers and curators isn't going to win him over.'

'Do you really think he's worth all this trouble?'

'Yes,' Vaughn said simply as he slowly did up the buttons on Grace's coat. 'He might well be a very important artist who'll reframe the British art scene. You don't?'

Grace shrugged. 'I can predict hemline lengths from season to season to the nearest centimetre, but this art stuff doesn't make sense. I like pictures that look like what they're meant to be.'

'Philistine,' Vaughn sniped, gently cuffing Grace's chin. 'So what do I do to bring Noah on side?'

'I should have said something before, but I wasn't sure how you'd take it,' Grace said hesitantly. Vaughn digested that with a wry dip of his head and gestured at her to continue. If he'd been this genial from the start, she thought, it would have simpled things up so much. 'Maybe you could have a party that's more Brick Lane than Belgravia, with a younger crowd – if one of the newer galleries was putting on a show, you could sponsor it and a ton of Noah-type people would turn up for free booze. Like, young fashion designers and I know loads of photographers and models.' Grace paused to ponder the scope of her social connections. 'And you can't serve poncy little canapés. Before I met you, I used to go to parties because I was broke and dinner was the finger buffet, so don't offer anything that's gone in one bite. But I don't think anyone will buy any art.'

'There's an interesting little gallery in Whitechapel I was thinking of investing in that would be perfect . . .' Vaughn began to slowly but definitely move them in the direction of the big swing doors. 'Maybe I should start creating a Zeitgeist instead of trying to second-guess where the next one will be.'

Grace eyed him warily. 'I'm talking about a low-key party, not a whole new art movement.'

'Just thinking out loud.' Vaughn visibly flinched as Noah called his name, but when he turned around he was smiling and his arm was back around Grace's waist, though she'd managed to get as far as the door without using him as a crutch. 'We're just leaving, Noah.'

Noah jiggled from foot to foot. 'Yeah, we have to clear out too, this place doesn't have a late licence.' Much as he liked to think that he was a sharp operator, he simply looked shifty, like a small boy caught with cake crumbs around his mouth, and Grace could feel Vaughn stiffen as he waited to hear what Noah really wanted. 'So, what are you two up to?'

'We're going to try and find a black cab with its light on,' Vaughn said blandly.

'So, I was wondering if you were a member of Shoreditch House? We could move on there. I'd really like to ask you about showing in New York and Lola wants to talk to Grace about something.' He gestured over his shoulder at a little group of people who were anxiously watching the proceedings. 'You could sign eight people in, right?'

Vaughn's plans to create a Zeitgeist weren't meant to start tonight. He'd already told Grace that he had to make a 6 a.m. call to Tokyo the next morning, but she could tell he was wavering by the way he nibbled on his bottom lip.

'Sorry, but we have to go now,' Grace said crisply, opening the door. 'I'm shooting really early tomorrow morning and I don't want to do it with a hangover.'

'Yeah, but Vaughn, you could put Gracie in a cab and come on your own?'

'Maybe some other time we could go there for lunch,' Vaughn said mildly, as if he wasn't the least bit annoyed at Grace ruining a perfect opportunity for him to cultivate Noah by sponsoring yet another bar tab. 'Your studio's just round the corner, isn't it?'

'You don't miss a fucking trick!' Noah wagged his finger in Vaughn's face. Vaughn really had to rate Noah's gynaecological daubings to suffer being baited with absolutely no finesse, Grace decided. 'Never let the whiff of big business sully my studio space, mate.'

It was just as well that Noah was so good looking otherwise his obnoxiousness would be unbearable, Grace thought as she followed Vaughn out of the door.

'Why on earth did you do that?' Vaughn demanded before they could even start to look for a cab. 'I had no choice but to agree with you.'

'He just wanted you there to buy the drinks,' Grace snapped. 'Then he'd impress his friends with a few more cracks about how dealers are destroying the art world.'

'You don't know anything about how this works, Grace.'

There was something coming down the road with a light on. Grace stepped off the kerb and flapped her arms wildly. 'I know about boys like Noah. I've dated enough of them, and the minute you act like you're interested, they treat you like shit.'

'You're trying to hail a road-sweeper, Grace, and it's about to mow you down.' Vaughn held out his hand. Once she was safely back on the pavement, he didn't let go. 'Where are your gloves?'

'I think I left them at work. We should walk up to the main road.'

They began to walk, Vaughn adjusting his long-limbed stride to match Grace's slower pace. 'So, going with your boy analogy, how should I woo Noah?'

'You're asking me? He can't be the first angry young artist who's refused to succumb to your charms.'

'Well, he is, which should have some novelty value but it's actually rather annoying. He doesn't even have an agent.'

'Maybe he's only in it for the art,' Grace suggested doubtfully. 'Or else he has a massive unearned income.'

'His family do actually own a huge estate in Devon – can probably trace their lineage back to William the Conqueror.'

'Typical,' Grace said sourly. 'I knew that he was just faking that Cockney accent. But if I were interested in Noah in that way, I'd flirt with his mates and give him some serious cold shoulder. That sometimes works.'

Vaughn made a non-committal noise, though Grace knew that first thing tomorrow morning he'd get someone to sniff around Noah's circle to see if they had any discernible talent and didn't object to being patronised by the Establishment.

'There's a cab going the other way!' Grace let go of Vaughn's hand so she could jump up and down, until the cab driver saw her and did a sharp U-turn.

Grace sighed gratefully when they were finally on their way back to North London. She shut her eyes, safe in the knowledge Vaughn would give directions to the driver and not rib her for drooling.

'You're not interested in Noah though, are you? Objectively speaking?'

Grace's eyes snapped open. 'No! Not objectively. Or subjectively. I'm so over that whole East London scene.'

'He thinks you're very attractive; he makes a point of mentioning it every time I see him,' Vaughn said, with an edge to his voice. 'And I was sure I interrupted something the night of my party. On the roof.'

'It was nothing.' Grace nudged Vaughn with her elbow because yes, she had a lot of personality defects but stringing Vaughn along while lusting after Noah wasn't one of them. 'He was drunk. Lola wasn't there. He made a half-hearted pass at me for the sake of it and I politely declined. That was it.'

It wasn't it. 'He reminds me slightly of that boy I saw you with in Liberty's the day we met. I just wondered if that was your usual type?'

'Liam? They look nothing like each other!' Grace frowned. Liam was a standard issue, snake-hipped, messy-haired indie boy who looked like all the other boys in bands who littered the pubs of Camden. Noah was an art boy and they had a whole different vibe. Grace pictured both of them in her head and was forced to admit to herself that maybe both Liam and Noah had the same cocksure swagger and arrogant charm that fooled a girl into thinking they were special. There was a time when Grace had always fallen for those boys with their careless smiles and studied disinterest and God, had they made her work for it.

She looked at Vaughn's clean profile and wondered when she'd stopped thinking of him as only handsome in a certain light. 'Maybe my type's changed.'

That was definitely a loaded statement and not one Grace was prepared to elaborate on, but Vaughn just patted her knee. 'If you promise not to dribble, I'll let you doze on my shoulder,' he offered magnanimously.

chapter twenty-eight

Vaughn had taken to calling Grace mid-afternoon if they weren't going out that evening. It wasn't a 'Hi, I was just thinking about you' call that couples in proper relationships made several times a day – but so they could discuss what Grace was making for dinner. The once-a-week home-made meal now happened every evening that they stayed in, and it was vital that Vaughn knew what was on the menu so he could call Gustav, his trainer, who'd adjust the next morning's workout accordingly. Then they'd decide on the evening's entertainment. The Ealing Films boxed set was finished and Grace was resisting all Vaughn's entreaties for a Wim Wenders retrospective.

'We don't have to watch a DVD,' Vaughn opined on the BlackBerry as Grace rooted through a box of costume jewellery at work. 'If you made it worth my while then I suppose I could see *Wings of Desire* on one of the nights you're doing something fashion-related. You still haven't modelled the last present I bought you from Agent Provocateur.'

'I'm not having that kind of conversation in the fashion cupboard,' Grace informed him primly. 'So, as I was saying, tonight I'm going to make a lasagne with wholewheat pasta, though it might just be salad if you insist on making me watch some boring black and white German film with subtitles.'

'There's nothing that would change your mind? I could go down on you because you seem to like that . . .'

There was a noise at the door and Grace turned her head to see Lily standing there.

'. . . and you make this adorable breathy noise . . .'

'I have to go now,' Grace said in her most efficient phone voice, as if Vaughn was some snooty PR giving her grief about the fashion credits.

'Why don't we take a raincheck and revisit the topic this evening, with a practical demonstration?'

'What*ever*. Send the car for six thirty; I'll pop to Tesco Metro first.'

Lily was still standing there with a martyred look. 'You're wanted in Kiki's office,' she said, with a put-upon air because pregnant women shouldn't have to deliver messages when there were non-pregnant interns about.

'OK,' Grace said equably. She hadn't made her daily attempt to mend the rift so now seemed as good a time as any. 'You look really glowy. Everything all right with the—'

'Was that *him*?'

'Yeah.' Grace searched desperately for something else to say on the subject that wasn't too controversial. 'Just for a chat about what I'm cooking for dinner. You remember that Jamie Oliver lasagne that I customised with . . .'

'You go around to his house and cook for *him*?' Lily rubbed her burgeoning bump anxiously.

'Yeah. Well, I've kind of moved in with him. With Vaughn. The bathroom pipes froze and the water in the toilet bowl iced up and someone still peed and turned the ice yellow,' Grace rambled, as she carefully squeezed past Lily who was motionless in the doorway. 'It was one of the grossest things I've ever seen.'

'Eeew,' leaked out of Lily's mouth before she could rein it back in. 'That's disgusting.'

'Vaughn has a guest sui— a spare room so I'm staying there

for a bit. Hey, I saw Laetitia the other night and she asked after you.'

'Oh, I haven't seen her for ages,' Lily said a little wistfully. But then she remembered that Grace was a terrible person who deserved all the yellow ice that God saw fit to send her way. 'She was more your mate than mine,' she clipped out. 'I don't want to get into anything with you, Gracie. I just came to give you the message.'

'I know,' Grace sighed. 'But nice to catch up.'

Lily rubbed her belly again, which seemed to have replaced tugging on a silky lock of her hair as her new nervous gesture. 'You've still got my blue tunic,' she said, before beetling off to the safety of the beauty department.

As Grace knocked quietly on Kiki's office door, she could feel panic welling up. What had she done wrong now? Actually she hadn't done anything wrong in weeks, which meant that Kiki must have been saving up all Grace's minor transgressions for one gigantic bollocking.

'You wanted to see me?' Grace stood at the door and tried hard not to shake, as Kiki, Lucie and Courtney all stared at her like she'd had a spider's web tattooed on to her face during her lunch-hour.

'We have a problem,' Kiki purred, and it was hard to judge what kind of mood she was in, though there was a cut-glass tumbler on her desk that would make a really good missile. 'And for once, you're actually the solution, hard as it is to believe.'

'I am?' Grace stood in front of Kiki's desk with her hands behind her back so no one could see her twisting her fingers nervously. 'Do you need me to call something in?'

'It's Nadja Stasova – we're trying to book her for the main May fashion story, but her agency says that she'll only shoot for *Vogue*.'

Grace pressed her lips together so she didn't start smiling. Nadja was constantly filling Grace in on her plans for total world domination and how they didn't include shooting for magazines without international editions. 'Is a waste of time if they not syndicate the pictures,' she'd sniffed after snubbing the editor of an American magazine at an opening in New York.

'That's a shame,' Grace said, trying to sound surprised. 'Do you want me to start pulling in comp cards for other girls with a similar look?'

'No, Grace, I don't,' Kiki said irritably. 'My sources tell me that you know this jumped-up little tart socially.'

Yes, but she lets me call her Nadja. 'Well, yeah, her boyfriend knows um . . . mine . . .' Grace ground to a halt as she always did when she tried to define exactly what Vaughn was, but Kiki's glare had managed to circumvent the Botox and was making her look positively demonic. A casual observer would never have guessed that only a few hours before, she'd been giving Grace a tutorial on cleavage and cocktail dresses. 'We've hung out a few times.'

'You have her personal number?'

Nadja had programmed it into Grace's BlackBerry under H for hot bitch. 'I don't know her that well,' Grace lied, because when her Vaughn life merged with her *Skirt* life, things always got complicated. 'Maybe you could try her booker again.'

Kiki didn't even blink. 'You phone her right now and get her to agree to the shoot and I'll let you style an advertorial. She's just bagged the new Prada campaign and they're making noises about only advertising with *Elle* and *Vogue* this year.'

It wasn't like Kiki to offer Grace any sweeteners. She was obviously desperate. Grace was all set to give serious phone, when she remembered Vaughn telling her that she had to make the most of opportunities that came her way, and this was an opportunity with a caps lock O.

Grace surreptitiously wiped her sweating palms on her arse, because hadn't Vaughn also said that she was crap at follow-through? 'I don't mind phoning Nadja, but I'd really like to style the pictures for the Hot Trends pages.' She tried to say this without a hint of anything that might sound like whining.

Kiki picked up the tumbler thoughtfully and Grace instinctively ducked but she just took a sip of water, then placed it safely back on its coaster. 'Are you trying to blackmail me, Grace?'

'No! I just . . . I thought . . .'

'I'm not letting you loose on actual models. You can shoot the accessories still-lifes for Snapshot and if you get Nadja Stasova, I'll let you assist and give you a styling credit.' She tapped her lacquered nails on the desk. 'Of course, if you don't get Nadja then that's a whole other conundrum, isn't it?'

But it turned out that when Grace phoned Nadja, she was in the midst of a very long hair appointment and only too happy to hear from 'my little Gracie with the coloured tights'.

Grace had to suffer a long diatribe about how the girl doing Nadja's hair had taken four attempts before she managed to mix the dye to the exact shade on the swatch Nadja had supplied, until it was time to plead, implore, and if that failed, cry loud noisy tears. Sometimes Grace found that having no dignity worked really well.

'I get the cover, yes?' Nadja wanted to know.

'Well, no, but it's the main fashion story, twenty pages, and we're shooting in Barcelona. We can hang out and drink Sangria and go shopping.'

Grace heard Nadja snapping at someone. 'They have Cavalli in Barcelona?'

'Lots of very cool shops and a great vintage market.' Grace tried to seal the deal.

'I never wear second-hand clothes. Make sure they fly me first class and I have best room in best hotel. We share and have a sleepover.'

Grace didn't know whether to feel elated or scared. 'You'll do it then?'

'Call my booker and she tell you my new day rate. Is very expensive. And Sergei and me we in London soon so you take me out to the cool places. I go now before this bitch ruins my hair. *Ciao*, like they say in Spain.'

Later, when Grace told Vaughn, he laughed and pinched her cheek. 'See? I knew you had it in you.' He was all smiles like she'd just discovered the next Damien Hirst. 'Leave it a couple of months and I'll give you some pointers on demanding a promotion and a pay rise.'

'I might cock up my shoots,' she said hastily. 'Probably will. Kiki's so picky about still-lifes and I'm going to have to juggle Lucie and Nadja when we—'

Vaughn clamped a hand over her mouth. 'I don't want to hear it. Your biggest downfall is your defeatism.' He pressed his thumb against Grace's bottom lip and his lashes swept down when Grace nibbled at the tip of it. 'You have an excellent eye, and if you can put together an outfit then I don't see the problem with shooting shoes or bags or whatever's in this month.'

Grace kissed his hand before pulling away. She prodded the little pile of DVDs on the coffee-table with her toe. 'You can watch your boring German film while I sketch out some rough layouts,' she decided, ignoring Vaughn's faint moan of protest. 'And then we need to talk about this party for Noah. I was thinking end of March, which is only three weeks away.' She picked up her notebook with the true fervour of the list geek that she was, and turned to a fresh page. 'How do you feel about sausage and mash instead of canapés?'

Her first shoot turned out to be rather an anti-climax for something that Grace had hungered for ever since she'd started at *Skirt*. There'd been a sticky moment when a courier had gone MIA with some really expensive purses, and Lucie had barely glanced at Grace's painstaking sketches, and didn't feel the need to come to the studio in case something went horribly wrong. But the photographer did what he was told, which was rarer than being fast-tracked up the queue for a Hermès Birkin, and though Grace waited anxiously to be bawled out for using cupcakes and fondant fancies as props to complement the new spring colours, it never happened. Instead the page layouts suddenly appeared on the gigantic flat-plan that took up a large part of one wall and Lucie decided that it would free her up to talk on the phone to her friends and book spa appointments, if Grace oversaw the accessory still-lifes for every issue. Grace had never thought getting ahead was so simple, but apparently she'd been wrong.

The party planning was going really well too, after Vaughn had loaned her Piers to run round East London looking at potential venues, interviewing DJs and commissioning graffiti artists to paint backdrops. Grace suspected that Vaughn was to Piers what Kiki was to her, but without the fashion advice. Either way, he was only too happy to do the heavy lifting and Vaughn was happy because Piers was out of his hair for a week or so and Grace was happy too.

Grace didn't like to dwell on her happiness, which she thought of as a Ready brek-style warm glow, encasing her in a little cocoon where the bad stuff couldn't get to her. But she was the happiest she'd ever been, not that she had a lot to compare it with. Life was good, really good – and Vaughn was a huge part of that. Grace could hardly believe that he'd become all things to her in a few short weeks: lover, confidant and friend. Maybe even her best friend, because the one not so good thing about her life was the Lily-shaped hole in the middle of it – but Lily would crack soon, Grace could tell. Then her happiness really would be complete, which was a scary thought, and as soon as she'd thunk it, Grace knew she'd jinxed her new-found joy.

It wasn't much of a surprise then to get a phone call later

that afternoon from her grandmother, demanding to know why a parcel of yarn she'd sent to Grace had been returned with *Not known at this address* stamped on it.

Having to tell her grandmother that she'd moved two months ago and had forgotten to tell her, made that little warm glow disappear pretty damn quick.

'I don't understand how we can speak every week and yet the fact that you'd moved house seemed to slip your mind. Really, dear, you met this man five minutes ago and now you're living with him,' her grandmother said, as if she understood only too well and didn't like it at all. 'I think it's very rash.'

'It's been five, nearly six months,' Grace pointed out. 'He had a spare room and he's away on business a lot so it just made sense when I had no hot water.'

'So you sleep in your own room, do you?' Scepticism fairly oozed down the phone line.

'Please, can we not even go there?' Grace begged, because her grandmother knew she was deflowered but chose to file it in her selective memory, along with the whole Rock Hudson turning out to be gay thing. 'I don't think either of us really wants to talk about that. Vaughn's place is huge and—'

'Vaughn?'

'Yes, Vaughn. That's his name, Gran.'

'It sounds like a surname.'

Grace put her hand over the mouthpiece so she could sigh. 'It *is* his surname. He goes by only one name, like Madonna.'

'But what's his first name?'

Vaughn's first name wasn't important, except that Grace didn't know what it was, and when she tried to explain that to her grandmother, it made Vaughn seem like some sketchy figure who could torture Grace for days, then bury her body in his back garden and nobody would ever find out. Her grandmother was the queen of worst-case scenarios.

'I don't like the idea of you living with *some man* that I've never even met, Gracie. And when I think of some of your previous boyfriends – well, you're not the best judge of character, are you?'

Grace hadn't introduced her grandmother to any boyfriends in the last five years so it was kind of unfair to bring up her teen romances. 'He's very nice,' she insisted. 'I'll bring him down for Sunday lunch some time soon.' Some time never.

'Not good enough,' her grandmother stated. 'Grandy's going on a golfing weekend this Friday so I'm coming to London.'

'This weekend is really tricky, and . . .'

'I'll get the eleven o'clock train on Saturday, and you and this Vaughn fellow will meet me for lunch. You can send me one of those text thingies on the phone to let me know the details.' It was her grandmother's 'don't fuck with me' voice that she'd used to great effect when the local cinema had tried to stop their Silver Screen concession rate for OAPs. There was no point in arguing.

chapter twenty-nine

Vaughn booked a table at J Sheekey because it had been his grandmother's favourite restaurant, but that didn't mean he was completely on board with the lunch arrangements. In fact, he'd tried his best to wriggle out of it. First he'd muttered something about possibly being in New York, before he remembered that he was an important art dealer who didn't have to deal with people's grandmothers if he didn't want to. 'It's out of the question, Grace,' he'd said flatly. 'In fact, it goes against the entire spirit of our agreement.'

'But she doesn't know we have an agreement. All she knows is that her beloved granddaughter is shacking up with some man who doesn't have a first name . . .'

'Of course I do. It's James.' Grace had simultaneously gaped at him and spilled tea down her new top. 'And if you ever call me by that name, I'll have you out on the street faster than you can blink.'

'James? I thought it was something really awful like Jethro or Jebediah. Don't know why you're so weird about it.'

'It was my father's name.' Five words, but there was a world of agony in Vaughn's absolutely deadpan delivery, like he didn't trust himself to put even an ounce of feeling into them. Grace had taken the hint and had launched into a whole series of inducements from sticky toffee pudding and blowjobs to watching back-to-back German films, until Vaughn had finally capitulated.

'I'll see you there against my better judgement,' he sighed unhappily on Saturday morning when Grace left to pick up her grandmother at Victoria because the thought of her braving the tube on her own and getting accosted by chuggers and dodgy Eastern European beggars made Grace break out in a cold sweat. It also meant her grandmother would have plenty of time to harangue her about living in sin, but them were the breaks.

Fortunately her grandmother had had an argy bargy with one of her rambling buddies, which meant she talked about that all the way to Leicester Square without pausing. Vaughn was waiting for them in the restaurant foyer, hanging back as her grandmother looked around suspiciously. Once she'd decided that the place passed muster, she allowed a server to take her coat. She was wearing the navy-blue Betty Barclay suit again – so she meant business. Grace threw Vaughn a sidelong glance, relieved that he was wearing a suit and not his usual weekend jeans and jumper combo.

'Gran, this is Vaughn. Vaughn, this is my grandmother, Jean.'

They shook hands, because her grandmother's generation didn't do air kisses, and then sized each other up like two dogs warily circling each other, before one of them decided to go for the throat.

'Grace has told me a lot about you,' Vaughn said politely, his face wearing a smiling Vaughn mask that didn't even look like him. 'It's good to finally meet you.'

'Well, she's told me very little about *you*,' her grandmother replied because she'd survived a war, one stillbirth, a daughter who'd got knocked up at seventeen and ten years of a Labour government, and she didn't take shit from anyone.

Vaughn did his best to be charming and deferential but Grace could tell from her grandmother's tightly pursed lips that she thought he was smarmy. When he suggested that they had caviar as a starter, that was profligate, which was right up there with adultery in her book.

Thankfully, the smoked haddock put her in a better mood and Grace carefully steered the conversation around to walking holidays abroad and what she should get her grandfather for his birthday. Vaughn remembered to adhere to Grace's list of strictly forbidden topics, which included politics and anything relating to Grace's degree (or lack thereof) and her job.

By the time they were waiting for their puddings, Grace allowed herself to relax slightly, leaning back in her chair until her grandmother folded her napkin, told Grace not to slouch and fixed Vaughn with the beadiest of eyes.

'So, how old are you?' she asked him baldly.

'I'm forty-one. Eighteen years older than Grace,' he added with the merest hint of a challenge, while Grace was forced to readjust the number in her head, which had hovered around thirty-seven. Forty-one seemed a lot older than thirty-seven, but then Vaughn *was* older than her. It was a simple truth – and the four extra years didn't matter that much.

'And I suspect you've been married at least once before?'

'Yes.'

'Children?'

'No.'

'Because if you have children with Grace you'll be in your sixties before they're even thinking of leaving home.'

Grace had decided to stay out of it because Vaughn was more than capable of taking care of himself, but she couldn't help the horrified, 'Gran! We're not having children. We're not even thinking of buying a house plant together, so just stop it.'

Vaughn patted Grace's hand, while her grandmother assessed the gesture to see if it was just a crafty trick to set her mind at ease.

'Someone has to say these things,' she insisted icily.

'No, they don't, Gran.'

This time Vaughn kept his hand on Grace's, the warmth of his fingers resting against hers a reminder that this time she wasn't defenceless in the face of her grandmother's most vociferous disapproval.

'Grace is a lovely girl and I don't see anything wrong in us being involved without having a five-year plan,' he said firmly.

Their puddings arrived just then, but her grandmother only gave her apple and rhubarb pie the most cursory of glances. 'A five-week plan would be something,' she said crisply. 'Grace *is* a lovely girl but she's very young and, quite frankly, she's always finding herself in these silly pickles and getting hurt. I don't want someone taking advantage of her.'

'Maybe she's taking advantage of *me*,' Vaughn suggested, and Grace had barely recovered from her grandmother's pithy summing-up of her failings before she was hurt and panicked all over again, because if Vaughn went where she thought he was going, then it was game over. 'I could be the one who gets hurt when she decides that she'd rather be with someone who's less likely to have a heart attack while he's running for the bus.'

'I don't think that's very likely.' At least her grandmother was smiling now, even if it was a pretty thin-lipped smile. 'You don't seem like the sort of man who takes buses.'

'He really doesn't,' Grace muttered, face pink because it was a sweet thing for Vaughn to say even though it was utter bullshit. 'Honestly, we're good and everything's fine and you don't need to worry about me.'

Her grandmother patted the hand that Vaughn wasn't holding. 'Someone has to worry about you, darling.' She paused as she came to a decision about something. 'I don't think we need to tell Grandy about this. Quite frankly, I can't see it lasting that long,' she said, plunging her spoon into the thick pastry crust.

After Vaughn had paid the bill, he insisted on taking her

grandmother back to Victoria Station and seeing her on to the platform safely. Grace was sure it was for her sake rather than her grandmother's. He stood over to one side, as Grace hugged her gran goodbye. 'Call me when you get home, OK?' she said.

Her grandmother stroked her cheek. 'You look well, Grace, but please have a little common sense. You wouldn't be the first girl to be taken in by a silver-tongued devil with a bulging wallet.'

It was a little too close to home for Grace to laugh it off. 'I know what I'm doing, Gran. Vaughn can seem a bit standoffish when you don't know him, but he's not like that at all. He can be really nice.'

'Nice is as nice does,' she said obliquely, checking her handbag was closed and looking down the platform. 'Well, I'd best be going. I don't want to leave it to the last minute and have to sit with my back facing the engine.'

She marched off, a sturdy but diminutive figure in the tweed coat that she'd had for years. Grace watched her until she got smaller and smaller, then turned and waved before she finally climbed on board.

'Grace, there's no need to look so upset,' Vaughn sighed when she trailed back to where he was waiting. 'I think the lunch went as well as it could. Honestly, did your grandmother say anything that came as a surprise?'

As they started walking in the direction of the taxi rank, Grace put her hands in her pockets and let her shoulders slump because there was no one to tell her off about it. 'Of course not. All that crap about five-year plans and our future children leaving for university while you wave them off from a bath-chair didn't bother me.' She came to a halt because she couldn't move her feet and try to articulate at the same time. 'As far as she knows, this is a proper relationship and we might really be in love, so it's very hurtful that she thinks it's just another mess that I've got myself into.'

Vaughn moved Grace out of the way of a family of tourists, and kept his hand on her arm. 'She's just being protective. You're her granddaughter so you'll always be a little girl to her.' He frowned. 'All your grandmother will ever see is an age gap.'

Grace made a tiny exasperated noise. 'And all *I* ever do is lie to her, and it cuts me up, but not enough to actually stop lying.'

'Secrets aren't the same as lying,' Vaughn commented, because they both had the muddiest of ethics, which was an odd thing to have in common. 'Look, it's done. We got lunch out of the way and we emerged fairly unscathed.' He walked with Grace through the narrow arch that led outside. 'As long as we're both happy with things, then there's nothing to worry about. You are happy, aren't you?'

Grace didn't have to hesitate. 'Of course I am!'

'Then it doesn't matter what anyone else thinks. Now – shall we go home? I'm sure I remember you promising me a whole afternoon in bed as payback.' Vaughn slid his hand down Grace's back and let it rest on the curve of her bottom for one meaningful second.

'I can't,' Grace sighed regretfully, as his hand tightened then moved away. 'I promised Piers we'd lock down the menu and then have a final look at the guest-list. Oh, don't frown at me like that, Vaughn. It will only take a couple of hours.'

He was definitely pouting. Or as close to pouting as he could get. 'Couldn't Piers do it on his own?'

'No! Everything has to be perfect and Piers is lovely but he doesn't get my whole low-rent Shoreditch vibe. He keeps trying to add lobster rolls to the menu when he thinks I won't notice.' Grace stood on tiptoe so she could kiss Vaughn's pursed mouth. 'Two hours, I promise, then I'm all yours.'

Grace had felt Vaughn smiling against her mouth but when she pulled away he was still sulking. 'Two hours and then I'm sending a search-party.'

'Two hours,' Grace repeated, clambering into the back of a taxi, which had just stopped in front of them. She looked out of the window at Vaughn standing there in his suit, appearing so proper and stiff if you didn't know him like she did. He caught her eye as the driver pulled away and smiled at her. One of those smiles that she didn't even know Vaughn had in his repertoire until a few weeks ago. Grace raised her hand and waggled her fingers and for the first time, Vaughn waved back.

chapter thirty

The Shoreditch party finally came to fruition on a cold, damp night at the beginning of March. Grace was still anxiously making additions to the guest-list at 8.30 p.m. and trying to pretend she wasn't bothered that the doors had opened half an hour earlier and that Vaughn, Piers and the gallery staff were still the only people there.

'How many people RSVP-ed?' Vaughn asked.

'We sent out Facebook invites,' Grace told him for the hundredth time – or it felt like the hundredth time. 'Nobody RSVPs on Facebook and no one ever turns up on time.'

Piers nodded. 'They really don't.' He came to a halt as Vaughn glared at him. 'I'm just going to make sure the bar's all set up.'

As soon as Piers scurried off, Vaughn turned to Grace. 'I knew it wasn't a good idea to have it on a Thursday evening. I told you that.'

'Thursday night is the new Friday night! Jesus, Vaughn, will you just stop? It's going to be fine. I know it all seems a bit chaotic compared to your usual parties, but everything's under control. People will come.'

Grace tried to smile comfortingly, but it felt more as if she was baring her teeth. She and Vaughn were both on edge, what with the party and the fact that she'd been on a lemon juice and cayenne pepper fast all week so she could fit into her new PPQ dress, but Vaughn really needed to lose the glower.

'Madeleine offered to help and you insisted that—'

Grace was saved by *Skirt's* fashion and beauty departments, minus Kiki, breezing through the door, still clutching the goodie bags from their previous engagement. The gallery was on three floors, all connected by a pretzel-like spiral staircase painted gold. The basement had been designated as a chill-out area, the ground floor had the free bar and the art, and the first floor was where people were meant to mill about, eating sausage and mash, while enjoying the pretentious black and white short films being projected on to the walls while they formed a new Zeitgeisty scene. It wasn't what the *Skirt* fashionistas were used to, and Grace could see the stragglers at the back hesitating on the threshold.

'Is there food? I'm starving,' Lucie announced, looking around suspiciously. She hated straying too far from West London.

There was a flurry of activity, people dumping coats behind the reception desk, snatching glasses of vodka and pomegranate juice and asking Grace, 'So where's the rich, older boyfriend, then?' like it was the only reason they'd come. Actually it probably was.

Vaughn had momentarily vanished, which Grace was grateful for as she saw Lily and Dan bringing up the rear.

'Oh hey, you made it,' she babbled, checking herself before she lunged forward to give Lily a hug, and froze herself when Dan put his arms around her and kissed her cheek. It was more affection than he'd ever shown her.

'Hello, stranger. Wow, you look really good,' he said. 'Very glossy.'

Grace ran a hand through her newly highlighted hair and grimaced. 'It's just smoke and mirrors,' she demurred. 'I'm so glad you both came. It's been ages . . .'

Dan grinned. 'Yeah, I can't remember the last time I saw you.'

'It was just before she bailed out on our wedding at the last moment,' Lily reminded him as she unbuttoned her coat to reveal her medium-sized baby bump. 'I need to pee,' she decided and wandered off.

'Is she ever going to stop hating me?' Grace asked Dan, who looked like he was over the whole bailing out on the wedding thing.

'You really hurt her feelings and she's got all these hormones making everything worse. Talking of which . . .' Dan whipped out a photo and proudly showed Grace a 3D ultrasound scan of something he called 'the peanut'.

'That's the heartbeat and you can just make out a leg,' he said, while Grace squinted at an amorphous blob.

'Grace doesn't want to see that,' Lily hissed, coming up behind them.

'Of course I do,' Grace insisted, rubbing her hands together nervously as Vaughn ventured out of the back office. He saw Grace, half-waved and started moving in her direction.

There was nothing Grace could do to stop the inevitable meeting between Lily and Vaughn. It was going to be like matter and anti-matter colliding, and the whole gallery would suddenly explode, leaving nothing behind but a lone flat cap worn by one of the DJ's mates.

'See? I knew people would turn up eventually,' Vaughn said, ruffling Grace's hair, though he hadn't known any such thing and she'd told him a million times to leave her hair alone. 'Isn't that your French friend Laetitia at the bar?'

'Yeah,' Grace muttered distractedly because Lily was scrutinising Vaughn with frightening intensity, like she'd had her eyes replaced with a bar-code reader. 'Do you want to go over and say hello?'

'In a minute.' Vaughn extended a hand. 'Aren't you going to introduce us, Grace?'

'Lily, Dan, this is Vaughn. Vaughn, this is Lily and Dan,'

Grace said limply, and she could see the light bulb pinging above Vaughn's head and Lily was opening her mouth and Grace knew exactly what she was going to say.

'You ruined my special day!' Lily pointedly rubbed her bump because it was the best prop ever for establishing the moral high ground.

'I did?' Vaughn looked more bemused than anything.

'Well, indirectly. Lily and Dan got married on Christmas Eve, when we were in Whistler.'

'Because you'd rather go skiing with *him* than stick around to see me get married!'

'Lils, you really need to start getting over it,' Dan said in a long-suffering way, like they'd discussed the Grace situation many times between them. 'Though to be fair, Gracie, we had to substitute Lily's inbred cousin and it really fucked up the group photos.'

'Oh yeah, and there was the wedding planner you had to fork out for instead of getting me to do it for free,' Grace said hotly, 'and by the way, Lily, what you said to me—'

Lily was squaring up to Grace, safe in the knowledge that she could probably throw a punch because Grace couldn't smack a woman in her condition, but Vaughn was clearing his throat.

'Well, I am somewhat responsible,' he said, though actually he was completely responsible. 'I booked our holiday as a surprise for Grace, because I wanted our first Christmas together to be memorable.'

Grace wanted to tell Vaughn that he needn't have bothered, because Lily knew about the arrangement. Knew about it, and thought it was sordid and tacky and one step up from selling her arse in King's Cross.

'But I'm her best friend and I was getting married,' Lily argued. 'I should have had first refusal.'

Vaughn put an arm around Grace, so he could pull her stiff body closer and brush her cheek with his lips, while Lily watched in disbelief. 'I'm sure Grace has already told you she was bedridden for most of Christmas with the most awful flu. Wasn't Christmas Eve the day you collapsed, darling?'

Grace almost missed her cue. 'Yup. How long was I out for? Maybe ten minutes. Right in front of Robert Simmons. Beyond embarrassing.'

Lily was vibrating, bump and all. 'Well, you never told me! And I had to find out from Beth in Features that you met Robert Simmons.'

'Lily, you were the one who wasn't talking to me. You can't have it both ways,' Grace said crossly.

'And she looked dreadful, if that's any consolation,' Vaughn continued, biting out the words as if he was relishing every moment of exacting revenge on Grace for making him eat salad all week. 'So even if Grace had been in the country, I don't think she'd have been able to make your wedding – *and* she'd have ruined the photos.'

'A grey complexion *would* have clashed with the dress,' Lily conceded, and Vaughn saw his advantage and pressed it home.

'But let's not rehash all this when I should be offering you congratulations. You must have been a very beautiful bride.'

Lily wasn't as impervious to Vaughn's charm as Grace's grandmother had been. She gave him one of those smiles that knocked most men into the middle of next week. To his credit, Vaughn didn't show any signs of being instantly smitten. 'Well, I looked OK in the photos.'

'You looked gorgeous, babe,' Dan insisted, stepping between Lily and Vaughn so he could mark his territory. 'You know, Grace used to go out with my friend, Liam. Great guy.'

Vaughn's work was done. 'Really?' he asked without much interest. 'There are some sofas downstairs if you want to sit down.' He took hold of Grace's hand. 'Will you excuse us?'

Grace had never been more pleased to be excused. The gallery had really filled out while Vaughn had been trying to broker the peace deal. There was a crush at the bar and even though she'd told the DJ that she wanted background music, Grace could hear Northern Soul booming down from the first floor so loudly that the bass made the walls vibrate. Some of the models Grace had invited from Nadja's agency were even dancing, gawky limbs flailing like wraiths caught in a stiff breeze. 'Well, at least people turned up.'

'Is Noah here? Did he say he was coming?'

'I'm sure he'll be here soon.'

'Well, he'd better,' Vaughn muttered darkly and strode off.

At ten thirty there was another swell of arrivals and Grace decided that she might as well call the party a success. The sausage and mash had run out, but there was still plenty of vodka and the upstairs space had become the unofficial dance floor. If nothing else, everyone seemed to be enjoying themselves and had merged into a seamless, heaving throng that might possibly cause a Zeitgeist. Fortunately, Piers had invited some proper grown-ups so Vaughn had people to talk to, but Grace could see him frowning as he failed to spot Noah.

Grace had officially given up on Noah, but as she came back from the loo, she was corralled by two of the gallery staff because someone on the guest-list had arrived with eleven people in tow. As Grace got nearer, she could hear Noah saying belligerently, 'Listen, sweetheart, I'm on the fucking list.' He looked up, saw Grace rushing over and waited with arms folded.

'It's OK, you can let him in,' Grace assured the girl on the door. 'He's on the list.' She lowered her voice so Noah wouldn't hear. 'He's Mr Vaughn's special guest.'

'The Fire Department could shut us down. We're way over capacity.' The door whore was very socially responsible for someone wearing a tutu.

Grace floundered, thought about stamping her foot, but wrung her hands instead, while Noah and friends went into a huddle like they were about to bolt and go somewhere else to keep their alcohol levels topped up.

Salvation appeared in the form of the *Skirt* posse who couldn't wait to get back to civilisation. 'Great party, Gracie,' Lucie trilled as she pushed her way towards the door. 'Really looking forward to the next one.'

The velvet rope was finally unclipped and Noah and his plus eleven bundled in, including Alex who gave Grace an ironic salute as he shouldered past her. Grace was immediately tackled by Noah, who pulled her into an enthusiastic and sweaty hug. 'Please tell me that there's still free booze.'

She wriggled free before she got Noah stains on her new dress. 'There's lots of vodka left but no sausage and mash. Where's Lola?'

Noah shrugged. 'Don't know. We're not together any more.' He didn't seem particularly bothered about it. 'Shall we go and sneak a fag?'

The gallery manager was snapping his fingers at Grace. 'I can't, but I have models. Upstairs. They're all dancing very badly and ruining my vibe so feel free to try and separate one from the herd.' She touched Noah's arm. 'When you see Vaughn, will you please be nice to him?'

'Gracie, that's no fun,' Noah said, wagging his shaven head from side to side as she looked at him imploringly. 'Oh look – if it means that much to you, I guess I could manage a hello.'

'It does, and if you could even muster a "good to see you and this is a great party" too, then that would be even better.'

The last guests left just before one, and after Grace had paid the DJ she wearily climbed the pretzel staircase to the first floor where Vaughn, Noah, Piers and a few stragglers had fetched up on a group of sofas. Grace pulled on a bright smile but she'd have much preferred to be back at Vaughn's having her last cup of tea of the day.

The whole evening had been one stress bomb after another, and now as Vaughn came back from fetching the remaining few bottles of vodka, Grace realised there was nowhere for him to sit. Vaughn cast his eyes over the sofas, realised he was out in social Siberia, and looked as if he might actually cry.

'I need the loo,' she hissed at him from her spot at the end of one of the couches. 'Sit here and I'll perch on the arm when I get back.'

It would have been a perfect solution achieved with minimum ease, except that when Grace stood up in her nosebleed-high heels, after far too much vodka, she pitched forward and ended up sprawling across the low table in front of them. Thank God she was wearing opaque tights.

There was a chorus of, 'Are you all right?' and Grace wished that everyone would shut the hell up and allow her to limp to the Ladies accompanied by what was left of her pride.

'Did you eat any dinner?' Vaughn asked.

'I had too much to do,' Grace said, rubbing her knee. 'And then it was all gone.'

'You can't drink on a stomach that's only got cayenne pepper and lemon juice in it.'

Grace was about to point out that her five-day detox was something that she didn't particularly want to share with the group, until someone piped up, 'Does that diet actually work? I really can't face doing Atkins again.'

'I lost four pounds in five days,' Grace admitted, though most of it had been water. That was the starter for ten. They were meant to be hipsters, scene kids, art iconoclasts and tastemakers, but they suddenly morphed into a bunch of housewives swapping diet stories. Grace was appalled. It was like being back at work.

Dieting was one subject that Vaughn excelled in, and when Grace finally hobbled away he had a rapt audience as he explained the benefits of weight training. 'Muscle actually weighs three times more than fat, but the more muscle you have, the more calories you burn.' Gustav had created a monster.

When Grace returned after trying to rescue her smoky-eye make-up, which was looking a little too racoon, they were well into the bottles of vodka.

'You must be starving,' Vaughn said, his arm automatically locking around Grace's waist as she settled on the arm of the couch. 'And are you going to be comfortable there?'

'I'm fine,' Grace assured him, and he smiled at her. Grace was used to Vaughn's smiles now. He had about twenty and she knew what each one meant, from the cold, wintry twist of his lips when he was trying to stay calm in the face of extreme provocation, to the dopey, dazed grin he'd give her when they had a lazy fuck on a Sunday morning. But Grace was sure that she hadn't seen this smile before. It creased his face, wrinkling his eyes and giving him two deep dimples as he looked at Grace like she was the reason the sun came up and flowers grew, and he was very pleased that she was currently leaning against him. It was *that* good a smile.

Some impulse that she wouldn't have given into if she hadn't drunk so much vodka made Grace bend her head and press her lips against Vaughn's forehead. Which just made his smile broaden so Grace leaned in even closer because she wanted to kiss the grin right off his face. She didn't even have time to pout her mouth into a perfect kiss-shape when Noah swapped places with the person who'd been sitting on Vaughn's other side, and the spell was broken.

'So, can I pick your brains about showing in New York?' he asked Vaughn, and Grace ceased to exist as they started this incomprehensible back and forth about galleries and dealers and the new curator at the Whitney Museum of American Art.

Grace started talking to Piers, who was shooting Vaughn these anxious looks like a little boy staying up way past bedtime who hoped that his daddy wouldn't notice, and Alex about their mutual love of Rodgers and Hammerstein musicals. It was far more interesting than the big group discussion about how all the original YBAs had 'sold out'. Grace really didn't see what the big deal was about selling out. Languishing in obscurity was all very well, but unless you were a Trustafarian, it led to bad things like not being able to pay the rent and yellow ice in your toilet bowl.

Vaughn was rhythmically stroking her hip, while he pleaded the case for the opposition and laughed at the howls of protest. Grace wondered if maybe they should do this once a month. Not another raucous party because her nerves couldn't take it, but hosting a low-key drinks and art salon, where Vaughn was at his best, rather than skulking on the sidelines as people pogo-ed to The Horrors. And he should always wear suits; he could become known for them. He did look so good in a suit.

The party ended when the gallery manager wandered up the stairs and stood there rattling his keys. Vaughn got up to settle the final bill and Grace clumsily slid on to the warm patch where Vaughn had been sitting.

Noah nudged her with his arm. 'He's not so bad, I guess.' He looked at Vaughn who was handing over a huge wad of notes. 'For a heartless, commerce-obsessed scumbag.'

'You're warming to him, I can tell.' Grace nudged him back. 'He's actually very sweet and kind, if you give him the chance.'

'Yeah, I'll take your word for it. Anyway, I thanked him for the invite and the booze and it's all good,' Noah said, stroking his bristly chin. 'You fancy going on somewhere else? There's a little bar around the corner with a late licence.'

Grace raised her eyebrows. 'Do they serve food?'

'I'll treat you to a kebab on the way,' Noah said with a mischievous grin, which suited him much better than his usual smirk.

'You've got yourself a deal.' Grace levered herself up and

walked over to Vaughn, who held out his arm so he could pull Grace in for a kiss.

'You're a very clever girl,' he murmured in her ear, looking over to where Noah was sprawled out on the sofa. 'I've never seen Noah smile so much.'

'It was nothing,' Grace insisted. 'Well, actually it's taken years off me but I think we pretty much rocked it. And Noah wants to carry on drinking so you might as well make the most of it while he's in such a good mood.'

Vaughn shook his head. 'Noah will keep. Let's get you home. You must be dead on your feet.'

Grace lifted up her leg. 'No, I'm wearing my eight-hour heels and actually I think I'm getting my second wind. There might even be dancing.'

She grabbed Vaughn's hand as a prelude to pulling him down the pretzel staircase after the others, but he stayed rooted to the spot. 'It's really late and I have an early conference call in the morning. Well, in a few hours actually.'

'Just half an hour then,' Grace begged, because she'd been on duty all night and the prospect of a relaxed little nightcap was just what she needed to decompress. Plus all she could think about was a kebab, with chips and the really hot sauce. 'Oh, come on, Vaughn, it will be fun.' She gave him the look that he always told her she should only use for the power of good because it was so persuasive. 'Please.'

'You go,' he said slowly, as if it was against his better judgement. 'Though you're not going to be in any fit state for work tomorrow if you pull an all-nighter.'

'It won't be an all-nighter. An hour. Or two hours, tops,' Grace promised as she carefully picked her way down the stairs, clinging tightly to the rail because pretzels and high heels and vodka were not a good combination.

'You always say two hours when you really mean at least four,' Vaughn sniffed, as they reached the ground floor. 'I'm not going to wait up for you and I'm definitely not going to phone in sick for you either when the hangover kicks in, in the morning.'

'I hardly ever get hangovers,' Grace said blithely, and Vaughn just laughed like it was the funniest joke she'd ever cracked before he disappeared out of the door, snapping over his shoulder at Piers that he wanted a word with him.

chapter thirty-one

How drunk did you have to be when a feckless reprobate like Noah Skinner decided that you needed to be put in a taxi? Very, very drunk indeed.

The after-hours drinking den hadn't been just round the corner but a half-hour's walk away, and had looked like someone's front room. Grace never did discover if it was someone's front room, but they'd had a cool collection of sounds, more vodka and although it was meant to close at two, they'd had a lock in.

After that, it had all become a bit of a blur, though Grace did remember buying a round of drinks for everyone in the house on Vaughn's credit card, possibly singing 'A Total Eclipse of the Heart' and there had finally been a trip to a kebab shop. When she'd tried to leap the counter so she could shave the elephant's leg, after much encouragement from Alex, Noah had marched her to the nearest minicab office.

Now she was standing outside the gates of Vaughn's ridiculously big house, unable to remember the security code and also having extreme difficulty in locating the buzzer.

Her fingers had turned into fat, stubby sausages so Grace hit as many buttons as she could see on the security panel until Vaughn's voice floated through the ether.

'Grace?'

'Lemme in! I'm freezing my arse off out here.'

The gates slowly swung open and Grace staggered up the drive. The front door opened, light spilling out, and there was Vaughn standing in the doorway.

'I didn't mean to wake you,' she bellowed when she was halfway up the drive. Her voice had sounded a lot less shouty and slurry in her head. 'Did you wait up for me? You didn't have to 'cause I was fine.'

She finally reached the front door and almost fell through it; only Vaughn's hand seizing her elbow stopped her from falling over for about the fifth time that night. 'Did you miss me? I missed you.'

Vaughn pulled Grace through the door and slammed it shut behind her, smiling thinly as she jumped. 'You're drunk,' was all he said, as she wobbled on one leg and tried to take off her shoe.

Grace gave up on the buckle and tugged the shoe off with great force, nearly toppling over again, before she attempted the same manoeuvre on the other foot. 'Maybe a little bit tipsy,' she corrected him. 'Just a little bit.'

She brushed back the curtain of her hair that was in her face, spitting out a few stray strands that had ended up in her mouth, and froze at the look on Vaughn's face. He was furious and she didn't know why.

'What the hell have you been doing?' he hissed, reaching her in a few short strides so he could grasp Grace's upper arms and haul her close. 'It's nearly four o'clock.'

She wriggled in his hold. 'It's not that late,' she insisted. 'It doesn't feel that late.'

'I've been calling you and calling you. I even called the car company and they hadn't heard from you. How did you get home? What the fuck have you been doing?' He was spitting questions at her and shaking her slightly when he got to the end of each one.

'Why are you so mad at me?' she whimpered. 'You said I

could go and I didn't hear my phone 'cause I couldn't find my phone. Noah got me a minicab because he said . . .' Grace closed her eyes because she couldn't bear to look at Vaughn's red face any more and she needed to think exactly what Noah had said '. . . I was too much of a princess to get the night bus.'

'Did you fuck him? You fucked that little shit, didn't you?' This time he shook Grace so hard she was sure that her teeth were no longer attached to her gums.

'What? No!' She tried to struggle free but Vaughn refused to ease the punishing grip that was going to leave bruises. 'I didn't fuck anybody! What are you talking about?'

'Then why is your lipstick so smeared and you're missing buttons. Ripped them off in the throes of passion, did he?'

Grace looked down at her dress, which was missing a few buttons, where she'd caught the hem on the edge of the table when she'd tried to get up and had fallen over. But even with her brain fogged with vodka she knew that it redefined the concept of a flimsy excuse. She stuck with the easy to explain. 'My lipstick's smudged because I had a bloody kebab. Here, smell!' And she breathed onion fumes in Vaughn's face, which was the secret code to make him let her go so she could rub her arms reproachfully. 'You think I fucked Noah?'

Vaughn folded his arms and looked at Grace like she'd just heaved her way out of some primordial swamp. 'Well, didn't you?'

'No, I didn't! How could you think that? I wouldn't do that – I'm with you!' She felt like she should be shouting but there was too much hurt in her voice to make it do anything other than throb.

'I don't believe you,' Vaughn said flatly, as if that was all there was to it.

'You don't believe me?' Grace didn't feel quite so drunk any more as she stood there in her stockinged feet with Vaughn towering over her, disappointment and disapproval etched into his face. It was one hell of a reality check. 'How could you? I would never do something like that! I was just drinking with him and about ten other people. Seriously!'

Vaughn was still staring at her, his eyes flickering from Grace's face to her body as if he had UV vision and could see Noah's fingertips all over her.

'Oh, for fuck's sake!' Grace wrenched up the skirt of her dress. 'You want proof I didn't shag him, be my guest.' She was already yanking down her tights and she didn't know how far she was going to go with this, how far Vaughn expected her to go, but she wasn't going to be found guilty of something so completely ludicrous.

'Stop it! Just stop it!' Vaughn snapped out of his funk and his hands were on Grace's, pulling up her tights, smoothing over her hips again and again as if he could brush away Noah's phantom touch. 'I swear, Grace, if you ever, ever fuck him, I'd kill you and then I'd kill him.'

It was such a silly, melodramatic thing to say in a fight that had already seen too much silliness and melodrama that Grace wanted to laugh, but Vaughn's voice was so low and urgent, his eyes blazing into hers, that all she managed to croak was, 'I haven't and I'm not going to, but if you think I'm the kind of person who would fuck someone else behind your back then I'm leaving.'

The onions in the kebab were repeating on her and Grace pulled a face as Vaughn cupped her cheek, wiping the corners of her mouth where her lipstick had bled. Five minutes earlier, she'd have smacked his hands away but now she curled her fingers round his wrist and stroked the spot where his pulse was thundering away.

Vaughn cleared his throat. 'Just in case you were wondering, Grace, this isn't an open relationship.'

She suddenly pulled away from him and flapped her hands ineffectually as she opened her mouth and then wished she hadn't.

'What's the matter?' Vaughn asked, as Grace turned a full 360 degrees because she couldn't decide the fastest way to get to the guest bathroom. Vaughn was already half-lifting her by the elbows and propelling her down the hall.

It was a three-second dash before Grace was on her knees and bringing up everything she'd put in her mouth in the last three hours.

Vaughn was much more helpful than he'd been in Whistler. He squatted down next to Grace as she hunched over the toilet bowl and gathered her hair up in a loose ponytail as he rubbed her back. 'You stupid, stupid girl,' he said over the retching.

Eventually there was nothing left in her stomach and Grace sat back with an exhausted little sigh. There was drool dribbling down her chin and she looked at her hand in dismay when she wiped her mouth and found it smeared with what was left of her lipstick.

'Are you all right now?' Vaughn ventured, all ready with a damp towel. For the life of her, Grace couldn't decide if it was the alcohol and the kebab that was responsible for her hurlathon or the violent argument they'd just had.

She stayed on her feet long enough to clean her teeth, then deliberately ignoring Vaughn's attempts to take her arm, she sank to the floor and star-fished her limbs.

'You can't be comfortable like that,' Vaughn protested, but he was sitting down and resting his back against the side of the bath. 'Wouldn't you like to lie on a bed, or a sofa?'

'How can you say that this isn't an open relationship, when it's not meant to be a relationship at all?' Grace demanded in a raspy voice.

'It's just an expression.'

'It's not a relationship, Vaughn. We're not having a relationship. It's an arrangement, we both know that.'

It sort of *was* a relationship, but if they started calling it that, slipping into bad habits, then, like all Grace's relationships, it would end prematurely and horribly. And she didn't want this to end – yet.

'I know it's an arrangement. It was just a slip of the tongue.' Vaughn gave an empty chuckle, which completely lacked anything approaching humour. 'Neither of us are cut out for a relationship, We don't play well with others, do we?'

'Well, you definitely don't! I stayed out way later than I said I would but I swear, Vaughn, if you think I'd shag Noah then come trotting back to you, I'm going. I mean it.' Grace could feel the anger welling up again.

'Would it make you feel better if I told you that I hated myself the whole time you were throwing up?'

'Not really.' Grace wondered if that might actually be the moment that Vaughn said the s-word, but he just reached over to stroke her foot, which was the only part of her within arm's reach. 'You could at least offer to make me some toast and tea – that would be a start.'

'I could do that,' Vaughn agreed gravely. He stood up and very gently helped Grace to her feet. Her ribs felt like they'd had a run-in with a cheese grater. 'What number does the toaster go on again?'

He wasn't joking either. Nor was he capable of getting the exact boiling-water-to-milk ratio right for a cup of tea that was halfway drinkable.

'I'll do it myself,' Grace sighed, using the wall to steady herself as she limped towards the kitchen.

They sat on opposite sides of the table drinking tea. Every time she looked at Vaughn from under her lashes as she took a sip of tea, he'd smile hesitantly at her like he was trying to make things right between them, though he obviously didn't have a clue where to start.

Grace looked out of the window where the sun was high up in the sky. 'There's no point in going to bed,' she said. 'I'll just feel worse when I have to get up in an hour's time.'

'Surely you're entitled to a sick day,' Vaughn suggested, but Grace shook her head.

'Kiki knows I had a big party last night so she's not going to believe any excuses about twenty-four-hour stomach bugs, and I have a ton of prep work for Nadja's shoot.' Grace slumped over the table. 'You should probably let Piers have the day off though.'

'Oh, bloody hell!' It took a huge effort but Grace raised her head to catch the shamed look on Vaughn's face. 'I fired Piers.'

'You did *what*?'

'I told him to keep an eye on you, and when you hadn't come home, I phoned him up and sacked him,' Vaughn admitted, running a hand through his hair. 'I don't know what gets into me sometimes.'

Grace could have done without the shouting and the shaking he'd subjected her to, but it had been a long time since anyone had been worried about her making it home in one piece. Not since she'd lived with her grandparents and their ridiculous 11 p.m. curfew. As Grace had tiptoed up the stairs, usually at least two hours after eleven, she'd always hear her grandmother call out, 'Is that you, dear? You're grounded for a month.' Happy days. Still, it didn't mean that Vaughn was forgiven.

'Piers lasted about ten minutes after you'd gone before he walked into a lamppost and had to go home. You'd better phone him up and unfire him,' Grace snapped.

'I'll do that,' Vaughn said quickly. 'He's had his eye on this Pop Art triptych that came in last month. It might do as a peace-offering.'

'You'd do that?'

'I would do that. I'm trying to make up for how unreasonable I've been, but you're sitting there with a look of dejection that I can't seem to shift.'

'I know.' Grace pulled a rueful face. 'Honestly, I could sulk for England.'

Vaughn reached across the table and took her hand. The spark between them that was always there, even when they were fighting, began to burn brightly again. Grace let her fingers coil around Vaughn's and none of it seemed to matter so much any more.

chapter thirty-two

Grace had had a lot of fights with a lot of boys, none of them coming even close to the ferocity of her fight with Vaughn, and it had always been the beginning of the end. They'd make up, but then they'd break up, usually within a week.

But that didn't seem to be the case with Vaughn – though it was hard to tell. The fight had been followed by a busy weekend of back-to-back brunches, lunches and dinners which hadn't left much time to prod at the wounds to see if they still hurt, then he'd flown to New York for the week, while Grace got the easyJet to Barcelona for five days' shooting main fashion with Nadja.

It was the first time Grace had been in the presence of Nadja as an almost-supermodel rather than as an almost-friend, and it had been a challenging experience. Although Grace had accompanied Nadja to McDonald's on three separate occasions on two different continents for a Quarter Pounder with cheese, fries and a full-fat Coke, on the job she insisted that, 'Every day I only eat thirty grams of cashew and an apple sliced eight times.' Every night, without fail, she'd eat the food right off Grace's plate, when she wasn't knocking back vodka and flirting shamelessly with any male aged between nine and ninety.

Nadja had also stuck to her plan that they'd share a room. The first thing Grace heard when she opened her eyes every morning was Nadja complaining about everything, from the birds singing too loudly to the sun coming through the drapes too brightly. The last thing Grace heard as she tried desperately to get some sleep was Nadja carping about her early call time or the girl in the club they'd just been to who wouldn't let Nadja queue jump in the Ladies.

But the shoot had had its upsides too. Grace had been left to her own styling devices as Lucie's husband had just been made redundant from his job in the City so she was spending all her time on the phone in tears because they might have to sell their holiday home in Cap Ferrat. And as the photographer was an egotistical cokehead, he spent most of his time in a drug-addled haze in the hotel bar, leaving his assistant to take the shots, which had turned out surprisingly well.

Nadja looked like a barely tamed wood nymph in a series of couture gowns cascading around her in a wash of saturated colour. Grace's favourite picture was Nadja skipping towards the camera on the beach at Sitges wearing a plunging red Viktor & Rolf dress, its skirt made entirely out of feathers, which seemed to float in the breeze. Nadja had her head back, toffee-coloured hair streaming behind her like she was about to throw down – possibly with someone who'd dared to look at her funny. Grace was usually the queen of quirk, but Kiki was all about the strong, sexy silhouette so she'd be happy, which was the important thing.

Still, Grace had never been more pleased to get on a 6 a.m. flight out of Barcelona on the Saturday morning, after promising Nadja that she couldn't wait for the next time they worked together.

Coming back to Vaughn's house felt very familiar now. Grace headed straight for the kitchen to put on the kettle and root through the fridge for something to eat. There was milk, so at least she could have a cup of tea, but apart from that the fridge was bare and there wasn't much in the cupboards except Vaughn's protein bars and some dried shiitake mushrooms.

Grace thought longingly of the two beds upstairs. Then she thought of the trip down to Waitrose on the Finchley Road so she could do a really big shop and have a proper Sunday roast waiting for Vaughn when he got home the next day. She drank her tea standing up because sitting down would be fatal, and was just about to haul her aching carcass to the front door when her phone rang.

It was Lily, which meant that it was a misdial. Had to be.

'Grace? You're back from Barcelona, right? Are you doing anything? I've just had the most massive row with Dan and he's stormed out!'

At any other time Grace would have been thrilled to hear from Lily, but she was seriously sleep-deprived and clutching the phone precariously between cheek and shoulder as she tried to put on her jacket.

'I've been back a couple of hours,' Grace mumbled. 'Why are you and Dan arguing?' It was too much to expect Lily to call because she'd been itching to get a debrief on Grace's trip. But at least she'd called.

'. . . he said that he didn't see why we should move his guitars out of the spare room if the baby was going to sleep in a crib in our room and I said that everyone gets a nursery ready when they're having a baby because it's just what you do, and he said—'

'Lily. Hey, *Lily*!' Grace repeated a bit louder so Lily would stop. Just stop. 'Do you want to meet for a coffee in Primrose Hill or something?'

'I can't drink coffee!'

'Decaff then or a herbal tea or an orange juice. I need fresh air before I fall into a coma.'

There was a moment's silence while Lily pondered this daring request. 'Well, OK. I suppose that would be all right,' she said graciously.

*

For someone who claimed to have been crying all day, Lily looked remarkably fresh-faced. Grace would even have said she was radiant but that could have been the pregnancy or because Lily's knowledge of skincare was encyclopaedic – she even knew what AHAs were.

Lily had already snagged a corner table in the Primrose Bakery as a water-soaked Grace, who'd got caught in a sudden shower on the way from the bus-stop, squelched her way to the table.

'I had your tunic dry-cleaned,' Grace said, carefully placing the precious package on the spare chair. 'Have you ordered?'

'I was waiting for you.' Lily looked coyly at the menu. 'If you were going to have a cupcake, then I'd have one too.'

After the lemon juice and cayenne-pepper detox and Nadja eating most of her meals, Grace's waistline could handle a cupcake or three. She'd barely licked the butter-cream frosting off her first one, before Lily was back to the fight she'd had with Dan, which sounded like an argument for the sake of having an argument. Throwing him out for his spirited defence against using a nappy delivery service for a baby who wasn't even born yet seemed a tad melodramatic.

Lily didn't really need much input from Grace, apart from the odd 'Really?' and, 'Yeah, that does sound annoying,' so Grace made short work of cupcake number two and realised that she was still furious with Lily and it was exponentially increasing as the minutes went by.

'And then he said it was just my hormones,' Lily spat and she'd obviously come to the end, because she folded her arms and looked at Grace expectantly.

'Yeah, sounds about right.' Lily was too shocked to do anything other than gasp, as Grace continued, 'Like, when I have PMS, I still have valid reasons to be irritated and pissed off but the hormones bring a side order of crazy to the table.'

'Well, thanks for the moral support,' Lily snapped, pushing away her half-eaten cupcake. 'Usually you're only too happy to slag Dan off.'

'Then the minute you make up, which you know you will, you tell him all the mean things I've said about him and he hates me a little bit more,' Grace reminded Lily waspishly. 'So what's the point?'

'Well, why did you bother asking me to meet you then, Grace?'

'I don't know,' Grace sighed. 'I'm sorry I never told you about Vaughn, I really am. And you don't even know how gutted I am that I missed your wedding, but half the reason why I never tell you stuff is because you're not interested.'

Lily sniffed contemptuously and Grace wondered why she'd even tried to explain or apologise. 'You didn't tell me because you knew what you were doing was totally wrong.'

'I'm not getting into that again. The real issue here is that you haven't even asked me how *I* am. You just called because you've had some bogus row with Dan and I'm meant to be the sympathetic best friend because it's your life and I just live in it.' Grace started shoving phone, purse and uneaten cupcake into her bag. 'Maybe I have been a shitty friend, Lils, but so have you, and what you called me was fucking unforgivable.'

There was meant to be a majestic storming out but the café was crowded and there was a pushchair blocking the exit so Grace ended up having to squeeze between the tables and was still within earshot when Lily burst into tears.

Grace could feel at least twenty pairs of disapproving eyes all cutting into her because she was an unfeeling bitch who shouted at pregnant women and made them cry. There was no way she was going back to their table, absolutely no way, except she was. But she was doing it with a really put-upon air to let Lily know she wasn't completely whipped.

'You have no idea what hard work it is being friends with

you,' Lily spluttered. 'You're, like, always moody and you never tell me what the matter is so in the end I don't ask.'

'I am not always moody. It's just the way my face looks.' Grace tipped her head back and opened her eyes really wide to stop the tears from spilling over. One girl crying in public was bad; two would have been ridiculous. 'I just felt like my life was always derailing in these hideous ways and you're just so fucking *perfect*. Everything you do is perfect and everyone loves you and you make me feel like a complete fuck-up.'

'I'm not perfect. I have problems too,' Lily insisted, wiping her eyes with a napkin. 'You always know exactly how to hurt me, Grace, and you totally nailed it when you said my life was over. I'm pregnant and I'm really scared I'm going to get stretchmarks and I'm only twenty-four and I had all this stuff I was going to do and I love Dan but what if he's not the one and, hello, I have *haemorrhoids*.'

It was the complete essence of Lily in one sentence. The sobs that Grace had been trying to hold back turned into giggles on the way out of her mouth. 'I'm sorry. That's not funny,' she choked, laughing so hard that tears poured down her cheeks again.

Lily was still crying but as Grace tried desperately to get herself under control, she gave a gurgly, hiccupy laugh, because the giggling was contagious. Like the time they'd both nearly been fired for having hysterics during an important company presentation because the publishing director's flies were undone. Grace and Lily sat at their corner table laughing and crying and flapping their hands in front of their faces, until the yummy mummy next to them got up and moved to a different table.

'I did really miss you, Gracie,' Lily said, when the giggles had quietened down. 'I've had nobody to talk to except Dan, and I don't think he can take much more.'

'You have loads of friends,' Grace pointed out gently. 'And most of them don't come with as much drama as I do.'

'I don't – not proper friends. Girls don't really want me as a friend because of this . . .' Lily waved a hand dismissively in front of her perfectly symmetrical face. 'Like they can't quite trust me not to steal their boyfriends or something. Don't get me wrong, I like being pretty but I feel I have to work extra hard to be nice and super-friendly all the time. And then when you didn't tell me about him, about Vaughn, it was like you didn't rate me as a friend as much as I rated you. That really hurt.'

Grace blinked back more tears. 'I didn't tell you because I knew it was a bit dodgy, and honestly, at the beginning I didn't think it was going to last more than about three months, and now . . .'

'And now?'

'It's good, really good. I feel that everything in my life is finally moving forward and I think I'm happy. The only thing that totally sucked was not having you.'

Lily reached across the table to squeeze Grace's hand so tightly that Grace thought she might have broken a couple of fingers. 'There were so many times when Beth in Features was wearing something really fashion backwards and I wanted to bitch about her.'

Grace nodded frantically. 'Are we talking about the high-waisted bootcut jeans with the orange ballet flats? Oh, poor Beth, she tries so hard but she never gets it right.' She scraped her chair around the corner so, just this once, she could give Lily a totally spontaneous hug. 'Can't we put all this shit behind us and be friends again?'

Lily wasn't drinking even the prescribed one glass of wine because it made her feel sick, but on the way to Hampstead she insisted they bought a bottle of wine, which Grace would drink while Lily got a vicarious thrill out of watching her.

But first she wanted the guided tour. Grace kept her out of

the places that she thought of as Vaughn's: the basement gym, his office and his bedroom, but Lily had more than enough square footage to keep her happy.

'Is that a poured resin floor?' she asked, as they started in the kitchen because interiors shows were her TV crack. 'You have a La Cornue range!'

Grace hadn't seen Lily this excited since the Chloé sample sale. Swigging out of the bottle of Pinot Grigio as she showed Lily around, Grace was secretly thrilled that she could finally show off – just a little bit. The last stop was her bedroom, though she didn't sleep in it so much lately. Lily made a beeline straight for the walk-in wardrobe and reverently stroked the garment bags, murmuring the names of designers under her breath.

She looked at Grace with an awed expression. 'You're dating so well, Gracie,' she breathed, and there wasn't a hint of censure in her voice now she saw the material benefits of sleeping with a really rich man. And just like that her gaze flickered to the huge bed, though actually Grace and Vaughn had only had sex in here the once. 'What's it like?'

'What's what like?' Graced asked archly, though she knew exactly what Lily meant.

'The doing it! What's he like in bed?'

Grace contemplated inventing a story about some weird fetish or telling Lily to mind her own business but the truth was that she'd been dying to tell someone. 'He's amazing. Seriously. We've done two things that I actually thought were illegal and Vaughn always makes sure I get off. Every single time.'

Lily's eyes were enormous circles of wonder. 'Really? Because you once said that you couldn't come unless you got on top and really, really wriggled.'

'Well, now I do,' Grace sighed, as she helped Lily to curl up beside her on the bed. 'I know you think it's a little weird but we went on a date in New York before all that other stuff and

I was dying to sleep with him then, just because of the way he kissed me.'

'He wasn't what I expected,' Lily mused. 'He's sort of handsome in a suity way.'

'I love his suits.' The combination of lack of sleep and half a bottle of wine was proving fatal. Any second now she'd start telling Lily about how Vaughn always said, 'Hello, gorgeous,' to her in the morning. Or how he'd lie on the sofa with his head in her lap and complain if she stopped stroking his hair. Or even how Vaughn would coax an orgasm out of her, when she was sure she couldn't come, by murmuring absolute filth in her ear. Well, maybe she wouldn't tell Lily that.

'You've gone bright red,' Lily noted. She brushed her hands over the covers and Grace could tell she was choosing her words carefully. 'When I saw you with him, it was odd. You looked like a proper couple.'

Sometimes Grace thought that she and Vaughn did have a proper relationship but it only existed in the space between things said and unsaid. 'I really like him, Lils,' Grace whispered because she didn't have the guts to say it any louder. 'He's funny and he looks out for me and no one's really done that before. And he's moody as fuck, but I am too so that works out. I never thought I'd be so into him.'

'Well, he must be into you too, 'cause otherwise he could have just set you up in your own place, instead of letting you move in here,' Lily said. 'I mean, you're really annoying to live with, Gracie. You have that whole clean freak thing going on.'

'Just because I objected to you leaving plates on the floor for three days in a row doesn't make me a clean freak,' Grace snapped automatically, before she took one deep breath and made a vow that she wasn't going to lose her cool with Lily. Not when they were almost made up. 'Vaughn has a housekeeper so dirty plates never become an issue. We just rub along really well.' It was all sounding a little too good to be true but Lily had missed the first few chapters. 'In the beginning though, not so much. I was really scared of him and the whole thing was so overwhelming, but we had this big *thing* blow up at the beginning of the year and since then Vaughn's been a sweetheart. Most of the time.'

Lily prodded Grace with her foot. 'You're sounding all kinds of smitten, Gracie. You sure you're not the tiniest bit in love?'

The l-word made Grace flinch. 'No,' she said immediately. 'I've told you before, I think love is a load of bollocks. People say they're in love just because they like shagging each other or they laugh at the same stuff or so they can use it as an excuse to fuck you over.'

'That is the most depressing thing I've ever heard,' Lily protested, sitting up, which took a lot of effort. 'And it's crap, Grace! I love Dan. I do. Even though I'm mad with him right now, all I can think about is that moment when he walks through the front door and he sees me and he gets this smile on his face, like – like I'm there and that's all he needs. He's my family as much as my mum and dad are. So, what you're saying – no. Love *is* real and it's the whole point of everything.'

Lily put up a good argument but Grace wasn't convinced at all. Love had been invented so there'd be something to write books and pop songs about. Or it was for people like Lily, but not for people like her.

'Well, put it this way,' she said. 'I'm not the kind of person who's capable of being in love. There's something missing from my hard wiring. So, this thing with Vaughn, it makes sense because he's like that too. It's the perfect arrangement for people like us.'

'You wouldn't know love if it was walking down the Prada runway in a really killer pair of heels.' Lily stopped rubbing her belly long enough to do air quotes. 'I just thought there was something "off" about Vaughn.'

'What do you mean by "off"?'

'Not sure.' Lily began rubbing her bump in an anti-clockwise fashion. 'He was all suave and stuff, but it was like he was trying to play me in this subtle way that I didn't get, but I still knew I was being played. I can't really explain it better than that. Did you know that the brain shrinks between three to five per cent during pregnancy?'

Grace seized upon the chance not to have to process or comment on what Lily had just said about Vaughn. He never made a good first impression. Besides, she had the perfect retort oven-ready. 'Your brain's shrinking? But how can you tell?'

Too much had happened for Grace and Lily to slot right back to where they'd been before the months of not talking, and maybe their friendship wouldn't be quite the same again, but Grace knew they were going to be all right because Lily tried to look offended for about a second, before she giggled and whapped Grace over the head with a pillow. Then, because she wanted to be a better friend, Grace persuaded Lily to give Dan a call to come and pick her up.

Which left Grace kicking it solo on a Saturday evening. It was only 8 p.m. and the whole of London was hers for the taking. Grace tapped in the security code so she wasn't murdered in the night by homicidal burglars and went to bed.

chapter thirty-three

When Grace had first started at *Skirt*, she thought 'appointments' was just fancy fashion speak for spending the morning in bed or going home early, which simply wasn't true. Or nine times out of ten, it wasn't true. On Monday morning, she spent a happy few hours visiting fashion PRs to look at their new summer accessories. It was hard to think about shooting pages for their summer issues when it was the middle of a very rainy March, Grace thought as she headed back to the office, her head full of the new wooden heels and jewellery adorned with anchors.

The first person she saw as she stepped out of the lift was Lily. Grace smiled because now Lily could smile back and even ask how the rest of Grace's weekend had been, but Lily was too busy squeaking. Then the two beauty-bots she was with joined in, emitting a pitch that was only audible to dogs.

'Where were you yesterday?' Lily finally said in a lower tone. 'I tried calling.'

'I was in bed – my phone was in another room,' Grace said, because Vaughn had got back at midday, just in time for a Sunday lunch of roast beef and all the trimmings. After the digestive process had been complete, Vaughn's plans for the rest of the day had mostly involved Grace naked in positions that had made her wish she still went to yoga classes.

'It's been the most exciting morning ever,' one of the

beauty girls breathed. 'Posy resigned because she's got a job at *Vogue* and Kiki had George from Security escort her out of the building.'

'You're kidding,' Grace gasped, because George escorting people from the premises was meant to be a *Skirt* urban myth. 'Oh shit! I bet Kiki's going to be in a filthy mood.'

'Don't you get what this means? They're going to have a vacancy for Posy's job and I think Courtney's pregnant too,' Lily whispered fiercely. 'She had a bag of crisps for breakfast. What more proof do you need?'

They lingered by the big swing doors that led to the *Skirt* office. 'There's no way Kiki would give me Posy's job,' Grace said morosely. 'I mean, she's been OK lately but she'll probably poach someone from *Vogue* just to pay them back. And she's always telling me how the fashion assistant on *ELLE* is wonderful and talented and everything that I'm not.'

Lily gave Grace a quick squeeze. 'You might get to do some of Posy's shoots while they're trying to find a replacement. Except, Kiki *is* mad at you,' she added with a guilty start. 'Sorry, I forgot to tell you. You really need to be in the same room as your phone.'

'Why? Why is she mad at me? I haven't done anything.' Grace racked her brains for anything she could have done lately to piss Kiki off, apart from simply existing. 'Was it the Barcelona shoot? She hated it – I knew it! Except I thought it was exactly what she wanted. And it was meant to be Lucie's shoot, though she spent 24/7 on the phone, and—'

'No, it's because you're all over the papers,' Lily said obliquely. 'It was all anyone could talk about until Posy came out of Kiki's office in tears.'

'But I'm not! I would know if I was all over the papers. What papers am I all over?'

'It might have been the *Sunday Express* or the *Mail On*

Sunday. That was why Kiki was so mad. She said it wouldn't have been so bad if it had been the *Observer* or *The Sunday Times*. But it was a nice picture.'

'There was a *picture*?' Grace gave a shudder of revulsion. When she and Vaughn had first been outed, Jake on the picture desk had had hours of fun sending jpegs round the office of Grace at various art happenings, which he got sent from the picture agencies every morning, along with photos of actual, genuine celebrities. Grace had threatened to do something with her giant stapler, a couple of bulldog clips and his dick until he'd promised to never do it again. It had been a salient reminder of just how unphotogenic Grace was, as Kiki had been at great pains to point out. 'Why would anyone want to put a picture of *me* in their paper?'

'It was one picture of you, lots of pictures of Vaughn,' Lily supplied helpfully. 'You never said he'd been married.'

'I'm going. Now. Can't talk.'

Back in the office, Grace tore through the Sunday papers until she found the piece in the *Mail On Sunday*, the paper of choice of her grandparents. It was part of a series of articles on businessmen who were weathering the current credit crisis and making hay while the rest of the country had to shop at Lidl. Grace's eye immediately went to the picture of her and Vaughn in Miami. She was wearing her Marc Jacobs dress and her face was half in profile as she leaned in to hear what Vaughn was saying in her ear. If memory served her right, it had been something disparaging about her purple tights. It could have been worse, Grace decided, as she began to skim through the copy. There wasn't much to skim through, as according to the reporter, *James Vaughn is notoriously reclusive and has never given an interview or even gone on record about any of his acquisitions or clients*. There was a reference to 'Vaughn's lost weekend' which, according to someone who'd been at Oxford with him, had lasted three years – but nothing about the ex-wife, just a list of Vaughn's past companions, whom Grace made a mental note to Google later.

Then it got to the good bit: *In recent months, Vaughn, 41, has been seen with Grace Reeves, 23, a London-based fashion editor on* Skirt *magazine. Although much younger than Vaughn's past girlfriends, Ms Reeves appears to be just as comfortable at a gala ball in New York as a warehouse party in East London. 'Gracie's a lovely girl but not the sharpest tool in the box. She's far more into fashion than art,' says gallery assistant, Alex Clark-Jones. 'I once asked her what she thought of Tracey Emin and the only thing she knew about her was that she was friends with Kate Moss.'*

Grace wanted to howl in outrage. She knew lots of dry art facts about Tracey Emin and could probably recite the names of at least ten of her works off the top of her head if she wanted to. She was in the middle of firing off a furious email to Alex telling him that, when her inbox pinged with a message from Kiki demanding her presence.

'Ah, it's our newly minted fashion editor,' Kiki said as Grace appeared in her doorway. 'It's funny, but I don't remember promoting you.'

'Yeah, well, I didn't know anything about that until I read it just now. And it was full of inaccuracies because I don't even—'

'So you've heard about Posy too, I take it?' Kiki looked as if she was plotting a world of pain for her former junior fashion editor. 'She couldn't even pronounce Givenchy properly when she first got here.'

Grace's pronunciation skills had always been first rate, but she wasn't sure if this was the right time to point that out. Or whether she should enquire politely if Kiki was going to put an ad for a junior fashion editor in Monday's *Guardian*, unless she had a strong internal candidate in mind. 'Did you see the Barcelona pictures?' she asked eventually, inwardly bracing herself for the inevitable invective.

'They were all right.' Kiki was really off her game to turn down the opportunity Grace had just given her. 'Neither Nadja nor Alessandro can take a bad picture but Lucie said you were very helpful. Put out a lot of fires. Just like a proper fashion editor.'

It was the single nicest thing Kiki had ever said, and even though the situation was far from ideal, Grace had to seize the next five minutes and hope she survived them without bodily harm. 'Actually, Kiki, I know Posy's only just gone but I'd really like to be considered for her job. I'd love the opportunity to—'

'You know, I had Kia from *ELLE* on the phone not even an hour ago saying exactly the same thing,' Kiki said brightly. 'We had a really good chat; she had some very interesting ideas about our High Street coverage.' She turned her attention back to Grace who was trying very hard not to look too pissed off. 'I expect you to pick up the slack with Posy gone.'

'I will, I will.'

'I need you to set up interviews back-to-back on Thursday at the Soho Hotel.' Kiki's smile had never been so malicious. 'And before you ask, we *are* putting an ad in the *Guardian* because we're legally required to advertise the job, but I already have a candidate in mind so there's not much point in applying. I'd really hate for you to waste your time when you have so much on already, Gracie.'

'Fine,' Grace said, although she didn't sound at all fine, but she wasn't getting paid for her acting skills.

'And I want ten ideas for new regular pages on my desk first thing tomorrow.' Kiki could never just quit while she was ahead, she had to stick around and twist the knife in a different direction. 'With some of those darling little illustrations you do.'

So she could show them to Posy's successor and they could have a good laugh before the new Posy completely ripped them off and pretended that they'd been her ideas all along, which was what the old Posy had done too.

It was a point of pride to produce ten ideas, complete with illustrations and tear sheets, and have them on Kiki's desk the next morning.

Vaughn was meant to be watching some turgid documentary on emerging Japanese underground artists, but it was in Japanese so he was more interested in watching Grace pull out her fibre-tip pens and start drawing a picture of a snooty girl walking an even snootier dog.

'Have you been holding out on me all this time, Grace?' he drawled, leaning over her shoulder to watch, which was distracting and very, very annoying. 'What would you say your influence is?'

Grace's influence was the stylised drawings on vintage sewing patterns, but she wasn't telling him that. 'Don't make fun of me,' she said shortly.

'But I'm *this* close to giving you your own exhibition,' Vaughn laughed. 'Seriously, you have a nice sense of whimsy and a good line.'

'I only got a B for my Art A-level so my line can't be that good.'

Vaughn ruffled Grace's hair, even though she was always telling him not to. 'You're very touchy tonight,' he murmured, kissing the side of her neck. Grace squirmed away, because there was one patch approximately three millimetres below her left ear that was so erogenous it made her want to crawl into Vaughn's lap and demand he fuck her right there and then. But if Kiki wanted these ideas on her desk, she was going to have them, and devoid of bodily fluids too.

'Is this business at work really bothering you?' Vaughn asked.

'Mostly, but that piece in the *Mail* didn't fill me with warm fuzzies either. I don't know why they quoted Alex, like he's an authority on me, and he made out that I was some empty-headed bimbo.'

'Poor Grace,' said Vaughn, as he stroked the back of her neck. 'If it would make you happy, I'm sure I could find some Russian mafia types who'd break his legs.'

Although she'd have sworn it wasn't possible, Grace giggled. 'No, you wouldn't.'

'Of course I would – just say the word. Really, Grace, Alex is just a vindictive little shit who can't resist stirring up trouble to take his mind off his own inadequacies, which are legion.' Vaughn could do a character assassination like no one else. 'Now, let's talk through your Kiki problem. Calmly and rationally,' he added, as Grace threw down her fibre-tip in a fit of pique.

'She could at least let me interview for the job,' Grace said, almost calmly and rationally. 'Even though it's a done deal. I thought I was getting on really well with her, or better anyway, and then she goes and pulls a stunt like this. It's just really unfair.'

'There are always other options,' Vaughn commented, turning Grace round so he could start kneading at her shoulders with his thumbs. He had an innate talent for back-rubs. 'I was reading in the *Financial Times* that sales of sewing machines are up by fifty per cent. You could open a shop that sells yarn and fabric or those odd things you put on the end of your knitting needles.'

For one second, Grace saw the name *Graceland* in a swirling apple-green cursive on black outside her very own shop. Then reality sank in. 'Yeah, but who'd give me the money to run amok sourcing hard-to-find Liberty prints?'

'Well, I would, of course.' Vaughn sounded surprised that she even had to ask. 'It's something to think about anyway.' His hands were kneading a particularly stubborn knot of tension on her left side so Grace couldn't twist around and look at his face to see if he was teasing.

'Do you really think I could be trusted with a business plan and a company chequebook?' Grace asked lightly, as if Vaughn had meant it as a joke and she was taking it in the spirit he'd intended.

'Well, there'd be people who'd look after that side of things for you,' Vaughn said very carefully, then he dug his thumb right under Grace's shoulder blade so she yelped. 'Like I said, it's just an idea. You don't seem particularly happy at work – or you don't today. Though tomorrow you'll probably be ecstatic about it.'

'The bits of my job that I like, I really like – and then there are the other bits that suck.' Grace leaned back against Vaughn's chest because her tension knots were now gone and she was halfway to gloop. 'I know I'm shallow, but I really think my life's vocation is dressing models in pretty clothes. It was probably because my grandmother made me give my Barbies to Oxfam because she said they encouraged antiquated gender roles.'

'Really? Your grandmother struck me as a woman who had no time for feminism.'

'She might bake a mean sponge cake but my gran's a firm believer in equal opportunities and being self-sufficient.' Grace pulled a face. 'The only time I ever saw her cry was when I failed my Latin GCSE and she realised that I wasn't going to be a lawyer.'

Vaughn laughed so hard at this that Grace felt a little miffed. She would have made a terrible lawyer who'd have constantly bitched about the wig ruining her hair and cried if she got a difficult judge, but Vaughn didn't have to find it quite so funny.

'It's really odd,' he said. 'I can't actually see your face, but I know you're pouting.'

Grace tried to rein in her lower lip as she struggled into a sitting position and picked up her sketchpad. 'I'm not pouting,' she denied. 'Go back to your boring Japanese documentary and stop disturbing me. I've still got eight more illustrations to do.'

Eventually, Vaughn went up to bed muttering about Grace's work ethic and left her hunched over her pad, ignoring the cramp in her right hand as she drew a troupe of Esther Williams-style bathing beauties. She didn't finish until two in the morning and it seemed that she'd only just crawled into bed and wrapped her cold, aching limbs around Vaughn, who was always toasty warm, when he was shaking her awake and telling her that she had half an hour before the car arrived.

Kiki didn't even look up when Grace placed the ideas on her desk and hurried out of her office because she couldn't bear to glance behind her to see her boss chucking the folder in the bin.

'Love the ensemble, Gracie,' Kiki cooed as Grace let the door accidentally hit her in the arse on the way out. 'Though I think head-to-toe black makes you look very pasty.'

Grace was in the cupboard with Lily trying on a different top to see if she could do that season's burnt orange (it turned out she couldn't) when Elise, the editor's PA, poked her head round the door.

'Lorna and Kiki want to see you at Soho Hotel in half an hour,' she announced cheerfully. 'They'll be in the private event room. You'd better run along, you don't want to be late.'

'Why do they want to see me?' Grace tried to sound curious rather than panicked.

'Haven't a clue,' Elise said peppily, because she was always full of pep. Grace and Lily suspected that she was either permanently on drugs or had accepted Jesus Christ as her personal lord and saviour.

'I have an awful feeling that I'm so very sacked,' Grace said, as she struggled to free herself from a burnt-orange cotton choke-hold.

'The only time I ever had a meeting with Lorna, it was to tell me off for poor timekeeping,' Lily reminisced in an extremely aggrieved tone. 'She threatened to put a warning on my file.'

Grace adjusted the bow on her blouse so it hung at a jauntier angle and turned to Lily with a helpless shrug. 'Do you think I should put on a really red lipstick to show that I'm a power player?'

Lily carefully surveyed Grace's raw goods. 'You haven't got time to do a base and without it you'll just be even paler.' She paused. 'I've got a nice muted rose from Stila you can try, and you can rub my bump for luck.'

chapter thirty-four

'Ah, so here's our little Gracie.' Lorna's voice came into the room approximately five seconds before she did. She was one of those women who made low maintenance look effortlessly chic. Handsome, rather than beautiful, she emphasised her patrician features with ruthlessly cropped hair and geek girl specs. She also never wore anything other than beautifully cut black trousers and crisp white shirts. 'I always think that if you have a statement bag and shoes, no one gives a good goddamn what you're actually wearing,' she was quoted as saying when she first became the editor of *Skirt* five years earlier – and the industry collectively wondered if a woman who'd spent most of her career as a serious journalist had the credentials to run a fashion magazine.

Grace's interaction with Lorna consisted of being treated as if she turned up every day as part of a community outreach programme. 'Our little Gracie,' she always cooed when they shared an elevator because Lorna was almost topping six foot and Grace was five foot three and a bona fide dwarf in the editor's eyes.

Grace stood up as Lorna and Kiki both came into the room and nervously rubbed the bilious-green stripes on the chair in front of her. 'No need to look so worried,' Lorna said, but Grace knew she liked the way Grace became instantly deferential in her presence. 'I've been hearing all about your adventures. You're mixing in some rarefied circles.'

'Grace's nabbed herself a very rich, very well-connected boyfriend,' Kiki elucidated with glee. 'It's all the fashion department talks about.'

'How very Jane Austen. I hear he's an art dealer. What did you think of the Turner Prize shortlist last year? I thought it was very uninspired.'

Grace wished that they could get to the firing or the dreaded news that an expensive piece of fashion merchandise had gone missing on Grace's watch and it was coming out of her wages. Anything rather than talking about art, which despite all of Vaughn's coaching and Madeleine's crib sheets, she was no better at, though not as bad as Alex would have it.

'I thought it was all too conceptual,' she said slowly, deciding to quote Vaughn verbatim. Then: 'I believe there's going to be a return to art that's figurative and *not* experiential.'

Kiki gave Grace a 'what the fuck?' look, while Lorna beamed. Hopefully it wasn't because she thought that she and Grace could start going to exhibitions together at the Haunch of Venison at lunch-time. If that were the case, then Grace would quite happily resign.

'This is a conversation that we should continue at a later date,' Lorna said, picking up some papers that looked horribly familiar. 'Now, let's talk about your ideas.'

Halfway through describing a regular High Street fashion section, shot on an actual High Street, Grace realised that this wasn't some new and obscure way to get a bollocking, but an actual interview. She momentarily faltered and wished she hadn't because Kiki glared furiously so she focused on Lorna's encouraging smile. 'So, if we were doing Saturday-night outfits,' Grace said, picking up her thread, 'we could do the photos in a bingo hall. Or if we were doing swimsuits, we could shoot it at Brockwell Lido or the Porchester Baths. I just think it would be a nice twist on the whole idea of doing a High Street fashion story every issue.'

'That's quite sweet,' Lorna remarked, tilting her head. 'The advertising department could use that to bring in some new revenue.'

'And we're all slaves to the advertising department,' Kiki sighed. 'What else have you got?'

Grace concluded with her thoughts on shooting up-and-coming designers' work on up-and-coming models shot by up-and-coming photographers and decided that she might as well go for broke. 'I was reading in the *Financial Times* the other day that sales of sewing machines have gone up by fifty per cent,' she volunteered, ignoring Kiki's snort of derision because she knew that Grace had never picked up a copy of the *FT* in her life. 'And I think it would be cool to have a page with little knitting patterns and things you could make yourself. We could even ask designers to do one-off patterns for us.'

'I think we've heard enough,' Kiki said crisply, turning to Lorna. 'Don't you?'

'Well, these ideas are really fresh, very left-field.' Lorna nodded decisively. 'Yes. I did have my reservations but I think you were right.'

Grace looked expectantly at Kiki, who spun it out as usual by slowly pouring some water into her glass and taking a sip. 'Posy's defected, as you know, and *entre nous* Courtney's pregnant and going back to the States,' Kiki explained, her lips curling as she described the current state of malaise of her fashion department. 'We're completely overhauling the fashion coverage in *Skirt* and launching a new section entirely devoted to the High Street. I know *I'm* very excited about that,' Kiki added in a monotone completely devoid of any excitement. 'How do you feel?'

'Sounds great,' Grace enthused, because she was still waiting for Kiki to get to the toy surprise. 'I've got loads of really good contacts in the press offices and they all wish we did more High Street stuff.'

'Good. I've decided to promote you to junior stylist and you can take full responsibility for it,' Kiki said briskly. 'I'm glad that's all settled. Now I can get on with the interviews for the new accessories editor.'

Grace gripped the sides of her chair and felt her throat close up. Lorna smiled benignly. 'Little Gracie is quite overwhelmed,' she announced. 'I have to say that Kiki has been your biggest champion. I heard good things about one of the *ELLE* girls but Kiki insisted that you'd be perfect. And, to be frank, the press coverage you're getting reflects well on the magazine. I like my staff to be seen in the right places with the right people. Just don't start dating footballers, please.'

'Er, thanks. Thank you. I won't let you down.' Reality was finally sinking in. At last her days as a fashion grunt were over. Grace wished there was more emphasis on what she knew rather than whom she knew, but it was still an upgrade. Besides, all the filing and coffee runs and being screamed at by Italian press officers had been getting her nowhere fast.

'I'll get HR to sort out the paperwork. Afraid I can't offer much money,' Kiki said blithely, going on to name a figure that, after tax, would buy Grace an extra packet of cigarettes a week.

'Actually, that doesn't work for me,' Grace found herself saying, in a repeat of all the times that she'd heard Vaughn use the exact same sentence. 'I'm going to take a few minutes to think about what I'd like in my package.' Kiki looked as if she might slide to the floor in a dead faint, as Grace grabbed her pad and hurried out of the room.

Neither Lorna nor Kiki came after her to ask what the hell she was playing at, and they were still sitting there talking about the publishing director's acrimonious divorce battle when Grace returned. If anything, they both looked amused, like Grace was wearing a pair of stilettos five sizes too big for her and playing dress-up.

'Obviously, this is open to negotiation,' Grace began hesitantly as she eyed the bullet points on her list.

'Obviously . . .' Kiki echoed with heavy irony.

'First, as I'm overseeing a section, I'd like an editor title. Posy was junior fashion editor and I have way more experience than she did. And I'd love the opportunity to style and write stories outside my section, and I really need you to find some more money. I can't live on that, Kiki. It would barely cover my rent and utilities after tax.' There was some other stuff about sharing an assistant and getting an assurance that she'd never have to fill in one of Kiki's expense forms ever again, but Grace decided that she'd fight those battles at a later date. 'I'm really happy to train up my replacement,' she added, just to show that she was a team player. 'I have this whole system for the cupboard and actually Celia would be perfect.'

It wasn't often that Kiki was lost for an acidic quip but right now was one of those moments and Grace savoured it for the whole ten seconds that it lasted. 'Of course, nothing's official yet, Gracie. I could still give Kia on *ELLE* a ring.'

'Look, I work really hard and I never stop having ideas and you'd get your money's worth out of me. You totally know that. Jeez, what Courtney spends on cabs in a month would cover the salary increase.' It popped out as soon as Grace thought it, but it was the absolute truth.

'If – and it's a big if – I decide to adjust the figures, you can explain to the rest of the fashion team why their expense budgets have been slashed,' Kiki said, before she relented. 'OK, I'll make you senior stylist but put an "edited by" on the opener to the new section and you can continue shooting the accessories still-lifes. We'll take other stories on an issue-by-issue basis.'

Grace didn't even have to think about it. 'Done!' she yelped, standing up because she couldn't sit still any longer. 'You won't regret this.' She turned to Kiki who had to smile in the face of

Grace's utter and unequivocal joy. 'Thank you so much for believing in me!'

'I don't think I've ever seen anyone quite so excited about a promotion before,' Lorna murmured, but she was smiling too. 'I take it you're not planning on jumping ship to *Vogue* any time soon?'

'No. God, I'd hate it there. They're all posh and apparently the HR woman checks your nails every Monday morning,' Grace said.

'I think that's everything. This has taken up far too much time already,' Kiki hissed, attempting to restore some semblance of control as Grace was almost dancing where she stood. 'I'll be back at the office later this afternoon.'

Grace took the hint. She floated through the hotel lobby, smiling blissfully at the man who held the door open for her and it seemed weird, almost miraculous, to feel the pavement hard beneath her feet, the sharp spring breeze lifting her hair.

She was already reaching for her phone, because good news had to be shared, quickly and immediately.

'I can tell you're in the middle of something but just so you know, I'm breaking into my bank account and taking you out for dinner tonight,' Grace said quickly, because Vaughn answered with a harried, 'Yes?' which meant that there were people in the room with him and that he was very busy. 'I have something to celebrate.'

'It's not your birthday, is it? No, that's July.' Vaughn sounded intrigued and not that bothered that Grace was interrupting his wheeler dealer-ing. 'Am I allowed a clue?'

'Patience, grasshopper,' Grace said, almost gurgling with glee. 'I'll see you at home at seven and don't be late.'

'I wouldn't dream of it,' Vaughn purred. 'Right, OK, I'll see you then,' he added, back in business mode, and Grace rang off so she could call her grandmother, who decided that the occasion merited turning off *Woman's Hour* so she could properly express her congratulations.

*

Grace was the kind of girl who often got told by complete strangers to 'Cheer up, love, it might never happen,' but by the end of the day her cheeks were actually sore from all the grinning and beaming. Even Lily had told Grace to, 'Stop smiling so much. It's freaking me out,' like she had the sole copyright on being the office sunbeam.

But what the hell. Life wasn't just good. It was *fucking* good. As soon as she thought that, as ever Grace tried to unthink it before she ruined it. 'Be more emo,' she told herself sternly as she opened the front door and called out, 'Anyone home?'

For a moment, she thought Vaughn might still be at the gallery, but he suddenly appeared in a doorway. 'Grace!' he exclaimed. 'I wasn't expecting you for at least another half-hour.'

'Kiki said I could go early because I was getting on her nerves.' Grace stretched her arms and by the time she'd worked out all her tube travel-related kinks, Vaughn was standing in front of her so she could wind them around his neck. 'Guess what?'

'What?' he asked suspiciously. 'You said something about a celebration. Has Coco Chanel come back from the grave with a new collection?'

Grace squeezed him tight until Vaughn actually whimpered as if she was hurting him. 'No, it's even better than that. I've been promoted. I'm *Skirt*'s new senior stylist!'

This feeling happy thing must be contagious because Vaughn looked like everything in his world was sunshine and frolicking puppies and ice cream. 'That's wonderful,' he said, taking her hands and kissing them. 'Tell me what happened and don't skip anything.'

They stood in the hall as Grace gave Vaughn a verbatim account, which consisted of a lot of, 'Well, then I said . . . and then she said . . . so I said . . .' but when Grace got to her favourite part where she'd renegotiated her salary and job title, Vaughn picked her up and spun her around as she shrieked in delighted surprise.

'I'm so proud of you,' he said, putting her down again but keeping his arms round her waist. 'And you're not taking me out to celebrate. This is my treat.'

'No, let me take you out,' Grace protested. 'Hey, I would never have argued my way to a better deal if I hadn't learned how to do it from you.'

Vaughn shook his head. 'Absolutely not. Where do you want to go? Shall I see if I can get us a table at The Wolseley? What are you in the mood for?' Then his hands slid down until they were cupping her arse and actually that was what she was in the mood for.

'I'd rather go to bed,' Grace said simply as she brushed against Vaughn slowly and deliberately, and felt him hardening, but when she glanced up to make sure that they were on the same page, he was giving her a quizzical look that wasn't at all convincing.

'Are you tired?' He stepped back and held Grace at arm's length, when she tried to follow. 'You should have said.'

Grace shrugged out of her jacket and let it fall to the floor. Then she started unbuttoning her blouse, Vaughn's eyes voraciously following the steady movement of her fingers. It wasn't until she slipped the blouse off her shoulders and threw it aside, that he took her hand.

'Maybe we both need a power nap,' he decided, his eyes darkening as he bent his head to kiss her.

Grace never understood how the mood could shift from teasing to a desperate frenzied need to get closer in the time it took for Vaughn to initiate that first kiss. That she'd be pulling at him and sliding her hand between the buttons of his shirt to curve her hand over the thrum of his heart, while her other hand stroked his cock and felt it quicken beneath her fingers. Vaughn would tug her the few short steps to the nearest sofa or bed, while drawing circles and glyphs on her skin with the tips of his fingers.

This time, both of them ended up in a tangle of limbs on the hall floor.

'I'll take you out tomorrow night,' Vaughn promised, when they were cuddled up on the couch in the lounge and both rooting around in the same Chinese takeout container for the last of the moo shu pork. He let Grace prise the last piece of meat out with her chopsticks and watched as she popped it into her mouth. 'Has it been like this before for you?'

Grace held up her hand as she chewed and swallowed. 'Has what?'

'The sex.'

She didn't blush any more when they talked about sex. Besides, the only light was coming from a lamp on each of the end-tables and she was still damp from the shower and her skin, hidden by one of Vaughn's shirts, was covered in red marks and not-quite bruises from his biting kisses. It was a post-sex intimacy that would last until morning when Grace woke up to find the other side of the bed empty because Vaughn was doing a complete circuit of Hampstead Heath as he worked off the noodles.

'No, but you know that,' Grace said. 'It didn't even come halfway as close.' She wasn't going to throw the question back at him because she always tried really hard not to think about the other women. Grace knew that Vaughn didn't have any complaints. He certainly gave her rave reviews during, anyway.

'We got off to a rather rocky start, but it always feels special with you,' Vaughn said quietly, placing the empty container on the coffee-table so he could lift Grace's legs on to his lap. 'Not just the sex.'

Now a definite blush crept into Grace's cheeks. 'Well, right back at you.' She scooched over so she was in his lap and tugged Vaughn's arms round her. 'I never thought I'd meet someone who'd find out about my heavy emotional baggage and still want to stick around.'

She rested her head against Vaughn's shoulder, feeling sleepy now that her tummy was full, and she was almost drifting into a doze and thought he was too from the steady rise and fall of his chest, when he cleared his throat. 'I just want you to know that I'm very glad that we found each other.'

Grace liked how he'd phrased it. Because they had both been alone and a little bit broken. Then they'd bumped into each other and something had finally stuck.

'Me too,' she said, and her eyelids were drooping now and she was fighting not to fall asleep because she had one last thing she wanted to say. 'Don't know about you, but I was so sick of feeling lost.'

chapter thirty-five

A couple of days later, Vaughn had to fly to New York. Grace hated it when he went overseas midweek, not just because she couldn't join him, but because yeah, she missed him when he wasn't there. It was a big house for just one person and it was hard to come home to all those empty rooms and no Vaughn to use as a body-sized pillow while she watched TV. They hadn't been going out so much lately, but Grace didn't mind. There was something very cosy about camping out in the den on the second floor while the April rain lashed against the huge windows.

Grace was cursing that same April rain the next afternoon as she stood on a beach in Dungeness and cast a baleful eye at the grey skies, which were bulging with the threat of an imminent downpour. It was her first solo shoot as a newly minted senior stylist; just Grace, Celia the intern and the photographer, Michael, who'd assisted on the New York shoot back in August. It was meant to be a jolly day out to shoot still-life beach accessories in a slightly gothic setting and possibly get in a couple of rounds of mini-golf if they finished early. However, finishing early wasn't on the agenda any more. They'd been there since eight that morning and hadn't managed to get a single shot in the poor light, which seemed to be fading by the minute.

After checking the weather forecast on her BlackBerry,

Grace made her first executive decision – that they'd find a cheap B&B, then get up hideously early to try again tomorrow, when the BBC promised clear skies and good visibility. There was nothing else to do but drive into Littlestone, hole up in a pub and sample the local scrumpy.

Several hours later, Grace was lying under a candlewick bedspread listening to Celia snoring in the bed next to her and wishing that the room would stop spinning, when her BlackBerry rang.

She answered the phone with a sleepy, 'Hey. What time is it in New York?'

'It's nearly seven,' Vaughn answered, and there was something about the way he said it, so even the transatlantic static couldn't mask the lifeless quality to his words, that had Grace wide awake and gripping the sheet in terror.

'What's wrong? Why do you sound like that? Shit, has someone died?'

'Nobody's died,' Vaughn snapped and it was his annoyed voice, which by now was like an old, familiar friend. 'I'm just in the middle of back-to-back meetings.'

Grace settled back down with a relieved sigh. 'Sucks to be you. You'll never guess where I am . . .' She waited for Vaughn to play along but there was silence, which was unnerving and needed to be filled. 'In this crappy little B and B. Celia's asleep in the next bed so I have to whisper. Anyway, it's been pissing down with rain so we're going to try and shoot tomorrow morning. What's the weather like in New York?'

'Warm.' Vaughn cleared his throat. 'Grace, I know this may come as a shock, but I've decided we should bring our arrangement to an end.'

'What do you mean?' Grace asked tremulously, because she really wasn't sure. Did he want the arrangement to become a relationship? Which it kind of already was, so what was the point of having to label it?

'I think it's best to quit while we're ahead, so I'm giving you a month's notice.'

'A month's notice of what? What the hell are you talking about?' Grace demanded, sitting up. She couldn't believe what Vaughn was saying. Not now. Not like this. Not when—

But all she heard was Vaughn mutter, 'How many more times do you want me to repeat it?'

'Why? What have I done wrong? Why are you doing this, because the other night you said you were glad that we'd found—'

'*Grace.*' Sometimes Vaughn could make the sound of her name last for hours. 'I haven't got the time to get into this now. I'm couriering over a letter; you'll have it tomorrow when you get back to my house.'

He hadn't said, 'When you get back home,' and it was all beginning to sink in with a horrible clarity. 'You can't just hit me with something like this. We need to talk—'

'I think in the circumstances, it's best if you don't fly out to join me this weekend,' Vaughn said in the same flat, unemotional voice. 'I really do have to go.'

'Stop interrupting me so you don't have to listen to what I'm saying,' Grace exclaimed in a fierce whisper because Celia was still snoring lightly and completely unaware that Grace's world was coming to an abrupt end. 'You can't just—'

'I have to go into my next meeting. Read the letter and we'll talk when I get back to London on Monday evening.'

Vaughn cut the connection before Grace could start screaming or crying or call him every swearword she knew. She had to settle for hurling her BlackBerry so hard across the room that she shattered the casing and woke Celia up with a startled cry.

There was a new BlackBerry waiting for Grace when she got back to London, along with a letter that had been propped against the kettle. That hurt the most, actually: Vaughn knew her so well that he'd told Madeleine or the housekeeper or one of his minions from the gallery to leave it there because the first thing Grace would do when she got home was make a cup of tea.

The letter told her even less than Vaughn's call.

Dear Grace

I regret to inform you that I have no choice but to formally dissolve our partnership. As per the contract between us dated 5 September 2008, your notice period is for 30 days from the date of this letter.
We'll discuss the finer details in due course.
Kind regards
Vaughn

It was so cold that Grace found herself shivering. Vaughn had held her when she cried and laughed at her lame jokes and always let her have the last spoonful of the puddings they'd shared – and he didn't care about any of it. He was ending everything they'd had and everything they still could have had, with three terse sentences. He was dumping her. Vaughn was no different from any of the other men who'd dumped her. In fact, he was just the same: a spineless wanker who couldn't even come up with a good reason for kicking Grace's sorry arse to the kerb.

Now she remembered that last evening they'd spent together and put a new spin on words that, at the time, had made her feel cherished, wanted. '*I just want you to know that I'm very glad that we found each other.*' I just want you to know that it was good while it lasted, but actually I'm done with you.

As Grace dunked her tea bag eleven times because she needed strong tea even more than she needed a stiff drink, she tried to quiet the angry questions that were ricocheting around her head and find some perspective. Because really, she'd always known that their arrangement was a temporary thing, but ever since she'd got her feet underneath Vaughn's Corbusier dining table, Grace had let herself get too comfortable. She had thought that changing her hair, wearing a few designer dresses and learning some key facts about Abstract Expressionism made a difference. But she was still the same Grace, and actually finding some perspective sucked and just made her feel even worse. Her time could be put to much better use, she decided. She could cry later.

Starting at the top of the house, Grace methodically worked her way down, looking for clues that would explain why Vaughn was ending things. After all, he was stuck in New York and not answering any of her increasingly abusive voice messages, so what other choice did she have than to hunt for traces of his other women? It was surprisingly easy because Vaughn didn't lock drawers or cabinets because he had nothing to hide, apart from a few bars of Green & Black's chocolate that she bet Gustav didn't know about.

Or was it just that Vaughn didn't do sentimentality? He bought art and sold it. Bought property, then gutted its insides and period details in favour of sleek lines and stark minimalism. He had arrangements with women and didn't keep photographs or keepsakes at the end of each affair. Because nothing and no one mattered to him.

As Grace refolded the freshly laundered pile of towels she'd dismantled in the basement gym, she knew she was acting like a certifiable crazy woman but felt powerless to stop. She needed a sign that all those nights spent in each other's arms, all the times they'd shared a glass of brandy or a bowl of chips or ruffled each other's hair hadn't just been empty gestures. She had to mean something to him, in the same way that Vaughn had stopped being simply an arrogant bastard who kept her in a style to which she'd very quickly become accustomed, and had become someone whom she was glad to have placed right in the very centre of her life.

When her snooping failed to turn up anything, even a receipt for the tomato-red Marc Jacobs bag that he'd bought her all those months ago, Grace did what anyone else would do in the same situation.

She called Alex.

chapter thirty-six

Alex wanted to have lunch at Cecconi's and he wanted Grace to book the table.

He was already there when Grace arrived, shamelessly rubbernecking a B-list actor on the next table and drinking a Bloody Mary. Grace noticed his red-rimmed eyes and wondered if he ever slept for more than four hours at a time. In a couple of years all the late nights and the morning afters would have eaten the pretty right off his face.

Grace kissed Alex's proffered cheek, handed over her jacket to the waiter and sat down. 'So, how have you been?' she asked, and she guessed that her question lacked sincerity because Alex wriggled in his chair.

'Just so you know, I was completely misquoted in the *Mail*,' he said quickly. 'I would never say anything like that about you.'

'I'd forgotten all about that,' Grace assured him, though she hadn't at all. But she wanted to establish a mood here – that she was in control of the situation and she could shut Alex down in a heartbeat if she needed to, so she opened her menu. 'Do you know what you want? The tuna salad is amazing but the gnocchi are really good too.'

They ordered lunch and a vodka martini each and swapped gossip about people they both knew, until they'd exhausted that topic of conversation because there was only so much you could say about people you'd only ever spoken to for five minutes at a time. Alex was fiddling with his cutlery when Grace folded her arms and said, 'I want to know about his other women.'

Alex rested his chin on his hand so Grace caught sight of grimy shirtcuffs and nails bitten down to the quick. It almost made her feel sorry for him. 'Bit late for that, isn't it, Gracie? I offered six months ago.'

Grace remembered then that she hated him, which made it easier to summon up a cool smile and pour herself a glass of water. No more martinis because she needed to keep everything in check: every fleeting emotion that glanced across her face, every nuance and inflection in her voice – and she really needed to stop twisting her hands nervously in her lap. Alex was a predator and the moment he got the faintest whiff of blood, he'd move in for the kill.

'I'm asking now and you know you can't wait to tell me.'

'And you promise you won't shoot the messenger?'

There was a waiter hovering at Grace's elbow. She turned to say that, no, they didn't need any more olives or bread or anything else, but he took one look at the frigid expression on her face and backed away mouthing apologies. 'Just tell me, Alex.'

'Of course, I can only go back two years or so, but that should do for starters. Now, where to begin . . . With Natalia, I think.'

Natalia had been with Vaughn when Alex first launched himself on an unsuspecting art world. She was a Russian socialite fallen on hard times as Vaughn was buying up Early Soviet art. Then there'd been Nancy, an American ex-model, who'd been the wrong side of thirty when her husband had traded her in for an eighteen year old. It just so happened that she had a circle of divorcée friends all working in galleries while they scouted around for husband number two. After Nancy had come a Japanese graphic artist, but she'd only lasted a few weeks because the bottom had fallen out of the Japanese market. Finally there had been Alex's particular chum, Lydia, the daughter of a painter who'd been the great white hope of the British art movement in the late sixties before he'd bought a farm in Wiltshire and hadn't been heard from since. Fast forward to Vaughn mounting a retrospective featuring his work of the last forty years, which had all been sold to museums and private collectors before the exhibition had even opened. In between those four of Grace's predecessors, there had been a number of perfectly groomed, perfectly coiffed thirty-somethings ('usually blondes – old Vaughn does seem to like his blondes – love the new lighter hair, by the way, Gracie') – but none of them had stuck around for longer than a month or so.

'And then we come to you, Gracie,' Alex said kindly. 'Not his usual type. Much younger. Not so polished. Normally that would be a bit of a problem for Vaughn; doesn't appreciate his ladies making social gaffes or fucking up the wine list, but it just so happens that he had a hunch about a new wave of Young British Artists.'

'Shut up,' Grace said through tightly clenched teeth. It was the first thing she'd said in half an hour.

'You wanted to be told and I'm telling you,' Alex snapped. 'You should be taking notes, not shooting me filthy looks.'

'Go on then,' Grace said, like she was daring him not to.

'As I was saying, Vaughn thought there was a new set of YBAs coming through, but none of them were that keen on corporate art raiders. He's got quite a reputation. And so . . .'

And so when Vaughn couldn't find a way in, he went looking for a new female friend to smooth his way, as he'd done so many times before. For a while he was hedging his bets and had been seen out with a woman starting up her own gallery on Hoxton Street and a semi-successful conceptual artist who rented space where Noah had his studio. Then he'd turned up at the party in Kensington with Grace.

Grace was only half-listening to Alex as she traced the pattern back like a trail of breadcrumbs and tried to remember the sequence of events leading up to that evening in Vaughn's office when he'd put the proposition to her. What he'd said. How he'd said it. If he'd actually meant any of it.

'I have to say, Gracie, none of the others managed to get so firmly entrenched. Moving in was a bold move and it's been what – six months now?'

'Seven,' Grace said automatically, because she knew right down to the day, even the hour, if she stopped to think about it.

'You've really lasted the course. Usually six months is Vaughn's cut-off point. He has a very low boredom threshold, and by that time his women have served their purpose. Be interesting to see what happens when he realises that Noah's not going to play. What are your plans?'

'What?' Grace blinked and the world swam back into focus and there was Alex sitting opposite her with a smile that wasn't edged with as much cruelty as usual.

'I mean, it was so obvious that Noah would fall for you. You're much prettier than Lola and Noah's always had a thing for small girls; makes him feel all big and manly,' Alex drawled, like the ways of heterosexual men would always be a mystery to him. 'How far were you prepared to go to bring Noah into the fold, or was that something Vaughn left up to you? Obviously, you chickened out because Noah would usually do anything for a blowjob and a bottle of vodka.'

'What do you mean, Noah's chickened out?'

'Well, he said that Vaughn went round to his studio before he flew to New York and Noah told him to fuck off in no uncertain terms, but our Mr Skinner seems very bitter for a man who claimed that he wasn't interested in being sponsored by a soul-sucking cunt. That's his pet name for Vaughn,' Alex confided. His eyes had lost a little of their morning-after glaze and were fairly sparkling with malice, though Grace couldn't tell who it was directed at. 'Reading between the lines, I'd say it was Vaughn who backed out. Noah's never managed to recreate the glories of his graduate show. But it does rather beg the question of where that leaves you, Gracie?'

Grace knew exactly where it left her: on one month's notice. She hadn't been special – she'd been totally expendable. God, she was so fucking stupid.

'Will you stop talking?' Grace begged, and she knew that she should be playing it cooler than this in front of Alex. She signalled frantically for a waiter. One was at her side and scribbling down her order for a large vodka tonic in an instant.

Grace was sure that Alex had been planning to extract every single ounce of Schadenfreude he could, but she must have looked like a cartoon character after an anvil had been dropped on its head because now he was trying hard to backtrack.

'Sweetie, it's not all bad. Noah's always speculating on what might have happened between you two if Vaughn hadn't got there first, and I'm sure Vaughn thinks you're a cracking girl. You've even been able to extract the stick from his arse, but please – tell me you're not in love with him?'

'No,' Grace declared thunderously, snatching her drink out of the waiter's hand before he could place it on the table. 'I am not in love with him. We have an arrangement. Love has got fuck all to do with it.'

'You'll be fine,' Alex said. 'Vaughn's filed away all your rough edges, and when you two decide to call it quits, there'll be plenty of other men lining up.'

It was a horrifying thought – making do with a succession of older, well-connected men who'd never love her but would line her bank account until her looks faded and her tits began to sag and she replaced gauche with jaded. Grace wasn't doing this ever again – pretending she was Cinderella – because when the clock struck midnight, all you were left with was a pumpkin and no way to get back home, to get back to the person you used to be. She'd had a glimpse of this brilliant, glittering world and tried hard to be a brilliant, glittering girl to match, and now she might just as well move back to Worthing, get a job in the haberdashery department of Beales and adopt some cats. Resign herself to being a spinster of the parish and cut out twenty miserable years of tawdry affairs with men who had too many issues to have serious, committed relationships because all the presents and the pretty things weren't worth the price you had to pay to get them.

Grace tried to tell herself that she should be relieved that, for once, the reasons for getting dumped had nothing do with her. It wasn't about Grace and Vaughn – it was about Vaughn and Noah. She'd just been the third wheel. But there was no relief, only pain, because she'd started feeling all these things that she'd had no right to feel.

'You're looking at me like I'm a complete bastard, Gracie.'

'What – and that's a new experience for you, is it?' Grace's smile was so brittle that she thought it might snap. 'If you breathe a word of this to anyone . . .'

Alex didn't bother to deny it. 'Haven't we already established that everyone already knows?'

But they didn't know about the car crash look on Grace's face as Alex had hit her with the highlights. 'If you have even a shred of decency I'd be grateful if you could keep your mouth shut about this.' Grace stared at the greying edges of Alex's cuffs and, with a sickening jolt of realisation, knew that they had more in common than she liked to think. 'Don't make me into some cautionary tale for any other wide-eyed little girls that come on to the scene.'

Draining the rest of her vodka tonic in one gulp, Grace crammed the three olives into her mouth and got up. Of course, it took her for ever to dig out her purse and throw a handful of ten-pound notes on the table while Alex stared studiously at his plate. Then she walked out without even a backward glance.

The depths of Grace's humiliation were inestimable. It wasn't just the thought of Noah and his friends laughing behind her back every time they'd seen her walk into a room, clutching on to Vaughn's arm. Or the politer smiles of people who'd sat around the dinner-table with them.

No, the single most humiliating part of the whole fucking humiliating exercise in abject humiliation was that somewhere between then and now, Grace had actually thought Vaughn was a nice guy, once she'd got past his emotional issues and bullshit. But secretly he must have been laughing at her too; at how gullible she was, how pathetically grateful for all the favours he saw fit to bestow on her. Every smile had been a mask. Each one of the words he'd whispered to her in the dark had been a lie. Her grandmother was right: she was a lousy judge of character.

But if Vaughn thought that Grace was going to meekly serve out her month's notice, then he was seriously deluded. That night when she got home, she even thought about sneaking away while Vaughn was still in New York, but that would involve a van and driver, a credit card that wasn't in his name and more balls than she currently had or would ever have. Besides, Vaughn owed her one *hell* of an explanation and Grace was going to collect in full. The five stages of being dumped were exactly the same as the five stages of grieving, and Grace had got to the angry part and didn't think she'd be leaving it any time soon.

But by Monday evening, she still hadn't come up with a plan that didn't involve detaching Vaughn's head from his neck, when he walked into the upstairs den where she was sitting stiff-backed on the sofa waiting for him. She'd expected him back hours ago and so she'd had plenty of time to let her rage simmer to a slow boil.

'There you are,' he said evenly as Grace stood up. 'Had a good weekend?'

For five seconds, Grace was shocked into speechlessness. Then, when Vaughn walked over and tried to kiss her cheek: 'You've got a fucking nerve!' she hissed, wrenching away. 'Don't touch me!'

Vaughn had started to unbutton his suit jacket as a prelude to throwing it on the back of the sofa, but he paused. 'Well, no need to ask if you got the letter. I can tell you're upset, but—'

'*Upset?*' She couldn't even bring herself to look at him, because she wanted to claw deep gouges on Vaughn's carefully contained face. Clenching her fists, she stared at her toes curling into the white wool rug.

'Look, Grace, I've just got off a plane that was delayed for several hours. I don't think this is the time or the place.'

It was typical of Vaughn to act as if Grace was having a snit for the sake of it. As though her emotions were clumsy, unseemly things and she should be able to control them. He was already halfway out of the room, mumbling something about needing a drink.

'You bastard! Don't you dare walk out on me!' Her words hauled him back.

'Don't you think you're overreacting slightly?' Vaughn wasn't giving her his poker face any more. He was pissed off now, but also a little wary as if, all of a sudden, Grace was an unknown quantity. 'You knew what you were getting into, so it's a little late to play the wronged woman.'

Grace tried to think of a plausible comeback that didn't mainly consist of 'You fucking wanker!' screamed over and over again, until she realised that this was one of the rare occasions when she could go with the truth. The truth was actually her friend. 'I had lunch with Alex,' she flung at Vaughn triumphantly, and he froze. 'Remember how I was absolutely forbidden from doing that? Well, now I know why.

In fact, I know all sorts of things about you and the women you have your little agreements with.'

'I was always honest with you about our arrangement and how it would work,' Vaughn said icily, folding his arms. 'And I fail to see how—'

'Bullshit! You made out like you were doing me some gigantic favour, lifting me out of the fucking gutter where you'd found me – but you were just using me to get to Noah! I wasn't even your first choice! And now you're chucking me because Noah wants nothing to do with you. All this time, you were just pretending that you cared about me!'

Grace had started crying, though she'd sworn she wouldn't. Vaughn looked like she'd coshed him on the head with the heavy glass paperweight on the coffee-table, and his hands hung limply at his sides. It gave her time to finish her speech which had been much more succinct and tear-free when she'd rehearsed it in her head. 'I'm not going to wait around for a month when I can't stand to be in the same room with you. I'm done. I'm finished. We're over!'

'I didn't tell you about my other attachments . . .'

'Mistresses!' Grace screeched now because all her carefully rehearsed speeches had abandoned her and she was considering inflicting some physical damage if Vaughn continued to act like she was being completely unreasonable. 'Call them what they were. Bangs for a fucking buck, and I bet what you paid them in allowances was a fraction of what you got in commission from the artists they threw at you.'

'Do not scream at me, Grace,' Vaughn suddenly snarled. 'I'm not in the mood for your cheap theatrics. Stop it, *now*!'

It shocked Grace out of her cheap theatrics so effectively that she bit her tongue as she clamped her mouth shut.

'I made you certain assurances about how our partnership would benefit you, which they have. My arrangements with previous partners really aren't any of your business.' Vaughn had the nerve to sigh in this long-suffering, put-upon way, like he couldn't believe Grace's temerity. 'Really, you've never understood how this was meant to work. It was a very simple arrangement but you always make things more complicated than they need to be.'

'It got complicated the first time we had sex,' Grace gritted in frustration because Vaughn had reined himself back in, was as implacable as ever. 'I remember all those assurances you made, and never once did you mention the fact that I was just there as bait. Noah didn't want anything to do with you so you tried to throw me in to sweeten the deal. Why did you get so angry when you thought I'd fucked him? Wasn't that part of your masterplan? Or was it some reverse psychology bullshit that I was just too stupid to—'

'Grace, *Grace* . . .' She was startled out of her rant, when Vaughn took her hands that had been flailing about wildly, so he could tug her towards the sofa. She didn't want to sit down next to him, his fingers still entwined with hers, because she wanted to pace angrily and gesture with her hands, but she found herself sitting so close to Vaughn that their thighs touched and he could stroke the hair back from her hot, angry face.

'I told you not to touch me!' she choked, but Vaughn ignored her, his hand slipping around to the back of her neck so he could start kneading the truly humungous tension knot for which he was solely responsible.

'You're very special to me,' he said in such a quiet voice that Grace had no choice but to lean closer so she didn't miss a word. 'And that hasn't changed. When I first saw you, I wasn't thinking about how useful you could be to my Machiavellian plans to take over the art world. I just thought about how pretty you were and how much I wanted to kiss you.'

'Yeah, I bet you said this stuff to your other women,' she said, wriggling her shoulders so she'd be free from Vaughn's treacherous hands because art dealer was just a fancy word for salesman and Vaughn was a really good salesman. She was sitting in a £5 million house that was a testament to how gifted he was with the hard sell.

'You're nothing like my other women. That's the whole point.'

'What's that supposed to mean? Maybe you should have stuck with your blonde thirty-somethings who knew how the game was played and when to keep their mouths shut. Sorry, Vaughn, you picked the wrong girl this time.' Grace forced herself to slide away from Vaughn so she could glare at him from a safe distance of twenty centimetres.

'They didn't drive me to despair on a daily basis,' Vaughn sighed, tipping his head back. 'I thought we agreed that we wouldn't talk about our others.'

'I didn't have anything to talk about, just a succession of creeps who treated me badly,' Grace said bitterly. 'Who dumped me within three months – and big whoop! – I made it all the way to seven months with you! I want you to tell me the truth. Tell me the reason you're dumping me has nothing to do with Noah or Young British Artists or . . .'

'It is what it is. You know I was – I am – attracted to you, but I can't let that factor into my business decisions.' Vaughn wouldn't look at her as he trotted out this statement, like he'd spent hours rehearsing his monotone delivery.

'You utter bastard!'

'I'm getting very bored with this,' Vaughn said, and Grace didn't know if that was another reason or if he was talking about her constant swearing. 'We had a few good months together and now it's time for us both to move on to new projects.'

'Oh my God, you've already got someone else all lined up,' Grace hissed incredulously, on her feet in an instant so she could loom over Vaughn for a change with her hands on her hips. 'No way am I sticking it out for another month so you can sweet-talk some other poor bitch into signing one of your contracts.'

'Talking of contracts, Grace,' Vaughn cut in coldly, 'you walk out now, I will sue you for breaching yours.'

'That's not fair!' she exclaimed.

'Life *isn't* fair,' Vaughn retorted, and he sounded disturbingly like her grandmother. 'It's over when I say it's over.' Then he stood up in a jerky, clumsy movement like he couldn't wait to get away from her. 'You were happy enough to sign the contract at the time, just remember that. We'll have any further discussions once you're done with the hysterics.'

Vaughn stalked out of the room with an angry toss of his head. If he'd had another X chromosome, it could even have been called a flounce.

chapter thirty-seven

Vaughn avoided her all night, which was cool with Grace. If he wanted to sulk, then he could just get on with it. She had plans of her own, things to do, people to see – except Lily was really put out when Grace called her before eight. She was even more put out when Grace said in an urgent voice, 'You *have* to meet me for breakfast and you absolutely *have* to come on your own.'

Lily was now nearly eight months' pregnant and didn't want brunch in some fancy shmancy Highgate café with scrambled eggs and smoked salmon and freshly squeezed orange juice. They had to meet at a greasy spoon on Junction Road so she could satisfy her cravings for bacon on a soft white roll smothered in ketchup that came from a red plastic tomato.

'He's dumping me,' Grace told Lily as she watched her trying to manoeuvre her hand to her mouth without dripping ketchup everywhere because Lily had the most ergonomically rounded bump Grace had ever seen. It didn't even look as if she was pregnant, but like she'd shoved a beach ball under her Topshop maternity dress for a laugh.

'Why is he dumping you?' Lily asked. 'I thought everything was going really well.'

'He's a bastard. A conniving, scheming bastard,' Grace spat, though she didn't really want to go into any more details and then have to listen to Lily's variations on the theme of 'I told you so'.

'What did he do?' Lily breathed, settling back for some lurid tale to add to the huge volume that was *Grace's Adventures in Dating*.

'He's given me a month's notice. How fucked up is that? Like, he's dumping me, but in thirty days' time and I'm just expected to suck it up and deal or he says he'll sue me for breach of contract. I mean, what the fuck?' Even with pretty much everything edited out, it was still a world of wrong.

'Oh, Grace.' Lily looked up at the ceiling and Grace knew she was trying to come up with a silver lining. 'I know you said you were into him and the sex was good and, my God, that house, but you knew it wasn't going to last for ever. You both agreed that it was an arrangement, not a love affair.'

'I know I did. But you can't live with someone and have little in-jokes and iron their shirts and not feel something for them, and all the time he was just playing me and—'

'You iron his shirts?' Lily looked appalled.

'Only when we go away. He can't pack for shit and then he hates unpacking too so everything's scrunched in his bag for ages and it's just wasteful to pay the hotel Housekeeping to do it.' Grace bristled under Lily's incredulous stare. 'What? I happen to like ironing.' She slumped over the table. 'When he found out about all my debts and paid them off, I thought he'd changed. I thought that *we'd* changed, but—'

'Hang on! He paid off your debts? *All* of them?' Lily wilted slightly as Grace glared at her. 'Didn't that make you feel weird? Like you had a "Sold" sticker slapped on you?'

Grace shrugged. 'Kind of, but mostly I was just relieved and he was so unbelievably nice about it; he wouldn't let me say thank you or try to pay him back. So, I started doing little things to show him that I was grateful. I'd cook him dinner and buy him little presents, and I did his bloody ironing, and the whole time he must have been laughing himself sick about how pathetic I was.'

'He was the pathetic one, taking advantage of you like that. Why shouldn't he pay off your debts? I've seen his house; he's loaded. I bet he only did it so he could lord it over you and make you do stuff you didn't want to. Sex stuff,' Lily added furtively.

'No, it wasn't like that. Not the sex stuff,' Grace mumbled. But now when she thought about it, had Vaughn really changed into a caring person or was it just that she'd been so humbled by gratitude that she'd started toeing the party line and hadn't given him cause to revert back to his Alpha bastard behaviour? Or maybe it was then that he'd really decided to put the squeeze on Noah and he'd needed Grace on side to make that happen. Grace put her head in her hands and groaned because she didn't know what to think or to believe any more. All that she knew was that the last four months, the so-called best months of her life, had been the most flimsy of illusions.

'Gracie, everything's going to be OK. God, if he were here right now, I'd have a thing or two to say to him. What a complete wanker,' Lily sniffed. Any lingering doubts that Grace had about the state of their friendship were gone. There was no judgement, no lectures on how stupid she'd been – just absolute belief that Grace was the injured party and Vaughn was overdue an arse-kicking. 'I never liked that bastard, ever since he ruined my special day.'

'He's not all bad,' Grace said quietly, because for some unfathomable reason she didn't want Lily to think quite so badly of Vaughn. 'He might have spun me a line but he also put up with a lot of my drama.'

As someone who'd had to put up with a good deal of Grace's drama in the past, Lily refrained from saying anything. Really, there wasn't much she could say, apart from the one thing that all good friends were contractually obligated to say in these circumstances. 'Well, I hope it doesn't work out as badly as you think it will. And if it does, you have first dibs on the sofa if I haven't given birth by then.'

When Grace got back to Hampstead that evening, after thinking up many pointless fashion-related tasks to delay leaving the office, she was relieved that there was no sign of Vaughn. She sped up the stairs for the safety of the guest suite and decided that reorganising her closet and maybe even starting to pack would be a great way to channel some of her restlessness.

She'd just reached for the first hanger when Vaughn tapped on the door.

For a moment, Grace contemplated telling him to piss off, but she wanted to see what mood Vaughn was in before she showed her hand.

'You can come in if you want,' she called out.

Vaughn didn't come in, but stuck his head cautiously round the door as if he half-expected to have something heavy thrown at him.

'You're back?'

'Looks like it,' Grace agreed, and Vaughn didn't even flinch at her flippant tone, which obviously meant he wanted to make up.

'I thought we could go to that little Italian on Parkway for dinner. You like it there, don't you?'

Situated in Camden Town, it was one of Grace's favourite places, though Vaughn hated it because it was every Italian restaurant cliché rolled into one, from the candles in Chianti bottles to the winking waiters brandishing alarmingly long pepper grinders.

'That would be nice.' Grace took a little beaded vintage cardie off its padded hanger and said casually, 'So, are you taking me out because you're hoping I won't scream at you in a public place?'

'Something like that,' Vaughn conceded with a small smile, stepping into the room. 'Let me help you.'

He was there in an instant, taking the cardigan from Grace so he could carefully ease her arms into the sleeves as if she suffered from brittle bones and wasn't likely to slug him if he made any sudden moves. Then, of course, he turned Grace round so he could do up all the buttons, hands brushing against her breasts, which had to be deliberate because Vaughn knew that when her blood was up, even the most incidental of touches could make her wet.

'We could just stay in?' Vaughn suggested with the faintest hint of a raised eyebrow. 'If you'd prefer.'

Grace deliberately stepped away. She was angry at her body for going into arousal mode because Vaughn had invaded her personal space bubble. And she was really angry at Vaughn for thinking all he had to do was get her naked and horizontal, so she'd pretty much agree to anything he wanted, just to get his hands and mouth on her.

'I could really fancy some cannelloni, how about you?' she said instead.

Stuffing Vaughn full of pasta was one of Grace's better ideas. It meant that she wasn't his sole focus as he wolfed down a plate of lasagne, so hot it bubbled at the edges. Sometimes Grace wondered why Vaughn was so fixated on money when really his pleasures were simple: food and sex. In that order.

They talked about Grace's Dungeness shoot and Gustav's latest diktat, which involved ankle weights, but though they skilfully avoided mentioning the elephant in the room, it was there, possibly by the dessert trolley wearing a tutu.

'Have you got plans for Friday evening?' Vaughn asked, when their plates had been cleared. 'There's a photography exhibition at Tate Modern that I thought you might enjoy.'

'So, what did you do today after you'd taken off your ankle

weights?' Grace asked, pointedly ignoring Vaughn's lame attempt to curry favour.

Vaughn smiled winsomely, which didn't suit him at all. 'I spent all day trying to buy you a tiara.'

Grace couldn't hold back a snort. 'Yeah, right.'

'I did! I knew Tiffany's was a no go but I tried Cartier, Van Cleef and Arpels, Asprey's, even a few dealers but I couldn't find one. Then I decided it wasn't the most practical piece of jewellery. Knowing you, you'd get mugged on the way to work.'

'True,' Grace said, deciding to play along and see where Vaughn was going with this.

He was going as far as his jacket pocket to pull out a small velvet box. 'So I got you this instead.'

Vaughn pushed the box across the table with one finger. Grace could see their waiter approaching, but as he caught sight of the box he stopped in his tracks. It was the kind of restaurant that dimmed the lights so all the waiters could line up to sing 'Happy Birthday' and force their victim to blow out a candle shoved into a piece of tiramisu. Grace could tell that their server thought an engagement was in the offing, in which case he was going to be sorely disappointed.

Still, she gasped when she opened the box with fumbling fingers and saw a brooch: a sheaf of flowers, their petals sparkling blue stones, the stems secured with a ribbon picked out in diamonds.

'Art Deco,' Vaughn said. 'I thought the aquamarines and platinum would go with the necklace and bracelet I bought you for Christmas.'

'It's beautiful,' Grace sighed, stroking it with the tip of one finger. 'Thank you.'

'So are we friends again?'

'No, we're not – and really, I don't think we ever were.' Grace closed the box. 'You know, you could just say sorry. It would be a lot cheaper.' Usually receiving expensive gifts made Grace go giddy around the gills, but this time she'd rather have had something else instead of jewellery. Reassurance, for instance.

'I could, but as far as I can remember, I didn't actually do anything wrong,' Vaughn said and it was his mildest voice, which always made Grace feel instantly defensive.

'Yeah, but . . .'

'Everything I said to you in my office that day was the truth. If you'd wanted to know more, you should have asked. And even though I've come to care for you – a lot – it doesn't change the fact that we have an agreement, which has reached a natural end.'

'But you said all those things to me about how happy you were and how good we are together. I didn't just imagine that – and then, two days later, it's suddenly just a business arrangement. *You gave me thirty days' notice!*'

'You've read far more into what I did or didn't say, than you should,' Vaughn said softly. 'The fact is, Grace, you've become too emotionally invested. You've begun to treat me like a boyfriend – buying me presents . . .'

Grace's jaw dropped. 'You buy *me* presents all the time!' she hissed, holding up the brooch and waving it in Vaughn's face.

'That's completely different,' Vaughn said quickly. 'You're my mistress, not my girlfriend. We had an agreement, not a relationship, but you kept blurring the lines until I don't think either of us even knew where the lines were any more.'

'But you called it a relationship first, and even if it isn't, there was still an *us* and I can't believe you would do this to *us*!'

'You need to grow up,' Vaughn told her ruthlessly. 'There's nothing to be gained from mistaking good sex for something more meaningful.'

It was so cold that all Grace could do was gape at Vaughn.

She felt as if something inside her had just curled up and died. As far as Vaughn was concerned, she'd just been a good lay and she was stupid to believe that he'd felt anything else for her.

'Y'know, every time I think I get you, I realise I don't. You give me jewellery when I'm really hating on you, and then when I think, Well, maybe I got Vaughn wrong, you open your mouth and ruin everything.' Grace folded her arms. 'I'm sick of it.'

'I don't think my personality stands up to close examination,' Vaughn said quietly. He waved away the waiter with a casual flick of his hand. 'Now, can we approach the subject of how we're going to dissolve our partnership without any temper tantrums?'

Grace nodded. She didn't feel as if she had the energy to even raise her voice.

'You'll keep all the gifts you've received and anything you purchased using the allowances or credit card,' Vaughn began. Grace hadn't even realised that not keeping them was an option, but apparently it was. She hadn't realised either that 'dissolving their partnership' was Vaughn-speak for negotiating her goodbye gift, though he probably had some fancy name for that as well, like a signing-off bonus or something.

'Vaughn, can we please just not do this?'

'I hadn't finished,' he said crisply. 'You can keep the credit card for one year with a monthly limit of five thousand pounds.'

So, it wasn't going to be a clean break then, because Vaughn would be in her life, or his fund manager would, for twelve more months. 'Oh great,' Grace said sarcastically. 'So when you're between arrangements, does that mean I can expect a visit, as I'm still on the payroll?'

'No,' Vaughn said so quickly that it would have completely crushed Grace's ego if he hadn't done such a thorough job of it five minutes ago. 'I'm also going to invest in some art for you. Nothing too abstract. How does that sound?'

Grace knew this was meant to be a negotiation, but quibbling over the details seemed so tacky and actually she didn't care about the state of her finances; she cared about the state of them – of her and Vaughn.

'Great,' she said listlessly.

'You are going to be fine, Grace. You must have known that I'd take care of you so I'm going to buy you your own flat. I was thinking of something near where you used to live, but more towards Dartmouth Park, though obviously you'll want to make that decision.'

'Are you kidding me?' Grace breathed. She felt a wave of shock slam into her so she had to clutch the edge of the table. 'No – it's too much. You can't and it's not—'

'We both know that you'll accept this . . . this token of my appreciation, so why don't we simply cut out the next ten minutes of self-flagellation,' Vaughn said, acid-drop sour. 'Isn't it obvious that I've always had your best interests in mind?'

'You totally played me and you can pretend that you've been honest with me from the start, but we both know that's a lie.' She shrugged, profoundly glad that she was dry-eyed for once and her voice was hardly shaking.

'I'm sure I don't need to tell you what happens to people who live in glass houses,' Vaughn reminded her, and she didn't know how he had the stones to look her in the eye and not wither from shame right where he sat. 'You were economical with the truth too, as I recall. Now shall we stop the recriminations and go back to discussing this like grown-ups?'

'If it's over, then why do you want me to stick around for another month?' Grace demanded. 'If you don't care about me, then you should be happy to get me out of your hair as quickly as possible, and God knows, I can't take thirty more days of being with someone who doesn't want to be with me.'

'Of course I care about you,' Vaughn said fiercely, and Grace wanted to believe him, but all evidence suggested just the opposite. 'That's why I insist that you see out the month so I have enough time to get your affairs in order,' he added, because he was oh so kind and considerate. 'We'll have a couple more dinners and invite some creative directors, designers and such. I'll even get Madeleine to set up a meeting with some agents who can rep you as a freelance stylist. There's really no need to worry.'

Grace gave a tiny bitten-off groan. 'Don't you see, you're putting me in an impossible position? You're offering me things – big, life-changing things – that I want to turn down, but I can't and then I'm, like, beholden to you. I owe you and I end up doing whatever it is you want, even if everything inside me is telling me not to.' She rested her elbows on the table so she could put her aching head in her hands. 'Please don't do this to me.'

She looked across at Vaughn and the flickering candle on the table cast shadows over his face, and for a moment Grace was sure she could see him struggling as much as she was. That all the complicated things she was overdosing on, doubt and uncertainty and sadness, because she was in mourning for something that hadn't even existed, was what he was feeling too. But it had to have been a trick of the light because Vaughn moved the candle so he could take her hand and his face was wearing that bland expression that made her want to scream.

'In a few months' time you'll look back on this and realise it was absolutely the right thing to do at absolutely the right time,' he said, trying to entwine Grace's fingers with his, until she snatched her hand back. 'That you're better off for this.'

'Better off because I've let myself be bought and sold?' Grace asked bitterly, and now it was easy to read Vaughn's face; he was suddenly and blisteringly angry.

'Don't say that,' he demanded. 'It's simply not true and I'm not talking about the material benefits of our arrangement.

I'm talking about us going our separate ways. It's the best thing for you.'

'You have no right to decide what's best for me,' Grace argued, but she'd given him that right, when she'd signed a contract which contained the clause *Other duties: as required*. 'You should have discussed it with me first.'

'I'm discussing it with you now.' Vaughn leaned back and Grace saw him take a deep breath before he adjusted his posture so his back was as stiff as his face. 'You'll accept what I've offered you.'

It was a statement, not a question, and Grace wished that she had the self-respect to tell Vaughn that he could stuff his flat and his credit card and his pieces of art. Her feet were firmly planted on the floor, all ready to push her chair back and do just that, but she wasn't moving, wasn't opening her mouth to do anything but take a frantic gulp of Chianti. He didn't want her any more but he was still giving her the chance to move forward, be someone other than the girl she used to be. And Grace knew she'd done many stupid things since she'd met Vaughn, but turning this down would be the most stupid.

'Yes,' she said in a voice so small it was almost a whisper. 'Thank you.'

'In that case the month's notice stands,' Vaughn said smoothly, because she'd just given him permission to be the selfish, autocratic bastard that he really was. 'No more tantrums and you'll keep the pouting and the snide remarks to a minimum?'

'I s'pose . . .' Grace said, not even attempting to dial down her sullen expression. 'Well, I'll try at least.'

'Good girl.' Vaughn smiled at her and when she stared back at him with a stony face he sighed and his eyes flicked down to her breasts, which to be fair, were heaving as Grace tried to get her emotions under control. 'Shall we order pudding or should I get the bill?'

Grace wanted to tell Vaughn to order something off the trolley because it was the only treat he'd be getting, but she just said diffidently, 'It's up to you. I'm not fussed either way.'

They hadn't talked about it, but Grace was one hundred per cent sure that she wasn't going to sleep with Vaughn any more, whether it was a breach of the contract or not.

Vaughn must have picked up on the telepathic messages Grace was sending out because he didn't even try to cop a feel in the taxi, so Grace assumed that there was a no-shagging clause for the notice period. One of these days she really needed to ask Madeleine for a copy of the contract, then sit down with a legal dictionary to work out exactly what it *did* say.

But it didn't really matter what the contract said, because once they got home and Grace dived for the front door as Vaughn paid the taxi driver, she'd only just got to her room when she heard him coming up the stairs. She waited to hear him continue the trek to the second floor where he could bloody well sleep alone, but he appeared in the open doorway.

She opened her mouth to tell him to leave, to get out because she had nothing left to say to him, but Vaughn leaned against the door jamb and the words dried up in her throat because he looked so beautiful standing there in the soft light. Or not beautiful, not exactly, he had too many angles, but the top button of his shirt was undone so Grace could see the long line of his neck, and his sleeves were rolled up so as Vaughn flexed his fingers she could see the play of muscle along his forearms and it made her remember what it felt like to be held by him, when she'd believed that he was hers.

They stood like that, not speaking for long moments, but the silence wasn't awkward. It was thick and charged until Vaughn crooked one long finger at her.

'Come here.' He used what Grace thought of as his sex voice, pitched low, and it seemed to vibrate under her skin.

So she went to him, not thinking of anything but closing the distance between them.

'Come on, Grace. Let's make up,' Vaughn whispered in her ear, and she didn't want to be a pushover, didn't want him to think he had a hold over her, but he did and it had nothing to do with the contract. Besides, she only had one month left to stock up on the kind of orgasms she'd probably never experience again.

She was in the mood for something urgent and wild, like it always was when they'd been arguing and matters were unresolved because their bodies were still in fight mode. But Vaughn was planting a row of soft kisses against her neck and it wasn't what Grace wanted. Not tonight when there was too much to think about and she didn't want to think at all.

'No,' she muttered, pulling away. 'Not like that.'

Vaughn looked supremely pleased with himself as he loosened his tie. 'Then how?'

Held down. Held open. Tied up. Bent over. Against the wall. On her knees. On her back. Grace didn't care.

'I don't know,' she whispered, because although Vaughn had annihilated most of her inhibitions, when she wanted him this badly she could hardly speak, let alone give him a list of action points.

'If you're capable of doing it, then you should be capable of saying it,' Vaughn drawled, and she got why he was so bloody smug – he hadn't thought she'd put out tonight. But her desire was written all over her burning cheeks and the way she had to struggle for every breath she took, so even the displacement of the air against her skin as she stepped away from Vaughn made Grace want to scream.

'Fuck me,' she ground out, and the desperation in her voice wiped the smile off Vaughn's face.

She was on her back before she'd even finished speaking, skirt pushed up and her knees somewhere around her ears. There was just a brief pause to tug down her knickers and then Vaughn's fingers were inside her, his thumb working her clit, and Grace came just like that, quickly, her mouth pressed against his shoulder, her breath dampening the shirt that he hadn't had time to take off.

It was intense, maybe even a little frightening, to feel so out of control that when Vaughn started moving inside her with a glacial slowness like they had world enough and time, she scratched and bit at him, until he slipped out of her, ignored her howls of protest and pinned her arms above her head.

'Why have you stopped?' she panted, wriggling frantically, fingernails trying to score Vaughn's wrists so he'd let her go and start moving again, start fucking her.

'I don't want to do it like that,' Vaughn murmured, dipping his head to lick across the damp hollow of her throat. 'I want to do it like this.'

Grace turned her head away when Vaughn tried to kiss her, so, still holding her down, his mouth moved over her cheeks, kissing the tip of her nose and her eyelids when she closed them so she wouldn't have to see the way he looked at her like she was his only reason for living. He placed soft kisses on her face, and with each touch of his lips Grace felt herself coming more undone until, when he let go of her wrists, her arms were around his neck and she was straining up for a kiss that Vaughn was only too happy to give.

Then he slid back inside her, her legs wrapping tight round his hips, and this time Grace let it be slow and soulful.

She lost count of the times she came, or perhaps she hadn't stopped coming, and even when Vaughn finished with a hoarse grunt and pulled out of her, her body was still humming with pleasure.

He rolled over, pulled Grace towards him and put his hand between her legs so he could coax one last orgasm from her, until she prised his fingers free. 'No more,' she begged, panting as she tried to come down, but all she could feel was the racing of her heart and the weals on her hands where she'd eventually wound them tight around the headboard because she'd thought she might float off the bed, the stinging in her eyes from tears she hadn't shed yet.

Vaughn pressed hot, open-mouthed kisses across her neck and shoulders. 'See? There's no reason why we can't be civilised about this,' he said throatily.

chapter thirty-eight

Grace had thought that getting through the next month would require guts and bravery and all sorts of other qualities she was sadly lacking. But it turned out she was wrong.

Acting like nothing had happened was easy because, apart from Vaughn's ultimatum, nothing had really happened. She still made him dinner, ironed his shirts and had sex with him every night.

'Really?' Lily queried, as they shopped for prams. 'You don't even do that thing when you snap, "Fine" even though you're not fine?'

'I know, it's very freaky,' Grace replied. 'It reminds me of when my parents were splitting up. Like, once they'd decided to get divorced, my dad was still around for a while and they got on really well. I guess they realised they'd be rid of each other pretty soon so there was no point in arguing any more.' Grace shook her head to clear the memory of her mother and father sitting in their tiny garden drinking tea and shooting her approving smiles as she pirouetted across the lawn. She'd been in the middle of her ballet phase.

'You hardly ever talk about your parents,' Lily noted, as she checked the price tag on a Bugaboo.

'There's nothing much to talk about. Just that carrying on as normal isn't that weird.' She prodded at the stroller with her foot. 'Are you going to get this one?'

'Well, really I wanted the three-in-one travel system with the detachable carry cot,' Lily said regretfully, 'but it is kinda expensive. My dad's had to close one of his garages and Dan says we need to be more self-sufficient.'

'My treat,' Grace said as she fished for her black Amex card. 'Officially sponsored by Vaughn for ruining your special day.'

'Really? Isn't it too much?' Lily tried to sound doubtful but if she hadn't been so pregnant, Grace suspected she'd have been jumping up and down with joy.

'Yeah, positive,' she said firmly. 'About time I used this card's power for good.'

'Are you sure you're OK, Grace?' Lily asked, pulling Grace away from the brightly coloured Bugaboo accessories she'd started to gather up. 'Even your fancy spa and the mineral make-up can't disguise the dark circles under your eyes.'

'Honestly, I'm fine,' Grace insisted, because if she said it enough times then it would be true.

'Whatever,' Lily said, waddling back to the Bugaboo section. 'But dark circles under the eyes never lie.'

Once they got back to the office, Grace began to work on the menu for her final dinner-party. She ran her eye over the guest-list and spotted two new names: an Australian artist called Tabitha Grey who apparently did something with silk-screening. Grace wondered if Vaughn was lining her up as a replacement, until she noted that Madeleine had helpfully supplied the information that Tabitha's plus-one was her 'lesbian life partner, married in 2005'. There was also a Japanese sculptor who might be a woman until Grace Googled the name and discovered that it was actually a man who'd been born and bred in Liverpool.

Maybe Vaughn had a period of quiet reflection between mistresses. Or maybe even he baulked at the thought of having outgoing and incoming women at the same table.

She was just trying to get more dirt on Tabitha, who could be bisexual, and just what kind of freak didn't have a Facebook, when Noah rang.

Noah had become a four-letter word, never spoken out loud, so it caught Grace off-guard when he said hesitantly, 'Hey, Grace? It's Noah, can you talk?' otherwise she'd have told him she was busy and hung up.

'What's up?' she asked, as she glanced at a sample menu and tried not to blame Noah for her current predicament. He couldn't help being an appalling artist.

'Look, this is going to sound weird, so I'll just come right out with it: could you drop round to mine this evening? I really need your advice.'

'About what? No one ever wants my advice about anything except hemlines.' Grace closed the menu binder so she could give Noah her full attention. 'Can't we do this over the phone?'

'It's more of a show than tell,' Noah said, and it was all very intriguing, but this was Noah and she was Grace and Vaughn wouldn't like it, even if Vaughn was probably at that very moment instructing Madeleine to book the movers for a week next Monday. Not that Grace cared what Vaughn did and did not like any more, but they'd had an agreement, which still had ten days left to run.

'I can't,' she sighed. 'It would be just too odd.'

'Half an hour, Gracie. I'll even pay for the taxi there and back,' Noah pleaded, and he never did that because cocky self-assurance was his default setting.

Grace looked up to see Celia, now newly promoted to fashion assistant, about to accept a package from the postroom without even bothering to ask for the delivery slip. 'I have to go,' she said distractedly. 'If you're in town soon, maybe we could meet for a coffee.' A coffee during daylight hours was innocent enough, after all.

'Yeah, I guess.' Grace didn't even know Noah could do dejected. 'I'll speak to you soon.'

It was a conversation that Vaughn didn't need to know about when he made his usual mid-afternoon call to ask her what she was making for dinner. But by five o'clock, Grace still hadn't heard from him and when she tried to phone him, the call was redirected to Madeleine's voicemail.

He finally picked up at five minutes after six. Grace would have been fuming if she wasn't making such a concerted effort to pretend she didn't care. 'Hey, what's happening?' she asked. 'Are you on your way over?'

From the noise coming down the other end of the line, it sounded like Vaughn was standing directly over a flight path. 'I meant to call,' he shouted over the din. 'Could you make your own way home?'

'Where are you? Don't you want dinner?' Grace winced – she sounded like the proverbial little wife worrying that the roast would spoil.

'I'm in the Covent Garden Hotel. I'm meeting someone, a client, before he flies back to New York tomorrow.'

That was fair enough. A little bit of notice would have been nice though. 'OK, I might go out too – some of the subs are going down the pub.'

'Fine,' Vaughn said testily, like he couldn't believe that they were still on the phone when he had an important client waiting.

'Or I might go shopping,' Grace added, just to keep Vaughn on the phone a little bit longer, because acting in a civilised manner didn't meant she'd called a complete halt to baiting Vaughn just a little.

'Don't start all that again,' Vaughn snapped. 'Haven't you got enough clothes, for God's sake? I'm not always going to be around to bail you out.'

Since Vaughn had paid her debts, there had been no more binges. OK, she hadn't had a reason to cane her credit card before now, but Grace had made a concerted effort to buy only what she needed in the way of going-out clothes each month.

Vaughn knew that and it was one of the things left unsaid. Or it should have been, like Noah. Or what an unmitigated bastard Vaughn really was.

'I'll get back to you on that one,' Grace snapped back, and it felt so good to unleash just a teensy little bit of the rage that had been simmering just under the surface for weeks. 'I have to go.'

'Don't drink too much. I'll see you later.' And Vaughn was gone before Grace could get a ballpark figure on how late 'later' was.

Grace did think about going shopping then, because it was better than spending hours in Vaughn's house repacking all her worldly goods and chattels for the umpteenth time. But going shopping was what the old Grace would have done, and Grace wasn't like that any more. Or she didn't want to be like that any more, didn't want to slide back into old habits and pretend it was a coping mechanism, when actually it just made her feel worse.

She sat at her desk for several minutes trying to fight the urge to leave the office because she knew that instead of taking the back road to get to the bus stop, she'd head straight down Oxford Street and find herself in Selfridges, probably in the Louis Vuitton concession on the ground floor.

She was saved by the ping of her email.

Gracie
Final offer: a cab here and back, all the red wine you can drink and my scintillating company.
Be there or be incredibly dull and boring.
Noah x

At exactly seven o'clock, Grace heaved herself up the fifth flight of stairs in a crumbling old warehouse in Dalston. Noah was waiting for her on the next landing and looking fairly thrilled to see her, which was a novelty these days. He held a bottle aloft. 'I have alcohol.'

'Those are my three favourite words in the English language.' Grace grinned.

His studio took up the entire sixth floor. From the splatters of paint on the worn floorboards to the sagging furniture and the smell of turps hanging in the air, it was exactly what Grace imagined an artist's studio to be – and Noah, in battered jeans, Japanese trainers and a holey T-shirt, was exactly what a Young British Artist should be, Grace thought as he hugged her.

'You all right?' he asked sharply, stepping back and looking at Grace with more intensity than she would have liked.

'I'm fine,' she said, shaking out her hair so it half-covered her face.

Noah shrugged and peered at her again. 'I don't know – you seem kind of sad.'

'Nothing a glass or three of wine won't put right,' Grace declared stoutly.

Noah poured a good half-bottle of Pinot Noir into chipped mugs stained with tannin and handed one to Grace. 'So, can I show you what I've been working on?' he asked eagerly.

Grace couldn't have heard him properly. 'You wanted me to come up and see your etchings? Really?'

'I'd have mentioned that in the email if I'd thought it would have been an incentive,' Noah said with a sly smile, and Grace punched him lightly on the arm. Her gran would have called him 'incorrigible' among other things, and the light, flirty banter that Grace and Noah always slipped into when there wasn't anyone else around was a welcome change after weeks of tense silences and stilted conversation.

Noah started pulling out canvases. 'The poppy paintings were deliberately designed to shock,' he confessed, like Grace hadn't already guessed. 'But I liked the idea of flowers; it's unexpected from a male artist, but it's more interesting to capture them decaying. They're still beautiful but there's something sinister in documenting their death. It's very voyeuristic.'

'Hmmm.' Grace looked at the canvases, relieved that none of them looked like bloody vulvas any more. Instead, she saw wilting flowers, their stems unable to bear the weight of drooping petals any longer, the water in the clear vases fetid. Just in case the visual wasn't working, the smell coming from a huge bunch of rotting lilies on the table next to Noah's easel caught at the back of her throat.

'Do you like them?' Noah asked, scrutinising Grace's face. 'How do they make you feel?'

'Well, they're OK, I guess. In a melancholy way.' She paused. 'Honestly, Noah? They just don't do it for me. Christ, I never want to get a bunch of mixed blooms again.' And she could hardly bear to look at them any more because – yes, she got it. Nothing lasted. Especially the good stuff. All you were left with were memories, and even they crumbled and faded over time.

Noah seemed delighted that his flowers were hurling Grace into an existential crisis. 'That's a really visceral reaction,' he announced with obvious satisfaction. 'I want people to look at them and become haunted by their own ghosts. Oh, but now I've made you look all sad again.'

'Really, I'm fine. This is just my thinking face.' Grace stepped away from the paintings and wandered across the floor so she could stare out of the window at the mean streets of East London below. 'What did Vaughn think of them?'

'Well, he said they'd be more powerful if I preserved the flowers, rather than painted them. Which is just tenth-rate Damien Hirst. Pickling a shark is one thing, but a bunch of tulips is just fucking stupid. Shall we finish the bottle?'

Grace looked at her mug, which was still half-full. She drained the contents, and held the mug out. 'Why not?'

Noah poured her another mug and stayed at her side.

'That should put a smile back on your face,' he said, chinking his mug against the side of hers.

'So, is this a live-work space?' Grace asked, looking around curiously. She was currently in the clutches of an eager estate agent who couldn't believe her luck that there were still cash buyers in the middle of a recession, but Grace was beginning to wonder if she wasn't done with North London and period conversions. Maybe she should think about loft living in East London – a complete change of scene.

'Yeah – I'll give you the tour.' He started walking her over to a collection of haphazard screens, stepped through a small gap and took Grace's hand to pull her through.

It wasn't as squalid as the studio, but it could have definitely done with an intensive spring clean, Grace thought as she stepped over a couple of take-out containers on the floor. There was a huge plasma TV mounted on the wall and underneath it a collection of games consoles, and to the side a huge, cracked leather sofa, a couple of interesting-looking lamps and more dirty crockery. 'Sorry about the mess,' Noah muttered guiltily. 'My mum came round last weekend and told me I lived like a pig.'

'What is it about boys living on their own and their complete inability to do the washing up?' Grace asked, flopping down on the sofa. Noah's place reminded her a lot of Liam's flat, though Liam had had a lot less high-tech gadgetry. It even had that same slightly musky smell of cigarettes and burned toast. It wasn't altogether unpleasant; it reminded Grace of the weeks when she and Liam had first got together and they'd stay up all night, smoking, drinking, listening to records and snogging for hours. Vaughn's house didn't smell of anything.

'So, like, shall we just talk about you and Vaughn, get it out of the way and then we can both chill out and get really pissed?' she went on, toeing off her sneakers and taking a cigarette from the pack that Noah was offering her.

'How did you know I wanted to talk about Vaughn?'

'Educated guess,' Grace said dryly. 'So, what's going on with you and him then? I take it he's cooled off.'

'Yup, he's so cool, he's got frostbite,' Noah said, and he sounded quite peeved about it. 'He barely looked at my pieces, said he wasn't quite sure that we were a good fit.'

'I thought you didn't want to be repped by him,' Grace reminded him a little bitterly. 'So, do you think you and Vaughn might still cut a deal?'

'Don't know. I said that I was going to work on some new stuff and he said he'd be in touch within the next few weeks.' Noah sat down next to Grace. 'There was nothing wrong with my work. Yeah, it's a little controversial, but that's better than playing it safe.'

'But, like I said, you weren't into the whole corporate art thing so it's no big deal.'

'Just because I was playing hard to get didn't mean I wouldn't have given in eventually. Vaughn only ever takes on one new artist at a time. It's a huge deal.' Noah cleared his throat nervously. 'So, Gracie, I have to ask you, why isn't Vaughn returning my calls?'

'You wanted to ask me that?' Grace nibbled on her bottom lip. 'I don't know.'

'Of course you know! Has he said anything to you – asked your advice?'

Grace snorted. 'Apart from letting me buy his shirts, no, Vaughn doesn't come to me for advice. I mean, really, can you imagine it?'

'I've been hearing rumours that he's interested in a couple of other artists and I haven't been invited to any of your parties for weeks.' Noah sounded as if his entire world had spun off its axis now that he'd been taken off the guest-list.

'Dude, you hated those parties.' Grace patted Noah's knee in what she hoped was a comforting manner. 'He really doesn't discuss this stuff with me.'

Noah's hand covered hers. 'You can't bullshit a bullshitter, Gracie. Just put me out of my misery and make it quick.' He finished the contents of his mug and gave Grace a doleful look that reminded her of those sad-eyed pictures of street urchins.

'Look, between you and me, there's a couple of new names floating around. Some Australian girl called Tabitha who's a silk-screening lesbian and a Japanese guy.' Grace frowned. 'His name's . . . I'm wanting to say "ruche" but that can't be right.'

'Fuck!' Noah knocked over his empty mug in his consternation. 'Ruichi . . . Roo! That wanker! He's a mate of mine. I saw him last night and he didn't say anything about Vaughn.'

Grace patted Noah's knee again. 'Sorry.'

'I knew I shouldn't have dicked Vaughn around for so long.' Noah took off his flat cap and rubbed his cropped hair. 'This is all your fault.'

'What did *I* do?' Grace leaned down and picked up the bottle so she could pour some more wine into Noah's mug. He looked like he needed it more than she did.

'Got hammered in the pub with me after your party,' Noah informed her. 'That was when Vaughn started cooling off. But first he read me the riot act, told me to keep away from you. In fact, he said that I was to imagine that there was a twenty-foot exclusion zone around you at all times.'

As they were currently thigh to thigh on the sofa, Noah hadn't taken Vaughn's warning to heart. Grace was all ready to start feeling hopeful that Vaughn going all caveman was a good thing when she remembered that it simply wasn't the case.

'I wouldn't even try to second-guess Vaughn,' she advised Noah sourly. 'Not if you want to actually stay sane.'

'But Gracie, he's really into you. Obviously. So couldn't you use your influence and persuade him to give me another chance?'

Grace sighed and decided she might as well come clean. 'Look, I have no influence. I'm on the outs too. About another week should do it,' she added, groping for the cigarettes, because lately her nicotine consumption had tripled. 'It was the only reason I was with him – to be pimped out to impressionable Young British Artists.'

'Well, Gracie, it's not exactly a newsflash,' Noah said, shifting closer so he was pressed against her. 'Everyone knew you were only with him for the money.' Now it was Noah's turn to pat her knee and keep his hand resting heavily on her leg, while Grace concentrated on smoking and drinking and pretending that Noah wasn't way too close for comfort. Light, flirty banter was one thing, but that was all she was in the mood for. 'I have to say though, he was really fucking scary when he told me to leave you alone. Guess he had a change of heart.'

'He doesn't have a heart,' Grace sneered. 'He probably had it removed, got Damien Hirst to cover it in Perspex and sold it to some Russian with more brains than taste.'

'You're so sexy when you get mad. Your face goes all pink, it's adorable,' Noah husked in her ear as his hand slowly and predictably travelled up her thigh. 'It must have been a fucking nightmare being stuck with him night after night.'

'You have no idea,' Grace said, calmly removing Noah's hand. 'Back off, Art Boy.' She looked around the room for a diversion from Noah who was huffing slightly. 'Oh, hey! I haven't played *Guitar Hero* in ages.'

'You want to play *Guitar Hero*?'

'Can we?' Grace begged, already off the sofa and crawling across the floor to pick up one of the guitars. 'Is it hooked up to your Nintendo or your PlayStation?'

It was the good, old-fashioned kind of fun that Grace dimly remembered from the days of Liam. Though even Liam had never let her climb on his sofa so she could jump off it in the middle of 'I Love Rock 'n' Roll'. She'd been so down on the old Grace that she'd forgotten how much fun she could be.

'You're such a dork,' Noah scoffed, when Grace insisted that they both stand back to back and brandish their guitars in unison to 'Sweet Child of Mine', but he didn't seem to mind, and when she got so giggly that she thought she might start to hyperventilate, Noah skinned up a couple of spliffs and made Grace a mug of tea exactly how she liked it. And toast with peanut butter because, unlike certain men she knew, Noah could operate a kettle and a toaster and knew how to have fun that didn't involve black and white subtitled foreign films or boring parties at embassies.

Grace sat cross-legged on the sofa sipping her tea and looking at Noah from under her lashes as he assembled another joint. He glanced up and grinned at her. 'I'm glad you don't look sad any more.'

'Me too. Being sad sucks.'

It occurred to Grace that once she was done and dusted with Vaughn and had given herself a suitable amount of time to get over him, Noah would be the perfect rebound romance. He was cute, ambitious, funny ha ha rather than funny peculiar, had his own place and he was really into her in this normal, unambiguous way. She'd have to tell him that she had zero tolerance for communist relationships, but apart from that wrinkle, Noah would make a great boyfriend.

'You know, it's probably a good thing that you and Vaughn are calling it quits,' Noah remarked as he expertly rolled the joint. 'He doesn't make you happy – anyone can see that. Don't you think you deserve to be happy, Gracie?'

'I am – I *was* happy. I just got in over my head and now . . .'

'You should be with someone who really gets you,' Noah whispered, and they were on the same page and that was another point in Noah's favour. No mixed signals. And in the end, though it wasn't quite what Grace had planned, which involved getting closer and closer to Noah so that the kissing was inevitable, Grace just turned her head and kissed him because really, what difference did ten more days make? She and Vaughn were done and there was no point pretending otherwise.

The kisses were all teeth and tongue. Not good kisses. Not even bad kisses. But kisses that were just a prelude so they could get to the next part, which was Noah pressing Grace back against the arm of the sofa so he could lie on top of her and grind his hard-on into her hip.

Grace shoved him away slightly so she could yank her sweater over her head, then lay back down so Noah could wrestle with her bra clip, and then he was cupping her breasts so he could lower his head and kiss them and it was nice. Super-nice, but it wasn't making Grace get that swoony feeling that weighed down her limbs and made her want to arch her hips and close her eyes and become short of breath.

'Kiss me again,' she murmured, pressing herself against Noah, and he was happy to oblige, sliding his tongue into her mouth and stroking her face even as his other hand delved between them.

'I wanted to fuck you the first time we met,' he muttered as he pulled down her zip. 'Couldn't you tell?'

'Not really. I'm crap at picking up on stuff like that,' Grace admitted, rubbing her knuckles against his cropped hair, which felt surprisingly soft, like goose down. She waited patiently for Noah to kiss her again but he was already fishing a condom out of his back pocket.

'You have the most fantastic tits,' Noah said, watching them shimmy as he pulled his jeans down, didn't even take them off and fisted his cock once, before he started pulling on the rubber. 'I can't wait to see the rest of you.'

Grace had thought that maybe they'd just have a little bit of a snog, maybe some dry humping, which wasn't so terrible in the grand scheme of being almost dumped. For a second, she thought about taking her jeans off because she'd started this, she'd kissed Noah, so she couldn't exactly back out . . .

'Come on, Gracie, get your jeans off and let's do this,' Noah urged her, squatting back on his haunches as he wanked himself off with slow strokes.

She'd already mentally listed all the reasons why Noah was the right boy for her, but she hadn't bothered to start on the reasons why he wasn't. Actually there was only one reason: he wasn't Vaughn and God help her, Vaughn was the only man she wanted. Even though having sex with Noah would be a spectacular 'fuck you' to Vaughn, Grace knew she couldn't go through with it, couldn't sully what she had – *what she'd had* – with Vaughn even though it had meant so little to him that he'd thrown it all away.

Pulling her knees up, she groped for her sweater, turning her head so she wouldn't have to look at Noah, at his dick.

'I have to go now,' she said in a tiny, tiny voice, which really showed that she could never go back to who she used to be. The old Grace, for all her fun-loving, dorky ways, wouldn't have been able to say that much – would have just taken off her jeans and got on with it because she didn't want to make a scene and get accused of being . . .

'Don't be a prick-tease. Come on, Gracie, do you want me to beg?' Noah was smiling, like he thought that Grace had had a last-minute attack of the playing-hard-to-gets.

'I'm sorry, I know I kissed you and everything, but I just can't.' Grace twisted away from Noah, and decided that it would be too awkward to get herself back into her bra. She pulled her sweater on and groped out a hand for her bra, which was lying on the coffee-table. 'Don't get me wrong – I think you're really cool and cute, and you've been so nice to me – but I just can't do this.'

'You can't start something and then back out,' Noah insisted, and he was starting to sound rather belligerent. A little bit like he wasn't used to being knocked back, though he probably wouldn't appreciate being told that disappointment was good for the soul.

'Look, I had too much to drink and I'm still with . . . technically I'm still with someone and maybe if I was single, things would be different, but I am and they're not.' The trick was to just keep talking. It didn't matter that it was word salad. If stuff kept pouring out of Grace's mouth then Noah would get the message.

But he sure wasn't getting it now.

'Gracie! Come on, I'll go down on you for a bit and get you back in the mood.'

'I don't think I ever was in the mood,' Grace sighed. 'I just wanted to be.'

'I thought you were cool and maybe you used to be, before you spent months with a supercilious wanker who probably can't even get it up.' Noah couldn't have been more wrong, but Grace realised that he was properly angry now, all ready to lash out so she quickly stuffed her feet into her Converses and breathed a sigh of relief as she heard the rasp of Noah's zip.

Grace stood up. She wanted to get out of there as quickly as possible, but she also felt the need to justify her behaviour. 'I'm sorry, Noah. It's just so complicated with me and Vaughn, and you just ended up in the middle of it and—'

Noah was walking away from her and Grace couldn't blame him. It was a really lame apology. 'Why the fuck did you kiss me then?' he threw over his shoulder as he walked back into the studio.

'I was looking for a way out and I thought you were it, so I'm sorry for that,' Grace said, following him.

Noah turned around with such a determined look on his face that Grace really hoped he wasn't going to smack her, or worse, try to kiss her again. But he just shoved her handbag at her. 'Get out.'

'Look, let's just put this down to a communication breakdown. It's not worth falling out over.'

'Is that your way of asking me not to tell Vaughn what a dirty little slapper you are?'

It struck Grace that she'd been so busy trying to force Noah into her perfect boyfriend mould, she'd forgotten what an arsehole he could be. 'Who do you think he'd believe, you or me?' she asked haughtily, though it felt like someone had her heart in a strangle-hold.

'I don't know, Gracie. What do *you* think?'

The invisible fingers let go of her heart so it could start beating in a fast and frantic rhythm. 'Vaughn trusts me,' Grace blustered, but even to her own ears, it sounded unconvincing. These last few weeks, she'd realised that she didn't have a clue how Vaughn really felt about her. Though he definitely knew about her propensity for lying when she was in a tight spot.

Noah was walking towards the door, Grace at his heels because the sooner he showed her the door, the sooner she could go and scour her brain free of the events of the last hour. Noah was already sliding back the bolt and Grace thought she was home and dry . . . when he turned round so she could get the full benefit of his spiteful smirk.

'Were you always this screwed up,' he said, 'or is it just since Vaughn's had his hands all over you?'

'I was fucked up in a completely different way,' Grace hurled at him venomously.

'Yeah well, remind me to cry into my beer for you.' Noah opened the door and with a mocking flourish showed Grace out. 'You sleep with dogs, you wake up with fleas.'

Grace ducked under his outstretched arm, which was holding the big metal door open, and once she was safely on the other side, she decided it was worth one last shot to see if Noah had a little piece of his heart that wasn't shrivelled up like his collection of dead flowers. 'Six months ago, if I'd come here, things would have worked out differently,' she said with this awful note of pleading that just made Noah's smile broaden. 'I didn't even realise how much I've changed but I have, and if you could just understand that and realise that

I wasn't trying to lead you on. I was just really confused . . .'

There was a ringing in Grace's ears as the heavy metal door slammed with such force that the reverb felt like it had perforated her eardrum. Nope, Noah's heart was as black as last season's nail varnish.

She couldn't go home, because Vaughn would take one look at her and *know* something was horribly and terribly wrong, so Grace took a cab to Hampstead and holed up in a bar nursing an orange juice for an hour. A succession of chancers, losers and the hopelessly looks-challenged paraded over and tried to chat her up. Sometimes Grace wondered if she emitted a pheromone that only men with severe emotional problems could pick up. Eventually the landlord rang the bell for last orders and she couldn't put off the long walk up the hill any longer.

It was raining torrentially, the kind of rain that you only got in pop videos, and Grace decided getting soaked to the bone was a suitable penance. She spat sodden rats' tails out of her mouth as the damp penetrated the soles of her sneakers with every step that she took.

Vaughn had left the upstairs landing light on, but the rest of the house was submerged in darkness. Grace quietly squelched up the stairs and slipped into her room. Tonight, there was a slideshow of images flickering behind her eyelids: the faces she'd put on Vaughn's faceless other women, the slug-like trail of pre-cum oozing out of Noah's dick, and Vaughn. Not the way he looked when he was really furious with her, but his softer faces. The sleepy smile when he first woke up, how he'd bliss out in rapture when he was eating something that Gustav had declared verboten and the way all the worry and stress was erased from his face when he came, and in that split second before he closed his eyes and let the rush overtake him, he'd look at Grace like maybe, just maybe, she was some kind of goddess.

Grace lay there for a long time on pillows that felt like rocks, every crease and wrinkle in the sheet underneath like razor blades, until she realised that she couldn't sleep on her own any more. That was how bad it had got. It was meant to be an arrangement – a simple, uncomplicated arrangement – and now she couldn't get to sleep unless she was lying next to a man who spent most of the night tossing and turning and annexing every inch of quilt that he could.

Vaughn was fast asleep when Grace crept into his room. He was sprawled across the bed so there wasn't much space for her as she carefully slid under the duvet and curled up against him. Vaughn stirred and muttered something that she couldn't make out, but his body knew she was there on some deeper level, because he turned over, made room for her and his arm slipped around her waist, drawing her closer and closer until he sighed and stopped moving.

She was so very, very screwed.

chapter thirty-nine

As Grace moved through her last week with an incipient dread of what would come next, the rainy weather suited her mood: dark, stormy, cold, lather, rinse, repeat. Also, there was guilt chewing up her insides, then spitting them back out, which was silly really, when she was almost back to being carefree and single. Well, the single part anyway.

It helped to be busy, organising the very last supper and being shown around flats, none of which were exactly right. They were either too far away from the tube or too close to Vaughn. Not enough closet space. Too dark. Too light. Too noisy. No roof terrace or . . .

'I just didn't get that feeling,' Grace said to Madeleine on the phone as she left work early to brief the caterers. 'You know when you walk in somewhere and you can tell right away if it feels like home?'

'Grace, you've seen twenty places in the last fortnight,' Madeleine reminded her tetchily.

'I know. I have the blisters to prove it,' Grace said. 'The flat in Tufnell Park was really nice but it's in the next street to my friend Lily, and when the baby arrives, she'll expect me round every time it burps.'

'Well, I'm going to organise a hotel for you until you find somewhere,' Madeleine said, and although Grace had known that Vaughn would want her out as soon as her notice period was up, Madeleine's confirmation made her breath hitch in her throat.

'I'm sorry that you're having to go to all this trouble,' Grace said as she slid into the back of the car that was waiting for her. 'I slummed it for two years in a bedsit in Archway so I don't know why I'm being so picky, but I just can't find the right place.'

Madeleine sighed. 'Can I give you some advice, Grace, strictly off the record?'

Over the last few months, Grace had started to think of Madeleine as another surrogate mother. If Kiki was her fashion mother, dispensing hemline diktats, then Madeleine was more of her social mother, issuing decrees about cheese plates and seating arrangements, but unsolicited, off-the-record advice sounded ominous. 'Well, yeah, I guess,' Grace replied doubtfully.

'I think that you're not going to find the perfect flat in your current state of mind,' Madeleine said slowly. Grace could tell she was picking her words with great delicacy. 'I'm sure you feel very upset at the moment, but you will get through this.'

'I'm fine, honestly.' As ever, the words tripped off her tongue with the greatest of ease and absolute zero sincerity.

'You're a very sweet girl, Grace, and you deserve much better than what Vaughn could give you. Much better. He had no right to . . . I've said too much,' Madeleine finished quickly.

'I'm not that sweet,' Grace disagreed. 'And Vaughn's been really generous. I'll always be grateful to him, even if I wish—'

'Well, let's not dwell on what-might-have-beens.' Madeleine was back to sounding brisk and efficient and Grace was left with the feeling that the other woman regretted everything she'd just said. 'I'll set up some more viewings for tomorrow. It's going to be an early start, I'm afraid.'

'OK,' Grace said without much enthusiasm.

'Also, where would you like to go this weekend?' Madeleine asked.

'I told you already, Tufnell Park, Dartmouth Park and the non-scuzzy bit of Kentish Town.'

'Vaughn wants to take you away,' Madeleine sounded exasperated, as if she wanted to get off the phone as soon as was humanly possible. 'Now where would you like to go?'

So he was sending her off in style? That was big of him. Since that evening with Noah, she'd barely seen Vaughn. He'd been working late, and Grace had been flat-hunting so there was only time for cursory enquiries before they had sex, every night. Then sex again in the morning, as Gustav buzzed Vaughn every five minutes. And in between, Vaughn slept and Grace stayed awake far longer than she should to watch him sleep.

'Really, I don't want to go anywhere,' Grace said imploringly. 'I have a ton of stuff to do and there's just no way to get it all done.'

It was pointless to spend the whole weekend on a romantic break in a foreign city, and pretend that it meant something, when it was just Vaughn having a last-minute pang of conscience.

'Grace, please. Vaughn was very insistent that he wanted to take you away, so *where would you like to go?*' Madeleine repeated manically, like she was on the verge of losing it. 'You know what he's like when he has a mind to do something.'

'I'll talk to him,' Grace offered. 'And I will think about what you said. About the flats, I mean. But I have to go now, I have a hamachi crisis looming.'

By the time the guests arrived, all crises had been averted, and in honour of the first truly warm night of the year, Grace opened the French windows so they could have champagne on the terrace. It was late April, so still a little chilly for *al fresco* drinking, but Vaughn had these huge outdoor burners emitting warm air and all sorts of carbon emissions, and Grace had bought armfuls of paper lanterns from Habitat so the overall effect was tropical. Almost.

It should have been a perfect night. The guest-list comprised her favourite Vaughn's people: George, the charming elderly curator from the V&A who'd let her try on the Vivienne Westwood, and his equally charming and elderly boyfriend who used to be a ballet dancer. Nadja and Sergei had flown in especially and, true to his word, Vaughn had also invited the creative director of a branding and trend-spotting agency who'd cornered Grace on her way to the kitchen and asked if they could do drinks next week.

Even the new faces, Tabitha and Ruichi, hadn't been what Grace had expected, which was variations on the Noah theme. Instead she got a straight-talking Amazon who looked like Lauren Hutton circa 1978 and an elfin, impish boy with a broad Liverpudlian accent. Even better, between the salad and the fish course, it had dawned on them that they were in an either/or situation and they'd tag-teamed Vaughn. He'd gone bright red when Tabitha had queried loudly, 'So, which one is it gonna be – me or Roo? The suspense is killing us.'

Grace had nearly snorted Sauvignon Blanc from her nostrils as Vaughn ran a finger between shirt collar and neck like he was slowly being strangled. Then he'd smiled wickedly. 'Actually, you should probably leave now. I have another batch of impoverished artists arriving for pudding.'

Everyone had laughed and the rest of the dinner had passed without a hitch. Grace was talking to Nadja about the new collections and waiting for Vaughn to give her the signal so she could start herding people into the drawing room for coffee and dessert, when he tapped his glass with the blade of his knife to get the table's attention.

Grace didn't know why – maybe one of the Chapman Brothers had suddenly died and he wanted a minute's silence.

'I'd like to propose a toast to Grace, who possesses all the

503

attributes that her name suggests,' Vaughn said, smiling at her. 'Thank you for hosting such an exquisite dinner – in fact, many exquisite dinners – and, well, for putting up with me for so long. I know we'll all miss you. To Grace . . .'

Nadja shot her a sympathetic look though Grace could have sworn that Nadja didn't have a single sympathetic bone in her body, and George patted her hand, as Grace sat there with a frozen smile on her face as the guests echoed Vaughn's toast. Except it wasn't a toast, but a little goodbye speech, so that everyone apart from Roo, Tabitha and their plus ones, knew that Grace was being terminated. She was in a state of termination.

They all looked at her expectantly and Grace guessed that she was meant to say something pretty and self-effacing, but she was no good at playing those kinds of games. Vaughn had all the rules memorised and a cheat sheet, and Grace hadn't even realised that she was in play. Her face ached with the effort of keeping her smile pinned on.

'Shall we have coffee next door?' she suggested, pushing back her chair. 'There's cake too.'

She didn't wait to see if anyone was following but marched out, Nadja close behind her. 'What's going on?' she demanded.

'We're splitting up,' Grace said heavily. 'As of next Monday.'
'But why?'

Grace was sick of asking herself the same question. 'It just wasn't working out,' she said woodenly.

'I can't believe that idiot would let you go!' Nadja exclaimed, making absolutely no effort to lower her voice as the other guests began to file into the drawing room. 'I have flat in Kensington if you need it. I never stay there. Is too far from Harvey Nicks.'

Vaughn kept his distance, probably because every time he glanced over at Grace, her eyes promised him a world of pain if he got too close. But eventually the last stragglers left,

George kissing her cheek and murmuring in her ear, 'Don't be a stranger, dear one. Keep in touch,' and it was just the two of them.

'I thought that went rather well,' Vaughn said casually, as Grace retrieved a stray glass from the foot of the stairs. 'What did you think of Roo and Tabitha?'

Grace turned on him. 'What does it matter what I think?' she hissed, putting the glass down again so she wouldn't throw it at him. 'How dare you pull that little farewell toast on me without any warning. It was absolutely fucking mortifying. Everyone knows!'

Vaughn shook his head. 'Grace, don't be so silly. Surely it's better that people find out from us . . .'

'From you, you mean!'

'As I was saying, better to hear it from us than for all sorts of rumours to start going round.' He raised his eyebrows at Grace who had her hands on her hips and a scowl on her face. 'Surely you're not going to spend our last five days together in a snit. Now stop pouting and tell me where you'd like to go this weekend.'

Grace wanted to stamp her foot in sheer frustration. 'You don't need to take me anywhere!' she said hotly. 'You can dress it up all you want, give your charming little speeches and toasts, but you're sick to death of me so I'll save you the bother of having to spend two whole days in a hotel suite with me.'

'What happened to being civilised and acting like a grown-up?' Vaughn demanded, his face tightening.

'I decided it was overrated,' Grace told him, one foot already on the stairs. 'I'm going to sleep in my room. Your fidgeting is really disturbing.'

They still weren't speaking a day later. Grace hadn't seen Vaughn at all the day before, as Madeleine had thoughtfully booked her first flat viewing at 7 a.m. She saw her last flat at 11 p.m. in Dartmouth Park and took it. It was on the top floor of a rambling Victorian house and had an actual turret. Besides, the estate agent had started to get tearful at the thought of looking at more flats over the weekend. When she finally got back to Hampstead it was to spend another fitful night in the guest room.

The next day wasn't much better. Grace had forgotten to set her alarm and arrived an hour late for a meeting with Kiki, who was due to brief her on the next issue's High Street section. It had been ages since she'd had such a vicious bollocking.

'You're still on probation as a section editor,' Kiki reminded Grace, once she'd reduced her to snivels that were almost sobs. 'Don't make me demote you, and don't you ever, *ever* come in late because you overslept.' She sniffed contemptuously. 'At least have the intelligence to pretend you were out on appointments. What the hell is going on with you, Gracie?'

Grace tried to give Kiki the edited highlights, but Kiki was having no truck with that. She wanted details: how generous was Vaughn being with his after-care service, where was she going to live, why was she still sticking around even though it was over? Kiki's face was truly something to behold when she heard about Vaughn threatening to sue Grace for breaching her contract. She managed to contort her forehead into a frown only through sheer force of will.

'I hope you've got a good lawyer,' she snorted.

'It was just a standard employment contract,' Grace explained. 'I don't even know where my copy is.'

'God, your stupidity never ceases to amaze me,' Kiki said. 'You don't give your mistress a standard employment contract. I bet it wouldn't stand up in a court of law. What you should have done was threaten to go to the papers. They'd have been all over the story. "London's richest art dealer gives his mistress a month's notice." '

'I would never do that.' Grace winced. 'I'd look like a twat and I couldn't do that to Vaughn. I'm not his biggest fan right now, but he has been very good to me, and if he doesn't want to be with me then dragging him through the courts and the gossip columns isn't going to change that, is it? He'd just hate me.'

'I know his type and you've had a lucky escape,' Kiki mused cryptically. 'You've done very well out of him and he's made you grow up a bit, which was long overdue, but men like that aren't keepers.'

'Yeah, but—'

'Grace, I'm not your mother,' Kiki snapped. 'I don't do hand-holding like I don't do wedge heels. Now get out and redo those ideas so they don't resemble anything I saw in last month's *ELLE*.'

Fridays weren't meant to suck so much, Grace thought morosely as she sat at her desk after lunch ostensibly looking at location houses on the web, but really playing online Scrabble. The weekend loomed large, like major surgery with only a fifty per cent chance of survival. She made a mental note to Google ulcer symptoms once she'd figured out a word that would use up four i's and two o's. Even the Scrabble gods had forsaken her.

As Grace looked up, hopeful of spotting Celia who could always be persuaded to go on a chocolate run, she saw Vaughn striding towards her. Except that was insane. Grace rubbed her tired eyes, took her hands away and yes, it was Vaughn! Or a Vaughn who had been abducted by aliens in the last twenty-four hours and had his memory wiped, because he was smiling.

'Isn't that your rich, older man, Gracie?' Lucie chirped as Grace got to her feet and rushed over to head Vaughn off at the pass.

'What are you doing here?' she hissed, grabbing Vaughn's arm so they could do this, whatever *this* was, in the privacy of the cupboard. There were whispers all around the open-plan office, rising in volume as every pair of eyes turned and swept over Vaughn. It was hideously embarrassing, but at least he was wearing a Prada suit and had been to his barber's since she last saw him so his hair wasn't as tufty as usual.

'This isn't at all what I was expecting,' Vaughn remarked, like he didn't care that every single one of Grace's colleagues had stopped what they were doing so they could gawp uninterrupted. 'I've been in the *Vanity Fair* offices and they're huge and—'

'What the *fuck* are you doing here?' Grace tried to drag Vaughn cupboardwards.

'Oh, are we going to the famous cupboard?' Vaughn peered through the open door. 'Much smaller than I imagined.' He turned back to Grace's anguished face. 'I was going to phone first, but we seem to be not speaking and anyway I wanted to surprise you.'

'Mission accomplished,' Grace said weakly, holding on to a clothes rail so she could stay upright. 'Why are you here?'

'I'm taking you to Paris for the weekend – the suite we stayed in at the Plaza Athenée that time. I even packed for you and cleared it with Kiki this morning. I don't think she likes me very much. Have you been telling tales on me?' Vaughn didn't seem that bothered if she had, and simply smiled when Grace flushed guiltily. 'She muttered something about you having to make the time up. Is she around?'

That at least Grace was spared. 'She always leaves early on Fridays.' She tried to swallow past the lump in her throat because he wanted to end it in Paris, the city of lovers. He could be so incredibly dense sometimes.

She raised her head, which had been drooping in dismay to see Vaughn watching her with that cool regard; making no bones about the fact that he was analysing her reaction and filing it away for later use.

'Vaughn . . .' Grace sighed. 'I don't want to go to Paris.'

'I know you don't, and we could stay in London and snarl at each other here,' Vaughn agreed tartly. 'But it's booked now and they'll clobber me with absolutely prohibitive cancellation fees. So, chop chop, get your coat . . . Oh Grace, don't do this.'

She was crying, or at least tears were streaming down her cheeks so she had to turn her back on Vaughn and try to wipe them on the sleeve of the first dress she could reach. 'How can you expect me to just carry on as normal?' she sobbed. 'Why are you acting like you don't even care?'

Vaughn's arms were round her before she'd even choked out the last sentence, forcing her to lean back against his chest so he could kiss the top of her head. 'We've been through this,' he said, the jovial tone wiped from his voice. 'You know I care, but it doesn't change the fact that this needs to end.'

He turned Grace round, although she tried to resist, and rather than look at him she pressed her face to his shoulder. 'I wish I wasn't going to miss you,' she mumbled against cashmere wool, and Vaughn's hand tightened in her hair so she guessed he understood. 'I absolutely hate you right now.'

Vaughn held Grace at arm's length. He didn't look particularly annoyed at such a damning indictment. If anything, he looked a little hurt. 'For the record, I'll miss you too.'

Grace squirmed in his grip, like a fish struggling on the end of a hook. 'No, you won't!'

'I will,' Vaughn said, so seriously that Grace's heart thudded painfully. Then he cuffed her chin and gave her just the tiniest, teensiest arch of an eyebrow. 'You've taught me at least seven new ways of saying "whatever", and the difference between Marc Jacobs and Marc by Marc Jacobs, and when you let your walls down, which isn't often, you're very, very sweet. Too sweet, Grace, that's the problem. There's a difference between what makes me happy and what's good for me.'

It took a huge effort but Grace managed to break free, mostly so she could check the cupboard door was firmly shut because some of the staff were finding excuses to congregate at that end of the office. 'All I ever get from you is riddles so I have to work hard to figure out what you're really trying to say.'

Vaughn's eyes were fixed on a row of sandals ready for a shoot on Monday morning. 'Believe me, you're better off not knowing,' he said in that same grave tone he'd used before. When he was like this, it made the prospect of Monday and being Vaughn-less seem too awful to contemplate. Then in the blink of an eye, Vaughn smiled like the confession Grace had forced out of him had never happened. 'Is that everything, because we do have a train to catch?'

Grace knew that she could tell him she wasn't going, and this time there'd be no more talk of breaching contracts; Vaughn would let her go. But it was one weekend out of her entire life. Two more days with Vaughn and she'd chalk it down to just another stupid thing to add to the already gargantuan list of all the other stupid things she'd already done, because of the way Vaughn was looking at her. He looked hopeful, but not entirely sure of himself, and Grace thought that maybe it was the first time she'd seen him show so much vulnerability. It made it impossible to refuse him anything.

'I'll just go and get my bag,' she told him.

Vaughn had booked them into a huge Art Deco suite at the Plaza Athenée with a view of the Eiffel Tower, especially if you stood out on the balcony and had a Carrie Bradshaw moment. Except it was the wettest April since records began, and all Grace could see when she looked out of the window was rain streaming down the glass like tears.

It wasn't an auspicious start to their last weekend, but they went out to dinner at Le Cinq in the Hotel Four Seasons George V for what Vaughn insisted was 'the best steak in Europe. Maybe even the world'. They made polite conversation about things that didn't really matter because talking about the things that did matter would have brought an end to the fragile truce they'd called. They didn't even talk when they had sex that night – not even the nonsensical words they'd usually murmur against each other's skin.

When Grace woke up on Saturday morning and all Vaughn had to say was that it was still raining and would she like breakfast in their suite or prefer to go down to the restaurant, she wanted to pull the covers over her head and stay there until it was time to check out on Sunday afternoon. It was a huge relief, after croissants and a half-hour conversation about whether it might or might not stop raining, that Vaughn suddenly discovered there was a work crisis that needed his immediate attention.

Although the weekend was turning out to be on a par with having root-canal treatment, Grace felt a tiny throb of irritation. It was the last time they'd spend together – now down to approximately thirty-six hours – and he was going to spend at least three of them working.

'Are you all right?' Vaughn eyed her anxiously.

She'd promised herself that she'd maintain a sunny disposition until Monday morning and she wasn't going to renege. 'I'm fine,' she said brightly. Too brightly. 'I think I'll go and run a few errands.'

'But it's raining!'

'I'm not going to dissolve.' Grace was already pulling on the sneakers she'd been wearing the day before. Vaughn's packing had been extremely light on practical items, and her first stop would be somewhere that sold anoraks. 'I'll be back for lunch,' she told him, and he didn't even look up when she kissed him goodbye. She suspected that he was beginning to regret his insistence on going away for the weekend. She also suspected that the art crisis could have waited until Monday.

Once she was outside, she didn't mind that it was raining. Anything was better than the fraught atmosphere in their suite. She stopped in what she guessed was the French version of New Look to buy a waterproof, then took a taxi to the little old-fashioned sweet shop on the Île St Louis. She had a feeling that on Monday, copious amounts of chocolate might be the only thing that would keep her sane.

She'd even bought a box of pralines for Vaughn and was rehearsing the little speech that would accompany them as she opened the door of their suite. Grace expected to see Vaughn hunched over his Airbook but the living room was empty. His coat was still thrown over the sofa so he hadn't gone out.

Grace walked into the living room, then paused. The room had a preternatural stillness to it that made her shiver and take a deep breath; a heavy tension seemed to thicken the air. She was suddenly certain, could feel it right in her frozen heart, that something was horribly wrong.

chapter forty

Vaughn appeared in the bedroom doorway, a tumbler of whisky in his hand. 'I wondered when you'd get back,' he said, and if you didn't know him, it would have sounded like a casual query. But Grace did know him, and she could hear the quiet rage underpinning each word. For the life of her, she didn't know why.

She steeled herself to walk towards Vaughn. He always got rumpled when he was fielding difficult work calls, but as she drew nearer Grace could see there was absolutely no colour to his face – just a grey pallor; the top button was missing from his shirt and his eyes ... God, his eyes. It was like he'd forgotten how to focus – his gaze skittered everywhere but her.

Then Vaughn pinned Grace in place and she wished he'd look away. She stopped moving and took a step back, as he said, 'Noah phoned. For someone so drunk, he was surprisingly lucid.'

Vaughn's sarcasm, as ever, verged on the sublime and Grace winced. It was as if he had been waiting for any reaction from her to snap him out of his fugue state because he was at her side in three angry strides, or would have been if Grace wasn't darting away in panic.

She made sure that the sofa was between them before she said, 'Vaughn, really, it's no big deal. If it had happened next week instead of this week, I'd have been out of your hair, or free from contractual obligation, y'know? OK, I should have—'

'Shut up!' Vaughn was at her side so fast that Grace wasn't sure how he'd managed it, his hands wrapping round her wrists in a bruising grip, so he could haul her closer in a parody of every time he'd done just that so he could kiss her. 'It's a bloody big deal, Grace, to kiss me and whisper all those breathy words as you wrapped yourself around me, then go to his bed and do the same tired, old routine. Or did you mean it when you told Noah that he was the best fuck you'd ever had? That no one had ever made you come so hard and so often?'

Grace tried to wrench her hands free so she could clamp them over her ears, but Vaughn refused to let her go, pressing down harder so she cried out as he dragged her towards the sofa and forced her into a sitting position. 'I never fucked him. I swear!'

'When did it start? After the party? Or was it going on before then?' Vaughn finally released her wrists, but it was just a momentary respite, so he could sit down next to her and cup her face in his hands. Grace could feel the tremor in his fingers, as if Vaughn was just itching to snap her neck. She forced herself to stay very still and look him right in the eyes.

That was when she started crying, because Vaughn's eyes weren't angry. She could see the hurt lodged there, and the way he cringed from her gaze, like a wounded animal. She'd been on the receiving end of that kind of agony often enough to know how wretched it felt. Like someone had taken out your heart, kicked it around for a few hours and then shoved it back in your chest.

'I didn't . . . I never have,' she began. 'Please, just listen to me and let me tell you what happened. Just be quiet and don't say anything, OK?'

Vaughn nodded and his hands fell away as if he couldn't bear to touch her, and that was all right. He was allowed to feel like that. Grace wiped her eyes with the back of her hand

and falteringly began to describe what had happened that evening, going into detail about the decaying flowers and drinking red wine out of tea-stained mugs because she needed to make Vaughn know that she wasn't lying. If there were silly, inconsequential details, not even a second left unaccounted for, he'd know she was telling the truth.

Vaughn put his head in his hands as Grace described what had happened on another sofa, the kisses and the clumsy groping and her top coming off. 'We didn't have sex. I thought about it but I couldn't go through with it because he wasn't you, and—'

'That's not quite true, though I applaud your efforts to try and make me feel included,' Vaughn said hollowly. 'If you really ran into the night, with your jeans around your ankles, which I very much doubt, it was because you realised that Noah wasn't going to be the meal-ticket that you thought he was. He was very clear about that. You told him he wasn't rich enough or useful enough.'

'That's not what happened! I told him why it was a bad idea and I apologised over and over again,' Grace insisted shrilly. 'Then he got really angry and threatened to tell you.'

'Well, he didn't share that part with me. He was too busy rhapsodising about your oral skills. Sadly, I have to agree with him on that score.'

'If he was such an expert on my technique, went into so much detail, then you have to know he was lying. Because I didn't even come close to doing that with him! But you . . . you know what I do. How I start, the noises I make, what I do with my hands when you first moan. Every time, Vaughn! So if Noah gave you a play by play, then you know it was bullshit because you've had enough blowjobs from me – and don't tell me you can't remember every single one.'

There was just the merest flicker of doubt in Vaughn's eyes but it was something, and Grace was just about to try and press her advantage when the light died. 'But you went round there in the first place, even after I'd made my feelings about you and Noah perfectly clear.'

'You utter fucking bastard!' It flew out of her mouth at the exact same moment that Grace remembered why she'd gone round to Noah's studio. Vaughn wasn't the injured party, *she* was. 'I went round there because I was miserable and I wanted to get some answers because you dumped me without any proper explanation. I've felt like shit these last few weeks, but you just expected me to deal with it, and when I couldn't you told me I was acting like a child. So fuck you, I wish I had fucked him!'

Vaughn opened his mouth to speak, then shut it again when the words deserted him. They sat there in silence for a while, broken only by an occasional sniff from Grace as she dabbed at her eyes until Vaughn got up and walked over to the mini-bar, took out a miniature of Absolut and started fixing Grace a vodka and tonic, which he handed to her along with a box of tissues.

Then he sat down and shot her an imploring glance. 'Grace, this is why we have to end things. You've become so emotionally attached. Really, you'll thank me for it one day.'

Grace glared at him, her eyes still glassy with unshed tears. 'I'm not emotionally attached,' she denied in a throbbing voice. 'I go through phases of liking you, but believe me, you *always* do something to make me change my mind.'

'So, it's just my money that you don't want to be parted from?' Vaughn asked harshly. 'Is that what's behind the hysterics and the inability to find a flat?'

It was lower than a snake's belly and a perfect example of how Vaughn could say the most hateful things and force Grace to change direction mid-course. 'So, when all else fails, you accuse me of being a whore? Well, what the hell does that make *you*?'

'I'm not . . . that's not what I meant.' Vaughn was floundering, on his feet again so he could pace. 'This is impossible. *You're* impossible.'

'Yeah, I'm impossible because I actually have feelings and opinions, instead of just smiling, organising place-settings and catering to your every whim,' Grace said bitterly. 'And FYI, I didn't fuck Noah but if you're not emotionally attached then why does the thought of it make you so angry? I'll tell you why: because you think I'm something you've bought, like one of your lame pieces of art, and God forbid anyone else should be allowed to play with it.'

'I don't know what you want from me,' Vaughn said, and she could hear the panic in his voice, as if he wasn't confronted by painful home truths very often. 'I can't do this,' he added, standing up and walking out.

Grace sat on the sofa and watched the hands of the ormolu clock on the mantelpiece slowly mark out an hour and knew that Vaughn wasn't coming back. It was probably just as well. There was nothing left to be said. In fact, they both needed to shut up and let an impartial third party knock some sense into them, because God knows, it seemed to be in very short supply.

She got to her feet, moving carefully, and started getting ready to leave Vaughn thirty-one hours ahead of schedule. Grace neatly folded clothes, put her shoes into dust bags and then took everything out and started again when she realised she'd neatly balled up all of Vaughn's clean socks and packed them too. She wasn't trying to split the atom here, just pack a freaking suitcase, but she was sinking to the floor because it was all too much. Just too much.

Grace was still lying there, staring into space and clutching one of her Louboutins like it was a favourite teddy bear because there didn't seem to be any room for it in her case, when Vaughn burst into the room, wild-eyed and sopping wet.

'You're absolutely soaked, what have you . . . ?'

'You're wrong, you know . . .'

They were both talking over each other. Grace struggled into a sitting position so she could get a proper look at Vaughn. He was dripping on to the carpet, the black shirt he was wearing was plastered to his chest, jeans stiff and water-logged, and his hair had flattened under the onslaught of a heavy shower. Grace glanced out of the window at the rain still streaming down so it was impossible to see anything other than grey.

'Where have you been?'

Vaughn grimaced as his wet shirt chafed against him. 'I went for a walk.'

'Without a coat in a bloody monsoon? You need a hot bath.' Grace let Vaughn pull her to her feet. 'You're going to catch your death.' She really hated it when she sounded like her grandmother.

Vaughn ignored her and prodded her case with his foot. 'You were planning your escape?'

'Well, yeah. I've booked a room at the Eldorado.' She tried to stand up straight and look purposeful, even though all of her wanted to slump. 'It's better to do it this way, instead of dragging it out and saying a whole bunch of stuff that we'll regret.'

Vaughn was already opening his mouth to probably say a whole bunch of stuff that Grace would definitely regret so she pressed her fingers to his lips. 'Christ, will you go and apply huge amounts of hot water to yourself? You're freezing.'

'I don't want you to go, Grace,' Vaughn insisted, trying to catch her hands as she stepped away. 'I need to talk to you.'

She was already rifling through the clothes she'd unpacked for him and sorting out a fresh outfit. 'I thought we were done talking,' Grace said, but she was following Vaughn into the bathroom as he turned on the taps and started pulling off his sodden clothes.

The only sound was the gushing taps, which filled up the

tub in record time so Vaughn could ease himself into the hot water, then immerse himself completely, ducking under the surface so Grace had time to put down the lid and sit on the toilet, before he emerged, spluttering and shaking his head. 'You have no idea how I really feel about you,' Vaughn said.

'You don't feel much of anything for me. Isn't that the whole point? I was part of a masterplan. Just convenient,' Grace said dully, and the pain that had died away got up and roared again.

'Hardly. You're the most inconvenient woman I've ever met.' Grace thought they were all set to start the next part of the Big Breaking Up Row. In her experience, there were usually several acts, but Vaughn suddenly sighed. 'I'm not doing this while I'm naked. Will you order me some coffee and stay put until I'm finished?'

'But I have a—'

'Just do as you're told.' Even naked in the tub, with his hair tuftier than usual, Vaughn could still get this you-will-obey-me edge to his voice that made Grace want to click her heels and salute. With a baleful glare, she left.

Grace was going to order coffee, then sneak out. But when Vaughn came out of the bathroom, dressed in the jeans and jumper she'd picked out, she was perched nervously on the very edge of one of the sofas. 'Coffee's here,' she said, her voice all squeaky, because Vaughn was looking more self-assured, less vulnerable. 'I ordered one of those giant eclairs you had last time.'

'I'll have mine black,' Vaughn said, sitting down next to her and crossing his legs. 'You should have a cup too. You look tired.'

Grace didn't want a cup of coffee and she didn't want to prolong the agony for a second longer than she had to, but she found herself carefully pouring out two cups, even nibbling on half the éclair, which Vaughn had cut in two. Really, they should have ended it like they started it, with champagne, she thought.

'You were right, you weren't my first choice,' Vaughn said, à propos of bloody nothing. 'You were just an amusing diversion one afternoon – a damsel in distress. I could tell from that first moment in Liberty's that you were too young. I should have left well alone and certainly not taken you to my club, and as for sending you that bloody Marc Jacobs bag, I don't know what I was thinking.'

Grace gasped in shock because she'd hoped Vaughn had asked her to stay so he could try to salvage what was left of the weekend, not start the post mortem. 'Gee, thanks,' she snapped.

'But you've made me so happy, Grace.' She looked at him warily. 'And that was never part of the agreement.'

It was such a bittersweet thing to say that Grace found herself clutching one of Vaughn's hands. He let her twine her fingers around his. 'I'm so sorry about the thing with Noah; that I hurt you.'

'I didn't even know I could be hurt. I thought I'd managed to rid myself of that nasty little habit,' Vaughn said, with a small smile that didn't reach his eyes. 'It's been quite a revelation to discover that the thought of you and him together can make me feel like . . .'

'But honestly, nothing happened,' Grace said desperately, because it was very important that Vaughn knew that. 'On paper, he's much more my type than you are, but when we kissed I didn't feel anything, because the only person I want to kiss is you. All Noah and I really have in common is that we both know what it's like to be rejected by you and it's horrible.'

'About that,' Vaughn said slowly. 'I meant what I said before: I don't want you to go.'

Grace felt her heart give a hopeful flutter. 'You don't?'

Vaughn shook his head and his eyes had never looked so

big, so blue, so guileless. 'I've been dreading the thought of next Monday.' He paused for a swift intake of breath. 'I'd like to lock you into our agreement for another year, put in some new clauses, set up a trust for you so you—'

'No!' It was the nicest possible thing he could have said, swiftly followed by the worst possible thing. 'We can both try and pretend we're not having a relationship but we are and you can't dictate a relationship with legally binding agreements and clauses, like I'm one of your employees. Why can't you see how insulting that is?'

'Sssh!' Vaughn put a hand on her shoulder and Grace let his touch calm her because she wanted to believe that they could work this out. That Vaughn would get his big, old brain on the case and realise that what he was saying was crazy talk. 'No, not like before. We should put all this nonsense behind us and work out a new contract. Together.'

'I won't be like your other women,' she said slowly, twisting her shoulder free from his hand. 'That's why you make us sign contracts so we come with an in-built expiration date.'

'Actually . . .' Vaughn rubbed his forehead. 'I never made any-one else sign a contract. I think they'd have laughed in my face if I'd suggested it. It was just you, Grace, because I knew you didn't know how this was meant to work and I couldn't run the risk that you'd lose your nerve once you realised what you'd got yourself into.'

'If I was such unsuitable mistress material, then why did you pick me?' Grace asked bitterly, though she wasn't sure she could bear to hear the answer.

Vaughn looked as though he really didn't want to tell her either. He leaned back against the cushions like he didn't have the energy to sit up straight. 'I was attracted to you, you know that, but the truth . . . the truth is I'd been turned down by two other women and I had a plan in place for Noah that was in danger of getting derailed. He was being very difficult, and in those instances I find it helpful if the woman I'm seeing can expedite things.'

'God, you totally played me,' Grace said, a hand to her heart because she had an ache in her chest every time she took a breath.

'And that's why this arrangement was doomed from the start,' Vaughn said, glancing at her briefly, then looking away. 'Because the others . . . my other women . . . they knew how this worked. Knew that it was a mutually beneficial arrangement that didn't need to be spelled out. We never mentioned money; they'd just send me their bills or ask to look through my inventory or contact Madeleine with the amount they'd like paid into their banks. And when it was time for the arrangement to end, there were no recriminations, no regrets. We'd enjoyed each other's company but it was never anything more than that. But you, Grace . . . you're worth so much more than I can give you, and you'll realise that soon enough. I can't do this – have a relationship without certain assurances. I just can't. You have to sign a contract.'

'You don't trust me because of what I did with Noah? I told you, *nothing happened*!' she choked out.

'I don't trust anyone,' he said simply. 'Especially not myself. And do you trust me? Really?'

She didn't, and Vaughn had given her no reason why she should, but if her three-month relationships had taught Grace anything, it was that you went into them full of hope and optimism that maybe this time things would be different. You had to leave it up to chance and a belief that you wouldn't make the same mistakes all over again. Relationships were about two people trying to make it work, not clauses and addenda written by lawyers.

Grace got to her feet because she couldn't sit next to Vaughn a moment longer without wanting to slap some sense into him. 'If you'd asked me to sign a new contract any time during this last month, I would have, but now everything's changed and I can't. This isn't the right way to do it. What about what *I* need? I need . . . Oh, fuck it!'

She was already moving towards the case, which she'd tried to repack while Vaughn was in the bath. What had taken so long before was now accomplished in a matter of seconds as Grace hurled her clothes in, shoving them viciously into place so she could get the zip done up.

'See, Grace? You don't know what you really need,' Vaughn said, as she picked up her case. He got up from the sofa and tried to intercept her as she practically ran to the door. 'I want you to stay, more than you could ever know, but we have to have a contract. If we're going to attempt a relationship, then a contract makes everything simple. We both know exactly where we stand.'

'No, it doesn't, it never did,' Grace told him. 'It won't be a relationship. It will be just like it was. So I'm going. Now.'

'I'm sorry.'

Vaughn couldn't have shocked Grace more if he'd accused her of shagging every aspiring artist in London. 'You don't apologise. Not ever,' she said, trying to step past him and get to the door, but he planted himself firmly in her path so that she had no choice but to look at him. He'd never looked like that, looked at her like that, his expression so unguarded that she could see everything: panic, fear and unholy amounts of desperation.

'There are a lot of things I should apologise for, which I'm not going to because I told you exactly the kind of man I was from the very beginning. But I am sorry that I can't change, be the man you want me to be. I'm sorry that I'm driving you away. Sorry that I've screwed this up in such a spectacular fashion. And I'm so sorry that I've hurt you.'

'Oh God, it doesn't even matter any more. None of it does. Look, I have to go.'

But Vaughn's hands were in her hair, tugging her head back so he could kiss her. Grace knew she should put up a struggle, maybe even aim her case in the direction of his knees, but she was already letting it fall to the floor with a dull thud so she could clutch his shoulders and kiss him back.

The shadows lengthened and dusk became dark became day again. They snatched brief periods of sleep, limbs tangled together, then one of them would wake and with a kiss, a caress or a muttered plea, it would start all over again.

The first time they'd made love slowly, bodies moving gently against each other as if every second were precious, but each time after that became more frantic and greedy, because the last time was getting nearer.

The very last time, Grace kept her eyes open and felt as if she was drowning in Vaughn; carving her nails into his back, her nostrils full of his scent, mouth biting into his shoulder.

Then he stopped, hands gripping her hips tightly as he dipped his head to kiss her neck. 'I wanted to make you happy, Grace,' he whispered in her ear. 'Whatever else I did or didn't do, that much is true.'

It pulled Grace out of her long, hard climb to orgasm so she was struggling in Vaughn's grasp, not to free herself but so she could use her hands to soothe away the strain she saw in his face as he frowned down at her. She wanted to tell Vaughn that she *had* been happy sometimes, but then he was kissing her so fiercely that her words got lost.

Afterwards he spooned against her, pressing hundreds of tiny kisses on her skin. 'You're leaving.' Finally it was a statement, not a question.

'I'm leaving.'

'If you stay, I'll give you ten thousand in cash every month, let you redecorate, anything you want. Just tell me and it's yours,' Vaughn murmured against her skin.

One month ago, Grace would have signed her soul away without a second thought. But it had been one hell of a month and all she wanted was to be the girl who'd finally managed to stick. 'I don't want those kinds of sweeteners. If you want me that badly, then the contract shouldn't matter. I'll stay because I want to stay, because I want to make this work. Honestly, Vaughn, that should mean more than signing my name on a contract.'

Vaughn didn't say anything at first then he sighed, his breath stirring up the baby hairs at the nape of her neck. 'I wish I could say yes, but that's not good enough.'

'Why isn't it?'

'It's just not. What else do you want me to say, Grace?'

She rolled over because she couldn't think straight with Vaughn's arms around her and she wanted to come up with a solution that would make both of them happy without feeling manipulated. Grace suddenly realised that one of them could break this impasse with those three little words, eight letters, but she could feel them sticking in her throat. Because if love was everything that people said it was, then Grace would be sure. She'd know in this absolutely certain, irrevocable way and as it was, she still didn't have a fucking clue what love felt like.

'But not that,' Vaughn said, because her face must have given her away. 'I don't think either of us even knows what love is.'

She wound her fingers through Vaughn's hair, so she could kiss the deep furrow that had appeared between his eyebrows. 'That's OK,' she said. 'I can't say it either.'

'Grace, it doesn't have to be this way,' Vaughn said heavily, tracing her jaw with the tips of his fingers.

'Yeah, it really does.' He had to stop touching her because it was making this impossible. 'Honestly, I'll be fine. I'll go and stay at Lil's until I sort something else out.'

'What about the place I was going to make an offer on? I thought you liked it.'

'I did,' Grace murmured. 'It had a turret, but God, if ever two people needed a clean break, it's us.'

'Grace, don't be so stupid. I'll buy a flat for you, put your name on the deed. No, let me finish.' Vaughn held her chin in an uncompromising grip. 'I need to know you'll be all right, that you're taken care of.'

Grace gently prised his hands off her. 'I started this because of the money, but I don't want it to end with that,' she insisted, stroking her thumbs along the high plane of his cheekbones. 'I can't believe I just said that. See what you've done to me?'

'Why don't you think about it?' Vaughn pressed a kiss to her forehead.

'I don't need to.' Grace pulled Vaughn in for one more kiss that was so final it almost made her cry, though she'd have sworn she didn't have any more tears left.

Vaughn didn't stop her when she pulled the covers back and got out of bed. She was sore and aching, from too much crying, too much fucking, not nearly enough sleep. Even a scalding hot shower didn't help – it just felt as if every last trace of Vaughn was being washed down the drain.

He was dressed and waiting for her when she came out of the bathroom, her jacket over his arm. 'I booked you the last seat on the Eurostar,' he said. 'I thought you'd prefer to go straight back to London.'

'Yeah, I do. Thanks.' The thought of spending the night just a cab ride away had been daunting. Grace had half-wondered if she wouldn't lose all her resolve and come crawling back to him before morning. This made it easier.

She let Vaughn help her into her jacket, then turn her around so he could do up the buttons, before handing her the suitcase. 'Be happy, Grace.'

'You too.' She ran the back of her hand over his cheek, catching her knuckles on his stubble. 'Don't let Gustav boss you about.'

'I'll try not to. What are you doing, you silly girl?'

Grace held her Amex card out. 'Giving this back to you.'

Vaughn held his hands up. 'Keep it. Honestly, Grace, I appreciate the big, dramatic gesture, but you really can't manage without it.'

'Well, I'm just going to have to learn, aren't I?' Grace said, tucking the card into Vaughn's shirt-pocket and letting her hand rest there for a second to feel the thud of his heart. 'I'll be fine.'

'If you need anything – *anything* – you're to come to me. Is that understood?'

Grace nodded and this would take for ever if she let it, both of them standing there with awkward smiles, hands still on each other. She wanted to think of some poignant but snappy last line that would commemorate the solemnity of the occasion, but all she could come up with was a heartfelt, 'God, this really sucks,' before she opened the door.

chapter forty-one

This time wasn't like the other times. Normally when Grace got to the end of another doomed relationship, there was only ever anger. Anger directed at whichever tousle-haired wanker had dumped her, and anger at herself for being stupid enough to get involved with yet another tousle-haired wanker.

But this time there was no anger. Just a bone-deep sadness that seeped into all the cracks and crevices so Grace felt weighed down with it. She hadn't cried since Paris, and actually she was kind of proud about that because it spoke of a quiet dignity. But still she woke up each morning gritty-eyed and aching, and sleepwalked through the day as if she really had spent the entire night sobbing.

And this time was also different to the other times, because Grace actually had options. In the past, being dumped was just one extra bad thing to put on the pile of all the other bad things that made up her life. Post-Vaughn, she had no debt and absolutely no wherewithal or credit cards to heal the hurt by shopping. She had a bulging contacts book she could hit up for freelance jobs, because now she totally got what people meant about throwing themselves into their work. And she had Lily's sofa until the end of the month, when Lily went on maternity leave and her mum came to stay. Nadja had been as good as her word and had offered Grace her flat, which was too far from Harvey Nicks, as long as Grace paid the truly astronomical service charges.

'Honestly, you can stay as long as you like,' Lily had said, when Grace had turned up late on that Sunday evening with her suitcase in her hand and a shell-shocked look on her face. But every spare inch of Lily and Dan's flat was filled up with baby paraphernalia, and when Dan got home from work each night, he'd smile bravely and say, 'You still here then, Gracie?'

Grace couldn't blame either of them, not really. As it was, Lily looked like she was gestating an elephant, and every time she carefully levered herself out of her chair at work, everyone held their breath in case her waters broke. They had just had the floor sanded, after all.

So Grace went out a lot. But getting dressed up to go to parties felt like an exercise in futility. Parties made people happy and she had to spend hours watching their stupid smiles and fending off the advances of men who didn't stand a chance because they weren't Vaughn. The cinema didn't help either. Rom-coms made her gag, anything with subtitles reminded her of Vaughn, so all that was left were smash 'em up action movies and the hero still got his girl and his happy ending. Her life had turned into a fucking Dusty Springfield song.

Not that anyone had much sympathy. The general consensus in the *Skirt* office was that it was a miracle it had lasted as long as it had. Grace was pretty sure they'd been running a book on it, though Lily swore that wasn't true. 'Really, you're well shot of him. He was a total wanker,' Lily proclaimed, as she supervised Grace's careful painting of the skirting board in the former spare room. 'But, God, Grace, would it have killed you to keep the credit card? I just don't get you sometimes.'

'It was a point of principle,' Grace insisted weakly. 'I couldn't keep living *off* him if I wasn't living *with* him.'

'I think you're bonkers,' Lily said. She rested her hands on her bump and gave Grace a thoughtful look. 'You know

Liam's not seeing anyone right now? He's always asking how you are. I think he's still sweet on you.'

'Oh God, just kill me now,' Grace snapped, slapping white paint on the polka-dot wallpaper in her irritation and hoping that Lily wouldn't notice. 'I was with Vaughn for seven months and I'm allowed to feel like shit for a while before I get screwed over by someone else – who definitely and never will be Liam. OK?'

Grace didn't point out that dating guys like Liam would be like shopping in Primark after getting used to Marc Jacobs. Actually she was shopping in Primark again because she had no credit cards and no overdraft, and seeing her bank account in credit was something that Grace had started to savour every month. Vaughn would be so proud of her.

'Grace!' Lily's peevish cry brought Grace back to reality where there was no Vaughn but an annoyed best friend who'd just noticed all the streaks of white emulsion liberally smeared on the wallpaper.

Generally Grace tried to avoid Liam when he popped over to take Dan to the pub, but on the Saturday, thirteen days since she last saw Vaughn, not that she was counting or anything, she was waiting for the minicab she'd ordered, sitting having a cigarette on the steps, when he was suddenly standing right in front of her.

'Hey,' he said, coming to a halt at the bottom of the steps. 'You all right?'

It was a warm day, they were well into May now, and the sunlight glinted off Liam's dirty-blond hair. As he lifted an arm to shield his eyes from the glare, his bicep bulged. Which was freaky because the only exercise Liam got was lifting pints and lugging crates of bootleg DVDs around.

'I'm fine,' Grace said, breathing smoke out through her nostrils, because she was only allowed cigarettes outside as Lily and Dan had got really paranoid about second-hand smoke.

'So is this moving day?'

Lily's mum had arrived the night before to take up residence in the nursery and to berate Grace for once again ruining Lily's special day. But then she'd given Grace a hug and said, 'Lily told me about that bloke you were with. His loss, Gracie.' It had been the first time since Paris that Grace thought she might cry. Generally she didn't miss having a mother, and wouldn't know what to do with hers if she suddenly turned up, but having Lily's mum around and fussing over Lily made her feel her own motherlessness very acutely. It didn't mean anything significant, Grace had decided. She felt everything very acutely these days.

'Yeah, just waiting for my cab.' It used to be that Grace and Liam could talk for hours without pause. This time, it was stilted and awkward, and though Grace thought she had a perfect photocopy of Liam in her head, now he seemed completely different. Though maybe it was the admiring look he was giving her, which was a new development.

'You look good,' he said. 'Shiny. I like your hair.'

Grace didn't look good. OK, she hadn't been crying herself to sleep every night, but that was because she hadn't been doing much in the way of sleeping, simply lying there wide-eyed, hands clawed into fists to stop herself picking up her phone to call Vaughn or to stop her from touching herself because her body was missing Vaughn too.

'Um, thanks,' she mumbled, and tried to smile. 'You look good too. You been working out?'

'As if. I've got a part-time delivery job at a printer's. I never knew paper was so heavy.' Liam gestured at Grace's weekend suitcase and laundry bags. 'Do you want me to help you with the rest of your stuff?'

'This is it,' Grace said. 'The rest of it is . . . it's at his place and I just haven't got round to collecting it yet. I've been busy,' she added vaguely.

'If you like, I could borrow my boss's van and get it for

you,' Liam offered. 'We could go for a drink after.'

Grace tried to think of a tactful way to turn Liam down but was saved by the tooting of a horn. She struggled to her feet. 'I have to go,' she yelped, almost knocking Liam over in her haste to reach the car.

Shoving her bags on the back seat, she clambered in after them. Really it was all Liam's fault, she thought. If he hadn't dumped her in Liberty's, on her birthday, then she'd never have met Vaughn and she wouldn't feel like fifty different shades of hell right now. But as Grace looked at Liam, who'd raced up the steps to retrieve a bag she'd forgotten, she knew that she needed to let her old resentments go. It was an unpleasant truth to suddenly confront, but Liam had been right to dump her when he did for the reasons that he did. She hadn't tried to make their relationship work. In fact, she'd gone into it with her mind already made up that it would combust within three months and so she'd just coasted along, marking time and putting in zero effort. Liam hadn't been a great boyfriend but she'd been a less than stellar girlfriend, Grace realised now, and so she smiled at Liam as he handed her the last bag.

'Look, I'm crappy company at the moment,' she said. 'Not fit for public consumption, y'know?'

'How about I ask you again in a month's time?' Liam asked, one hand on the door so Grace couldn't close it.

'Three months,' she countered. 'At least.'

Grace didn't know what Nadja's problem was because when the taxi got to Knightsbridge and stopped outside a redbrick mansion block on a tree-lined avenue, Harvey Nicks was near enough to be her new corner shop. Not that she wanted to start thinking of it like that; Sainsbury's Central would have to do.

Although Nadja's booker had couriered over a set of keys and a tenancy agreement, that wasn't good enough for the porter, who seemed to think that his peaked cap and clipboard automatically made him God. Grace was red-faced and flustered by the time she'd dug out her passport and her driving licence as proof of ID and had her laundry bags sneered at as she was finally ushered into the lift.

Arriving at the fifth floor, Grace found the right flat at the end of a corridor that smelled of beeswax and a faint lingering scent of industrial-strength disinfectant. She wrestled with the keys, then stepped through the door and gazed flatly into the large sunny living room. Normally she'd have been delighted with the fireplace's original Art Deco tiling and the huge picture windows, especially as Nadja had never met a glitter-encrusted piece of clothing that she didn't like. She'd obviously never even moved in once she realised that she'd have to walk a whole two minutes to get to the shops, otherwise the flat would have been redecorated to resemble the inside of a disco ball.

Grace slowly turned round and blinked a couple of times. Just to be sure, she ran to the kitchen and started pulling open drawers and cupboard doors. There wasn't a stick of furniture or utensil in the place, not even a teaspoon or a dishcloth.

It meant that on the Monday morning, Grace finally had to steel herself to call Madeleine Jones and arrange to have her stuff sent over. She'd been ignoring Madeleine's increasingly fractious phone messages and had decided to abandon all her belongings, but beggars couldn't be choosers and Grace had a set of Le Creuset saucepans and some Tiki shot glasses that she really needed. Besides, she'd been wearing the same weekend's worth of clothes for the last fortnight.

Grace knew that she and Vaughn were broken, with no hope of repair, but phoning Madeleine to organise the removal of all traces of herself from Vaughn's world seemed so . . . final.

'Grace! I was on the verge of sending your things to the

Skirt offices,' Madeleine said when Grace rang, as if she no longer had to pretend to be friendly. 'Give me your address, and I'll get everything sent over by the end of tomorrow.'

Grace strained her ears in case she'd be able to hear Vaughn barking at someone in the background but there was nothing except an impatient sigh from Madeleine.

'I still have the BlackBerry,' Grace added, after some serious tutting from Madeleine because she couldn't remember the name of the mansion block. 'What shall I do with it?'

'Oh, you can keep it.'

'I can?' Grace asked hopefully because Vaughn was the only person who called her on the BlackBerry and maybe he couldn't bear to sever all ties . . .

'Well, the calling plan runs out in September and then you can either take it over yourself or throw it away. It's your choice.' Grace had forgotten how frosty and officious Madeleine could be, but it was all coming back to her now. It made sense that she'd be on Vaughn's side.

'Well, if you're sure that's OK,' Grace started to say, but Madeleine had already hung up.

Madeleine might not be so friendly any more but she was still a stickler for efficiency. When Grace got back from work the next evening she had to climb over a mountain of packing crates to get from the lift to her front door. As an added bonus, she got a dressing down from the night porter, who seemed to hate her as much as his daytime colleague did. 'Please be considerate of the other residents, Miss Reeves,' he hissed, as Grace was dragging the last of the crates through the door and making a hell of a racket about it. It wouldn't have killed him to help, but he just adjusted his stupid peaked cap and went off muttering.

As Grace started going through the crates, she found that she couldn't bear to look at most of the contents. There was the expensive shit she'd bought on her shopping binges and there was the expensive shit that Vaughn's money had paid for, and she didn't want either kinds of expensive shit in her life. Too many memories, both bad and good, and the good ones hurt the most.

EBaying would have taken too long and required too much effort, so Grace arranged for a buyer from a second-hand designer boutique to come round later in the week. It was an edifying experience, to watch Barb rifle through her belongings. 'You've got a good eye,' she told Grace, who was only slightly flattered, as Barb had the leathery look that came from years of sunbed abuse and was wearing a tight pair of white jeans that wouldn't have worked on a woman even half her age. 'Pity you didn't go for the Versaces and the Guccis, I can't get rid of them fast enough. Anything you want to keep?'

Grace gave her ill-gotten gains a cursory onceover. 'Just this,' she said, unearthing the tomato-red Marc Jacobs Hobo from the bottom of the pile. It was heavier than she expected and when she opened it, she found three jewellery boxes inside. She handed the two smaller ones over – somehow she didn't think Barb would be interested in Claire's Accessories' tiaras and she couldn't bear to be parted from it. 'These are from Tiffany's,' she said. 'You can take them too.'

'Either you owe big on the credit cards or it was a bad break-up,' Barb said knowingly, holding the aquamarine, pearl and diamond necklace up to the light. 'You got a hallmark certificate for this? Oh, it's in the box. So, which was it?'

'Break-up,' Grace said shortly, swallowing hard. 'And credit-card debt. It's complicated.'

A smile passed fleetingly across Barb's deeply tanned face. 'Best not to have any reminders lying about then,' she said, looking like it was sheer torture to stop herself from rubbing her manicured hands together in glee. 'I'll give you a couple of minutes to change your mind. No other mementoes you want to keep?'

Grace shook her head. 'No, I want you to take it all.'

So Barb took everything, except the Fendi shearling boots, which had tidemarks, and a couple of dresses by designers that she didn't know. Grace was happy to see it all hefted out of the door by Barb's husband and her two hulking teenage sons. In return, she got a cheque for an amount that was barely twenty per cent of what the items had originally cost. It still added up to a hell of a lot of money.

Then she hurried out to get some food so she could feed her grandparents lunch the next day.

chapter forty-two

'Well, it's hardly a surprise,' her grandmother said. Grace was amazed that she'd been able to restrain herself for that long. After all, they'd arrived a full hour ago with three deckchairs, an airbed and a card-table, which her grandmother had bullied the porter into ferrying in from the car. Talking about little Coco, who'd finally arrived in the world three days ago, and two weeks late, had only taken half an hour. Most of that thirty minutes had been spent with her grandmother voicing her disapproval at Lily and Dan for naming their daughter after Lily's favourite perfume. 'You've had a lucky escape,' she concluded.

How is it a lucky escape when I feel so fucking miserable that I want to crawl into bed and stay there for ever, Grace wanted to ask, but she just speared a pea with her fork and said, 'Yeah, I suppose.'

'But really, dear, was that any reason to dye your hair that awful colour again? It's very draining.'

Grace fingered the ends of her back-to-black hair. It was part of her new economy drive, because once-a-month hair appointments to have her highlights retouched were a thing of the past. And it was also an attempt to make her outside match her mood, which was darker than a coal mine in a black-out. 'I just fancied a change,' she muttered. 'You're always telling me change is good.'

'This is a lovely place though, dear,' her grandmother remarked. 'You don't see dado rails much these days.'

This warranted her grandfather putting down his knife and fork so he could give Grace a disapproving look through his bifocals. 'Why did no one tell me you were living with this fellow?'

'I was thinking of maybe buying somewhere,' Grace said quickly, because the cheque from Barb was just about enough to put down a deposit on a flat in the scrag-end of London's outer boroughs if she never bought another item of clothing ever again. 'Can you explain the whole mortgage thing, Grandy?'

As diversions went, this was a winner. Her grandfather almost bounced on his seat in anticipation. 'Were you thinking of a fixed rate or a tracker?' he asked eagerly.

'Huh? Just a normal mortgage where I pay lots of money every month and in twenty-five years I finally get to own my own place.'

Her grandfather patted her hand. 'I'll explain it and then you'll understand.'

Her grandmother beamed at her because Grace was out of the clutches of the sinister older man and had miraculously saved enough money to take her first faltering steps on the property ladder. Deep down, she must have known that rich, forty-something boyfriends came with their own rewards, but she'd obviously decided not to dwell on that detail.

She sat on a deckchair and nodded approvingly as Grace and her grandfather discussed mortgages. Actually, there was very little discussion because Grace couldn't get her head round base rates and interest-only repayment schemes. Her grandfather started drawing graphs and pie-charts, while Grace listened with one ear. Or maybe just half of one ear. Being fiscally responsible was deathly boring, she thought, as her grandmother got up to put on the kettle and said, 'I made some cheese scones last night. I thought they might cheer you up.'

Her grandfather was now rattling on about interest rates and Grace slipped her arm through his so she could give him a quick kiss on the cheek. 'I love you so much, Grandy. You're always there for me. Both of you,' she added, as her grandmother returned with the tea tray.

'We love you too,' her grandmother said fondly. Then: 'Of course, we're not going to be around for ever.'

'Oh, don't even go there, Gran,' Grace scoffed. 'You've got years ahead of you.'

'Well, you say that, but one of Grandy's golfing chums – you remember Stan? – went into hospital for a minor procedure on an ingrown toenail, caught one of those superbugs and was dead within a week!'

'Yeah, but that doesn't mean that—'

'And Jean from two doors down, she's been diagnosed with cancer of the colon, and Barney from the pensioners' group is booked in for a triple bypass.' Her grandmother unconcernedly took a sip of tea. 'I expect to go to bed one evening and not wake up the next day.'

'When you get to our age, your social activities revolve around hospital appointments and friends' funerals,' her grandfather chimed in.

'Can we not talk about this?' Grace implored, but it was too late. Her grandfather was already pulling a file out of a Waitrose carrier bag. 'We were glad you called because we wanted to go through this with you,' he said, handing a stack of papers to Grace.

She stared at the top sheet in horror. It was a bullet-pointed action plan in the event that her grandparents died within a week of each other. And then they were off with talk about life insurance policies and solicitors and who was getting what.

They'd always been there with unconditional love, unheeded advice and a stoic disposition as Grace managed to disappoint their expectations at every stage of her emotional development. And now, according to them, they could be dead before Christmas.

'I don't even want to look at this. God, if anything happened to either of you, let alone both of you, I'd be devastated,' Grace told them, because her heart was currently on the critical list but it wasn't completely broken. 'It would be the absolute worst thing in the world.'

'Nonsense,' her grandmother said stoutly. 'Soon you'll be married and have your own family.'

'I don't think that's ever going to happen. You *have* to put up with me, but no one else does.'

'Silly old pickle.' Her grandfather pulled out even more papers. 'Now, like we said, we don't have favourites but you can have first choice of the Royal Doulton figurines. Just don't tell your Aunt Alison. It will be our little secret.'

'I don't want the figurines!' Which was true enough, though their collection of Clarice Cliff pieces was another matter. 'Let's drop this, please. I'll read through the papers but I don't want to talk about it. It's horrible and morbid.'

Her grandparents exchanged an amused glance. 'There's no need to get so emotional, Grace. Honestly, you can be so highly strung sometimes. You're just like your mother.'

There had been a lot of things said lately that Grace didn't want to hear, but that took first prize. 'I am nothing like her at all.'

'She said the same thing when we talked about this on the phone,' her grandmother said. 'Practically word for word.'

'Well, it's not like *she's* going to be all on her own,' Grace pointed out venomously. 'Anyway, she's the one who does the leaving, not the other way round.'

'You're just being melodramatic now, Grace. Why don't we get all this paper off the table and have a nice game of Scrabble? We packed the travel set just in case.'

Her grandparents left at four to beat the traffic, though

Grace wasn't sure how many cars there were rushing off to Worthing from Kensington on a Saturday afternoon. Wandering back into the living room, whose period vibe was completely ruined by the deckchairs, she started clearing away the papers. The worst thing about living here wasn't the lack of furniture, but the lack of people. It was hard being on her own again. Of all the things Grace missed, from making her come so hard that it took quarter of an hour for her breathing to get back to normal, to his huge house and chauffeur-driven black cars, mostly she just missed Vaughn. Missed all those quiet, unspectacular moments that, when added up, showed how entwined their lives had become. And right now, she missed being able to phone him, because it would be so easy to tap in the eleven digits that would put his voice on the line. 'Grace, about bloody time,' he'd say, and make it sound like an endearment.

But she couldn't call Vaughn, because she'd left him. Which was a novelty, until Grace remembered that he'd have left her eventually if she hadn't done it first. She was never the one. She was never even the one before the one. She was the girl who seemed like a good idea at the time, but ultimately was just a phase that people went through.

That was the way it had always been. Friends and lovers came and went because there was something about her which repelled them, and she didn't have a clue what it was. It was a mystery that she couldn't solve on her own, and there wasn't a single person in the world who could help . . .

Grace glanced down at the papers she was holding until a name leaped out at her, and even when she put the papers in a shoe-box and shoved it into a kitchen cupboard, the name remained stuck in her head, which was just great.

She needed alcohol. If she was going to do what she feared she was about to do, then she needed a glass of wine, at least.

A quick trip to Oddbins and half a bottle of Pinot Grigio later, Grace's hand reached for the phone and she dialled the number that she had memorised, even though she'd never, ever called it.

The line clicked and whirred, then rang with a hollow echo. It rang and rang, and just as Grace was about to admit defeat, someone picked up.

'Hello?'

'Caroline . . . Mum – it's Grace.'

There was the weird delay that happened when you were calling someone who was half a world away. Factor in a shocked silence and Grace wondered if the phone was still working.

'Hi.' Caroline sounded just a little freaked out. Then: 'Mum and Dad are OK, aren't they?' she asked sharply.

There was no other reason for Grace to call her. 'They're fine. Apart from being obsessed with dying and their funeral arrangements, though Grandy's hip is playing up again.'

'They're not still on about all that, are they?'

'Yeah. There's an action plan and letters that have to be posted and, just so you know, they don't want flowers, just donations to the local Red Cross,' Grace said dryly. And that was *that* covered, and all she had left to ask her mother was, 'So, how's the weather?'

Apparently it was starting to get really cold, with the odd thunderstorm, and Gary had taken Kirsty to her ballet class and Caroline was waiting in for someone to fix the washing machine because it was making this strange rattle when it went into spin cycle and . . .

'Why did you leave?' There was no easy way to broach it so Grace found herself simply spitting it out.

'I beg your pardon?'

'Why did you leave me? What did I do wrong?' Grace croaked because her throat was suddenly dry as if all the moisture had been sucked out of her body.

'You didn't do anything wrong, Gracie. What's the point of dragging this up after all this time?'

'Because I have to know. I need to figure out why everyone gets sick of me and leaves, because then I can change and make it stop. And you were the first one to go so you must have seen something, like, rotten in me. What was it?'

'It wasn't you, it was me,' Caroline said, which was too ironic for words. 'You didn't want to stay with me. The judge asked you, and you said you didn't want to live with me.'

'But I was eight! Who asks an eight year old something like that? And if you'd loved me, you wouldn't have just given up and gone to Australia and left me behind.'

'Grace, the judge asked you again and again. The social worker took you out of the court and you were gone ages and when you came back, all you would say is that you didn't want to live with me or your father.'

That wasn't right. 'No, it didn't happen like that. She asked me one time.'

'That's exactly what happened. And that's what happened when we went back a week later too. And every week for a whole month.'

Grace could picture it so clearly. Rubbing her finger on the polished wooden table and leaving greasy smears. The portrait of the Queen behind the judge, and afterwards how her grandfather had bought her a lolly from the ice-cream van parked outside. 'I don't remember any of that,' she snapped.

'Well, I do because it was the worst fucking month of my life and it's been etched in my memory ever since,' Caroline snapped right back.

'That can't be right. She asked me and you looked at Dad and then you looked at me, really glared like you hated me, and so I said it just the once and it felt like I'd said the worst swear word ever, and then you weren't there and it was all my fault.' Grace curled her legs under her and rested one hand against her burning cheek. 'You could still have stayed though, couldn't you?'

Caroline's voice, when she spoke, was thick with tears. 'Grace, you don't know how much I regret not staying and fighting for you. I think about you all the time; what would have happened if I'd just dragged you back home with me. I know things got really bad with the divorce but I thought we were happy together. Do you remember how, in the summer we'd spend all day on the beach and we'd collect shells together and you'd nag me to paint your toenails pink like mine?'

'Every time I tried to think about you, I'd get so angry and all I could remember was you and Dad rowing all the time because you wouldn't have got married if you hadn't got pregnant. Neither of you really wanted me and that's the story of my life. That I'm just not fucking good enough.'

'That's absolute rubbish, Grace,' Caroline snorted with a half-laugh, half-sob. 'The divorce was about us, not you. In fact, you were the only good thing that came out of our marriage. I guess you haven't had this conversation with your dad?'

That hadn't even occurred to Grace. 'No, he's a wanker. I hate him.'

'And you don't hate me?'

'It's more complicated than that. I just shoved everything about you away so I wouldn't have to think about it. Then you got back in touch, and I had to deal with it all again. Except I didn't.' Grace could hear her voice starting to quiver but she was determined to get through this. 'The day I got your first email about Kirsty, I walked out of my degree. I had two weeks to go and I just bailed on it. Like, it reminded me there was no point. I wasn't going to be good enough again so I might just as well give up.'

'I felt exactly like that after the divorce,' Caroline said. 'I was walking past the travel agent's and they were advertising cheap flights and I thought, Everything is just too hard and Grace doesn't want me so I'll leave.'

'I wish you'd stayed. I feel like life happens to other people, and I drift in and out of their lives without ever making any kind of impact. I want to matter to someone. Like, they'll put up with all my bad shit because my good stuff makes up for it, you know?' The tension had shifted, almost evaporated, and for the first time, Grace wished that Caroline was there, that they could go for a drink together or something. 'Do you love Gary?'

'Yeah, I do,' Caroline said gently. 'He bugs me like you wouldn't believe, but I couldn't imagine being without him.'

'But how do you know that you love him?' Grace persisted. ''Cause people say that they love each other, but what does it mean? That you can't live without someone? Because you can – you won't die if they're not there, even if you feel like you might for a while and—'

'What's with all the soul-searching, Gracie? Is it that guy you were seeing? Mum didn't like him at all. Said he was no better than he ought to be, which wasn't much.'

'He's not like that at all,' Grace hissed, instinctively springing to Vaughn's defence. 'He was really nice to her but she was determined to think he was being smarmy.'

'So, you're still together?' Caroline prompted.

'No, it wasn't going to work out. We just couldn't come to an agreement.' It was so unintentionally funny that Grace started laughing, though it turned into sobs halfway through, and then she was choking it all out. All of it. Not the carefully edited version she'd told her grandmother or the abridged edition she'd given Lily. Caroline got the full *Ballad of Grace and Vaughn*; she even had to get rid of the washing repairman halfway through.

'God, how did you manage to get yourself into such a mess?' Caroline asked when Grace had got to the end, which was the part where she'd sold all of Vaughn's gifts and Barb would only give them back if Grace paid their resale value.

'Am I meant to give you a stirring pep-talk about seizing the day and being mistress of your own destiny, because I'd be really crap at that.'

'I probably wouldn't listen. Or I'd agree with you and then do completely the opposite.' Grace stretched out her right leg, which was getting crampy, and yawned. 'If he'd really wanted me to stay, he'd have shut up about the contract or found a way that we could have worked round it, but he didn't.'

'Well, neither did you,' Caroline pointed out.

'Yeah, but that's what Vaughn does. He's Solution Guy. I don't do that, I can't do that because—'

'Your job is just to drift? Yeah, you said.' Caroline's voice was Sahara dry. 'But maybe it's up to you to find a way to make it work. He sounds like he doesn't know his arse from his elbow.'

'He really doesn't. God, he just kept going on and on about the bloody contract and locking me in for another year. I just don't get him. I never did, I suppose.'

Caroline made an impatient sound. 'What's to get? Of course he wants a watertight contract. From what you've said, he's probably worried you'll wake up one morning, come to your senses and get the hell out of there.' Grace heard Caroline light a cigarette and exhale deeply. 'I mean, he's not exactly a catch, is he?'

'He is!' Grace said indignantly. 'He's handsome and he's funny – well, sarcastic funny so sometimes you're not quite sure if he's joking – and he's rich and good in bed and—'

'—Divorced, has issues up the wazoo, addictions, serious commitment phobia,' Caroline recited. 'Why can't you find a nice boy your own age?'

'Have you *seen* the boys who are my own age? They're pathetic and they walk around with their jeans slung so low, you can see their pants. Anyway, I don't want anyone else, I just want Vaughn.' It was good to finally say it, as if Grace said it out loud then maybe the universe would get the message and send him back to her. 'I should probably go now. It's really late.'

'I'm not going to make any big demands, but next time I email you, you could always email me back,' Caroline suggested. 'Just to let me know how you are and whether Mum has reached a decision about the sandwiches at her wake re: crusts or no crusts.'

'I might be coming to Australia for Fashion Week,' Grace revealed casually. It wasn't a done deal but Kiki seemed keen to pack her off as she said she couldn't bear to look at Grace's miserable face much longer. 'If it happened I'd be working a lot, but y'know, we'd be on the same continent,' she tailed off.

'Well, let me know either way,' Caroline said just as casually, but then she sighed. 'It's so good to hear from you, Gracie. If you ever need to talk, about Vaughn or anything, well, you know where I am. No pressure or anything. I know I haven't been the greatest mother in the world, but we could be friends or work towards being friends.'

Grace put the phone down, her hand shaking slightly. She couldn't even begin to sort out how she felt about maybe having Caroline back in her life as far as the odd email and phone call went. After finishing the bottle of wine, she concluded that it was a good thing, though she knew that she'd always have a momentary flash of panic when she saw Caroline's name in her inbox. It was too late to do the mother/daughter bonding thing – Grace never even thought of herself as someone's daughter – but you could never have too many friends. Or, and it was a big or, Caroline could be an honorary older sister – she seemed really adept at sniffing out Grace's bullshit. And there was only one other person in the world who was able to do that.

Grace just wished that Caroline had been a little less effusive about Vaughn's failings. And that she gave better advice, because how could she go to Vaughn now? She couldn't. She'd walked out and she couldn't walk back in. Not without a really big sign that let her know she'd be welcome, because Vaughn's unpredictability was the most predictable thing about him.

So, it was stalemate. No way was she signing another one of his contracts. Even if it wasn't an employment contract, it would be something that Vaughn had got his really expensive team of lawyers to draw up, and he wouldn't be able to stop himself from including a few sneaky clauses that would bite her on the arse later. He might have said that a contract would protect them from each other, but really it was something Vaughn could hide behind, rather than admit that a relationship was something he couldn't control. That *she* was something he couldn't control because he'd never really believe that Grace would want to be with him if the bottom fell out of the global art market and the only good time he could show her was a once-a-week trip to the cinema. There was no way Grace would be able to persuade him otherwise, and signing a contract would just confirm all of Vaughn's worst suspicions. She was damned if she did and doubly damned if she didn't because she still wouldn't have Vaughn.

It was time to think about a future that didn't have Vaughn in it, but a one-bedroom flat in North Finchley with too many cats instead. Because Grace had no talent for coming up with cunning plans and she also had no follow-through and was too keen on big, dramatic gestures . . . and all of a sudden she knew exactly what she was going to spend her money on.

chapter forty-three

A couple of weeks later, Grace spent the last of her Barb money at Liberty's on a little black dress, a pair of bright red tights and shoes that should have had *Fuck Me* stamped on their soles. With the last ten pounds, she took a cab over to Thirlestone Mews.

'I'm here to see Vaughn,' she said, when Piers answered the intercom. 'It's Grace.'

'Hey Grace . . . I'm really sorry, um, but I don't seem to have you on his schedule.'

'Can you just tell Vaughn that I need to see him, Piers,' Grace said sharply because she'd replayed this scene in her head again and again, and sitting on the doorstep hadn't featured too highly.

'He's busy right now.'

Busy was better than not being there at all. 'He said if I needed anything, I was to get in touch – so stop being difficult and let me in!'

Doubt was setting in fast because maybe that was what Vaughn had said to the others. It could be part of his boilerplate goodbye speech and not mean a thing.

Just then the door opened and Piers was standing there, all flustered and twitchy. 'It's good to see you, but you should have called first.'

'Good to see you too.'

They eyed each other warily. Grace tried to look stern because she knew Piers would cave under pressure, but he was still barring her way. 'He's in a meeting.'

'I'll wait,' Grace replied implacably, stepping right up to the threshold and not stopping so Piers had to move aside before Grace mowed him down. She brandished her Marc Jacobs bag, which was a perfect match for her tights. 'I even brought something to read.'

Grace managed to get through another five chapters of *Kavalier & Clay* while she waited. Or she turned the pages and pretended not to notice that each member of the gallery staff found a reason to wander into Reception, stare at her like she was an apparition, then scurry away.

At six on the dot, Piers came hurrying down the stairs looking even more twitchy and flustered. 'I'm really sorry, Grace, but he's already left.'

Grace eyed Piers, then the stairs, which she hadn't seen Vaughn tripping down. 'No, he hasn't.'

'He went out the back,' Piers said, his face florid because being the bearer of really bad news probably wasn't on his job description.

'You haven't *got* an out the back,' Grace reminded him, and then light dawned. 'He went down the fire escape to avoid me? Well, that's bloody great, isn't it?' She'd never felt more foolish in her life, even though there were plenty of examples to choose from.

'He has got a dinner,' Piers said helplessly.

Grace turned on him with unblinking eyes. 'Where?'

'You know I can't tell you, Grace,' Piers said carefully, like he suspected she was a heartbeat away from a truly monumental hissy fit and he didn't want to trigger the explosion. 'I could make you an appointment, but I'm afraid he's really booked up . . .'

'Yeah, and he couldn't fit me in much before Christmas,' Grace supplied.

She could feel all her bravado leaking away. She'd had two weeks to convince herself that she was a genius and everything was going to be all right, and with one quick scuttle down the fire escape, Vaughn had let her know that he never wanted to see her again. 'It's OK. I'm going.'

'Did you want to leave a message?'

For a second, Grace contemplated handing over the envelope, but there was no point. Vaughn had made his feelings perfectly clear. She was never to darken his lobby again.

'No, it's OK.' It was hard to make a dignified exit so Grace settled for leaving with a mid-level flounce.

She looked up and down the road carefully for a telltale sign of a big black car and when there wasn't one, she turned left and started the long walk home. Walking to the *Skirt* offices and back to Nadja's flat was another facet of her new economical lifestyle, but walking long distances wasn't meant to be done in four-inch heels, especially when it was June and far too warm for opaque tights.

Grace arrived home a fretful, sweaty mess. As luck would have it, her arch nemeses, the day and night porters, were changing shifts, but Grace hurried past them with her head down, as one harsh word about abusing the rubbish chute or playing her radio too loud after 10.30 p.m. and she'd start crying.

She waited until she was safely inside her flat, sank to the floor and *then* she started crying. It was the first time since Paris and it wasn't good to let it all out. It hurt – a physical, rib-aching, throat-throbbing ache that was no match for the pain in her heart because so much for big, dramatic gestures and newfound maturity and being optimistic for once in her sorry life. Vaughn wouldn't even see her. They were so finished, that 'finished' ceased to have any meaning.

Grace cried as she ran a bath. Cried as she towelled herself off. Cried as she tried to eat toast, then cried her way down a bottle of wine before she cried herself to sleep.

It was the deep sleep of the hopeless and Grace should have stayed that way until morning, possibly sleeping through her alarm and arriving at work with a tear-induced and alcohol-enabled headache. But she came to with a jolt a few scant hours later as someone buzzed on the door. Grace muttered, rolled over and went back to sleep as the buzzing started again and after a while was replaced by a sharp knock.

Grace attempted to get up from the airbed, which was always a tricky manoeuvre. In the end, she slid on to the floor and made her way upright from there, stumbling to the door with a tremulous, 'Who is it?'

'Miss Reeves? You have a visitor.'

Grace fumbled with the deadbolt and stuck her head out of the door, only to retreat immediately as she saw the night porter and a shadowy figure standing behind him.

'This fellow says he knows you,' the porter said, and for once he wasn't sounding angry but concerned, like his duties included protecting his residents from potential rapists.

Grace pushed her hair out of her eyes and peered out again. Vaughn stepped forward and into the dim glow of the hall's uplighters. His face looked so grim and unapproachable that Grace wanted to deny all knowledge of him, but she was opening the door a little wider. 'He did . . . he does.' She hesitated, long enough that the night porter bristled as if he was getting ready to come to Grace's aid if Vaughn made any sudden movements.

'I really don't see why it's necessary to go through this rigmarole,' Vaughn drawled, and Grace understood why the porter was so chary. He was drunk. Or he'd had enough to drink that he was slurring his words slightly. 'We can do this in the hall, Grace, but I think it would be better if you just let me in.'

'Or you could just leave?' the porter suggested, squaring his shoulders though he was twenty portly years older than Vaughn and Grace didn't fancy his chances.

'It's all right, you can come in,' she said quickly before they could throw down right there and then. She'd be evicted for sure.

Vaughn stalked through the door as Grace smiled apologetically at the porter, who beckoned her closer. 'Any sign he's going to get nasty, just press the star key on the intercom and I'll be up in a flash,' he whispered, one eye on Vaughn who was already in the living room.

'Thanks,' Grace whispered back. 'It's not at all what it looks like.'

She wasn't sure exactly what it *did* look like – but it was probably nothing good.

He'd lost weight. That was the first thing Grace noticed when she hurried back into the lounge to see Vaughn eyeing her deckchairs and card-table with a curled lip. He'd gone past the rangy that he used to be and was heading towards gaunt. Gustav probably had him running for two hours every morning and eating nothing but protein bars.

'It's all right,' he said, still standing with his back to her. 'I know why you came to the office today and I'll spare you the little speech you've rehearsed. Here. I can see you've found it hard to manage without it.' He held out his hand and nestling there was her black Amex card.

The old Grace would have snatched it from him with some impassioned words about how he owed her. But Grace version 2.0 simply stood there and felt grateful that she was all cried out because otherwise tears would have started cascading down her cheeks at that very moment.

'And what? You couldn't see me without sneaking down the fire escape so you could have a stiff drink first?' she hissed. 'I was waiting for hours!'

Grace sank down heavily on one of the deckchairs. Vaughn was staring at her, his eyes travelling from head to toe and not missing a thing in between. If only he'd seen her six hours ago, all gussied up. Now her hair was sticking up because she'd gone to bed with it damp, and she was wearing pyjama bottoms adorned with skulls and crossbones and a ratty T-shirt. Still, she wasn't wearing a bra and Vaughn's gaze was now fixed on the shape of her breasts underneath the soft, thin cotton. He still wanted her, so that was something. Not much, but it was something.

'Just take the card,' he said mechanically, holding it out again.

'I don't want it,' Grace protested. 'That wasn't why I came round to see you. Look, could you just sit down?'

'You want me to sit on one of those?' Vaughn asked sceptically, staring at the deckchair like he'd never seen one before. Then he lowered himself carefully down and looked surprised when it didn't collapse under him. 'What do you want, Grace?'

She took a deep breath. 'I miss you. Have you missed me?'

'You mean you missed my money,' Vaughn corrected. He rapped his knuckles against the card-table. 'I can see why.'

'How can you think that all you meant to me was just a blank cheque? Why are you selling yourself so short?'

Vaughn didn't reply. Just looked at Grace and then at the room with so much disdain that she decided this wasn't her Vaughn, but his evil twin that Grace had never liked very much. For a second she wondered if she should abandon her plan altogether, or if she should just go for it. Because, really, what had she left to lose? 'I'm not going to lie,' she began, but Vaughn snorted derisively at that.

'Why change the habits of a lifetime?' he drawled, and he could stop acting so superior when he was sitting on a deckchair and he'd had to get pissed before he could come and see her.

'I'm not going to lie,' she repeated, glaring him furiously into silence. 'I do miss your money. I miss getting chauffeured to work and I miss not having to look at the price tag before I buy something, and I even miss your poured resin floor.' Vaughn's lips twisted wryly but he hadn't taken his eyes off Grace's face. 'But I have my own money now and this great place to live and work's going OK, but everything just feels horrible without you. Worse than horrible. I can manage fine without you but I don't want to—'

'Grace – please . . .' Vaughn dropped the disaffected air so he could put his elbows on the card-table and rub his eyes. 'You were the one who left. It was your decision and your decision alone.'

'*Have* you missed me though?'

'Yes.' He made it sound as if Grace had dragged the confession from him with some electrodes and a pair of rusty pliers. 'Of course I have. If you remember, I asked you to stay.'

Then Vaughn scraped his chair back and stood up, so he could loom over her again. Grace had even missed the looming, but not the withering stare.

'Five minutes to get to the bloody point and then I'm leaving.' Vaughn sounded like he meant it, but he couldn't stop himself from freeing a strand of her hair that was tucked into the collar of her T-shirt. His fingers brushed against her neck for one fleeting, glorious second, and it was the final push Grace needed.

'I've had a lot of time to think,' she said. 'And you're not such a prize, you know? Like, you're a divorcé and you used to be a drug addict, and you have a serious eating disorder. Plus you're controlling and you've hurt me in ways I didn't think I could be hurt.'

'And why did you feel the sudden need to tell me this?' Vaughn asked, his voice shaky, and Grace could see him swallowing compulsively as if nothing she was saying came as a surprise but he didn't particularly like hearing it said out loud. 'You're far from perfect yourself.'

Grace nodded. 'I know. I lie all the time. In fact, I lie so much that I have a hard job remembering what happened and what didn't. I'm shallow and a neat freak, and sometimes I don't actually think I'm that smart.'

Vaughn tilted his head. 'You forgot to mention that you whine a lot and you're the most passive-aggressive person I've ever met. Fine, we're both thoroughly objectionable people, can I go now?'

'We're not objectionable,' Grace contradicted. 'We're broken. It's like we have all these jagged edges that scare other people off, but when we're with each other, our jagged edges fit together and we're almost whole.' It had been a much better analogy when she'd just been thinking it in her head. But Vaughn wasn't running for the door or telling her not to be stupid, he was still standing there and there was no good reason not to get up and take his hands. So she did.

'Don't,' Vaughn murmured, but he didn't pull away as Grace gripped his wrists tightly and felt his pulse positively galloping. 'We had a good innings, but six months is just about my limit.'

'So you let me have a month for free, then?' Grace was getting a contact high from being this near to him, able to smell the faint citrus tang of his aftershave and the whisky he'd been drinking, could press her head against his chest to hear his heart beating. 'And three months was all I ever normally got, but now I realise that three months was all I could deal with so I didn't bother to put any effort in. And neither did you. You liked having your little arrangements because you thought you'd be safe that way. It meant you didn't have to try, you could just give them money and cut your losses after six months because you were worried that they'd start to see the real you and they wouldn't like him very much.'

'Just so we're clear, I didn't push you away,' Vaughn said, and he was stroking her hair and Grace wondered if he'd reach down and kiss her, but then he stepped away. 'I begged you not to leave.'

'You offered me a new contract. It's a big difference.'

Vaughn had never used to look this old. Older, yes. But now he seemed to have aged and be ageing before Grace's eyes. 'Maybe I did think six months was what it took until the novelty of the money wore off,' Vaughn admitted heavily. 'But I saw that moment when the realisation hit them that all the presents and the parties didn't go far enough to compensate for having to put up with me. Obviously I miscalculated what an incentive my money would be to a girl like you.'

Grace dropped his hands and stepped away to the other side of the room. 'Jesus, Vaughn, you're not listening to a single word I've been saying!'

'I don't know what you are saying, Grace, apart from assassinating my character and dredging up the same tired conversation that we've had before.'

'I wanted you to make this big extravagant gesture that we didn't need agreements or contracts, because we had something that was deeper than that.' Grace paused because she didn't want to simply have the words fly out of her mouth with their usual lack of precision. 'I thought it meant that you didn't care about me.'

'That's not what I meant at all,' Vaughn said furiously, and the anger was better than the sarcastic voice he'd been using. 'It means that we both know where we stand so there can't be any confusion or disappointment later on.'

'Didn't work out so well for us though, did it?' Grace wanted to reach across and touch Vaughn, or maybe hit him over the head – she wasn't sure. 'We're both crap at relationships and we've both done terrible things to each other. I know I've given you no reason to trust me and I want to trust you. I want to believe that we can make this work, but you're so sure that we need a contract to do that. I don't, I still don't, but if this is what you need for us to be together, then so be it. I had a new one made . . .'

'A new what?'

'I need to get something. Don't go,' Grace pleaded, as she scurried to the hall where she'd dumped her Marc Jacobs bag. 'Hang on.' She eased the folder out, opened it and handed Vaughn a copy of the agreement she'd had her lawyer draw up.

It was another of those big life-changing moments when you didn't know what the next ten seconds would bring but you knew that nothing would ever be the same after. Grace sat down as she wasn't sure her legs could hold her any longer.

Vaughn stared at the top page like it was written in Dolphin. 'Is this meant to be some kind of joke?'

'No, it's me wanting to be with you so much that I've found a way that we can both get what we want, even though I'm absolutely fucking terrified of being rejected.'

'But this is a pre-nup.' Vaughn pointed at the words with his index finger, as if Grace might need some help deciphering them. 'You do know it's not legally binding in this country, don't you?'

'And you do know that making your mistress sign an employment contract and then threatening to sue her for breaching it would never have stood up in court?' Grace asked sweetly.

Vaughn narrowed his eyes and in the old days Grace would have recoiled from the scowl on his face, but she just sat and waited until Vaughn realised she wasn't going to back down. 'Well, yes, but I was relying on the fact that you didn't,' he admitted slowly.

Grace tapped the address on the top sheet. 'You're sneaky, Vaughn, but I can be sneakier. That's why I had this drawn up in New York. Of course, we'd have to get married there too, which will really annoy my grandparents, but it means this will be one hundred per cent legally binding.'

'You're unbelievable.'

'In a good way or a bad way?'

'I'm not sure.' Vaughn's voice was as soft as feathers and

the harsh lines of his face finally relaxed. 'Oh Grace, what am I going to do with you?'

Grace really didn't know, but then Vaughn was squatting down in front of her so he could rest his hands on her knees and look at her so she was drowning in the blue of his eyes. 'Hey,' she said softly. She guessed it was all right to touch him now and let one finger trail across a pronounced cheekbone. 'You've got so thin.'

Vaughn smiled in a lopsided way that made Grace itch to kiss the crooked corners of his mouth. 'It turns out that when I'm really miserable, I don't want to comfort eat. Gustav's very worried about me. He's letting me have carbs again.'

'I don't expect you to sign it, you know.' Grace shrugged. 'But it was the only thing I could think of to make things right between us. Like, you might appreciate a big extravagant gesture. Sometimes, I do actually have some follow-through, you know.'

'Do you have something to sit on that's not made of canvas?' Vaughn enquired, as he thumbed through the sheaf of papers.

'Not right now. But our interiors editor has said I can borrow her Habitat discount card,' Grace said, and Vaughn smiled again. 'Don't take this the wrong way but there's the airbed . . .'

Vaughn pulled Grace out of the deckchair. 'What way would I take it?'

'I'm not putting out,' Grace said firmly as she led Vaughn into the bedroom. 'Not like this, not when everything is so up in the air and I still don't even know if you're going to leave and I'm never going to see you again.'

He kissed the top of her head. 'I've missed you, Grace. There were so many times that I wanted to tell you to come back, that the contract didn't matter, but I convinced myself you were better off without me.'

Grace wanted him to say more, a whole lot more about

how, as well as not eating, he didn't sleep and wandered round his big empty house trying to catch the lingering scent of her perfume, but he just gingerly approached the airbed and sat down with a little moue of distaste. 'God, I can't believe you sleep on this contraption.'

'It's not so bad,' Grace said, and let him tug her down, though she wasn't sure that the bed would take both of them. She could already feel the floor hard against her hip, but Vaughn was lying with his head in her lap and she could play with his hair while he read her contract.

He started laughing when he got to the top of the second page. 'You're going to take me out on a date every week?'

'Yup. Nothing fancy. It will probably be ten-pin bowling and a pizza, but you need to start realising that there's a whole world out there that doesn't involve the buying and selling of art.'

'And you're going to cook me dinner at least once a week,' Vaughn continued, his mouth curving into a smile. 'How did you manage to get any lawyer to agree to draft this agreement?'

Vaughn had a point. Her lawyer, and his boss, and even his boss's boss had told Grace that she was insane, although they'd couched it more politely than that. It was the first clause of the second section that had really rocked their stuffy worlds. If they did break up, no matter whose fault it was, Grace would take nothing except the items that she'd brought with her or separately purchased with her own income.

When Vaughn got to that part, Grace watched his eyebrows knit together and his eyes flicker from left to right so rapidly she wondered if he was about to have an aneurism. 'Exactly what items were you planning to bring to our union?'

'I've got some really cool Tiki shot glasses and a lot of vintage dresses. That's in the next section.'

'I see.' Grace could have sworn Vaughn was smiling, but as if he knew she was scrutinising his face for hidden clues, he thinned his lips and read through to the end without further comment.

'Really, Vaughn, I know it's crazy but it's the only way to make you realise I'm in this for a long, long time and I'm going to do everything I can to make it work. If you want to start investing in Young Berlin Artists then I'll learn to speak German. You decide that collage is where it's at, I'll swot up on that.' There wasn't much else to say and Grace was starting to feel a little angry. She was the only one giving here and making impassioned speeches and doing everything she could to show Vaughn that she wanted to be with him, and he wasn't doing much of anything.

'You'd do that to be with me?' Vaughn asked doubtfully. 'And it doesn't have anything to do with my money?'

Grace was ready to throw in the towel or throw Vaughn out because really, what was the point ... but something in his voice stopped her. She could sense the fear underpinning his words and she was able to slot in the last piece of the puzzle. It was far too much responsibility for this to be all about him, when he didn't like himself very much, and he couldn't understand why anyone else would.

'Vaughn, you wouldn't be you without your money,' Grace sighed. 'It's part of who you are. So, yeah, I'd say it's ninety per cent about wanting to be with you and ten per cent about the fact that you're absolutely loaded.' She took a moment to reassess. 'Thirty–seventy when you're being an arsehole, though.'

She looked down to see a satisfied smile appear on Vaughn's face. 'My turn, I think. Are you going to do something about your hair?' he asked, sitting up. 'And promise never to wear those pyjama bottoms ever again?'

'What has that got to do with anything?' Grace snapped.

'You'll need to work on the pout too,' Vaughn added, as Grace's lower lip began to jut. 'Do you promise?'

Grace rolled her eyes. 'What*ever*.'

'Well, it's a start, I suppose,' Vaughn said, producing a pen from the inner pocket of his jacket and starting to flick through the pre-nup. 'This won't do at all,' he said, scoring through the section where Grace agreed to relinquish all claims on his estate and initialling it, then moving on to the dotted line that was waiting for his signature.

'What are you doing?' Grace tried to snatch the pen away from him, but Vaughn warded her off with one arm, which was infuriating. 'You can't just cross out my big, extravagant gesture. And you need to get your lawyer to look at it and—'

'I know,' Vaughn said, and signed his name with a flourish. He put the contract down and turned to Grace with a smile that made her stupid heart start beating again. 'I'm glad we've cleared that up, will you put out now?'

It was, Grace thought, a strange way to say, I love you.

NINE USES FOR AN EX-BOYFRIEND
By Sarra Manning

Hope Delafield hasn't always had an easy life.

She has red hair and a temper to match, as her mother is constantly reminding her. She can't wear heels, is terrified of heights and being a primary school teacher isn't exactly the job she dreamed of doing, especially when her class are stuck on the two times table.

At least Hope has Jack, and Jack is the God of boyfriends. He's sweet, kind, funny, has really good hair, a cool job on a fashion magazine and he's pretty (in a manly way). Hope knew that Jack was The One ever since their first kiss after the Youth Club Disco and thirteen years later, they're still totally in love. Totally. They're even officially pre-engaged. And then Hope catches Jack kissing her best friend Susie . . .

Does true love forgive and forget?
Or does it get mad . . . and get even?

YOU DON'T HAVE TO SAY YOU LOVE ME
By Sarra Manning

Sweet, bookish Neve Slater always plays by the rules.

And the number one rule is that good-natured fat girls like her don't get guys like gorgeous William, heir to Neve's heart since university. But William's been in LA for three years, and Neve's been slimming down and reinventing herself so that when he returns, he'll fall head over heels in love with the new, improved her.

So she's not that interested in other men. Until her sister points out that if Neve wants William to think she's an experienced love-goddess and not the fumbling, awkward girl he left behind, then she'd better get some, well, experience.

What Neve needs is someone to show her the ropes, someone like Max. Wicked, shallow, *sexy* Max. And since he's such a man-slut, and so not Neve's type, she certainly won't fall for him. Because William is the man for her . . . right?

HORSE PLAY
By Jo Carnegie

Churchminster village – picturesque,
quaint, sleepy – OR NOT . . .

A place where women know exactly what they want,
and it's not cream tea with the vicar.

A place where anything can happen . . . so be careful
what you wish for

And a place where the men had better behave . . .
because the ladies won't take it lying down
(well not unless they want to)!

'The new SATC (Sex and the Countryside)'
Heat

'Sexy, sassy and scandalous'
Glamour